D1045229

THORNTON WILDER

Thornton Wilder

THE BRIDGE OF SAN LUIS REY AND OTHER NOVELS 1926–1948

The Cabala
The Bridge of San Luis Rey
The Woman of Andros
Heaven's My Destination
The Ides of March
Selected Stories and Essays

THE LIBRARY OF AMERICA

Volume compilation, notes, and chronology copyright © 2009 by
Literary Classics of the United States, Inc., New York, N.Y.
All rights reserved.
No part of this book may be reproduced commercially
by offset-lithographic or equivalent copying devices without
the permission of the publisher.

Copyright © 1924, 1926, 1927, 1928, 1930, 1935, 1936, 1941, 1947, 1948,
1954, 1967, 1973 by the Wilder Family LLC. Reprinted by
permission of the Wilder Family LLC, c/o The Barbara
Hogenson Literary Agency, Inc. All rights reserved.

The paper used in this publication meets the
minimum requirements of the American National Standard for
Information Sciences—Permanence of Paper for Printed
Library Materials, ANSI Z39.48—1984.

Distributed to the trade in the United States
by Penguin Group (USA) Inc.
and in Canada by Penguin Books Canada Ltd.

Library of Congress Control Number: 200923634
ISBN 978-1-59853-045-2

First Printing
The Library of America—194

Manufactured in the United States of America

J. D. McClatchy
SELECTED THE TEXTS AND
WROTE THE CHRONOLOGY AND NOTES
FOR THIS VOLUME

Contents

The Cabala . I

The Bridge of San Luis Rey III

The Woman of Andros 193

Heaven's My Destination 249

The Ides of March . 409

Early Stories
 The Marriage of Zabett 607
 "Spiritus Valet" . 610
 Eddy Greater . 621
 Précautions Inutiles . 631
 A Diary: First and Last Entry 635
 The Warship . 638

Essays on Fiction
 On Reading the Great Letter Writers 645
 James Joyce, 1882–1941 657
 Gertrude Stein's *Four in America* 661
 Joyce and the Modern Novel 686

Chronology . 697
Note on the Texts . 711
Notes . 714

THE CABALA

First Encounters

THE train that first carried me into Rome was late, over-
crowded and cold. There had been several unexplained
waits in an open field, and midnight found us still moving
slowly across the Campagna toward the faintly-colored clouds
that hung above Rome. At intervals we stopped at platforms
where flaring lamps lit up for a moment some splendid
weather-moulded head. Darkness surrounded these platforms,
save for glimpses of a road and the dim outlines of a mountain
ridge. It was Virgil's country and there was a wind that seemed
to rise from the fields and descend upon us in a long Virgilian
sigh, for the land that has inspired sentiment in the poet ulti-
mately receives its sentiment from him.

The train was overcrowded, because some tourists had dis-
covered on the previous day that the beggars of Naples smelt
of carbolic acid. They concluded at once that the authorities
had struck a case or two of Indian cholera and were disinfecting
the underworld by a system of enforced baths. The air of Naples
generates legend. In the sudden exodus tickets for Rome be-
came all but improcurable, and First Class tourists rode Third,
and interesting people rode First.

In the carriage it was cold. We sat in our overcoats meditating,
our eyes glazed by resignation or the glare. In one compart-
ment a party drawn from that race that travels most and de-
rives least pleasure from it, talked tirelessly of bad hotels, the
ladies sitting with their skirts whipped about their ankles to
discourage the ascent of fleas. Opposite them sprawled three
American Italians returning to their homes in some Apennine
village after twenty years of trade in fruit and jewelry on upper
Broadway. They had invested their savings in the diamonds on
their fingers, and their eyes were not less bright with anticipa-
tion of a family reunion. One foresaw their parents staring at
them, unable to understand the change whereby their sons had
lost the charm the Italian soil bestows upon the humblest of its
children, noting only that they have come back with bulbous

features, employing barbarous idioms and bereft forever of the witty psychological intuition of their race. Ahead of them lay some sleepless bewildered nights above their mothers' soil floors and muttering poultry.

In another compartment an adventuress in silver sables leaned one cheek against the shuddering windowpane. Opposite her a glittering-eyed matron stared with challenging persistency, ready to intercept any glance the girl might cast upon her dozing husband. In the corridor two young army officers lolled and preened and angled for her glance, like those insects in certain beautiful pages of Fabre, who go through the ritual of flirtation under futile conditions, before a stone, merely because some associative motors have been touched.

There was a Jesuit with his pupils, filling the time with Latin conversation; a Japanese diplomat reverently brooding over a postage-stamp collection; a Russian sculptor sombrely reading the bony structure of our heads; some Oxford students carefully dressed for tramping, but riding over the richest tramping country in Italy; the usual old woman with a hen and the usual young American, staring. Such a company as Rome receives ten times a day, and remains Rome.

My companion sat reading a trodden copy of the London *Times*, real estate offers, military promotions and all. James Blair after six years of classical studies at Harvard had been sent to Sicily as archaeological adviser to a motion picture company bent on transferring the body of Greek mythology to the screen. The company had failed and been dispersed, and Blair thereafter had roamed the Mediterranean, finding stray employment and filling immense notebooks with his observations and theories. His mind brimmed with speculation: as to the chemical composition of Raphael's pigments; as to the lighting conditions under which the sculptors of antiquity wished their work to be viewed; as to the date of the most inaccessible mosaics in Santa Maria Maggiore. Of all these suggestions and many more he allowed me to make notes, even to the extent of copying some diagrams in colored inks. In the event of his being lost at sea with all his notebooks—a not improbable one, as he crosses the Atlantic on obscure and economical craft, not mentioned in your paper, even when they founder—it would be my confusing duty to make a gift of this material to the

Librarian of Harvard University where its unintelligibility might confer upon it an incomputable value.

Presently discarding his paper, Blair decided to talk: You may have come to Rome to study, but before you settle down to the ancients you see whether there aren't some interesting moderns.

There's no Ph.D. in modern Romans. Our posterity does that. What moderns do you mean?

Have you ever heard of the *Cabala*?

Which one?

A kind of a group living around Rome.

No.

They're very rich and influential. Everyone's afraid of them. Everybody suspects them of plots to overturn things.

Political?

No, not exactly. Sometimes.

Social swells?

Yes, of course. But more than that, too. Fierce intellectual snobs, they are. Mme. Agaropoulos is no end afraid of them. She says that every now and then they descend from Tivoli and intrigue some bill through the Senate, or some appointment in the Church, or drive some poor lady out of Rome.

Tchk!

It's because they're bored. Mme. Agaropoulos says they're frightfully bored. They've had everything so long. The chief thing about them is that they hate what's recent. They spend their time insulting new titles and new fortunes and new ideas. In lots of ways they're medieval. Just in their appearance for one thing. And in their ideas. I fancy it's like this: you've heard of scientists off Australia coming upon regions where the animals and plants ceased to evolve ages ago? They find a pocket of archaic time in the middle of a world that has progressed beyond it. Well, it must be something like that with the Cabala. Here's a group of people losing sleep over a host of notions that the rest of the world has outgrown several centuries ago: one duchess' right to enter a door before another; the word order in a dogma of the Church; the divine right of kings, especially of Bourbons. They're still passionately in earnest about stuff that the rest of us regard as pretty antiquarian lore. What's more, these people that hug these notions aren't just hermits and ignored eccentrics, but members of a

circle so powerful and exclusive that all these Romans refer to them with bated breath as the Cabala. They work with incredible subtlety, let me tell you, and have incredible resources in wealth and loyalty. I'm quoting Mme. Agaropoulos, who has a sort of hysterical fear of them, and thinks they're supernatural.

But she must know some of them personally.

Of course she does. So do I.

One isn't afraid of people one knows. Who's in it?

I'm taking you to meet one of them tomorrow, this Miss Grier. She's leader of the whole international set. I catalogued her library for her,—oh, I couldn't have got to know her any other way. I lived in her apartment in the Palazzo Barberini and used to get whiffs of the Cabala. Besides her there's a Cardinal. And the Princess d'Espoli who's mad. And Mme. Bernstein of the German banking family. Each one of them has some prodigious gift, and together they're miles above the next social stratum below them. They're so wonderful that they're lonely. I quote. They sit off there in Tivoli getting what comfort they can from one another's excellence.

Do they call themselves the Cabala? Are they organized?

Not as I see it. Probably it never occurred to them that they even constituted a group. I say, you study them up. You ferret it out, the whole secret. It's not my line.

In the pause that followed, fragments of conversation from the various corners of the compartment flowed in upon our minds so recently occupied with semi-divine personages. I haven't the slightest desire to quarrel, Hilda, muttered one of the Englishwomen. Naturally you made the arrangements for the trip as best you could. All I say is that that girl did *not* clean off the washstand every morning. There were rings and rings.

And from an American Italian: I says it's none of your goddam business, I says. Take your goddam shirt the hell outta here. He run, I tell you; he run so fast you don't see no dust for him he run so.

The Jesuit and his pupils had become politely interested in the postage stamps and the Japanese attaché was murmuring: Oh, most exclusively rare! The four-cent is pale violet and when held up to the light reveals a water-mark, a sea-horse. There are only seven in the world and three are in the collection of the Baron Rothschild.

Symphonically considered, one heard that there had been no sugar in it, that she had told Marietta three mornings running to put sugar in it, or bring sugar, although the Republic of Guatemala had immediately cut them, a few had leaked out to collectors, and that more musk-melons than one would have thought possible were sold annually at the corner of Broadway and 126th Street. Perhaps it was in revulsion against such small change that the impulse first rose in me to pursue these Olympians, who though they might be bored and mistaken, had at least, each of them, "one prodigious gift."

It was in this company then, and in the dejected airs of one in the morning that I first arrived in Rome, in that station that is uglier than most, more hung with advertisements of medicinal waters and more redolent of ammonia. During the journey I had been planning what I should do the moment I arrived: fill myself with coffee and wine, and in the proud middle of the night, run down the Via Cavour. Under the hints of dawn I should behold the tribune of Santa Maria Maggiore, hovering above me like the ark on Ararat, and the ghost of Palestrina in a soiled cassock letting himself out at a side door and rushing home to a large family in five voices; hurry on to the platform before the Lateran where Dante mixes with the Jubilee crowd; overhang the Forum and skirt the locked Palatine; follow the river to the inn where Montaigne groans over his ailments; and fall a-staring at the Pope's cliff-like dwelling, where work Rome's greatest artists, the one who is never unhappy and the one who is never anything else. I would know my way about, for my mind is built upon the map of the city that throughout the eight years of school and college had hung above my desk, a city so longed for that it seemed as though in the depth of my heart I had never truly believed I should see it.

When I arrived finally, the station was deserted; there was no coffee, no wine, no moon, no ghosts. Just a drive through shadowy streets to the sound of fountains, and the very special echo of travertine pavements.

During the first week Blair helped me find and fit out an apartment. It consisted of five rooms in an old palace across the river and within stone's-throw of the basilica of Santa Maria in Trastevere. The rooms were high and damp and bad

Eighteenth Century. The ceiling of the salone was modestly coffered and there were bits of crumbling stucco in the hall, still tinted with faint blues and pinks and gilt; every morning's sweeping carried off a bit more of some cupid's curls or chips of scroll and garland. In the kitchen there was a fresco of Jacob wrestling with the angel, but the stove concealed it. We passed two days in choosing chairs and tables, in loading them upon carts and personally conducting them to our mean street; in haggling over great lengths of gray-blue brocade before a dozen shops, always with a view toward variety in stains and unravellings and creases; in selecting from among the brisk imitations of ancient candelabra those which most successfully simulated age and pure line.

The acquisition of Ottima was Blair's triumph. There was a trattoria at the corner, a lazy casual talkative wine-shop, run by three sisters. Blair studied them for a time, and finally proposed to the intelligent middle-aged humorous one that she come and be my cook "for a few weeks." Italians have a horror of making long-term contracts and it was this last clause that won Ottima. We offered to take on any man she recommended to help her with the heavier work, but she clouded at that and replied that she could very well do the heavier work too. The removal to my rooms must have arrived as a providential solution to some problem in Ottima's life, for she attached herself passionately to her work, to me, and to her companions in the kitchen, Kurt the police dog and Messalina the cat. We each winked at the others' failings and we created a home.

The day following our arrival, then, we called upon the latest dictator of Rome and found a rather boyish spinster with an interesting and ailing face, fretful bird-like motions and exhibiting a perpetual alternation of kindness and irritability. It was nearly six when we walked into her drawing-room in the Palazzo Barberini and found four ladies and a gentleman seated a little stiffly about a table conversing in French. Mme. Agaropoulos gave a cry of joy at seeing Blair, the absent-minded scholar to whom she was so attached; Miss Grier echoed it. A thin Mrs. Roy waited until something had been dropped into the conversation about our family connections before she could relax and smile. The Spanish Ambassador and his wife wondered how on earth America could get on without

a system of titles whereby one might unerrably recognize one's own people, and the Marquesa shuddered slightly at the intrusion of two coarse young redskins and began composing mentally the faulty French sentence with which she would presently excuse herself. For a time the conversation blew fitfully about, touched with the formal charm of all conversation conducted in a language that is native to no one in the group.

Suddenly my attention was caught by a tension in the room. I sensed the tentatives of an intrigue without being able to gather the remotest notion of the objectives. Miss Grier was pretending to babble, but was in reality quite earnest, and Mrs. Roy was taking notes, mentally. The episode resolved itself into a typical, though not very complicated, example of the Roman social bargain, with its characteristic set of ramifications into religious, political and domestic life. In the light of information received much later, I call your attention to what Mrs. Roy wanted Miss Grier to do for her; and what Miss Grier asked in return for her services:

Mrs. Roy had narrow eyes and a mouth that had just tasted quinine; while she spoke her ear-pendants rattled against her lean clavicles. She was a Roman Catholic, and in her political activity a Black of the Blacks. During her residence in Rome she had occupied herself with the task of bringing the needs of certain American charitable organizations to the attention of the Supreme Pontiff. Slander attributed a diversity of motives to her good works, the least damaging of which was the hope of being named a Countess of the Papal States. The fact is that Mrs. Roy was pressing audiences in the Vatican with the hope of inducing His Holiness to commit a miracle, namely to grant her a divorce under the Pauline Privilege. This consummation, not without precedent, depended upon a number of conditions. Before taking any such step the Vatican would ascertain very carefully how great the surprise would be in Roman Catholic circles; American cardinals would be asked in confidence for a report on the matron's character, and the faithful in Rome and Baltimore, without their being aware of it, would be consulted. This done it would be well to gauge the degree of cynicism or approval the measure would arouse in Protestants. Mrs. Roy's reputation happened to be above reproach, and her right to a divorce indisputable (her husband had offended

under every category: he had been unfaithful; he had lapsed from a still greater faith; and he had become an *animae periculum*, that is, he had tried to draw her into an irreverent argument over the liquefaction of the blood of St. Januarius); but the Protestant *imprimatur* was needed. Whose opinion would be more valuable for this purpose than that of the austere directress of the American Colony? Miss Grier would be approached—and both women knew it—through channels exquisite in their delicacy and resonance; and if an uncertain note were sounded from the Palazzo Barberini, the familiar verdict Inexpedient would be returned to the petitioner, and the question never reopened.

Mrs. Roy having so much to ask from Miss Grier, wanted to know if there were any service she could render in return.

There was.

No Italian work of art of the classic periods may leave the country without an enormous export tax. How then did Mantegna's "Madonna between St. George and St. Helen" ever arrive at the Alumnae Hall of Vassar College without passing through the customs? It was last seen three years before in the collection of the poor Principessa Gaeta; it was so ascribed in the reports of the Minister of Fine Arts for the following years, in spite of the rumor that it was being offered to the museums of Brooklyn, Cleveland and Detroit. It changed hands six times, but the dealers, savants and curators were so taken up with the problem as to whether or not St. Helen's left foot had been retouched by Bellini (as Vasari affirms) that it had never occurred to them to ask if it had been registered at the border. It was finally bought by a mad old Boston dowager in a lavender wig who, dying, bequeathed it (along with three spurious Botticellis) to that college with which her vicious spelling alone would have prevented her association in any capacity save that of trustee.

The Minister of Fine Arts at Rome had just heard of the donation and was in despair. When the thing became known his position and reputation would be gone. All his vast labors for his country (*exempli gratia*: he had obstructed the disinterment of Herculaneum for twenty years; he had ruined the façades of twenty gorgeous Baroque churches in the hope of finding a Thirteenth-Century window; etc., etc.) would avail

him nothing in the storms of Roman journalism. All loyal Italians suffer at the sight of their art treasures being carried off to America; they are only waiting for some pretext to rend an official and appease their injured honor. The Embassy was already in agonies of conciliation. Vassar could not be expected to give up the picture, nor to pay a smuggler's duty. Tomorrow morning the Roman editorials would picture a barbarous America stealing from Italy her very children and references would be made to Cato, Aeneas, Michelangelo, Cavour and St. Francis. The Senatus Romanus would sit on every bit of delicate business that America was endeavoring to recommend to Italian favor.

Now Miss Grier, too, was a trustee of Vassar. She had a flattering position in the long processions that formed in June among the sun-dials and educative shrubs. She was ready to pay the fine, but not until she had placated the city fathers. This could be done by obtaining the favorable votes of the committee that was to sit that very evening. This committee was composed of seven members, four of whose votes she already commanded; the other three were Blacks. For the matter to be dropped in the interest of the Princess Gaeta a unanimous verdict was necessary.

If Mrs. Roy descended at once to her car, she would have time to drive to the American College in the Piazza di Spagna and confer with dear omniscient Father O'Leary. Marvellous are the acoustics of the Church! Before ten that evening the three Black votes would be decently cast for conciliation. It was Miss Grier's task over the tea-table to convey this long exposition to Mrs. Roy and to intimate the ineffable return she, Miss Grier, would be able to make for any favors. This was complicated by the necessity of making sure that neither Mme. Agaropoulos nor the Ambassadress (men don't matter) suspected the least collusion. Fortunately the Ambassadress could not understand rapid French, and Mme. Agaropoulos, being sentimental, could be continually distracted from the main issue by little sops of prettification and pathos.

Miss Grier played these several cards with the economy and precision of a faultless technique. She had that quality which is a peculiar part of the genius that invests great monarchs, and which we see notably in Elizabeth and Frederick, the power of

adjusting threats to just the degree that stimulates, yet does
not antagonize. Mrs. Roy understood at once what was ex-
pected of her. She had been packing committees and concili-
ating soured Papal chamberlains and Italian political *dévotés*
these many years; trading in influence was her daily portion.
Moreover joy can exert the happiest sort of influence on the
intelligence and she felt her divorce was at hand. She rose
hastily.

Will you excuse me if I run? she murmured. I told Julia
Howard I would call for her at Rosali's. And I have an errand
in the Piazza di Spagna.

She bowed to us and fled. What emotion is it that lends
wings to such matter-of-fact feet and blitheness to such thin
dispositions? The next year she married a young French
yachtsman, half her age; she settled down in Florence and gave
birth to a son. The Blacks no longer talked votes when she en-
tered their drawing-rooms. Vassar retains the painting and in
its archives a letter from the Italian Secretary for Foreign Af-
fairs which reads like a deed of gift. The influence of a work of
art upon the casual passerby is too subtle for determination,
but one has faith to believe that the hundreds of girls who pass
beneath the Mantegna daily draw from it impulses that make
them nobler wives and mothers. At least that is what the Min-
istry promised the College.

When the others had gone, Miss Grier made a face after
them, lowered the lights and bade us talk about New York. She
seemed to take some pleasure in such exotic company as our-
selves, but her mind strayed until suddenly jumping up, she
smoothed out the folds of her gown and bade us hurry off,
dress, and come back to dinner at eight. We were surprised but
equal to it, and dashed off into the rain.

At once I harried Blair for more facts about her. He could
give me little; the portrait of her mind and even of her features
lies in the following account of her ancestry that I made out
for myself by reading between the lines and by studying the
photographs of a history of the Griers, written by a second
cousin, for considerations.

It seems that her great-grandfather had gone to New York
in 1800, suffering from ill-health. He took an old house in the
country and intended spending his days like a hermit, studying

the prophetic passages of the Bible and encouraging the multi-
plication of four pigs that he had brought across the water in a
basket. But his disposition improving with his affairs, he soon
discovered himself to be married to the heiress of Dawes Cor-
ners, Miss Agatha Frehestocken, the death of whose parents,
ten years later, united two farms of considerable extent. Their
children, Benjamin and Anne, were brought up with such ed-
ucation as fell to them on rainy afternoons at the caprice of
their father. Our Miss Grier's grandfather, a crafty single-minded
country boy, disappeared for many years into a whirlpool of
obscure activity in town, becoming in turn potboy, newspaper
devil and restaurant manager. At last he revisited his parents
and forced them to permit his using their land as security for
some railroad investments. We have his picture at this stage:
the daguerreotype of the Dutch yokel with the protruding
lower lip and grinning pugnacious eyes is reproduced in any
history of the great American fortunes. Probably the gentle
art of horsewhipping one's parents was revived that Sunday
evening at Dawes Corners for Anne intimates that she was di-
rected to take her knitting into the feed-house and sit on sacks
until she was recalled. The old father cursed the son roundly
from the imprecatory psalms and had his curious revenge: the
worm of religious introspection was stirred in the brain of Ben-
jamin Grier and a strain of ill-health in his body. Success came
of it: he became a deacon and a millionaire at about the same
time; he was presently directing five railroads from a wheel-
chair. His parents died in a Washington Square mansion, un-
forgiving to the end.

Benjamin married the daughter of another magnate, a girl
who in another age and faith would have retired to a convent
and eased the poverty of her mental and spiritual nature in a
perpetual flow of damp unexplainable tears. She bore a sickly
son to the world of brownstone, a son in whom the esthetic
impulse, stifled during so many generations of Griers and Hal-
letts, attained a piteous flowering, a passion for the operas of
Rossini, and for things he fondly took to be Italian, garish
rosaries, the costumes of the peasants of Capri, and the painting
of Domenichino. He married a firm sharp woman, older than
himself, who had deliberately chosen him in the vestry of the
Presbyterian Church. They were incredibly wealthy, with that

wealth that increases in the dark and, untended, doubles in a year. With the affiliation of this determined Grace Benham one last offspring was made possible to the Grier line,—our Miss Grier. To the score of governesses that trod sobbing on one another's heels, she appeared a monster of guile and virulence. She was dragged without rest from New York to Baden-Baden, from Vevey to Rome, and back again; and she grew up without forming any attachment to place or person. Her parents died when she was twenty-four and finally sheer solitude did what exhortation could not do: her character softened in an attempt at piteously luring people to talk to her, live with her, to fill somehow the moneyed emptiness of her days.

Such an account of her extraction, if she read it, would have neither interested her nor embarrassed her. Her mind lay under the hot breath of a great fretfulness; she lived to ridicule and insult the fools and innocents of her social circle. In this fretfulness floated all the enthusiasms and frustrations of her line: her great-grandfather's gloom, her grandfather's whip and his dread of the Valley of Bones, her grandmother's red eyes and her father's repressed loves for the Normas and Semiramides of the Academy of Music. She was restless too, with the masculine capacities inherited from her grandfather, the capacities of a business magnate, that given her sex and situation could find their only outlet in a passion for making women tremble and a mania for interfering in the affairs of others. She was with all this a woman of intelligence and force; she ruled her eccentric and rebellious parish with acrid pleasure and at her death the drawing-rooms of Rome resounded with a strange wild murmur of muted joy.

Her portrait is not complete without an account of her strangest habit, due partly to the sleepless nights of a lifetime of illness, and partly to the fear of ghosts instilled in her by governesses when she was a girl. She was never able to sleep until the coming on of dawn. She feared to be alone; toward one in the morning she could be found urging her last callers to stay a little longer; *c'est l'heure du champagne*, she would say, offering them that untimely inducement. When finally they went away she would devote the rest of the night to music, for like the German princes of the Eighteenth Century she maintained her own troupe of musicians.

These sessions before dawn were not vaguely and sentimentally musical; they were to the last degree eclectic. In one night she would hear all the sonatas of Scriabin or the marches of Medtner; in one night both volumes of the Well-Tempered Clavichord; all the Handel fugues for organ; six Beethoven trios. Gradually she won away from the more easily appreciated music altogether and cultivated only what was difficult and cerebral. She turned to music that was interesting historically and searched out the forgotten rivals of Bach and the operas of Grétry. She paid a group of singers from the Lateran choir to sing her endless Palestrina. She became prodigiously learned. Harold Bauer would listen meekly to her directions on phrasing Bach—he averred that she had the only truly contrapuntal ear of the age—and the Flonzaleys acceded to her request to take certain pages of Loeffler a little faster.

In time I encountered a number of people who for one reason or another were unable to sleep between midnight and dawn, and when I myself tossed sleepless or when I returned late to my rooms through the deserted streets—at the hour when the parricide feels a cat purring against his feet in the darkness—I pictured to myself old Baldassare, in the Borgo, former Bishop of Shantung, Apostolic Visitor to the Far East, rising at two to study with streaming eyes the Church Fathers and the Councils, marvelling, he said, at the continuous blooming of the rose-tree of Doctrine; or of Stasia, a Russian refugee who had lost the habit of sleeping after dark during her experience as nurse in the War, Stasia playing solitaire through the night and brooding over the jocose tortures to which her family had been subjected by the soldiers of Taganrog; and of Elizabeth Grier listening the length of her long shadowed room to some new work that d'Indy had sent her or bending over the score while her little troupe revived the overture to *Les Indes Galantes.*

When we remounted the steps an hour later, then, we found the guests already arrived and awaiting their hostess. Among other privileges Miss Grier had long reserved to herself a prerogative of royalty, that of being the last arrival at one's own parties. In the hall the maître-d'hôtel gave me a note reading: Please take in Mlle. de Morfontaine, a high Merovingian

maiden who may invite you to her villa at Tivoli. In a few mo-
ments Miss Grier had slipped in and was greeting her guests in
a hurried zigzag across the room. She was dressed after a cos-
tume-plate by Fortuny, conceived in salamander red and black.
About her neck hung a rare medal of the Renaissance, much
larger than any other woman would have ventured to wear.

As this woman wanted to be in a position to hear every
word spoken at her table Rome had long had good reason to
complain of the crowded arrangements of her dinners; we
were packed together like the hurried diners at Modane. But
she had still other conventions to challenge: she discussed the
food; she reversed the direction of conversation from the right
to the left hand at the least convenient opportunities; she
talked to the servants, chattily; she shifted the conversation
from French to English or Italian capriciously; she referred to
guests who had been invited but had not been able to come.
One suddenly became aware that she was not eating the
courses that were served to us. She began with a little bowl of
breadcrumbs and walnuts; to this she added later—while we
confronted a *faisan Souvaroff* dressed with truffles and *foie gras*
and graced with that ultimate dark richness which it is the priv-
ilege of Madeira to confer on game—an American cereal, soaked
in hot water and touched with butter. Nor could she restrain
herself from teasing her guests in a dangerous way, and with
almost inspired precision: a political Duke on his dull speeches;
Mrs. Osborne-Cady on the career as a concert-pianist that she
had sacrificed to a more than usually disappointing home-life.
For a moment at the beginning of the meal her electric eyes
paused at my place and she began to murmur ominously, but
thinking better of it she ordered the servant to offer me some
more *oeufs cardinal* adding with a sort of insolence that they
were the only *oeufs cardinal* that one could eat in Europe and
that Mémé (the elder Princess Galitzine) was a little fool to
vaunt her chef, who had received his training in railway-stations,
etc., etc.

The high Merovingian maiden at my left was Mademoiselle
Marie-Astrée-Luce de Morfontaine, daughter of Claude-Elzéar
de Morfontaine and Christine Mézières-Bergh; her grandfather
Comte Louis Mézières-Bergh had married Rachel Krantz, the
daughter of the great financier Maxi Krantz, and had been the

French ambassador to the Vatican in 1870. She was then, excessively rich, for she owned, they said, more shares in the Suez Canal than the Rothschilds. She was tall, large-limbed and bony, without somehow being too thin. Her high white face, framed between two carnelian ear pendants, recalled some symbolical figure in a frieze of Giotto, out of drawing, but radiating gaunt spiritual passions. She had a hoarse voice and a rapt manner, and for the first ten minutes said many foolish things because her mind was afar off; one felt vaguely that it would come around in its own time. This it presently did and with considerable impact. She outlined to me the whole Royalist movement in France. She seemed to believe as passionately in its aim as she depised its practice. There can be no king in France, she cried, until catholicism has had a great revival there. France cannot be great save through Rome. We are Latins; we are not Goths. They are forcing alien systems upon us. Eventually we shall find ourselves, our kings, our faith, our Latin hearts. I shall see France return to Rome before I die, she added clasping her hands before her chin. I replied faintly that both the French and Italian temperaments seemed to me singularly unrepublican, whereupon she laid her long pale hand upon my sleeve and invited me to come that week-end to her villa.

You will hear the whole argument, she said. And the Cardinal will be there.

I asked which Cardinal? The pain on her face showed me that at least for the circle in which she moved there were not seventy cardinals, but one.

Cardinal Vaini, of course. The College at present is singularly free of uninteresting priests, but surely the only cardinal with learning, with distinction, with charm, is Cardinal Vaini.

I had so often encountered learning, distinction and charm (to say nothing of piety) in the lower reaches of the Church that I was shocked to learn that these qualities were so rare higher up.

Besides she added, what other is friendly to France, the rebellious daughter? You have not yet met the Cardinal? Such knowledge! And to think that he will not write! If I may say it without disrespect His Eminence is afflicted with a sort of— inertia. The whole world is waiting for an explanation of

certain contradictions in the Fathers; he is the only man who can do it; yet he remains silent. We beg him with prayers. It is in his power to effect the re-entry of the Church into literature. Perhaps he might singlehanded carry through the cause we all have so at heart.

I asked shyly what cause this might be.

She turned toward me with some surprise. Why, the promulgation of the Divine Right of Kings as a dogma of the Church. We hope to have an Ecumenical Council called for that purpose within the next twenty-five years. I thought that of course you knew; in fact I assumed that you were one of our workers.

I replied that I was both an American and a Protestant, an answer that I felt relieved me of the burden of being a catholic royalist.

Oh, she said, we have many adherents who at first glance would appear to have no interest in the movement: we have Jews and agnostics, artists, and, yes, even anarchists.

I now felt quite sure that I was sitting beside an insane person. They don't lock you up when you have millions, I said to myself. The idea of trying to collect a Council, in the Twentieth Century, to give crowns a supernatural sanction and to enroll the sanction among the articles of obligatory belief, was no mere pious revery; it was lunacy. We were prevented from returning to the subject that evening, but several times I found her spacious half-mad glance resting on me with greater implication of intimacy than I was quite ready to acknowledge.

I will send the car for you at eleven, she murmured as she passed me in leaving the table. You must come. I shall have a great favor to ask of you.

On returning to the drawing-rooms I found myself beside Ada Benoni, daughter of a popular senator. Although she seemed almost too young to go out in the evening, she had that soft cautious sophistication of well-brought-up Italian girls. I asked her almost at once if she would tell me about the Cabala.

Oh, the Cabala's only some people's joke, she answered. There is no Cabala, really. But I know what you mean. And the young girl's eyes carefully estimated the distance between us

and the company on all sides. By Cabala they mean a group of people that are always together and have a lot in common.

Are they all rich? I asked.

No . . . she answered thoughtfully. We mustn't speak so loudly. Cardinal Vaini can't be rich, nor the Duchess d'Aquilanera.

But they're all intellectual?

The Princess d'Espoli isn't intellectual.

Then what have they in common?

Oh, they haven't anything in common, except . . . except that they despise most people, you and me and my father and so on. They've each got one thing, some great gift, and that binds them together.

Do you believe that they work together and plan trouble here and there?

The girl's forehead wrinkled and she reddened slightly. No, I don't think they mean to, she said softly.

But they *do?* I insisted.

Well, they sit over there in Tivoli and talk about us and somehow, without knowing it, they then *do* something.

How many of them do you know?

Oh, I know all of them a little, she replied quickly. Everybody knows all of them. Except, of course, the Cardinal. I love them all, too. They're only bad when they're together, she explained.

Mlle. de Morfontaine has asked me to spend the week-end at her villa in Tivoli. Will I see them there?

Oh, yes. We call that the hotbed.

Is it all right? Have you any advice to give me before I go?

No.

Yes, you have.

Well, she admitted, drawing her eyebrows together, I advise you to be . . . to be stupid. It's hard. You must expect them to be very cordial at first. They have a way of getting very excited about people and then getting tired of them and dropping them. Except every now and then they find someone they like and they adopt him or her for good, and there's a new member of the Cabala. Rome's full of people who went through the rapids and didn't stick. Miss Grier's especially that way. She's just met you lately, hasn't she?

Why, yes,—just this afternoon.

Well, she'll have you around every minute of the day for a while. She's coming over in a minute to ask you to stay to her midnight supper. She has famous midnight suppers.

But I can't. I was here to tea and immediately asked to dinner. It would be ridiculous to stay to midnight. . . .

It's not ridiculous in Rome. You're just getting into the rapids, that's all. Everybody cultivates their friendships in rushes. It's very exciting. Don't try and fight against it. If you do that you lose the best of everything. Do you want to know how I know about your being in the rapids? Well, I'll tell you. My fiancé was to have come to the dinner tonight, and an hour before, a note was brought to his house asking him to come next Friday instead and go to the Opera also. She does that often and it only means that she has found some new friend she insists on keeping by her that evening. Of course the second invitation, the consoling one, is always bigger and more showy than the first, but we get angry.

I should say so. I'm sorry I was the one to prevent . . .

Oh, that's all right, she answered. Vittorio's out waiting for me in the car now.

So it was that when Blair and I presented ourselves before Miss Grier to take our leave, she drew me aside with an irresistible vehemence and standing against my ear said: You are to come back here tonight. There will be some people in to a late supper whom I want you to meet. You can, can't you?

I made some show of protest, and the effect was appalling. But, my dear young man, she cried, I'll have to ask you to trust me. There is something of the first importance that I want to put to you. The fact is I have already telephoned a very dear friend of mine. . . . Please now, just as a favor to me, put off what you had planned. There's a very great service we want to ask you.

Of course with that I fairly folded up, as much with surprise as compliance. Apparently the whole Cabala wanted me to do favors.

Thank you, thank you so much. About twelve.

It was then about ten. Two hours to kill. We were about to go to the Circus, when Blair exclaimed:

Say, do you mind if I drop in and see a friend of mine for a minute. If I'm going Tuesday I ought to say goodbye and see how he is. Do you hate sick people?

No.

He's a nice fellow, but he hasn't long to live. He's published some verse in England; one of the thousand, you know. It got an awful rap. Maybe he's quite a poet, but he can't get over that diction. He's awfully adjectival.

We climbed down the Spanish Steps and turned in at the left. On the stairs Blair stopped and whispered: I forgot to tell you that he's watched over by a friend, a sort of water-colourist. They're dead-poor and it's all they can do to get a doctor. I meant to lend them some more money—what have you with you?

We assembled a hundred lire and knocked at the door. Receiving no answer we pushed it open. There was a lamp burning in the further of two mean rooms. It stood beside a bed and cast its light on the remorseless details of a barricade built during the last stages of consumption against a light vaulter; bowls and bottles and stained cloths. The sleeping invalid was sitting high in bed, his head turned away from us.

The artist must have gone out for a minute to look for some money, said Blair. Let's stay around a bit.

We went into the other room and sat in the dark looking at the moonlight that filled the Fountain of the Boat. There were fireworks on the Pincian Hill in memory of some battle on the Piave and the tender green of the sky seemed to tremble behind the Chinese blooms that climbed the night. A friendly tram entered the square at intervals, stopped inquiringly, and bustled out again. I tried to remember whether Virgil had died in Rome . . . no, buried near Naples. Tasso? Some piercing-sweet pages of Goethe, the particular triumph of Moissi who brings to them his wide-open eyes and elegiac voice. Presently we heard a call from the next room: Francis. Francis.

Blair went in: I guess he's gone out a minute. Can I do something for you? I'm going in a day or two and I called around to see how much better you are. Would it tire you if we sat with you a bit? . . . Come on in, say!

For the moment Blair had forgotten the poet's name and our introduction was slurred over. The sick man looked his

extremity, but his fever gave to his eyes an eager and excited air; he seemed willing to listen or to talk for hours. My eye fell upon a rough pencilled note that lay on the table beyond the invalid's reach: Dear Dr. Clarke: he spat up about two cupfuls of blood at 2 P.M. He complained so of hunger that I had to give him more than you said. Be back at once. F.S.

Have you been able to write anything lately? Blair began.

No.

Do you read much?

Francis reads to me. He pointed to a Jeremy Taylor on his feet. You're Americans, aren't you? I have a brother in America. In New Jersey. I was to have gone over there.

The conversation lapsed, but he kept staring at us, smiling and bright-eyed, as though it were swift and rare.

By the way, are there any books you'd like us to lend you?

Thank you. That would be fine.

What, for instance?

Anything.

Think of one you'd like especially.

Oh, anything. I'm not particular. Only I suppose it would be hard to find any translations from the Greek?

Here I offered to bring in a Homer in the original and stammer out an improvised translation.

Oh, I should like that most of all, he cried. I know Chapman's well.

I replied, unthinking, that Chapman's was scarcely Homer at all, and suddenly beheld a look of pain, as of a mortal wound, appear upon his face. To regain control of himself he bit his finger and tried to smile. I hastened to add that in its way it was very beautiful, but I could not recall my cruelty; his heart seemed to have commenced bleeding within him.

Blair asked him if he had almost enough poems for a new book.

I don't think about books any more, he said. I just write to please myself.

But the insult to Chapman had been working in him; he now turned his face away and great tears fell upon his hands. Excuse me. Excuse me, he said. I'm not well, and I seem to . . . to do this about nothing.

There was a search for a handkerchief, but none being found he was persuaded to use mine.

I don't want to go away without seeing Francis, said Blair. Do you know where I might find him?

Yes, yes. He's around the corner at the Café Greco. I begged him to go and get some coffee; he'd been here all day.

So Blair left me with the poet, who seemed to have forgiven me and was ready for the hazards of further conversation. Feeling it was better I did the talking, I began to discourse upon everything, on the fireworks, on the wildflowers of Lake Albano, on Pizzetti's sonata, on a theft in the Vatican library. His face showed clearly what matter pleased him; I experimented on it, and discovered that he was hungry for hearing things praised. He was beyond feeling indignant at abuses, beyond humor, beyond sentiment, beyond interest in any bits of antiquarian lore. Apparently for weeks together in the wretched atmosphere of the sick-room Francis had neglected to speak highly of anything and the poet wanted before he left the strange world to hear some portion of it praised. Oh, I laid it on. His eyes glowed and his hands trembled. Most of all he desired the praise of poetry. I launched upon a history of poetry, calling the singers by name, getting them wrong, assigning them to the wrong ages and languages, characterizing them with the worn epithets of an encyclopedist, and drawing upon what anecdotage I could,—all bad, but somehow marshalling the glorious throng. I spoke of Sappho; of how a line of Euripides drove mad the citizens of Abdera; of Terence pleading with audiences to come to him rather than to the tight-rope walkers; of Villon writing his mother's prayers before the great picture-book of a cathedral wall; of Milton in his old age, holding a few olives in his hand to remind himself of his golden year in Italy.

Quite suddenly in the middle of the catalogue he burst out fiercely: I was meant to be among those names. I was.

The boast must have revolted me a little and my face have shown it, for he cried again: I was. I was. But now it's too late. I want every copy of my books destroyed. Let every word die, die. When I'm dead I don't want a soul to remember me.

I murmured something about his getting well.

I know more about it than the doctor, he replied, staring at me with stern fury. I studied to be a doctor. And I watched my mother and brother die, just as I am dying now.

There was no answer for that. We sat silent. Then in a gentler voice he said:

Will you promise me something? My things weren't good enough; they were just beginning to be better. When I am dead I want you to make sure that Francis does what he promised. There must be no name on my grave. Just write: Here lies one whose name was writ in water.

There was a noise in the next room. Blair had returned with the water-colourist. We withdrew. The poet was too sick to see us again and when I came back from the country he had died and his fame had begun to spread over the whole world.

Marcantonio

L A DUCHESSA D'AQUILANERA was a Colonna and came from the conservative wing of a family that cannot forget its cardinalitial, royal and papal traditions. Her husband had come of a Tuscan house that had received its illustration by the Thirteenth Century, was praised in the histories of Machiavelli and execrated in Dante. Neither family had counted a misalliance in twenty-two generations, and even in the twenty-third incurred only such stigma as attaches to marriage with an illegitimate Medici or a Pope's "niece." The Duchess could never forget—among a thousand similar honors—that her grandfather's grandfather, Timoleo Nerone Colonna, Prince of Velletri, had carried many an insulting message to the ancestors of the present King of Italy, the old but apologetic house of Savoy; and that her father had refused a Grandeeship at the court of Spain because it had been withheld from his father; and that through herself she carried to her son the titles of Chamberlain of the Court of Naples (if there were one), Prince of the Holy Roman Empire (if that superb organization had only survived) and Duke of Brabant, a title which unfortunately reappears among the pretensions of the royal families of Spain, Belgium and France. She had the best of claims to an Altesse, and even to an Altesse Royale; at least to the Sérénissime, for her mother had been the last member of the royal family of Craburg-Hottenlingen. She had the largest cousinage outside the Buddhist priesthood. The heralds of the European courts bowed to her with a particular distinction, realizing that by some accident many diverse and lofty lines converged in her odd person.

She was fifty when I met her, a short, black-faced woman with two aristocratic wens on the left slope of her nose, yellow, dirty hands, covered with paste emeralds (an allusion to her Portuguese claims; she was Archduchess of Brazil, if Brazil had only remained Portuguese), lame with the limp that pursues the Della Quercia, just as her aunt had been epileptic with the

epilepsy of the true Vani. She lived in a tiny apartment in the Palazzo Aquilanera, Piazza Araceli, from the windows of which she watched the sumptuous weddings of her rivals, ceremonies to which she had been invited, but dared not attend, foreseeing that she would be assigned to places that fell below her pretensions; to accept a humble seat would be to admit that one had relinquished the whole bundle of vast historic claims. She had left many a great function abruptly on discovering that her chair was behind some of those Colonna cousins who had cast away all right to aristocratic distinction by marrying theatre women or Americans. She refused to be seated behind pillars among dubious Neapolitan titles—in the shadow of her own family tombs; to be left among the footmen at the door of a musicale; to be invited at the eleventh hour; and to be kept waiting in antechambers. For the most part she clung to her ugly stuffy rooms, brooding on the disregarded glories of her line and envying the splendors of her richer relatives. The fact is that from the point of view of a middle-class Italian she was not really poor; but she was too poor to afford the limousine and livery and great entertainments; to be without these and yet invested with her pretensions was to be poorer than the last nameless body fished out of the Tiber.

Recently however she had begun to receive unexpected and thrilling recognitions. Little though she went out, when she did appear in society, her austere face, her majestic limp, and her strange jewels carried conviction. People were afraid of her. The arbiters of precedence in Rome dared at last to intimate to the Odescalchi and Colonna and Sermoneta that this almost shabby little woman whom they snubbed and shoved like some half-wit poor relation, had every right to precede them at a formal function. French circles, such as had not lost all seigneurial deferences under the sponge of republicanism, recognized her ultramontane alliances. She was the first to notice the improvement in her reception, and if a bit bewildered it did not take her long to set her sails to the unexpected breeze. She had a son and daughter to advance and it was for them that she now resolved to immolate her pride. From the earliest signs of her rehabilitation she forced herself to sally out into the world, and finding that her stock was higher in the international colony she stooped distastefully to call upon the

American peeresses and on the South American represen-
tatives. Eventually she found herself at Miss Grier's midnight
suppers. The reflection of the consideration she received in
such places finally reached her own people and she was gradu-
ally spared the more obvious humiliations.

It became necessary for her now to drop her former friends,
the dull soured old women, more plaintive than herself, and
with less reason, with whom she had been accustomed to fret
away the long afternoons and evenings behind the drawn
blinds of the Piazza Araceli. She was obliged likewise to aban-
don a sordid habit that linked her no less surely to the previous
centuries, namely that of rushing into law-suits. The innate ca-
pacity for affairs which abounded in this woman had found
during the days of her obscurity this extraordinary outlet. She
went about scenting out old claims and deeds, the slips of
tradesmen and the subtle omissions of lawyers. She was always
protecting her shyer friends from imposition, and she was
always successful and often made a good deal of money. She
employed obscure boy-lawyers and when she was called upon
as a witness, relying on her distinctions to prevent her being
interrupted, she used the occasion as an opportunity to sum
up the whole case. The middle classes seeing in the morning
paper that S. A. Leda Matilda Colonna duchessa d'Aquilanera
was attacking the City of Rome over the valuation of property
near a railroad, or contesting the bill of some popular stationer
or fruiterer on the Corso, suffered willingly the inconvenience
of holding a seat in court for hours in order to see the malig-
nant resourceful woman and to hear her trenchant sarcasms
and her irresistible accumulation of evidence. Yet her relatives
had always sneered at this passion, failing to see that she rep-
resented more clearly than themselves the qualities that had
always gone to characterize the aristocracy.

It was this woman then whom we confronted when we re-
turned at midnight for our third engagement that day in the
old palace. Supper was served in a larger, brighter apartment
than I had yet seen. As I entered the huge doorway my eyes
fell upon a strange figure that I knew at once must be a Cabal-
ist. A short, dark, ugly woman, holding a cane between her
knees was staring at me with magnificent fierce eyes. With the

bodiced dress and eagle's head I became aware of her jewels, seven huge lumpy amethysts strung about her neck on a golden rope. I was presented to this witch who at once, and by the blackest art, made one like her. On hearing that Blair was leaving Rome shortly she centered her attention on me.

For a moment she sat before me, sliding the end of her stick nervously about on the floor, drawing in her upper lip, and gazing hard into my eyes. She asked me my age. I was twenty-five.

I am the Duchess d'Aquilanera, she began. What language shall we speak? I think we will talk English. I do not talk it good, but we must be plain. It must be so you must understand me quite perfectly. I am a great friend of Miss Grier. I have often talked over with her a great problem—a sorrow, my young friend—that is in my home. Suddenly tonight at seven o'clock she call me up on the telephone and told me she have found someone who could help me: she mean you. Now listen: I have a son of sixteen. He is important because he is somebody. How you say?—he is a personage. We are of a very old house. Our family has been in the front of Italy, everyone in her triumph and in her trouble. You are not sympathetic to that kind of greatness in America, no? But you must have read history, no? ancient times and the middle times and like that? You must realize how important the great families are . . . have always been to . . . countries . . .

(Here she grew nervous, and blew several bubbles and expended herself in those splendid Italian gestures denoting difficulty, perhaps futility, and resignation before the impossible. I hastened to assure her that I had great respect for the aristocratic principle.)

Perhaps you have and perhaps you haven't, she said at last. In all events, think of my son as a prince whose blood contains all sorts of kings and noble people. Well, now I must tell you he has fallen in bad ways. Some women have got hold of him and I do not know him any more. All our boys in Italy go that way when they are sixteen, but Marcantonio, my God, I do not know what is the matter with him and I shall go crazy. Now in America you are all descended from your Puritans, are you not, and your ideas are very different. There is only one thing to do, and that is: you must save my boy. You must talk

to him. You must play tennis with him. I have talked to him; the priest has talked to him, and a good friend of mine, a Cardinal, has talked to him and still he does nothing but go to that dreadful place. Elizabeth Grier says that most boys in America at your age are just . . . naturally . . . good. You are *vieilles filles*; you are as temperate as I do not know what. It's very strange, if it's true, and I do not think I believe it; at all events it's not wise. At all events you must talk to Marcantonio and make him stay away from that dreadful place or we shall go mad. My plan is this: next Wednesday we are going for a week to our beautiful villa in the country. It is the most beautiful villa in Italy. You must come with us. Marcantonio will begin to admire you, you can play tennis and shoot and swim and then you can have long talks and you can save him. Now, won't you do that for me, because no one has ever come to you in such trouble as I have come to you in today?

Hereupon, in sudden fear that all her efforts had been in vain, she began waving her stick to attract Miss Grier's attention. That lady had been watching us from a corner of her eye and now came running up. The Duchess burst into a flood of tears, crying into her pocket handkerchief: Elisabetta, speak to him. Oh, my God, I have failed. He not want us and all is lost.

I was divided between anger and laughter and kept muttering into Miss Grier's ear: I'd be glad to meet him, Miss Grier, but I can't lecture the fellow. I'd feel like a fool. Besides what would I do with a whole week. . . .

She's put it to you wrongly, said Miss Grier. Let's not say anything more about it tonight.

At this the Black Queen began rolling about in her chair, the motions preparatory to rising. She rammed her stick against my shoe for leverage on the polished floor and stood up. We must pray to God to find another way. I am a fool. I do not blame the young man. He cannot realize the importance of our family.

Nonsense, Leda, said Miss Grier, firmly in Italian. Be quiet a moment. Then turning to me: Would you like to pass a weekend at the Villa Colonna-Stiavelli, or not? There's no stipulation about lecturing the Prince. If you like him, you'll feel like talking to him anyway, and if you don't like him, you're welcome to leave him alone.

Two Cabalists were begging me to take a glimpse of the most famous of Renaissance villas, one moreover that was obstinately closed to the public and that had to be peered at from the road half a mile away. I turned to the Duchess and bowing low accepted her invitation. Whereupon she kissed the shoulder of my coat, murmured with a beautiful smile: Christiano! Christiano! and bidding us goodnight, passed bowing from the room.

I shall see you Sunday at Tivoli, said Miss Grier, and tell you all about it there.

During the next few days my mind lay under the dread of the two engagements that lay ahead of me: the week-end at the Villa Horace and the missionary enterprise at the Villa Colonna. I stayed in my rooms, depressed, reading a little, or took long walks through the Trasteverine underworld, thinking about Connecticut.

The car that called for me Saturday morning already contained a fellow-guest. He introduced himself as M. Léry Bogard, adding that Mlle. de Morfontaine had offered to send for us separately, but that he had taken the liberty of requesting that we be called for together, not only because any company in crossing the Campagna is better than none, but because he had heard many things of me that led him to believe that we would not be uncongenial. I replied in that language wherein all courtesy sounds sincere, that the possibility of being congenial to so distinguished a member of the French Academy and to so profound a scholar was a greater honor than I dared hope for. These overtures did not tend to chill the encounter. M. Bogard was a fragile elderly gentleman, immaculately dressed. His face was delicately tinted by exquisite reading and expensive food, russet and violet about the eyes, his cheeks a pale plum from which rose the ivory-white of his nose and chin. His manner was soft and conciliatory, expressed for the most part in the play of his eyelids and hands, both of which fluttered in unison like petals about to fall upon the breeze. I spoke hesitantly of the pleasure I had derived from his works, especially from those pages, so faintly tinctured with venom, on Church History. But now he cried out at once: Do not mention them! My early indiscretions! Horrible! What would

I not give to withdraw them. Can that nonsense have reached as far as America? You must let your friends know, young man, that those books no longer represent my attitude. Since then I have become an obedient son of the Church and nothing would give me greater comfort than to hear that they had been burned.

What may I tell my friends now represents your real views? I asked.

Why read me at all? he cried in mock grief. There are too many books in the world already. Let us read no more, my son. Let us seek out some congenial friends. Let us sit about a table (well-spread, pardi!) and talk of our church and our king and perhaps of Virgil.

My face must have shown a trace of the suffocation I experienced at this plan of life, for M. Bogard became at once more impersonal. The country we are traversing now, he said, has known stirring times . . . and he began an instructive travelogue, as though I were some stupid acquaintance, his hostess' son, and as though he were not, nor ever had been, a distinguished scholar.

On arriving at the Villa we were met by the steward and shown to our rooms. The Villa had been a monastery for many years and in purchasing it Mlle. de Morfontaine had obtained likewise the adjoining church which still served the peasants of the hillside. She claimed that the Villa was the very one that Maecenas had given to Horace: local tradition affirmed it; the foundations were of the best opus reticulatum; and the location fulfilled the rather vague requirements of classical allusion; even onomatopoeia testified, declared our hostess, asserting that from her window the waterfall could be literally heard to lisp

". . . domus Albuniae resonantis
Et praeceps Anio ac Tiburni locus et uda
Mobilibus pomaria rivis."

In furnishing her monastery our hostess had combined, as best she could, a delight in esthetic effects and a longing for severity. A long low rambling plaster building, without grace of line, was the Villa Horace. Disordered rose gardens surrounded it, with intentionally neglected gravel paths, and chipped marble benches. One entered a long hall at the end of

which several steps descended to a library. The hall was lined
with doors at regular intervals on both sides, doors to what
had once been cells now thrown together into reception
rooms. Many of these doors stood open during the day and
the long corridor, paved with russet tile, was striped with the
sunshine that fell across it. The ceiling had been coffered, and
like the doors touched with dark green and gilt, and with that
rich wasted brick-red that is the color of Neapolitan tiles. The
walls were yellow white, of caked and crumbling plaster, and
the beauty of the view with the optical illusion of distance and
the depth and the lightness of the library seen like some great
green-golden well at the further end, appealed to that sense of
balance and one's tactile imagination as do the vistas in the
paintings of Raphael whose spell is said to reside in that secret.
To the left lay the reception rooms, carpeted in one color,
hung with tabernacles and Italian primitives, while huge can-
delabra, pots of flowers and tables covered with brocades and
crystals and uncut jewels, relieved the severity of unfreshened
walls. Towards the end of the hall at the right one ascended a
few steps to the refectory, the barest room in the house. By
day the refectory was a meaningless casual club-room. Lunch-
eon was a negligible affair at the Villa; one's conversation
must be saved for dinner; at luncheon one barely looked at one
another, one talked about the last rains and the next drought,
or any subject that did not faintly allude to the devouring pas-
sions of the house, religion and aristocracy and literature. The
beauty of the refectory was purely a matter of lighting and at
eight o'clock the greatness of the room lay in the pool of wine-
yellow light that was shed on the red table cloth, the dark
green crested plates, the silver and the gold, the wineglasses,
the gowns and decorations of the guests, the ambassadorial
ribbons, the pontifical violets, and the little army of satin-clad
footmen that suddenly appeared from nowhere.

 On the night of my arrival the Cardinal was the last to ap-
pear at dinner, and entered directly into the refectory where
we stood waiting for him. His expression was benignant, even
beaming. While he blessed the meal, Mlle. de Morfontaine
knelt on her admirable yellow gown and M. Bogard dropped
on one knee and shaded his eyes. The grace was in English, a

strange affair discovered by our erudite guest among the literary remains of some disappointed Cambridge parson.

Oh, pelican of eternity,
That piercest thy heart for our food,
We are thy fledglings that cannot know thy woe.
Bless this shadowy and visionary food of substance,
Whose last eater shall be worm,
And feed us rather with the vital food of
Dreams and grace.

The Cardinal, though unimpaired in mind and body, looked all of his eighty years. The expression of dry serenity that never left his yellow face with its drooping moustache and pointed beard gave him the appearance of a Chinese sage that has lived a century. He was born of peasants on the plain between Milan and Como, and had begun his education at the hands of the local priests who soon discovered in him a veritable genius for latinity. He was passed upward from school to school gaining in his progress all the prizes the Jesuits had to offer. The attention of a large body of influential churchmen was gradually drawn to him and at the time of his graduation from the great college on the Piazza Santa Maria sopra Minerva (presenting a thesis of unparalleled brilliance and futility on the forty-two cases in which suicide is permissible and the twelve occasions on which a priest may take up arms without danger of homicide) a choice between three great careers was offered to him. The details of each had been prepared under the highest patronage: he might become a fashionable preacher; or one of the courtier-secretaries of the Vatican; or a learned teacher and disputant. To the amazement and grief of his professors he suddenly announced his intention of following a road that to them meant ruin; he declared for Missions. His foster-fathers raged and wept and called on heaven to witness his ingratitude; but the boy would hear of nothing less than the Church's most dangerous post in Western China. Thither in due time he departed with scarcely a blessing from his teachers who had already turned their attention to more docile if less brilliant pupils. Through fire, famine, riots, and even torture, the young

priest labored for twenty-five years in the province of Sze-
chuen. This missionary fever however did not entirely spring
from piety. The boy, conscious of the great powers raging
within him, had been throughout his youth insolent, con-
temptuous of his teachers and of his companions. He knew
and despised every type of a churchman to be found in Italy;
never had he seen a thing adequately done by them, and now
he dreamed of a field of work where he would be answerable
to no fool. In the whole realm of the Church there was only
one region that filled his requirements; a month's travelling by
crude wagon separates one from the next priest in Sze-chuen.
There, then, after a shipwreck, some months of slavery, and
other experiences that he never related, but which reached the
world from his native helpers, he settled in an inn, dressed as a
native, grew a pigtail, and lived among the villagers for six
years without mentioning his faith. He passed the time studying
the language, the classics, the manners, ingratiating himself with
the officials and so perfectly identifying himself with the daily
life of the city that in time he all but lost the odor of foreign-
ness. When at last he began to declare his mission to those
merchants and officials in whose homes he had become an
almost nightly visitor his work was rapid. Perhaps the greatest of
all the Church's missionaries since the Middle Age, he turned
many a compromise that was destined to shock Rome pro-
foundly. He somehow achieved a harmonization of Chris-
tianity and the religions and accepted ideas of China that had
its parallel only in those daring readings that Paul discovered
in his Palestinian cult. So subtle were the priest's adaptations
that it never occurred to his first converts to be even conscious
of repudiating their old faith until at last after twenty lectures
he showed them how far they had gone and how charred were
the bridges that lay behind them. Once he had them baptized
however, he could give them only the bitterest bread to eat:
the foundations of his cathedral lay squarely on a score of mar-
tyrs' graves, but once built suffered no further assault and grew
slowly and irresistibly. Finally sheer statistics did what envy
could not prevent and he was made a bishop. At the end of his
fifteenth year in the East he returned to Rome for the first time
and was received with cold dislike. His health had been partly
undermined, and he was granted a year's repose, during which

he worked in the Vatican library on a thesis relative to nothing in China, the donation of Constantine. This was considered shocking in a missionary and when it was published its learning and impersonality won it the neglect of the ecclesiastical reviewers. He was treated with condescension by the courtiers of the Palace; by implication they described to him their idea of his great creation in Western China: a low mud-brick meeting-house and a congregation of beggars who pretended to a conversion in order to be fed. He did not trouble to describe to them the stone cathedral with two awkward but lofty towers, the vast porch, the schools and library and hospital; the processions on Feast days carrying garish but ardent banners entering the great cavern of the Church and singing the correctest Gregorian; nor of the governmental honors, the tax-exemptions, the military respect during revolutions, the co-operation of the city.

At last he returned, willingly enough, to sink himself for another ten years into the remote interior. His visit to Rome had not altered his boyish attitude toward his fellowmen. He had heard strange tales about himself,—how he had amassed a huge fortune by taking bribes from the Chinese merchants, how he had interpreted the atonement in Buddhist terms and had allowed pagan symbols to be stamped upon the Host itself.

The ecclesiastical honors that eventually arrived must have been extravagantly deserved, for they came without his or any friend's negotiation. Sheer accomplishment must so have stared the Vatican in the face that it had felt torn from its hands the trophies it was accustomed to relinquish only on the receipt of petitions bearing ten thousand signatures or at the instance of wealth or power. To receive these new distinctions, the Bishop returned to Rome again after an absence of ten years. This time he meant to remain in Italy, having decided that henceforth his work would be better in the hands of natives. The ecclesiastics viewed this return with considerable trepidation, for if he returned as a scholar eager for doctrinal debates they dreaded seeing exposed their lack of interest or equipment; if he came as a critic of the Propaganda, they were all in danger. They watched him settle down with two Chinese servants and an absurd peasant woman whom he insisted on referring to as his sister, in a tiny villa on the Janiculum, join the Papal

Archaeological Society and apply himself to reading and gardening. Within five years his retirement had become a greater embarrassment to the Church than his pamphlets might have been. His fame among Romanists outside Rome was unbounded; every distinguished visitor rushed from the station to get an introduction to the recluse of Janiculum; the Pope himself was a little tried by the zeal of visitors who imagined that His Holiness enjoyed nothing better than discussing the labors, the illness, and the modesty of the Cathedral Builder of China. English Catholics and American Catholics and Belgian Catholics who did not understand the exquisite subtlety of these matters and should let them alone, kept crying: Why isn't something being done for him? He humbly refused a high honorary Librarianship in the Vatican, but his refusal was not accepted and his name crowned the stationery; the same thing happened with the great committees on Propaganda; he did not appear at the meetings, but no speech was so influential as the report of chance words let fall in conversation with disciples at the Villino Wei Ho. His very lack of ambition frightened the Churchmen; they supposed it must arise from a similar emotion to that which kept Achilles sulking in his tent, and dreaded the moment when he would ultimately arise, swinging his mighty prestige and crush them for the honors they begrudged him; finally he was offered the Hat, by a committee from the College all in a perspiration lest he refuse it. This time he accepted their offer and went through the forms with a rigid decorum and with an observance of traditional minutiae that had to be elaborately explained to his Irish American colleagues.

It would be hard to say what his thoughts were those clear mornings as he sat among his flowers and rabbits, a volume of Montaigne fallen on to the gravel path from the tabouret beside him, what were his thoughts as he gazed at his yellow hands and listened to the hushed excitement of the Aqua Paola exclaiming in eternal praise of Rome. He must surely have asked himself often in what year his faith and joy had fled. Some said that he had become attached to a convert who had relapsed into paganism; some said that one day under torture he had renounced Christianity to save his life from the hands of brigands. Perhaps it was only that he had attempted the hardest

task in the world and found it not so difficult after all; and reflecting that he could have built up a huge fortune in the financial world with half the energy and one-tenth the gifts; that he was the only person living who could write a Latin that would have entranced the Augustans; that he was the last man who would be able to hold in his head at one moment all the learning of the Church; and that to become a Prince of the Church required nothing but a devoted indifference to its workings,—reflecting on these things he may well have felt the world not to be worth the thunder of admiration and applause that was so continually mounting to Heaven in its praise. Perhaps one of the other stars is more worthy of one's best efforts.

Grace concluded, the meal could not be begun until the Cardinal was informed as to Alix. But where's Alix?

Alix is always late.

Are you sure she's coming?

She telephoned this afternoon, that . . .

Now isn't that too bad of her! She's coming in panting when the dinner's half over. Then apologies. Father, you're too kind to her. You always forgive her directly. You must act cross.

We must all act cross.

Everybody look angry when Alix comes in.

I had assumed that the conversation of the Cabala *in camera* would be vertiginous. If I anticipated the wit and eloquence of its table-talk I dreaded their gradual discovery that I was tongue-tied or doltish. When, therefore, the conversation at last broke forth I had the mixed sensation of discovering that it was not unlike that of a house party on the Hudson. Wait, I told myself, they will warm up. Or perhaps it is my presence here that prevents them from being at their best. I recalled the literary tradition that the gods of antiquity had not died but still drifted about the earth shorn of the greater part of their glory—Jupiter and Venus and Mercury straying through the streets of Vienna as itinerant musicians, or roaming the South of France as harvesters. Casual acquaintances would not be able to sense their supernaturalism; the gods would take good care to dim their genius but once the outsider had gone would lay aside their cumbersome humanity and relax in the reflections of their ancient godhead. I told myself that I was the

obstacle, that these Olympians chattered and chaffed for a sea-
son until my departure, when the air would change,—what di-
vine conversation. . . .

Presently in burst their Alix, the Princess d'Espoli, panting
and a-flutter with apologies. She knelt to the Cardinal's sap-
phire. No one looked the least bit cross. The very servants
beamed. We are to know a great deal about the Princess later;
suffice it to say that she was a Frenchwoman of the utmost
smallness and elegance, sandy-haired, pretty, and endowed
with a genius for conversation in which every shade of wit,
humor, pathos and even tragic power followed in close succes-
sion. Within a few moments she was enchanting the company
with a lot of nonsense about a horse who had started talking
on the Pincian Hill and the efforts of the Police Force to sup-
press such an aberration of nature. As I was presented to her
she murmured quickly: Miss Grier told me to tell you that she
will be here at about ten-thirty.

After dinner Mme. Bernstein played the piano for a time.
She was still the power behind the great German banking house.
Without ever venturing into her sons' offices or directors'
meetings she yet disposed of all the larger decisions of the firm
by curt remarks at their dinner tables, by postscripts to her
letters and by throaty injunctions at the moment of saying
goodnight. She wanted the sensation of having retired from its
direction; her whole middle life had been expended in a mag-
nificent display of generalship and financial imagination, yet
she could not keep her mind off its problems. The friendship
of the Cabala was beginning to reconcile her to advancing age,
and drawing her further and further into her love for music.

As a girl she had often heard Liszt and Tausig in her
mother's home; by dint of never playing Schumann or Brahms
she had kept her fingers all silver and crystal, and even now,
practically in her old age, she evoked the great era of virtuosi,
a time when the orchestra had not led piano technique into a
desperate imitation of brass and strings. Mlle. de Morfontaine
sat holding in the cup of her hand the muzzle of one or other
of her splendid dogs. Her eyes were filled with tears, but
whether they were the facile tears of her half-mad nature or the
witness of memories brought back on the tide of Chopin's
sonata, we cannot know. The Cardinal had retired early and

the Princess sat in the shadows, not listening to the music, but pursuing some of the phantoms of her most secretive mind.

Barely had the army with banners ceased drilling in the wintry sunlight of the last movement when a servant whispered to me that the Cardinal wished to see me.

I found him in the first of the two small rooms that had been set aside for him at the Villa. He was writing a letter, standing up to it at one of those high desks known to the clerks of Dickens and the illuminators of the Middle Age. I was later to receive many of those famous letters, never more nor less than four pages long, never falling short of their amazing suavity, never very witty nor vivid yet never untouched from beginning to end by the quality of their composer's mind. Whether he declined an invitation or suggested a reading of Freud's book on Leonardo, or gave suggestions on the feeding of rabbits, always from the first sentence he foresaw his last and always like a movement from Mozart's chamber-music the whole unit lay under one spirit and the perfection of details played handmaid to the perfection of the form. He seated me in a chair that suffered all the light that was in the room, treating himself to a fine shadow.

He began by saying that he had heard that I was to keep an eye on Donna Leda's son for a while.

I became warm and unintelligible in an effort at protesting that I could guarantee nothing; that I was most reluctant; and that I still reserved the right to withdraw at any moment.

Let me tell you about him, he began. Perhaps I should say first that I am a sort of old uncle in the family, and their confessor for many years. Well,—this Marcantonio. What shall I say? Have you seen him?

No.

The boy is full of good things. He . . . he . . . Full of good things. Perhaps that's his trouble. You say you haven't met him yet?

No.

Everything seemed to start well. He was good in his studies. He made a lot of friends. He was particularly good in the ceremonial that his rank requires, his attendance at Court and at the Vatican. His mother was a little anxious about his boyish dissipations. She had his father in mind, I suspect, and wanted

the boy to get over them as soon as possible. Donna Leda is a more than usually foolish woman. She was very pleased when he set up his own apartment off on the Via Po and became very secretive about it.

Here the Cardinal began to grope about again, perhaps surprised at his own awkwardness. Presently however he gathered up the reins with new determination and said: And then, my dear young man, something went wrong. We thought he would go through the usual experience of a Roman young man of his class and come out. But he has never come out. Perhaps you can tell me why this young fellow couldn't have had his five or six little affairs and gotten over it?

I showed myself as quite unequal to answering this question. In fact I was so amazed at the five or six little liaisons for a boy of sixteen, that it was all I could do to keep my face casual. I wanted badly not to appear shocked and endeavored by a lift of an eyebrow to imply that the boy might have a score if he liked.

Marcantonio, continued the priest, went around with a group of boys older than himself. His greatest wish was to be like them. You could see them at the races, in the music-halls, at Court, in the tea-rooms and hotel lobbies. They wore monocles and American hats, and all they talked about was women and their own successes. Euh . . . perhaps I should begin at the beginning.

There was a pause.

He was first initiated—perhaps I should use a stronger word —on Lake Como. He used to play tennis with some very warm little South American girls, heiresses from Brazil, I believe, from whom no secrets were hid. I fancy our Tonino merely meant to pay them a shy compliment or two, a sudden kiss under the laurel-bushes. But he soon found himself with a little . . . a sort of Rubens riot on his hands. Well, it began in imitation of his older friends. From imitation it went to an exercise of vanity. What was Vanity became Pleasure. Pleasure became a Habit. Habit became a Mania. And that's where he is now.

There was another pause.

You must have heard of how certain insane persons become enormously intelligent—that is, they become sly and secretive

—trying to conceal their delusion from their guards? Yes; and I am told that vicious children perform feats of duplicity worthy of the most expert criminals, in an effort to conceal their tricks from their parents. You have heard of such things? Well, that is where Marcantonio is now. What can be done? Some people would say that we should let him go and make himself thoroughly sick. Perhaps they are right, but we should like to step in before that, if possible. Especially since there has come a new development into the story.

My mood at that moment was overwhelmingly against new developments. In the distance I could hear that Mme. Bernstein had resumed her Chopin. I would have given a lot for the power of being rude enough to leap for the doorknob and bid my host goodnight, a long goodnight to the wallowing little Prince and his mother.

Yes, continued the Cardinal, his mother has at last found a marriage for him. To be sure she does not believe there is a house in the world that can bring any new distinction to her own, but she has found a girl with an old name and some money and expects me to do the rest. But the girl's brothers know Marcantonio. They are in the group I described to you. They refuse to permit the marriage until Marcantonio has, well —been quiet for a while.

Now my face must have shown a rich mixture of horror and amusement and anger and astonishment, for the Cardinal became perplexed. You never can tell what will surprise an American, he probably said to himself.

No, no. Excuse me, Father. I can't, I can't.

What do you mean?

You want me to go to the country to hold him down to a few weeks of temperance. I don't understand how you can mean such a thing, but you do. He's a sort of Strassburg goose whom you want to stuff with virtue, don't you, against his marriage. Don't you see . . . ?

You exaggerate!

Excuse me if I sound rude, Father: No wonder you couldn't make an impression on the boy,—you didn't believe in what you were saying. You don't really believe in temperance.

Believe in it. Of course I do. Am I not a priest?

Then why not make the boy . . . ?

But after all, *we are in the world.*

I laughed. I shouted with a laughter that would have been insulting, if it hadn't contained a touch of hysteria. Oh, I thank thee, dear Father Vaini, I said to myself. I thank thee for that word. How clear it makes all Italy, all Europe. *Never try to do anything against the bent of human nature.* I came from a colony guided by exactly the opposite principle.

Excuse me, Father, I said at last. I can't go on with it. Under any conditions I should feel an awful hypocrite talking to the boy. But if I knew it were only a measure to keep him good a month or two I should feel ten times more so. It can't be argued; it's just a matter one feels. I must tell Miss Grier I cannot visit her friend. She is driving out here at ten-thirty. If you will excuse me I shall go and find her in the music-room now.

Do not be angry with me, my son. Perhaps you are right. Probably I do not believe these things.

Hardly had I re-entered the music-room with my revolt written all over me when the Princess d'Espoli came forward. By that telepathy which the Cabala employed in its affairs she already knew that I had to be persuaded all over again. She made me sit down beside her and with the briefest outlay of those gifts of suppliance and enchantment of which she held the secret, she won my promise. In two minutes she had made it seem the most natural thing in the world that I should play stern older brother to a gifted drifting friend of hers.

As by the click of some invisible stage-manager Miss Grier entered.

How are you, how are you? she said, trailing her russet draperies across the tiles toward me. You can't guess who drove me out. I must hurry back. The Lateran choir is coming to sing Palestrina to me about twelve,—perhaps you know the motets from the Song of Songs? No? Marcantonio brought me here. He loves high-powered cars, and as his mother can't give him one I let him play with mine. Can you come out and meet him now? You'd better get your coat. Do you like night rides?

She led me out to the road where behind two blinding headlights a motor was humming impatiently. Antonino, she called. This is an American friend of your mother's. Do show him the car for half an hour, will you? Don't kill anybody.

An incredibly slight and definite little elegant, looking exactly his sixteen years, with spark-like black eyes bowed stiffly to me in the faint light over the wheel. Italian princes do not rise at the approach of ladies.

Don't hurt my car or my friend, Marcantonio.

No.

Where are you going?

But he did not choose to answer and the aroused motor drowned out the lady's questions. For ten minutes we sat in silence while the road rose to the headlights. After a harrowing struggle with his own selfishness Don Marcantonio asked me if I wanted to take the wheel. Assured that nothing would alarm me more, he settled down to driving with an almost voluptuous application. He made nice distinctions with grades and corners, took long descents cantabilemente, and played scherzi on cobblestones. The outlines of the Alban hills stood out against the stars that like a swarm of golden bees recalled that haughty Barberini who had declared that the sky itself was the scutcheon of his house. All lights were out on the farms, but occasionally we passed through a village whose francobollo shop showed a lantern and a group of card players. Many a wakeful soul in those enormous family beds must have turned over, crossing himself, at the sighing whistle of our flight.

Presently however the driver wanted to talk. He asked a great many questions about the United States. Could one plunge into the life of the Wild West any minute? Were there many big cities as big as Rome? What language was spoken in San Francisco? in Philadelphia? Where did our athletes train for the Olympic Games? Was the public allowed to watch them? Did I know about such things? I replied that at school and college one couldn't help picking up hints on form and training. He then disclosed the fact that at the Villa Colonna he had directed the gardeners to make a running-track, cinders and hurdles and pit and shed and embanked corners. And that we were to use it every morning. He dreamed of himself doing incredible distances in incredible time. He outlined a plan to me whereby under my direction he would begin by running a mile every morning, and should add a half-mile daily for weeks. This would go on for years and then he would be ready to enter the Paris Olympics of 1924.

In my head the nerves of astonishment had been a little fatigued lately, what with Mlle. de Morfontaine and her Ecumenical Council, the Cardinal and his tolerances, Miss Grier and her cereals. But I confess they received no small twinge when this frail and emptied spirit announced his candidacy for a world's record in long runs. Not without sly intention I began to outline the sacrifices that such an ambition would entail. I touched on diet and early hours and early rising; he accepted them eagerly. I then skirted those self-denials that would touch him more particularly, and now with a mounting exaltation, with an almost religious fire, he pledged himself to all temperance. The fact that I was astonished shows my immaturity. I thought I was witness to a great conversion. I told myself that he wanted to be saved; that he was rolling up outside forces that might protect himself from his weakness; and that he hoped to find in athletics a deliverance from despair.

Returning to the Villa we found the company still listening to music. As we entered the room all eyes were turned towards us and I knew that for the present the Cabala had laid aside all activity and was brooding over one thing, the rescue of Donna Leda's son.

On arriving at my rooms in Rome I found several notes from a Mr. Perkins of Detroit, a successful manufacturer who had crossed with me. Mr. Perkins, descending upon Italy for the first time, was resolved to see it at its best. There were no collections so private but that he was able to secure letters of admittance; no savants too occupied but that he obtained their services as ciceroni; audiences he obtained with the Pope were, as he called them, "super-special"; excavations not yet open to the public suffered his disappointed peerings. Some secretary at the Embassy must have mentioned that I had already made some Italian acquaintances, for there were these notes from him reminding me that he wanted to know some real Italians. He wanted to see what they were like in their homes, and he expected me to show him some. Mind, real Italians. I wrote him at once that all the Italians I knew were half French or half American, but assured him that when I had actually isolated a native I would bring them together. I added that I was leaving for the country, but would return in a week or two and see what could be done.

*

To the country then I went, being driven for the greater
part of a day by Marcantonio himself. His enthusiasm for run-
ning had by no means abated; in fact it seemed to have gone
from strength to strength, probably because of some lapses
from strict training in the interval. It was late afternoon and a
red sunset was filtering through a blue dusk when we entered
the great gates of the park. There was first a forest of oaks;
then a mile of open lawn with some hurrying sheep; then a
pineta with a brook; the farmhouses in a cloud of doves; the
upper terrace with a perspective of fountains; and at last the
casino with the Black Queen trailing her garments of dusty
serge across the driveway of powdered shell. There was little
time to admire the orange-brown front of the villa roughened
with wreaths and garlands that were crumbling away before the
sun and rain, or the famous frieze of the women in Ariosto's
poems, recalling the days when Pope Sylvester Lefthand held
here his academy and invented the Sylvestrian sonnet-form. All
I could do was to conceal my pleasure at the discovery that I
was to live by candle-light in rooms that though the originals
of hundreds of bad copies on Long Island, were here the
secret shame of their owners. My hosts' ideal of residence was
a hotel on the Embankment and they all but breathed an apol-
ogy for the enormous rooms to which I was conducted, and in
which I stood transfixed, lost in antiquarian dreams until Mar-
cantonio knocked on the door to call me to supper.

At table I was presented to Donna Julia, Marcantonio's half-
sister, and to a spinster cousin of the family, always present,
always silent and whose lips never ceased moving, as solitaries'
must, to the measure of her inner thoughts. Like all girls of her
class Donna Julia had never been alone for more than a half-
hour in all her life. Her immense talents for being bad had been
balked at every turn; they had been forced to take refuge in her
eyes. She had never even been allowed to read anything more
inflammatory than the comedies of Goldoni and *I Promessi
Sposi*, but she guessed at a criminal world and presently when
marriage suddenly opened up to her every freedom she played
her part in it. Donna Julia was a little stiff, almost ugly with her
level baleful regard. She kept silent most of the time, was ut-
terly incurious of me, and seemed chiefly occupied in angling

for her brother's evasive glance so as to plant into it a triumphant significant idea.

One retired early at the Villa Colonna. But Marcantonio, for whom my simplest remarks were astonishing, would stop in at my room and talk for hours over some glasses of Marsala. No doubt his mother, noting the visits through her half-opened door down the hall, assumed with great satisfaction that I was reading lectures on hygiene. But, especially as the week advanced, we were chiefly taken up with a diagram that showed day by day how the little champion had run and in what time.

It must have been at the end of a week of this that in one of our late conversations his friendliness suddenly turned into contempt. A week's preoccupation with unsentimental matters now took its revenge. Back into his mind flooded the images of passion, and he wanted to boast. Perhaps he saw that prowess on the field was not to be his, and his egoism being athirst for all possible superlatives, he must replace it with a catalogue of the first prizes he had won in another arena. He recalled the Brazilian girls under the arbors of Como. He described how he had returned to Rome after that initiation bent on seeing whether the game was as easy as it had seemed. Suddenly his eyes had been opened to a world he had not dreamed of. So it was true that men and women were never really engaged in what they appeared to be doing, but lived in a world of secret invitations, signals and escapes! Now he understood the raised eyebrows of waitresses and the brush of the usher's hand as she unlocks the loge. It is not an accident that the wind draws the great lady's scarf across your face as you emerge from the door of the hotel. Your mother's friends happen to be passing in the corridor outside the drawing-room, but not by chance. Now he discovered that all women were devils, but foolish ones, and that he had entered into the true and only satisfactory activity in living—the pursuit of them. One minute he was exclaiming at the easiness of it; the next he described its difficulties and subtlety. Now he sang the uniformity of their weakness and now the endless variety of their temperaments. Next he boasted of his utter indifference and his superiority to them; he knew their tears but he did not believe they really suffered. He doubted whether they had souls.

To incidents that were true he added others that he wished

had been true. To his acquaintance with a corner of Rome he added a fourteen-year-old's vision of a civilization where no one thought about anything but caresses. This fantasy took him about two hours. I listened without a word. It must have been this that undermined his exhilaration. He had been talking to impress me. Impressed I certainly was; no New Englander could help it; but I knew that a great deal depended on my not showing it. Perhaps it was his sudden realization that, seen through my eyes, these adventures were not enviable; perhaps it was that the black tide of reaction licked close on the heels of such pride; perhaps it was just truth finding room for utterance in his mounting fatigue,—at all events, there was strength left for one more outburst: I hate them all! I hate it. There's no end to it all. What shall I do? And he fell on his knees beside the bed and buried his face in the side of the mattress, his hands feverishly pulling at the cover.

Priests and doctors must often hear the cry Save me! Save me! I was destined to hear it from two other souls before my Roman year was over. Who now thinks it uncommon?

I scarcely know what I said when my turn at last came around. All I know is that my mind whipped up to its subject with a glee. Heaven only knows what New England divines lent me their remorseless counsels. I became possessed with the wine of the Puritans and alternating the vocabulary of the Pentateuch with that of psychiatry I showed him where his mind was already slipping: I pointed out wherein he already resembled his uncle Marcantonio, no mean warning; I made him see that even his interest in athletics was a symptom of his disintegration; how that he was incapable of fixing his mind on the general interests of man, and how everything he thought and did—humor, sports, ambition—presented themselves to him as symbols of lust.

My little tirade was effective beyond all expectation and for a number of reasons. In the first place, it had the energy and sincerity which the Puritan can always draw upon to censure those activities he cannot permit himself,—not a Latin demonstration of gesture and tears, but a cold hate that staggers the Mediterranean soul. Again, all my words had already their dim counterpart in the boy's soul. It is the libertine and not the preacher who conceives most truly of the ideal purity and

soundness, because he pays it out, coin by coin, regretfully, knowingly, unpreventably. All my words went to rejoin their prototypes in Marcantonio's mind. Again, how could I know that he had arrived but recently at that stage of failure when one's whole being reverberates, as with some bell of despair, with the words: I shall never get out of this. I am lost. Again, I found out later that Marcantonio had a streak of religious frenzy in him, that for a year he had watched himself alternating communion and dissipation, the exaltation of the former itself betraying him into the latter and the despair of the latter driving him in anguish to the former. At last in sheer cynicism, after watching himself fail so often, he had missed Mass for several months. All these reasons go toward explaining the prostrating effect my brief and vindictive speech had. He cowered against the carpet, begging me to stop, gasping out his promises of reform. But having brought him to a conviction he might never attain again, I thought it unwise to let go. I had reserves of indignation left. But now he knelt crying on the carpet, covering his ears with his hands and shaking his wet face at me with all its terror and suppliance. I stopped and we stared at one another, darkly, trembling under our several headaches. Then he went to bed.

The next morning he seemed etherealized, made almost transparent by his new resolutions. He walked lightly and with an air of humility. No reference was made to the scene of the evening before, but his glances over the tennis net implied an obedience and a deference that were more annoying than impudence. After two sets we wandered over to the lower fountain and here stretched out on the semi-circular bench he slept for three hours. It seemed to me as I watched morning advance to noon and the sun penetrate his thin body in the delicious fatigues that follow hysterical outbursts, it seemed that it would not be rash to wonder if possibly we may have succeeded. I day-dreamed. From the formal terrace below the casino came the click of topiary shears; from the field where the ancient altar had been placed, drum-shaped and bearing an almost effaced frieze, came the shouts of some divinity students (to whom a little villa on the estate had been offered as a vacation house) playing football, their cassocks tucked up about their knees; from the pine wood the exclamations of two shepherds who

sat whittling while their flock drifted almost imperceptibly to the road beyond. The fountain before me gave forth its varied sounds: the whir of its initial jet and the tinkle as it fell back into the first bowl; the drumtaps as this overflowed and slipped into the second; and the loud loquacity with which the lowest basin received all that came to it from every level. Tacitus lay unread upon my knee while my eyes followed the lizards that flashed in and out of the brilliant sunshine on the gravel, noting their confusion when a sudden breeze bent the poised veil of the fountain and swept us all with a fine mist. The monotony of light and the noise of water, of insects, and of doves in the farmhouses behind me, combined to recall those tremulous webs of sound that modern composers set shimmering above their orchestra, to draw across it presently on the oboes their bleating melody in thirds.

While I sat there a note was brought me from the house. Mr. Perkins of Detroit had heard I was at the Villa and from the hotel in the nearby town announced his intention of calling on me,—lucky in having a pretext for entering the most inaccessible villa in Italy. I scribbled on the back of his envelope that an unfortunate event in the family prevented my asking him to the house at present.

The hot sunlight of the morning had gathered its storm and all afternoon we sat indoors. Marcantonio and Donna Julia attempted teaching me the Neapolitan dialect, while the silent cousin sat by, deeply shocked. But my lesson soon descended into a subtle and barbed quarrel between the teachers. It was conducted for the most part in rapid and hate-laden parentheses, far above my head, in their thick *argot*. What she taunted him about I can only guess. He was invariably beaten; he grew loud and angry. Twice he leaped around the table to strike her; she waited for the blow, stretching herself sleekly and looking up at him from her magnetic eyes. At length he urged me to come away from her and to go upstairs, and the two parted much as children of seven would with a bout of grimaces and a competition to have the last ugly word.

After dinner the war was resumed. The Duchess was nodding by the fire; the cousin was mumbling opposite her. And the two children sat in the shadows exchanging invective. I was made strangely uneasy by their curious quarreling. I excused

myself and went to bed. The last thing I saw was an infuriated blow that Marcantonio directed at his sister's shoulder and the last sound I heard was the tremolo of her provocative laughter as they tussled on the carved wooden chest in the corner. I debated with myself on the stairs: surely I had imagined it; my poor sick head was so full of the erotic narratives of the week; surely I imagined the character of mixed love and hate in those blows that were savage caresses, and that laughter that was half sneer and half invitation.

But I had not imagined it.

At about three I was awakened by Marcantonio. He was still dressed. He poured at my drowsy head a torrent of whirling words in which I distinguished nothing but a feverish reiteration of the phrase: You were right. Then he left the room as abruptly as he had come.

What luck Mr. Perkins had always had! Even now when he brought to bear all his American determination and broke into the gardens of the forbidden Villa, what guardian angel arranged that he should see the Villa at its most characteristic? Surely a rich old Italian villa is at its most characteristic when a dead prince lies among the rosebushes. When Frederick Perkins of Detroit leapt the wall in the crystal airs of seven in the morning, he discovered at his feet the body of Marcantonio d'Aquilanera, 14th prince and 14th duke of Aquilanera and Stoli, 12th duke of Stoli-Roccellina, marquis of Bugnaccio, of Tei, etc., baron of Spenestra, of Gran-Spenestra, seigneur of the Sciestrian Lakes; patron of the bailie of the order of San Stephano; likewise prince of Altdorf-Hottenlingen-Craburg, intendant elector of Altdorf-H-C.; prince of the Holy Roman Empire, etc., etc.; chamberlain of the court of Naples; lieutenant and cousin of the Papal Familia; order of the Crane (f. class); three hours cold, and with a damp revolver clutched in his right hand.

Alix

THE Cabalists received the news of Marcantonio's death philosophically. The account of it which the bereaved mother gave to Miss Grier was a miracle of misunderstanding. According to her I had done wonders; in fact it was the suddenness and thoroughness of the boy's reformation that had broken his health. She, *she*, was to blame. She should have foreseen that continence was not to be expected of a mere lad; he had gone insane from an excess of virtue and shot himself from too much sanctity. These things are out of our hands, dear Leda, murmured Miss Grier. The Cardinal made no comment.

The Cabala went back to its usual occupations. Being the biographer of the individuals and not the historian of the group I shall not take up much space here with details of the discomfiture of Mrs. Pole (she had been impudent to Miss Grier), nor of the Renan performance (*L'Abbesse de Jouarre* was effectively not given as a benefit at the Constanzi). From a purely disinterested love of Church tradition they blocked the canonization of several tiresome nonentities that had been proposed to gratify the faithful in Sicily and Mexico. They saved the taxpayers of Rome the purchase of hundreds of modern Italian paintings, and the establishment of a permanent museum for them. They interested public opinion in the faint smell of drains that is wafted through the Sistine Chapel. When an oak forest fell ill in the Borghese Gardens no one but the Cabala had the sense to send to Berlin for a doctor. To tell the truth their achievements were not very considerable. I soon saw that I had arrived on the scene in the middle of the decline of their power. At first they thought they could do something about the strikes, and about the Fascismo, and the blasphemies in the Senate; and it was only after a great deal of money had been spent and hundreds of persons ineffectually goaded that they realized that the century had let loose influences they could not stem, and contented themselves with less pretentious assignments.

I came to see more and more of them. My youth and

foreignness never ceased to amuse them and they were made almost uncomfortable by the knowledge that I so liked them. They thought they had outgrown being susceptible to being liked. From time to time they would point their fingers to where I sat staring at them in sheer wonder.

He's like an eager dog with his tongue out of his mouth, Alix d'Espoli would cry. What does he see in us?

He never loses hope that we will suddenly say something memorable, said the Cardinal looking at me musingly,—the look of a great talker who knows that for lack of a Boswell his greatness must die with him.

He comes from the rich new country that will grow more and more splendid while our countries decline to ruins and rubbish heaps, said Donna Leda. That's why his eyes shine so.

Why, no, cried Alix. I believe he loves us. Just simply loves us in a disinterested new world way. Once I had a most beautiful setter, named Samuele. Samuele spent all his life sitting around on the pavement watching us with a look of most intense excitement.

Did he bite? asked Donna Leda who had a literal mind.

You didn't have to give Samuele a sandwich to win his devotion. He liked to like. You won't be angry with me if every now and then I call you Samuele to remind me of him?

You mustn't talk about him in front of him, muttered Mme. Bernstein who was playing solitaire. Young man, get me my furs from the piano until these people remember themselves.

The Princess explained me. What fairer service can one render another? How could I do other than attach myself to one with so quick and gracious an interpretation.

The Princess was not really modern. As scientists gazing at certain almost extinct birds off Australia are able to evoke a whole lost era, so in the person of this marvellous princess we felt ourselves permitted to glimpse into the Seventeenth Century and to reconstruct for ourselves what the aristocratic system must have been like in its flower.

The Princess d'Espoli was exceedingly pretty in a fragile Parisian way; her vivacious head, surmounted by a mass of sandy reddish hair, was forever tilted above one or other of her thin pointed shoulders; her whole character lay in her sad laughing eyes and small red mouth. Her father came of the Provençal

nobility and she had spent her girlhood partly in provincial convent schools and partly climbing like a goat the mountains that surrounded her father's castle. At eighteen she and her sister had been called in from the cliffs, dressed up stiffly and hawked like merchandise through the drawing-rooms of their more influential relatives in Paris, Florence, and Rome. Her sister had fallen to an automobile manufacturer and was making the good and bad weather of Lyons; Alix had married the morose Prince d'Espoli who had immediately sunk into a profounder misanthropy. He remained at home sunk in the last dissipations. His wife's friends never saw or referred to him; occasionally we became aware of him, we thought, in her late arrivals, hurried departures and harassed air. She had lost two children in infancy. She had no life, save in other people's homes. Yet the sum of her sufferings had been the production of the sweetest strain of gaiety that we shall ever see, a pure well of heartbroken frivolity. Wonderful though she was in all the scenes of social life, she certainly was at her finest at table, where she had graces and glances that the most gifted actresses would fall short of conceiving for their Millamants, and Rosalinds and Célimènes; nowhere has been seen such charm, such manners, and such wit. She would prattle about her pets, describe a leave-taking seen by chance in a railway station, or denounce the Roman fire departments with a perfection of rendering of Yvette Guilbert, a purer perfection in that it did not suggest the theatre. She possessed the subtlest mimicry, and could sustain an endless monologue, but the charm of her gift resided in the fact that it required the collaboration of the whole company; it required the exclamations, contradictions, and even the concerted shouts as of a Shakespearean mob, before the Princess could display her finest art. She employed an unusually pure speech, a gift that went deeper than a mere aptitude for acquiring grammatical correctness in the four principal languages of Europe; its source lay in the type of her mind. Her thought proceeded complicatedly, but not without order, in long looping parentheses, a fine network of relative clauses, invariably terminating in some graceful turn by way of climax, some sudden generalization or summary surprise. I once accused her of speaking in paragraphs and she confessed that the nuns to whom she had gone to school in Provence had required

of her every day an oral essay built on a formula derived prin-
cipally from Madame de Sévigné and terminating in a *concetto.*

Such rare personalities are not able to derive nourishment
from ordinary food. Rumors of the Princess's strange stormy
loves reached us continually. It seems that she was doomed to
search throughout the corridors of Rome a succession of at-
tachments as brief and fantastic as they were passionate and
unsatisfied. Nature had decided to torment this woman by
causing her to fall in love (that succession of febrile interviews,
searches, feints at indifference, nightlong solitary monologues,
ridiculous visions of remote happiness) with the very type of
youth that could not be attracted by her, with cool impersonal
learned or athletic young Northerners, a secretary at the
British Embassy or Russian violinist or German archaeologist.
As though these trials were not sufficient, society had added to
them this aggravation, that her Roman hostesses, conscious of
this failing and wishing to make sure that at their tables the
Princess would display her finest flights, would intentionally
include among their guests the Princess's latest infatuation to
whom throughout the evening she would sing, like a swan, her
song of defeated love.

As a mere girl, if I may presume to reconstruct the growth
of her personality, she sensed the fact that there was in her
something that a little prevented her making friends, namely,
intelligence. The few intelligent people who truly wish to be
liked soon learn, among the disappointments of the heart, to
conceal their brilliance. They gradually convert their keen per-
ceptions into more practical channels,—into a whole tech-
nique of implied flattery of others, into felicities of speech, into
the euphemisms of demonstrative affection, into softening for
others the crude lines of their dullness. All the Princess's per-
fection was an almost unconscious attempt at making friends
of those who would first be her admirers, yet realizing that if
she were too artistic they would be dazzled but repelled, and
that if she were less than perfect they would dismiss her as a
trivial bright hysteric. For many years she had practiced this
babbling speech on her friends, unconsciously noting on their
faces which tones of the voice, which appropriate fleck of the
hands, which delayed adjectives were more and which less suc-
cessful. In other words she had achieved mastery of a fine art,

the all but forgotten art of conversation, under the impetus of love. Like some panic-stricken white mouse in the trap of a psychologist's experiment she had been seeking her ends by the primitive rules of trial and error, only to learn that at the last one is too bruised by the mistakes to enjoy the successes. The exquisite and fragile mechanism of her temperament had not been able to stand the strain laid upon it, the double exhaustion of inspiration and woe; and the lovely being was already slightly mad. She grew daily more light-headed and could be caught from time to time in moods that were variously foolish and pathetic. But her deepest wound was still to come.

James Blair and his notebooks were staying over in Rome after all. He had come upon some new veins of research. For him ten lifetimes would be all too short to pursue the horizons of one's curiosity. Think, he would say, it would take about ten years to work up the full critical apparatus to attack the historical problems surrounding the life of St. Francis of Assisi. It would take almost as many to get up the Roman road-system, the salt roads and the wheat roads,—God, the whole problem as to how the Rome of the Republic was fed. Another day he would be dreaming about starting on the eight or ten books in French and German on Christina of Sweden and her life in Rome; then one studied up Swedish and read the diaries and the barrels-full of notes; when one knew more about her than did anyone alive one passed on to her father and buried oneself for months in libraries to master the policies and the military genius of Gustavus Adolphus. Thus life stretched . . . bindings . . . bindings . . . catalogues . . . footnotes. One studied the saints and never thought about religion. One knew everything about Michelangelo yet never felt deeply a single work. James spent weeks of fascinated attention on the women of the Caesars and yet could scarcely be dragged to dinner at the Palazzo Barberini. He found all moderns trivial, and was the dupe of the historians' grand style which fails to convey the actuality (for Blair, the triviality) of their heroes. The present casts a veil of cheapness over the world: to look into any face, however beautiful, is to see pores and the folds about the eye. Only those faces not present are beautiful.

The fact is that quite early James Blair had been frightened

by life (in a way which the Princess, in a moment of misery and inspiration, was to divine later with the cry: What kind of a stupid mother could he have had?) and had forever after bent upon books the floodtides of his energy. At times his scholarship resembled panic; he acted as though he feared that raising his eyes from the page he would view the world, or his share in the world, dissolving in ruin. His endless pursuit of facts (which had no fruit in published work and brought no intrinsic esthetic pleasure) was not so much the will to do something as it was the will to escape something else. One man's release lies in dreams, another's in facts.

All this resulted in a real unworldliness, which with his youth and learning and faintly *distrait* courtesy especially endeared him to older women. Both Miss Grier and Mme. Agaropoulos hovered about him with mothering delight and sighed with vexation at his obstinate refusal to come and see them. He reminded me of the lions that stare, unwinking and unseeing, at the crowd about their cage, the crowd that grimaces and waves admiring parasols, though the beast disdains to pick up even a biscuit from such vulgar givers.

At the time that the Princess's story begins he was engaged in establishing the exact location of the ancient cities of Italy. He was reading mediaeval descriptions of the Campagna and tracing through place-names, through dried water-courses, through cracked old paintings the exact position of disused roads and abandoned towns. He was learning about the country's former plants and animals: he was quite happy. Sometimes he made notes of all this, but for the most part he preferred to learn the truth and then forget it.

When it began to get cold in his room he serenely made use of mine, covering my tables with his vellum-bound folios, standing his pictures against my wall, and strewing my floors with his maps. He had dazzled one of the librarians at the Collegio Romano with his allusions and had obtained the privilege of bringing the material home.

One day the Princess d'Espoli came to see me. Ottima admitted her. She came in upon James Blair who was kneeling on the floor crawling from city to city on some yellow crested maps. His coat was off; his hair was in a tangle, and his hands were gray with dust. He had never met her and did not like her

clothes. He did not want to be drawn into a conversation and stood, handsome and sulky, his glances stealing to the maps on the floor. Explained that I was out. Might not be back before. Would not forget to tell that.

Alix didn't mind. She even asked for some tea.

Ottima had just come in to begin thinking about dinner. While tea was making Alix asked to have the maps explained to her. Now the Princess was more capable of entering into an enthusiasm for old cities than most of the several hundred women of her acquaintance; but short of a doctorate in archaeology one does not enter upon such ground with James Blair. Coldly, haughtily, and with long quotations from Livy and Virgil, he harangued my guest. He dragged her remorselessly up and down the seven hills; he wrung her in and out of all the shifting beds of the Tiber. When I finally returned I found her sitting gazing at him over the edge of her teacup with a faintly mocking expression. She had not known that such a man was possible. Throughout the whole episode Blair had acted like nothing so much as a spoiled boy of seven interrupted in a game about Indians. It would be hard to say what had most captivated the Princess, but it was probably that trace of sturdy spoiled egotism. It might have been, in part, the cold douche of being unwelcome,—she who was the delight of the most delightful people in Europe, who had never entered a door without arousing a whirlpool of welcome, who had never come too early nor left too late,—suddenly she had tasted the luxury of being resented.

As soon as I arrived Blair took a swift and awkward departure.

But he's charming! He's charming! she cried. Who is he?

I told her briefly of his home, his progress through the universities, and his habits of study.

But he's extraordinary. Tell me: is he—shy, is he *boudeur* with everybody? Now perhaps I did something to annoy him? What could I have said, Samuele?

I hastened to reassure her. He's that way with everyone. And most people like him all the more for it. Especially older women. For example, Miss Grier and Mme. Agaropoulos adore him and all he does is to sit on their chairs inventing excuses for not coming to dinner.

Well, I'm not old and I like him. Oh, he is so rude! I could

have slapped him. And he only looked at me once. He will have a hard time in life, Samuele, unless he learns to be more gracious. Isn't there anybody he likes, no? besides you?

Yes, he's engaged to a girl in the United States.

Dark hair or light?

I don't know.

Mark my words, he will be very unhappy, unless he learns to be more amiable. But think! what intelligence, what an eye! And how wonderful it is to see such an absence of trickery, you know, such simplicity. Does he live here?

No, he just brings his books in here when it's too cold in his own room.

He is poor?

Yes.

He is poor!

Not very poor, you know. When he really gets down to his last cent he can always find things to do at once. He's happy to be poor.

And he lives quite alone?

Yes. Oh, yes.

And he is poor. (This caused her a moment's astonished reflection, until she burst out:) But you know, that is not right! It is society's duty . . . that is, society should be proud to protect such people. Someone very gifted should be appointed to watch over such people.

But, Princess, James Blair values his independence above everything. He doesn't want to be watched over.

They should be watched over in spite of themselves. Look, you will bring him to tea some day. I am sure my husband's library has some more old maps of the Campagna. We have the bailiff's reports of the Espoli back into the Sixteenth Century. Wouldn't that bring him?

Even surprised at herself, the Princess tried for a time to talk of other things, but presently she returned to praise what she called Blair's single-mindedness; she meant his self-sufficiency, for while we are in love with a person our knowledge of his weaknesses lies lurking in the back of our minds and our idealization of the loved one is not so much an exaggeration of his excellences as a careful "rationalization" of his defects.

When next I saw Blair he wasted two or three hours before

he got up courage to ask me who she was. He listened darkly
while I spoke my enthusiasm. At last he showed me a note in
which she asked him to drive with her to Espoli, look over the
estate, and to examine the archives. He was to bring me if I
wanted. James wished greatly to go; but he was suspicious of
the lady. He liked her and yet he didn't. He was trying to tell me
that he only liked ladies who didn't like him first. He twisted
the letter about trying to decide, then going to the table wrote
a note of refusal.

Then began what it is merely brutal to call a siege. Driving
in the Corso Alix would say to herself: There's nothing uncon-
ventional in my stopping at his room to see if he wants to drive
in the Gardens. I could do as much for a dozen men and it
would be perfectly natural. I am much older than he is, so
much so, that it would merely be an act of . . . thoughtful-
ness. When she stood on the platform before his door (for she
was not content to send up the chauffeur) she would experi-
ence a moment of panic, wishing to recall her ring, imagining
when no one answered that he was in hiding behind the closed
door, listening, who knows, in anger or contempt to her loud
heartbeats. Or she would debate all evening among the gilt
chairs of her little salon as to whether she might drop him a
note. She would count the days since last she had spoken to
him and gauge the propriety (the inner, the spiritual propriety,
not the worldly propriety: for the Cabalists the latter had ceased
to exist) of a new meeting. She was always coming upon him
by accident in the city (she called it her proof of the existence
of guardian angels) and it was with these chance meetings that
she had generally to content herself. She would attract his at-
tention the length of the Piazza Venezia and carry him to
whatever destination he confessed to. No one has ever been
happier than Alix on these few occasions when she sat beside
him in her car. How docilely she sat listening to his lecture;
with what tenderness she secretly noticed his tie and shoes and
socks: and with what intensity she fixed her gaze upon his face
trying to imprint upon her memory the exact proportions of
his features, the imprint that indifference retains so much
better than the most passionate love. There was a possibility
that they might have become the most congenial of friends, for
he dimly sensed that there was something in her that allied her

to the great ladies of his study. If she had only succeeded in concealing her tenderness. At the first signs of his liking for her she would become so intoxicated with the intimation of cordiality that she would make some shy little remark with a faintly sentimental implication; she would comment on his appearance or ask him to lunch. And lose him.

One day he gave her a book that had been mentioned in their conversations. He did not stop to think that it was the first move he had made spontaneously in the whole relation. Hitherto every suggestion, every invitation, had proceeded from her (from her, trembling, presuffering a rebuff, lightly) and she longed for a first sign of his interest. When this book was brought to her, then, she lost her balance; she thought it justified her in pushing the friendship on to new levels, to almost daily meetings, and to long comradely lazy afternoons. She never realized that in his eyes she was, first, an enemy to his studies, and second, that strange hedged monster which all his wide reading had not been able to humanize: a married woman. She called once too often. Suddenly he changed; he became rude and abrupt. When she climbed his stairs he *did* hide behind the door and the bell rang in vain and with a menacing sound, though she had her ways of knowing he was in. She became terrified. Again she confronted that cavern of horror in her nature: she seemed always to be loving those that did not love her. She came to me, distraught. I was cautious and offered her philosophy until I could sound Blair in the matter.

Blair came to me of his own accord. He paced up and down the room, bewildered, revolted, enraged. His stay in Rome had become impossible. He no longer dared remain in his room and when he was out he clung to the side streets. What should he do?

I advised him to leave town.

But how could he? He was in the middle of some work that. Some work that. Damn it all. All right, he'd go.

I begged him before he went to come to dinner with me once when the Princess would be present. No, no. Anything but that. I, in turn, became angry. I analyzed the different kinds of fool he was. An hour later I was saying that the mere fact of being loved so, whether one could return it or not, put one

under an obligation. More than an obligation to be merely kind, an obligation to be grateful. Blair did not understand, but consented at last on the difficult condition that I was not to reveal to the Princess that he was leaving for Spain on the very night of the dinner.

Of course, the Princess arrived early, so enchantingly dressed that I fairly floundered in admitting her. She held tickets for the opera; one no longer cared to hear *Salome*, but *Petrushka* was being danced after it, at ten-thirty. Blair's train left at eleven. He arrived and played his most gracious. We were really very happy, all of us, as we sat by the open window, smoking and talking long over Ottima's excellent *zabaglione* and harsh Trasteverine coffee.

It was a continual surprise to me to see that in Blair's presence she was always a proud detached aristocrat. Even her faintly caressing remarks were such as would not be noticed if one had let them fall to someone with whom one was not secretly in love. Her fastidious pride even drove her to exaggerating her impersonality; she teased him, she pretended she did not hear when he addressed her, she pretended she was in love with me. It was only when he was not present that she became humble, even servile; only then could she even imagine calling on him unasked. At last she rose: It's time to go to the Russian Ballet, she said.

Blair excused himself: I'm sorry I must go back and work.

She looked as though a sword had gone through her. But surely, three-quarters of an hour with Stravinsky is a part of your work. My car's right here.

He remained firm. He too had a ticket for that night.

For a moment she looked blank. She had never met obstinacy under such conditions and did not know what to do next. After a moment she bent her head and pushed back her coffee-cup. Very well, she said lightly. If you can't, you can't. Samuele and I shall go.

Their parting was grim. During the drive to the Constanzi she remained silent, fingering the folds of her coat; during the ballet she sat at the back of the box thinking, thinking, thinking, with staring dry eyes. At the close scores of friends pressed about her in the corridor. She became gay: Let's go to the cabaret run by the Russian refugees, she said. At the door of

the cabaret she dismissed her chauffeur, telling him that her maid need not sit up for her. We danced for a long time in silence, her depression stealing back upon her.

When we left the hall the unfriendliest moonlight in the world was flooding the street. We found a carriage and started towards her home. But falling into the most earnest conversation in all our acquaintance we failed to notice that the carriage had reached her door and had been standing there for some time.

Look, Samuele, do not make me go to bed now. Let me go in and change my clothes quickly. Then let us drive about and watch the sun come up over the Campagna. Would that make you angry with me?

I assured her that it was just what I wanted and she hurried into the house. I paid off the driver who was drunk and quarrelsome and when she rejoined me we strolled through the streets talking and gradually inviting a resigned drowsiness. We had experimented with vodka at the cabaret and the alcohol conferred upon our minds the same mood that the moonlight was shedding upon the icy bubble of the Pantheon. We strayed into the courtyard of the Cancelleria and criticized the arches. We returned to my rooms for cigarettes.

Last night I wasn't at all brave, she said, lying back in the darkness on the sofa. I was desperate. That was before I received your invitation. Could I go to see him or couldn't I? A week had gone by. I asked myself would he feel . . . well, insulted, if a lady knocked on his door at ten o'clock. It was about ten o'clock. Really, there's nothing peculiar about a lady's paying a perfectly impersonal call at about nine-thirty. There's nothing self-conscious, Samuele, about my being here now, for instance. Besides I had a perfectly good reason for going. He asked me what I thought of *La Villegiatura*, and since then I had read it. Now tell, my dear friend, would it have been ridiculous from the American point of view if I had . . . ?

Beautiful Alix, you are never ridiculous. But wasn't your meeting with him tonight all the fresher, all the happier, just because you hadn't seen him for so long?

Oh, how wise you are! she cried. God has sent you to me in my trouble. Come by me and let me hold your hand. Are you ashamed of me when you have seen me suffer so? I suppose I

should be ashamed. You see me without any dignity. You have kind eyes and I am not ashamed in front of you. I think you must have loved too, for you take all my foolishness as a matter of course. Oh, my dear Samuele, every now and then the thought comes over me that he despises me. I have all the faults that he hasn't. When I have this nightmare that he not only dislikes me but laughs at me, yes, laughs at me, my heart stops beating and I blush for hours at a time. The only way I can save myself then is by remembering that he has said many kind things to me; that he sent me that book; that he has asked after me. And then I pray God very simply to put into his mind just a bit of regard for me. Just a bit of respect for those things . . . those things that other people seem to like in me.

We sat in silence for a time, her feverish hand plunged deep into mine and her bright eyes gazing into the darkness. At last she began speaking again in a lower voice:

He is good. He is reasonable. When I am analytical this way I unfit myself for his loving me. I must learn to be simple. Yes. Look, you have done so much for me, may I ask for one more favor. Play to me. I must get out of my mind that wonderful music where Petrushka wrestles with himself.

I felt ashamed of playing before her who played far better than any of us, but I drew out my folios and started right through Gluck's *Armide*. I had hoped that the inept performance would awaken an esthetic annoyance and so shake her out of her dejection, but I presently saw that she had fallen asleep. After a long and adroit diminuendo I left the piano, turned on a shaded light near her, and stole off into my own room. I changed my clothes and lay down ready for the walk in which we were to see the sun rise. I was trembling with a strange happy excitement, made up partly of my love and pity for her, and partly from the mere experience of eavesdropping on a beautiful spirit in the last reaches of its pride and suffering. I was lying thus, proud and happy in the role of guardian, when my heart suddenly stopped beating. She was weeping in her sleep. Sighs welled up from the depths of her slumber, hoarse protests, obstinate denials and moans followed one upon another. Suddenly her broken breathing ceased and I knew she was awake. There was a half-minute of silence; then a low call: Samuele.

Hardly had I appeared at the door before she cried: I know he despises me. He runs away from me. He thinks me a foolish woman who pursues him. He tells the servant to tell me he is out, but he stands behind the door and hears me go away. What shall I do? I'd better not live. I'd better not live any more. It's best, dear Samuele, that I go out right now, in my own way, and stop all this mistaken, this, this, futile suffering of mine. Do you see?

She had arisen and was groping for her hat. I really have courage enough tonight, she muttered. He is too good and too simple for me to worry him as I do. I'll just slip out . . .

But Alix, I cried. We love you so. So many people love you.

You can't say that people love me. They like to greet me on the stairs. They like to listen and smile. But no one has ever watched under my window. No one has secretly learned what I do every hour of the day. No one has . . .

She lay back on the sofa, her cheeks flushed and wet. I talked to her for a long time. I said that her genius was social, that she was made for the delight of company, that she relieved others of the weight of their own boredom, their disguised self-hatred. I promised her that she could find happiness in the exercise of her gift. I could see by a glimpse of her wet cheek turned away that it calmed her to be told so, for she possessed the one form of genius that is almost never praised to its face. She grew more tranquil. After a pause she began talking in a dreamy tone:

I will leave him alone. I will never see him again, she began. When I was a girl and we lived on the mountains, Samuele, I had a pet goat named Tertullien that I loved very much. One day Tertullien died. I would not be comforted. I was hateful and obstinate. The nuns with whom I went to school could do nothing with me and when it was my turn to recite I refused to speak. At last my dear Mother Superior called me into her room and at first I was very bad, even with her. But when she began to tell me of her losses I flung my arms about her and wept for the first time. As a punishment she made me stop everyone I met and say to them twice: *God is sufficient! God is sufficient!*

After a pause she added: I know that it can be true for other people, but I still wanted Tertullien. When is your patience with me coming to an end, Samuele?

Never, I said.

The windows were beginning to show the first light of dawn. Suddenly a little bell rang out nearby, a tinkle of purest silver.

Hush, she said. That's the earliest mass at some church.

Santa Maria in Trastevere is just around the corner.

Hurry!

We let ourselves out of the palace and breathed the cold gray air. A mist seemed to hang low about the street; puffs of blue smoke lay in the corners. A cat passed us. Shivering but elated we entered the church joining two old women in wadded clothes and a laborer. The basilica loomed above, the candles of our side-chapel picking out reflections in the curious marbles and the gold of the mosaics in the vast black cave. The service of the Mass was enrolled with expedition and accuracy. When we came out a milky light had begun to fill the square. The shutters of several shops were being lowered; drowsy passers-by made the diagonals staggering; a woman was lowering her chickens in a basket from the fifth story for a long day's scratching.

We walked over to the Aventine, crossing the Tiber which twisted like a great yellow rope under a delicate fume. We stopped for a glass of sour blue-black wine and a paper bag of peaches.

For the time at least the Princess seemed to herself to have forever closed her mind to even the remotest hope that she would ever see Blair again. Sitting on a stone bench on the gloomy Aventine while the sun shouldered its way up through plunging orange clouds, we mused. She seemed for a time to have fallen back into her old despondency; I resumed the arguments that spoke more glowingly of her gifts.

Suddenly she straightened up. All right. I will try it for you. I must do something. Where are you going today?

I murmured that Mme. Agaropoulos was giving a sort of a musicale: that she was introducing a young compatriot who claimed to have discovered the secret of ancient Greek music.

Write her a note. Telephone her. Ask her if I may come. I too shall learn about ancient Greek music. I shall be introduced to everyone there. I shall be asked to everyone's house. Listen, Samuele, since you say it is my talent I shall get to know everyone in Rome. I shall die of social engagements: Here lies

the woman who never refused an invitation. I shall meet two thousand people in ten days. I shall lay myself out to please anybody on earth. And mind you, Samuele, if that does not nourish me, we shall have to finish trying, you know. . . .

Mme. Agaropoulos was staggered with joy when she discovered that the unhoped for, the improcurable Princess was coming to her house. Mme. Agaropoulos was not the slave of social categories, but she longed to frequent the Cabala, as some long for the next world. She assumed that in that company all was wit and love and peace. There one would find no silly people, none envious, none quarrelsome. She had met the Princess d'Espoli once and had ever since taken her as the type of person she would herself have been if she had been better-looking, thinner and had had more time to read, little realizing that all these had been more in her power than in Alix', and that she had spoiled her own progress by a lazy kindliness, great kindliness but lazy.

The Princess called for me in her car at five o'clock. It would be impossible for me to describe her clothes; it is enough to say that she had the most incredible power of supplying new angles, shades, lines, that interpreted her character. This aptitude received added éclat from her residence in Italy, for Italian women, though often more beautiful, lack both figure and judgment. They anxiously spend enormous sums in Paris and achieve nothing but bundles of rich stuffs that bulge or trail or blow about them in effects they half guess to be unsuccessful, and seek to repair with a display of stones.

We pursued the Via Po for a mile or two and alighted at the ugliest of its houses, an example of that modern German architecture that has done so much for factories. As we mounted the stairs she kept muttering: Watch me! Watch me! In the hall we found a host of latecomers standing with their fingers on their lip while from the drawing rooms there issued the sound of passionate declamation accompanied by the plucking of a lyre, the desolate *moto perpetuo* of an oriental flute and a rhythmic clapping of hands. In other words we had arrived too early; our campaign for meeting two thousand souls in ten days was being balked at the outset. Fretted we pushed on into the garden behind the house. Sitting down on a stone bench, with the tragic ode still faintly sounding in our ears we gave our atten-

tion to the spectacle in the middle distance of a white-haired
gentleman in a wheel-chair overflowing with brightly-colored
shawls. This was Jean Perraye; I told the Princess of how Mme.
Agaropoulos had found the saintly old French poet at the
point of death, wrapt in shawls in a wretched little hotel at
Pisa, and how by supplying him with tender interest, whole milk
and a group of pet animals she had restored his muse, com-
forted his last years and effected his entrance into the French
Academy. At this moment he was engaged in addressing a cir-
cle of attentive cats. These six cats, intermittently licking the
fine silk of their shoulders, and casting polite glances at their
patron, were gray angoras, the color of cigarette ash. We had
read the poet's latest book and knew their names: six queens of
France. We practically dozed on the bench—the hot sunlight,
the choruses of the *Antigone* behind and Jean Perraye's ex-
ordium to the queens of France and Persia before, would have
made drowsy even those who had not passed a night of con-
fession and tears.

When we came to ourselves the audition was over and the
company, doubly noisy after music, was shouting its apprecia-
tion. We re-entered the house, hungry for pastry and encoun-
ters. A sea of hats, with scores of self-conscious eyes staring
about in perpetual search of new salutations, marking down
the Princess for their own; occasionally the large stomach of a
senator or an ambassador swathed in serge and bound with a
golden chain.

Who's the lady in the black hat? whispered Alix.

Signora Daveni, the great engineer's wife.

Fancy! Will you bring her to me or should you take me to
her. No, I'll go to her. Take me.

Signora Daveni was a plain little woman presenting the high
lifted forehead and fresh eyes of an idealistic boy. Her husband
was one of Italy's foremost engineers, an inventor of many
tremendous trifles in airplane construction and a bulwark of
conservative methods in the rising storm of labor agitation.
The Signora was on every philanthropic committee of any
importance in the whole country and during the War had di-
rected incalculable labors. The consciousness of her responsi-
bilities combined with a touch of brusqueness from her humble
extraction had brought her into many a short triumphant

struggle with cabinets and senates and there are stories of her having sharply rebuked the vague, well-intentioned interferences of the royal ladies of Savoy. Yet these distinctions had only made her manners the simpler and her quick cordiality was continually deflating the deference that was paid to her. She dressed badly; she walked badly, her large feet pushing before her like those of some jar-carrier in an upland village. It had been rather fine in uniform, but now that she must return to hats and gowns and rings the consciousness of her lack of grace caused her much depression. Her home was in Turin, but she lived a great deal in Rome out among the open lots of the Via Nomentana and knew everyone. The Princess with the unexpectedness that lies in the very definition of genius turned the conversation upon the use of sphagnum moss as a surgical dressing. The diverse excellence of the two women glimpsed one another; the Princess was astonished to find such quiet mastery in a woman without a *de* and the Signora was amazed to find the same quality in a noblewoman.

I drifted off, but presently the Princess rejoined me. She is real, that woman. I am going to dinner with her Friday; so are you. Find me some more. Who is that blonde with the voice?

You don't want to know her, Princess.

She must be important with that voice; who is she?

She is the woman in the whole world who is most your opposite.

Then I must know her. Will she give me tea and introduce me to a dozen people?

Oh, yes, she'll do that. But you haven't a thing in common. She is a narrow British woman, Princess. Her only interest is in the Protestant Church. She lives in a little British hotel. . . .

But where does she get that *authority*—and the Princess made a gesture of perfect mimicry.

Well, I admitted, she has received the highest honors an Englishwoman can receive. She wrote a hymn and they made her a Dame of the British Empire.

You see I must be caught out of myself. I must meet her right now.

So I led her up to Dame Edith Steuert, Mrs. Edith Foster Prichard Steuert, author of "Far From Thy Ways, I Strayed," the greatest hymn since Newman's. Daughter, wife, sister, what

not, of clergymen, she lived in the most exciting currents of Anglicanism. Her conversation ran on vacant livings and promising young men from Shropshire, and on the editorials in the latest *St. George's Banner* and *The Anglican Cry*. She sat on platforms and raised subscriptions and got names. She seemed to be forever surrounded by a ballet of curates and widows who, at her word, rose and swayed and passed the scones. For she was the author of the greatest hymn of modern times and gazing at her one wondered when the mood could have struck this loud conceited woman, the mood that had prompted those eight verses of despair and humility. The hymn could have been written by Cowper, that gentle soul exposed to the flame of an evangelism too hot even for Negroes. For one minute in her troubled girlhood all the intermittent sincerity of generations of clergymen must have combined in her, and late at night, full of dejections she could not understand, she must have committed to her diary that heartbroken confession. Then the fit was over, and over for ever. It was a telling example of that great mystery in religious and artistic experience: the occasional profundity of nobodies. Dame Edith Steuert on being presented, straightened visibly to show that she was not impressed by the title. With a candor that was another surprise, Alix asked her if she might use her name as reference on her nephew's application for entrance into Eton College. To be sure the nephew was in Lyons, but if Dame Edith would permit the Princess to call upon her some afternoon she would bring some of the boy's letters, photographs and sufficient apparatus to convince her that he was a student recommendable. Friday afternoon was agreed upon, and the Princess rejoined me for new introductions.

So it went on for an hour. The Princess had no method; each new encounter was a new problem. Within three minutes the meeting became an acquaintance, and the acquaintance a friendship. Little did the new friends guess how strange it was to her. She kept asking me what their husbands "did." It delighted her to think that their husbands did anything; she had never guessed that one could meet such people and smiled amazedly like a girl about to meet a real printed poet. A doctor's wife, the wife of a man in rubber, fancy. . . . Toward the end of the afternoon her enthusiasm waned. I feel a little

dusty, she whispered. I feel very Bovary. To think that all this
has been going on in Rome without my knowing it. I'll go and
say goodbye to Mme. Agaropoulos,—*tiens*, who is that beauti-
ful lady. That is an American, isn't it? Quick.

For the only time in my life I saw the beautiful and unhappy
Mrs. Darrell who had come to take leave of her Roman friends.
As she entered the room a silence fell upon the company; there
was something antique, something Plato would have seized
upon in the effect of her beauty. She made much of it, with
that touch of conceit that we allow to a great musician listening
exaggeratedly to his own perfect phrasing, or to the actor who
sets aside author, fellow-players and the fable itself, in order to
improvise the last excessive moments of a death scene. She
dressed, she glanced, she moved and spoke as only uncon-
tested beauties may: she too revived a lost fine art. To this vir-
tuosity of appearing, her illness and suffering had added a
quality even she could not estimate, a magic of implied melan-
choly. But all this perfection of hers was unapproachable; none
of her dearest friends, not even Miss Morrow, dared to kiss
her. She was like a statue in a solitude. She presuffered her
death, and her spirit was set in defiance. She hated every atom
of a creation where such things were possible. The next week
she was to retire to her villa at Capri with her collection of
Mantegnas and Bellinis and to live through four months with
their treacherous love-affair and to die. But this day in the
serenity of the selfishness that was her perfection and the self-
ishness that was her illness she effaced the room.

He would have loved me if I had looked like that, breathed
Alix into my ear, and sinking into a retired chair covered her
mouth with her hand.

Mme. Agaropoulos took Helen Darrell's fingertips a little
timidly and led her to the finest chair. No one seemed able to
say anything. Luigi and Vittorio, sons of the house, went up
and kissed her hand; the American ambassador approached to
compliment her.

She is beautiful. She is beautiful, muttered Alix to herself.
The world is hers. She will never have to suffer as I must. She
is beautiful.

It would not have consoled the Princess if I had explained to
her that Helen Darrell, having been admired extravagantly

from the cradle, had never been obliged to cultivate her intelligence to retain her friends and that, if I may say it respectfully, her mind was still that of a school-girl.

Fortunately the flautist was still there to play and during the performance of the Paradise music from *Orpheus* scarcely a pair of eyes in the room left the newcomer's face. She sat perfectly straight, allowing herself none of the becoming attitudes which music suggests to her kind, no ardent attention, no starry-eyed revery. I remember thinking she marked too deliberately the anti-sentimental. When the music was over she asked to be taken to say goodbye, for the present, to Jean Perraye. From the window I could see them alone together, with the gray cats, queens of France, moving meaninglessly about them. One wonders what they said to one another as she knelt beside his chair: as he said later, they loved one another because they were ill.

Alix d'Espoli would not stir until she knew that Mrs. Darrell had left the house and garden. All her suffering had rushed back upon her. She pretended to be sipping a cup of tea while she gathered herself together. I understand now, she murmured hoarsely. God has never meant me to be happy. Others may be happy with one another. But I shall never be. I know that now. Let us go.

Then began what was ever after known to the Cabala as Alix aux Enfers. She would lunch at a tiny pension with some English spinsters; stop in at some studio in the Via Margutta; pass through a reception at an Embassy; dance till seven at the Hotel Russie as the guest of some cosmetic manufacturer's wife; dine with the Queen Mother; hear the last two acts of the Opera in Marconi's box. Even after that she might feel the need of finishing the day at the Russian cabaret, perhaps contributing herself a monologue to the program. She no longer had any time to see the Cabala and it watched her progress with terror. They begged her to come back to them, but she only laughed at them with her bright febrile eyes and dashed off into her new-found whirlpools. Long after when some Roman name arose in their conversation they would all cry: Alix knows them! To which she would reply coolly: Of course I know them, and a roar would arise from the table. The acquaintances she was now pursuing for distraction, I had long

since pursued for study or from simple liking; but she soon
outstripped me by the hundreds. I went to a few engagements
with her, but often enough we would come upon one another
in ludicrous situations; whereupon we would retire behind a
door and compare notes as to how we got there. Did Com-
mendatore Boni ask a few people to the Palatine? she was there.
Did Benedetto Croce give a private reading of a paper on
George Sand? we glimpsed one another gravely in that solemn
air. She lost a comb in defense of Reality at the stormy opening
of Pirandello's *Sei Personaggi in Cerca d'Autore*; at Casella's
party for Mengelberg, who had been surpassing himself at the
Augusteo, dear old Bossi stood on her train and the sound of
ripping satin caught the enraptured ear of a dozen organists.

When the bourgeoisie discovered that she was accepting in-
vitations there was a tumult as of many waters. Most of her
hostesses assumed that she would not have come to them were
it not for the fact that better doors were beginning to be
closed against her, but fair or foul they would accept her. And
they had her at her best; the faint touch of frenzy that was
driving her on only rendered her gift the more dazzling.
People who had spent their lives laughing at tiresome jokes
were now given something to laugh at. She would be begged
to do this or that "bit" which had become famous. Have you
heard Alix do the Talking Horse? No, but she did the Kron-
prinz in Frascati for us last Friday. Oh, aren't you lucky!

For the first time she was seeing something of artists and
among them she was enjoying her liveliest successes. The under-
painting of her misery which especially these days rendered her
wit so magical was much clearer to them than to the manufac-
turers. They never failed to mention it and their love led them
to paying her the strangest tributes which at the time she was
in too great a daze to stop and value.

For a while I thought she was enjoying all this. She would
laugh so naturally over some of the accidents of the days. More-
over I noticed that she was forming some very rare attach-
ments and I hoped that the friendship of Signora Daveni or of
Duse or of Besnard would be able to comfort and finally rec-
oncile her. But one evening I was suddenly shown how utterly
ineffectual this plunging about the jungle was.

After a month's absence James Blair wrote me from Spain

that he had to come back to Rome, even if it were only for a week. He promised to see no one, to keep up side streets and to get out as soon as it was possible.

I wrote him back in the strongest profanity that it was impossible. Go anywhere else. Don't fool with such things.

He replied, no less angry, that he could move about the earth as freely as everybody else. Whether I liked it or not he was coming to Rome the following Wednesday and nothing would stop him. He was on the traces of the Alchemists. He wanted to know all that was left of the old secret societies and his search was leading to Rome. Since I could do nothing to prevent his coming I could at least devote my energies to concealing it. I took almost ridiculous precautions. I even saw to it that Mlle. de Morfontaine had Alix in Tivoli over the weekend and that Besnard had her sitting for a portrait most of the mornings. But there is a certain spiritual law that requires our tragic coincidences. Which of us has not felt it? Take no precautions.

The seer whom Blair had returned to visit, Sareptor Basilis, lived in three rooms on the top floor of an old palace in the Via Fontanella di Borghese. Rumor had it that he could make lightning play about his left hand and that when his meditations approached ecstasy he could be seen sitting among the broken arcs of a dozen rainbows; and that as you mounted the dark stairs you fought your way through the welcoming ghosts as through a swarm of bees. In the front room where the meetings were held (Wednesdays for adepts, Saturdays for beginners) one was awed by discovering a circular hole in the roof that was never closed. Under it had been laid a zinc-lined depression that carried off the rain water and in this depression stood the master's chair.

Long meditation and ecstatic trances had certainly beautified his face. His blue-green eyes, not incapable of sudden acuteness, drifted vaguely about under a smooth pink forehead; he had the bushy white eyebrows and beard of Blake's Creator. Except for his long walks he seemed to have no private life, but sat all day and night under the hole in the roof, lending an ear to a whispering visitor, writing slowly with his left hand, or gazing up into the sky. A host of people from every walk of life sought him out and held him in reverence.

He gave no thought to practical necessities, for his admirers, spiritually prompted, were continually leaving significant looking envelopes beside him on the zinc-lined depression. Some left bottles of wine and bars of bread, and brown silk shirts. The only human occupation that arrested his attention was music, and it is said that he would stand by the door of the Augusteo on the afternoon of a symphony concert and wait for some passerby, spiritually prompted, to buy him a ticket. If none came, he would continue on his way without bitterness. He composed music himself, hymns for unaccompanied voices which he affirmed he had heard in dream. They were written in a notation resembling our own, but not sufficiently so to allow of transcription. I have puzzled for hours over the score of a certain *Lo, where the rose of dispersion empurples the dawn*. This motet for ten voices, a chorus of angels on the last day, began plainly enough with the treble clef on five staves, but how was one to interpret a sudden shrinkage of the horizontal lines to two in all parts? I humbly approached the master on this subject. He replied that the effect of the music at that point could only be expressed by a radical departure from standard notation; that the economy of staves denoted an acuity of pitch; that the note on which my thumb was reposing was an E, a violet E, an E of the quality of a lately-warmed amethyst . . . music powerless to express . . . ah . . . the rose of dispersion empurples. At first the nonsense in which he moved and thought enraged me. I invented opportunities for provoking his absurdity. I improvised a story about a pilgrim who had come up to me in the nave of the Lateran and told me it was God's will that I should return with him to a leper colony in Australia. Dear Master, I cried, how shall I know if this be my real vocation? His answer was not clear. I was told that destiny herself was the mother of decision, and that my vocation would be settled by events not by consideration. In the next breath I was bidden to do nothing rashly; to lay my ear over the lute of eternity and to plan my life in harmony with the cosmic overtones. During the course of a year thousands of women visited him, of every rank, and in every sort of perplexity, and to each one he offered the comforts of metaphor. They came away from him with shining faces; these phrases were beautiful and profound to them; they wrote them

in their diaries and murmured them over to themselves when
they were tired.

Basilis was attended by two homely sisters, the Adolfini girls.
Lise must have been thirty and Vanna about twenty-eight. They
say that he ran across them in the Italian quarter of London
where they were serving as attendants in a ballet school.
Penury and abuse had left them scarcely the human sem-
blance. Every evening at eleven when they had unlaced the last
slipper of the night class, treated the floor with tallow, polished
the bars and tied up the chandelier, they went around the cor-
ner to the Café Roma for a thimbleful of coffee to sip with their
bread. Here Basilis was to be found, a photographer's assistant
with grandiose pretensions. He was vice-president of the Rosi-
crucian Mysteries, Soho Chapter, a group of clerks, waiters
and idealistic barbers who found compensation for the humili-
ations they underwent by day in the glories they ascribed to
themselves by night. They met in darkened rooms, took oaths
with one hand resting on the works of Swedenborg, read papers
on the fabrication of gold and its metaphysical implications,
and elected one another with great earnestness to the offices of
arch-adept and *magister hieraticorum.* They corresponded
with similar societies in Birmingham, Paris and Sydney, and
sent sums of money to the last of the magi, Orzinda-Mazda of
Mount Sinai. Basilis first discovered his power over the minds
of women when he fell into the habit of talking to the two mute
sisters in the café. They listened wide-eyed to his stories of
how some workmen near Rome, breaking by chance into the
tomb of Cicero's daughter, Tulliola, discovered an ever-burning
lamp suspended in mid-air, its wick feeding on Perpetual Prin-
ciple; of how Cleopatra's son Caesarion was preserved in a
translucent liquid "oil of gold," and could be still seen in an
underground shrine at Vienna; and of how Virgil never died,
but was alive still on the Island of Patmos, eating the leaves of
a peculiar tree. The wonder-stories, the narrator's apocalyptic
eyes, the excitement of being spoken to without anger, and the
occasional offer of Vermouth bewitched the sisters. They be-
came his unquestioning slaves; with the money they had saved
up he opened a Temple where his gift met extraordinary suc-
cess. The girls left the ballet school and became doorkeepers
in the house of their lord. The new leisure into which they

entered, the sufficient food, the privilege of serving Basilis, his confidence and his love, combined to constitute a burden of happiness almost too great to be borne. Happiness is in proportion to humility: the humility of the Adolfini girls was so profound that there was in it no room for the expression of gratitude or surprise; in the face of it food could not fatten them nor love soften their bony features; not even when after some altercation with the London police Basilis and his handmaidens removed to their native Rome. To be sure the master in turn never confessed his indebtedness to the girls for their silent and skillful ministration. Even in love he was impersonal; they merely provided him with that mood of gentle satiety of the senses which is an indispensable element of the philosopher's meditation.

It was under this skylight then that Blair and I sat at about eleven-thirty, waiting for the public séance to begin. We were early, and leaning back against the wall we watched the little group of visitors that one by one moved up to the unboxed confessional that was the master's ear. A clerk with watery eyes and trembling hands; a stout lady of the middle class, gripping a large shopping purse and talking with great rapidity about her *nepote*; a trim little professional woman, probably a lady's maid, stuffing a tiny handkerchief into her mouth as she sobbed. Basilis' eyes seldom strayed to his visitors' faces; while he dismissed them with a few measured grave sentences his glance revealed nothing but its serene abstraction. Presently a younger woman, heavily veiled, crossed the floor swiftly to the empty chair beside him. She must have been there before, for she lost no time in greetings. Under deep emotion she pleaded with him. A little surprised by her vehemence he interrupted her several times with the words *Mia figlia*. The reproaches only increased her energy, and brushing back her veil with her hand in order to thrust her face into the sage's she revealed herself as Alix d'Espoli. Terror went through me; I seized Blair's arm and made signs that we were to escape. But at that moment the Princess with a gesture of anger, as though she had come, not so much to ask the sage's counsel, as to announce a determination, rose and turned to the door. Unerringly her eyes met ours, and the rebellious light died out, to be replaced by fear. For a

moment the three of us hung suspended on one cord of hor-
ror. Then the Princess collected herself long enough to tinc-
ture the despairing contraction of her mouth with a smile; she
bowed to us deliberately in turn and passed almost majestically
from the room.

At once I returned home and wrote her a long letter, using
the whole truth as a surgeon in an extremity would resort to a
wholesale guesswork with the knife. I never received an answer.
And our friendship was over. I had often to meet her again,
and we even came finally to have agreeable conversations to-
gether, but we never mentioned the affair and there was a
glaze of impersonality over her eyes.

From the night she had seen us in Basilis' rooms the Princess
gave up her social researches as abruptly as she had begun
them. Nor did she ever go to the Rosicrucian again. I heard
that she was attempting the few remaining consolations that
lie open to affliction: she took to the fine arts; she climbed up
ladders respectfully placed for her in the Sistine Chapel and
stared at the frescos through magnifying glasses; she resumed
the culture of her voice and even sang a little in public. She
started off on a trip to Greece, but came back without any ex-
planations a week later. There was a hospital phase during
which she cut off her hair and tiptoed about among the wards.

At last the beating of the wings, the darting about the cage,
subsided. She had come to the second stage of convalescence:
the mental pain that had been so great that it had to be passed
into the physical and that expressed itself in movement, had
now sufficiently abated to permit her to think. All her vivacity
left her and she sat about in her friends' homes listening to
their visitors.

Little by little then her old graces began to reappear. First a
few wry sarcasms, gently slipping off her tongue; then some
rueful narratives in which she appeared in a poor light; then
ever so gradually the wit, the energy, and last of all the humor.

The whole Cabala trembled with joy, but pretended to have
noticed nothing. Only one night when for the first time at
table she had returned to her gorgeous habit of teasing the
Cardinal on his Chinese habits, only once on leaving the table
did he take her two hands and gaze deep into her eyes with a

significant smile that both reproached her for her long absence
and welcomed her back. She blushed slightly and kissed the
sapphire.

I, who know nothing about such things, assumed that the
grand passion was over and dreaded any moment seeing her
interesting herself in some new Northerner. But one little inci-
dent taught me how deep a wound may be.

One afternoon at the villa in Tivoli we were standing on the
balcony overlooking the falls. Whenever she was left alone with
me her charm abated; she seemed to be fearing that I might at-
tempt a confidence; the muscles at the corners of her mouth
would tighten. We were joined from the house by a well-
known Danish archaeologist who began to discourse upon the
waterfall and its classical associations. Suddenly he stopped and
turning to me, cried:

Oh, I have a message for you. How could I have forgotten
that! I met a friend of yours in Paris. A young American named
Blair—let me see, was it Blair?

Yes, Doctor.

What a young man! How many of you Americans are like
that? I suppose you never met him, Princess? . . .

Yes, replied Alix, I knew him too.

Such intelligence! He is surely the greatest instinctive
scholar I have ever met, and, believe me, perhaps he is all the
greater for never putting anything down on paper. And such
modesty, Princess,—the modesty of the great scholar that
knows that all the learning one human head can hold is but a
grain of dust. I spent two whole nights over his notebooks and
I honestly felt as though I had brushed against a Leonardo,
really, a Leonardo.

We both stood rapt, listening to the waves of happy praise
when suddenly I became aware that the Princess had fainted
beside me with a happy smile upon her face.

Astrée-Luce and the Cardinal

THERE was a vague understanding among the members of
the Cabala that I was engaged upon the composition of a
play about Saint Augustine. None of my friends had ever seen
the manuscript (even I was surprised to come upon it every
now and then at the bottom of my trunk), but it was treated
with enormous respect. Mlle. de Morfontaine especially kept
asking about it, kept walking about on tiptoes and glancing at
it sideways. It was to this that she was alluding in the note I re-
ceived soon after Blair's frightened departure: Try and arrange
to come up to the Villa for a few weeks. It is perfectly quiet
until five o'clock every afternoon. You can work on your poem.

It was my turn for a little peace. I had so recently passed
through the desperations of Marcantonio and Alix. I sat holding
the note for a long while, my wary nervous system begging me
to be cautious, begging me to make sure that no hysterical
evenings could possibly lie behind it. Here was a place where it
was perfectly quiet until five o'clock every afternoon. It was
five o'clock every morning that I wanted to be reassured about.
You can work on your poem. Surely the only vexation that
could proceed from that wonderful lady lay exactly there,—
she would be asking me every morning about the progress on
the Third Act. It would be good for me to be hectored about
my play. And what wonderful wines she stored. To be sure the
lady was mad, indubitably mad. But mad in a nice way, with
perfect dignity; decently mad on a million a year. I wrote her I
would come.

What could have been more reassuring than the first days?
Mornings of sunlight when the dust settled thicker on the olive-
leaves; when the terraced hillside seemed to be powdering
away; when no sound reached the garden but the cry of a carter
in the road, the cooing of doves, stepping high along the eaves
of the gardener's shed, and the sound of the waterfall with its
mysterious retardations, a sound of bronze. I ate luncheon
alone under a grape arbor. The rest of the day was spent in

roaming over the hills or among the high chairs of Astrée-
Luce's rich and curious library.

From the middle of the afternoon one sensed the approach
of dinner. One felt the gradual tightening of the chord of for-
mality until, like the bursting of some pyrotechnical bomb, full
of dazzling lights and fascinating detail, the ceremony began.
For hours there had come a hum as of bees from the wing of
the house that contained the kitchen; there followed the flights
of maids and hairdressers through the corridors, the candle-
lighter, the flower-bearers. The crushing of gravel under the
window announces the arrival of the first guests. The major-
domo clasps on his golden chain and takes his place with the
footmen at the door. Mlle. de Morfontaine descends from her
tower kicking her train about to teach it its flexibility. A string
quartet on the balcony begins a waltz by Glazounov as sub-
dued as a surreptitious rehearsal. The evening takes on the air
of a pageant by Reinhardt. One passes to the saloon. At the
head of the table behind peaks of fruits and ferns, or cascades
of crystal and flowers, sits the hostess, generally in yellow satin,
her high ugly face lit with its half-mad surprise. She generally
supports a headdress of branching feathers and looks like
nothing so much as a bird of the Andes blown to that bleak-
ness by the coldest Pacific breezes.

I have described how Miss Grier brooded over her table and
placed herself to hear every word whispered by her remotest
guest. Astrée-Luce followed a contrary procedure and heard
so little of what was said that her very guest of honor was often
obliged to resign all hope of engaging her attention. She would
seem to have been caught up into a trance; her eyes would be
fixed on some corner of the ceiling as though she were trying to
catch the distant slamming of a door. Generally some Cabalist
held the opposite end of the table: Mme. Bernstein, huddled
up in her rich fur cape, looking like an ailing chimpanzee and
turning from side to side the encouraging amiability of her gri-
mace; or the Duchess d'Aquilanera, a portrait by Moroni, her
dress a little spotty, her face a little smudged, but somehow
evoking all the passionate dishonest splendid barons of her
line; or Alix d'Espoli making passes with her exquisite hands
and transforming the guests into witty and lovable and enthu-
siastic souls. Miss Grier seldom came, having festivals of her

own to direct. Nor was it often possible to invite the Cardinal, since any company to meet him must be chosen with infinite discretion.

Almost every evening after the last guest had left the hill or retired to bed, and the last servant had finished finding little things to adjust, Astrée-Luce and I would descend into the library and have long talks over a drop of *fine*. It was then that I began to understand the woman and to see where my first judgments had been wrong. This was not a silly spinster of vast wealth nourishing a Royalist chimaera; nor the sentimental half-wit of the philanthropic committees; but a Second-Century Christian. A shy religious girl so little attached to the things about her that she might awake any day and discover that she had forgotten her name and address.

Astrée-Luce has always illustrated for me the futility of goodness without intelligence. The dear creature lived in a mist of real piety; her mind never drifted long from the con-templation of her creator; her every impulse was goodness it-self: but she had no brains. Her charities were immense but undigested; she was the prey of anyone who wrote her a letter. Fortunately her donations were small, for she lacked the aware-ness to be either avaricious or prodigal. I think she would have been very happy as a servant; she would have understood the role, have seen beauty in it, and if her position had been full of humiliation and trials it would have deeply nourished her. Sainthood is impossible without obstacles and she never could find any. She had heard over and over again of the sins of pride and doubt and anger, but never having felt even the faintest twinge she had passed through the earlier stages of the spiri-tual life in utter bewilderment. She felt sure that she was a wicked sinful woman, but did not know how to go about her own reform. Sloth? She had been on her knees an hour every morning before her maid appeared. So difficult, so difficult is the process of making oneself good. Pride? At last after intense self-examination she thought she had isolated in herself some vestiges of pride. She attacked them with fury. She forced her-self to do appalling things in public in order to uproot the propensity. Pride of appearance or of wealth? She soiled her sleeves and bodice intentionally and suffered the silent con-sternation of her friends.

She read the lessons so literally that I have seen her give away her coat time after time. I have seen her walk miles with a friend who asked her to go as far as the road. Now I was to learn that her fits of abstraction were withdrawals into herself for prayer and adoration, and often caused by almost ludicrous incidents. I was no longer left to wonder why all references to fish and fishing sent her off into the clouds; I realized that the Greek word for fish was the monogram of her Lord and acted upon her much as a muezzin's call acts upon a Mohammedan. A traveller spoke flippantly of the pelican; at once Mlle. de Morfontaine repaired to her mental altar and besought its guest not to grieve at the disrespect paid to one of His most vivid symbols. Strangest illustration of all was shown me a little later. One day she chanced to notice on my hall table an envelope which I had addressed to Miss Irene H. Spencer, a teacher of Latin in the High Schools at Grand Rapids, who had come over to put her hand on the Forum. At once Astrée-Luce insisted on meeting her. I never told Miss Spencer why she had been tendered so amazing a luncheon, why her hostess had listened so breathlessly to her trivial travelogues, nor why on the following day a golden chain hung with sapphires had been left at the pension for her. In fact Miss Spencer was a devout Methodist and would have been shocked to learn that IHS meant anything.

Strange though Mlle. de Morfontaine was, she was never ridiculous. Such utter refusal of self can by sheer excess become a substitute for intelligence. Certainly she was able to let fall remarkably penetrating judgments, judgments that proceeded from the intuition without passing through the confused corridors of our reason. Though she was exasperating at times, at others she would abound in almost miraculous perceptions of one's needs. People as diverse as Donna Leda and myself had to love her, one moment almost with condescension as to an unreasonable child, and the next with awe, with fear in the presence of something of infinite possibility. Whom were we entertaining unawares? Might this, oh literally! be an . . . ?

This then was the being whom I came to know during those late conversations in the library over a drop of *fine*. The talk was leisurely, full of pauses and to no point, but my bruised in-

stinct could no longer escape the conviction that there was some deeply important matter that she wished to submit to me. I soon foresaw that I was not to rest. My dread of the revelation however was heightened by the obvious difficulty Astrée-Luce found in coming to the point. Finally instead of trying to avoid the discussion I tried to provoke it; I thought I could help here and there by opening veins of conversation that might surprise her problem. But no. The happy moment hung off.

One evening, she asked me abruptly whether it would greatly interfere with my work if we were to move to Anzio for a few days. I replied that I should like nothing better. All I knew of Anzio was that it was one of the resorts on the sea, a few hours from Rome, the site of one of Cicero's villas, and near Nettuno. She added a little anxiously that we should have to go to a hotel, a very poor hotel at that, but that it was out of season and there were ways in which she could supply some of the deficiencies of the service. A little foresight could prevent my being too uncomfortable.

So one morning we climbed into the large plain car she reserved for travelling and drove westward. The back seat served as a warehouse. One glimpsed a maid, a prie-dieu, a cat, a real panel by Fra Angelico, a box of wines, fifty books and some window curtains. I found out later that there had been a lavish assortment of caviare, pâté, truffles and ingredients for rare sauces by which, with a discouraging failure to understand me, she intended to supplement the resources of a tourists' hotel. She drove, herself, and in nothing did Heaven's interest in her reveal itself more clearly. First we stopped at Ostia so that I might see the veritable spot where the last scene of my wretched play took place. We read aloud the page of Augustine and I silently vowed to renounce forever any notion of rephrasing it.

On our first evening at Anzio a cold wind blew in from the sea. The vines and shrubs whipped the houses; the lamps of the cafés about the square swung cheerlessly over wet tables; one could not escape the desolate slip-slap of the waves against the sea-wall. But we both had a taste for such weather. We decided at about six o'clock to walk to Nettuno returning for dinner at half-past nine. We wrapped ourselves in rubber and started off, leaning against the wind and spray and feeling

strangely exhilarated. For a time we walked in silence, but entering at last that portion of the road that lies between the high walls of the villas, Astrée-Luce began to talk:

I have told you before, Samuele (the whole Cabala had followed the Princess in calling me Samuele), that the hope of my life is to see a king reigning in France. How impossible such a thing seems now! No one knows it better than I. But everything I love most is improbable. And it is the fact that it seems so untimely that will help us most when we come to prepare the Divine Right of Kings as a dogma of the Church. What anger there will be, what sneers! Even important Churchmen will rush down to Rome and beg us not to upset the progress of Catholicism by such a move. There will be controversies. All the newspapers and the reviews will be shouting and weeping and laughing and the whole basis of democratic government, the folly of republics, will be aired. Europe will be cleansed of the poison in its side. We have nothing to fear from debates. The people will turn to God and ask to be ruled by those houses of His choosing.—However, I am not trying to convince you of it now, Samuele; I am only stating it so as to lead up to something else. You are a Protestant; does this make you impatient? Are you tired of me?

No, no, please. I am very interested, I replied.

At that moment our road brought us again to the water's edge. We stood for a moment on a parapet looking down on the loud sea that plunged about on the washing stones of a village. It began to rain. Astrée-Luce was gripping the iron railing watching the steam that rose from the waves; she was crying silently.

Perhaps, she continued, as we returned to our journey, you can imagine the tenth part of my disappointment as I watch the Cardinal getting older, and myself, and the nations falling deeper and deeper into error, and so little done. He can help us. He seems to me to have been especially created to help us. I do not forget his work in China. It was heroic. But what a greater work remains for him in Europe. Year follows year and still he sits up there on the Janiculum, reading and walking in the garden. Europe is dying. He will not stir.

At the time I was deeply moved. The rain and her tears and the puddles and the slapping noises of the water against the

sea-wall had begun to affect me. All the voices of nature kept repeating: Europe is Dying. I would have liked to stop and have a good meaningless cry myself, but I had to listen to the voice beside me:

I cannot understand why he does not write. Perhaps I am not meant to understand. I know he believes that the universality of the Church is imminent. I know that he believes that a Catholic Crown is the only possible rule. But he does not stir to help us. All we ask from him is a book on the Church and the States. Think, Samuele, his learning, his logic, his style— but you have never heard him preach? His irony in controversy and his amazing perorations! What would be left of Bosanquet? The constitutions of the republics of the world would be tossed about—you will forgive me if I seem disrespectful to your great country—tossed about like eggshells. His book would not be just a book fallen from the press: it would be a force of nature; it would be the simultaneous birth of an idea in a thousand minds. It would be placed at once in the canon and bound up with the Bible. And yet he spends his day among rose bushes and rabbits and reading histories of this and that. I want to do this in my lifetime; I want to arouse this great man to his task. And you can help me.

I was excited. The air was full of a divine absurdity. Here was someone who was not afraid of using superlatives. This was being mad on a great scale. It would be hard to come down to ordinary living after these intoxicating threats against the presidents of this world and the binderies of the British Bible Society. I tried to think of something to say. I mumbled something about willingness.

She did not notice my inadequacy. It seems to me, she continued, that I have at last discovered one of the causes of his reluctance to join us. But first, tell me how he is regarded by the various Romans whom you have met. What is his legend among people who do not know him?

Here I was frightened. Could *she* have heard? How could any of those strange rumors have reached her?

But she would learn nothing from me. I took leave of good faith and told her all the favorable reports I had heard. Simple souls were captivated by the thought that apart from a few major obligations he lived on sixty-five lire a week; that he

spoke twelve languages; that he enjoyed polenta; that he visited in certain Roman homes (her own, in particular) without ceremony; that he was translating the Confessions and the Imitation into exquisite Chinese. I knew Romans who so loved the very thought of him that they took walks to the Janiculan Hill solely to peer between his garden gates and lurked about the house in the hope of giving their children an opportunity to kiss his ring.

Astrée-Luce waited in silence. At last she said with only a trace of reproach:

You are trying to spare me, Samuele. But I know. There are other stories about him. His enemies have been at work systematically poisoning his prestige. We know that there is no one in Rome who is kinder, more humble, higher-minded; but among the common people he has almost the reputation of a monster. Some people have been at work spreading such rumors deliberately. And the Cardinal has heard of them: through the whispering of servants or by cries in the road, or by anonymous letters, in all sorts of ways. He exaggerates this attitude. He feels that he is in a hostile world. It has made his old age tragic. And that is why he will not write. Yet it is within our power to save him still.—But look! There is a francobollo shop. Let us get some cigarettes and find some place to sit down. It makes me so happy to talk of this!

Provided with cigarettes we looked about for a wine shop. Our wish evoked one at the next curve in the road, a smoky uncordial tunnel, but we sat down before the glasses of sour inky wine and continued our conspiracy. Astrée-Luce confessed that if the ill-odor had become attached to the Cardinal's name through any real delinquencies on his part, we could not have hoped to dissipate it. Truth in such subtle regions as rumor would be unalterable. But she knew that the aspersions in this case were the result of a clever campaign and she felt sure that a countercampaign could still sweeten his reputation. In the first place our enemies had taken advantage of the Italians' prejudice against the Orient. An Italian enjoys the same delicious shudder at the sight of a Chinaman that an American boy does at the mention of a trapdoor over a river. The Cardinal had returned from the East yellow, unwrinkled. His walk troubled them. It was easy to build upon this, to pass

the whisper along the Trasteverine underworld that he kept strange images, that animals (his gardenful of rabbits and ducks and guinea fowl) could be heard shrieking late at night, that his faithful Chinese servant had been seen in all sorts of terrifying attitudes. Next, his frugal life stirred their imaginations. Every one knew he was fabulously wealthy. Rubies as big as your fist and sapphires like doorknobs, where were they? Did you ever go up to the gate of the Villino Wei Ho? Come with me Sunday. If you sniff hard enough you can get the strangest odor, one that will leave you drowsy for days and give you dreams.

We were to change all this. We sat there choosing a committee of rehabilitation. We were to have magazine articles, newspaper paragraphs. His eightieth birthday was approaching. There would be presentations. Mlle. de Morfontaine was donating a Raphael altar piece to his titular church. But most of all we would send out agents among the people, telling them of his goodness, his simplicity, his donations to their hospitals, and ever so faintly his sympathy with socialistic ideas; he was to be the People's Cardinal. We had anecdotes of his snubbing the arrogant members of the College, of his defending a poor man who had stolen a chalice from his church. China was to be re-created for the Trasteverines. And so on. We were to prop up the Cardinal so that the Cardinal could prop up Europe.

When we returned to the hotel that night Astrée-Luce seemed to have grown ten years younger. Apparently I was the first person to whom she had outlined her vision. She was so eager to be at work that she suddenly asked me if I minded packing up again and going back to Tivoli that night. We could the better start work in the morning. What she really wanted was the exhilaration and fatigue of driving (her terrible driving) before she went to bed. So we put back into the car the maid, the Fra Angelico, the ingredients for sauces and the cat, and returned to the Villa Horace at about two in the morning.

The Cardinal was not to know that we were putting up a scaffolding about his good name and freshening the colors; but we were to persuade him not to do some of the things that particularly antagonized the public. The very next morning Astrée-Luce shyly begged me to go and see him. She did not

know why, but she had a vague idea that now I knew her hopes my eyes would be open to significant details.

I found him as one could find him every sunny day the year round, seated in the garden, a book on his knee, a reading glass in his left hand, a pen in his right, a head of cabbage and a Belgian hare at his feet. A pile of volumes lay on the table beside him: *Appearance and Reality*, Spengler, *The Golden Bough*, *Ulysses*, Proust, Freud. Already their margins had begun to exhibit the spidery notations in green ink that indicated a closeness of attention that would embarrass all but the greatest authors.

He laid aside his magnifying glass as I came up the path of shells. *Eccolo, questo figliolo di Vitman, di Poe, di Vilson, di Guglielmo James,—di Emerson, che dico!* What do you want?

Mlle. de Morfontaine wants you to come to dinner Friday night, just the three of us.

Very good. Very nice. What else?

What do you want, Father, for your birthday? Mlle. de Morfontaine wants me to sound you tactfully . . .

Tactfully!—Samuelino, walk to the back of the house and tell my sister you will stay to lunch. I am to have a little Chinese vegetable dish. Will you have that or a little risotto and chestnut-paste? You can buy yourself something solid on the way down hill. How is Astrée-Luce?

Very well.

A little illness would be good for her. I am uncomfortable when I am with her. There are certain doctors, Samuele, who are not happy when they are talking to people in good health. They are so used to the supplicating eyes of patients that say: Shall I live? In the same way I am ill at ease in the company of persons who have never suffered. Astrée-Luce has eyes of blue porcelain. She has a fair pure heart. It is sweet to be in the company of a fair pure heart, but what can one say to it?

There was St. Francis, Father . . . ?

But he had been libertine in his youth, or thought he had.— Senta! Who can understand religion unless he has sinned? who can understand literature unless he has suffered? who can understand love unless he has loved without response? *Ecc!* The first sign of Astrée-Luce's being in trouble was last month. There is a certain Monsignore who wants her millions for his churches

in Bavaria. Every few days he climbs the hill to Tivoli and breathes into her ear: *And the rich He hath sent empty away.* The poor child trembles and pretty soon Bavaria will have some enormous churches, too ugly for words. Oh, you know, there is for every human being one text in the Bible that can shake him, just as every building has a musical note that can overthrow it. I will not tell you mine, but do you want to know Leda d'Aquilanera's? She is a great hater, and they say that during the Pater Noster she closes her teeth tight upon: *Sicut et nos dimittimus debitoribus nostris.*

At this he laughed for a long time, his body shaking in silence.

But was not Astrée-Luce devoted to her mother? I asked.

No, she has had no losses. That was when she was ten. She has poetized her, that is all.

Father, why did not that literal faith of hers carry her to a convent?

She promised her dying mother she would stay alive to put a Bourbon on the throne of France.

How can you laugh, Father, at her devotion to . . .

We old men are allowed to laugh at things that you little students may not even smile about. Oh, oh, the house of Bourbon. Would you be surprised if I gave up my life to reviving the royal brother-and-sister marriages of Egypt? Well! It is not more impossible.

Dear Father, won't you write one more book? Look, you have about you all the greatest books of the first quarter of my century . . .

And very stupid they are, too.

Won't you make us one. Such a great book, Father Vaini. About yourself, essays like Montaigne,—about China and about your animals and Augustine . . .

Stop! No! Stop at once. You frighten me. Do not you see that the first sign of childhood in me will be the crazy notion that I should write a book? Yes, I could write a book better than this ordure that your age has offered us (and with a sharp blow he pushed over the tower of books; the Belgian hare gave a squeal as he barely escaped being pinned under Schweitzer's *Skizze*). But a Montaigne, a Machiavelli . . . a . . . a . . . Swift, I will never be. How horrible, how horrible it would be

if you should come here some day and find me writing. God preserve me from the last folly. Oh, Samuele, Samuelino, how bad of you to come here this morning, and awaken all the vulgar prides in an old peasant. No, don't pick them up. Let the animals soil them. What is the matter with this Twentieth Century of yours . . . ? You want me to compliment you because you have broken the atom and bent light? Well, I do, I do.— You may tell our rich friends, tactfully, that I want for my birthday a small Chinese rug now reposing in the window of a shop on the Corso. It would be unbecoming for me to say more than that it is on the left as you approach the Popolo.— The floor of my bedroom is getting colder every morning, and I always promised myself that when I became eighty I might have a rug in my bedroom.

What went wrong?

The first hour was delightful. The Cardinal always ate very little (never meat) and that with preposterous slowness. If his soup took him ten minutes his rice required half an hour. To be sure the elements of trouble were present merely in these friends' characters. They were so different that just to hear them talking together had an air of high comedy. First, Astrée-Luce made the mistake of referring to the Bavarian Monsignore. She suspected that the Cardinal was out of sympathy with any plans she might have of helping the Church in that direction; she longed to talk over with him the problem of her wealth and its disposition, but he refused to give her the least advice. He had endless resources of ingenuity in evading the subject. As Rome was arranged at that time it was most important that he should exercise no influence on that aspect of his friend's life. Yet he allowed it to be seen that he knew she would handle the matter foolishly. It ailed him to see such an enormous instrument for progress drift down the wind of ecclesiastical administration.

Now we must remember that it was the eve of his eightieth birthday. We have already seen that the event had precipitated a flood of amused bitterness. As he said later, he should have died at the moment of leaving his work in China. The eight years that had elapsed since then had been a dream of increasing confusion. Living is fighting and away from the field the most

frightening changes were taking place in his mind. Faith is fighting, and now that he was no longer fighting he couldn't find his faith anywhere. This vast reading was doing something to him. . . . But most of all we must remember his terror at the thought that the people of Rome hated him. He would leave in dying a memory without affection and without dignity. An anonymous letter had told him that even in Naples children were kept in good behavior with threats that the Yellow Cardinal would skin them. If one were young one would laugh at such a rumor, but being old one grew cold. He was leaving a world where he was shuddered at for a world that was no longer as distinct as it had been, but which might yet have this consolation that he would not be able to look down from it and see the people surreptitiously spitting on the endings in *issimus* that would compose his epitaph.

Before I knew it we were in the middle of a wrangle about prayer. Astrée-Luce had always longed to hear the Cardinal discourse upon abstract matters. She had often tried to draw him into arguments on the frequent communion and on the invocation of the saints. He had once whispered to me that she was trying to extract from him the materials for a calendar, such sweet manuals as she could buy in the Place Saint Sulpice. Every word of his was sacred. She would not have hesitated to put him in a Church window with St. Paul. It was only after a few moments that she became aware that he was saying some rather strange things. Could that be Doctrine? If anything he said was difficult all she had to do was to try hard to grasp it. Truth, new truth. So she listened, first with surprise, then with mounting terror.

He was launched upon the paradox that in prayer one should never ask for anything. His dialectic was doing an incredible work. He had decided to be Socratic and was asking Astrée-Luce questions. He wrecked her on several orthodox assumptions. Twice she fell into heresy and was condemned by the councils. She seized hold of St. Paul but the epistle broke in her hand. She came to the surface for the third time but was struck by a Thomist fragment. The previous week the Cardinal had been called to the deathbed of a certain Donna Matilda della Vigna, and it was poor Donna Matilda who was now dragged forth to point the argument. Exactly what had the survivors

been praying for? Astrée-Luce was easily routed from the more obvious positions. She became frightened. Presently she rose:

I don't understand. I don't understand. You are joking, Father. Aren't you ashamed of saying such things to bewilder me, when you know how I value everything you say.

Look, then, continued the Cardinal. I shall ask Samuele about this. As he is only a Protestant it will be very easy to entangle him. Samuele, may I assume that God may have intended Donna Matilda to die before long anyway?

Yes, Father, for she died that very night.

But we thought that if we prayed very sincerely we might change His mind.

Why . . . there is authority for our hoping that in extremities our prayer may. . . .

But she died. Then we were not sincere enough! Or persevering enough! Good! Sometimes He grants and sometimes He doesn't, and Christians are expected to pray hard on the chance that this is one of the times He might relent. What a notion! Astrée-Luce, what a thought!

Father, I can't stay and hear you talk this way . . .

What a view of these things. Listen. It is incredible that He should change His mind. Because we frightened mortals are on the carpet? Oh! You are a slave to the idea of bargain. The money changers are still in the temple!

Here Astrée-Luce, gone quite white, returned to the arena with one more brave venture: But, Father, you know He answers the requests of a good Catholic. Then she added in a lower voice with tears in her eyes: But you were there, dear Father. If you had deeply wished it you could have altered the . . .

Here he half rose from his chair crying with terrible eyes: Insane child! What are you saying? I? *Have I no losses?*

Now she flung herself upon the floor before him. You have been saying these things to prove me. What is the answer? I will not let you go until you tell me. Dear Father, you know that prayer is answered. But your clever questions have upset all my old . . . old . . . What is the answer?

Come, sit down, my daughter, and tell me yourself. Think!

This went on for another half-hour. I grew more and more astonished. Mere prayer as a problem was soon left far behind.

It was the idea of a benignant power behind the world that was being questioned now. For the Cardinal it was an exercise in rhetoric, sharpened by his temperamental scepticism on the one hand and by his latent resentment against Astrée-Luce on the other. It was a kind of questioning that would have had no effect on sound intellectual believers. It was disastrous for Astrée-Luce because she was a woman without a reason who just this once was trying to reason. She would so have liked to have been a deep thinker, and when she fell it was through her desire to be a different person.

It went on and on. At every fresh proposal he would now cry Bargain! A Bargain! and point out that her prayers sprang from fear or the greed for comfort. Astrée-Luce was going to pieces. I moved over behind her chair and pleaded with the Cardinal by gesture. Was he tormenting her out of caprice? Did he realize her devotion to himself?

At last she seemed to have a light:

My head is in a whirl. But I know now what you mean me to answer. We may not ask for things, or people, or relief from sickness, but we may ask for spiritual qualities; for instance for the advancement of the Church . . . ?

Vanity! Vanity! How many years have we been praying for a certain good thing? What have statistics shown us?—I refer to the conversion of France.

With a cry Astrée-Luce rose and left the room. I took upon myself to protest to him.

She is foolish, Samuelino. You cannot call those convictions deep that were overturned with straws. No, trust me. This is for her good. I have been a confessor too long to go astray here. She has the spiritual notions of a school-girl. She must be fed on some harsher bread. Understand that she has never suffered. She is good. She is devout. But as I told you the other day, just by accident she has never known trouble.

Just the same, Eminence, I know her well enough to know that this very moment she is in her chapel, clinging to the altar-rails. She will be depressed for weeks.

But just at that moment Astrée-Luce returned. Her manner was agitated and artificially gracious. Will you excuse me if I go to bed now? she asked. (She never called him Father again.) Please stay and talk with Samuele.

No, no. I must be going. But before I go let me tell you one thing. The real truths are difficult. At first they are forbidding. But they are worth all the others.

I shall be thinking over what we have said.—I . . . I . . . Excuse me, if I ask you something?

Yes, my child, what is it?

Promise me you weren't joking.

I wasn't joking at all.

Did I really hear you say that the prayers of good men are of no . . . ? However. Goodnight. You will forgive my slipping away now?

So they took their leaves.

I went to bed worried. I was worrying about Astrée-Luce. Was she going to lose her faith? What do bystanders do in such a case? The loss of one's faith is always comic to outsiders, especially when the loser is in fine health, wealth, and a fairly sound mind. The loss of any one or all of these has a sort of grandeur; Astrée-Luce should have the loss of her faith depend on one of the others. It's not a thing one loses in fine weather.

I was wakened from a troubled sleep by a discreet but continuous knocking upon my door. It was Alviero, the major-domo.

Madame says will you please dress and come to her in the library, please.

What's the matter, Alviero?

I do not know, Signorino. Madame have not sleeped all night. She have been in the church hitting the floor.

All right, Alviero, I'll be there in a minute. What time is it?

Three o'clock and one-half, Signorino.

I dressed rapidly and hurried to the library. Astrée-Luce was still in her gown. Her face was white and drawn; her hair was disheveled. She came toward me with both hands extended: You will forgive my sending for you, won't you? I want you to help me. Tell me: were you made unhappy by the strange things Cardinal Vaini said after dinner?

Yes.

Have you Protestants ideas on these things?

Oh, yes, Mlle. de Morfontaine.

Were his ideas new? Is that what everyone is thinking?

No.

Oh, Samuele, what has happened to me! I have sinned. I have sinned the sin of doubt. Shall I ever have peace again? Can the Lord take me back after I have had such thoughts? Of course, of course, I believe that my prayers are answered, but I have lost . . . the . . . the reason why I believe it. Surely, there is a key here. Perhaps it's just one word. All you have to do is find the one little argument that makes the whole thing natural. Isn't it strange! I've been looking here (and she pointed at the table which was covered with open books, the Bible, Pascal, the Imitation) but I don't seem to be able to put my finger on the right place. Sit down and try and tell me, my dear friend, what arguments there are that God hears us speak and will answer us.

I talked to her for quite a long while, but achieved nothing. Perhaps I even made it worse. I told her that I was sure that she still believed. I showed her that the very fact that she was distressed about it proved that she was furiously believing. After an hour of this wrestling she seemed a little comforted, however, and picking up a fur coat went back to her cold chapel and prayed diligently for faith until the morning.

At about ten she appeared in the garden and asked me to read a note that she was sending to the Cardinal. I was to pass on it. Dear Cardinal Vaini, I will always honor you above all my friends. I think you love me and wish me well. But in your great learning and multiple interests you have forgotten that we who are not brilliant must cling to our childhood beliefs as best we may. I have been inexpressibly troubled since yesterday evening. I want to ask a favor of you: that you indulge my weakness to the extent of not touching upon matters of belief when I am with you. It gives me great pain to have to ask you this. I beg of you to understand it as apart from any personal feelings of unfriendliness. I hope that I may grow strong enough to talk of these matters with you again.

It was a very bad letter, but that was perhaps due to the content. I suggested shyly that she omit the last sentence. So she copied it and sent it off by a special messenger.

Soon the day came for the end of my stay in the Villa. She came up to my room for a last talk.

Samuele, you have been with me during the saddest days of my life. I cannot deny that all interest has gone out of living

for me. I still believe, but I don't believe as I used to. Perhaps
it was not right that I went through life as I did. Now I know
that I rose up every morning full of unspeakable happiness. It
seldom left me. I had never thought before that my beliefs in
themselves were unbelievable. I used to boast that they were,
but I did not know what I was saying. Now hours come to me
when I hear a voice saying: There is no prayer. There is no
God. There are people and trees, millions of them both, every
moment dying.—You will come and see me again, won't you,
Samuele? Have I made it very unpleasant for you in the house?

When I reached my rooms in Rome I found three letters
from the Cardinal asking me to come and see him at once. As
I entered the gate he came toward me eagerly:

How is she? Is she well?

No, Father, she is in great trouble.

Come inside, my son. I must speak to you.

When we entered his study, he closed his door behind him,
and said with great emotion: I want to say to you that I have
sinned, greatly sinned. I cannot rest until I have tried to re-
pair the harm I have done. Look, look at this letter she has
written me.

Yes, I have seen it.

Her letter forbids my explaining what I meant. Is there no
way I can reassure her?

There is only one way now. You must regain all her confi-
dence before you touch on such matters again. You must come
and go about her house as though nothing had happened—

Oh, but she will never ask me again!

Yes, she is having you all to dinner quite soon, Alix, Donna
Leda, and M. Bogard.

Thanks be to God! I thank Thee, I thank Thee, I thank
Thee, I thank Thee . . .

May I speak quite boldly, Eminence?

Yes. I am a poor old man, all mistakes. Speak to me as you
like.

If you go, take great care not to let slip any remark on reli-
gious matters. I beg of you, do *not* try to reinstate yourself
with some orthodox comments. She might misunderstand one
little word and think you were attacking her faith again. It is

very serious. Your ideas are not orthodox, Father, and if you said an orthodox thing it would not sound sincere and that would be worst of all. But if you come and go simply and affectionately, she will lose her horror of you—

Horror of me!

Yes, and very gradually, perhaps after a year, you may be able—

But I may not live a year!

Es muss sein!

This struck him as humorous and ruefully he sang Beethoven's phrase, adding: All the avenues of life lead to that.

Es muss sein. I should have stayed in China. (Here he fell silent for a while, heaving deep sighs and staring at his yellow hands.) God has chosen to take away my reason. I am an idiot, falling into every ditch. Oh, that I had died long ago—and yet I cannot die until I have righted myself. Hand me that red book behind you. There are two plays about old men, Samuelino, that grow dearer every day to an old man. There is your Lear, and—and opening *Oedipus at Colonus* he translated slowly:

Generous son of Aegeus, to the gods alone old age and death come never. But all else is confounded by all-mastering time. The strength of earth decays and the strength of the body. Faith dies. Distrust is born. Among friends the same spirit does not last true . . . and bowing his head he let the book fall to the floor. *Es muss sein.*

I did not go to that dinner. I dined alone with Miss Grier in the city, but at about ten we drove out to Tivoli to sit with the company. As we went I outlined to her discreetly the relations that now existed between two of her best friends: Oh, how stupid he is, she cried. How cruel! What a lot he has forgotten. Don't you see that the whole thing rests, not on the abstract question as to whether her prayers may be answered, but on

the question as to whether ONE prayer may be answered? Her prayer for France . . . Doesn't he believe such things are real to other people?

He thinks that a little doubt will be good for her. He describes her as the woman who has never suffered.

He is in his dotage. I am so angry I am ill.

At this moment our car drew aside to let pass another hurrying by towards Rome. This was Mlle. de Morfontaine's great ugly travelling car and the Cardinal was in it.

There he is now, cried Miss Grier. They must have broken up early.

Something's happened, I said.

Yes, something has very likely happened, God forgive us. If everything were all right, Alix would be driving back with him. Our wonderful company is dissolving. Alix no longer trusts us. Leda is losing her good old commonsense. Astrée-Luce has quarrelled with the Cardinal. I'd better leave Rome and go back to Greenwich.

As we approached the Villa we became aware that something indeed must have happened. The front door was open. The servants were gathered in the hall whispering in front of the closed doors of the drawing rooms. As we entered these opened and Alix, Donna Leda and Mme. Bernstein appeared supporting a sobbing Astrée-Luce. They led her up the stairs to her tower. Miss Grier without questioning the servants as to what had happened, gently urged them to return to their rooms. We passed into the drawing room just in time to see M. Bogard leaving by another door and looking considerably shaken. We sat down in silence, our thoughts full of foreboding. Simultaneously we became aware of a faint odor of powder and smoke and glancing about my eye fell upon a rent near the ceiling beneath which a little pile of white dust had collected on the floor. Mme. Bernstein hurried in and after closing the door carefully behind her, came toward us:

Not a soul must hear of this. Oh, this must be kept so quiet. What a thing to happen! Anything is possible after this. What a blessing that no servants were in the room when . . .

Miss Grier asked her several times what had happened.

I know nothing. I can hardly believe my own senses, she cried. Astrée-Luce must have gone mad. Elizabeth, will you

believe me when I tell you that we were sitting here quietly over our coffee—Look, look! I didn't see that hole in the ceiling before!—Isn't it all frightful?

Please, Anna, please tell us what happened!

I am.—There we were sitting over our coffee, talking in low voices of this and that, when suddenly Astrée-Luce went over to the piano, picked up a revolver from among the flowers and shot at the good Cardinal.

Anna! is he hurt?

No. It didn't even come near him. But what a thing to happen! What on earth could have made her do such a thing! We were friends—we were all such good friends. I do not understand anything.

Try and think, Anna: did she say anything when she fired at him, or before she fired?

That's the strangest of all. You won't believe me. She called out: The Devil is here. The Devil has come into this room. At the Cardinal!

What had he been saying?

Nothing! Merely everyday things. We had been telling stories about the peasants. He had been telling us about some peasants he had come across on his walks outside S. Pancrazio.

Suddenly Alix appeared: Elizabeth, go to her quickly. She wants to see you. She is alone.

Miss Grier hurried out.

Alix turned to me:

Samuele, you know the majordomo better than we do. Will you go and tell him that Astrée-Luce has had a nervous breakdown. That she thought she saw a burglar at the window, and that she fired at him. It is so important for the dear Father's sake that no hint of this gets about.

I went out and found Alviero. He knew the explanation was insufficient, but utterly devoted to the whole Cabala he could be trusted to dress the story at exactly the points that would most convince the other servants.

Alix did not understand what lay back of the shot, but she was able to recall the conversation that had led up to it. The Cardinal had told the following simple story, an incident he had witnessed in one of his walks outside the city wall:

A farmer wished to break his six-year-old daughter of crying.

One afternoon he led her by the hand to the center of a marshy waste, thickly grown with wiry reeds well above the child's head. There he had suddenly flung away her hand, saying: Now are you going to cry any more? The child, with a last rush of contrary pride and with a beginning of fear, started to cry. All right, shouted the father, we don't want any bad children in our house. I'm going to leave you here with the tigers. Goodbye. And jumping out of the child's sight, repaired to a wine shop at the edge of the waste and sat down for an hour's cardplaying. The child strayed about from hummock to hummock, wailing. In due time the father reappeared and taking her affectionately by the hand led her home.

That was all.

But Astrée-Luce had never learned, as the rest of us have, to harden her heart slightly before stories of cruelty or injustice. She may have had no losses of her own, but she had always been ready to expose her imagination to the full force of other people's wrongs. Such an anecdote would have drawn from others a sigh, a swift protective contraction of the lips and a smile of gratitude for its safe conclusion. But to Astrée-Luce it was the vividest reminder that the God whose business it was to brood over the world ministering to the discouraged and the mistreated, was no more. The Cardinal had killed him. There was no one left to soothe the horse that has been beaten to death. The kittens that the boys fling against the wall have no one to speak for them. The dog in torment that keeps his eyes upon her face, and licks her hands even while his eyes grow dim, shall have no comforter but her. This was not a casual story the Cardinal was telling: it concealed a covert allusion to their conversation of the preceding week. It was a taunt. It was a sort of curse. Look at the world without God, he was saying. Get used to it. If she had lost God, oh how clearly she had gained the Devil. Here he was triumphing in this lacerating story. Astrée-Luce went over to the piano, picked up a revolver from the flowers and shot at the Cardinal, crying: The Devil has come into this room!

As the Cardinal drove back that night he kept repeating to himself the words: Then these things are real! It had required Astrée-Luce's shot to show him that belief had long since become for him a delectable game. One piled syllogism on syl-

logism, but the foundations were diaphanous. He strained to remember what faith was like when he had had it. He kept dragging before his mind's eye the young priest in China exhorting the families of the Mandarins. That was himself. Oh, to retrace the way. He would go back to China. If he could look again on the faces that were serene with a serenity he had given them, perhaps he could steal it back. But side by side with this hope was a terrible knowledge: no words could describe the conviction with which he saw himself guilty of the greatest of all sins. Murder was child's play compared to what he had done.

The firing of the shot had done as much for Astrée-Luce. On awaking, her terror lest she had harmed him, later her fear that she had fallen out of reach of his forgiveness was greater than had been her misery in a world without faith. It was given to me to carry from each to the other the first messages of anxious affection. When Astrée-Luce and the Cardinal discovered that they were living in a world where such things could be forgiven, that no actions were too complicated but that love could understand, or dismiss them, on that day they began their lives all over again. This reconciliation was never put into words, in fact it remained to the end merely in a state of hope. They longed to see one another again, but it would have been impossible. They dreamed of one of those long conversations that one never has on earth, but which one projects so easily at midnight, alone and wise; words are not rich enough nor kisses sufficiently compelling to repair all our havoc.

He received permission to return to China, and sailed within a few weeks. Several days after leaving Aden he fell ill of a fever and knew that he was to die. He called the Captain and the ship's doctor to him and told them that if they buried him at sea they would have to face the indignation of the Church, but that they would be fulfilling his dearest wish. He took what measures he could to shift upon himself the blame for such an irregularity. Better, better to be tossing in the tides of the Bengal Sea and to be nosed by a passing shark, than to lie, a sinner of sinners, under a marble tomb with the inevitable *insignis pietate*, the inescapable *ornatissimus*.

The Dusk of the Gods

WHEN my time came to leave Rome I set aside several days for the last offices of piety, piety in the Roman sense. I wrote a note to Elizabeth Grier arranging for a long late talk on the eve of my departure. There are some questions I want to ask you, I said, which no one can answer. Then I went to the Villino Wei Ho and sat for an hour with the Cardinal's sister. The guinea fowl were less vocal than formerly and the rabbits were still hobbling about the garden looking for a gleam of violet. I went to Tivoli and peered through the iron gates of the Villa Horace. Already it looked as though no one had lived there for years. Mlle. de Morfontaine had returned to her estates in France and was living in the closest retirement. They said that she opened no letters, but I wrote her a note of farewell. I even spent an afternoon in the stifling rooms of the Palazzo Aquilanera, where Donna Leda imparted to me in great confidence the news of her daughter's engagement. Apparently the young man was unable to produce any cousins from among the draughty courts of Europe; his family was merely Italian; but he owned a modern palace. At last a bathroom was to make its appearance in the house of Aquilanera. How time flies! ·

My most considerable observance was a trip to Marcantonio's grave. I found it by the village cemetery near the Villa Colonna-Stiavelli. Consecrated ground had been denied the boy, but in her bewilderment and love the mother had contrived a false wall of stones and briars that seemed to include his grave among those of souls that the Church felt safe in recommending at the Judgment Day. Here I sat down and prepared to think about him. I was perhaps the only person in the world who understood what had brought him there. The last office of friendship would be to think about him. But some birds were singing; a man and his wife were cultivating the ground in the next field; the sunlight was heavy. Hard as I tried I could not keep my thoughts on my friend; it was not

difficult to recall his features or to meditate about dissipation; but really elegiac reflection escaped me, Marcantonio. I drove back to Rome ashamed of myself. But it had been a delightful day in the country, unforgettable June weather.

There was one association I could not renew; I could not go to see Alix. Whenever I met her by chance the barrier of her lowered eyelids told me that we would never have long talks again.

Closing the apartment was melancholy enough. Ottima and I spent hours in packing, our heads bent over our boxes and full of our imminent farewells. She was going back to her wine-shop at the corner. Long before I bought a ticket she had begun to pray for those in peril on the sea and to notice the windy days. After an exhausting struggle with myself I decided to give her the police dog. Kurt's affections were equally divided between us; in Europe or in America he would pine for an absent friend. Ottima and Kurt would grow old together in a life filled with exquisite mutual attentions. I could swear that before I went to the hotel on that last night Kurt knew I was taking leave of him. There was a grandeur I fell short of in the way he faced an inevitable situation. He placed one paw on my knee and looked to the right and left in deep embarrassment. Then lying down he placed his muzzle between his paws and barked twice.

I found Elizabeth Grier at midnight sitting in the library that Blair had catalogued. Her small neat head looked tired and after some desultory conversation I made a move to go. She reminded me that I had intended asking her some questions.

My questions are harder to put than to answer.

Try.

Miss Grier, did you know that you and your friends were called the Cabala?

Yes, of course.

I shall never know such a company again. And yet there seems to be some last secret about you that I've never been able to seize. Haven't you anything to tell me that will show me what you all meant, how you found one another, and what made you so different from anyone else?

Miss Grier took a few minutes off to think this over. She sat smiling strangely and stroking with her fingertips the roots of

her hair beside her left temple. Yes, she said, but it will only make you angry if I tell you. Besides it's very long.

It's not long, Miss Grier, but you will insist on making it long because you hate to have your guests leave before dawn. However, I shall listen to you for hours if you promise to throw some light on the Cabala and the dinners at the Villa Horace.

Well, first you must know, Samuele, that the gods of antiquity did not die with the arrival of Christianity.—What are you smiling at?

You're adorable. You have resolved to make your explanation last forever. I asked about the Cardinal and you have gone back to Jupiter. What became of the gods of antiquity?

Naturally when they began to lose worshipers they began to lose some of their divine attributes. They even found themselves able to die if they wanted to. But when one of them died his godhead was passed on to someone else; no sooner is Saturn dead than some man somewhere feels a new personality descending upon him like a strait-jacket, do you see?

Now, Miss Grier!

I told you it would make you angry.

You don't pretend this is true?

I won't tell you whether this is true, or an allegory, or just nonsense.—Next, I am going to read you a strange document that came into my hands. It was written by a certain Hollander who became the god Mercury in 1912. Will you listen?

Has it anything to do with the Cabala?

Yes. And with you. For I sometimes think that you are the new god Mercury. Take some of that claret and listen quietly.

I was born in a Dutch parsonage in 1885. I was the despair of my home and the terror of the village, a little liar and thief in the full enjoyment of my health and wit. My real life began one morning of my twenty-seventh year when I experienced the first of a series of violent pains in the center of my head. This was my deification. Some untender hand was emptying the cup of my skull of its silly gray brains and filling it with the divine gas of instinct. My body too had its part in this; each microscopic cell had to be transformed; I was not to fall sick or grow old or die, save when I chose. As historian of the gods I

have to keep record of an accident whereby, through some monstrosity in spiritual law, an Apollo of the Seventeenth Century failed to completely deify: one arm remained corruptible.

It was then that I discovered the first great attribute of our nature, namely that to wish for a thing is to command it. It does not suddenly fall into your hand or descend in a rosy mist upon your carpet. But circumstances start a discreet ballet about you and the desired thing comes your way through the neatest possible imitation of natural law and probability. Scientists will tell you that they have never seen the sequence of cause and effect interrupted at the instance of prayer or of divine reward or retribution. Do they think, the fools, that their powers of observation are cleverer than the devices of a god? The poor laws of cause and effect are so often set aside that they may be said to be the merest approximations. I am not merely a god but a planet and I speak of things I know. So I stole my mother's savings from under her pillow and went to Paris.

But it is at Rome that we were last worshiped under our own names, and it is thither that we are irresistibly called. During the journey I gradually discovered further traits of my new being. I woke up mornings to discover that bits of information had been deposited in my mind overnight, the enviable knowledge for instance, that I had the power of "sinning" without remorse. I entered the Porta del Popolo one midnight in June, 1912. I ran the length of the Corso, leapt the fence that surrounds the Forum, and flung myself upon the ruins of my temple. All night in the fine rain I tore my clothes in joy and anguish, while up the valley came an interminable and ghostly procession singing my hymns and hiding me in a tower of incense. With the coming of dawn my worshipers vanished and wings no longer fluttered at my heels. I climbed out of the sunken ruins and went out into the misty streets in search of some coffee.

Godlike I never reflect; all my actions arrive of themselves. If I pause to think I fall into error. During the next year I made a great deal of money on the races at Parioli. I speculated in motion pictures and African wheat. I went into journalism and the misrepresentations I sowed will have deferred Europe's recovery from the War many scores of years. I love discord

among gods and men. I have always been happy. I am the happiest of the gods.

I had been called to Rome to serve as the gods' messenger and secretary, but more than a year had passed before I recognized even one. The Church of Santa Maria sopra Minerva is built over an ancient temple to that goddess and there one day I found her. So impatient was I to discover the others that I disobeyed the laws of my nature and went hunting for them. I spent hours hanging about the station in search of newly arrived divinities. One night I strode the platform waiting for the Paris Express. I was trembling with premonition. I had donned a silk hat and its complements, a coral camellia, and a little blonde moustache. Plumed with blue smoke and uttering splendid cries the train rushed into the station. The travelers descended from their compartments into a sea of *facchini* and relatives. I bowed to a Scandinavian diplomat and a Wagnerian prima donna. They returned my greeting hesitantly; a glance into their eyes showed me that they were brilliant but not supernatural. There was no incipient Bacchus among the Oxford students on vacation; the Belgian nuns on pilgrimage discovered me no Vesta. I scanned faces for half an hour until the length of pavement was deserted and a long line of old women with pails appeared. I stopped by the engine to ask a guard if another section of the train was to follow. I turned to see a strange face looking at me from the small window of the locomotive— misshapen, black with coal-dust, gleaming with perspiration and content, and grinning from ear to ear, was Vulcan.

Here Miss Grier raised her head: There follow fifty pages describing his encounters with the others. Have you anything to say? Do you recognize anything?

But, Miss Grier, I've had no headaches! I don't receive what I want!

No?

What am I to understand? You've made it twice as confused. Explain some more.

He goes on to say that the gods were afraid of being laughed at for what they had lost. Flight, for instance, and invisibility, and omniscience and freedom from care. People

would forget that they still had a few enviable powers: their strange elation; their command over matter; their ability to live or die when they chose and to live beyond good and evil. And so on.

What became of him?

Finally he decided to die, as they all do. All gods and heroes are by nature the enemies of Christianity—a faith trailing its aspirations and remorses and in whose presence every man is a failure. Only a broken will can enter the Kingdom of Heaven. Finally tired out with the cult of themselves they give in. They go over. They renounce themselves.

I was astonished at the desolation in her voice. It held me back from eagerly demanding of her the application to the Cabala of all these principles. We went into the next room where her musicians were waiting to offer us some English madrigals. The applications still occur to me, especially when I am depressed. They give in. They go over.

On the night that my steamer left the bay of Naples I lay sleepless in my deck-chair until morning. Why was I not more reluctant at leaving Europe? How could I lie there repeating the Aeneid and longing for the shelf of Manhattan? It was Virgil's sea that we were crossing; the very stars were his: Arcturus and the showery Hyades, the two Bears and Orion in his harness of gold. All these passed before me in a cloudless sky and in the water, murmuring before a light wind, the sliding constellations were brokenly reflected.

Mercury is not only the messenger of the gods; he is the conductor of the dead as well. If in the least part his powers had fallen to me I should be able to invoke spirits. Perhaps Virgil could read my mood for me, and raising my two palms I said in a low voice (not loud enough to reach the open portholes behind me):

Prince of poets, Virgil, one of your guests and the last of barbarians invokes you.

For an instant I thought I saw the shimmer of a robe and the reflection of the starlight on the shiny side of a laurel leaf. I pressed my advantage:

O *anima cortese mantovana*, greatest of all Romans, out of

the eternity of that limbo to which the Florentine, perhaps wrongly, consigned you, grant me a crumb of time.

Now indeed the shade stood in mid-air just above the hand-rail. The stars were glittering and the water was glittering, and the great shade, picked out in sparks, was glittering furiously. But the image must become clearer. There was one title that might avail more with him than those of poet or Roman.

Oh, greatest spirit of the ancient world and prophet of the new, by that fortunate guess wherein you foretold the coming of Him who will admit you to His mountain, thou first Christian in Europe, speak to me!

Now indeed the gracious spirit became completely visible with pulsations of light, half silver and half gold, and spoke:

Be brief, importunate barbarian. Except for this last salutation wherein you have touched my only pride, I would not delay here. Detain me not from the absorbing games of my peers. Erasmus is in debate with Plato, and Augustine has descended from the hill and sits among us, though the air is gray. Be brief, I pray you, and give heed to your Latin.

At this I realized that I had no definite question to put to my guest. In order to mark time and prolong so uncommon an interview, I engaged him in conversation:

Was I then right, Master, in assuming that Dante was not completely in God's confidence?

Indignation infused a saffron stain into the noble figure in silver-gold: Where, where is he, that soul of vinegar, that chose to assign the souls of the dead more harshly than God? Tell him that though a pagan I too shall see bliss. It is nothing that I must first pay the penalty of ten thousand years. Behold this moment I exhibit the sin of anger; where is *he* in pain for the sin of pride?

I was a little shocked to discover that neither genius nor death removed us beyond the temptation to asperity, but said: Master, have you met the poets of the English tongue that have come into your groves?

Let us be brief, my friend.—One came that had been formerly blind and did me much honor. He spoke a noble Latin. Those that stood by assured me that in his lines mine were not seldom reflected.

Milton was indeed your son. . . .

But before him came another, greater than he, a writer of pieces for a theatre. He was proud and troubled and strode among us unseeing. He made me no salutation. Vanity no longer exists among us, but it is sweet to exchange greetings among the poets.

He knew but little Latin, Master, and perhaps had never read your page. Moreover in life he was neither the enemy nor advocate of grace and being arrived in your region his whole mind may well have been consumed with anxiety as to his eternal residence. Is he among you still?

He sits apart, his hand over his eyes, and only raises his head when, in the long green evenings, Casella sings to us, or when on the wind there drifts from Purgatory the chorus that one Palestrina prepares.

Master, I have just spent a year in the city that was your whole life. Am I wrong to leave it?

Let us be brief. This world where Time is, troubles me. My heart has almost started beating again,—what horror! Know, importunate barbarian, that I spent my whole lifetime under a great delusion,—that Rome and the house of Augustus were eternal. Nothing is eternal save Heaven. Romes existed before Rome and when Rome will be a waste there will be Romes after her. Seek out some city that is young. The secret is to make a city, not to rest in it. When you have found one, drink in the illusion that she too is eternal. Nay, I have heard of your city. Its foundations have knocked upon our roof and the towers have cast a shadow across the sandals of the angels. Rome too was great. Oh, in the pride of your city, and when she too begins to produce great men, do not forget mine. When shall I erase from my heart this love of her? I cannot enter Zion until I have forgotten Rome.—Dismiss me now, my friend, I pray thee. These vain emotions have shaken me. . . . (Suddenly the poet became aware of the Mediterranean:) Oh, beautiful are these waters. Behold! For many years I have almost forgotten the world. Beautiful! Beautiful!—But no! what horror, what pain! Are you still alive? Alive? How can you endure it? All your thoughts are guesses, all your body is shaken with breath, all your senses are infirm, and your mind

ever full of the fumes of one passion or another. Oh, what misery to be a man. Hurry and die!

Farewell, Virgil!

The shimmering ghost faded before the stars, and the engines beneath me pounded eagerly toward the new world and the last and greatest of all cities.

THE BRIDGE OF
SAN LUIS REY

To my Mother

Perhaps an Accident

O N Friday noon, July the twentieth, 1714, the finest bridge
in all Peru broke and precipitated five travellers into the
gulf below. This bridge was on the highroad between Lima
and Cuzco and hundreds of persons passed over it every day. It
had been woven of osier by the Incas more than a century
before and visitors to the city were always led out to see it. It
was a mere ladder of thin slats swung out over the gorge, with
handrails of dried vine. Horses and coaches and chairs had to
go down hundreds of feet below and pass over the narrow tor-
rent on rafts, but no one, not even the Viceroy, not even the
Archbishop of Lima, had descended with the baggage rather
than cross by the famous bridge of San Luis Rey. St. Louis of
France himself protected it, by his name and by the little mud
church on the further side. The bridge seemed to be among
the things that last forever; it was unthinkable that it should
break. The moment a Peruvian heard of the accident he signed
himself and made a mental calculation as to how recently he
had crossed by it and how soon he had intended crossing by it
again. People wandered about in a trance-like state, muttering;
they had the hallucination of seeing themselves falling into a
gulf.

There was a great service in the Cathedral. The bodies of the
victims were approximately collected and approximately sepa-
rated from one another, and there was great searching of
hearts in the beautiful city of Lima. Servant girls returned
bracelets which they had stolen from their mistresses, and
usurers harangued their wives angrily, in defense of usury. Yet
it was rather strange that this event should have so impressed
the Limeans, for in that country those catastrophes which
lawyers shockingly call the "acts of God" were more than usu-
ally frequent. Tidal waves were continually washing away cities;
earthquakes arrived every week and towers fell upon good
men and women all the time. Diseases were forever flitting in
and out of the provinces and old age carried away some of the

most admirable citizens. That is why it was so surprising that the Peruvians should have been especially touched by the rent in the bridge of San Luis Rey.

Everyone was very deeply impressed, but only one person did anything about it, and that was Brother Juniper. By a series of coincidences so extraordinary that one almost suspects the presence of some Intention, this little red-haired Franciscan from Northern Italy happened to be in Peru converting the Indians and happened to witness the accident.

It was a very hot noon, that fatal noon, and coming around the shoulder of a hill Brother Juniper stopped to wipe his forehead and to gaze upon the screen of snowy peaks in the distance, then into the gorge below him filled with the dark plumage of green trees and green birds and traversed by its ladder of osier. Joy was in him; things were not going badly. He had opened several little abandoned churches and the Indians were crawling in to early Mass and groaning at the moment of miracle as though their hearts would break. Perhaps it was the pure air from the snows before him; perhaps it was the memory that brushed him for a moment of the poem that bade him raise his eyes to the helpful hills. At all events he felt at peace. Then his glance fell upon the bridge, and at that moment a twanging noise filled the air, as when the string of some musical instrument snaps in a disused room, and he saw the bridge divide and fling five gesticulating ants into the valley below.

Anyone else would have said to himself with secret joy: "Within ten minutes myself. . . !" But it was another thought that visited Brother Juniper: "Why did this happen to *those* five?" If there were any plan in the universe at all, if there were any pattern in a human life, surely it could be discovered mysteriously latent in those lives so suddenly cut off. Either we live by accident and die by accident, or we live by plan and die by plan. And on that instant Brother Juniper made the resolve to inquire into the secret lives of those five persons, that moment falling through the air, and to surprise the reason of their taking off.

It seemed to Brother Juniper that it was high time for theology to take its place among the exact sciences and he had long

intended putting it there. What he had lacked hitherto was a laboratory. Oh, there had never been any lack of specimens; any number of his charges had met calamity,—spiders had stung them; their lungs had been touched; their houses had burned down and things had happened to their children from which one averts the mind. But these occasions of human woe had never been quite fit for scientific examination. They had lacked what our good savants were later to call *proper control.* The accident had been dependent upon human error, for example, or had contained elements of probability. But this collapse of the bridge of San Luis Rey was a sheer Act of God. It afforded a perfect laboratory. Here at last one could surprise His intentions in a pure state.

You and I can see that coming from anyone but Brother Juniper this plan would be the flower of a perfect skepticism. It resembled the effort of those presumptuous souls who wanted to walk on the pavements of Heaven and built the Tower of Babel to get there. But to our Franciscan there was no element of doubt in the experiment. He knew the answer. He merely wanted to prove it, historically, mathematically, to his converts, —poor obstinate converts, so slow to believe that their pains were inserted into their lives for their own good. People were always asking for good sound proofs; doubt springs eternal in the human breast, even in countries where the Inquisition can read your very thoughts in your eyes.

This was not the first time that Brother Juniper had tried to resort to such methods. Often on the long trips he had to make (scurrying from parish to parish, his robe tucked up about his knees, for haste) he would fall to dreaming of experiments that justify the ways of God to man. For instance, a complete record of the Prayers for Rain and their results. Often he had stood on the steps of one of his little churches, his flock kneeling before him on the baked street. Often he had stretched his arms to the sky and declaimed the splendid ritual. Not often, but several times, he had felt the virtue enter him and seen the little cloud forming on the horizon. But there were many times when weeks went by . . . but why think of them? It was not himself he was trying to convince that rain and drought were wisely apportioned.

Thus it was that the determination rose within him at the

moment of the accident. It prompted him to busy himself for six years, knocking at all the doors in Lima, asking thousands of questions, filling scores of notebooks, in his effort at establishing the fact that each of the five lost lives was a perfect whole. Everyone knew that he was working on some sort of memorial of the accident and everyone was very helpful and misleading. A few even knew the principal aim of his activity and there were patrons in high places.

The result of all this diligence was an enormous book, which as we shall see later, was publicly burned on a beautiful Spring morning in the great square. But there was a secret copy and after a great many years and without much notice it found its way to the library of the University of San Marco. There it lies between two great wooden covers collecting dust in a cupboard. It deals with one after another of the victims of the accident, cataloguing thousands of little facts and anecdotes and testimonies, and concluding with a dignified passage describing why God had settled upon that person and upon that day for His demonstration of wisdom. Yet for all his diligence Brother Juniper never knew the central passion of Doña María's life; nor of Uncle Pio's, not even of Esteban's. And I, who claim to know so much more, isn't it possible that even I have missed the very spring within the spring?

Some say that we shall never know and that to the gods we are like the flies that the boys kill on a summer day, and some say, on the contrary, that the very sparrows do not lose a feather that has not been brushed away by the finger of God.

PART TWO:

The Marquesa de Montemayor

A NY Spanish schoolboy is required to know today more about Doña María, Marquesa de Montemayor, than Brother Juniper was to discover in years of research. Within a century of her death her letters had become one of the monuments of Spanish literature and her life and times have ever since been the object of long studies. But her biographers have erred in one direction as greatly as the Franciscan did in another; they have tried to invest her with a host of graces, to read back into her life and person some of the beauties that abound in her letters, whereas all real knowledge of this wonderful woman must proceed from the act of humiliating her and of divesting her of all beauties save one.

She was the daughter of a cloth-merchant who had acquired the money and the hatred of the Limeans within a stone's-throw of the Plaza. Her childhood was unhappy: she was ugly; she stuttered; her mother persecuted her with sarcasms in an effort to arouse some social charms and forced her to go about the town in a veritable harness of jewels. She lived alone and she thought alone. Many suitors presented themselves, but as long as she could she fought against the convention of her time and was determined to remain single. There were hysterical scenes with her mother, recriminations, screams and slamming of doors. At last at twenty-six she found herself penned into marriage with a supercilious and ruined nobleman and the Cathedral of Lima fairly buzzed with the sneers of her guests. Still she lived alone and thought alone, and when an exquisite daughter was born to her she fastened upon her an idolatrous love. But little Clara took after her father; she was cold and intellectual. At the age of eight she was calmly correcting her mother's speech and presently regarding her with astonishment and repulsion. The frightened mother became meek and obsequious but she could not prevent herself from persecuting Doña Clara with nervous attention and a fatiguing love. Again there were hysterical recriminations, screams and slamming of

doors. From the offers of marriage that fell to her, Doña Clara deliberately chose the one that required her removal to Spain. So to Spain she went, to that land from which it takes six months to receive an answer to one's letter. The leave-taking before so long a voyage became in Peru one of the formal services of the Church. The ship was blessed and as the space widened between the vessel and the beach both companies knelt and sang a hymn that never failed to sound weak and timid in all that open air. Doña Clara sailed with most admirable composure, leaving her mother to gaze after the bright ship, her hand pressing now her heart and now her mouth. Blurred and streaked became her view of the serene Pacific and the enormous clouds of pearl that hang forever motionless above it.

Left alone in Lima the Marquesa's life grew more and more inward. She became increasingly negligent in her dress and like all lonely people she talked to herself audibly. All her existence lay in the burning center of her mind. On that stage were performed endless dialogues with her daughter, impossible reconciliations, scenes eternally recommenced of remorse and forgiveness. On the street you beheld an old woman, her red wig fallen a little over one ear, her left cheek angry with a leprous affection, her right with a complementary adjustment of rouge. Her chin was never dry; her lips were never still. Lima was a city of eccentrics, but even there she became its jest as she drove through the streets or shuffled up the steps of its churches. She was thought to be continuously drunk. Worse things were said of her and petitions were afloat that she be locked up. She had been denounced three times before the Inquisition. It is not impossible that she might have been burned had her son-in-law been less influential in Spain and had she not somehow collected a few friends about the viceregal court who suffered her for her oddity and her wide reading.

The distressing character of the relations between mother and daughter were further embittered by misunderstandings over money. The Condesa received a handsome allowance from her mother and frequent gifts. Doña Clara soon became the outstanding woman of intelligence at the Spanish court. All the wealth of Peru would have been insufficient to maintain her in the grandiose style she fancied for herself. Strangely enough her extravagance proceeded from one of the best traits

in her nature: she regarded her friends, her servants and all the interesting people in the capital, as her children. In fact there seemed only one person in the world towards whom she did not expend herself in kind offices. Among her *protégés* was the cartographer De Blasiis (whose *Maps of the New World* was dedicated to the Marquesa de Montemayor amid the roars of the courtiers at Lima who read that she was the "*admiration of her city and a rising sun in the West*"); another was the scientist Azuarius whose treatise on the laws of hydraulics was suppressed by the Inquisition as being too exciting. For a decade the Condesa literally sustained all the arts and sciences of Spain; it was not her fault that nothing memorable was produced in that time.

About four years after Doña Clara's departure Doña María received her permission to visit Europe. On both sides the visit was anticipated with resolutions well nourished on self-reproach: the one to be patient, the other to be undemonstrative. Both failed. Each tortured the other and was on the point of losing her mind under the alternations of self-rebuke and the outbursts of passion. At length one day Doña María rose before dawn, daring no more than to kiss the door behind which her daughter was sleeping, took ship and returned to America. Henceforth letter-writing had to take the place of all the affection that could not be lived.

Hers were the letters that in an astonishing world have become the text-book of schoolboys and the ant-hill of the grammarians. Doña María would have invented her genius had she not been born with it, so necessary was it to her love that she attract the attention, perhaps the admiration, of her distant child. She forced herself to go out into society in order to cull its ridicules; she taught her eye to observe; she read the masterpieces of her language to discover its effects; she insinuated herself into the company of those who were celebrated for their conversation. Night after night in her baroque palace she wrote and rewrote the incredible pages, forcing from her despairing mind those miracles of wit and grace, those distilled chronicles of the viceregal court. We know now that her daughter barely glanced at the letters and that it is to the son-in-law that we owe their preservation.

The Marquesa would have been astonished to learn that her

letters were immortal. Yet many critics have accused her of keeping one eye on posterity and point to a number of letters that have all the air of being bravura pieces. To them it seems impossible that Doña María should have put herself to the same pains to dazzle her daughter that most artists expend on dazzling the public. Like her son-in-law they misunderstood her: the Conde delighted in her letters, but he thought that when he had enjoyed the style he had extracted all their richness and intention, missing (as most readers do) the whole purport of literature, which is the notation of the heart. Style is but the faintly contemptible vessel in which the bitter liquid is recommended to the world. The Marquesa would even have been astonished to learn that her letters were very good, for such authors live always in the noble weather of their own minds and those productions which seem remarkable to us are little better than a day's routine to them.

This was the old woman who hour by hour would sit upon her balcony, her odd straw hat casting a purple shadow across her lined and yellow face. How often as she turned her pages with her gemmed hands, she would ask herself, almost with amusement, whether the constant pain at her heart had an organic seat. She wondered whether a subtle doctor cutting through to that battered throne could at last discover a sign and lifting his face to the amphitheatre cry out to his students: "This woman has suffered, and her suffering has left its mark upon the structure of her heart." This idea had so often visited her that one day she wrote it into a letter and her daughter scolded her for an introspective and for making a cult of sorrow.

The knowledge that she would never be loved in return acted upon her ideas as a tide acts upon cliffs. Her religious beliefs went first, for all she could ask of a god, or of immortality, was the gift of a place where daughters love their mothers; the other attributes of Heaven you could have for a song. Next she lost her belief in the sincerity of those about her. She secretly refused to believe that anyone (herself excepted) loved anyone. All families lived in a wasteful atmosphere of custom and kissed one another with secret indifference. She saw that the people of this world moved about in an armour of egotism, drunk with self-gazing, athirst for compliments, hearing little of what was said to them, unmoved by the accidents that

befell their closest friends, in dread of all appeals that might interrupt their long communion with their own desires. These were the sons and daughters of Adam from Cathay to Peru. And when on the balcony her thoughts reached this turn, her mouth would contract with shame for she knew that she too sinned and that though her love for her daughter was vast enough to include all the colours of love, it was not without a shade of tyranny: she loved her daughter not for her daughter's sake, but for her own. She longed to free herself from this ignoble bond; but the passion was too fierce to cope with. And then on that green balcony a strange warfare would shake the hideous old lady, a singularly futile struggle against a temptation to which she would never have the opportunity of succumbing. How could she rule her daughter when her daughter saw to it that four thousand miles lay between them? Nevertheless Doña María wrestled with the ghost of her temptation and was worsted on every occasion. She wanted her daughter for herself; she wanted to hear her say: "You are the best of all possible mothers"; she longed to hear her whisper: "Forgive me."

About two years after her return from Spain there took place a series of inconspicuous events that had a great deal to tell about the inner life of the Marquesa. Only the faintest allusion to them occurs in the Correspondence, but as that is found in Letter XXII which contains other signs I shall do my best to give a translation and commentary of the first part of the letter:

"*Are there no doctors in Spain? Where are those good men from Flanders that used to help you so? Oh, my treasure, how can we punish you enough for letting your cold endure so many weeks? Don Vicente, I implore you to make my child see reason. Angels of Heaven, I implore you to make my child see reason. Now that you are better, I beg of you, resolve that when the first warning of a cold comes you will steam yourself well and go to bed. Here in Peru I am helpless; I can do nothing. Do not be self-willed, my beloved. God bless you. I am enclosing in today's packet the gum of some tree which the sisters of San Tomás peddle from door to door. Whether it be of much use I know not. It can do no harm. I am told that in the convent the silly sisters inhale it so diligently that one cannot smell the incense at Mass. Whether it be worth anything I know not; try it.*

"*Rest easy, my love, I am sending His Most Catholic Majesty the perfect gold chain.*" (Her daughter had written her: "*The chain arrived in good condition and I wore it at the christening of the Infante. His Most Catholic Majesty was gracious enough to admire it and when I told Him that you had given it me He sent you His compliments upon your taste. Do not fail to send Him one as like it as possible; send it at once, by way of the Chamberlain.*") "*He need never know that in order to obtain it I had to walk into a picture. Do you remember that in the sacristy of San Martin there is a portrait by Velasquez of the Viceroy who founded the monastery and of his wife and brat? and that his wife is wearing a gold chain? I resolved that only that chain would do. So one midnight I slipped into the sacristy, climbed upon the robing-table like a girl of twelve and walked in. The canvas resisted for a moment, but the painter himself came forward to lift me through the pigment. I told him that the most beautiful girl in Spain wished to present the finest gold chain that could be found to the most gracious king in the world. It was as simple as that, and there we stood talking, we four, in the gray and silvery air that makes a Velasquez. Now I keep thinking about a more golden light; I keep looking at the Palace: I must pass the evening in a Titian. Would the Viceroy let me?*

"*But His Excellency has the gout again. I say 'again' because the flattery of the court insists that there are times when he is free of it. This being Saint Mark's day His Excellency started out to visit the University where twenty-two new doctors were being brought into the world. He had hardly been carried from his divan to his coach when he screamed and refused to go any farther. He was carried back to his bed where he broke a most delicious cigar and sent for the Perichole. And while we listened to long doctrinal addresses, more or less in Latin, he heard all about us, more or less in Spanish, from the reddest and cruellest lips in town.*" (Doña María permitted herself this passage, although she had just read in her daughter's last letter: "*How many times must I tell you to be more cautious in the things you say in your letters? They often show signs of having been opened on the journey. Nothing could be more ill-judged than your remarks on the you-know-what-I-mean at Cuzco. Such remarks are not funny, even though Vicente did compliment you upon them in his postscript, and they might get us into a great deal of trouble with*

Certain Persons here in Spain. I continue to be astonished that your indiscretions have not long since led to your being ordered to retire to your farm.")

"*There was a great press at the Exercises and two women fell from the balcony, but God in His goodness saw that they fell on Doña Merced. All three are badly hurt, but will be thinking of other things within a year. The President was speaking at the moment of the accident and being short-sighted could not imagine what the disturbance of cries and talk and falling bodies could be about. It was very pleasant to see him bowing, under the impression that he was being applauded.*

"*Speaking of the Perichole, and of applause, you should know that Pepita and I decided to go to the Comedia this evening. The public still idolizes its Perichole; it even forgives her her years. We are told that she saves what she can, every morning, by passing alternate pencils of ice and fire across her cheeks.*" (Translation falls especially short of this conceit which carries the whole flamboyance of the Spanish language. It was intended as an obsequious flattery of the Condesa, and was untrue. The great actress was twenty-eight at this time; her cheeks had the smoothness and polish of dark yellow marble and would certainly have retained that quality for many years. Apart from the cosmetics required by her performances the only treatment Camila Perichole afforded her face was to throw cold water at it twice a day, like a peasant woman at a horse trough.) "*That curious man they call Uncle Pio is by her all the time. Don Rubío says that he cannot make out whether Uncle Pio is her father, her lover, or her son. The Perichole gave a wonderful performance. Scold me all you like for a provincial ninny, you have no such actresses in Spain.*" And so on.

It is on this visit to the theatre that further matter hangs. She decided to go to the Comedia where the Perichole was playing Doña Leonor in Moreto's *Trampa Adelante*; perhaps some material could be derived from the visit for her daughter's next letter. She took with her Pepita, a little girl about whom later we shall learn much. Doña María had borrowed her from the orphanage connected with the Convent of Santa María Rosa de las Rosas to be her companion. The Marquesa sat in her box gazing with flagging attention at the brilliant stage. Between the acts it was the Perichole's custom to lay aside the

courtly rôle and appear before the curtain to sing a few topical songs. The malicious actress had seen the Marquesa arrive and presently began improvising couplets alluding to her appearance, her avarice, her drunkenness, and even to her daughter's flight from her. The attention of the house was subtly directed to the old woman and a rising murmur of contempt accompanied the laughter of the audience. But the Marquesa, deeply moved by the first two acts of the comedy, scarcely saw the singer and sat staring before her, thinking about Spain. Camila Perichole became bolder and the air was electric with the hatred and glee of the crowd. At last Pepita plucked the Marquesa's sleeve and whispered to her that they should go. As they left the box the house arose and burst into a roar of triumph; the Perichole flung herself into a frenzied dance, for she saw the manager at the back of the hall and knew that her salary had been increased. But the Marquesa remained unaware of what had taken place; in fact she was quite pleased, for during the visit she had contrived a few felicitous phrases, phrases (who knows) that might bring a smile to her daughter's face and might make her murmur: "Really, my mother is charming."

In due time the report reached the Viceroy's ears that one of his aristocrats had been openly baited in the theatre. He summoned the Perichole to the Palace and ordered her to call upon the Marquesa and to apologize. The trip was to be made barefoot and in a black dress. Camila argued and fought, but all she gained was a pair of shoes.

The Viceroy had three reasons for insisting. In the first place the singer had taken liberties with his court. Don Andrés had contrived to make exile endurable by building up a ceremonial so complicated that it could be remembered only by a society that had nothing else to think about. He nursed his little aristocracy and its minute distinctions and any insult paid to a Marquesa was an insult to His Person. In the second place, Doña María's son-in-law was an increasingly important personage in Spain, laden with possibilities of injury to the Viceroy, nay with the possibility of supplanting him. The Conde Vicente d'Abuirre must not be vexed, even through his half-wit mother-in-law. Finally, the Viceroy was delighted to humble the actress. He suspected that she was deceiving him with a matador, perhaps with an actor,—between the flattery of the court and the

inertia of gout he could not quite make out who it was; at all events, it was clear that the singer was beginning to forget that he was one of the first men in the world.

The Marquesa, beside not having heard the scurrilous songs, was in other ways unprepared for the actress's visit. You should know that after the departure of her daughter, Doña María had lighted upon a certain consolation: she had taken to drinking. Everyone drank *chicha* in Peru and there was no particular disgrace in being found unconscious on a feast day. Doña María had begun to discover that her feverish monologues had a way of keeping her awake all night. Once she took a delicate fluted glassful of *chicha* on retiring. Oblivion was so sweet that presently she stole larger amounts and tried dissimulating their effects from Pepita; she hinted that she was not well, and represented herself as going into a decline. At last she resigned all pretense. The boats that carried her letter to Spain did not leave oftener than once a mouth. During the week that preceded the making of the packet she observed a strict regimen and cultivated the city assiduously for material. At last on the eve of the post she wrote the letter, making up the bundle towards dawn and leaving it for Pepita to deliver to the agent. Then as the sun rose she would shut herself up in her room with some flagons and drift through the next few weeks without the burden of consciousness. Finally she would emerge from her happiness and prepare to go into a state of "training" in preparation for the writing of another letter.

Thus on the night following the scandal in the theatre she wrote Letter XXII and retired to bed with a carafe. All next day Pepita moved about the room, glancing anxiously at the figure on the bed. The next afternoon Pepita brought her needlework into the room. The Marquesa lay staring at the ceiling with wide-open eyes, talking to herself. Towards dusk Pepita was called to the door and informed that the Perichole had come to see the mistress. Pepita remembered the theatre very well and sent back word angrily that the mistress refused to see her. The man carried the message to the street door, but returned awestruck with the news that the Señora Perichole was armed with a letter from the Viceroy presenting her to the lady. Pepita tiptoed to the bed and started talking to the Marquesa. The glazed eyes moved to the girl's face. Pepita shook

her gently. With great effort Doña María tried to fix her mind on what was being said to her. Twice she lay back, refusing to seize the meaning, but at last, like a general calling together in a rain and by night the dispersed division of his army she assembled memory and attention and a few other faculties and painfully pressing her hand to her forehead she asked for a bowl of snow. When it was brought her, she long and drowsily pressed handfuls of it against her temples and cheeks; then rising she stood for a long time leaning against the bed and looking at her shoes. At last she raised her head with decision, she called for her fur-trimmed cloak and a veil. She put them on and tottered into her handsomest reception room where the actress stood waiting for her.

Camila had intended to be perfunctory and if possible impudent, but now she was struck for the first time with the dignity of the old woman. The mercer's daughter could carry herself at times with all the distinction of the Montemayors and when she was drunk she wore the grandeur of Hecuba. For Camila the half-closed eyes had the air of weary authority and she began almost timidly:

"I come, señora, to make sure that you could not have misunderstood anything I said on the evening that Your Grace did me the honour to visit my theatre."

"Misunderstood? Misunderstood?" said the Marquesa.

"Your Grace might have misunderstood and thought that my words were intended to be disrespectful to Your Grace."

"To me?"

"Your Grace is not offended at her humble servant? Your Grace is aware that a poor actress in my position may be carried beyond her intentions . . . that it is very difficult . . . that everything. . . ."

"How can I be offended, señora? All that I can remember is that you gave a beautiful performance. You are a great artist. You should be happy, happy. My handkerchief, Pepita. . . ."

The Marquesa brought out these words very rapidly and vaguely, but the Perichole was confounded. A piercing sense of shame filled her. She turned crimson. At last she was able to murmur:

"It was in the songs between the acts of the comedy. I was afraid Your Grace . . ."

"Yes, yes. I remember now. I left early. Pepita, we left early, did we not? But, señora, you are good enough to forgive my leaving early, yes, even in the middle of your admirable performance. I forget why we left. Pepita . . . oh, some indisposition. . . ."

It was impossible that anyone in the theatre could have missed the intention of the songs. Camila could only assume that the Marquesa, out of a sort of fantastic magnanimity, was playing the farce of not having noticed it. She was almost in tears: "But you are so good to overlook my childishness, señora,—I mean Your Grace. I did not know. I did not know your goodness. Señora, permit me to kiss your hand."

Doña María held out her hand astonished. She had not for a long time been addressed with such consideration. Her neighbors, her tradespeople, her servants—for even Pepita lived in awe of her,—her very daughter had never approached her thus. It induced a new mood in her; one that must very likely be called maudlin. She became loquacious:

"Offended, offended at you, my beautiful, . . . my gifted child? Who am I, a . . . an unwise and unloved old woman, to be offended at you? I felt, my daughter, as though I were— what says the poet?—*surprising through a cloud the conversation of the angels.* Your voice kept finding new wonders in our Moreto. When you said:

> '*Don Juan, si mi amor estimas,*
> *Y la fe segura es necia,*
> *Enojarte mis temores*
> *Es no quererme discreta.*
> *¿Tan seguros. . . .'*

and so on,—that was true! And what a gesture you made at the close of the First Day. There, with your hand *so.* Such a gesture as the Virgin made, saying to Gabriel: *How is it possible that I shall have a child?* No, no, you will begin to have resentment at me, for I am going to tell you about a gesture that you may remember to use some day. Yes, it would fit well into that scene where you forgive your Don Juan de Lara. Perhaps I should tell you that I saw it made one day by my daughter. My daughter is a very beautiful woman . . . everyone thinks. Did . . . did you know my Doña Clara, Señora?"

"Her Grace often did me the honour of visiting my theatre. I knew the Condesa well by sight."

"Do not remain so, on one knee, my child.—Pepita, tell Jenarito to bring this lady some sweet-cakes at once. Think, one day we fell out, I forget over what. Oh, there is nothing strange in that; all we mothers from time to time. . . . Look, can you come a little closer? You must not believe the town that says she was unkind to me. You are a great woman with a beautiful nature and you can see further than the crowd sees in these matters.—It is a pleasure to talk to you. What beautiful hair you have! What beautiful hair!—She had not a warm impulsive nature, I know that. But, oh, my child, she has such a store of intelligence and graciousness. Any misunderstandings between us are so plainly my fault; is it not wonderful that she is so quick to forgive me? This day there fell one of those little moments. We both said hasty things and went off to our rooms. Then each turned back to be forgiven. Finally only a door separated us and there we were pulling it in contrary ways. But at last she . . . took my . . . face . . . thus, in her two white hands. So! Look!"

The Marquesa almost fell out of her chair as she leaned forward, her face streaming with happy tears, and made the beatific gesture. I should say the mythical gesture, for the incident was but a recurring dream.

"I am glad you are here," she continued, "for now you have heard from my own lips that she is not unkind to me, as some people say. Listen, señora, the fault was mine. Look at me. Look at me. There was some mistake that made me the mother of so beautiful a girl. I am difficult. I am trying. You and she are great women. No, do not stop me: you are rare women, and I am only a nervous . . . a foolish . . . a stupid woman. Let me kiss your feet. I am impossible. I am impossible. I am impossible."

Here indeed the old woman did fall out of her chair and was gathered up by Pepita and led back to her bed. The Perichole walked home in consternation and sat for a long time gazing into her eyes in the mirror, her palms pressed against her cheeks.

But the person who saw most of the difficult hours of the Marquesa was her little companion, Pepita. Pepita was an orphan and had been brought up by that strange genius of Lima,

the Abbess Madre María del Pilar. The only occasion upon which the two great women of Peru (as the perspective of history was to reveal them) met face to face was on the day when Doña María called upon the directress of the Convent of Santa María Rosa de las Rosas and asked if she might borrow some bright girl from the orphanage to be her companion. The Abbess gazed hard at the grotesque old woman. Even the wisest people in the world are not perfectly wise and Madre María del Pilar who was able to divine the poor human heart behind all the masks of folly and defiance, had always refused to concede one to the Marquesa de Montemayor. She asked her a great many questions and then paused to think. She wanted to give Pepita the worldly experience of living in the palace. She also wanted to bend the old woman to her own interests. And she was filled with a sombre indignation, for she knew she was gazing at one of the richest women in Peru, and the blindest.

She was one of those persons who have allowed their lives to be gnawed away because they have fallen in love with an idea several centuries before its appointed appearance in the history of civilization. She hurled herself against the obstinacy of her time in her desire to attach a little dignity to women. At midnight when she had finished adding up the accounts of the House she would fall into insane vision of an age when women could be organized to protect women, women travelling, women as servants, women when they are old or ill, the women she had discovered in the mines of Potosí, or in the workrooms of the cloth-merchants, the girls she had collected out of doorways on rainy nights. But always the next morning she had to face the fact that the women in Peru, even her nuns, went through life with two notions: one, that all the misfortunes that might befall them were merely due to the fact that they were not sufficiently attractive to bind some man to their maintenance and, two, that all the misery in the world was worth his caress. She had never known any country but the environs of Lima and she assumed that all its corruption was the normal state of mankind. Looking back from our century we can see the whole folly of her hope. Twenty such women would have failed to make any impression on that age. Yet she continued diligently in her task. She resembled the swallow in the fable who once every thousand years transferred a grain of

wheat, in the hope of rearing a mountain to reach the moon. Such persons are raised up in every age; they obstinately insist on transporting their grains of wheat and they derive a certain exhilaration from the sneers of the bystanders. "How queerly they dress!" we cry. "How queerly they dress!"

Her plain red face had great kindliness, and more idealism than kindliness, and more generalship than idealism. All her work, her hospitals, her orphanage, her convent, her sudden journeys of rescue, depended upon money. No one harbored a fairer admiration for mere goodness, but she had been obliged to watch herself sacrificing her kindliness, almost her idealism, to generalship, so dreadful were the struggles to obtain her subsidies from her superiors in the church. The Archbishop of Lima, whom we shall know later in a more graceful connection, hated her with what he called a Vatinian hate and counted the cessation of her visits among the compensations for dying.

Lately she had felt not only the breath of old age against her cheek, but a graver warning. A chill of terror went through her, not for herself, but for her work. Who was there in Peru to value the things she had valued? And rising one day at dawn she had made a rapid journey through her hospital and convent and orphanage, looking for a soul she might train to be her successor. She hurried from empty face to empty face, occasionally pausing more from hope than conviction. In the courtyard she came upon a company of girls at work over the linen and her eyes fell at once upon a girl of twelve who was directing the others at the trough and at the same time recounting to them with great dramatic fire the less probable miracles in the life of Saint Rose of Lima. So it was that the search ended with Pepita. The education for greatness is difficult enough at any time, but amid the sensibilities and jealousies of a convent it must be conducted with fantastic indirection. Pepita was assigned to the most disliked tasks in the House, but she came to understand all the aspects of its administration. She accompanied the Abbess on her journeys, even though it was in the capacity of custodian of the eggs and vegetables. And everywhere, by surprise, hours would open up in which the Directress suddenly appeared and talked to her at great length, not only on religious experience, but on how to manage women and how to plan contagious wards and how to beg for money.

It was a step in this education for greatness that led to Pepita's arriving one day and entering upon the crazy duties of being Doña María's companion. For the first two years she merely came for occasional afternoons, but finally she came to the palace to live. She never had been taught to expect happiness, and the inconveniences, not to say terrors, of her new position did not seem to her excessive for a girl of fourteen. She did not suspect that the Abbess, even there, was hovering above the house, herself estimating the stresses and watching for the moment when a burden harms and not strengthens.

A few of Pepita's trials were physical: for example, the servants in the house took advantage of Doña María's indisposition; they opened up the bedrooms of the palace to their relatives; they stole freely. Alone Pepita stood out against them and suffered a persecution of small discomforts and practical jokes. Her mind, similarly, had its distresses: when she accompanied Doña María on her errands in the city, the older woman would be seized with the desire to dash into a church, for what she had lost of religion as faith she had replaced with religion as magic. "Stay here in the sunlight, my dear child; I shall not be long," she would say. Doña María would then forget herself in a reverie before the altar and leave the church by another door. Pepita had been brought up by Madre María del Pilar to an almost morbid obedience and when after many hours she ventured into the church and made sure that her mistress was no longer there, still she returned to the street-corner and waited while the shadows fell gradually across the square. Thus waiting in public she suffered all the torture of a little girl's self-consciousness. She still wore the uniform of the orphanage (which a minute's thoughtfulness on the part of Doña María could have altered) and she suffered hallucinations wherein men seemed to be staring at her and whispering—nor were these always hallucinations. No less her heart suffered, for on some days Doña María would suddenly become aware of her and would talk to her cordially and humorously, would let appear for a few hours all the exquisite sensibility of the Letters; then, on the morrow she would withdraw into herself again and, while never harsh, would become impersonal and unseeing. The beginnings of hope and affection that Pepita had such need to expend would be wounded. She tiptoed about the

palace, silent, bewildered, clinging only to her sense of duty
and her loyalty to her "mother in the Lord," Madre María del
Pilar, who had sent her there.

Finally a new fact appeared that was to have considerable
effect on the lives of both the Marquesa and her companion:
"My dear mother," wrote the Condesa, *"the weather has been
most exhausting and the fact that the orchards and gardens are
in bloom only makes it the more trying. I could endure flowers if
only they had no perfume. I shall therefore ask your permission to
write you at less length than usual. If Vicente returns before the
post leaves he will be delighted to finish out the leaf and supply you
with those tiresome details about myself which you seem to enjoy so.
I shall not go to Grignan in Provence as I expected this Fall, as
my child will be born in early October."*
What child? The Marquesa leaned against the wall. Doña
Clara had foreseen the exhausting importunities that this news
would waken in her mother and had sought to mitigate them
by the casualness of her announcement. The ruse did not suc-
ceed. The famous Letter XLII was the answer.

Now at length the Marquesa had something to be anxious
about: her daughter was to become a mother. This event,
which merely bored Doña Clara, discovered a whole new scale
of emotions in the Marquesa. She became a mine of medical
knowledge and suggestion. She combed the city for wise old
women and poured into her letters the whole folk-wisdom of
the New World. She fell into the most abominable superstì-
tion. She practiced a degrading system of taboos for her child's
protection. She refused to allow a knot in the house. The
maids were forbidden to tie up their hair and she concealed
upon her person ridiculous symbols of a happy delivery. On
the stairs the even steps were marked with red chalk and a
maid who accidentally stepped upon an even step was driven
from the house with tears and screams. Doña Clara was in the
hands of malignant Nature who reserves the right to inflict
upon her children the most terrifying jests. There was an eti-
quette of propitiation which generations of peasant women
had found comforting. So vast an army of witnesses surely im-
plied that there was some truth in it. At least it could do no
harm, and perhaps it did good. But the Marquesa did not only

satisfy the rites of paganism; she studied the prescriptions of Christianity as well. She arose in the dark and stumbled through the streets to the earliest Masses. She hysterically hugged the altar-rails trying to rend from the gaudy statuettes a sign, only a sign, the ghost of a smile, the furtive nod of a waxen head. Would all be well? Sweet, sweet Mother, would all be well?

At times, after a day's frantic resort to such invocations, a revulsion would sweep over her. Nature is deaf. God is indifferent. Nothing in man's power can alter the course of law. Then on some street-corner she would stop, dizzy with despair, and leaning against a wall would long to be taken from a world that had no plan in it. But soon a belief in the great Perhaps would surge up from the depths of her nature and she would fairly run home to renew the candles above her daughter's bed.

At last the time came to satisfy the supreme rite of Peruvian households looking forward to this event: she made the pilgrimage to the shrine of Santa María de Cluxambuqua. If there resided any efficacy in devotion at all, surely it lay in a visit to this great shrine. The ground had been holy through three religions; even before the Incan civilization distraught human beings had hugged the rocks and lashed themselves with whips to wring their will from the skies. Thither the Marquesa was carried in her chair, crossing the bridge of San Luis Rey and ascending up into the hills toward that city of large-girdled women, a tranquil town, slow-moving and slow-smiling; a city of crystal air, cold as the springs that fed its many fountains; a city of bells, soft and musical, and tuned to carry on with one another the happiest quarrels. If anything turned out for disappointment in the town of Cluxambuqua the grief was somehow assimilated by the overwhelming immanence of the Andes and by the weather of quiet joy that flowed in and about the side-streets. No sooner did the Marquesa see from a distance the white walls of this town perched on the knees of the highest peaks than her fingers ceased turning the beads and the busy prayers of her fright were cut short on her lips.

She did not even alight at the inn, but leaving Pepita to arrange for their stay she went on to the church and knelt for a long time patting her hands softly together. She was listening to the new tide of resignation that was rising within her. Perhaps

she would learn in time to permit both her daughter and her gods to govern their own affairs. She was not annoyed by the whispering of the old women in padded garments who sold candles and medals and talked about money from dawn to dark. She was not even distracted by an officious sacristan who tried to collect a fee for something or other and who, from spite, made her change her place under the pretext of repairing a tile on the floor. Presently she went out into the sunshine and sat on the steps of the fountain. She watched the little processions of invalids slowly revolving about the gardens. She watched three hawks plunging about the sky. The children who had been playing by the fountain stared at her for a moment, and went away alarmed, but a llama (a lady with a long neck and sweet shallow eyes, burdened down by a fur cape too heavy for her and picking her way delicately down an interminable staircase) came over and offered her a velvet cleft nose to stroke. The llama is deeply interested in the men about her, is even fond of pretending that she too is one of them and of inserting her head into their conversations as though in a moment she would lift her voice and contribute a wan and helpful comment. Soon Doña María was surrounded by a number of these sisters who seemed on the point of asking her why she clapped her hands so and how much her veiling cost a yard.

Doña María had arranged that any letters arriving from Spain should be brought to her at once by a special messenger. She had travelled slowly from Lima and even now as she sat in the square a boy from her farm ran up and put into her hand a large packet wrapped in parchment and dangling some nuggets of sealing-wax. Slowly she undid the wrappings. With measured stoic gestures she read first an affectionate and jocose note from her son-in-law; then her daughter's letter. It was full of wounding remarks rather brilliantly said, perhaps said for the sheer virtuosity of giving pain neatly. Each of its phrases found its way through the eyes of the Marquesa, then, carefully wrapped in understanding and forgiveness it sank into her heart. At last she arose, gently dispersed the sympathetic llamas, and with a grave face returned to the shrine.

While Doña María was passing the late afternoon in the Church and in the Square, Pepita was left to prepare their lodging. She showed the porters where to lay down the great

wicker hampers and set about unpacking the altar, the brazier, the tapestries and the portraits of Doña Clara. She descended into the kitchen and gave the cook exact instructions as to the preparations of a certain porridge upon which the Marquesa principally subsisted. Then she returned to the rooms and waited. She resolved to write a letter to the Abbess. She hung for a long time over the quill, staring into the distance with trembling lip. She saw the face of Madre María del Pilar, so red and scrubbed, and the wonderful black eyes. She heard her voice as at the close of supper (the orphans sitting with lowered eyes and folded hands) she commented on the events of the day, or as, by candlelight, she stood among the beds of the hospital and announced the theme for meditation during the night. But most clearly of all Pepita remembered the sudden interviews when the Abbess (not daring to wait until the girl was older) had discussed with her the duties of her office. She had talked to Pepita as to an equal. Such speech is troubling and wonderful to an intelligent child and Madre María del Pilar had abused it. She had expanded Pepita's vision of how she should feel and act beyond the measure of her years. And she had unthinkingly turned upon Pepita the full blaze of her personality, as Jupiter had turned his upon Semele. Pepita was frightened by her sense of insufficiency; she hid it and wept. And then the Abbess had cast the child into the discipline of this long solitude, where Pepita struggled, refusing to let herself believe that she had been abandoned. And now from this strange inn in these strange mountains, where the altitude was making her lightheaded, Pepita longed for the dear presence, the only real thing in her life.

She wrote a letter, all inkstains and incoherence. Then she went downstairs to see about fresh charcoal and to taste the porridge.

The Marquesa came in and sat down at the table. "I can do no more. What will be, will be," she whispered. She unbound from her neck the amulets of her superstition and dropped them into the glowing brazier. She had a strange sense of having antagonized God by too much prayer and so addressed Him now obliquely. "After all it is in the hands of another. I no longer claim the least influence. What will be, will be." She sat for a long time, her palms against her checks, making a blank

of her mind. Her eyes fell on Pepita's letter. She opened it me-
chanically and started to read. She had read a full half of it
before her attention was aware of the meaning of the words:
"*. . . but all this is nothing if you like me and wish me to stay
with her. I oughtn't to tell you but every now and then the bad
chambermaids lock me up in rooms and steal things and perhaps
My Lady will think that I steal them. I hope not. I hope you are
well and not having any trouble in the hospital or anywhere.
Though I never see you I think of you all the time and I remem-
ber what you told me, my dear mother in God. I want to do only
what you want, but if you could let me come back for a few days
to the convent, but not if you do not wish it. But I am so much
alone and not talking to anyone, and everything. Sometimes I do
not know whether you have forgotten me and if you could find a
minute to write me a little letter or something, I could keep it,
but I know how busy you are. . . .*"

Doña María read no further. She folded the letter and put it
aside. For a moment she was filled with envy: she longed to
command another's soul as completely as this nun was able to
do. Most of all she longed to be back in this simplicity of love,
to throw off the burden of pride and vanity that hers had
always carried. To quiet the tumult in her mind she picked up
a book of devotion and tried to fix her attention upon the
words. But after a moment she suddenly felt the need to
reread the whole letter, to surprise, if possible, the secret of so
much felicity.

Pepita returned bringing the supper in her hands, followed
by a maid. Doña María watched her over the top of her book
as she would have watched a visitor from Heaven. Pepita tip-
toed about the room laying the table and whispering direc-
tions to her assistant.

"Your supper is ready, My Lady," she said at last.

"But, my child, you are going to eat with me?" In Lima
Pepita generally sat down at the table with her mistress.

"I thought you would be tired, My Lady. I had my supper
downstairs."

"She does not wish to eat with me," thought the Marquesa.
"She knows me and has rejected me."

"Would you like me to read aloud to you while you are eating,
My Lady?" asked Pepita, who felt that she had made a mistake.

"No. You may go to bed, if you choose."

"Thank you, My Lady."

Doña María had risen and approached the table. With one hand on the back of the chair she said haltingly: "My dear child, I am sending off a letter to Lima in the morning. If you have one you can enclose it with mine."

"No, I have none," said Pepita. She added hastily: "I must go downstairs and get you the new charcoal."

"But, my dear, you have one for . . . Madre María del Pilar. Wouldn't you . . . ?"

Pepita pretended to be busy over the brazier. "No, I'm not going to send it," she said. She was aware during the long pause that followed that the Marquesa was staring at her in stupefaction. "I've changed my mind."

"I know she would like a letter from you, Pepita. It would make her very happy. I know."

Pepita was reddening. She said loudly: "The innkeeper said that there would be some new charcoal ready for you at dark. I'll tell them to bring it up now." She glanced hastily at the old woman and saw that she had not ceased from staring at her with great sad inquiring eyes. Pepita felt that these were not things one talked about, but the strange woman seemed to be feeling the matter so strongly that Pepita was willing to concede one more answer: "No, it was a bad letter. It wasn't a good letter."

Doña María fairly gasped. "Why, my dear Pepita, I think it was very beautiful. Believe me, I know. No, no; what could have made it a bad letter?"

Pepita frowned, hunting for a word that would close the matter.

"It wasn't . . . it wasn't . . . brave," she said. And then she would say no more. She carried the letter off into her own room and could be heard tearing it up. Then she got into bed and lay staring into the darkness, still uncomfortable at having talked in such a fashion. And Doña María sat down to her dish amazed.

She had never brought courage to either life or love. Her eyes ransacked her heart. She thought of the amulets and of her beads, her drunkenness . . . she thought of her daughter. She remembered the long relationship, crowded with the

wreckage of exhumed conversations, of fancied slights, of inopportune confidences, of charges of neglect and exclusion (but she must have been mad that day; she remembered beating upon the table). "But it's not my fault," she cried. "It's not my fault that I was so. It was circumstance. It was the way I was brought up. Tomorrow I begin a new life. Wait and see, oh my child." At last she cleared away the table and sitting down wrote what she called her first letter, her first stumbling misspelled letter in courage. She remembered with shame that in the previous one she had piteously asked her daughter how much she loved her, and had greedily quoted the few and hesitant endearments that Doña Clara had lately ventured to her. Doña María could not recall those pages, but she could write some new ones, free and generous. No one else has regarded them as stumbling. It is the famous letter LVI, known to the Encyclopedists as her Second Corinthians because of its immortal paragraph about love: "Of the thousands of persons we meet in a lifetime, my child . . ." and so on. It was almost dawn when she finished the letter. She opened the door upon her balcony and looked at the great tiers of stars that glittered above the Andes. Throughout the hours of the night, though there had been few to hear it, the whole sky had been loud with the singing of these constellations. Then she took a candle into the next room and looked at Pepita as she slept, and pushed back the damp hair from the girl's face. "Let me live now," she whispered. "Let me begin again."

Two days later they started back to Lima, and while crossing the bridge of San Luis Rey the accident which we know befell them.

PART THREE:

Esteban

ONE morning twin boys were discovered in the foundlings' basket before the door of the Convent of Santa María Rosa de las Rosas. Names were found for them almost before the arrival of the wet-nurse, but the names were not as useful to them as our names are to most of us, for no one ever succeeded in telling the boys apart. There was no way of knowing who their parents were, but Limean gossips, noticing as the boys grew older how straight they held themselves and how silent and sombre they were, declared them to be Castilian and laid them in turn at all sorts of crested doorways. The person in the world who came nearest to being their guardian was the Abbess of the Convent. Madre María del Pilar had come to hate all men, but she grew fond of Manuel and Esteban. In the late afternoon she would call them into her office, send for some cakes from the kitchen, and tell them stories about the Cid and Judas Maccabeus and the thirty-six misfortunes of Harlequin. She grew to love them so, that she would catch herself gazing deep into their black and frowning eyes, looking for those traits that would appear when they grew to be men, all that ugliness, all that soullessness that made hideous the world she worked in. They grew up about the convent until they were a little past the age when their presence began to be a slight distraction to the dedicated sisters. From thence they became vaguely attached to all the sacristies in town: they trimmed all the cloister hedges; they polished every possible crucifix; they passed a damp cloth once a year over most of the ecclesiastical ceilings. All Lima knew them well. When the priest rushed through the streets carrying his precious burden into a sickroom either Esteban or Manuel was to be seen striding behind him, swinging a censer. As they grew older, however, they showed no desire for the clerical life. They gradually assumed the profession of the scribe. There were few printing presses in the New World and the boys soon made a fair living transcribing comedies for the theatre, ballads for the crowds,

and advertisements for the merchants. Above all they were the copyists of the choirmasters and made endless parts of the motets of Morales and Vittoria.

Because they had no family, because they were twins, and because they were brought up by women, they were silent. There was in them a curious shame in regard to their resemblance. They had to live in a world where it was the subject of continual comment and joking. It was never funny to them and they suffered the eternal pleasantries with stolid patience. From the years when they first learned to speak they invented a secret language for themselves, one that was scarcely dependent on the Spanish for its vocabulary, or even for its syntax. They resorted to it only when they were alone, or at great intervals in moments of stress whispered it in the presence of others. The Archbishop of Lima was something of a philologist; he dabbled in dialects; he had even evolved quite a brilliant table for the vowel and consonant changes from Latin into Spanish and from Spanish into Indian-Spanish. He was storing up notebooks of quaint lore against an amusing old age he planned to offer himself back on his estates outside Segovia. So when he heard one day about the secret language of the twin brothers, he trimmed some quills and sent for them. The boys stood humiliated upon the rich carpets of his study while he tried to extract from them their *bread* and *tree* and their *I see* and *I saw*. They did not know why the experience was so horrible to them. They bled. Long shocked silences followed each of the Archbishop's questions, until finally one or the other mumbled an answer. The priest thought for a while that they were merely in awe before his rank and before the luxury of his apartment, but at last, much perplexed, he divined the presence of some deeper reluctance and sadly let them go.

This language was the symbol of their profound identity with one another, for just as resignation was a word insufficient to describe the spiritual change that came over the Marquesa de Montemayor on that night in the inn at Cluxambuqua, so *love* is inadequate to describe the tacit almost ashamed oneness of these brothers. What relationship is it in which few words are exchanged, and those only about the details of food, clothing

and occupation; in which the two persons have a curious re-
luctance even to glance at one another; and in which there is a
tacit arrangement not to appear together in the city and to go
on the same errand by different streets? And yet side by side
with this there existed a need of one another so terrible that it
produced miracles as naturally as the charged air of a sultry day
produces lightning. The brothers were scarcely aware of it
themselves, but telepathy was a common occurrence in their
lives, and when one returned home the other was always aware
of it when his brother was still several streets away.

Suddenly they discovered that they were tired of writing.
They went down to the sea and found an occupation in load-
ing and unloading vessels, not ashamed of working side by side
with Indians. They drove teams across the provinces. They
picked fruit. They were ferrymen. And always they were silent.
Their sombre faces took on from these labors a male and gypsy
cast. Their hair was seldom cut and under the dark mat their
eyes looked up suddenly surprised and a little sullen. All the
world was remote and strange and hostile except one's brother.

But at last the first shadow fell across this unity and the
shadow was cast by the love of women. They had returned to
the city and resumed the copying of parts for the theatre. One
night the manager, foreseeing a thinning house, gave them a
free admission. The boys did not like what they found there.
Even speech was for them a debased form of silence; how
much more futile is poetry which is a debased form of speech.
All those allusions to honour, reputation, and the flame of
love, all the metaphors about birds, Achilles and the jewels of
Ceylon were fatiguing. In the presence of literature they had
the same darkling intelligence that stirs for a time behind the
eyes of a dog, but they sat on patiently, gazing at the bright
candles and the rich clothes. Between the acts of the comedy
the Perichole stepped out of her rôle, put on twelve petticoats
and danced before the curtain. Esteban had some copying still
to do, or pretended so, and went home early; but Manuel stayed
on. The red stockings and shoes of the Perichole had made
their impression.

Both brothers had fetched and carried their manuscripts up
and down the dusty stairs behind the stage. There they had

seen an irritable girl in a soiled bodice mending her stockings before a mirror while her stage director read aloud her lines for memorization. She had let fall upon the boys for a moment the detonation of her amazing eyes, immediately dissipated in her amused recognition that they were twins. Forthwith she had dragged them into the room and placed them side by side. Carefully, amusedly and remorselessly she had peered into every square inch of their faces, until finally laying one hand on Esteban's shoulder she had cried out: "This one is the younger!" That had been several years before and neither brother had thought of the episode again.

Henceforth all Manuel's errands seemed to lead him past the theatre. Late at night he would drift about among the trees beneath her dressing-room window. It was not the first time that Manuel had been fascinated by a woman (both brothers had possessed women, and often, especially during their years at the waterfront; but simply, latinly), but it was the first time that his will and imagination had been thus overwhelmed. He had lost that privilege of simple nature, the dissociation of love and pleasure. Pleasure was no longer as simple as eating; it was being complicated by love. Now was beginning that crazy loss of one's self, that neglect of everything but one's dramatic thoughts about the beloved, that feverish inner life all turning upon the Perichole and which would so have astonished and disgusted her had she been permitted to divine it. This Manuel had not fallen in love through any imitation of literature. It was not of him, at all events, that the bitterest tongue in France had remarked only fifty years before: that many people would never have fallen in love if they had not heard about it. Manuel read little; he had only been once to the theatre (where above all there reigns the legend that love is a devotion) and the Peruvian tavern-songs that he might have heard, unlike those of Spain, reflected very little of the romantic cult of an idealized woman. When he said over to himself that she was beautiful and rich and fatiguingly witty and the Viceroy's mistress, none of these attributes that made her less obtainable had the power to quench his curious and tender excitement. So he leaned against the trees in the dark, his knuckles between his teeth, and listened to his loud heart-beats.

But the life that Esteban was leading had been full enough for him. There was no room in his imagination for a new loyalty, not because his heart was less large than Manuel's, but because it was of a simpler texture. Now he discovered that secret from which one never quite recovers, that even in the most perfect love one person loves less profoundly than the other. There may be two equally good, equally gifted, equally beautiful, but there may never be two that love one another equally well. So Esteban sat up in their room by a guttering candle, his knuckles between his teeth, and wondered why Manuel was so changed and why the whole meaning had gone out of their life.

One evening Manuel was stopped on the street by a small boy who announced to him that the Perichole wished him to call upon her at once. Manuel turned in his path and went to the theatre. Straight, sombre and impersonal, he entered the actress's room and stood waiting. Camila had a service to ask of Manuel and she thought a few preliminary blandishments were necessary, but she scarcely paused in combing a blond wig that was dressed upon the table before her.

"You write letters for people, don't you? I want you to write a letter for me, please. Please come in."

He came forward two steps.

"You never pay me the least visit either of you. That's not Spanish of you."—meaning 'courteous.'—"Which are you, Manuel or Esteban?"

"Manuel."

"It doesn't matter. You are both unfriendly. Neither of you ever comes to see me. Here I sit learning stupid lines all day and no one ever comes to see me but a lot of peddlers. It is because I am an actress, no?"

This was not very artful, but for Manuel it was unspeakably complicated. He merely stared at her from the shadows of his long hair and left her to improvise.

"I am going to engage you to write a letter for me, a very secret letter. But now I can see that you don't like me and that to ask you to write a letter would be as good as reading it aloud in all the wine-shops. What does that look mean, Manuel? Are you my friend?"

"Yes, señora."

"Go away. Send me Esteban. You do not even say *Yes, señora* as a friend would say it."

Long pause. Presently she raised her head: "Are you still there, Unfriendly?"

"Yes, señora . . . you can trust me to do anything for you . . . you can trust . . ."

"If I ask you to write one letter for me, or two letters, you promise never to mention to a human being what is in them, or even that you wrote them?"

"Yes, señora."

"What do you promise by?—by the Virgin Mary?"

"Yes, señora."

"And by the heart of Saint Rose of Lima?"

"Yes, señora."

"Name of the Name, Manuel, anyone would think you were as stupid as an ox. Manuel, I am very angry with you. You are not stupid. You don't look stupid. Please don't say just *Yes, señora* again. Don't be stupid or I'll send for Esteban. Is anything the matter with you?"

Here Manuel cast himself upon the Spanish language and exclaimed with unnecessary vigor: "I swear by the Virgin Mary and the heart of St. Rose of Lima that all that has to do with the letter will be secret."

"Even from Esteban," prompted the Perichole.

"Even from Esteban."

"Well, that's better." She motioned him to sit down at a table where writing materials were already laid out. As she dictated she strode about the room, frowning, swinging her hips. With her arms akimbo, she hugged her shawl about her shoulders defiantly.

"Camila Perichole kisses the hands of Your Excellency and says —No, take another piece of paper and begin again. *The señora Micaela Villegas, artist, kisses the hands of Your Excellency and says that, being the victim of the envious and lying friends that Y.E.'s goodness permits about Him, she can no longer endure Y.E.'s suspicions and jealousy. Y.E.'s servant has always valued Y.E.'s friendship and has never committed, nor even thought, an offense against it, but she can no longer fight against the calumnies that Y.E. believes so readily. Señora Villegas, artist, called the Perichole,*

therefore returns herewith such of Y.E.'s gifts as have not been placed beyond recall, since without Y.E.'s confidence, Y.E.'s servant can take no pleasure in them."

Camila continued walking about the room for several minutes, consumed by her thoughts. Presently without so much as glancing at her secretary, she commanded: "Take another leaf. *Have you gone mad? Do not ever think of dedicating another bull to me again. It has caused a frightful war. Heaven protect you, my colt. Friday night, the same place, the same time. I may be a little late, for the fox is wide-awake.* That will be all."

Manuel rose.

"You swear that you have made no errors?"

"Yes, I swear."

"There is your money."

Manuel took the money.

"I shall want you to write me more letters from time to time. My uncle Pio generally writes my letters; these I do not wish him to know about. Good night. Go with God."

"Go with God."

Manuel descended the stairs and stood for a long time among the trees, not thinking, not moving.

Esteban knew that his brother was continually brooding over the Perichole, but he never suspected that he saw her. From time to time during the next two months a small boy would approach him in great haste and ask whether he were Manuel or Esteban, and being informed that he was only Esteban, the boy would add that Manuel was wanted at the theatre. Esteban assumed that the call was for copyist's work and was therefore utterly unprepared for a visit that they received one night in their room.

It was almost midnight. Esteban had gone to bed, and lay gazing out from under the blanket at the candle beside which his brother was working. There was a light tap at the door and Manuel opened to admit a lady heavily veiled, out of breath and nervous. She threw back the scarf from her face and said hurriedly:

"Quick, ink and paper. You are Manuel, yes? You must do a letter for me at once."

For a moment her glance fell on the two bright eyes that glared at her from the edge of the cot. She murmured: "Eu . . . you

must excuse me. I know it is late. It was necessary . . . I must come." Then turning to Manuel, she whispered into his ear: "Write this: *I, the Perichole, am not accustomed to wait at a rendez-vous.* Have you finished that? *You are only a cholo, and there are better matadors than you, even in Lima. I am half Castilian and there are no better actresses in the world. You shall not have the opportunity*—Have you got that?—*to keep me waiting again, cholo, and I shall laugh the last, for even an actress does not grow old as fast as a bullfighter.*"

To Esteban in the shadows the picture of Camila leaning over his brother's hand and whispering into his ear was complete evidence that a new congeniality had formed such as he would never know. He seemed to shrink away into space, infinitely tiny, infinitely unwanted. He took one more glance at the tableau of love, all the paradise from which he was shut out, and turned his face to the wall.

Camila seized the note the moment it was done, pushed a coin along the table and in a last flurry of black lace, scarlet beads and excited whispers left the room. Manuel turned from the door with his candle. He sat down, put his hand over his ears, his elbows on his knees. He worshipped her. He murmured to himself over and over again that he worshipped her, making of the sound a sort of incantation and an obstacle to thought.

He emptied his mind of everything but a sing-song, and it was this vacancy that permitted him to become aware of Esteban's mood. He seemed to hear a voice that proceeded from the shadows saying: "Go and follow her, Manuel. Don't stay here. You'll be happy. There's room for us all in the world." Then the realization became even more intense and he received a mental image of Esteban going a long way off and saying good-bye many times as he went. He was filled with terror; by the light of it he saw that all the other attachments in the world were shadows, or the illusions of fever, even Madre María del Pilar, even the Perichole. He could not understand why Esteban's misery should present itself as demanding a choice between him and the Perichole, but he could understand Esteban's misery, as misery. And at once he sacrificed everything to it, if it can be said we ever sacrifice anything save what we know we can never attain, or what some secret wisdom tells us it would be uncomfortable or saddening to possess. To be

sure there was nothing on which Esteban could base a com-
plaint. It was not jealousy, for in their earlier affairs it had never
occurred to either of them that their loyalty to one another
had been diminished. It was merely that in the heart of one of
them there was left room for an elaborate imaginative attach-
ment and in the heart of the other there was not. Manuel
could not quite understand this and, as we shall see, he nour-
ished a dim sense of being accused unjustly. But he did under-
stand that Esteban was suffering. In his excitement he groped
for a means of holding this brother who seemed to be receding
into the distance. And at once, in one unhesitating stroke of
the will, he removed the Perichole from his heart.

He blew out the candle and lay down on his bed. He was
trembling. He said aloud with exaggerated casualness: "Well,
that's the last letter I write for that woman. She can go and
find a pander somewhere else. If ever she calls here or sends for
me when I'm out, tell her so. Make it plain. That's the last I
have to do with her," and with that he began reciting his
evening psalm aloud. But he had hardly reached *A sagitta
volante in die* when he became aware that Esteban had risen
and was lighting the candle.

"What's the matter?" he asked.

"I'm going out for a walk," replied Esteban sombrely, fas-
tening his belt. After a moment, he broke out with an assump-
tion of anger: "You don't have to say . . . what you just said,
for me. I don't care whether you write her letters or not. You
don't have to change for me. I haven't anything to do with that."

"Go to bed, you fool. God, you're a fool, Esteban. What
made you think I said that, for you? Don't you believe I mean
it when I say I'm through with her? Do you think I want to
write any more of her dirty letters and get paid for them like
that?"

"It's all right. You love her. You don't have to change
because of me."

"'*Love* her?' *Love* her? You're crazy, Esteban. How could I
love her? What chance would there be for me? Do you suppose
she'd give me those letters to write if there were any chance?
Do you suppose she'd push a piece of money across the table
every time. . . . You're crazy, Esteban, that's all."

There was a long pause. Esteban would not go to bed. He

sat by the candle in the middle of the room, tapping with his hand on the edge of the table.

"Go to bed, you fool," shouted Manuel, rising on one elbow under the blanket. He was talking in their secret language and the new pain at his heart gave a greater ring of reality to his assumption of rage. "I'm all right."

"I won't. I'm going out for a walk," replied Esteban picking up his coat.

"You can't go out for a walk. It's two o'clock. It's raining. You can't go and walk about for hours like that. Look, Esteban, I swear to you there's nothing left to all that. I don't love her. I only did for a time."

By now Esteban stood in the dark of the open door. In the unnatural voice with which we make the greatest declarations of our lives, he muttered: "I'm in your way," and turned to go.

Manuel leapt out of his bed. His head seemed to be full of a great din, a voice crying out that Esteban was going away forever, was leaving him alone forever. "In the name of God, in the name of God, Esteban, come back here."

Esteban came back and went to bed and the matter was not mentioned again for many weeks. The very next evening Manuel had an opportunity of declaring his position. A messenger arrived from the Perichole and was told harshly to inform the actress that Manuel would write no more letters for her.

One evening Manuel tore open the flesh on his knee against a piece of metal.

Neither brother had ever been ill for as much as a day in his life, and now Manuel, utterly bewildered, watched his leg swell and felt the waves of pain rise and fall in his body. Esteban sat by and stared at his face trying to imagine what great pain was. At last one midnight Manuel remembered that the signboard of a certain hair-dresser in the city described the proprietor as an experienced barber and surgeon. Esteban ran through the streets to fetch him. He pounded on the door. Presently a woman leaned out of a window and announced that her husband would be back in the morning. During the fearful hours that followed, they told one another that when the doctor had seen the leg all would be well. He would do something about it, and Manuel

would be out around the town in a day or two, even in a day perhaps, even less than a day.

The barber arrived and prescribed various draughts and ointments. Esteban was instructed to lay cold cloths on his brother's leg every hour. The barber withdrew and the brothers sat down to wait for the pain to subside. But while they continued staring into one another's face waiting for the miracle of science the pain grew worse. Hour after hour Esteban approached with his dripping towel and they discovered that the moment of its application was the worst of all. With all the fortitude in the world Manuel could not prevent himself from shouting and from flinging himself about upon the bed. Night came on and still Esteban stolidly waited and watched and worked. Nine, ten, eleven. Now when the time drew near to apply the cloths (the hour struck so musically from all those towers) Manuel would plead with Esteban not to do his work. He would resort to guile and declare that he scarcely felt it. But Esteban, his heart bursting with pain and his lips a line of iron, would roll back the blanket and bind the towel fiercely in its place. Manuel gradually became delirious and under this application all the thoughts he did not permit himself in his right mind would burst magnified from his mouth.

Finally at two o'clock, out of his mind with rage and pain, and flinging himself half out of the bed until his head struck the floor, Manuel cried: "God condemn your soul to the hottest hell there is. A thousand devils torture you forever, Esteban. God condemn your soul, do you hear?" At first, the air gone out of his body, Esteban went out into the hall and leaned against the door, his mouth and eyes wide open. Still he heard from within: "Yes, Esteban, may God damn your beastly soul forever, do you hear that? For coming between me and what was mine by right. She was mine, do you hear, and what right had you. . . ." and he would go off into an elaborate description of the Perichole.

These outbursts recurred hourly. It was some time before Esteban was able to realize that his brother's mind was not then clear. After some moments of horror, in which his being a devout believer had its part, he would return to the room and go about his duties with bent head.

Towards dawn his brother became serener. (For what human ill does not dawn seem to be an alleviation?) It was in one of these intervals that Manuel said quite calmly:

"God's son! I feel better, Esteban. Those cloths must be good after all. You'll see. I'll be up and around tomorrow. You haven't slept for days. You'll see I won't cause you any more trouble, Esteban."

"It's no trouble, you fool."

"You mustn't take me seriously when I try and stop you putting on the old cloths, Esteban."

A long pause. At last Esteban brought out, barely audible:

"I think . . . don't you think it would be fine if I sent for the Perichole? She could just come and see you for a few minutes, I mean. . . ."

"Her? You still thinking about her? I wouldn't have her here for anything. No."

But Esteban was not content yet. He dragged up a few more phrases from the very centre of his being:

"Manuel, you still feel, don't you, that I came between you and the Perichole and you don't remember that I told you it was all right with me. I swear to you I'd have been glad if you'd gone away with her, or anything."

"What are you bringing that up for, Esteban? I tell you, in God's own name, I never think of that. She's nothing to me. When are you going to forget that, Esteban? I tell you I'm glad things are as they are. Look, I got to get angry when you keep going back to that."

"Manuel, I wouldn't speak of it again, only when you get angry at me about the cloths . . . you, you get angry at me about that, too. And you talk about it and you . . ."

"Look, I'm not responsible what I say. My old leg hurts then, see."

"Then you don't damn me to hell because . . . it looks like I came between you and the Perichole?"

"Damn you to . . . ? What makes you say that? You're going crazy, Esteban; you're imagining things. You haven't had any sleep, Esteban. I been a curse to you and you're losing your health because of me. But you'll see, I won't trouble you much more. How could I damn you to hell, Esteban, when you're all I've got? Understand, see, that when the cold cloths

go on, I just lose myself, see. You know. Don't think about it twice. It's time to put them on now. I won't say a word."

"No, Manuel, I'll skip this time. It won't do you any harm, I'll just skip this time."

"I've got to get well, Esteban. I've got to get up soon, you know. Put them on. But one minute—give me the crucifix. I swear by the blood and body of Christ that if I say anything against Esteban, I don't mean it and it's just the foolish words when I'm dreaming because of the pain in my leg. God make me well again soon, amen. Put it back. There. Now I'm ready."

"Look, Manuel, it won't hurt if I skip just this once, see. It'll be good for you, sure, to not get it all stirred up just this once."

"No, I've got to get well. The doctor said it had to be done. I won't say a word, Esteban."

And it would begin all over again.

During the second night a prostitute in the next room started beating on the wall, outraged at such language. A priest in the room on the other side would come out into the hall and beat on the door. The whole floor would gather before the room in exasperation. The innkeeper came up the stairs, loudly promising his guests that the brothers would be dumped into the street the very next morning. Esteban, holding his candle, would go into the hall and permit them to rage at him for as long as they pleased; but after that he took to pressing his hand firmly over his brother's mouth during the moments of greatest stress. This increased Manuel's personal rage at him and he would babble all through the night.

On the third night, Esteban sent for the priest and amidst the enormous shadows Manuel received the sacrament, and died.

Thereafter Esteban refused to come near the building. He would start off upon long walks, but presently drifting back, would hang about, staring at passers-by, within two streets of where his brother lay. The innkeeper failing to make any impression upon him and remembering that the boys were brought up at the Convent of Santa María Rosa de las Rosas, sent for the Abbess. Simply and soundly she directed all that was to be done. At last she went down to the street corner and spoke to Esteban. He watched her approach him, a glance mixed

of longing and distrust. But when she stood near him he turned sideways and looked away.

"I want you to help me. Won't you come in and see your brother? Won't you come in and help me?"

"No."

"You won't help me!" A long pause. Suddenly as she stood there full of her helplessness there flashed through her mind an incident of many years before: the twin brothers about fifteen years old were sitting at her knee and she was telling them the story of the crucifixion. Their large grave eyes were fixed upon her lips. Suddenly Manuel had cried out loudly: "If Esteban and I had been there we would have prevented it."

"Well, then, if you won't help me, will you tell me which you are?"

"Manuel," said Esteban.

"Manuel, won't you come and sit with me up there for just a short time?"

After a long pause: "No."

"But Manuel, dear Manuel, can't you remember as children how you did so many things for me? You were willing to go across the town on some little errand. When I was ill you made the cook let you bring me my soup?" Another woman would have said: "Do you remember how much I did for you?"

"Yes."

"I, too, Manuel have lost. I too . . . once. We know that God has taken them into His hands. . . ." But this did not do at all. Esteban turned vaguely and walked away from her. When he had gone about twenty paces he stopped and stared down a side-street, like a dog who wants to go away, but is reluctant to offend the master who calls him back.

That was all they could get out of him. When the fearful procession passed through the city, with its black hoods and masks, its candles in broad daylight, its display of heaped-up skulls, its terrifying psalms, Esteban followed it in the parallel streets, catching glimpses of it from a distance, like a savage.

All Lima was interested in this separation of the brothers. Housewives whispered together sympathetically about it as they unfurled their carpets from the balconies. The men in the wine-shops, alluding to it, shook their heads and smoked in silence

for a while. Travellers from the interior told of seeing Esteban
as he strayed with eyes like coals along the dried-up beds of
rivers or through the great ruins of the old race. A herder of
llamas had come upon him standing upon a hilltop, asleep or
dazed, wet with dew under the stars. Some fishermen surprised
him swimming far out from shore. From time to time he would
find work to do, he would become a shepherd or a carter, but
after a few months he would disappear and stride from prov-
ince to province. But he always returned to Lima. One day he
appeared at the door of the Perichole's dressing-room; he made
as though to speak, gazed earnestly at her and vanished. One day
a sister came running into the office of Madre María del Pilar
with the news that Esteban (whom the world called Manuel)
was lingering about the door of the convent. The Abbess hur-
ried out into the street. For months she had been asking her-
self what strategy could reconcile this half-demented boy to
living among them again. She assembled as grave and calm a
manner as she was able and appearing at the street door mur-
mured "My friend" and looked at him. He gazed back at her
with the same glance of longing and distrust that he had
shown her before, and stood trembling. Again she whispered
"My friend" and moved a step forward. Suddenly Esteban
turned and breaking into a run disappeared. Madre María del
Pilar rushed stumbling back to her desk and fell upon her
knees, exclaiming angrily: "I have prayed for wisdom and You
have given me none. You have not chosen to give me the least
grace. I am a mere scrubber of floors. . . ." But during the
penance she set herself for this impudence the thought came
to her to send for Captain Alvarado. Three weeks later she had
a ten-minute conversation with him. And the next day he
started for Cuzco where, it was said, Esteban was doing some
copying for the University.

There was this strange and noble figure in Peru during these
years, the Captain Alvarado, the traveller. He was blackened
and cured by all weathers. He stood in the Square with feet
apart as though they were planted on a shifting deck. His eyes
were strange, unaccustomed to the shorter range, too used to
seizing the appearances of a constellation between a cloud and
a cloud, and the outline of a cape in rain. His reticence was

sufficiently explained for most of us by his voyages, but the Marquesa de Montemayor had other light on the matter. *"Captain Alvarado is bringing you this letter in person,"* she wrote to her daughter. *"Introduce him to some of your geographers, my treasure, though it may make them a little uncomfortable, for he is the diamond of sincerity. They will never see anyone who has travelled so far. Last night he described to me some of his voyages. Imagine him pushing his prow through a sea of weeds, stirring up a cloud of fish like grasshoppers in June; or sailing between islands of ice. Oh, he has been to China and up the rivers of Africa. But he is not merely an adventurer and he seems to take no pride in discovering new places; nor is he a mere merchant. One day I asked him narrowly why he lived so, and he avoided my question. I found out from my laundress what I think is the reason of his wandering: My child, he had a child; my daughter, he had a daughter. She was just old enough to cook a holiday meal, and do a little sewing for him. In those days he merely sailed between Mexico and Peru and hundreds of times she waved him farewell or welcome. We have no way of knowing whether she was more beautiful or intelligent than the thousands of other girls that lived about him, but she was his. I suppose it seems ignoble to you that a great oak of a man should go about the world like a blind man about an empty house merely because a chit of a girl has been withdrawn from it. No, no, you cannot understand this, my adored one, but I understand and grow pale. Last night he sat with me and talked of her. He laid his cheek against his hand and looking into the fire, he said: 'It sometimes seems to me that she is away upon a voyage and that I shall see her again. It seems to me that she is in England.' You will laugh at me, but I think he goes about the hemispheres to pass the time between now and his old age."*

The brothers had always entertained a great respect for Captain Alvarado. They had worked for him a short time and the silence of the three of them had made a little kernel of sense in a world of boasting, self-excuse and rhetoric. So now when the great traveller came into the dark kitchen where Esteban was eating the boy drew his chair farther into the shadow, but at a distance, he was glad. The Captain gave no sign of recognizing or even of seeing him until he had finished his meal. Esteban had finished long before, but not wishing to be spoken to,

waited until the Captain should have left the cave. At last the Captain walked over to him and said:

"You are Esteban or Manuel. You helped me once with some unloading. I am Captain Alvarado."

"Yes," said Esteban.

"How are you?"

Esteban muttered something.

"I am looking for some strong fellows to go on my next trip with me." Pause. "Would you like to come?" Longer pause. "England. And Russia. . . . Hard work. Good wages. . . . A long way from Peru.—Well?"

Apparently Esteban had not been listening. He sat with his eyes on the table. At last the Captain raised his voice, as to a deaf person:

"I said: Do you want to go on my next trip with me. . . ."

"Yes, I'll go," answered Esteban suddenly.

"Fine. That's fine. I want your brother, too, of course."

"No."

"What's the matter? Wouldn't he want to come?"

Esteban mumbled something, looking away. Then half rising, he said: "I got to go now. I've got to see somebody about something."

"Let me see your brother myself. Where is he?"

". . . 'dead," said Esteban.

"Oh, I didn't know. I didn't know. I'm sorry."

"Yes," said Esteban. "I got to go."

"Hmm.—Which are you? What's your name?"

"Esteban."

"When did Manuel die?"

"Oh, just a . . . just a few weeks. He hit his knee against something and . . . just a few weeks ago."

They both kept their eyes on the floor.

"How old are you, Esteban?"

"Twenty-two."

"Well, that's settled then, you're coming with me?"

"Yes."

"You may not be used to the cold."

"Yes, I'm used to it.—I've got to go now. I got to go in the city and see somebody about something."

"Well, Esteban. Come back here for supper and we'll talk

about the trip. Come back and have some wine with me, see. Will you?"

"Yes, I will."

"Go with God."

"Go with God."

They had supper together and it was arranged that they were to start for Lima the next morning. The Captain got him very drunk. At first they poured and drank and poured and drank in silence. Then the Captain began to talk about ships and their courses. He asked Esteban questions about tackle and about the guide-stars. Then Esteban began to talk about other things, and to talk very loudly:

"On the ship you must give me something to do all the time. I'll do anything, anything. I'll climb up high and fix ropes; and I'll watch all night,—because, you know, I don't sleep well anyway. And, Captain Alvarado, on the ship you must pretend that you don't know me. Pretend that you hate me the most. So that you'll always give me things to do. I can't sit still and write at a table any more.—And don't tell the other men about me . . . that is, about . . ."

"I hear you went into a burning house, Esteban, and pulled someone out."

"Yes. I didn't get burned or anything. You know," cried Esteban, leaning across the table, "you're not allowed to kill yourself; you know you're not allowed. Everybody knows that. But if you jump into a burning house to save somebody, that wouldn't be killing yourself. And if you became a matador and the bull caught you that wouldn't be killing yourself. Only you mustn't put yourself in the bull's way on purpose. Did you ever notice that animals never kill themselves, even when they're sure to lose? They never jump into a river or anything, even when they're sure to lose. Some people say that horses run into bonfires. Is that true?"

"No, I don't think that's true."

"I don't think it's true. We had a dog once. Well, I mustn't think of that.—Captain Alvarado, do you know Madre María del Pilar?"

"Yes."

"I want to give her a present before I go away. Captain

Alvarado, I want you to give me all my wages before I start—I won't need any money anywhere—and I want to buy her a present now. The present isn't from me only. She was . . . was . . ." Here Esteban wished to say his brother's name, but was unable to. Instead he continued in a lower voice: "She had a kind of a . . . she had a serious loss, once. She said so. I don't know who it was, and I want to give her a present. Women can't bear that kind of a thing like we can."

The Captain promised him that they would choose something in the morning. Esteban talked about it at great length. At last the Captain saw him slip under the table, and himself, rising up, went out into the square before the inn. He looked at the line of the Andes and at the streams of stars crowding forever across the sky. And there was that wraith hanging in mid-air and smiling at him, the wraith with the silvery voice that said for the thousandth time: "Don't be gone long. But I'll be a big girl when you get back." Then he went within and carried Esteban to his room and sat looking at him for a long while.

The next morning he was waiting at the bottom of the stairs when Esteban appeared:

"We're starting when you're ready," said the Captain.

The strange glitter had returned to the boy's eyes. He blurted out: "No, I'm not coming. I'm not coming after all."

"Aïe! Esteban! But you have promised me that you would come."

"It's impossible. I can't come with you," and he turned back up the stairs.

"Come here a moment, Esteban, just a moment."

"I can't come with you. I can't leave Peru."

"I want to tell you something."

Esteban came down to the foot of the stairs.

"How about that present for Madre María del Pilar?" asked the Captain in a low voice. Esteban was silent, looking over the mountains. "You aren't going to take that present away from her? It might mean a lot to her . . . you know."

"All right," murmured Esteban, as though much impressed.

"Yes. Besides the ocean's better than Peru. You know Lima and Cuzco and the road. You have nothing more to know about

them. You see it's the ocean you want. Besides on the boat you'll have something to do every minute. I'll see to that. Go and get your things and we'll start."

Esteban was trying to make a decision. It had always been Manuel who had made the decisions and even Manuel had never been forced to make as great a one as this. Esteban went slowly upstairs. The Captain waited for him and waited so long that presently he ventured half the way up the stairs and listened. At first there was silence; then a series of noises that his imagination was able to identify at once. Esteban had scraped away the plaster about a beam and was adjusting a rope about it. The Captain stood on the stairs trembling: "Perhaps it's best," he said to himself. "Perhaps I should leave him alone. Perhaps it's the only thing possible for him." Then on hearing another sound he flung himself against the door, fell into the room and caught the boy. "Go away," cried Esteban. "Let me be. Don't come in now."

Esteban fell face downward upon the floor. "I am alone, alone, alone" he cried. The Captain stood above him, his great plain face ridged and gray with pain; it was his own old hours he was reliving. He was the awkwardest speaker in the world apart from the lore of the sea, but there are times when it requires a high courage to speak the banal. He could not be sure the figure on the floor was listening, but he said "We do what we can. We push on, Esteban, as best we can. It isn't for long, you know. Time keeps going by. You'll be surprised at the way time passes."

They started for Lima. When they reached the bridge of San Luis Rey, the Captain descended to the stream below in order to supervise the passage of some merchandise, but Esteban crossed by the bridge and fell with it.

PART FOUR:

Uncle Pio

IN one of her letters (the XXIXth) the Marquesa de Montemayor tries to describe the impression that Uncle Pio *"our aged Harlequin"* made upon her: *"I have been sitting all morning on the green balcony making you a pair of slippers, my soul,"* she tells her daughter. *"As the golden wire did not take up my whole attention I was able to follow the activity of a coterie of ants in the wall beside me. Somewhere behind the partition they were patiently destroying my house. Every three minutes a little workman would appear between two boards and drop a grain of wood upon the floor below. Then he would wave his antennae at me and back busily into his mysterious corridor. In the meantime various brothers and sisters of his were trotting back and forth on a certain highway, stopping to massage one another's heads, or if the messages they bore were of first importance, refusing angrily to massage or to be massaged. And at once I thought of Uncle Pio. Why? Where else but with him had I seen that very gesture with which he arrests a passing abbé or a courtier's valet, and whispers, his lips laid against his victim's ear? And surely enough, before noon I saw him hurry by on one of those mysterious errands of his. As I am the idlest and silliest of women I sent Pepita to get me a piece of nougat which I placed on the ant's highway. Similarly I sent word to the Café Pizarro asking them to send Uncle Pio to see me if he dropped in before sunset. I shall give him that old bent salad fork with the turquoise in it, and he will bring me a copy of the new ballad that everyone is singing about the d—q—a of Ol—v—s. My child, you shall have the best of everything, and you shall have it first."*

And in the next letter: *"My dear, Uncle Pio is the most delightful man in the world, your husband excepted. He is the second most delightful man in the world. His conversation is enchanting. If he weren't so disreputable I should make him my secretary. He could write all my letters for me and generations would rise up and call me witty. Alas, however, he is so moth-eaten by disease and bad company, that I shall have to leave him to his underworld."*

*He is not only like an ant, he is like a soiled pack of cards. And I
doubt whether the whole Pacific could wash him sweet and fra-
grant again. But what divine Spanish he speaks and what exqui-
site things he says in it! That's what one gets by hanging around
a theatre and hearing nothing but the conversation of Calderón.
Alas, what is the matter with this world, my soul, that it should
treat such a being so ill! His eyes are as sad as those of a cow that
has been separated from its tenth calf."*

You should know first that this Uncle Pio was Camila Peri-
chole's maid. He was also her singing-master, her coiffeur, her
masseur, her reader, her errand-boy, her banker; rumor added:
her father. For example, he taught her her parts. There was a
whisper around town that Camila could read and write. The
compliment was unfounded; Uncle Pio did her reading and
writing for her. At the height of the season the company put
on two or three new plays a week, and as each one contained a
long and flowery part for the Perichole the mere task of mem-
orization was not a trifle.

Peru had passed within fifty years from a frontier state to a
state in renaissance. Its interest in music and the theatre was
intense. Lima celebrated its feast days by hearing a Mass of
Tomás Luis da Vittoria in the morning and the glittering
poetry of Calderón in the evening. It is true that the Limeans
were given to interpolating trivial songs into the most exquisite
comedies and some lachrymose effects into the austerest music;
but at least they never submitted to the boredom of a mis-
placed veneration. If they had disliked heroic comedy the
Limeans would not have hesitated to remain at home; and if
they had been deaf to polyphony nothing would have pre-
vented their going to an earlier service. When the Archbishop
returned from a short trip to Spain, all Lima kept asking: "What
has he brought?" The news finally spread abroad that he had
returned with tomes of masses and motets by Palestrina,
Morales and Vittoria, as well as thirty-five plays by Tirso de
Molina and Ruiz de Alarcón and Moreto. There was a civic
fête in his honor. The choir-boys' school and the green room
of the Comedia were swamped with the gifts of vegetables and
wheat. All the world was eager to nourish the interpreters of so
much beauty.

This was the theatre in which Camila Perichole gradually made her reputation. So rich was the repertory and so dependable the prompter's box that few plays were given more than four times a season. The manager had the whole flowering of the 17th Century Spanish drama to draw upon, including many that are now lost to us. The Perichole had appeared in a hundred plays of Lope de Vega alone. There were many admirable actresses in Lima during these years, but none better. The citizens were too far away from the theatres of Spain to realize that she was the best in the Spanish world. They kept sighing for a glimpse of the stars of Madrid whom they had never seen and to whom they assigned vague new excellences. Only one person knew for certain that the Perichole was a great performer and that was her tutor Uncle Pio.

Uncle Pio came of a good Castilian house, illegitimately. At the age of ten he ran away to Madrid from his father's hacienda and was pursued without diligence. He lived ever after by his wits. He possessed the six attributes of the adventurer— a memory for names and faces, with the aptitude for altering his own; the gift of tongues; inexhaustible invention; secrecy; the talent for falling into conversation with strangers; and that freedom from conscience that springs from a contempt for the dozing rich he preyed upon. From ten to fifteen he distributed handbills for merchants, held horses, and ran confidential errands. From fifteen to twenty he trained bears and snakes for travelling circuses; he cooked, and mixed punches; he hung about the entries of the more expensive taverns and whispered informations into the travellers' ears—sometimes nothing more dubious than that a certain noble house was reduced to selling its plate and could thus dispense with the commission of a silversmith. He was attached to all the theatres in town and could applaud like ten. He spread slanders at so much a slander. He sold rumors about crops and about the value of land. From twenty to thirty his services came to be recognized in very high circles—he was sent out by the government to inspirit some half-hearted rebellions in the mountains, so that the government could presently arrive and whole-heartedly crush them. His discretion was so profound that the French party used him even when they knew that the Austrian party used him also. He had long interviews with the Princesse des Ursins, but he

came and went by the back stairs. During this phase he was no longer obliged to arrange gentlemen's pleasures, nor to plant little harvests of calumny.

He never did one thing for more than two weeks at a time even when enormous gains seemed likely to follow upon it. He could have become a circus manager, a theatrical director, a dealer in antiquities, an importer of Italian silks, a secretary in the Palace or the Cathedral, a dealer in provisions for the army, a speculator in houses and farms, a merchant in dissipations and pleasures. But there seemed to have been written into his personality, through some accident or early admiration of his childhood, a reluctance to own anything, to be tied down, to be held to a long engagement. It was this that prevented his thieving, for example. He had stolen several times, but the gains had not been sufficient to offset his dread of being locked up; he had sufficient ingenuity to escape on the field itself all the police in the world, but nothing could protect him against the talebearing of his enemies. Similarly he had been reduced for a time to making investigations for the Inquisition, but when he had seen several of his victims led off in hoods he felt that he might be involving himself in an institution whose movements were not evenly predictable.

As he approached twenty, Uncle Pio came to see quite clearly that his life had three aims. There was first this need of independence, cast into a curious pattern, namely: the desire to be varied, secret and omniscient. He was willing to renounce the dignities of public life, if in secret he might feel that he looked down upon men from a great distance, knowing more about them than they knew themselves; and with a knowledge which occasionally passed into action and rendered him an agent in the affairs of states and persons. In the second place he wanted to be always near beautiful women, of whom he was always in the best and worst sense the worshipper. To be near them was as necessary to him as breathing. His reverence for beauty and charm was there for anyone to see and to laugh at, and the ladies of the theatre and the court and the houses of pleasure loved his connoisseurship. They tormented him and insulted him and asked his advice and were singularly comforted by his absurd devotion. He suffered greatly their rages and their meannesses and their confiding tears; all he asked was to be

accepted casually, to be trusted, to be allowed like a friendly and slightly foolish dog to come and go in their rooms and to write their letters for them. He was insatiably curious about their minds and their hearts. He never expected to be loved by them (borrowing for a moment another sense of that word); for that, he carried his money to the obscurer parts of the city; he was always desperately unprepossessing, with his whisp of a moustache and his whisp of a beard and his big ridiculous sad eyes. They constituted his parish; it was from them that he acquired the name of Uncle Pio and it was when they were in trouble that he most revealed himself; when they fell from favour he lent them money, when they were ill he outlasted the flagging devotion of their lovers and the exasperation of their maids; when time or disease robbed them of their beauty, he served them still for their beauty's memory; and when they died his was the honest grief that saw them as far as possible on their journey.

In the third place he wanted to be near those that loved Spanish literature and its masterpieces, especially in the theatre. He had discovered all that treasure for himself, borrowing or stealing from the libraries of his patrons, feeding himself upon it in secrecy,—behind the scenes, as it were, of his mad life. He was contemptuous of the great persons who for all their education and usage, exhibited no care nor astonishment before the miracles of word order in Calderón and Cervantes. He longed himself to make verses. He never realized that many of the satirical songs he had written for the vaudevilles passed into folk-music and have been borne everywhere along the highroads.

As the result of one of those quarrels that arise so naturally in brothels his life became too complicated and he removed to Peru. Uncle Pio in Peru was even more versatile than Uncle Pio in Europe. Here too he touched upon real-estate, circuses, pleasures, insurrections and antiques. A Chinese junk had been blown from Canton to America; he dragged up the beach the bales of deep-red porcelain and sold the bowls to the collectors of virtú. He traced down the sovereign remedies of the Incas and started a smart trade in pills. Within four months he knew practically everyone in Lima. He presently added to this acquaintance the inhabitants of scores of sea-coast towns, mining camps

and settlements in the interior. His pretensions to omniscience became more and more plausible. The Viceroy discovered Uncle Pio and all this richness of reference; he engaged his services in many affairs. In the decay of his judgment Don Andrés had retained one talent, he was a master of the technique of handling confidential servants. He treated Uncle Pio with great tact and some deference; he understood which errands the other should not be asked to undertake and he understood his need for variety and intermission. Uncle Pio in turn was perpetually astonished that a prince should make so little use of his position, for power, or for fantasy, or for sheer delight in the manipulation of other men's destinies; but the servant loved the master because he could quote from any of Cervantes' prefaces and because his tongue had a little Castilian salt about it still. Many a morning Uncle Pio entered the Palace through corridors where there was no one to cross but a confessor or a confidential bully and sat with the Viceroy over his morning chocolate.

But for all his activity nothing made Uncle Pio rich. One would have said that he abandoned a venture when it threatened to prosper. Although no one knew it, he owned a house. It was full of dogs that could add and multiply and the top floor was reserved for birds. But even in this kingdom he was lonely, and proud in his loneliness, as though there resided a certain superiority in such a solitude. Finally he stumbled upon an adventure that came like some strange gift from the skies and that combined the three great aims of his life: his passion for overseeing the lives of others, his worship of beautiful women, and his admiration for the treasures of Spanish literature. He discovered Camila Perichole. Her real name was Micaela Villegas. She was singing in cafés at the age of twelve and Uncle Pio had always been the very soul of cafés. Now as he sat among the guitarists and watched this awkward girl singing ballads, imitating every inflection of the more experienced singers who had preceded her, the determination entered his mind to play Pygmalion. He bought her. Instead of sleeping locked up in the wine bin, she inherited a cot in his house. He wrote songs for her, he taught her how to listen to the quality of her tone, and bought her a new dress. At first all she noticed was that it was wonderful not to be whipped, to be offered hot soups,

and to be taught something. But it was Uncle Pio who was really dazzled. His rash experiment flourished beyond all prophecy. The little twelve-year-old, silent and always a little sullen, devoured work. He set her endless exercises in acting and mimicry; he set her problems in conveying the atmosphere of a song; he took her to the theatres and made her notice all the details of a performance. But it was from Camila as a woman that he was to receive his greatest shock. The long arms and legs were finally harmonized into a body of perfect grace. The almost grotesque and hungry face became beautiful. Her whole nature became gentle and mysterious and oddly wise; and it all turned to him. She could find no fault in him and she was sturdily loyal. They loved one another deeply but without passion. He respected the slight nervous shadow that crossed her face when he came too near her. But there arose out of this denial itself the perfume of a tenderness, that ghost of passion which, in the most unexpected relationship, can make even a whole lifetime devoted to irksome duty pass like a gracious dream.

They travelled a great deal, seeking new taverns, for the highest attribute of a café singer will always be her novelty. They went to Mexico, their odd clothes wrapped up in the self-same shawl. They slept on beaches, they were whipped at Panama and shipwrecked on some tiny Pacific islands plastered with the droppings of birds. They tramped through jungles delicately picking their way among snakes and beetles. They sold themselves out as harvesters in a hard season. Nothing in the world was very surprising to them.

Then began an even harder course of training for the girl, a regimen that resembled more the preparation for an acrobat. The instruction was a little complicated by the fact that her rise to favor was very rapid; and there was some danger that the applause she received would make her content with her work too soon. Uncle Pio never exactly beat her, but he resorted to a sarcasm that had terrors of its own.

At the close of a performance Camila would return to her dressing room to find Uncle Pio whistling nonchalantly in one corner. She would divine his attitude at once and cry angrily:

"Now what is it? Mother of God, Mother of God, what is it now?"

"Nothing, little pearl. My little Camila of Camilas, nothing."

"There was something you didn't like. Ugly fault-finding thing that you are. Come on now, what was it? Look, I'm ready."

"No, little fish. Adorable morning star, I suppose you did as well as you could."

The suggestion that she was a limited artist and that certain felicities would be forever closed to her never failed to make Camila frantic. She would burst into tears: "I wish I had never known you. You poison my whole life. You just think I did badly. It pleases you to pretend that I was bad. All right then, be quiet."

Uncle Pio went on whistling.

"The fact is I know I was weak to-night, and don't need you to tell me so. So there. Now go away. I don't want to see you around. It's hard enough to play that part without coming back and finding you this way."

Suddenly Uncle Pio would lean forward and ask with angry intensity: "Why did you take that speech to the prisoner so fast?"

More tears from the Perichole: "Oh God, let me die in peace! One day you tell me to go faster and another to go slower. Anyway I shall be crazy in a year or two and then it won't matter."

More whistling.

"Besides the audience applauded as never before. Do you hear me? *As never before.* There! Too fast or too slow is nothing to them. They wept. I was divine. That's all I care for. Now be silent. Be silent."

He was absolutely silent.

"You may comb my hair, but if you say another word I shall never play again. You can find some other girl, that's all."

Thereupon he would comb her hair soothingly for ten minutes, pretending not to notice the sobs that were shaking her exhausted body. At last she would turn quickly and catching one of his hands would kiss it frantically: "Uncle Pio, was I so bad? Was I a disgrace to you? Was it so awful *that you left the theatre?*"

After a long pause Uncle Pio would admit judiciously: "You were good in the scene on the ship."

"But I've been better, Uncle Pio. You remember the night you came back from Cuzco——?"

"You were pretty good at the close."

"Was I?"

"But my flower, my pearl, *what was the matter in the speech to the prisoner?*"

Here the Perichole would fling her face and arms upon the table amid the pomades, caught up into a tremendous fit of weeping. Only perfection would do, only perfection. And that had never come.

Then beginning in a low voice Uncle Pio would talk for an hour, analyzing the play, entering into a world of finesse in matters of voice and gesture and tempo, and often until dawn they would remain there declaiming to one another the lordly conversation of Calderón.

Whom were these two seeking to please? Not the audiences of Lima. They had long since been satisfied. We come from a world where we have known incredible standards of excellence, and we dimly remember beauties which we have not seized again; and we go back to that world. Uncle Pio and Camila Perichole were tormenting themselves in an effort to establish in Peru the standards of the theatres in some Heaven whither Calderón had preceded them. The public for which masterpieces are intended is not on this earth.

With the passing of time Camila lost some of this absorption in her art. A certain intermittent contempt for acting made her negligent. It was due to the poverty of interest in women's rôles throughout Spanish classical drama. At a time when the playwrights grouped about the courts of England and France (a little later, of Venice) were enriching the parts of women with studies in wit, charm, passion and hysteria, the dramatists of Spain kept their eyes on their heroes, on gentlemen torn between the conflicting claims of honour, or, as sinners, returning at the last moment to the cross. For a number of years Uncle Pio spent himself in discovering ways to interest the Perichole in the rôles that fell to her. Upon one occasion he was able to announce to Camila that a granddaughter of Vico de Barrera had arrived in Peru. Uncle Pio had long since communicated to Camila his veneration for great poets and Camila never questioned the view that they were a little above the kings and not below the saints. So it was in great excitement that the two of them chose one of the master's plays to perform before

his granddaughter. They rehearsed the poem a hundred times, now in the great joy of invention, now in dejection. On the night of the performance Camila peering out between the folds of the curtain had Uncle Pio point out to her the little middle-aged woman worn with the cares of penury and a large family; but it seemed to Camila that she was looking at all the beauty and dignity in the world. As she waited for the lines that preceded her entrance she clung to Uncle Pio in reverent silence, her heart beating loudly. Between the acts she retired to the dusty corner of the warehouse where no one would find her and sat staring into the corners. At the close of the performance Uncle Pio brought the granddaughter of Vico de Barrera into Camila's room. Camila stood among the clothes that hung upon the wall, weeping with happiness and shame. Finally she flung herself on her knees and kissed the older woman's hands, and the older woman kissed hers, and while the audience went home and went to bed the visitor remained telling Camila the little stories that had remained in the family, of Vico's work and of his habits.

Uncle Pio was at his happiest when a new actress entered the company, for the discovery of a new talent at her side never failed to bestir the Perichole. To Uncle Pio (standing at the back of the auditorium, bent double with joy and malice) it seemed that the body of the Perichole had become an alabaster lamp in which a strong light had been placed. Without any resort to tricks or to false emphasis, she set herself to efface the newcomer. If the play were a comedy she became the very abstraction of wit, and (as was more likely) if it was a drama of wronged ladies and implacable hates, the stage fairly smouldered with her emotion. Her personality became so electric that if she so much as laid her hand upon that of a fellow actor a sympathetic shudder ran through the audience. But such occasions of excellence became less and less frequent. As her technique became sounder, Camila's sincerity became less necessary. Even when she was absent-minded the audience did not notice the difference and only Uncle Pio grieved.

Camila had a very beautiful face, or rather a face beautiful save in repose. In repose one was startled to discover that the nose was long and thin, the mouth tired and a little childish, the eyes unsatisfied—a rather pinched peasant girl, dragged from the

cafés-chantants and quite incapable of establishing any har-
mony between the claims of her art, of her appetites, of her
dreams, and of her crowded daily routine. Each of these was a
world in itself, and the warfare between them would soon have
reduced to idiocy (or triviality) a less tenacious physique. We
have seen that in spite of her discontent with her parts, the
Perichole knew very well the joy that might reside in acting
and warmed herself from time to time at that flame. But that
of love attracted her more often, though with no greater assur-
ance of happiness, until Jupiter himself sent her some pearls.

Don Andrés de Ribera, the Viceroy of Peru, was the rem-
nant of a delightful man, broken by the table, the alcove, a
grandeeship and ten years of exile. As a youth he had accom-
panied embassies to Versailles and Rome; he had fought in the
wars in Austria; he had been in Jerusalem. He was a widower
and childless of an enormous and wealthy woman; he had col-
lected coins a little, wines, actresses, orders and maps. From the
table he had received the gout; from the alcove a tendency to
convulsions; from the grandeeship a pride so vast and puerile
that he seldom heard anything that was said to him and talked
to the ceiling in a perpetual monologue; from the exile, oceans
of boredom, a boredom so persuasive that it was like pain,—he
woke up with it and spent the day with it, and it sat by his bed
all night watching his sleep. Camila was passing the years in
the hard-working routine of the theatre, savoured by a few un-
tidy love-affairs, when this Olympian personage (for he had a
face and port fit to play gods and heroes on the scene) sud-
denly transported her to the most delicious midnight suppers
at the Palace. Contrary to all the traditions of the stage and state
she adored her elderly admirer; she thought she was going to
be happy forever. Don Andrés taught the Perichole a great
many things and to her bright eager mind that was one of the
sweetest ingredients of love. He taught her a little French; to
be neat and clean; the modes of address. Uncle Pio had taught
her how great ladies carry themselves on great occasions; he
taught her how they relax. Uncle Pio and Calderón had
trained her in beautiful Spanish; Don Andrés furnished her
with the smart slang of *El Buen Retiro*.

Uncle Pio was made anxious by Camila's invitation from the
Palace. He would have much preferred that she continue with

her little vulgarian love-affairs in the theatrical ware-house. But when he saw that her art was gaining a new finish he was well content. He would sit in the back of the theatre, rolling about in his seat for sheer joy and amusement, watching the Perichole intimate to the audience that she frequented the great world about whom the dramatists wrote. She had a new way of fingering a wine-glass, of exchanging an adieu, a new way of entering a door that told everything. To Uncle Pio nothing else mattered. What was there in the world more lovely than a beautiful woman doing justice to a Spanish masterpiece?—a performance (he asks you), packed with observation, in which the very spacing of the words revealed a comment on life and on the text—delivered by a beautiful voice—illustrated by a faultless carriage, considerable personal beauty and irresistible charm. "We are almost ready to take this marvel to Spain," he would murmur to himself. After the performance he would go around to her dressing-room and say "Very good!" But before taking his leave he would manage to ask her where, in the name of the eleven thousand virgins of Cologne, she had acquired that affected way of saying *Excelencia*.

After a time the Viceroy asked the Perichole whether it would amuse her to invite a few discreet guests to their midnight suppers, and he asked her whether she would like to meet the Archbishop. Camila was delighted. The Archbishop was delighted. On the eve of their first meeting he sent the actress an emerald pendant as big as a playing-card.

There was something in Lima that was wrapped up in yards of violet satin from which protruded a great dropsical head and two fat pearly hands; and that was its archbishop. Between the rolls of flesh that surrounded them looked out two black eyes speaking discomfort, kindliness and wit. A curious and eager soul was imprisoned in all this lard, but by dint of never refusing himself a pheasant or a goose or his daily procession of Roman wines, he was his own bitter jailer. He loved his cathedral; he loved his duties; he was very devout. Some days he regarded his bulk ruefully; but the distress of remorse was less poignant than the distress of fasting and he was presently found deliberating over the secret messages that a certain roast sends to the certain salad that will follow it. And to punish himself he led an exemplary life in every other respect.

He had read all the literature of antiquity and forgotten all about it except a general aroma of charm and disillusion. He had been learned in the Fathers and the Councils and forgotten all about them save a floating impression of dissensions that had no application to Peru. He had read all the libertine masterpieces of Italy and France and reread them annually; even in the torments of the stone (happily dissolved by drinking the water from the springs of Santa María de Cluxambuqua), he could find nothing more nourishing than the anecdotes of Brantôme and the divine Aretino.

The Archbishop knew that most of the priests of Peru were scoundrels. It required all his delicate Epicurean education to prevent his doing something about it; he had to repeat over to himself his favourite notions: that the injustice and unhappiness in the world is a constant; that the theory of progress is a delusion; that the poor, never having known happiness, are insensible to misfortune. Like all the rich he could not bring himself to believe that the poor (look at their houses, look at their clothes) could really suffer. Like all the cultivated he believed that only the widely-read could be said to *know* that they were unhappy. On one occasion, the iniquities in his see having been called to his notice, he almost did something about it. He had just heard that it was becoming a rule in Peru for priests to exact two measures of meal for a fairly good absolution, and five measures, for a really effective one. He trembled with indignation; he roared to his secretary and bidding him bring up his writing materials, announced that he was going to dictate an overwhelming message to his shepherds. But there was no ink left in the inkwell; there was no ink left in the next room; there was no ink to be found in the whole palace. This state of things in his household so upset the good man that he fell ill of the combined rages and learned to guard himself against indignations.

The addition of the Archbishop to the suppers was so successful that Don Andrés began to think of new names. He had grown increasingly dependent upon Uncle Pio, but waited until Camila should propose his inclusion of her own accord. And in due time Uncle Pio brought with him that courser of the seas, the Captain Alvarado. Generally the reunion had been several hours under way before Camila was able to join them

after her performance at the theatre. She would arrive towards one o'clock, radiant and bejewelled and very tired. The four men received her as they would a great queen. For an hour or so she would carry the conversation, but gradually reclining more and more against Don Andrés' shoulder she would follow the talk as it flitted from one humorous lined face to the other. All night they talked, secretly comforting their hearts that longed always for Spain and telling themselves that such a symposium was after the manner of the high Spanish soul. They talked about ghosts and second-sight, and about the earth before man appeared upon it and about the possibility of the planets striking against one another; about whether the soul can be seen, like a dove, fluttering away at the moment of death; they wondered whether at the second coming of Christ to Jerusalem, Peru would be long in receiving the news. They talked until the sun rose, about wars and kings, about poets and scholars, and about strange countries. Each one poured into the conversation his store of wise sad anecdotes and his dry regret about the race of men. The flood of golden light struck across the Andes and entering the great window fell upon the piles of fruit, the stained brocade upon the table, and the sweet thoughtful forehead of the Perichole as she lay sleeping against the sleeve of her protector. There would ensue a long pause, no one wishing to make the first move to go, and the glances of them all would rest upon this strange beautiful bird who lived among them. But Uncle Pio's glance had been upon her all night, a quick glance from his black eyes, full of tenderness and anxiety, resting on the great secret and reason of his life.

But Uncle Pio never ceased watching Camila. He divided the inhabitants of this world into two groups, into those who had loved and those who had not. It was a horrible aristocracy, apparently, for those who had no capacity for love (or rather for suffering in love) could not be said to be alive and certainly would not live again after their death. They were a kind of straw population, filling the world with their meaningless laughter and tears and chatter and disappearing still lovable and vain into thin air. For this distinction he cultivated his own definition of love that was like no other and that had gathered all its bitterness and pride from his odd life. He regarded love as a sort of cruel malady through which the elect are required to

pass in their late youth and from which they emerge, pale and wrung, but ready for the business of living. There was (he believed) a great repertory of errors mercifully impossible to human beings who had recovered from this illness. Unfortunately there remained to them a host of failings, but at least (from among many illustrations) they never mistook a protracted amiability for the whole conduct of life, they never again regarded any human being, from a prince to a servant, as a mechanical object. Uncle Pio never ceased watching Camila because it seemed to him that she had never undergone this initiation. In the months that followed her introduction to the Viceroy he held his breath and waited. He held his breath for years. Camila bore the Viceroy three children, yet remained the same. He knew that the first sign of her entrance into the true possession of the world would be the mastery of certain effects in her acting. There were certain passages in the plays that she would compass some day, simply, easily, and with secret joy, because they alluded to the new rich wisdom of her heart; but her treatment of such passages became more and more cursory, not to say embarrassed. He presently saw that she had tired of Don Andrés and had returned to a series of furtive love-affairs with the actors and matadors and merchants of the town.

She became more and more impatient of acting and another parasite found its way into her mind. She wanted to be a lady. She slowly contracted a greed for respectability and began to refer to her acting as a pastime. She acquired a duenna and some footmen and went to church at the fashionable hours. She attended the prize days at the University and appeared among the donors of the great charities. She even learned to read and write a little. Any faint discrimination against her as a bohemian she challenged with fury. She led the Viceroy a horrible life with her passion for concessions and her gradual usurpation of privileges. The new vice displaced the old and she became noisily virtuous. She invented some parents and produced some cousins. She obtained an undocumented legitimatization of her children. In society she cultivated a delicate and languid magdalenism, as a great lady might, and she carried a candle in the penitential parades, side by side with ladies who had nothing to regret but an outburst of temper and a furtive glance into Descartes. Her sin had been acting and everyone knows

that there were even saints who had been actors,—there was
Saint Gelasius and Saint Genesius and Saint Margaret of Anti-
och and Saint Pelagia.

There was a fashionable watering place in the hills not far
from Santa María de Cluxambuqua. Don Andrés had travelled
in France and had thought to build himself a little mock Vichy;
there was a pagoda, some drawing-rooms, a theatre, a little
arena for bull-fights and some French gardens. Camila's health
had never known a shadow, but she built herself a villa in the
vicinity and sipped the hateful waters at eleven o'clock. The
Marquesa de Montemayor has left a brilliant picture of this
opéra bouffe paradise with the reigning divinity parading her
fierce sensitiveness along the avenues of powdered shell and
receiving the homage of all those who could not afford to
offend the Viceroy. Doña María draws a portrait of this ruler,
stately and weary, gambling all through the night in sums that
would have raised another Escurial. And beside him she sets
the portrait of his son, Camila's little Don Jaime. Don Jaime,
at seven years, was a rachitic little body who seemed to have in-
herited not only his mother's forehead and eyes, but his father's
liability to convulsions. He bore his pain with the silent bewil-
derment of an animal, and like an animal he was mortally
ashamed when any evidences of it occurred in public. He was
so beautiful that the more trivial forms of pity were hushed in
his presence and his long thoughts about his difficulties had
given his face a patient and startling dignity. His mother dressed
him in garnet velvet, and when he was able he followed her
about at a distance of several yards, extricating himself gravely
from the ladies who tried to detain him in conversation. Camila
was never cross to Don Jaime and she was never demonstra-
tive. When the sun was shining the two could be seen walking
along those artificial terraces in silence, Camila wondering
when the felicity would begin that she had always associated
with social position, Don Jaime rejoicing merely in the sun-
light and anxiously estimating the approach of a cloud. They
looked like figures that had strayed there from some remote
country, or out of an old ballad, that had not yet learned the
new language and had not yet found any friends.

Camila was about thirty when she left the stage and it re-
quired five years for her to achieve her place in society. She

gradually became almost stout, though her head seemed to grow more beautiful every year. She took to overdressing and the floors of the drawing-rooms reflected a veritable tower of jewels and scarves and plumes. Her face and hands were covered with a bluish powder against which she drew an irritable mouth in scarlet and orange. The almost distraught fury of her temper was varied by the unnatural sweetness of her address in the company of the dowagers. In the earliest stages of her progress upward she had intimated to Uncle Pio that he was not to be seen with her in public, but finally she became impatient even of his discreeter visits. She conducted the interviews with formality and evasion. Her eyes never crossed his and she angled for pretexts to quarrel with him. Still he ventured out once a month to try her patience and when the call had become impossible he would climb the stairs and finish the hour among her children.

One day he arrived at her villa in the hills and, through her maid, begged for an opportunity to talk with her. He was told that she would see him in the French gardens a little before sunset. He had come up from Lima on a strange sentimental impulse. Like all solitary persons he had invested friendship with a divine glamour: he imagined that the people he passed on the street, laughing together and embracing when they parted, the people who dined together with so many smiles,—you will scarcely believe me, but he imagined that they were extracting from all that congeniality great store of satisfaction. So that suddenly he was filled with the excitement of seeing her again, of being called "Uncle Pio," and of reviving for a moment the trust and humour of their long vagabondage.

The French Gardens were at the southern end of the town. Behind them rose the higher Andes and before them there was a parapet overlooking a deep valley and overlooking wave after wave of hills that stretched toward the Pacific. It was the hour when bats fly low and the smaller animals play recklessly underfoot. A few solitaries lingered about the gardens, gazing dreamily into the sky that was being gradually emptied of its colour, or leaned upon the balustrade and looked down into the valley, noting in which village a dog was barking. It was the hour when the father returns home from the fields and plays for a moment in the yard with the dog that jumps upon him, holding his

muzzle closed or throwing him upon his back. The young girls look about for the first star to fix a wish upon it, and the boys grow restless for supper. Even the busiest mother stands for a moment idle-handed, smiling at her dear and exasperating family.

Uncle Pio stood against one of the chipped marble benches and watched Camila coming towards him:

"I am late," she said. "I am sorry. What is it you wish to say to me?"

"Camila,—" he began.

"My name is Doña Micaela."

"I do not wish to offend you, Doña Micaela, but when you let me call you Camila for twenty years, I should think——"

"Oh, do as you like. Do as you like."

"Camila, promise me that you will listen to me. Promise me that you will not run away at my first sentence."

At once she burst out with unexpected passion: "Uncle Pio, listen to me. You are mad if you think you can make me return to the theatre. I look back at the theatre with horror. Understand that. The theatre! The theatre, indeed! The daily payment of insults in that filthy place. Understand that you are wasting your time."

He answered gently: "I would not have you come back if you are happy with these new friends."

"You don't like my new friends, then?" she answered quickly. "Whom do you offer me in their stead?"

"Camila, I only remember . . ."

"I will not be criticized. I don't want any advice. It will be cold in a moment, I must go back to my house. Just give me up, that's all. Just put me out of your mind."

"Dear Camila, don't be angry. Let me talk to you. Just suffer me for ten minutes."

He did not understand why she was weeping. He did not know what to say. He talked at random: "You never even come to see the theatre, and they all notice it. The audiences are falling away now, too. They only put on the Old Comedy twice a week; all the other nights there are these new farces in prose. All is dull and childish and indecent. No one can speak Spanish any more. No one can even walk correctly any more.

On Corpus Christi Day they gave *Belshazzar's Feast* where you were so wonderful. Now it was shameful."

There was a pause. A beautiful procession of clouds, like a flock of sheep, was straying up from the sea, slipping up the valleys between the hills. Camila suddenly touched his knee, and her face was like her face twenty years before: "Forgive me, Uncle Pio, for being so bad. Jaime was ill this afternoon. There's nothing one can do. He lies there, so white and . . . so surprised. One must just think of other things. Uncle Pio, it would be no good if I went back to the theatre. The audiences come for the prose farces. We were foolish to try and keep alive the Old Comedy. Let people read the old plays in books if they choose to. It is not worth while fighting with the crowd."

"Wonderful Camila, I was not just to you when you were on the stage. It was some foolish pride in me. I grudged you the praise that you deserved. Forgive me. You have always been a very great artist. If you come to see that you are not happy among these people you might think about going to Madrid. You would have a great triumph there. You are still young and beautiful. There will be time later to be called Doña Micaela. We shall be old soon. We shall be dead soon."

"No, I shall never see Spain. All the world is alike, Madrid or Lima."

"Oh, if we could go away to some island where the people would know you for yourself. And love you."

"You are fifty years old and you are still dreaming of such islands, Uncle Pio."

He bent his head and mumbled: "Of course I love you, Camila, as I always must and more than I can say. To have known you is enough for my whole life. You are a great lady now. And you are rich. There is no longer any way that I can help you. But I am always ready."

"How absurd you are," she said smiling. "You said that as boys say it. You don't seem to learn as you grow older, Uncle Pio. There is no such thing as that kind of love and that kind of island. It's in the theatre you find such things."

He looked shamefaced, but unconvinced.

At last she rose and said sadly: "What are we talking about! It is growing cold. I must be going in. You must be resigned.

I have no heart for the theatre." There was a pause. "And for the rest? . . . Oh, I do not understand. It is just circumstance. I must be what I must. Do not try to understand either. Don't think about me, Uncle Pio. Just forgive, that's all. Just try to forgive."

She stood still a moment, searching for something deeply felt to say to him. The first cloud reached the terrace; it was dark; the last stragglers were leaving the gardens. She was thinking of Don Jaime, and of Don Andrés and of himself. She could not find the words. Suddenly she bent down and kissed his fingers and went quickly away. But he sat for a long time in the gathering clouds trembling with happiness and trying to penetrate into the meaning of these things.

Suddenly the news was all over Lima. Doña Micaela Villegas, the lady that used to be Camila the Perichole, had the small-pox. Several hundred other persons had the small-pox also, but popular interest and malignity were concentrated upon the actress. A wild hope ran about the town that the beauty would be impaired that had enabled her to despise the class from which she sprang. The news escaped from the sick-room that Camila had become ludicrous in homeliness and the cup of the envious overflowed. As soon as she was able she had herself carried from the city to her villa in the hills; she ordered the sale of her elegant little palace. She returned her jewels to their givers and she sold her fine clothes. The Viceroy, the Archbishop, and the few men at court who had been her sincerest admirers besieged her door still with messages and gifts; the messages were ignored and the gifts were returned without comment. No one but her nurse and maids had been permitted to see her since the commencement of her illness. As an answer to his repeated attempts Don Andrés received a large sum of money from her with a letter compounded of all that is possible in bitterness and pride.

Like all beautiful women who have been brought up amid continual tributes to her beauty she assumed without cynicism that it must necessarily be the basis of anyone's attachment to herself; henceforth any attention paid to her must spring from a pity full of condescension and faintly perfumed with satisfaction at so complete a reversal. This assumption that she need look for no more devotion now that her beauty had passed

proceeded from the fact that she had never realized any love save love as passion. Such love, though it expends itself in generosity and thoughtfulness, though it give birth to visions and to great poetry, remains among the sharpest expressions of self-interest. Not until it has passed through a long servitude, through its own self-hatred, through mockery, through great doubts, can it take its place among the loyalties. Many who have spent a lifetime in it can tell us less of love than the child that lost a dog yesterday. As her friends continued in their efforts to draw her again into society she grew more and more angry and dispatched insulting messages to the city. It was said for a time that she was retiring into religion. But new rumours that all was fury and despair on the little farm contradicted the old. For those near to her the despair was fearful to behold. She was convinced that her life was over, her life and the children's. In her hysterical pride she had given back more than she owed and the approach of poverty was added to the loneliness and the gloom of her future. There was nothing left for her to do but to draw out her days in jealous solitude in the center of the little farm that was falling into decay. She brooded for hours upon the joy of her enemies and could be heard striding about her room with strange cries.

Uncle Pio did not allow himself to be discouraged. By dint of making himself useful to the children, by taking a hand in the management of the farm and by discreetly lending her some money he obtained his entrance into the house and even into the presence of its veiled mistress. But even then Camila, convinced in her pride that he *pitied* her, lashed him with the blade of her tongue and derived some strange comfort from heaping him with sneers. He loved her the more, understanding better than she did herself all the stages in the convalescence of her humiliated spirit. But one day an accident befell that lost him his share in her progress. He pushed open a door.

She thought she had locked it. For just one hour a foolish secret hope had come to her; she wondered whether she could make a paste of chalk and cream to spread upon her face. She who had sneered so often at the befloured grandmothers of the court wondered for a few moments whether she had learned anything on the stage that would aid her now. She thought she had locked the door and with hurried hands and beating heart

she laid on the coat, the grotesque pallor, and as she gazed into the mirror and recognized the futility of her attempt she caught the image of Uncle Pio standing in the door amazed. She rose from the chair with a cry and covered her face with her hands.

"Go away. Go away out of my house forever," she screamed. "I never want to see you again." In her shame she drove him out with blasphemy and hatred, she pursued him down the corridor and hurled objects down the stairs. She gave her farmer orders that Uncle Pio was forbidden to come into the grounds. But he continued for a week trying to see her again. At last he went back to Lima; he filled in the time as best he could, but he longed to be by her as a boy of eighteen would long. At last he devised a stratagem and returned up into the hills to put it into effect.

One morning before dawn he arose and lay on the ground below her window. He imitated in the darkness the sound of weeping, and, as nearly as he could, of a young girl's weeping. He continued in this for the whole quarter of an hour. He did not let his voice rise above that degree of loudness which Italian musicians would represent by the direction *piano*, but he frequently intermitted the sound trusting that if she were asleep it would insinuate itself into her mind as well by duration as by degree. The air was cool and agreeable. The first faint streak of sapphire was appearing behind the peaks and in the east the star of morning was pulsating every moment with a more tender intention. A profound silence wrapped all the farm buildings, only an occasional breeze set all the grasses sighing. Suddenly a lamp was lit in her room and a moment later the shutter was thrown back and a head wrapped in veils leaned far out.

"Who is there?" asked the beautiful voice.

Uncle Pio remained silent.

Camila said again in a tone edged with impatience:

"Who is there? Who is there weeping?"

"Doña Micaela, my lady, I beg of you to come here to me."

"Who are you and what do you want?"

"I am a poor girl. I am Estrella. I beg of you to come and help me. Do not call your maid. I pray you, Doña Micaela, to come yourself."

Camila was silent a moment, then said abruptly: "Very well,"

and closed the shutter. Presently she appeared around the corner of the house. She wore a thick cloak that dragged in the dew. She stood at a distance and said: "Come over here to where I am standing,—Who are you?"

Uncle Pio rose up. "Camila, it is I,—Uncle Pio. Forgive me, but I must speak to you."

"Mother of God, when shall I be free of this dreadful person! Understand: I want to see no one. I don't want to speak to a soul. My life is over. That is all."

"Camila, by our long life together, I beg of you to grant me one thing. I shall go away and never trouble you again."

"I grant you nothing, nothing. Stay away from me."

"I promise you I shall never trouble you again if you listen to me this once." She was hurrying around to the door on the other side of the house and Uncle Pio was obliged to run beside her to make sure that she heard what he was saying. She stopped:

"What is it then? Hurry. It is cold. I am not well. I must go back to my room."

"Camila, let me take Don Jaime for a year to live with me in Lima. Let me be his teacher. Let me teach him the Castilian. Here he is left among the servants. He is learning nothing."

"No."

"Camila, what will become of him? He has a good mind and he wants to learn."

"He is sick. He is delicate. Your house is a sty. Only the country is good for him."

"But he has been much better these last few months. I promise you I shall clean out my house. I shall apply to Madre María del Pilar for a housekeeper. Here he is in your stables all day. I shall teach him all that a gentleman should know,—fencing and Latin and music. We shall read all. . . ."

"A mother cannot be separated from her child like that. It is impossible. You are crazy to have thought of it. Give up thinking of me and of everything about me. I no longer exist. I and my children will get on as best we can. Do not try to disturb me again. I do not want to see any human being."

Now it was that Uncle Pio felt obliged to use a hard measure. "Then pay me the money that you owe me," he said.

Camila stood still, confounded. To herself she said: "Life is too fearful to bear. When may I die?" After a moment she

answered him, in a hoarse voice: "I have very little money. I will pay you what I can. I will pay you now. I have a few jewels here. Then we need never see one another again." She was ashamed of her poverty. She took a few steps, then turned and said: "Now I see that you are a very hard man. But it is right that I pay you what I owe you."

"No, Camila, I only said that to enforce my request. I shall take no money from you. But lend me Don Jaime for one year. I shall love him and take every care of him. Did I harm you? Was I a bad teacher to you in those other years?"

"It is cruel of you to keep urging gratitude, gratitude, gratitude. I was grateful,—good, good! but now that I am no longer the same woman there remains nothing to be grateful for." There was a silence. Her eyes were resting on the star that seemed to be leading forth the whole sky in its wonder. A great pain lay at her heart, the pain of a world that was meaningless. Then she said: "If Jaime wishes to go with you, very well. I shall talk to him in the morning. If he wishes to go with you, you will find him at the Inn about noon. Good night. Go with God."

"Go with God."

She returned to the house. The next day the grave little boy appeared at the Inn. His fine clothes were torn and stained now and he carried a small bundle for change. His mother had given him a gold piece for spending-money and a little stone that shone in the dark to look at in his sleepless nights. They set off together in a cart, but soon Uncle Pio became aware that the jolting was not good for the boy. He carried him on his shoulder. As they drew near to the bridge of San Luis Rey, Jaime tried to conceal his shame for he knew that one of those moments was coming that separated him from other people. He was especially ashamed because Uncle Pio had just over-taken a friend of his, a sea-captain. And just as they got to the bridge he spoke to an old lady who was travelling with a little girl. Uncle Pio said that when they had crossed the bridge they would sit down and rest, but it turned out not to be necessary.

PART FIVE:

Perhaps an Intention

A NEW bridge of stone has been built in the place of the old, but the event has not been forgotten. It has passed into proverbial expressions. "I may see you Tuesday," says a Limean, "unless the bridge falls." "My cousin lives by the bridge of San Luis Rey," says another, and a smile goes around the company, for that also means: under the sword of Damocles. There are some poems about the accident, classics to be found in every Peruvian anthology, but the real literary monument is Brother Juniper's book.

There are a hundred ways of wondering at circumstance. Brother Juniper would never have arrived at his method had it not been for his friendship with a certain master in the University of San Martin. This student's wife had stolen away one morning on a boat for Spain, following a soldier, and had left him the care of two daughters in their cradle. He was possessed of all the bitterness that Brother Juniper lacked and derived a sort of joy from the conviction that all was wrong in the world. He whispered into the Franciscan's ear such thoughts and anecdotes as belied the notion of a guided world. For a moment a look of distress, almost of defeat, would come into the Brother's eyes; then he would begin patiently explaining why such stories held no difficulty for a believer. "There was a queen of Naples and Sicily," the student would say, "who discovered that she was carrying an angry tumor in her side. In great dismay she commanded her subjects to fall to their prayers and ordered that all the garments in Sicily and Naples be sewn with votive crosses. She was well loved by her people and all their prayers and embroideries were sincere, but ineffectual. Now she lies in the splendor of Monreale, and a few inches above her heart may be read the words: *I shall fear no evil.*"

It was by dint of hearing a great many such sneers at faith that Brother Juniper became convinced that the world's time had come for proof, tabulated proof, of the conviction that

was so bright and exciting within him. When the pestilence visited his dear village of Puerto and carried off a large number of peasants, he secretly drew up a diagram of the characteristics of fifteen victims and fifteen survivors, the statistics of their value *sub specie aeternitatis.* Each soul was rated upon a basis of ten as regards its goodness, its diligence in religious observance, and its importance to its family group. Here is a fragment of this ambitious chart:

	Goodness	Piety	Usefulness
Alfonso G.	4	4	10
Nina	2	5	10
Manuel B.	10	10	0
Alfonso V.	−8	−10	10
Vera N.	0	10	10

The thing was more difficult than he had foreseen. Almost every soul in a difficult frontier community turned out to be indispensable economically, and the third column was all but useless. The examiner was driven to the use of minus terms when he confronted the personal character of Alfonso V., who was not, like Vera N., merely bad: he was a propagandist for badness and not merely avoided church but led others to avoid it. Vera N. was indeed bad, but she was a model worshipper and the mainstay of a full hut. From all this saddening data Brother Juniper contrived an index for each peasant. He added up the total for victims and compared it with the total for survivors, to discover that the dead were five times more worth saving. It almost looked as though the pestilence had been directed against the really valuable people in the village of Puerto. And on that afternoon Brother Juniper took a walk along the edge of the Pacific. He tore up his findings and cast them into the waves; he gazed for an hour upon the great clouds of pearl that hang forever upon the horizon of that sea, and extracted from their beauty a resignation that he did not permit his reason to examine. The discrepancy between faith and the facts is greater than is generally assumed.

But there was another story of the master of San Martín (not so subversive, this one) that probably gave to Brother Juniper the hint for his procedure after the fall of the bridge of San Luis Rey.

This master was one day walking through the Cathedral of Lima and stopped to read the epitaph of a lady. He read with an increasingly prominent lower lip that she had been for twenty years the centre and joy of her home, that she had been the delight of her friends, that all who met her went away in astonishment at her goodness and beauty, and that there she lay awaiting the return of her Lord. Now on the day that he read these words, the master of San Martín had had much to fret him, and raising his eyes from the tablet he spoke aloud in his rage: "The shame of it, the persecution of it! Everyone knows that in the world we do nothing but feed our wills. Why perpetuate this legend of selflessness? Why keep this thing alive, this rumour of disinterestedness?"

And so saying he resolved to expose this conspiracy of the stone-cutters. The lady had been dead only twelve years. He sought out her servants, her children and her friends. And everywhere he went, like a perfume, her dear traits had survived her and wherever she was mentioned there arose a suffering smile and the protest that words could not describe the gracious ways of her. Even the eager youth of her grandchildren, who had never seen her, was made more difficult by the news that it was possible to be as good as that. And the man stood amazed; only at last he muttered: "Nevertheless, what I said was true. This woman was an exception, perhaps an exception."

In compiling his book about these people Brother Juniper seemed to be pursued by the fear that in omitting the slightest detail he might lose some guiding hint. The longer he worked the more he felt that he was stumbling about among great dim intimations. He was forever being cheated by details that looked as though they were significant if only he could find their setting. So he put everything down on the notion perhaps that if he (or a keener head) reread the book twenty times, the countless facts would suddenly start to move, to assemble, and to betray their secret. The Marquesa de Montemayor's cook told him that she lived almost entirely on rice, fish and a little fruit and Brother Juniper put it down on the chance that it would some day reveal a spiritual trait. Don Rubío said of her that she used to appear at his receptions without invitation in order to steal the spoons. A midwife on the edge of the town declared that Doña María called upon her with morbid questions until

she had been obliged to order her away from the door like a beggar. The bookseller of the town reported that she was one of the three most cultivated persons in Lima. Her farmer's wife declared that she was absent-minded, but compact of goodness. The art of biography is more difficult than is generally supposed.

Brother Juniper found that there was least to be learned from those who had been most closely associated with the subjects of his inquiry. Madre María del Pilar talked to him at length about Pepita, but she did not tell him of her own ambitions for her. The Perichole was at first difficult of approach, but presently even liked the Franciscan. Her characterization of Uncle Pio flatly contradicted the stores of unsavory testimonies that he had acquired elsewhere. Her allusions to her son were few and conceded with pain. They closed the interview abruptly. The Captain Alvarado told what he could of Esteban and of Uncle Pio. Those who know most in this realm, venture least.

I shall spare you Brother Juniper's generalizations. They are always with us. He thought he saw in the same accident, the wicked visited by destruction and the good called early to Heaven. He thought he saw pride and wealth confounded as an object lesson to the world, and he thought he saw humility crowned and rewarded for the edification of the city. But Brother Juniper was not satisfied with his reasons. It was just possible that the Marquesa de Montemayor was not a monster of avarice, and Uncle Pio of self-indulgence.

The book being done fell under the eyes of some judges and was suddenly pronounced heretical. It was ordered to be burned in the Square with its author. Brother Juniper submitted to the decision that the devil had made use of him to effect a brilliant campaign in Peru. He sat in his cell that last night trying to seek in his own life the pattern that had escaped him in five others. He was not rebellious. He was willing to lay down his life for the purity of the church, but he longed for one voice somewhere to testify for him that his intention, at least, had been for faith; he thought there was no one in the world who believed him. But the next morning in all that crowd and sunlight there were many who believed, for he was much loved.

There was a little delegation from the village of Puerto, and Nina (Goodness 2, Piety 5, Usefulness 10) and others stood

with drawn puzzled faces while their little friar was given to the congenial flames. Even then, even then, there remained in his heart an obstinate nerve insisting that at least St. Francis would not utterly have condemned him, and (not daring to call upon a greater name, since he seemed so open to error in these matters) he called twice upon St. Francis and leaning upon a flame he smiled and died.

The day of the service was clear and warm. The Limeans, their black eyes wide with awe, poured through the streets into their Cathedral and stood gazing at the mound of black velvet and silver. The Archbishop enclosed in his wonderful and almost wooden vestments perspired upon his throne, lending from time to time a connoisseur's ear to the felicities of Vittoria's counterpoint. The choir had restudied the pages that, as his farewell to music, Tomás Luis had composed for his friend and patron, the Empress of Austria, and all that grief and sweetness, all that Spanish realism filtering through an Italian mode, rose and fell above the sea of mantillas. Don Andrés, under the colours and feathered hangings of his office, knelt, ill and troubled. He knew that the crowd was furtively glancing at him, expecting him to play the father who has lost his only son. He wondered whether the Perichole was present. He had never been obliged to go so long without smoking. The Captain Alvarado pushed in from the sunny square for a moment. He looked across the fields of black hair and lace at the trooping of the candles and the ropes of incense. "How false, how unreal," he said and pushed his way out. He descended to the sea and sat on the edge of his boat, gazing down into the clear water. "Happy are the drowned, Esteban," he said.

Behind the screen the Abbess sat among her girls. The night before she had torn an idol from her heart and the experience had left her pale but firm. She had accepted the fact that it was of no importance whether her work went on or not; it was enough to work. She was the nurse who tends the sick who never recover; she was the priest who perpetually renews the office before an altar to which no worshippers come. There would be no Pepita to enlarge her work; it would relapse into the indolence and the indifference of her colleagues. It seemed to be sufficient for Heaven that for a while in Peru a disinterested

love had flowered and faded. She leaned her forehead upon her hand, following the long tender curve that the soprano lifts in the Kyrie. "My affection should have had more of that colour, Pepita. My whole life should have had more of that quality. I have been too busy," she added ruefully and her mind drifted into prayer.

Camila had started from the farm to attend the service. Her heart was filled with consternation and amazement. Here was another comment from the skies; that was the third time she had been spoken to. Her small-pox, Jaime's illness, and now the fall of the bridge,—oh, these were not accidents. She was as ashamed as though letters had appeared on her forehead. An order from the Palace announced that the Viceroy was sending her two daughters to a convent-school in Spain. That was right. She was alone. She gathered a few things together mechanically and started to the city for the service. But she fell to thinking of the crowds gaping over her Uncle Pio and over her son; she thought of the vast ritual of the church, like a chasm into which the beloved falls, and of the storm of the *dies irae* where the individual is lost among the millions of the dead, features grow dim and traits fade. At a little more than half the journey, at the mud church of San Luis Rey she slipped in and knelt against a pillar to rest. She wandered through her memory, searching for the faces of her two. She waited for some emotion to appear. "But I feel nothing," she whispered to herself. "I have no heart. I am a poor meaningless woman, that's all. I am shut out. I have no heart. Look, I won't try and think of anything; let me just rest here." And scarcely had she paused when again that terrible incommunicable pain swept through her, the pain that could not speak once to Uncle Pio and tell him of her love and just once offer her courage to Jaime in his sufferings. She started up wildly: "I fail everybody," she cried. "They love me and I fail them." She returned to the farm and carried for a year the mood of her self-despair. One day she heard by accident that the wonderful Abbess had lost two persons whom she loved in the same accident. Her sewing fell from her hand: then *she* would know, she would explain. "But no, what would she say to me! She would not even believe that such a person as I could love or could lose."

Camila decided to go to Lima and look at the Abbess from a distance. "If her face tells me that she would not despise me, I will speak to her," she said.

Camila lurked about the convent church and fell humbly in love with the homely old face, though it frightened her a little. At last she called upon her.

"Mother," she said, "I . . . I . . ."

"Do I know you, my daughter?"

"I was the actress, I was the Perichole."

"Oh, yes. Oh, I have wished to know you for a long while, but they told me you did not wish to be seen. You too, I know, lost in the fall of the bridge of San. . . ."

Camila rose and swayed. There! again that access of pain, the hands of the dead she could not reach. Her lips were white. Her head brushed the Abbess's knee: "Mother, what shall I do? I am all alone. I have nothing in the world. I love them. What shall I do?"

The Abbess looked at her closely. "My daughter, it is warm here. Let us go into the garden. You can rest there." She made a sign to a girl in the cloister to bring some water. She continued talking mechanically to Camila. "I have wished to know you for a long while, señora. Even before the accident I had wished much to know you. They told me that in the *autos sacramentales* you were a very great and beautiful actress, in *Belshazzar's Feast.*"

"Oh, Mother, you must not say that. I am a sinner. You must not say that."

"Here, drink this, my child. We have a beautiful garden, do you not think so? You will come and see us often and some day you will meet Sister Juana who is our gardener-in-chief. Before she entered religion she had almost never seen a garden, for she worked in the mines high up in the mountains. Now everything grows under her hand.—A year has gone by, señora, since our accident. I lost two who had been children in my orphanage, but you lost a real child of your own?"

"Yes, Mother."

"And a great friend?"

"Yes, Mother."

"Tell me. . . ."

And then the whole tide of Camila's long despair, her lonely obstinate despair since her girlhood, found its rest on that dusty friendly lap among Sister Juana's fountains and roses.

But where are sufficient books to contain the events that would not have been the same without the fall of the bridge? From such a number I choose one more.

"The Condesa d'Abuirre wishes to see you," said a lay-sister at the door of the Abbess's office.

"Well," said the Abbess, laying down her pen, "who is she?"

"She has just come from Spain. I don't know."

"Oh, it is some money, Inez, some money for my house for the blind. Quick, bid her come in."

The tall, rather langorous beauty entered the room. Doña Clara, who was generally so adequate, seemed constrained for once. "Are you busy, dear Mother, may I talk to you for a while?"

"I am quite free, my daughter. You will excuse an old woman's memory; have I known you before?"

"My mother was the Marquesa de Montemayor. . . ." Doña Clara suspected that the Abbess had not admired her mother and would not let the older woman speak until she herself had made a long passionate defense of Doña María. The languor fell away in her self-reproach. At last the Abbess told her of Pepita and Esteban, and of Camila's visit. "All, all of us have failed. One wishes to be punished. One is willing to assume all kinds of penance, but do you know, my daughter, that in love—I scarcely dare say it—but in love our very mistakes don't seem to be able to last long?"

The Condesa showed the Abbess Doña María's last letter. Madre María dared not say aloud how great her astonishment was that such words (words that since then the whole world has murmured over with joy) could spring in the heart of Pepita's mistress. "Now learn," she commanded herself, "learn at last that anywhere you may expect grace." And she was filled with happiness like a girl at this new proof that the traits she lived for were everywhere, that the world was ready. "Will you do me a kindness, my daughter? Will you let me show you my work?"

The sun had gone down, but the Abbess led the way with a

lantern down corridor after corridor. Doña Clara saw the old and the young, the sick and the blind, but most of all she saw the tired, bright old woman who was leading her. The Abbess would stop in a passageway and say suddenly: "I can't help thinking that something could be done for the deaf-and-dumb. It seems to me that some patient person could, . . . could study out a language for them. You know there are hundreds and hundreds in Peru. Do you remember whether anyone in Spain has found a way for them? Well, some day they will." Or a little later: "Do you know, I keep thinking that something can be done for the insane. I am old, you know, and I cannot go where these things are talked about, but I watch them sometimes and it seems to me . . . In Spain, now, they are gentle with them? It seems to me that there is a secret about it, just hidden from us, just around the corner. Some day back in Spain, if you hear of anything that would help us, you will write me a letter . . . if you are not too busy?"

At last after Doña Clara had seen even the kitchens, the Abbess said: "Now will you excuse me, for I must go into the room of the very sick and say a few words for them to think about when they cannot sleep. I will not ask you to come with me there, for you are not accustomed to such . . . such sounds and things. And besides I only talk to them as one talks to children." She looked up at her with her modest rueful smile. Suddenly she disappeared a moment to return with one of her helpers, one who had likewise been involved in the affair of the bridge and who had formerly been an actress. "She is leaving me," said the Abbess, "for some work across the city and when I have spoken here I must leave you both, for the flour-broker will not wait for me any longer, and our argument will take a long time."

But Doña Clara stood in the door as the Abbess talked to them, the lamp placed on the floor beside her. Madre María stood with her back against a post; the sick lay in rows gazing at the ceiling and trying to hold their breaths. She talked that night of all those out in the dark (she was thinking of Esteban alone, she was thinking of Pepita alone) who had no one to turn to, for whom the world perhaps was more than difficult, without meaning. And those who lay in their beds there felt that they were within a wall that the Abbess had built for them;

within all was light and warmth, and without was the darkness they would not exchange even for a relief from pain and from dying. But even while she was talking, other thoughts were passing in the back of her mind. "Even now," she thought, "almost no one remembers Esteban and Pepita, but myself. Camila alone remembers her Uncle Pio and her son; this woman, her mother. But soon we shall die and all memory of those five will have left the earth, and we ourselves shall be loved for a while and forgotten. But the love will have been enough; all those impulses of love return to the love that made them. Even memory is not necessary for love. There is a land of the living and a land of the dead and the bridge is love, the only survival, the only meaning."

THE WOMAN OF ANDROS

The first part of this novel is based upon the *Andria*, a comedy of Terence who in turn based his work upon two Greek plays, now lost to us, by Menander.

THE Earth sighed as it turned in its course; the shadow of night crept gradually along the Mediterranean, and Asia was left in darkness. The great cliff that was one day to be called Gibraltar held for a long time a gleam of red and orange, while across from it the mountains of Atlas showed deep blue pockets in their shining sides. The caves that surround the Neapolitan gulf fell into a profounder shade, each giving forth from the darkness its chiming or its booming sound. Triumph had passed from Greece and wisdom from Egypt, but with the coming on of night they seemed to regain their lost honors, and the land that was soon to be called Holy prepared in the dark its wonderful burden. The sea was large enough to hold a varied weather: a storm played about Sicily and its smoking mountains, but at the mouth of the Nile the water lay like a wet pavement. A fair tripping breeze ruffled the Aegean and all the islands of Greece felt a new freshness at the close of day.

The happiest, and one of the least famous of the islands, Brynos, welcomed the breeze. The evening was long. For a time, the sound of the waves, briskly slapping against the wall of the little harbor, was covered by the chattering of women, by the shouts of boys, and by the crying of lambs. As the first lights appeared, the women retired; as the air was filled with the clangor of the shop fronts being put into place, the boys' voices ceased; and finally only the murmur of the men in the wineshops, playing at games with ivory counters, mingled with the sounds from the sea. A confused starlight, already apprehensive of the still unrisen moon, fell upon the tiers of small houses that covered the slope and upon the winding flights of stairs that served as streets between them.

The wineshops stood about the roughly paved square at the water's edge and in one of them the five or six principal fathers of the island sat playing. By the time the moon had risen, two of these, Simo and Chremes, had outstayed their companions. Simo was the owner of two warehouses; he was a trader and had three ships that passed continually to and fro among the islands. The men had finished playing; the counters lay on the

table between them and they sighed into their beards as they thought of the long walk through the ghostly olive trees to their homes. Simo was more tired than usual: whereas the law of moderation teaches us that the mind cannot be employed for more than three hours daily over merchandise and numerals without soilure, he had that day spent five hours in argument and traffic.

"Simo," said Chremes suddenly, with the air of a man bracing himself to an unpleasant and long deferred task, "your boy is twenty-five now—"

Simo groaned as he saw the subject arising that he was never able to look in the face.

"It's four years," continued Chremes, "since you first said that a young man mustn't be forced into marriage by his old people. And certainly no one has been trying to force Pamphilus. But what is he waiting for? He helps you in the warehouse; he exercises in the field; he dines at the Andrian's. How many years must that kind of life go on before you agree with me that he would be better off married to my daughter?"

"Chremes, he must come to me of his own accord. I will not be the first one to speak about it to the boy."

"First! It won't be speaking of it first, Simo. It has been understood between our families for years that he will marry Philumena. It's being spoken of all the time. The young people tease him about it from morning to night. He knows perfectly well that my daughter is ready to marry him. It's sheer laziness on his part. It's sheer unwillingness to take on the responsibilities of being a husband and a father and the foremost young householder on the island."

"He's a young man who knows what he means to do. I will not coerce him."

"Then it's settled that he doesn't want to marry my daughter. It's a humiliation for her to be waiting all these years for him to make up his mind, and her mother's been after me to close the matter for a long time. Perhaps I shouldn't say it, but you'll be throwing away a good thing through sheer hesitancy, both of you. Philumena is by far the healthiest and the prettiest girl on any of these islands. And she's clever at everything that is expected of a woman in the home. The uniting of our two families has advantages, Simo, that I don't have to point

out to you. But this lapse of time has made it clear that your son is going to wait until his fancy has been caught by some other girl, I suppose. So be it! From this very night my wife is going to start looking about for some other young man."

"Chremes, Chremes, he's only twenty-five. Let him play about a little longer. Why must they become husbands and fathers so soon? He's good and he's happy. So is your daughter. Let them be awhile."

"Grandchildren!—that's what I want to see. There shouldn't be a long step between the generations. It's bad for customs and manners."

"You'll make a greater mistake by hurrying than by delaying."

"Well," Chremes continued, "there's another reason why I want the matter settled soon. And that is this: we don't like the visits that Pamphilus is paying to the Andrian woman. Naturally, Simo, it's hard for me to be severe about it, because my own son goes there too. But it's natural that a father should be more exacting in regard to his son-in-law than in regard to his son."

Simo looked more uncomfortable than ever and remained silent. Chremes went on:

"I don't think you like this resort to foreign women any more than I do. Our islands have always been famous for strict and good behavior. If the devil was in us as boys we could always follow some shepherdess up a dark road. But this Andrian has brought the whole air of Alexandria to town with her, perfumes and hot baths and late hours."

Simo stroked his cheeks a moment and then replied in a low grunting voice: "Well, if it isn't one thing, it's another, I suppose. I don't know anything about this Andrian. The women seem to talk of nothing else from morning to night, but one can't believe what they say."

Thus invited, Chremes launched into his exposition with considerable relish, examining Simo's face from time to time to see if the details were arousing in him the interest they held for himself. "Her name is Chrysis, and I don't know what she means by calling herself Andrian. The island of Andros was never famous for such airs and graces as she puts on. She's flitted from Corinth and Alexandria, you may be sure. She should have stayed in her cities instead of burying herself in our town

and reciting poetry to our young men. Yes, yes, she recites poetry to them like the famous ones. She has twelve or fifteen of them to dinner every seven or eight days,—the unmarried ones, of course. They lie about on couches and eat odd food and talk. Presently she rises and recites; she can recite whole tragedies without the book. She is very strict with the young men, apparently. She makes them pronounce all the Attic accents; they eat in the Athenian mode, drinking toasts and wearing garlands, and each in turn is elected King of the Banquet. And at the close, hot towels are passed around for them to wipe their hands on."

Simo did not concede to Chremes the pleasure of his close interest; his eyes were lowered and his face wore the same bored expression that it brought to all island gossip. Chremes decided to be less expansive and added with easy indignation: "As for me, Alexandria is Alexandria and Brynos is Brynos. A few more imported notions and our island will be spoiled forever. It will become a mass of poor undigested imitations. All the girls will be wanting to read and write and declaim. What becomes of home life, Simo, if women can read and write? You and I married the finest girls of our time and we've been happy. We can at least provide one more generation of good sense and good manners on this island before the age arrives when all the women will have the airs of dancers and all the men go about waiting on them."

Simo knew the answer to this, but he repressed it. Chremes, more than any man on the island, was ruled by his wife. In fact from her loom in the shadow, Chremes's wife tried to rule the whole island, using her harassed husband as her legislative and punitive arm. Simo asked:

"What happens after the banquet?"

"Each boy pays for his plate, and pays right smartly too, and from time to time one or another is graciously permitted to stay until morning. That's all I know."

"Is your son at all these dinners?"

"He was quarreling or something,—or perhaps he drank too much, I don't know. At all events, he was expelled for a time. Thrown right out into the street, he was, by the other guests. But he's made his peace with her again."

"Do you talk to him about this . . . this Chrysis?"

"Why, no. I pretend to know nothing about it."

"Is my son always there?"

"They say he's practically always there."

There was a long pause. The boy who attended in the wine-shop went out into the moonlight and started putting up the shutters. Presently he returned and whispered to Simo that an old woman was waiting outside to speak to him and that she had been waiting there for some time. This was unusual on Brynos, but Simo took pride in never betraying any surprise. He nodded slightly and continued staring before him.

"Are there any other women at the Andrian's?" he asked.

"I don't know. Some say there are and some say there aren't. But there's a houseful of some sort. In fact it's a kind of hospital for the old and the lame and the . . . all kind of old battered pensioners. The house is way up at the edge of the town . . ."

"I know where it is."

". . . and the people, whoever they are, never come into town. They never even go out on the road by day. Oh, you can be sure the townspeople talk of nothing else."

Chremes rose and put on his cloak. He saw that Simo was as far as ever from committing himself. "Well, that's how it stands," he said. "I hope that in another ten days you can give me a more definite answer. My wife is after me a good deal, Simo, and she says that I'm to tell you this, that unless Pamphilus stops those visits all idea of a marriage between himself and Philumena is impossible. And that any such marriage must be definitely settled pretty soon or you'll have to start finding some other girl one-tenth as good."

For the first time Simo bestirred himself and said slowly: "You and your wife will be throwing away a good thing too, Chremes. It's precisely because Pamphilus is a great deal more than an ordinary island boy that I can't speak to him as I could to another son. There are more sides to Pamphilus than you imagine."

"Yes, Simo, we know that he's a fine young man. But we also know, if you will forgive me, that there's a strain in Pamphilus of the . . . the undecided, the procrastinating. To do his best and to take his place, Pamphilus must be urged on by someone, like yourself, whom he admires. And he's not as interested in

this island and in what it stands for as he should be. Do you know the young priest of Æsculapius and Apollo? Well, there is something of the priest in Pamphilus. Such people aren't interested in putting their foot forward. They haven't yet come to see what life is about."

Chremes went out and plodded home along the rocky road. Simo sat on a minute longer. What a bad ending to a bad day, he thought. The two men had grown up on the island together. For thirty years they had been its leading citizens. They knew one another too well. In their conversation they had let play the faint antagonism that always lay between them. This boasting about their children,—how vulgar, how unhellene. How unphilosophic. Yet that was true: there was something of the priest in Pamphilus.

Simo turned to the old woman who was hiding in the shadow by the door. "You wanted to speak to me?" he asked roughly.

Between fright and suspense—for she had been waiting there for the greater part of two hours—Mysis was barely able to find her voice. "My mistress wishes to speak to you, sir,—Chrysis, the Andrian," and she pointed with both hands towards the waterfront.

Simo grunted. Looking up he saw the beautiful woman leaning against the parapet at the water's edge fifteen paces away. Her head and body were wrapped in veils, and she waited calmly and impersonally in the moonlight as though two hours were but a moment in her serenity. Below her in the little protected harbor the boats knocked against one another in friendly fashion, but all else was still under the melancholy and peace of the moon. Simo approached her without deference and said: "Well?"

"I am—" she began.

"I know who you are."

She paused and began again. "I am in an extremity. I am driven to ask a service of you." Simo pushed his lips forward, raised his eyebrows, and lowered his eyes wearily. She continued in an even voice without anxiety or suppliance: "A friend of mine is very ill on the island of Andros from which I come. Twice I have sent this friend money by the hands of various

sea-captains going between the islands. I know now that the
captains are dishonest and that my money never reaches him.
All that I ask is that you put your frank upon the package of
money and it will reach him."

Simo did not like to see women carrying themselves, as this
Andrian did, with dignity and independence. His antagonism
was increased; he asked abruptly: "Who is this friend?"

"He was formerly a sea-captain," she replied, still without
servility. "But now he is not only ill; he is insane. He is insane
by reason of the hardships he endured in the war. I have put
him in charge of some people, but they will only be kind to
him as long as I send them money for it. Otherwise they will
put him away on a small island nearby with the others. You
know such islands . . . where basins of food are left for them
every few days . . . and where—"

"Well," said Simo harshly, "since your friend has lost the use
of his reason and since he cannot realize the conditions under
which he lives, it is best that you leave him upon the island
with the others. Is that not so?"

Chrysis tightened her lips and looked far out over his head.
"I have no answer for that," she replied. "It may be true for
you, but it is not true for me. This man was once a very fa-
mous sea-captain. You may have known him. His name was
Philocles. Now I think I am his only friend, unless you choose
to help him also."

Simo did not acknowledge having known him, but the tone
in his next words was less vindictive. "When would you like
this money to go?"

"I . . . I have some money ready now, but I would prefer
to send some in ten days."

"What is your name?"

"My name is Chrysis, daughter of Arches of Andros."

"Chrysis, I will do this for you, and I will even add to the
sum. In return you will do a favor for me. You will refuse my
son entrance into your house."

Chrysis moved slightly to one side and stretching her arm
along the parapet looked down into the harbor. "Favors cease
to be favors when there are conditions attached to them, Simo.
Magnanimity does not bargain with its powers." These max-
ims were almost murmured; then she raised her head and said

to him: "I cannot do that, unless I tell your son that it is because you have ordered it."

Simo's slightly cynical superiority over the rest of the world reposed on the fact that he had gone through life without ever having been surprised as unjust, untruthful, or ungenerous. Angry, but with himself, for having been caught at this disadvantage, he replied: "That is not necessary. It would be quite simple for your servant to tell him that you do not wish him to come into the house."

"I could not do that. There are several young men on the island to whom my door, for one reason or another, is closed. I cannot do that to Pamphilus without giving him a reason. If you understood the spirit of our group you would not wish me to do that; I think that there we are not lacking in respect for one another. I hardly know your son; I have scarcely exchanged twenty words with him; but I know that he is by far the first young man among my guests." Suddenly the image of Pamphilus rose up before her and she was filled with an excitement and joy in praising him, and for that very reason she subdued herself and added in a lower voice: "He is old enough to make decisions for himself. And if I do this, he must understand."

Simo was aware that some strange wise praise of his son hovered between them and his heart almost stopped beating for pleasure, but from his lips there rushed the brutal phrase he had prepared a moment before: "Then you must send your money to Andros some other way."

"Very well," she said.

They stood looking at one another. Simo suddenly realized that he lived among people of thin natures and that he was lonely; he was out of practice in conversing with sovereign personalities whose every speech arose from resources of judgment and inner poise. With his wife, with Chremes, with the islanders one could talk with half one's mind and still hold one's authority, but here in a few moments this woman had caught him twice at a disadvantage. Chrysis saw this and came to his aid; she broke the silence that was leaving him obstinate, angry, and small.

"It is perhaps his younger brother whose life can be arranged for him; your Pamphilus deserves to be better under-

stood than that." And her tone implied: "You and he are of one measure and should stand on the same side."

Simo preferred talking about his sons to any other activity in the world, but his emotions were very mixed as he assembled an answer to this remark:

"Well, well . . . Andrian, I will frank your money for you. I have boats going to Andros every twelve days. One went off today."

"I thank you."

"Could I ask you . . . euh . . . not to mention this to Pamphilus?"

"I shall not."

"Well . . . well, good night."

"Good night."

Simo trudged home in an unaccustomed elation. It made him happy to hear Pamphilus praised and "probably this woman was an exceptional judge of persons." He had made a fool of himself, but in good hands one does not mind. "Life . . . life . . . ," he said to himself, hunting for a generalization that would describe its diversity, its power of casting up from time to time on the waves of tedious circumstance such star-like persons. The generalization did not arrive, but he walked on in a bright astonishment. How he would like to hear her read a play; he used to be interested in such things and when his journeys took him to an island that was large enough to have a theatre he never missed an opportunity to hear a good tragedy.

As he entered the courtyard of his farm he saw Pamphilus standing alone, looking at the moon.

"Good evening, Pamphilus," he said.

"Good evening, father."

Simo went to bed, deeply moved with pride, but for form's sake he repeated anxiously to himself: "I don't know what I'll do with him. I don't know what I'll do with him."

And Pamphilus stood looking at the moon and thinking about his father and mother. He was thinking about them in the light of a story that Chrysis had told. As the banquets drew to a close she liked to move the conversation away from local comment and to introduce some debate upon an abstract principle. (She cited often the saying of Plato that the true philosophers

are the young men of their age. "Not," she would add, "because they do it very well; but because they rush upon ideas with their whole soul. Later one philosophizes for praise, or for apology, or because it is a complicated intellectual game.") Pamphilus remembered that on one evening the conversation had turned upon the wrong that poets do in pretending that life is heroic. And a boy from the other end of the island had said, half-mockingly and half-hopefully: "Well, you know, Chrysis . . . you know, life in a family is not in the same world as life in Euripides."

Chrysis sat a moment searching for her answer, then she lifted her hand and said: "Once upon a time—"

The table burst out laughing, but with an affectionate laugh of mock-repudiation, because they knew that she liked to cast her remarks into the form of fables and to begin them with this childish formula. Pamphilus heard again her beautiful voice saying:

"Once upon a time there was a hero who had done a great service to Zeus. When he came to die and was wandering in the gray marshes of Hell, he called to Zeus reminding him of that service and asking a service in return: he asked to return to earth for one day. Zeus was greatly troubled and said that it was not in his power to grant this, since even he could not bring above ground the dead who had descended to his brother's kingdom. But Zeus was so moved by the memory of the past that he went to the palace of his brother and clasping his knees asked him to accord him this favor. And the King of the Dead was greatly troubled, saying that even he who was King of the Dead could not grant this thing without involving the return to life in some difficult and painful condition. But the hero gladly accepted whatever difficult or painful condition was involved, and the King of the Dead permitted him to return not only to the earth, but to the past, and to live over again that day in all the twenty-two thousand days of his lifetime that had been least eventful; but that it must be with a mind divided into two persons,—the participant and the onlooker: the participant who does the deeds and says the words of so many years before, and the onlooker who foresees the end. So the hero returned to the sunlight and to a certain day in his fifteenth year.

"My friends," continued Chrysis, turning her eyes slowly

from face to face, "as he awoke in his boyhood's room, pain filled his heart,—not only because it had started beating again, but because he saw the walls of his home and knew that in a moment he would see his parents who lay long since in the earth of that country. He descended into the courtyard. His mother lifted her eyes from the loom and greeted him and went on with her work. His father passed through the court unseeing, for on that day his mind had been full of care. Suddenly the hero saw that the living too are dead and that we can only be said to be alive in those moments when our hearts are conscious of our treasure; for our hearts are not strong enough to love every moment. And not an hour had gone by before the hero who was both watching life and living it called on Zeus to release him from so terrible a dream. The gods heard him, but before he left he fell upon the ground and kissed the soil of the world that is too dear to be realized."

It was with such eyes that Pamphilus now saw his father pass into the house and that he had seen his mother moving about, covering the fire and going about the last tasks of the day. And it was in the light of that story that his eyes had been opened to the secret life of his parents' minds. It seemed suddenly as though he saw behind the contentment and the daily talkativeness into the life of their hearts—empty, resigned, pathetic and enduring. It was Chrysis's reiterated theory of life that all human beings—save a few mysterious exceptions who seemed to be in possession of some secret from the gods—merely endured the slow misery of existence, hiding as best they could their consternation that life had no wonderful surprises after all and that its most difficult burden was the incommunicability of love. Certainly that explained the humorous sadness of his father and the fretful affection of his mother. And now as his father passed him in the courtyard this interpretation shook him more forcibly than ever. What can one do for them? What —to be equal to them—can one do for oneself? He was twenty-five already, that is—no longer a young man. He would soon be a husband and a father, a condition he did not invest with any glamour. He would soon be the head of this household and this farm. He would soon be old. Time would have flowed by him like a sigh, with no plan made, no rules set, no strategy devised that would have taught him how to save these others

and himself from the creeping gray, from the too-easily accepted frustration.

"How does one live?" he asked the bright sky. "What does one do first?"

Chrysis's view of human experience expressed itself, as we have seen, in fables, in quotations from literature, in proverbs and in mottoes. Herself she summed up in a word: she regarded herself as having "died." Dead then as she was, the inconveniences of her profession, the sneers of the villagers, the ingratitude of her dependents, no longer had the power to disturb her. The only thing that troubled her in her grave was the recurrence, even in her professional associations, of a wild tenderness for this or that passerby, brief and humiliating approaches to love. These experiences and any others that were able to depress her, she now dismissed as weakness, as pride, as an old, rebellious and unwhipped vanity. The morning after the conversation with Simo at the water's edge she awoke strangely troubled; but she resolved not to examine the new dejection. It floated all day above her head,—a voice repeating: "I am alone. Why have I never seen that before? I am alone." Indeed the profession she followed was one of those that emphasize the dim notion that lies at the back of many minds: the notion that we are not necessary to anyone, that attachments weave and unweave at the mercy of separation, satiety and experience. The loneliest associations are those that pretend to intimacy.

But she had discovered two ways of mitigating this unresponsiveness and instability in the world she lived in. The first was the development she brought to the institution of the hetaira's banquet. She took endless pains over these reunions and to the wide-eyed guests they seemed indeed all that one could conceive of wit and eloquence and aristocratic ease. Great talkers are so constituted that they do not know their own thoughts until, on the tide of their particular gift, they hear them issuing from their mouths. Chrysis gave herself that luxury, the luxury of talking to these young men from her whole mind. Much of it lay beyond their reach; but her refusal to condescend, her assumption that the analysis of ideas and of masterpieces was their natural element, excited them. She knew that apart from

her beauty she was not particularly fitted for her calling; she lacked the high spirits that please the customers of middle age; but younger men, who still approach love with a touch of awe, are not so disappointed with those common exercises when they find them invested with melancholy, dignity and literature. Perhaps the maturity of a civilization can be judged by this trait, by observing whether the young men first fall in love with women older or younger than themselves; if in their youth their imaginations pass their time in hallowing the images of prattling unnourishing girls their natures will be forever after the thinner. But even at their best Chrysis's guests seemed remote and immature to her and finally she discovered a second way of making life more stable and her friends more constant: she adopted stray human beings that needed her.

In the inner monologue of her thoughts Chrysis called these dependents her "sheep." And although they were gathered into her shelter from places and moments of fearful extremity, they became accustomed to their new comfort with extraordinary rapidity. In fact their past trials began to take on a romantic color and when anything in the present situation did not suit them they had been known to regret the lost felicities of the slave-markets, the mills and the massacred villages. For Chrysis human nature no longer had many surprises and the manner in which the sheep scolded and even condescended to their shepherd did not deject her. She loved them and was sufficiently repaid by occasional hours of a late afternoon when the odd group would sit in the garden, weaving in amity and humor. Such hours almost resembled life in a home.

There was to be a banquet that evening, so shaking her head at the shadow that hovered above her she descended into the town to do the marketing. She was accompanied by Mysis and the porter,—Mysis carrying a net to hold the fruit and the salad-greens, and the porter a large jar to be filled with saltwater and then with fish and shell-fish. Chrysis moved slowly down the long twisting flights of stairs. She was wrapped about by a great scarf of antique finely-wrinkled material and wore a broad-brimmed Tanagran hat of woven straw. The one hand that appeared outside the folds of her scarf carried a small wooden fan. It was her business to be invested with the remoteness and glamour of a legend, for at that time Greek taste

turned upon a nostalgia for the antique; it was her business to
be as different from other women as possible and to convert
that difference into money. The shops and temporary booths
were all on the open square at the water's edge and there in
the bright sunlight the most excitable and loquacious of races
was enjoying its morning tumult; but as this calm and day-
dreaming figure appeared above them a hush fell upon the
bargainers. This was the very deportment the Greek women
lacked and sighed for. They were short and swarthy and shrill,
and their incessant conversation was accompanied by the in-
cessant play of their hands. The whole race was haunted by a
passionate admiration for poise and serenity and slow motion,
and now for an hour the Andrian's every move was followed
by the furtive glances of the islanders, with mingled awe and
hatred. The Brynians, when she appeared, felt themselves to
be provincial and commercial. From time to time some of the
young men who had been guests at her house approached her
and spoke to her. Then it was that the unmarried girls and the
young wives of the island gazed with consternation and fallen
jaw at the way she smiled and talked and dismissed their brothers
and their future husbands. Philumena, in the shadow of an
awning, leaned back against a wall and watched the stranger;
turning her head slightly she could see Pamphilus at the tally-
desk in the door of his father's warehouse. Her eyes fell on her
rough gown and her red arms and a long slow blush mounted
to her face. But all the while Chrysis's heart had been growing
heavier. "I have lived alone and I shall die alone," it said, and
groaned within her.

As she returned to her house from the market she fell into a
feverish monologue. "The fault is in me. It's my lack of perse-
verance in affection. I know that. Now, Chrysis, you must begin
your life over again; you must assemble some plan. You must
devote yourself with all your mind to your sheep. You must break
down all their coldness and wilfulness. You must make yourself
love them again. You must bring back the happiness you felt
with each one of them when you first knew them. It is routine,
it is the daily contact that has spoiled all that. It's cowardly of
me to be able to love people only when they are new. Now, now,
Chrysis!—arise!" For the hundredth time she was visited by

hope and courage. She would win in this thing. As she approached the house she was all but stumbling in her eagerness; she would create a home. "If I love them enough, I can understand them," she muttered. "One never learns how to live, or one's lights on living arrive too late, when one has spoiled the surrounding situation, spoiled it beyond repair. But I am to be on the earth for fifty years, and I must do it."

Chrysis did not realize what took place in the house during her absences, and that when she left it the house was empty. The personalities of her flock were extinguished. They fretted; they hovered about the gates peering in the direction from which she would return, and their minds ceased to act save in terms of that resentment which is the complement of devotion. She did not realize that this wasting of love in fretfulness was one of the principal activities on the planet. When she was away fear descended upon them; their dependence upon her was so great that even her temporary absences reminded them of the destitution from which they had been lifted,—circumstances so fearful that their conscious minds never revisited them, but which hovered in the distance enriching their present ease and hardening their self-centredness. All this antagonism therefore met her in a flood as she stumbled across the threshold of her home. By the middle of the afternoon she was saying to herself, almost in a panic: "It is impossible. I can do nothing. They even hate me. But fortunately I am dead. It is not my pride that is hurt. I am at peace in the ground. Yet oh! if only we had some help in these matters. If only the gods were sometimes present among us. To have nothing to go by except this idea, this vague idea, that there lies the principle of living!"

During the banquet she looked about her for comfort. "It is also cowardly of me to be happy only at the banquets where I can lead the conversation and display my thoughts and be admired." But tonight even that exhilaration was wanting; her guests seemed younger and remoter than ever, and she in turn was capricious and all but irritable. It was to be expected, therefore, that the conversation would take turns little likely to comfort her.

Niceratus, one of the more assured of her guests, asked her what life would be like in two thousand years.

"Why," she said at once, "there will be no more war."

"I should not wish to be alive in a world where there was no war," he replied. "That would be an age of women."

Now Chrysis was jealous of the dignity of women and lost no occasions to combat such hasty disparagements. She leaned forward and asked encouragingly:

"You wish to serve the state, Niceratus?"

"I do."

"And you admire courage?"

"I do, Chrysis."

"Then go bear children," she replied, turning away.

Niceratus found this remark unseemly and left the house. (He absented himself from the two successive banquets, but later returned and asked her pardon for making a personal grievance out of a difference of opinion. Confessions of error always gave Chrysis great pleasure. "Happy are the associations," she would say, "that have grown out of a fault and a forgiveness.")

The conversation then turned upon the plays concerning Medea and Phaedra which she had read to them at an earlier banquet and upon all manifestations of extravagant passion. The young men declared that the problem was not as complicated as it appeared to be and that such women should have been whipped like disobedient slaves and shut up in a room with a jar of water and a little plain food until their pride was subdued. They then recounted to her, almost in whispers, the story of a girl from a village on the further side of the island whose behavior had thrown her family and her friends into consternation. The girl had continued for a time, glorying in her disorders, until one morning, rising early, she had climbed a high cliff near her home and thrown herself into the sea. A silence fell on the company as all turned inquiringly to Chrysis asking for the explanation of such a reversal.

To herself she said: "Do not try to explain to them. Talk of other things. Stupidity is everywhere and invincible." But their continued expectancy prevailed upon her. She seemed to struggle with herself for a moment, deeply troubled, and then began in a low voice: "Once upon a time the great army of women came together to a meeting. And they invited to this meeting one man, a tragic poet. They told him that they wished

to send a message to the world of men and that he was to be their advocate and mouthpiece. 'Tell them,' said the women eagerly, 'that it is only in appearance that we are unstable. Tell them that this is because we are hard-pressed and in bitter servitude to nature, but that at heart, only asking their patience, we are as steadfast, as brave and as manly as they.' The poet smiled sadly, saying that the men who knew this already would merely be ashamed to be told it again, and the men who did not know it would learn nothing through the mere telling; but he consented to deliver the message. The men at first were silent, then one by one they broke out into laughter. And they sent the poet back to the army of women with these words: 'Tell them not to be anxious and not to trouble their pretty heads with these matters. Tell them that their popularity is not dying out, and let them not endanger it through heroics.' When the poet had repeated these words to the women, some blushed with shame and some with anger; some rose with a weary sigh: 'We should never have spoken to them,' they said. They went back to their mirrors and started combing their hair and as they combed their hair they wept."

Chrysis had barely finished this story when a young man who had hitherto taken little part in the conversation suddenly launched into a violent condemnation of her means of livelihood. This youth was of that temper that seeks to mould the lives of others abruptly to certain patterns of its own choosing. He now commanded Chrysis to become a servant or a sempstress. The other guests began to whisper among themselves and to avert their faces from confusion and anger, but Chrysis sat gazing at his flashing eyes and admiring his earnestness. There was a certain luxury in having an external mortification added to an inner despair. She was already troubled by her recent discomfiture of Niceratus and now chose to be magnanimous. She arose and approached the young fanatic; taking his hand she smiled at him with grave affection, saying to the company: "It is true that of all forms of genius, goodness has the longest awkward age."

But these incidents were not of a nature to distract her mind from the protracted oppression of the day. "Vain. Empty. Transitory," the voice within her repeated. But just as she was about to finish the day with the comprehensive summary that she had

nothing to lend to life and no place to fill, her eyes fell upon Pamphilus. It was his custom, through lack of self-confidence, to take the last seat at the remote end of the room. The guests acknowledged his preëminence among them, but when one evening they had wished to elect him King of the Banquet he had furtively and savagely intimated to them his refusal and the votes had passed to another. But Chrysis's eyes had often, as now, rested upon that head bent forward to receive her every word and that received each one with so earnest a frown.

"That is something!" she said to herself suddenly and for a moment her heart stopped beating.

She had intended to recite to them *The Clouds* of Aristophanes that evening, but she now changed her mind. She felt the need to nourish her heart and those watchful eyes with something lofty and deeply felt. Perhaps what she called the "lofty" was in this world merely a beautiful form of falsehood, cheating the heart. But she would try again tonight and see whether, after so dejected a day, it woke any stir of conviction. "What shall I read?" she asked herself as the tables were being removed. "Something from Homer?—Priam begging of Achilles the body of Hector? No. . . . No. . . . Nor would they understand the *Oedipus at Colonus*. The *Alcestis*? The *Alcestis*?"

One of the shyer guests, seeing her deliberating over the choice of the evening's declamation, timidly asked her to read the *Phaedrus* of Plato.

"Oh, my friend," she said, "I have not seen the book for several years. I should be obliged to improvise long stretches in it. . . ."

"Could you . . . could you read the opening and the close?"

"I shall try it for you," she replied and rising slowly disposed the folds of her robe about her. The servants withdrew and silence fell upon the company. This was the moment (on happier evenings) that she loved; this hush, this eagerness, this faintly mocking affection. What drives them—she would ask herself—in the next fifteen years to become so graceless . . . so pompous, or envious, or so busily cheerful?

At first all went well. The boys listened with delight to the account of how other young men gathered in the streets and

palaestra of Athens to hear the arguments of Socrates. Listening, they agreed that nothing in the world was more to be prized than a beautifully ordered speech. Then followed the description of the walk that Socrates and Phaedrus took into the country. *"This is indeed a rare resting-place. This plane-tree is not only tall, but thick and spreading. And this agnus castus is at the very moment of flowering and its shade and its fragrance will render our stay the more agreeable. These images and these votive-offerings tell us that the place is surely sacred to some nymphs and to some river-god. . . . Truly, Phaedrus, you are an admirable guide."*

From there she passed to the close:

"But let us go now, as the heat of the day is over.

"Socrates: Would it not be well before we go to offer up a prayer to the gods of this place?

"Phraedus: It would, Socrates.

"Socrates: Beloved Pan, and all ye other gods who haunt this place, grant that I may become beautiful in the inner man and may whatever I possess without be in harmony with that which is within. May I esteem the wise men alone to be rich. And may my store of gold be such as none but the good may bear. Phaedrus, need we say anything more? As for myself I have prayed enough.

"Phaedrus: And let the same prayer serve for me, for these are the things friends share with one another."

All went well until this phrase. Then Chrysis, the serene, the happily dead, seeing the tears that stood in the eyes of Pamphilus, could go no further, and before them all she wept as one weeps who after an absence of folly and self-will returns to a well-loved place and an old loyalty. It was true, true beyond a doubt, tragically true, that the world of love and virtue and wisdom was the true world and her failure in it all the more overwhelming. But she was not alone; he too saw the long and failing war as she did, and she loved him as though she were loving for the first time and as one is never able to love again. That was sealed; that was forever assigned.

After a few moments she collected herself and quieted the guests who had risen in concern about her. "Sit down, my friends. I am ready now," she said smiling. "I shall read you *The Clouds* of Aristophanes."

But it was some time before the laughter rose among the

couches, the laughter that was a just tribute to the divine wit
of the poet of *The Clouds.*

Brynos rose with the dawn, and it was not many hours later
that the morning's work was over. Several days after the con-
versation recorded above, Pamphilus, having helped his father
in the warehouse and being in no mood for exercising in the
field, started out to walk to the highest point on the island. It
was early Spring. A strong wind had blown every cloud from
the sky and the sea lay covered with flying white-tipped waves.
His garments leapt and billowed about him and his very hair
tugged at his head. The gulls themselves, leaning upon the
gusts, were caught unawares from time to time and blown
with ruffled feathers and scandalized cries towards the violet-
blue zenith. Pamphilus led his life with much worry and self-
examination and all the exhilaration of wind and sun could not
drive from his mind the anxious affection with which he now
turned over his thoughts of Chrysis and Philumena and of the
four members of his family. He was straying among the rocks
and the lizards and the neglected dwarfed olive-trees, when his
attention was suddenly caught by an incident on the hillside to
his left. A group of boys from the town was engaged in tor-
menting a young girl. She was retreating backwards up the
slope through a disused orchard, shouting haughtily back at
her pursuers. The boys' malice had turned to anger; they were
retorting hotly and letting fly about her a few harmless stones.
Pamphilus strode over to the group and with a gesture
ordered the boys down the hill. The girl, her face still flushed
and distrustful, stood with her back against a tree and waited
for him to come towards her. They looked at one another for a
moment in silence. Finally Pamphilus said:

"What is the matter?"

"They're just country fools, that's all. They've never seen
anyone before who didn't come from their wretched Brynos."
And then from rage and disappointment she began to cry un-
controllably and despairingly.

Pamphilus watched her for a time and then asked her where
she had been going.

"Nowhere. I was just going for a walk and they followed
me from the town. I can't do anything. I can't go any-

where. . . . I wasn't hurting them. I was just going for a walk alone and they called names after me. They followed me way up here; I called names at them and then they started throwing things at me. That's all."

"I thought I knew everyone on the island," said Pamphilus thoughtfully, "but I have never seen you before. Have you been here long?"

"Yes, I've been here almost a year," she replied, adding indistinctly, ". . . but I hardly ever go out or anything."

"You hardly ever go out?"

"No," and she fumbled with her dress and stared at the sea, frowning.

"You should try to know some of the other girls and go out for walks with them."

This time she turned and looked into his face. "I don't know any of the other girls. I . . . I live at home and they don't let me go out of the house, except when I go out for walks nights with . . . well, with Mysis." She continued to be shaken with sobs, but she was adjusting her hair and the folds of her dress. "I don't see why they have to throw stones at me," she added.

Pamphilus looked at her in silence, gravely. Presently he collected himself and said: "There's a big smooth stone over there. Will you go over there and sit down?"

She followed him to the stone, still busy with her hair and drawing her fingers across her eyes and cheeks.

"I have a sister just about your age," said Pamphilus. "You can begin by knowing her. You can go for walks with her and then you wouldn't be a stranger any more. Her name is Argo. You'd like one another, I know. My sister is weaving a large mantle for my mother and she'd like you to help her with it and she could help you with yours. Are you making a mantle?"

"Yes."

"That would be fine," said Pamphilus, and from that moment Glycerium loved him forever.

"I probably know your father, don't I?" he asked.

"I have no father," she replied, looking up at him weakly, "I am the sister of the woman from Andros."

"Oh . . . oh . . . ," said Pamphilus, more astonished than he had ever been in his life. "I know your sister well."

"Yes," said Glycerium. Her bright wet eyes strayed over the streaked sea and the blown birds. "She doesn't want anyone to know that I'm there. All day I stay up on the top of the house or work in the court. Only at night I'm allowed to go for a walk with Mysis. Even now I'm supposed to be in the house, but I broke my promise. She has gone to the market and so I broke my promise. I wanted to see what the island and the sea look like by day. And I wanted to look across to Andros where I come from. But the boys followed me here and threw stones at me and I can never come again."

Here she fell to weeping even more despairingly than before and Pamphilus could do nothing but say "Well" several times and "Yes." At last he asked her what her name was.

"Glycerium. Chrysis went away from home a long time ago and I was living with my brother and he died and I couldn't live with him any more. And I had nowhere to go or anything, and one day she came back and took me to live with her. That's all."

"Have you any brothers or sisters?"

"Oh, no."

"Who is Mysis?"

"Mysis isn't Greek. She is from Alexandria. Chrysis found her. All of them in the house,—she just found them somewhere. That's what she does. Mysis was a slave in the cloth mills. Sometimes she tells me about it."

Pamphilus still gazed at her, and bringing back her wandering evasive glance from the sea she looked at him from her thin face and enormous hungry eyes. Even a long glance did not now embarrass them.

"Do you want me to ask Chrysis to let you go about the island by day?" he asked.

"If she doesn't want it, we mustn't change her. Chrysis knows best." She turned away from him and said in a lower voice, dreamy and embittered: "But what can become of me? Am I always to stay locked up? I am fifteen already. The world is full of wonderful things and people that I might never know about. I know it was wrong of me to break my promise; but to live for years without ever knowing new people,—to hear them passing the door all day, and to see them a long ways off. Do you think I did very wrong?"

"No."

"I don't know anyone. I don't know anyone."

"Well . . . well, you'll come to know my sister. That will be a beginning," he said, taking her fingertips thoughtfully and wonderingly in his.

"Yes," she said.

"Everything is beginning over again. I'm your friend. Then my sister. Soon you will have a great many. You'll see."

"But where will I be five years from now and ten years from now," she cried, staring about her wildly. "I don't know. I'm afraid. I'm unhappy. Everyone in the world is happy except me."

The caress of the hands in first love, and never so simply again, seems to be a sharing of courage, an alliance of two courages against a confusing world. As his hand passed from her hair to her shoulder, she turned to him with parted lips and hesitant eyes, then suddenly bound both her arms about his neck. Into his ears her lips wildly and all but meaninglessly repeated: "Yes. Yes. Yes. I can't stay there forever. I should never know anyone. I should never see anybody."

"She will let you come to see me," he said.

"No," said Glycerium. "But I'll come by myself. I mustn't ask her. She would not let me come. She always knows best. And the boys can throw their stones. I don't mind if you're here. What . . . what is your name?"

"My name is Pamphilus, Glycerium."

"Can . . . can I call you by it?"

It was not at this meeting, nor at their next, but at the third, beneath the dwarfed olive-trees, that those caresses that seemed to be for courage, for pity and for admiration, were turned by Nature to her own uses.

These conversations took place in the early Spring. One afternoon in the late Summer Chrysis slipped out of her house and climbed the hill behind it. She was filled with a great desire to be alone and to think. She looked out over the glittering sea. The winds were moderate on that afternoon and before them the innumerable neat waves hurried towards the shore, running up the sands with a long whisper, or discreetly lifting against the rocks a scarf of foam. In the distance a school of dolphins engaged at their eternal games led the long procession of curving backs. The water was marbled at intervals with

the strange fields and roadways of a lighter blue; and behind all she beheld with love the violet profile of Andros. For a time she strayed about upon the crest of the hill, making sure that no one was watching or following her, then descending the further side she sought out her favorite retreats, a point of rock that projected into the sea and a sheltered cove beside it. As she drew near the place, she stumbled forward, almost running, and as she went she murmured soothingly to herself: "We are almost there. Look, we are almost there now." At last, climbing over the boulders she let herself down into an amphitheatre of hot dry sand. She started unbinding her hair, but stopped herself abruptly: "No, no. I must think. I should fall asleep here. I must think first. I shall come back soon," she muttered to the amphitheatre, and continuing her journey she reached the furthermost heap of stones and sat down. She rested her chin upon her hand and fixing her eyes upon the horizon she waited for the thoughts to come.

The first thing to think about was her new illness. Several times she had been awakened by a wild fluttering in her left side that continued, deepening, until it seemed to her as though a great stake were being driven into her heart. And all the day the sensation would remain with her as of a heavy object burdening the place where this trouble lay. "Probably . . . very likely," she said to herself, "the next time I shall die of it." At the thought a wave of anticipation passed over her. "I shall probably die of it," she repeated cheerfully and became interested in some crayfish in the pool at her feet. She plucked some grasses behind her and started dragging them before the eyes of the indignant animals. "Nothing in life could make me abandon my sheep, but if I die they will have to fall back on Circumstance as I did. Glycerium, what will become of you? Apraxine, Mysis . . . ? There are times when we cannot see one step ahead of us, but five years later we are eating and sleeping somewhere." (It was humorous, pretending that one's heart was as hard as that.) "Yes," she said aloud, to the pain that trembled within her, "only come quickly." She leaned forward still dragging the stems before the shellfish: "I have lived thirty-five years. I have lived enough. *Stranger, near this spot lies Chrysis, daughter of Arches of Andros: the ewe that has strayed from the flock lives many years in one day and dies at*

a great age when the sun sets." She laughed at the deceptive comforts of self-pity and taking off a sandal put her foot into the water. She drew herself up for a moment, asking herself what there was left in the house for the colony's supper; then recollecting some fish and some salad on the shelf, she returned to her thoughts. She repeated her epitaph, making it a song and emphasizing, for self-mockery, its false sentiment. "O Andros, O Poseidon, how happy I am. I have no right to be happy like this. . . ."

And she knew as she gazed at the frieze of dolphins still playing in the distance that her mind was avoiding another problem that awaited her. "I am happy because I love this Pamphilus,—Pamphilus the anxious, Pamphilus the stupid. Why cannot someone tell him that it is not necessary to suffer so about living." And the low exasperated sigh escaped her, the protest we make at the preposterous, the incorrigible beloved. "He thinks he is failing. He thinks he is inadequate to life at every turn. Let him rest some day, O ye Olympians, from pitying those who suffer. Let him learn to look the other way. This is something new in the world, this concern for the unfit and the broken. Once he begins that, there's no end to it, only madness. It leads nowhere. That is some god's business." Whereupon she discovered that she was weeping; but when she had dried her eyes she was still thinking about him. "Oh, such people are unconscious of their goodness. They strike their foreheads with their hands because of their failure, and yet the rest of us are made glad when we remember their faces. Pamphilus, you are another herald from the future. Some day men will be like you. Do not frown so. . . ."

But these thoughts were very fatiguing. She arose and, returning to the amphitheatre, laid herself down upon the sand. She murmured some fragments from the Euripidean choruses and fell asleep. She had always been an islander and this hot and impersonal sun playing upon a cold and impersonal sea was not unfriendly to her. And now for two hours the monotony of sun and sea played about her and wove itself into the mood of her sleeping mind. As once the gray-eyed Athena stood guarding Ulysses—she leaning upon her spear, her great heart full of concern and of those long divine thoughts that are her property—even so, now, the hour and the place all but

gathered itself into a presence and shed its influence upon her. When her eyes finally opened she listened for a time to the calm in her heart. "Some day," she said, "we shall understand why we suffer. I shall be among the shades underground and some wonderful hand, some Alcestis, will touch me and will show me the meaning of all these things; and I shall laugh softly for hours as I do now . . . as I do now."

She arose and binding up her hair prepared to ascend the slope. But just as she turned to leave the place, there visited her the desire to do something ceremonial, to mark the hour. She stood up straightly and held out her arms to the setting sun: "If you still hear prayers from the lips of mortals, if our longings touch you at all, hear me now. Give to this Pamphilus some assurance—even some assurance such as you have given to me, unstable though I am—that he is right. And oh! (but I do not say this from vanity or pride, O Apollo,—but perhaps this is weak, this is childish of me, perhaps this renders the whole prayer powerless!) if it is possible, let the thought of me or of something I have said be comforting to him some day. And . . . and . . ."

But her arms fell to her side. The world seemed empty. The sun went down. The sea and sky became suddenly remote and she was left with only the tears in her eyes and the longing in her heart. She closed her lips and turned her head aside. "I suppose there is no god," she whispered. "We must do these things ourselves. We must drag ourselves through life as best we can."

Chrysis had made the mistake of accustoming the members of her household to her invariable presence and now while she slept they became increasingly indignant at the length of her absence. In twos and threes they hovered about the door peering to the right and to the left with mingled scorn and alarm.

"When she comes in, see that no one says a word to her," directed Apraxine, a tall lame woman whom Chrysis had found beaten and left for dead at the edge of the desert below the terraces of Alexandria.

"Pretend you don't see her."

". . . to go sallying off a whole day without a word to a soul."

"I'm sure I don't wish to stay in a house where I count for nothing."

". . . less than nothing, it seems."

Presently however something happened that distracted their minds from their resentment. A new sheep arrived at the fold.

Simo's frank had carried to Andros the money that Chrysis intended for the support of the stricken sea-captain. But Philocles's guardians had long since tired of their charge and become discontented with the intermittent payments. They decided to take advantage of this sum of money to ship him off to Brynos. It was necessary for this purpose to wait for a lucid interval in the patient's condition. Such a moment finally arrived; they hurriedly made up his bundle, brushed his hair, and led him down to the waterfront, where they found the captain of a boat sailing between the Cyclades who was willing to undertake the commission. And thus it was that on the afternoon of Chrysis's retreat to solitude Philocles arrived on Brynos. A boy who attended at one of the wineshops in the town was directed to escort him to her house, and suddenly the childlike sea-captain was thrust into the courtyard among the conspiring pensioners.

Ten years before Philocles had been the greatest navigator on the Mediterranean, first in skill and experience and first in fame. He had been many times to Sicily and to Carthage; he had passed through the Gates of Hercules and visited the Tyrian mines in Britain. He had sailed westward for months across the great shelf of water, seeking new islands, and had been forced to turn back by the visible anger of the gods. In the present age men were captains or merchants or farmers, but in the great age men had been first Athenians or Greeks, and the islanders regarded Philocles as of that order, a belated giant. He was already in middle life when Chrysis first knew him—she had been a passenger on one of his trips to Egypt—and it astonished her to find someone laconic in a chattering world and with quiet hands in a gesturing civilization. He was blackened and cured by all weathers. He stood in the squares of the various ports of call, his feet apart as though they were forever planted on a shifting deck. He seemed to be too large for daily life; his very eyes were strange—unaccustomed to the shorter range, too used to seizing the appearances of a

constellation between a cloud and a cloud, and the outlines of a headland in rain. Wind, salt and starvation had moulded his head, and his mind had been rendered, not buoyant, but rich and concentrated by the enforced asceticisms of a prolonged duty and of long sea voyages. He had been one of the persons whom Chrysis had most loved in all her life and it was she who had discovered his secret, the secret that it was neither adventure nor gain that drove him along his adventurous life. He was passing the time and filling the hours in anticipation of release from a life that had lost its savor with the death of his daughter. These two saw in one another's eyes the thing they had in common, the fact that they had both died to themselves. They lived at one remove from that self that supports the generality of men, the self that is a bundle of self-assertions, of greeds, of vanities and of easily-offended pride. Three years before, Philocles had been forced to captain some ships of a city at war. He had been captured and mutilated and what was left of so kingly a person was a timorous child.

The sheep examined the newcomer who had been thrust so abruptly into their midst. They questioned him and amused themselves with his answers. Then they gave him a bench in the sunlight where he might whisper to his heart's content.

The sun set and soon after Chrysis came stumbling through the door, laughing apologetically and pushing back her hair. "Forgive me, O my dear friends, forgive me. I fell asleep on the sand and I'm very sorry I'm so late." (The men and women raised their eyebrows cynically and went on with their work.) "Apraxine, has anything happened?" (Apraxine cleared her throat with Alexandrian hauteur and became absorbed in looking for a thread on the ground.) "Now we must find something particularly rare for supper."

The sheep exchanged pitying glances over all this tawdry artifice and when Chrysis passed into the house they burst into laughter. The laughter was condescending, but the soul had returned to the community. Finally at a signal from Apraxine, Glycerium went to the door and announced to Chrysis that Philocles had arrived from Andros. He had seen her pass and some twinge of memory had set him trembling. He rose and walked unsteadily to the middle of the court. She saw him

standing before her, haggard, with hollow puzzled eyes and with untrimmed beard.

She went forward repeating, "My dear friend, my friend!" but as she embraced him a loud voice within her seemed to say: "Something is going to happen. The threads of my life are drawing together."

That night Chrysis was awakened from a light and feverish sleep by the instinctive knowledge that someone was near her. She raised herself on one elbow and peered towards the faint glimmer of the door.

"Who is it? Who is there?" she said.

A figure seemed suddenly to rise from the threshold. "It's I, Chrysis. It's Glycerium."

"Is something the matter? Is someone ill?"

"No . . . it's only . . ."

"Light a lamp, my child. What do you want?"

"Chrysis, are you angry with me for waking you up? I couldn't sleep, Chrysis, and I had to come into your room."

"But why are you crying, my dear, my dove? Come now and sit on the edge of the bed. Of course I'm not angry with you." Glycerium sank upon the floor beside her. "No, no,—the floor is cold. Come sit up here. Your hair is wet! Tell me now, what is making you unhappy?"

"Nothing."

"What? Then you have something to tell me?"

"No . . . I don't know what . . . I just want you to talk to me."

"Well, I have something to tell you." Chrysis was stroking Glycerium's hair, delicately following with her finger-tips the strands as they passed above and behind the ear, when suddenly Glycerium threw her arms about her sister's neck and sobbed uncontrollably. Chrysis continued gravely with her caress, thinking that she was merely dealing with one of the meaningless accesses of despair that descend upon adolescence when the slow ache of existence is first apprehended by the growing mind. "There!" she murmured in a rhythmic undertone, "Sh . . . sh . . . sh . . . sh. . . . We love you. We all love you in this house. Our beautiful Glycerium, our gentle, our very beautiful Glycerium . . . sh . . . sh . . . there! Are you

comfortable now? I have some good news for you. (No, no, there is plenty of room.) This is it: Beginning tomorrow you are going to lead an altogether different life. I am going to let you wander all over the island alone. And when Mysis and I go to market you can go with us. You may climb the hills if you like, and you may explore along the water's edge,—I shall even show you the secret of the secrets of my heart,—a beautiful hidden shelter by the sea where one can be perfectly alone. . . . Well? are you pleased? Doesn't this news make you happy?"

"Yes, Chrysis."

"Now! I thought it would make you very happy and all you say is: Yes, Chrysis!"

"Chrysis, tell me: what will become of me?"

Chrysis changed her position and in the dark shut her eyes a moment. "Oh, my dear, my dear . . . that's what everyone asks, everyone on earth. Well, first you tell me: what do you want to become?"

"I want to marry someone and . . . and be in his home. Chrysis, tell me: can I marry someone? Without a father and a mother and without anything, is it possible that I can marry someone?"

"My dear, there is always . . ."

"Chrysis, I'm grown-up now. I'm fifteen. Please tell me the truth. I must know. Don't say something merely to quiet me. I must know the truth. Can a man ever ask me to marry him? Why are you waiting so long to answer me?"

"I have been planning to have a long talk with you about all these things. But not now. Wait a short time; wait until you have had a week, two weeks, of this new life when you will be free to wander all over the island. Then you will be able to understand better what I have to say."

Glycerium paused a moment. "I know, I know," she said, her face against Chrysis's shoulder. "That means that no one will ever be able to marry me."

"No, no, I don't say that. . . ."

Glycerium rose and stood in the middle of the room. "I understand," she said in the darkness.

Chrysis raised herself again on one elbow and said slowly: "We are not Greek citizens. We are not people with homes. We are considered strange, only a little above the slaves. All

those others live in homes and everyone knows their fathers and their mothers; they marry one another. They think we would never fit into their life. Although all that is true,—"

"But there are stories," said Glycerium, "of men who even married girls that had been slaves."

"Yes, if a young man should fall in love with you, it is possible that he would take you into his home. That is why I have tried to take such care of you and why I have kept you hidden here in the house. Through the young men who come to the banquets, the island knows that you are here and that you have been carefully protected. And now that you are to walk about the island freely you must be a hundred times more careful than other girls. You are beautiful and you are good, and before all their unfriendly eyes you must show them your modesty and your goodness. That is all there is to say and to hope, my child."

"Perhaps, Chrysis . . . it is best that I do not go about the island freely, after all."

"No, no. You will feel like going out. It will come gradually. But now you must go to bed and to sleep, my darling. All these things will solve themselves as best they can. All you can do for the present is to be yourself, your very self, my Glycerium."

Glycerium moved unsteadily towards the bed: "Chrysis, I must tell you something."

"Yes? . . ."

"You will be angry with me, Chrysis."

"Why . . ."

"May the gods protect me, I . . . I have been talking with Mysis and now I know that I am going to be the mother of a child."

There was silence for a moment followed by the sound of Chrysis putting her feet upon the floor. "Where is Mysis? Let me get up."

"It is true, Chrysis. I broke my promise the times when you were away. I used to go out over the hills."

"Oh, my child, my child!"

"But he loves me. He will marry me. He loves me, I know."

"Who is it? What is his name?"

"It is Pamphilus, son of Simo."

Chrysis grew rigid in the darkness. Then she slowly put her

feet back into the bed. Glycerium continued wildly: "He loves me. He will take care of me. He has told me so a hundred times. Chrysis, what shall I do? What shall I do? I am afraid."

A low moan at the door revealed the fact that Mysis had accompanied her younger mistress to this interview and was kneeling outside the door without the courage to enter.

After a moment Chrysis said in a light impersonal voice: "Well, you . . . go off to bed now and go to sleep. Yes. We'll both be catching cold here. It's late. I think it must be almost morning."

"I cannot sleep."

"Everything will be all right, Glycerium. I can't talk any more now. I'm not well. We'll talk about it in the morning."

Glycerium left the room, trembling.

In her darker hours Chrysis carried on what she called a "dialogue with Fate." And now as she turned to the wall she said: "I hear you. You have won again."

Before long the pain in her side became fixed and unremitting, and Chrysis knew that her life was drawing to a close. She took to her bed and her thoughts no longer clung to the world about her. Now when her courage was being undermined by her pain she dared not ask herself if she had lived and if she were dying, unloved, in disorder, without meaning. From time to time she peered into her mind to ascertain what her beliefs were in regard to a life after death, its judgments or its felicities; but the most exhausting of all our adventures is that journey down the long corridors of the mind to the last halls where belief is enthroned. She resigned herself to the memory of certain moments when intuition had comforted her and she quieted her heart with Andrian cradle-songs and with fragments from the tragic poets. She saved her strength to fulfill a last desire, one that may perhaps seem unworthy to persons of a later age. Her mind had been moulded by formal literature, by epics and odes, by tragedies and by heroic biography, and from this reading she had been imbued with the superstition that one should die in a noble manner, and in this high decorum even the maintenance of her beauty played a part. The only terror left in the world was the fear that she might leave it with cries of pain, with a torn mind, and with discomposed features.

The news spread about the island that the Andrian was gravely ill. The young men who had been her guests were confused by the discrepancy between their mothers' sarcasms and the respect that Chrysis had inspired in themselves, but some brought shy offerings of wine and cheese to her door. For such brief interviews she raised herself on one elbow and sought to recover her light-spoken graciousness. But most of the young men stayed away; it required a maturer mind than they could summon to hold side by side their memories of sensual pleasure and their respect due to the dying.

Pamphilus had other reasons for staying away. It seemed more and more unlikely that he would ever be permitted to marry Glycerium. But one morning he appeared at Chrysis's house and asked to see her. He traversed the court, picking his way among her motley and dismayed pensioners, and his eyes fell upon Glycerium. She was seated beside Philocles at her sister's door, silent and without hope. Pamphilus stopped for a moment on one knee before her and took her hands in his. "Do not be afraid," he said in a low voice. "No harm will come to you." She derived no courage from his words; she lifted her eyes and scanned his face. Her mouth trembled, but no words came and her eyes returned to the ground. Pamphilus passed into the room where Chrysis lay; for a moment he could distinguish nothing in the darkness. Presently he became aware of the priest of Æsculapius and Apollo bending over a brazier in the corner, and finally he saw Chrysis smiling at him gravely from the bed. He sat down beside her in silence; each waited for the other to begin.

"We are sorry, all of us are sorry, Chrysis," he said at last, "to hear that you have been so ill."

"Thank you, Pamphilus. Thank them all."

"There . . . there has been so much rain. When the sunlight returns you will feel better at once."

"Yes, it has always been the sunlight that has done me the most good. You are all well on your farm?"

"Yes, the gods be praised."

"The gods be praised. I shall never forget a favor your father did for me."

Pamphilus was struck with amazement. "My father?"

"Oh, forgive me . . . I remember now I promised him not

to mention it to you. Oh, my illness has made me forget that. I am ashamed, I am ashamed. But now I had better add that it was a small commission he did for me by one of his boats going to Andros. I would not have him think me unfaithful to my promise. I beg of you earnestly not to tell him that I spoke of it."

"Indeed, I shall not tell him, Chrysis."

There fell another pause between them, while her strengthless hands lightly pressed upon the bed in her self-reproach.

"Yes," said Pamphilus. "When there is more sunlight you will feel better at once. The sky has been overcast for a long time. I cannot remember when it has been overcast so long."

To themselves they both cried: "How shall we ever get out of this?"

"We have missed the banquets. I would like to tell you again, Chrysis, what great pleasure they gave me. I have been looking forward to the next one when you promised to read us I forget what play."

"It was to have been the *Ion* of Euripides."

"Yes."

"This," said Chrysis, glancing towards the priest with a smile, "this is my Ion."

But perhaps the words were ill-chosen. She thought she saw the priest frowning as he bent over his work. "Forgive me," she said to him abruptly, "if I have offended you. I did not mean it ill."

But the tears were rolling down her cheeks. "Life, Pamphilus," she said, "is full of mistakes, but the wrongs we do to those we love and honor are more than we can endure." The priest approached the further side of the bed and adjusted the pillows; he whispered a few words into her ear and went back to his brazier.

"Am I tiring you?" Pamphilus asked.

"No, no. I am very happy that you have come." To herself she thought: "Time is passing, and what are we saying! Is there not something heartfelt that I can find to say to him, something to remember, for him and for me?" But she distrusted the emotion that filled her heart. It was perhaps mere excitement and pain; or a vague and false sentiment. Probably the best thing to do was to be stoic; to be brave and inarticulate; to talk of trivial things. Or was it a greater bravery to sur-

mount this shame and to say whatever obvious words the heart dictated? Which was right?

Pamphilus was thinking: "She is dying. What can I say to her? But I have never been able to place words rightly. I am dull. I am nothing to her but the man who has wronged her sister." Aloud he said in a low voice: "I shall marry Glycerium if I can, Chrysis. At all events you may be sure that no harm will come to her."

"Though I love her dearly," replied Chrysis, finding her words with great difficulty, "I shall not urge you. I . . . I no longer believe that what happens to us is important. You will marry Glycerium or another. The years will unfold these things. It is the life in the mind that is important."

"I shall do what I can for her."

"You have only to be yourself without fear, without doubting, Pamphilus."

"Chrysis, you will forgive me for having spoken to you so little at the banquets . . . and for having sat at the further end and . . . that is the way I am. It was not because I did not respect you. I cannot talk as those others can. I am only a listener. Even now I cannot say what I mean. But I followed all that you said."

The pain in Chrysis's side seemed to increase beyond all endurance. "Oh, friend," she said, "do not distrust. These things are not so unsatisfactory . . . so interrupted as they seem to be." The priest had been watching her; she made a slight sign to him. "I do not wish you to go away," she continued to Pamphilus, almost in a whisper, "but it is best that I sleep now." Then raising herself on one elbow she breathed in anguish: "Perhaps we shall meet somewhere beyond life when all these pains shall have been removed. I think the gods have some mystery still in store for us. But if we do not, let me say now . . ." her hands opened and closed upon the cloths that covered her, ". . . I want to say to someone . . . that I have known the worst that the world can do to me, and that nevertheless I praise the world and all living. All that is, is well. Remember some day, remember me as one who loved all things and accepted from the gods all things, the bright and the dark. And do you likewise. Farewell."

Simo arose early to witness Chrysis's funeral. The Greeks,

for reasons that lay deep in their sense of the fitness of things
and in their superstition, conducted their funerals in the hour
before dawn, and it was therefore still profound night when
the little procession of her household prepared to pass through
the streets of the town. When Simo arrived at the square he
found that many of the men of Brynos had already gathered
there and, drawing the folds of their rough cloaks about them,
were standing talking together in low voices. The men of his
own age had brought their curiosity and contempt with them
and were congratulating themselves on the island's happy de-
liverance from the foreign woman; but the younger men who
had known Chrysis stood with sullen faces, their throats rigid
with antagonism at the glee of their elders. Simo took his place
in silence beside Chremes, but refused to respond to the latter's
animated comment. Presently as the sounds of the flute and
the mourners were heard approaching he discovered Pam-
philus standing beside him, as silent as himself.

Mysis herded the shuffling and stumbling company before
her as best she could. Philocles walked with lifted knees, as
children do in a procession. In one hand he held some grasses
and with the other he clutched the mantle of his companion,
the old doorkeeper; but he was continually straying off, or
standing still to gaze with wide dazzled eyes at the torches that
preceded him or at the laughing by-standers. Behind him the
deaf and dumb Ethiopian girl could scarcely be restrained
from running forward to walk beside her sleeping friend,
Chrysis, whose rebuke had been so terrible when she had done
wrong and whose smile had been sufficient compensation for
her imprisonment in silence. Glycerium walked with lowered
eyes, lost to hope and lost to the decorum that now required
of her the wailing and the distraught gestures of a conspicuous
mourner. All these passed forward under the bright stars that
had received the first intimation of day and shone with a last
heightened brilliance, and under the long garlands of smoke
that hung above the company in that windless air.

As the onlookers accompanied the procession into the open
country, Simo's attention was fixed upon Glycerium, by reason
of her condition, which was apparent to all, of her resemblance
to her sister, of the dejection that invested her, and of the
beauty and modesty of her bearing. And he became aware that

his son also was watching the girl. In fact, during the whole
journey, Pamphilus bent upon her his burning eyes, trying to
intercept her glance and to communicate to her his encour-
agement and his love. But not until they reached the heaped-
up wood whereon the bodies of a goat and a lamb were laid
beside that of Chrysis, and not until the fire had touched it,
did she raise her eyes. Then as the sound of the wailing in-
creased in shrillness and the sound of the flute floated pierc-
ingly above all, she turned to Mysis and began to speak wildly
into her ear. But the words of her vehemence were not heard
in that din, nor were Mysis's words of encouragement. Gly-
cerium was trying to draw herself away from the supporting
arm of the other and the slow faltering struggle of the two
women was lighted up by the rising flames. Pamphilus, in the
intensity of his concentration upon the suffering of the girl,
moved slowly forward, his hands held out before him. And
now he heard the words that she was repeating: "It's best. It's
best so!" Suddenly Glycerium pushed the older woman away
from her and with a loud cry of "Chrysis!" stumbled forward
to fling herself upon the body of her sister.

But Pamphilus had foreseen this attempt. Running across
the sand, he seized her by her disheveled hair and drew her
back and into his arms. The touch of that encircling arm re-
leased her tears. She laid her head against his breast as one who
had been there before and was returning home.

The scandal of this embrace was felt at once by all the by-
standers and chiefly by Chremes, who turned upon Simo with
his protest and astonishment. But Simo had moved away and
was walking slowly home through the breaking dawn. Now he
understood the Pamphilus of the last months.

The islanders discussed interminably the surprising event
that had taken place at Chrysis's funeral. They watched with
hushed excitement the chill that had fallen across the relations
between the families of Simo and of Chremes. Rumor presently
asserted that Pamphilus had promised to acknowledge the
child, though no one, naturally, even discussed the possibility
of a marriage. Readers of a later age will not be able to under-
stand the difficulties that beset the young man. Marriage was
not then a sentimental relation, but a legal one of great dig-
nity, and the bridegroom's share in the contract involved not

so much himself as his family, his farm, and his ancestors. Without the support of his parents and without a residence in their home a young man was a mere adventurer, without social, economic or civil standing. A marriage was only possible if Simo declared it to be so. The customs of the islands encouraged fathers in the luxuries of blustering and tyranny, but Simo's relations with his son had always been strangely impersonal. He was confused by his own deference for his son, by what he thought was his own weakness. Yet Simo's silence did not have the air of a final refusal; it even seemed to imply that the decision, with all its possibilities of lifetime regret and of a lifetime's contention on the farm, rested with Pamphilus.

One day several months after Chrysis's funeral Pamphilus betook himself to the palaestra for some exercise. He entered the low door and, nodding to a group of friends that sat scuffling under an awning at the edge of the enclosure, he walked across the hot red sand. The old attendant at the door who had won a laurel wreath in his youth came trotting across the burning ring after him and as soon as Pamphilus had seated himself on a marble bench began kneading his calves and ankles. In the centre of the field Chremes's son was going through the motions of hurling an imaginary discus; thirty and fifty times he turned with lifted knee, trying to fix in his muscular memory the perfect synchronization of the gestures. Two other young men were practicing a festival dance, interrupting their work from time to time to criticize one another's slightest deviation from a harmonious balance. The young priest of Æsculapius and Apollo was running around the course. Pamphilus sent the attendant away and lying down on his cloak let the sunlight beat upon him. He did not think about his problem, but left his mind a blank, suffused with a dull misery that identified itself with the drowsy heat. Presently he placed his elbow on the ground and raising his head rested his cheek upon his hand and watched the priest of Apollo.

The priest never entered the competitive games, but he was undoubtedly first upon the island for endurance and second only to Pamphilus in swiftness. Save on the days of festival he appeared for exercise daily and ran six miles. He preserved a perfect temperance: he drank no wine; he lived on fruit and vegetables; he awoke with the sun and unless there was some

call to attend the sick he went to sleep with it. He had taken the vow of chastity, the vow that forever closes the mind to the matter, without wistful back-glancing and without conceding the possibility that circumstance might yet present a harmless deviation, the vow which, when profoundly compassed, fills the mind with such power that it is forever cut off from the unstable tentative sons of men. His office required his passing so much time among the sick and the distressed that he had become inadequate to the cheerful and the happy and no one on the island knew him very well. But he had a strange power over the sick and the demented and only in their hours of confession and despair was the shutter of his impersonality lifted; such as had known him then followed him ever after with their eyes, in gratitude and in astonishment. He was only twenty-eight, but he had been sent to Brynos by the priests that attended the great mysteries of Athens and Corinth as a signal honor; for the shrine on Brynos was one of particular significance in the legend of Æsculapius and his father Apollo. Pamphilus had never spoken to him beyond the salutations of the field, but he would rather have known him than anyone in the world, and he in turn watched Pamphilus with grave interest. Now Pamphilus lay following him with his eyes and wishing he had his own life to live over again.

Suddenly he became aware that someone was shaking him by the shoulder. It was one of his companions. "Here comes your father," said the boy and went back to the awning. Pamphilus rose to his feet and waited respectfully as Simo approached, preceded by the old attendant.

"Stay where you are. Lie down again," said Simo; "I'll sit here on this bench. I want to talk to you."

Pamphilus lay down, his face turned away towards the track.

Simo wiped his face with the hem of his skirt. "I won't be long, my boy. . . . But we must consider this matter somehow . . . after all." He was not sure of himself. He blew his nose. He coughed several times and roughly adjusted the folds of his gown. He repeated "Very well" and "Now" and waited in vain for Pamphilus to say something. At last he launched forth among his prepared introductions:

"Well now, my boy, I assume you want to marry the girl. Hm . . ."

Pamphilus put his head down between his folded arms as though he were going to sleep. He sighed in anticipation of all the irrelevancies he was about to hear. In his heart he knew he had only to say yes or no and his father would accede to his wish.

"I don't wish to coerce you. I think you are old enough to see the good and the bad for yourself. But for a few moments now I want to talk all around the matter. I want to put the other side of the case in its plainest terms and leave it there for a while. May I do that?"

"Yes," said Pamphilus.

"Well, to begin with, it's only right to face the fact that there is no outward obligation to marry the girl. I've looked into the matter. She is not a Greek citizen. She happens to have been brought up in a sheltered manner, or so I take it. This Chrysis seems to have tried to prevent the girl's falling into her way of life; but that does not alter the fact that she is a mere dancing girl. Now, mind you, I can see that she is modest and well-mannered. She appears to be just such a person as our own Argo. But she could never have hoped for anything above the situation she is now in. The world is full of just such likable stray girls as this Glycerium, but we cannot be expected to welcome them into the fabric of good Greek family life. You may be sure that Chrysis knew perfectly well that Glycerium must some day become a hetaira like herself, or a servant."

Simo paused. He could see the back only of his son's head, but he was able to imagine upon his face the set unhappy expression they had all been obliged to watch there for the last weeks. He coughed again and abruptly flung himself upon another of his openings:

"No doubt you feel yourself fairly bound to her by a promise—but a promise, Pamphilus, in which you failed to consider the rest of us, and especially your mother. If you decided to marry the girl, your mother and sister would try to live with her as peaceably as possible, we know; but it would be a good deal to ask of them. You know them. This girl does not understand the first thing about our island manners. She doesn't know how simple and monotonous our women's lives are. I expect that life with the Andrian and with that strange company at the house on the hill was an odd affair. She'd be un-

happy with us. And even if she didn't contradict your mother all day . . . and worse . . . she'd become silent and sullen. Pamphilus, they would never grow fond of one another. It would be better to be cruel to her now and let her alone, than to set up discord, a lifetime of discord on our farm."

For a moment his memory failed him, but he rallied and continued:

"Well, even assuming that your mother and sister came to like her and to accept her cordially in the home, all her life she would have to endure something insulting in the manner of the other women on the island. We men do not take that interest in social discrimination, my son, but women . . . women with their few interests and . . . and so on . . . they enjoy having someone to ignore or to stare down. It warms them. Glycerium is not a Greek citizen. Her sister was a hetaira. All her life she would be obliged to endure their looking at her with straight lips and (I can see them) with half-closed eyes. But even that is not the chief thing."

He hoped that the suspense in this splendid transition would be reflected in some change in his son's position, but the young man lay motionless. Simo's weary eyes turned slowly about the palaestra.

"The girl is not strong. The women of the village seem to know something about it. She's a quick nervous high-strung girl and she'd bring you a series of thin and sickly children. You and I know those homes. She's not unlike our neighbor Douro's wife; isn't she? and the uneven health of such women —even though they're often more likable, yes, more likable, than the Philumenas—takes the shape of complaining and quarrelsomeness. And in their children. One has no right to bring into the world those children that cannot join others in their games, silent children who go through life regularly subject to fevers and coughs and pains. The most important thing in life is a houseful of strong healthy boys. Take Philumena, now. You do not 'love' Philumena, as the poets use the word. Well, when I married your mother perhaps I did not 'love' her in that sense. But I grew to love her and . . . euh . . . now I cannot imagine myself as having been married to anyone else, as satisfactorily married to anyone else. Philumena is handsome. But most important of all, Philumena is strong.

So . . . so, Pamphilus, does what I am saying seem to have
some truth in it? . . . Pamphilus?"

But Pamphilus had fallen asleep.

His last thought had been the recollection of one of Chry-
sis's maxims, an ironic phrase which he had chosen to take lit-
erally: *The mistakes we make through generosity are less terrible
than the gains we acquire through caution.*

Simo was not vexed. He sighed. Looking up he saw the
priest of Æsculapius and Apollo running around the course.
He recalled the day several months before when he and So-
strata had taken Pamphilus's sister to the temple. For two days
and two nights, Argo had been suffering from an ear-ache, and
although they knew that the priest was often ungracious when
his attention was asked on smaller ills they ventured to present
her to him. The hour at which he was accustomed to receive the
sick was a little after sunrise and there they found his colony.
There were invalids brought to him on beds; there were suf-
ferers from tumors, from protracted languors, from sore eyes;
there were the possessed. Simo and Sostrata had passed their
lives without ailments. They regarded them, like poverty, like
uncleanliness, as mere bad citizenship; they were on the point
of returning home, so great was their distaste for such mani-
festations. The priest required that the guardians who had
brought their sick to him should retire to a distance during his
interviews, and Simo and Sostrata had withdrawn with an ill
grace to a nearby grove. Argo seemed not to share her parents'
revulsion from these matters; even before she approached the
place (her fingers pressed upon her ear) she had been subdued
to awe and when her turn came she told her little story with
caught breath. The priest gently touched her ear, reciting a
charm. He poured in some oil and looked deeply into her shy
eyes. And gradually as he gazed at her a smile appeared upon
his lips and slowly she smiled in return. True influence over an-
other comes not from a moment's eloquence nor from any
happily chosen word, but from the accumulation of a lifetime's
thoughts stored up in the eyes. And there is one thing greater
than curing a malady and that is accepting a malady and sharing
its acceptance. The ear-ache did not abate at once, but Argo
pretended to her parents that it did, for the other healing they
would not have understood; and all night long instead of com-

plaining she pressed against her ear the little bag of laurel leaves he had given her and talked to herself, rehearsing that interview and that glance. Thereafter she never had any conversation with the priest, but when she happened to meet him upon the road, her heart was filled with excitement; she gave him a shy greeting and her eyelids fluttered in a quick intimate glance and he in turn let fall upon her a faint allusion to his smile. Her parents were amused by this bond; the priest had brought out in their daughter a side they had never known in her, and one that sent messages all along her life. Henceforth she even stood up straighter. One day a cousin who lived on the other side of the island came to a meal with them and let fall a remark in disparagement of the priest, saying that he was a comfort chiefly to old women who imagined themselves to be ill. Argo's eyes grew dark and her lips straight with anger. She refused to eat another mouthful and forever after the poor foolish cousin could never draw a word from her and never knew why. All this now returned to Simo's mind as he watched the priest.

"People like that," he thought to himself, "have some secret about living. Why don't they tell it to us outright, instead of wrapping it up in mystery and ceremonial? They know something that prevents their blundering about, as we do. Yes, what am I doing here," he added, pushing out his lower lip, "but playing the fool? Blundering, advising in things I know nothing about." He looked long at his sleeping son. "Pamphilus has some of that secret, too. And that woman from Andros had it, too. Chremes was right, though he meant it ill: there is something of the priest in Pamphilus, something of the priest trying to make its way in him. Let me get up and go away before I say anything more."

So he arose and a little guiltily left the field.

Pamphilus's mind was all but made up, yet still under the burden of perplexity and self-reproach he decided to seek still more light on his problem and a last reassurance by reviving a custom that had been in frequent use among the Greeks of the great age, but which had fallen off at the time of the events of this story. It consisted merely in abstaining from speech and from food from one sunrise to the next and in either passing the night in the temple enclosure or in arriving there before

the dawn that closed the watch. There was not thought to be any particular magic in the practice: it cleared the mind of bodily fumes, it removed it from the commerce of the day and prepared it perhaps for a significant dream. The watcher guarded his fast and his silence, but the Greek mind did not approve of heightening the experience by any further self-denial. One moved about the home as usual, exercised in the palaestra or worked at the loom; one slept. If some uninformed person spoke to the watcher, he drew his finger across his lips and the condition of the vow was understood. Athletes still observed it several days before a race; brides on the eve of their wedding; old ladies who hoped to recover some lost trinket, or to recapture in a dream the features of some all-but-forgotten love; and devout soldiers about to set forth upon an expedition. It was indeed little short of odd that a healthy young man in the even current of life should revive this custom, but the islanders were still sufficiently religious to respect the habits that had expressed the spiritual life of their glorious grandfathers, and made no comment.

By mid-afternoon hunger had gained upon him and his dejection had increased a hundred-fold. Whichever choice he made would involve the unhappiness of others. Under the weight of the alternatives even the memory of Glycerium lost for a time any tender association. He climbed over the remoter parts of the island, gazing absently out to sea and idly plucking the grasses among the rocks where he sat. He came to the spot where he had first seen Glycerium and stood for a time, quiet as the stones about him, asking himself whether the associations in life are based upon an accidental encounter or upon a profound and inner necessity. When he returned to the farm his mother and sister felt the desolation that invested him and moved about with hushed steps. The very slaves went about their tasks on tiptoe and finally withdrew in silence and in alarmed interrogation. During the evening meal Pamphilus sat by the door with closed eyes. His brother, returning, stepped over his feet with awed circumspection (he too had made the watch only a few months before, but in pomp, with twelve other youths on the occasion of their enrollment in the League) and held himself at a distance, rendered uncomfortable by so much seriousness in a good athlete. Of her own accord Argo

brought Pamphilus a bowl of water which he drank, smiling the while intimately into her grave eyes; she returned to her place at the table with great dignity and with secret excitement, as though she had done something conspicuous. When Simo finally told her and her brother to go to bed she slipped up to her father and laid her lips against his ear: "What is it, father?" she whispered. "No, tell me, what is the matter?" He took her hands and played with them a moment; he raised his eyebrows wisely and told her to go to bed and sleep well. From her bed in the darkness she noted the movements of the family: that her mother took a cloak and went out into the garden by the cliff, and that later her father did the same. With wide eyes and cautious lifted ear she followed this unaccustomed nocturnal roaming. She was filled with loving excitement; she kissed her doll many times with violence and wept. She became aware that her younger brother was venturing on hands and knees towards the moonlight in the court: she too ventured out and they stared at one another, but Pamphilus suddenly loomed up from the shadows and waved them back to their beds.

Pamphilus wandered about the outer court. Again the moon was at the full, throwing a milky blue mist over the tiers of olive trees that climbed the hill across the road and casting black shadows among the farm buildings. Its serenity contrasted strangely with the mysterious excitement it awakened among the human beings it fell upon. Pamphilus had seen his parents go into the garden, but he saw them now without emotion, without pity. He returned to the house and lay down upon his bed. Never had he been possessed by mood further from illumination. Lying on his face he traced outlines upon the floor with his finger.

The shells gleamed on the path as Simo walked up and down; from time to time he cast a furtive glance at his wife. She was sitting on a bench of chipped and stained marble that had been his mother's favorite seat. It had been placed there generations before, under a fig arbor blown down long since on a night of legendary storm. It stood at the very end of the garden where a cliff broke down to the sea, and from it one could hear forever the long spreading whispers of the ebbing and the rising waves below. From that seat his mother had directed the bringing up of five children, had dried their tears and listened with

nodding head to the absurd procession of their shifting enthu-
siasms. "Viewed from a distance," Simo said to himself, "life is
harmonious and beautiful. No doubt the years when my
mother smiled to us from that bench were as full of crossed
wills and exasperations as today, but how beautiful they seem
in memory! The dead are wrapped in love; in illusion, perhaps.
They go underground and slowly this tender light begins to
fall upon them. But the present remains: this succession of
small domestic vexations. I have lived such a life for sixty years
and I am still upset by its ephemeral decisions. And I am still
asking myself which is the real life: the present with its discon-
tent, or the retrospect with its emotion?" He looked again
guardedly at Sostrata, who sat fingering the folds of her cloak
and expressing in every line of her position her unfriendliness
and her rebellion. "The fault is in me," he continued. "If I
were wiser, I could do this thing. As the head of the family I
should be firmer. I should say 'yes' or 'no' clearly and let Pam-
philus bring in his little girl. I should weed out all these hesita-
tions. Even now she is waiting for me to make up her mind for
her; if I spoke distinctly, even against her will, she would adjust
herself without great effort. The house would find a way of ac-
cepting the new member and things would run on smoothly
enough." He was thinking of going towards her with smiling
affection, suggesting that at sixty they had earned the right to
remain tranquil though the house fell; but he foresaw that her
pride would not accommodate itself to any such resignation,
and he continued up and down the garden.

Indeed Sostrata did not wish Simo to speak to her. Her
mind was filled with one long obstinate exclamation at the stu-
pidity of men. Only a woman's mind could foresee all the harm
that would result from such a marriage as the one now being
weighed. It was the women of the island that had measured all
danger that came with the arrival of the Alexandrian woman;
and now she, the first matron of Brynos, was being ordered to
receive into her home the last offscouring of that dispersed
colony. She had anticipated all her life the rich satisfactions of
being a mother-in-law and a grandmother, though what she
anticipated was a daughter-in-law of straw. A Greek HOME, she
knew, was the only breakwater against the tide of oriental man-
ners, of financial fluctuation, and of political chaos. The high-

est point towards which any existence could aspire was to be a member of an island family, living and dying on one farm, respected, cautious, and secretly wealthy; of a family stretching into the past as far as the mossy funerary urns could record, and into the future as far as the imagination could reach, that is to one's grandchildren. Society was similarity. These things she repeated to herself, and under the waves of her indignation and self-pity—though the greater part of the time she stood in awe of her husband and her son—all her gracious traits disappeared, her beautiful eyes became harsh that for three days had been bright with the angry tears of her inner monologue.

When after a long stretch of time Simo paused in his walk and approached her with deferential hesitation, she arose abruptly and walked past him into the house, breathing hard and trembling with excitement.

At last Pamphilus arose and throwing his fleece-lined cloak over his shoulder slowly and musingly walked through the little garden in the court and passed through the outer gates of the farm. He was strangely light-headed from hunger and dejection. He paused for a moment to gaze at the rising hillside before him and its silvered olive trees. To his eyes they seemed to be pulsating in even waves of intensity, as though the whole earth and sky were on fire and burning with a pale slow silver flame, the whole earth and sky, unconsumed yet incessantly feeding the countless tongues of flame. He was gazing at this serene conflagration when he became aware of two dim figures in a pool of profound shadow at his right, leaning against the pillar of the gate. Glycerium was pressing her cheek against the stone and breathing her prayer towards the house within and beside her Mysis, distraught and helpless, stood urging her mistress to return home and to leave the ominous vapors of the night and the jealous chill of the moon.

When Glycerium saw that Pamphilus was standing in the road and that he had recognized her, she drew back into Mysis's arms overcome with shame; but slowly collecting herself she stretched forward a hand to him and fixed her great eyes imploringly on his face.

Mysis whispered to her: "We must go home, my bird, my treasure."

"Pamphilus," said Glycerium, "help me!"

His heart contracted within him as he realized the extremity of suffering that had led her thus far. He laid his finger gravely across his lips. He did not smile, but approaching her he looked down into her face with earnest reassurance and beckoned her to accompany Mysis toward the town.

Glycerium pushed back the scarf from her forehead and fell upon one knee before him, babbling incoherently: "I love you. I love you, Pamphilus. You promised me that you loved me. What am I to do? What is to become of me?"

Pamphilus looked at Mysis and again drew his finger across his mouth.

"Hush, my darling," she said. "You see he has taken the vow and cannot speak to us. And we must not speak to him. Look, he wants you to start home with me." She put her arm about the girl's waist and they began to move slowly toward the road.

"He promised me that he loved me," muttered Glycerium, unable to see for her tears, but permitting herself to be led forward. After a few steps, however, she turned and, pushing Mysis aside, said: "No, no! I wish to see him again." She pressed her scarf against her mouth for a moment and gazed at him, her whole soul in her eyes: "Pamphilus, do not marry me, if it is not right. But do not leave me alone. Do not leave me so long alone. Remember Chrysis. Remember the day you found me being stoned by the boys. No, no, do not marry me, if your father and your mother do not wish it, but let me know that . . . that I am still loved by you."

At last he nodded and smiled and waved to her slowly.

"He is nodding his head, Mysis!" cried Glycerium.

"Yes, my treasure."

"Look, Mysis, he is smiling at me. Can you see? Look very hard, Mysis."

"See, now he is waving to you. Wave to him again."

Glycerium waved eagerly, like a child, until Pamphilus was out of sight. It was a long walk home over uneven stones. Glycerium talked excitedly of the smile, trying to estimate the exact shade of intention and affection that lay in his waving to her and in the nod of his head. They discussed the significance of his taking the vow and they talked in general of the custom of taking the vow and recalled all the occasions they could remember of this usage and the results of each occasion. "All will

be well, Mysis," she repeated feverishly. "You will see, believe me, all will be well." But finally they fell silent, and in the silence their fears returned and an overwhelming weariness. As they reached the door of their house, Glycerium paused with tight-drawn lower lip and with fear in her eyes: "There is nothing to hope for," she said. "The gods are angry because I thought for a time that I was happy and that the world was easy to live in. At that time I did not understand anything about life and I said cruel things to Chrysis, because I thought the world was easy to live in. And the gods are right. Oh, if I could speak to her for only one moment and could tell her that now I understand her goodness, her goodness. But Chrysis is dead!" She turned to Mysis, but at these words Mysis had withdrawn from her and, beating upon her forehead with the knuckles of her two hands, had fallen upon the threshold of the house.

Pamphilus continued in the opposite direction. He wandered about the upland pastures as he had done all day, and climbed to the highest point on the island to gaze upon the moon and the sea. He tried to lift his mind out of the narrow situation of his problem by thinking of things not before him. He thought of the ships that under that magical flowing light were making their way from port to port, each one casting aside at its prow two glistening murmurous waves. It was the hour when the helmsman in the security of the course falls into a reverie, remembers his childhood or reckons up his savings. Pamphilus thought of the thousands of homes over all Greece where sleeping or waking souls were forever turning over the dim assignment of life. "Lift every roof," as Chrysis used to say, "and you will find seven puzzled hearts." He thought of Chrysis and her urn, and remembered her strange command to him that he praise all life, even the dark. And as he thought of her his depression, like a cloud, drifted away from him and he was filled with a tremulous happiness. He too praised the whole texture of life, for he saw how strangely life's richest gift flowered from frustration and cruelty and separation. Chrysis living and Chrysis dying in pain; the thoughtful glance that his father so often let rest upon him and the weary expression on his father's face when he thought himself unobserved; the shy

mystery of Glycerium. It seemed to him that the whole world did not consist of rocks and trees and water nor were human beings garments and flesh, but all burned, like the hillside of olive trees, with the perpetual flames of love,—a sad love that was half hope, often rebuked and waiting to be reassured of its truth. But why then a love so defeated, as though it were waiting for a voice to come from the skies, declaring that therein lay the secret of the world. The moonlight is intermittent and veiled, and it was under such a light that they lived; but his heart suddenly declared to him that a sun would rise and before that sun the timidity and the hesitation would disappear. And as he strode forward this truth became clearer and clearer to him and he laughed because he had been so long blind to what was so obvious. He strode forward, his arms raised to the sky in joyous gratitude, and as he went he cried: "I praise all living, the bright and the dark."

The exhilaration gave place finally to a tranquil fatigue. As he entered the shadowy temple he saw the priest sleeping before the altar he tended. The priest opened his eyes a moment and above the curve of his arm he watched the young man spread his cloak upon the marble pavement and lie down upon it and fall asleep.

Simo was awakened a little before dawn by the sounds of shrill voices and of unaccustomed movement in the outer courtyard. On approaching he discovered that a clamorous old woman had entered the gates and that a number of his slaves were trying in vain to quiet her and to drive her back into the road. He recognized Mysis. With a gesture he commanded the men to release her. "What is the matter?" he asked.

"I must see Pamphilus."

"He is not here."

"I cannot go away until I have seen him," she replied, her voice rising in feverish insistence. "A life depends upon it. I do not care what happens to me, but Pamphilus must know what they have done to us."

Simo said quietly: "I shall have you whipped; I shall have you shut up in a room for three days, if you continue to make this noise. Pamphilus will be able to listen to you later in the morning."

Mysis was silent a moment, then she raised her eyes and said sombrely: "Later in the morning will be too late, and all will be lost. I beg of you to let me see him now. He would wish it. He would not forgive you for turning me away now."

"Come, tell me what is the matter and I will help you."

"No, it is you who have done this harm and now he alone can save us."

Simo sent the slaves back to their quarters. Then he turned to her again: "In what way have I harmed you?"

"You do not wish to help us," she said. "The Leno's boat has arrived at the island and my mistress Glycerium and all the household of Chrysis have been sold to him as slaves. We were awakened in the middle of the night by the herald of the village and told to gather our clothes together and to go down to the harbor. Glycerium is not well now; she must not be driven so. I myself escaped through the rows of a vineyard and have come to find Pamphilus. It was you who have done this, for it was the Fathers of the Island who ordered that we should be sold as slaves to pay our debts."

This was true. He remembered having listened without interest to a discussion of the matter, assuming that it would be carried out with sufficient warning and delay to admit of Glycerium's being separated from the rest of the destitute company. The Leno's boat visited Brynos so seldom that it seemed to the Fathers of the Island that they might yet be under the necessity of providing for the household through many months while awaiting the arrival of this purchaser.

Suddenly a light dawned upon Mysis: "He is at the temple! How could I have forgotten that he was under the vow of silence and that he must be there!" And turning she started to enter the road.

"You must not go to him at the temple," said Simo sharply. "I shall come down to the harbor with you now and buy your mistress from the Leno."

He returned to the house for his cloak, then walked into the town with Mysis hurrying at his heels. Dawn was breaking as he descended the winding stairs to the square. Against the streaked sky he saw the mast of the Leno's boat. The Leno was not only a dealer in slaves; he was a wandering bazaar and sold foreign foods and trinkets and cloths. If an island were large

enough he came ashore and conducted a fair and a circus. And now in the first cold light of morning Simo could see on the raised portion of the deck a brightly colored booth, a chained bear, an ape, two parrots, and other samples of the Leno's stock in trade, including the household of Chrysis. Philocles had remained on shore and for two hours had been standing at the parapet uttering short broken cries towards his companions. Being a Greek citizen he could not be sold into slavery and was to be transported later to Andros.

Simo descended the steps of the landing with Mysis and was rowed out to the boat. While he concluded his transaction with the black and smiling Leno Mysis sank upon her knees before Glycerium, telling her of this good fortune. But Glycerium derived no joy from the news. She sat between Apraxine and the Ethiopian girl, amid the bundles of their clothes, and for weariness she could scarcely raise her eyes or move her lips. "No," she said, "I shall stay here with you. I do not wish to go anywhere."

Simo approached them. "My child," he said to Glycerium, "you are to come with me now."

"Yes, my beloved," Mysis repeated into her ear, "you must go with him. All will be well. He is taking you ashore to Pamphilus."

Still Glycerium remained with bent head. "I do not wish to move. I do not wish to go anywhere," she said.

"I am the father of Pamphilus. You must come with me and good care will be taken of you."

At last and with great difficulty she arose. Mysis supported her to the side of the boat and there taking her farewell she whispered to her: "Goodbye, my dear love. Now may the gods bring you happiness. I shall never see you again, but I pray you to remember me, for I have loved you well. And wherever we are, let us remember our dear Chrysis."

The two women embraced one another in silence, Glycerium with closed eyes. At last she said: "I would that I were dead, Mysis. I would that I were long dead with Chrysis, my dear sister."

"You are to come with us too," said Simo to Mysis, who having known even greater surprises obediently followed him. The little group was rowed in silence to the shore. The Leno's

oarsmen struck the water, his bright colored sails were raised, and his merchandise left the harbor for other fortunes.

The sun had already risen when Pamphilus returned with swift and happy steps to his home. There he discovered Glycerium sleeping peacefully under his mother's care. There was not a sound to be heard on the farm, for his mother, already invested with the dignity of her new duties as guardian and nurse to the outcast girl, had ordered a perfect quiet. Argo was sitting before the gate, her eyes wide with wonder and pleasure at the arrival of this new friend. Simo had gone to the warehouse and when he returned, for all his happiness, he moved about with lowered eyes, driven by the constraint in his nature to act as though nothing had happened.

In the two days that followed, all their thoughts were centred about the room where the girl lay and all their hearts were renewed under the fragile claims that Glycerium's beauty and shyness made upon them. Simo seemed, after Pamphilus, to have best understood her reticence and to have been understood by her; a friendship beyond speech had grown up between them. This flowering of goodness, however, was not to be put to the trial of routine perseverance, nor to know the alternations of self-reproach and renewed courage; for on the noon of the third day Glycerium's pains began and by sunset both mother and child were dead.

That night after many months of drought it began to rain. Slowly at first and steadily, the rain began to fall over all Greece. Great curtains of rain hung above the plains; in the mountains it fell as snow, and on the sea it printed its countless ephemeral coins upon the water. The greater part of the inhabitants were asleep, but the relief of the long-expected rain entered into the mood of their sleeping minds. It fell upon the urns standing side by side in the shadow, and the wakeful and the sick and the dying heard the first great drops fall upon the roofs above their heads. Pamphilus lay awake, face downward, his chin upon the back of his hand. He heard the first great drops fall upon the roof over his head and he knew that his father and mother, not far from him, heard them too. He had been repeating to himself Chrysis's lesson and adding to it his Glycerium's last faltering words: "Do not be sorry; do not be afraid," and he had been remembering how with the faintest movement of her

eyes to one side, she had indicated her child and said: "Wher-
ever we are, we are yours." He had been asking himself in as-
tonishment wherein had lain his joy and his triumph of the few
nights before: how could he have once been so sure of the
beauty of existence? And some words of Chrysis returned to
him. He recalled how she had touched the hand of a young
guest who had returned from an absence, having lost his sister,
and how she had said to him in a low voice, so as not to em-
barrass those others present who had never known a loss: "You
were happy with her once; do not doubt that the conviction at
the heart of your happiness was as real as the conviction at the
heart of your sorrow." Pamphilus knew that out of these frag-
ments he must assemble during the succeeding nights sufficient
strength, not only for himself, but for these others,—these
others who so bewilderingly now turned to him and whose
glances tried to read from his face what news there was from
the last resources of courage and hope, to live on, to live by.
But in confusion and with flagging courage he repeated: "I
praise all living, the bright and the dark."

On the sea the helmsman suffered the downpour, and on
the high pastures the shepherd turned and drew his cloak closer
about him. In the hills the long-dried stream-beds began to fill
again and the noise of water falling from level to level, warring
with the stones in the way, filled the gorges. But behind the
thick beds of clouds the moon soared radiantly bright, shining
upon Italy and its smoking mountains. And in the East the
stars shone tranquilly down upon the land that was soon to
be called Holy and that even then was preparing its precious
burden.

HEAVEN'S MY DESTINATION

George Brush is my name;
America's my nation;
Ludington's my dwelling-place
And Heaven's my destination.
> *(Doggerel verse which children of the*
> *Middle West were accustomed to*
> *write in their schoolbooks.)*

Of all the forms of genius,
goodness has the longest awkward age.
—THE WOMAN OF ANDROS

Chapter I

George Brush tries to save some souls in Texas and Oklahoma. Doremus Blodgett and Margie McCoy. Thoughts on arriving at the age of twenty-three. Brush draws his savings from the bank. His criminal record; Incarceration No. 2.

ONE morning in the late summer of 1930 the proprietor and several guests at the Union Hotel at Crestcrego, Texas, were annoyed to discover Biblical texts freshly written across the blotter on the public writing-desk. Two days later the guests at McCarty's Inn, Usquepaw, in the same state, were similarly irritated, and the manager of the Gem Theater near by was surprised to discover that a poster at his door had been defaced and trampled upon. The same evening a young man passing the First Baptist Church, and seeing that the Annual Bible Question Bee was in progress, paid his fifteen cents and, taking his place against the wall, won the first prize, his particular triumph being the genealogical tables of King David. The next night, several passengers on the Pullman car "Quarritch," leaving Fort Worth, were startled to discover a young man in pajamas kneeling and saying his prayers before his berth. His concentration was not shaken when he was struck sharply on the shoulder by flying copies of the *Western Magazine* and *Screen Features*. The next morning a young lady who had retired to the platform of the car to enjoy a meditative cigarette after breakfast, returned to her seat to discover that a business card had been inserted into the corner of the window pane. It read:

George Marvin Brush, Representing the Caulkins Educational Press. New York, Boston, and Chicago. Publishers of Caulkins' Arithmetics and Algebras, and other superior textbooks for school and college. Across the top of the card the following words had been neatly added in pencil: *Women who smoke are unfit to be mothers.* The young lady reddened slightly, tore the card into flakes and pretended to go to sleep. After a few moments she sat up and, assuming an expression of weary scorn, looked about the car. None of the passengers seemed capable of such

a message, least of all a tall, solidly built young man whose eyes, nevertheless, were gravely resting on her.

This young man, feeling that he had made his point, picked up his briefcase and went forward to the smoking-car. There almost every seat was filled. The day was already hot and the smokers, having discarded coat and collar, lay sprawled about in the blue haze. Several card games were in progress, and in one corner an excitable young man was singing an interminable ballad, alternately snapping his fingers and stamping his heel to mark the beat. An admiring group was gathered about him, supplying the refrain. Congeniality already reigned in the car and remarks were being shouted from one end of it to the other. Brush looked about him appraisingly, and chose a seat beside a tall leather-faced man in shirt sleeves.

"Sit down, buddy," said the man. "You're rocking the car. Sit down and lend me a match."

"My name is George Brush," said the younger man, seizing the other's hand and looking him squarely and a little glassily in the eye. "I'm glad to meet you. I travel in school books. I was born in Michigan and I'm on my way to Wellington, Oklahoma."

"That's fine," said the other. "That's fine, only relax, sonny, relax. Nobody's arrested you."

Brush flushed slightly and said, with a touch of heaviness, "In beginning a conversation I like to get all the facts on the table."

"What did I tell you, buddy?" said the other, turning a cold and curious eye on him. "Relax. Light up."

"I don't smoke," said Brush.

The conversation did the rounds of the weather, the crops, politics, and the business situation. At last Brush said:

"Brother, can I talk to you about the most important thing in life?"

The man slowly stretched out his full lazy length on the reversed seat before him and drew his hand astutely down his long yellow face. "If it's insurance, I got too much," he said. "If it's oil-wells, I don't touch 'em, and if it's religion, I'm saved."

Brush had an answer even for this. He had taken a course in college entitled "How to approach strangers on the subject of Salvation"—two and a half credits—generally followed the next semester by "Arguments in Sacred Debate"—one and a

half credits. This course had listed the openings in such an encounter as this and the probable responses. One of the responses was this, that the stranger declared himself already saved. This statement might be either (1) true, or (2) untrue. In either case the evangelist's next move was to say, with Brush:

"That's fine. There is no greater pleasure than to talk over the big things with a believer."

"I'm saved," continued the other, "from making a goddam fool of myself in public places. I'm saved, you little peahen, from putting my head into other people's business. So shut your damn face and get out of here, or I'll rip your tongue out of your throat."

This attitude had also been foreseen by the strategists. "You're angry, brother," said Brush, "because you're aware of an unfulfilled life."

"Now listen," said the other, solemnly. "Now listen to what I'm saying to you. I warn you. One more peep of that stuff and I'll do something you'll be sorry for. Now wait a minute! Don't say I didn't warn you: one more peep——"

"I won't trouble you, brother," said Brush. "But if I stop, don't think it's because I'm afraid of anything you'd do."

"What did I tell you," said the man, quietly. He leaned over, and picking up the briefcase that was lying between Brush's feet, he threw it out of the window. "Go and get it, fella, and after this learn to pick your man."

Brush rose. He was smiling stiffly. "Brother," he said, "it's lucky for you I'm a pacifist. I could knock you against the roof of this car. I could swing you around here by one leg. Brother, I'm the strongest man that was ever tested in our gym back at college. But I won't touch you. You're rotted out with liquor and cigarettes."

"Haw-haw-haw!" replied the man.

"It's lucky for you I'm a pacifist," repeated Brush, mechanically, staring at the man's eyes, the yellow strings of his throat, and the blue stain his collar button had left.

By now the whole car was interested. The leather-faced man threw his arm over the back of the seat and included his neighbors in his pleasure. "He's nuts," he said.

Voices in the car began to rise in a threatening tide: "Get the hell out of here." . . . "Put him out."

Brush shouted into the man's face: "You're full of poisons—Anybody can see that. You're dying. Why don't you think about it?"

"Haw-haw-haw!" said the man.

The noise in the car rose to a roar. Brush went down the aisle and entered the toilet. He was trembling. He put his hand on the wall and laid his forehead against it. He thought he was going to throw up. He muttered over and over again, "He's rotten with liquor and cigarettes." He gargled a mouthful of cold water. When his breathing had become regular again, he returned to the car "Quarritch." He walked with lowered eyes and, sitting down, he held his head in his hands and stared at the floor. "I shouldn't hate anybody," he said.

The train reached Wellington an hour later. Brush went to the hotel, engaged an automobile, and retrieved the briefcase. He spent the day calling on the department heads in the high school. On coming out of the dining-room after dinner he went to the writing-desk, printed a Bible text neatly on the blotter, and went early to bed.

The next morning brought his twenty-third birthday. He rose early and started to leave the hotel for a walk before breakfast. In one hand he held a rough draft of his resolutions for the year, along with a list of his virtues and faults. As he passed through the lobby he noticed that a fresh blotter had been placed on the writing-desk. He went up to it, took out his fountain pen, and stood a moment irresolute. Then without sitting down he printed across the top the words, "Thou, Lord, seest me."

A negro who was crouched on the floor, polishing spittoons, raised his eyes slowly and said, with guarded animosity: "You'd better not write on that blotter. Mr. Gibbs is awful mad about that. He's had to change it once already and he's awful mad."

"Does it do any harm to anybody?" asked Brush, calmly, returning the pen to his pocket.

"The folks don't like it. Mr. Blodgett, who's stayin' here, 's all roused up."

"Well, tell Mr. Blodgett to speak to me about it. I'd like to meet him," replied Brush, crossing to the water-cooler and

starting to draw himself a drink of water. At that moment the manager of the hotel came down the stairs, followed by a man and a woman. The man was short and fat; he had a round red face and a pair of mobile black bushy eyebrows. He crossed the room to the writing-desk and picked out a piece of stationery.

"Look't this!" he cried, suddenly, pointing at the blotter. "Look't this! Now that's the second time. God! it gives me a pain."

"You can't stop'm, Mr. Blodgett," said the manager, sadly. "Why, last year, there was a fellow——"

"Well, I'd like to meet one. I'd like to tell'm what I think."

The manager whispered a few words to Blodgett and indicated Brush with his thumb.

Blodgett whistled. "You don't say!" he said.

The woman interposed loudly: "Now Reme, you're always picking up some crazy galoot or other. You'll get into trouble one of these days. Come in to breakfast and let'm be."

"Well, sister, you gotta have some fun when you're on the road, don't you?" said Blodgett. "This is a chance. Watch me now."

As Brush started to go to the street Blodgett put out his hand. "Say, buddy," he said, quietly, one eyebrow subtly raised, "where are you holding meetings?"

"I'm not holding any meetings," replied Brush, seizing his hand and looking dynamically into his eyes. "I think your name is Blodgett. Mine is George Brush. George Marvin Brush. I travel in textbooks. Glad to know you, Mr. Blodgett."

"Yes, sir, every time," said Blodgett. "Doremus Blodgett, Everlast Hosiery. So you travel, do you?"

"Yes."

"Well, then, what's the idea of writing all over these blotters? You're young and healthy. See what I mean?"

"I'm glad to talk about it," said Brush.

"That's the way. Now look here, Brush. I'm glad to see you're a reasonable fella. We were afraid you were going to be one of these faynatics. See what I mean? Brush, I want you to meet the finest little girl in the world, my cousin, Mrs. Margie McCoy."

"Glad to know you," said Brush.

Mrs. McCoy had a large puffy face heavily covered with powder. It was surmounted by a fine head of orange, brown, and black hair. She did not acknowledge the introduction.

"Fella to fella," continued Blodgett, "what's the idea of writing over all these blotters, eh? I don't say it isn't all right for preachers. They get paid for it."

"Mr. Blodgett, I've found a good thing and I want to tell everybody about it."

"Let'm be, Reme. Let'm be," said Mrs. McCoy, beckoning her cousin toward the dining-room door with jerks of her head and the movements of her sullen eyes.

"Well, I don't like it," continued her cousin, suddenly belligerent.

"If you don't like it," continued Brush, "that's because you're aware of an unfulfilled life."

Blodgett began to shout. "That's the trouble with you stinking reformers, you think everybody——"

Here Margie McCoy flung herself between them: "Have some breakfast first, for Gawd's sake! Now stop it! Stop it, I say! You're always trying to get into a fight. Besides, the doctor told you you gotta keep calm."

"I don't fight, Mrs. McCoy," said Brush. "Let him say what he wants to say."

Blodgett began again in a calmer tone. "I don't say it isn't all right for preachers, but what gripes me is when some . . . Goddam it! everything has its place."

"Aw, come on and get some cawfee," said Mrs. McCoy, adding, under her breath: "He's just a nut. Let'm be."

"Say, why aren't you a preacher, anyway? Why aren't you in a church, where you belong?"

"There's a reason for that," replied Brush, staring fixedly at the wall behind Blodgett.

"Couldn't you get enough money?"

"No, that wasn't the trouble. . . . I had a very personal reason."

"Stop right there!" cried Blodgett. "I don't want to hear anything that's not my business. All I say is that it looks to me like you had a still more personal reason for going in."

Brush stared at him somberly. "I'm not afraid to tell," he

said. "I did something . . . I did something that a minister can't do."

"Oh, I see!" said Blodgett, out of his depths. "Well . . . of course, that makes a difference."

"What did he *say*?" asked Mrs. McCoy.

"He said . . . he did something that a minister can't do." Then turning to Brush, Blodgett took on a conspiratorial air; lowering his voice, he inquired, "What was it?"

"I wouldn't like to tell that with a lady here," said Brush.

Blodgett raised his eyebrows and whistled compassionately: "Ain't that terrible! There's a woman in it, eh?"

"Yes."

"Tchk-tchk-tchk! You know you ought to marry the poor girl."

Brush looked at him sharply. "Of course I want to marry her. Only I can't find her."

"I gotta get out of here," cried Margie McCoy, abruptly. "I'm going cuckoo. Let'm be, Reme. He's crazy. He's nuts," and she hurried into the dining-room.

Blodgett's manner took on the hushed and prudent manner he would have assumed had Brush informed him that he was talking to Napoleon. "Say, ain't that terrible! How did it happen?"

"I'd rather not talk about it," said Brush.

Blodgett asked some questions about the road and about business conditions in Texas. Then he said: "How about coming up to the room tonight, eh?—little talk?"

"I'd like to, but I'm leaving this morning for Oklahoma City."

"What? We'll be there tomorrow. Where do you put up, boy?"

It seemed that they both planned to stay at the McGraw House and a meeting was planned for the following evening. "Good! About eight, see? Come up to the room and have a little drink."

"I don't drink, but I'd like a little talk."

"Oh, you don't drink?"

"No."

"Sure, I realize it's against the law," said Blodgett, generously.

"It undermines the nervous system and impairs the efficiency," added Brush.

"Damn it, you're right. You're right. I'm going to stop it one of these days. You never said a truer word. But you won't mind if the little lady and I have something while you're there?"

"No."

Mrs. McCoy appeared at the door. "Reme, you come here," she cried. "Come here. He might shoot or something."

"Marge, what do you mean, shoot. He's all right. He's a fine fella." He slapped Brush on the back, then lowering his voice, added, confidentially: "No ill-feelings, see? The little girl's always that way when you first know her."

Blodgett winked intimately and followed his cousin in to breakfast.

Brush left the hotel and walked down the street in the shade of the cottonwood trees. He listened enviously to the domestic sounds that came from the houses to his right and his left. Housewives were shaking rugs out of windows or shifting saucepans upon a stove. Children were heard calling in shrill voices, every sentence beginning and ending with a querulous "Ma." A few men had taken advantage of the early coolness and were cutting the lawn; others were flinging open the doors of their garages and casting a first reassuring glance at their car. At the edge of town Brush left the road and followed a path through some deep grass; passing some rubbish-heaps and a deserted sawmill he came upon a clear stream that, flowing rapidly, seemed to carry a load of tangled weeds towards a pond. He lay down beside the pond, face downward, and gazed at the scene. Two water snakes glided by, weaving in and out of each other's shadow. In the middle of the pond a turtle, with two small turtles on her back, climbed out upon a rotting plank. More turtles followed and, settling themselves squarely, drew their heads partly into their shells and closed their eyes. The very bird calls announced a hot day.

Brush had come out to think. This was his twenty-third birthday, and birthdays were solemn occasions for him. Two years before he had risen up from a swinging hammock on his father's porch, had crossed the town of Ludington, Michigan, and proposed marriage to a widow ten years older than himself. He had been refused, but he never forgot the exhilaration

of having done it, nor the look in her eyes as she stood drying her hands on her apron, while her children crawled about on the floor, untying his shoestrings. One year before he had spent the evening in the Public Library at Abilene, Texas, reading the life of Napoleon in the Encyclopædia Britannica. When he finished he had taken a pencil from his pocket and written in the margin, "I am a great man, too, but for good," and had signed his initials. The perspiration had stood out on his forehead.

And now before the pool near Wellington, Oklahoma, he prepared to examine himself on his twenty-third birthday. Tremendous were the good resolutions adopted that morning. It was to be a great year. He never forgot the solemnity of that hour, even though, at the end of it, still on an empty stomach, he fell asleep.

As a result of one of the decisions made by the pool near Wellington, Brush found himself towards noon on the same day in Armina, forty miles away, whither he had come to draw his savings from a bank in that town. The bank consisted of one big room, high and well lighted, with a pen in the middle, walled in with a show of marble and of bright steel gratings. Beside the door the president sat in his smaller pen, filled with despair. Short of a miracle his bank had little over a week to live. Banks had been failing all through these states for months, and now even this bank, which had seemed to him to be eternal, would be obliged to close its doors.

Brush glanced at the president, but, resisting the temptation to go and talk to him, went to a desk and, drawing out his bankbook, made out a slip. He presented himself at the cashier's window.

"I'm closing up my account," he said. "I'll draw out everything except the interest."

"I beg your pardon?"

"I'll take out the money," he repeated, raising his voice as though the cashier were deaf, "but I'll leave the interest here."

The cashier blinked a moment, then began fumbling among his coins. At last he said, in a low voice, "I don't think we'll be able to keep your account open for so small a sum."

"You don't understand. I'm not leaving the interest here as an account. I don't want it. Just turn it back into the bank. I don't believe in interest."

The cashier began casting distraught glances to right and left. He paid out both sum and interest across the grating, mumbling: "I . . . the bank . . . you must find some other way of disposing of the money."

Brush took the five hundred dollars and pushed the rest back. He raised his voice sharply and could be heard all over the room saying, "I don't believe in interest."

The cashier hurried to the president and whispered in his ear. The president stood up in alarm, as though he had been told that a thief was entering the vaults. He went to the door of the bank and stopped Brush as he was about to leave.

"Mr. Brush?"

"Yes."

"Might I speak to you for a moment, Mr. Brush? In here."

"Certainly," said Brush, and followed him through a low gate into the presidential pen. Mr. Southwick had a great unhappy sheep's head rendered ridiculous by a constant fluttering adjustment of various spectacles and pince-nez and black satin ribbons. His professional dignity reposed upon an enormous stomach supported in blue serge and bound with a gold chain. They sat down on either side of this monument and gazed at one another in considerable excitement.

"Mm . . . mm . . . ! You feel you must draw out your savings, Mr. Brush?" said the president, softly, as though he were inquiring into an intimate hygienic matter.

"Yes, Mr. Southwick," replied Brush, reading the name from a framed sign on the desk.

". . . And you're leaving your interest in the bank?"

"Yes."

"What would you like us to do with it?"

"I have no right to say. The money isn't mine. I didn't earn it."

"But your money, Mr. Brush—I beg your pardon—your money earned it."

"I don't believe that money has the right to earn money."

Mr. Southwick swallowed. Then in the manner he had once used while explaining to his daughter that the earth was round, he said: "But the money you deposited here, that money has been earning money for us. The interest represents those profits, which we share with you."

"I don't believe in profits like that."

Mr. Southwick edged his chair forward and asked another question: "Mm . . . mm . . . ! May I ask why you have thought it best to withdraw your money at this time?"

"Why, I'm glad to tell you, Mr. Southwick. You see, I've been thinking about money and banks a lot lately. I haven't quite thought the whole matter through yet—I'll be able to do that when my vacation comes in November—but at least I see that for myself I don't believe in saving money any more. Up till now I used to believe that you were allowed to save *some* money—like five hundred dollars, for instance, for your old age, you know, or for the chance your appendix burst, or for the chance you might get married suddenly—for what people call a rainy day; but now I see that's all wrong. I've taken a vow, Mr. Southwick; I've taken the vow of voluntary poverty."

"Of what?" asked Mr. Southwick, his eyes starting out of his head.

"Of voluntary poverty, like Gandhi. I've always followed it somewhat. The point is to never have any money saved up anywhere. Do you see?"

Mr. Southwick mopped his forehead.

"When my pay check comes every month," continued Brush, earnestly, "I immediately give away all money that's left over from the month before, but I always knew that at bottom that wasn't honest. Honest, with myself, I mean, because all this time I had five hundred dollars hidden away in this bank here. But from now on, Mr. Southwick, I won't need any banks. You see, the fact that I had this money here was a sign that I lived in fear."

"Fear!" cried Mr. Southwick. He rapped the bell on his desk so hard that it crashed to the floor.

"Yes," said Brush, his voice rising as the truth became clearer to him. "No one who has money saved up in a bank can really be happy. All the money locked up here is being saved because people are afraid of a rainy day. They're afraid, as they say, that worst may come to worst. Mr. Southwick, may I ask if you're a religious man?"

Mr. Southwick was deacon in the First Presbyterian Church and had passed a red velvet collection bag for twenty years, but at this question he jumped as though he had been struck sharply in the ribs. A clerk approached him. "Go out at the

corner and get Mr. Gogarty at once," he commanded, hoarsely. "Get him at once!"

"Then you know what I'm talking about," continued Brush. His voice could now be heard throughout the hall. Clerks and depositors had stopped what they were doing and were listening in consternation. "There is no worst coming to worst for a good man. There's nothing to be afraid of. To save up money is a sign that you're afraid, and one fear makes another fear, and that fear makes another fear. No one who has money in banks can really be happy. It's a wonder your depositors can really sleep nights, Mr. Southwick. There they lie, wondering what'll happen to them when they get old and when they get sick and when banks have troubles——"

"Stop it! Stop what you're saying!" cried Mr. Southwick, very red in the face. A policeman entered the bank. "Mr. Gogarty, arrest this man. He's come here to make trouble. Get him out of here at once."

Brush faced the policeman. "Arrest me," he said. "Here I am. What have I done? I haven't done anything. I'll tell the judge. I'll tell everybody what I've been saying."

"Come on along. You come on quiet."

"You don't have to push me," said Brush. "I'm glad to come."

He was taken to the jail.

"My name is George Marvin Brush," he said, seizing the warden's hand.

"Take your dirty hand away," said the warden. "Jerry, get the fellow's prints."

Brush was led into another room to record his finger-prints and to be photographed.

"My name's George M. Brush," he said, seizing the photographer's hand.

"How are yuh?" said the other. "Glad to see yuh. My name's Bohardus."

"I didn't catch it," said Brush, politely.

"Bohardus—Jerry Bohardus."

Jerry Bohardus was a retired policeman with a kindly disposition and a dreamy, fumbling manner. A shock of long gray hair fell into his eyes. "Kindly step up in front of this glass table for me," he said. "It's fine weather we're having."

"Oh, fine," said Brush. "It's fine, outside."

"Now put your hand down lightly on this pad, Mr. Brown. That's the ticket. That's right. That's fine." He lowered his voice and added, confidentially: "Don't feel badly about this business, Mr. Brown. It's just a form we gotta go through, see? It don't mean anything. They send these here prints to Washington, where there are eighty-five thousand others; some of them belong to sheriffs and mayors, too, yes, sir. I wouldn't be surprised if there were a few senators. Now the other hand, my boy. That's the ticket. So you never had this done before?"

"No," said Brush. "The other town I was arrested in didn't seem to care about it."

"Probably they didn't have the ay-paray-tus," replied Bohardus, complacently knocking the glass table with his knuckles. "We give two thousand dollars for all this, and it's a dandy."

Brush earnestly examined the result. "That thumb's not very clear, Mr. Bohardus," he said. "I think I'd better do it over again."

"No, that's clear enough. You've got a fine thumb. See them spirals?"

"Yes."

"They're just about the finest spirals I ever saw. Some say they stand for character."

"Do they?"

"That's what they say. Now we'll take your picture. Will you kindly put your head in this frame? . . . That's the ticket. It's funny about finger-prints," continued Bohardus, placing a board of numerals against Brush's chest. "Even if there were a trillion contrillion of them no two'd be alike."

"Isn't that wonderful!" replied Brush, his voice lowered in awe. Bohardus retired under a dark cloth. "Do you want me to smile now?" called Brush.

"No," answered Bohardus, emerging and adjusting his lenses. "We don't generally ask for a smile in this work."

"I suppose you've seen lots of criminals in your day, Mr. Bohardus?"

"I? I certainly have. I've bertillioned people that have killed their folks and that have poisoned their wives and that have spat on the flag. You wouldn't believe what I've seen. . . . Now we'll get your side face, Mr. Brown. . . . That's the

ticket." He came forward and turned Brush's head. He took the occasion to ask, delicately, "May I inquire what they think you did, Mr. Brown?"

"I didn't do anything. I just told a bank president that banks were immoral places and they arrested me."

"You don't say. . . . Chin up, Mr. Brown."

"My name isn't Brown. It's Brush—George Brush."

"Oh, I see. Well, what's a name, anyway? . . . There, now I guess we got some good pictures."

"Do you sell copies of these, Mr. Bohardus?"

"We're not allowed to, I reckon. Leastways, there never was no great demand."

"I was thinking I could buy some extra. I haven't been taken for more than two years. I know my mother'd like some."

Bohardus stared at him narrowly. "I don't think it shows a good spirit to make fun of this work, Mr. Brown, and I tell you I don't like it. In fifteen years here nobody's made fun of it, not even murderers haven't."

"Believe me, Mr. Bohardus," said Brush, turning red, "I wasn't making fun of anything. I knew you made good photos, and that's all I thought about."

Bohardus maintained an angry silence, and when Brush was led away refused to return his greeting. The chief of police, Mr. Southwick, and other dignitaries were in earnest conference when Brush was led into the warden's office. At once he approached Mr. Southwick.

"I still don't see what was wrong in the things I said. Mr. Southwick, I can't apologize for a mistake I don't understand. I can see that you might feel hurt because I haven't a very high opinion of the banking business, but that's not a thing you can put me in prison for, and it's not a thing I can change my mind about, either. Anyway, all I ask is a fair trial and I think I can clear myself in half an hour. And I hope there are as many people in the courtroom as possible, because in these depression times a lot of people ought to know what Gandhi thinks of money."

The chief of police came toward him threateningly. "Now stop this foolishness!" he said. "Stop it right now. What's the matter with you, anyway?" He turned back to his men. "Jerry thinks this guy's screwy. Perhaps we ought to take him up to

Monktown for some tests. . . . How about it, young fella? What's the matter with you, anyway? Are you nuts?"

"No, I'm not," cried Brush, violently, "and I'm getting tired of this. You can see perfectly well I'm not crazy. Give me any old test you like—memory, dates, history, Bible. I'm an American citizen, and I'm of sound mind, and the next person that calls me crazy will have to answer for it, even if I am a pacifist. I told Mr. Southwick that his bank and every other bank is a shaky building of fear and cowardice. . . ."

"All right, dry up, pipe down," said the chief. "Now looka here, Brush, if you aren't out of this town in an hour you get the strait-jacket and a six-months' sanity test upstate. Do you hear?"

"I'd like to take it," said Brush, "but I can't spare six months."

"Gogarty," said the chief, "see him to the depot."

Gogarty was a tall man with a great bony jaw and pale blue eyes.

"Boy, are you coming along quiet?" asked Gogarty.

"Of course I'll be quiet," said Brush.

After they had gone a number of blocks in silence Gogarty stopped, turned, and putting one forefinger on Brush's lapel, asked in a confidential tone:

"Say, boy, where did you get that idea about the Armina Savings Bank bein' shaky? Who told yuh?"

"I didn't mean that bank only. I meant all banks."

This answer did not satisfy Gogarty. Lost in thought, he continued to peer over his spectacles into Brush's face. Then he turned and stared up the street.

"Looks to me like there's a lot of people at the door of that bank now," he said. Suddenly he was roused to action. "Boy, you stick by me," he said. He dashed into the house before which they were standing. A woman was washing the dishes. "Mrs. Cowles," said Gogarty, severely, "as constable in this town I am obliged to use your telephone."

"Why, certainly, Mr. Gogarty," said Mrs. Cowles, nervously.

"And I'll have to ask you, ma'am, to go out on the front porch while I'm talking here."

Mrs. Cowles obeyed. When Gogarty had received a reply he said: "Mary, put on your hat. Do what I tell you. Go down and

draw out all the savings, down to the last cent. And run. Only got half an hour. And don't tell nobody what you're doing."

He left the house with Brush and allowed Mrs. Cowles to return to her work. He again peered up the street, and deciding that his duty lay there, trusted Brush to reach the railway station by himself.

Mr. Southwick went home and lay down in a darkened room. From time to time he moaned, whereupon his wife, moving about on tiptoe, would rise and change the damp cloths on his forehead, whispering: "Sh, Timothy dear! There's nothing to worry about. You just take a nap. Sh!"

Chapter II

Oklahoma City. Chiefly conversation. The adventure in the barn. Margie McCoy gives some advice.

B RUSH arrived at the McGraw House in Oklahoma City on the same evening. The following morning he set about putting in a hard day's work. He called on all manner of school superintendents, principals, and heads of departments. He drove out to a reformatory and was persuaded to address the assembled student body.

At eight o'clock in the evening he knocked at Blodgett's door. For a moment there was the sound of voices in loud altercation, then Blodgett came out into the hall and closed the door behind him.

"Say, Brush," he said, "about tonight. I just want to ask you to be a little careful. You know. My cousin's kind of nervous. Just keep off subjects that might upset her. You get the idea."

"All right. I'll try and remember."

"Yeah. She's had a lot of fuss lately. She only got a divorce last month, and you know how it is."

"She's a . . . divorced woman?" asked Brush, softly.

"Yeah, yeah. So you see!" and Blodgett winked with fraternal complicity. Then he opened the door and announced, with nervous cordiality: "Well, Marge, look who's here."

Margie McCoy was sitting on the bed, her feet on a newspaper, her back against the iron bed-stead. Her face was still sullen. She held a tall glass in one hand, and a cigarette in the other. She acknowledged Brush's greeting by only the slightest movement of her eyes, after which she continued gazing implacably at the wall before her.

The conversation proceeded with the greatest difficulty. Brush went carefully, not sure which subjects were likely to unnerve a woman who had recently passed through the harrowing experience of obtaining a divorce. After forty minutes of this discomfort he rose to go.

"Well, thank you very much for letting me come around,"

he said, backing to the door. "I'd better be going. I still have some reports to draw up, and . . ."

To the surprise of both the men, Mrs. McCoy spoke: "What's the hurry? What's the hurry?" she asked, irritably. "Sit down. Don't you smoke, either? No wonder you feel like a fool, just sitting and talking. Remus, give 'm some ginger ale, anyway. That way he can at least hold something in his hand, my-God!"

A second attack was made on conversation. Brush let fall the news that he had been arrested and taken to jail since last he saw them. He was encouraged to tell the story and was soon recounting his conversation with Mr. Southwick. He explained the theory of voluntary poverty. Now Mrs. McCoy's eyes were resting on him in astonishment. At the end of his exposition the same question rose simultaneously to the lips of both the listeners.

"What would you do if you lost your job?" they asked.

"Well, I don't know exactly. I never really thought about it. I guess I'd find something. Leastways, it doesn't seem very likely. I keep getting raises all the time. They even make me nervous."

"The raises make you nervous?" asked Mrs. McCoy.

"Yes."

"What would you do if you got sick?" she asked.

"What are you going to do when you get old?" asked Blodgett.

"I already explained that to you," he said.

Mrs. McCoy solemnly put her feet on the floor and, placing her hands on her hips, she leaned forward: "Listen, baby," she said. "Let me look at you. Are you trying to kid me?"

"Why, no, Mrs. McCoy. I'm serious."

She just as solemnly returned to her position on the bed. "Well, something's the matter," she muttered, looking distrustfully into her glass.

"Buddy," said Blodgett, "why did you say that it made you nervous to get raises?"

"Because hardly anybody else's getting raises these days. I think everybody ought to be hit by the depression equally. You see?"

Mrs. McCoy said dryly: "Sure I see. Your ideas aren't the same as other people's, are they?"

"No," said Brush, "I should think not. I didn't put myself

through college for four years and go through a difficult religious conversion in order to have ideas like other people's."

"I see. Now answer me another: When you get married what are you going to use for money?"

"I beg your pardon?"

"How do you know your wife'll be willing to throw away all your money every month, and how do you know she'll be willing to look forward with a big thrill to the poorhouse, like you do?"

"Oh, she will," said Brush.

"You're engaged, are you?" asked Blodgett.

"I'm . . . I'm practically engaged. Well, I don't know whether I'm engaged or not."

"Is she a . . . she's a nice girl, eh?"

"I don't know that, either—not for sure." Brush glanced at Blodgett. "I'd better not talk about it," he said. "It's all a part of that big mistake I made. You said you didn't want me to mention things like that tonight."

"I can stand anything now," said Mrs. McCoy. "After the big poverty idea I can stand anything. The other morning was different. I couldn't stand it on an empty stummick, that's all. Come on and tell us what happened."

Again Brush looked at Blodgett.

"Sure," said Blodgett. "Go ahead."

"I know it's a pretty intimate thing to tell people . . . people that I've only known a short time. But you'll see how badly I need advice on it. Before I begin I think I ought to explain to you how I feel about women."

"Just a minute, buddy," said Blodgett, trimming a cigar. "You're sure you can stand it, sister?"

"What did I tell you? I can stand anything."

Brush looked up in surprise. "There's nothing hard to stand about this. I just wanted you to know that until this thing happened I was looking everywhere for a wife. Really, everywhere. It was almost the only thing I thought about. You see, I'm twenty-three years old; in fact, that was my birthday when you met me yesterday."

"Well, well!" said Blodgett. "Many happy returns of the day."

"Thank you a lot . . . and I should have settled down long ago . . ."

"I see."

". . . and founded an American home."

"What?"

Brush leaned forward earnestly. "You know what I think is the greatest thing in the world? It's when a man, I mean an American, sits down to Sunday dinner with his wife and six children around him. Do you know what I mean?"

"Six, eh?"

"Yes, and the more the better. Well, that's the thing I want most of all, so everywhere I go I keep looking for a wife. And every now and then I used to think I'd found her. For instance, I was singing in church one day—I guess I never told you I had a very good tenor voice——"

"No."

"Well, I have; so when I come to a town where I have to stay over Sunday I go to the minister of a church and offer to sing at the service. It makes the service more inspiring. And one day I was singing and I saw a girl in the congregation that looked perfect to me. I was singing 'The Lost Chord,' and when I came to the loud part you can imagine how I put everything into it. After service everybody came up and asked me to go home to dinner with them. That's what always happens. And the father of this girl came up and asked me to go home with them. All during dinner I sat by her and I thought she was the finest girl I'd ever seen in my life, even though she didn't say hardly a word. But all the time I was afraid something would spoil it. I brought the conversation around to evolution and I found she was all right there; they didn't believe any of that about monkeys. Well, you can guess what happened."

"No," said Blodgett, "I don't know as I can."

"We were sitting around after dinner and she asked her brother for a cigarette."

"You don't say!"

"Her mother was pretty disappointed in her and said so, but she wasn't as disappointed as I was. I guess she wanted to show off, with a singer in the house, that she wasn't just a village girl. That was in Sulphur Falls, Arkansas. Now I can never hear about Sulphur Falls without a funny feeling in my stomach."

"That's quite a story," said Blodgett. "Eh, Margie?"

"Did she ever know what she lost?" asked Mrs. McCoy.

Brush smiled. "It wasn't only me she lost, Mrs. McCoy," he said.

Blodgett broke in hurriedly. "Do they ever refuse to let you sing?"

"Sometimes they give me a test, but after a few notes they know it's all right."

"You ought to be able to pick up some handy money, that way."

"No, I don't believe in taking money for it. Once in Plata, Missouri, a man came up and offered me two hundred dollars to sing at the Elks' convention in St. Louis, but I couldn't. I would have done it for them free of charge, only my route didn't go anywhere near St. Louis at that time. That's another of my theories. A voice like mine is just a gift, that's all. It's not to anybody's credit to have a fine voice. It's just a thing of nature, like any other. Niagara Falls and the caves of Kentucky and John McCormack are just gifts to the public. It's like strength. I happen to have that, too. I'll help you move your trunk or your piano all day, but I wouldn't take money for it. Do you see?"

"Yes," said Mrs. McCoy, "I see something. Only, when are you going to get back to the other story?"

"It's a hard story to tell. It was in the vacation before my senior year at college——"

"What college was that?" asked Blodgett.

"Shiloh Baptist College, in South Dakota, a very good college. Summers I used to cover Missouri, Illinois, and some parts of Ohio, selling the Children's Encyclopædia. I walked and hitch-hiked from one place to another. And one day I got lost. I must have been about twenty miles from Kansas City, sort of southwest. It got dark and began to rain. So I stopped at a farmhouse to ask if I could sleep in the barn. The farmer and his wife took me into their kitchen and gave me some coffee and bread and butter. They said they were Methodists and I could see there were three or four beautiful daughters moving around; but I couldn't see them very well because they stayed out of reach of the lamplight. But I noticed them and they all seemed to be quiet, beautiful girls. I said to myself that I'd make a good note of the house in the morning and come back again some day. Then I thanked them and said

good night and went to the barn and went to sleep." Here Brush took out his handkerchief and wiped his forehead. "From now on it's kind of delicate," he said, "and I don't want to hurt your feelings, but I guess you've both been married."

"Yes," said Blodgett, "we know the worst."

"I woke up in the pitch dark and heard a girl's voice laughing, and then later it was half laughing and half crying. She asked me if I wanted something to eat. Well, I can always eat something——"

"Have an apple?" asked Mrs. McCoy.

"No, thank you, not now. . . . We had a long talk. She said she wasn't happy on the farm. I asked her what her name was and she said 'Roberta.' Anyway, it sounded like Roberta. And that's important, because maybe it was Bertha. And one day in the newspaper I saw that there was a girl's name called Hertha. It might have been any one of those names."

"What does it matter what her name was?" cried Mrs. Mc-Coy.

"You'll see. Anyway, she cried and I tried to comfort her. So I decided she was the person I was going to marry."

There was a pause; the others looked at him inquiringly.

He repeated with emphasis, "So I decided she was the person I was going to marry."

Blodgett leaned forward and asked in a low, shocked voice, "You mean you ruined the girl?"

Brush turned pale and nodded.

"Give him a drink!" cried Mrs. McCoy, abruptly. "Give him a drink, for Gawd's sake!"

"I don't drink," said Brush.

"Remus, you give'm a drink," she cried, still more violently. "He's gotta take it. I can't stand seeing him act like a big baby. Now you drink that down and stop being a fool."

Brush accepted the glass and made a pretense of sipping at it. To his surprise, a weak sweetish taste lingered on his lips.

"Hurry up," said Mrs. McCoy. "How does it end?"

"That's about all," he continued. "I tried to tell this girl I'd be back the next day to marry her, but she ran back into the house. So I went down the road in the rain and walked all night. I walked for hours, planning what I'd say to her father and everything. But, you know, I've never been able to find that

house again. I've been up and down every road that side of
Kansas City a dozen times. I asked everybody about a farm-
house with daughters that were Methodists. I talked to all the
R.F.D. postmen, but it was no good. Now you know why I
can't think of being a minister."

There was a pause.

"And you love the girl, huh?" asked Blodgett.

Brush was displeased with the question. "It's not important
if I love her or not," he said. "All I know is that I'm her hus-
band until she or I dies. When you've known anybody as well
as that, it means that you can never know anybody else as
well as that until one of the two of you dies."

Mrs. McCoy leaned out of the bed and peered at the glass in
his hand vindictively. "You're not drinking that drink!" she
cried. "Drink it up. Don't you fool with it. Drink it up."

"I don't drink, Mrs. McCoy."

"I don't care whether you do or don't. I tell you to."

Blodgett himself was alarmed at her intensity. He raised one
eyebrow expressively as a signal to Brush who took another
swallow. Mrs. McCoy watched him belligerently. Then again she
lowered her feet solemnly to the floor. She said, slowly, "Do
you want advice?"

"Yes, I do."

"Naw, naw. I'm *asking* you, do you want some advice?"

"Yes."

"From who? From me?"

"Yes."

"Then listen! Now listen! Since you've tried as hard as you
can; since you can't find the girl; since the girl let herself in for
it, anyway—see?—since all these things are so, *forget it*. You're
clear. You're free. Begin again. Begin all over."

"I can't do that. Don't you see I'm married already?"

"What are you talking about? You're not *married*. You have
no license. You're not married."

"Mrs. McCoy, if you say I'm not married you're just quib-
bling with words, because I certainly am."

Mrs. McCoy stared at him wrathfully, then, shaking her
head, returned to her former position.

Brush continued with lowered eyes: "Anyway, it's perfectly
clear to me. And maybe it means that I can't settle down and

found an American home. Sometimes I think I may get so discouraged that I may fall sick—or worse. Because that's all sickness is—discouragement. That's one of my theories, too. I have a theory that all sickness comes from having lost hope about something. If they find out they're not as good as they thought they were—in business or in anything else—or if they've done wrong and can't undo it, then they gradually fall sick. They really want to die. They haven't any real interest left in wanting to see the sun come up on the next day. They *think* they want to live, but secretly they don't. Anyway, I'm going to think it through next November when I get my vacation. In the meantime I'm a good example of it. Look at me; I'm so worried about this that I got influenza last Spring. I've never been sick in my life. And another thing—if you'll excuse my mentioning it—I never used to have to take laxatives; but now I have to take laxatives all the time. I know what causes it, too. It means that I don't want to live unless I can settle down and have an American——"

At this point Margie McCoy became distraught. "Can't you stop him? Name-a-God, is this going on forever! Seems like we been here hours talking about this one thing. Change the subject. I'm going nuts. And you there, take another drink. No-o-o, none of those bird-sips."

Brush took another swallow and then rose. "I guess I'd better be going," he said. "I have to leave on a two-o'clock train for Camp Morgan. Thank you for letting me come to see you."

He stood lamely in the middle of the room, waiting to see whether Mrs. McCoy intended shaking hands with him. She rose and strolled towards the door, swinging her hips as she went. She leaned against the wall by the door. The two men looked at her in some trepidation.

"Now, listen! Listen to me!" she said, emphatically. "You make me sick. Where do they get yuh, your the'ries and your ideas? Nowhere! Live, kid,—live! What'd become of all of us sons-a-bitches, if we stopped to argue out every step we took? Stick down to earth."

Brush looked at her with furrowed brow and said in a low voice, "It seems to me I live."

To the astonishment of both men, she placed her hand on his shoulder. "I mean, look around you. We'll all be dead

soon. Thinking doesn't change anything. It only makes you twice as blue."

"It doesn't make me blue," he said.

Mrs. McCoy turned back angrily into the room and lit another cigarette. "Oh, go to hell!" she said.

Blodgett followed Brush into the hall.

"I wish she'd at least shaken hands with me," said Brush.

"Don't get her wrong," said Blodgett, confusedly. "That's the way she is when you first know her. She'll be all right when you know her better."

Brush returned slowly to his room. Before beginning to pack, he stood at the window and looked out into the rain. "I talk too much," he said to himself in a whisper. "I must watch that. I talk too damn much."

Chapter III

*Good times at Camp Morgan. Dick Roberts' night-
mares. Dinner with Mississippi Corey.*

GEORGE BRUSH'S trip to Camp Morgan was in obedience
to a telegram he had received on his arrival in Oklahoma
City. The telegram came from his superior in the publishing-
house and read: JUDGE LAKE MORGAN CAMP SETTLE GUTEN-
BERG ALDUS CAXTON GIVE HIM THE WORKS SKIES THE LIMIT
EINSTEIN. This message was not so difficult of interpretation
as it appears to be. Howells, the sender, was a debonaire soul
who signed his official communications with any signature that
occurred to him as being improbable. "Judge Lake Morgan
Camp" meant that Representative Corey, judge by inheritance
from his father, was spending the week-end at the Lake Mor-
gan Chautauqua and Recreation camp, Morganville, Okla-
homa. Judge Corey was the most influential member of the
educational committee at the legislature; the choice of the text-
books for the public-school system lay largely in his hands.
"Settle Gutenberg Aldus Caxton" meant that Brush was to
persuade him to recommend certain textbooks published by
his house. The names of the great printers served as code con-
vention for Caulkins' *First Year Algebra*, Mademoiselle Des-
fontaines' *Les Premiers Pas*, and Professor Grubb's *A Soldier
with Cæsar*. "Give him the works skies the limit" referred to an
elaborate joke between Howells and Brush, a joke that re-
posed on the pretense that representatives could be bribed. It
implied that Brush was empowered to offer Judge Corey an
honorary directorship in the League for the Improvement of
Secondary Education. This post carried with it a retaining fee
of seven hundred dollars a year. The joke had long since lost its
freshness for Brush, but Howells returned to it month after
month. Howells even insisted that a rival publishing-house
practiced such a device in all seriousness, offering certain legis-
lators a seat on the advisory council of an Education for Better
Citizenship Union, carrying a retaining fee of a thousand dol-

lars a year. Brush knew that Caulkins and Company would be incapable of such strategy, and, besides, he was unable to see how one opened the conversation that would lead to such an offer. At all events, he was able to place textbooks before millions of school children without such aids, and he was highly regarded by his firm in spite of his eccentricities.

In fact, his eccentricities gave the publishing-house no little pleasure. Brush's expense-account statements were unlike any others ever received in the office. He recorded every nickel and expended a large amount of ingenuity in saving the firm's money. He never doubted that the great Mr. Caulkins examined his reports in person, and he was right. Mr. Caulkins not only read them; he took them home to his wife, and carried them about with him in his pocket to show his friends at the club. There was only one point on which Brush and Howells came to strife. Brush not only refused to accept appointments with school officials on Sunday; however pressed his time, he refused to travel by train or bus on Sunday in order to reach an appointment on Monday morning. At a pinch he would consent to walk and hitch-hike. To ride a train on Sunday broke the Sabbath and prevented the trainmen from going to church and from passing the day in meditation. Howells pointed out to him that trains ran on Sunday anyway, "to carry sons and daughters to the bedside of their parents who had suddenly been taken ill." Brush replied that most parents would be willing to wait another day.

Brush left Oklahoma City at two and, employing a complicated chain of trains, buses, trolleys and taxicabs, crossed the greater part of the state and arrived at Morganville the next afternoon. During the journey he approached no one on the subject of salvation, but he reasoned with a Greek proprietor of a lunch-wagon on the matter of profanity, urged a farmer's boy to work his way through college, persuaded a garage proprietor to adopt a famished cat, and "thought through" the matter of capital punishment and the life sentence.

At Morganville he climbed into a bus hung with Chinese lanterns and banners that read: "Good times at Camp Morgan." He faced an advertisement on the back of the seat before him that read: "Girls, extend your acquaintance. Our Name-Badge

Dances introduce everyone." The bus, advancing wildly through a pine wood, first passed a company of women in bloomers who were being instructed in nature lore, then a shoal of men in underwear who staggered by, their eyes starting out of their heads, their heels rapped by the cane of a sneering athletic coach. The road skirted a lake that was dotted with canoes and rowboats. In the middle of the lake a great balloon, advertising an automobile gasoline, was moored to a projecting rock. Brush dismounted at the administration shed and bought a registration card accompanied by a handful of tickets—bed assignment, meal coupons, and admission to a performance of "The Rivals" by the Normal School Forest of Arden Players.

His cot was one of six in a tent named "Felix." It belonged to the Oranges. His tentmates greeted him cheerfully, for the next morning the Oranges were to have a tug of war with the Blues, and Brush looked as though he could pull six men off their feet. He took a walk around the grounds, without enthusiasm. Seeing there was to be a camp-fire sing and marshmallow roast, he sought out the entertainment director, offered his services as soloist, and was accepted. Then he called upon the manager of the dining-hall, and had a place reserved for him at Judge Corey's table.

Returning to his tent, he began to unpack. He arranged his tooth-brush and shaving-outfit on the shelf above his bed. On the cot next to his a man of forty lay, recovering from his exertions on the reducing squad. He opened an eye from time to time to observe Brush as he went about his work. Presently he raised himself up and, putting his feet on the floor, sat forlornly on the edge of his bed, his head in his hands.

Brush glanced at him sharply. "Don't you feel right?" he asked. "Did you overdo it?"

"Oh, I feel all right," said the man. A silence fell on his dejection. Brush glanced at him again and found the man looking at him with an absurd woe in his eyes. To recover himself the man said: "I don't know why I came to this place. I wish I were back in the office."

"It's Friday already," said Brush. "You wouldn't be doing anything in the office over the week-end, would you?"

"No, nor any other time. But I got the habit; I just go and sit there. I'm in real estate, and let me tell you we get heart

failure every time the phone rings. I go and sit there and fool around the desk. I don't know."

"Sundays?"

"Yes, I manage to be there Sundays, too. There isn't anything else to do."

There was another pause. Brush began putting on a clean shirt for dinner.

"My wife dragged me here. She said it was good for the kids to get these lectures and shows. Yeah, she said it was good for the kids to take in these shows and concerts. Say, fella, my name's Dick Roberts of Meyrick."

"Glad to meet you. My name's George Brush. I travel in school books. My home's in Ludington, Michigan."

"Michigan, eh? Is there anything doing in your line?"

"Yes . . . yes," said Brush, tying his tie and frowningly studying Roberts' face in the mirror. "We keep selling pretty well."

Roberts struggled with himself and finally said, with effort: "Brush . . . mm. I may have to ask you to do a little favor for me."

"Sure. What can I do?"

"It may not be necessary, see, but just on the chance it is. I see as you've got the next cot to mine. My wife tells me I talk in my sleep. Just wake me up if I do."

"You mean that you snore?"

"No, I don't snore. She says that sometimes I sort of shout. Not very often, but sometimes. If I do it these nights, just hit me, see? Then I'll get up and go and sleep by the lake where I won't trouble anybody."

"Sure I'll do that."

"I just mentioned it. I don't sleep very well, anyway," continued Roberts, staring at the ground. "I guess I haven't slep' for weeks, not what you'd call slep'. That's why I went on that damned running squad. I wanted to get tired out."

The tent "Felix" stood beside the road that led through the camp-ground to the water's edge. Brush became aware of a woman standing in the road and calling: "Oh, Dick! Dick Roberts!"

"There's your wife calling you now," he said.

Roberts went out to her. Brush could hear her saying: "Lillian

wants you to come in swimming and hold her up. Perhaps you're too tired now, though. I think there's just time before dinner and it might do you good."

"Yes, I'll be right along."

"Are you going to be comfortable, Dick?" she asked, peering anxiously towards the tent.

"Yes, it's fine. Everything's fine," he said, adding, "Wait a minute."

Roberts came back into the tent. "I'd like you to shake hands with my wife, if you're not busy," he said.

"I'd like to," replied Brush.

Mrs. Roberts was a short, slight woman with a manner that was at once vivacious and shy. After the introduction the three started walking slowly down the hill. Mrs. Roberts' eyes returned frequently with concern to her husband's face; his rested on the ground or affected to be interested in some object across the lake.

"We're so glad we came," said Mrs. Roberts. "The children are just as happy as they can be. You'd think they'd been here all summer, and of course they simply love it. I suppose you've come for a good rest and change."

"No," said Brush. "I don't like this kind of place. I've come on business to contact a man."

"Oh!" said Mrs. Roberts, glancing quickly at his face. "Well, I hope I see you again, Mr. Brush. Now I expect you'll be wanting to talk to some of these pretty girls around here."

"I'll get my suit on," said Roberts, and left them.

Brush did not move away. He continued walking gravely by Mrs. Roberts. She again glanced nervously at his face, and, stopping, said with great effort:

"Mr. Brush, since you're in my husband's tent, I think I ought to tell you something."

"I know. He told me."

"About his nightmares, you mean?"

"Yes."

"Perhaps it won't happen. But it would be very good of you to wake him up at once. I'm afraid he worries about that business too much. He just sits all day and all evening in that office, and I think he broods, that's a fact. That's why I came here to Camp Morgan—though it's quite expensive—to give

him a change. Oh, I don't know what to do and I'm just sick about it!"

Here Mrs. Roberts began groping feverishly in her handbag for a handkerchief. Brush glanced down at her hands out of the corners of his eyes, standing ready to offer her his own, then continued solemnly looking at the lake.

"And what's more," added Mrs. Roberts, ". . . six weeks ago he had a kind of awful experience and he's never been the same since. And very likely he broods about that, too."

"Was he in an automobile accident?"

"No; it wasn't that. I'd like to tell you about it, if you're not . . . if you're not going any place. You see, Mr. Roberts and I were at one of those foolish amusement parks and we were riding on a roller-coaster, and a man in the same car as we were fell out and was killed. While he was dying, though, he wanted to dictate a letter to his family in Fort Wayne, Indiana, and Mr. Roberts, being an Elk, too, volunteered to take it. It was a simply awful accident. This man—though I hate to say it— was a perfect fool, Mr. Brush. He was one of that show-off kind and I guess he was trying to catch the attention of some girls in the same car. Mr. Roberts and I just hated him and there wasn't anybody that thought his jokes were funny. But the more people were disgusted with him the more he cut up. And the second trip, going around a curve, he stood right up in the car and pretended to dive. And sure enough, naturally, he fell. He fell hitting all those girders and things. Then while he was on the ground, waiting for the ambulance, he kept calling: 'Is anybody here an Elk? Is anybody here an Elk?' Seems he wanted to talk to an Elk, so Mr. Roberts volunteered. It made a terrible impression on him."

"I'll be glad to watch out for him tonight, Mrs. Roberts," said Brush. "I didn't think he looked very happy."

She turned and said, quickly, with nervous emphasis: "You know, that's a fact—he's *not* happy. I suppose I really oughtn't to tell you anything about this . . . you being so young and everything . . . but, Mr. Brush, I think he was going to commit suicide last week."

"Do you?"

"I don't know. I don't know. And I've never mentioned it to a soul. But one night I got up. I saw a light in the bathroom,

and he was standing there just thinking . . . and with such a look on his face, Mr. Brush, such a sad look. And now when he calls out in his sleep I think it's about *that*. There's no business at his office any more, not to speak of, and he worries about me and the children." Here she suddenly lowered her head and whispered, passionately: "I don't mind if we're going to be poor. I don't care if we're as poor as dirt. I don't care if the town pays for us, only I don't want him to be so miserable."

"You ought to tell him that," said Brush.

"I can't. Somehow I can't. He's real proud. He thinks so much of having a nice home in a good neighborhood. He's real proud. Sometimes it seems like he thinks the depression's his own fault. You know, he'd kill himself for the insurance. I know he would. And I'm just sick about it."

"Apart from the nightmares, does he sleep very well?"

"I . . . I don't know. I listen to his breathing and sometimes I think he just imitates sleeping, so as not to worry me."

At this minute a boy of nine, dripping wet, came running up the slope, calling: "Mamma, I gotta turtle. I gotta turtle, mamma. Look't." But as his eyes caught sight of the tears on his mother's face the words stuck in his throat. He glanced from his mother to Brush, then back again, then continued in a low voice; "Look, mamma, I gotta turtle. See."

"George, this is Mr. Brush. He rooms in the same tent with your father and you. Can you say how-do-you-do?"

A queenly woman with a badge on her chest approached them. "Don't forget the costume ball tomorrow night," she said. "You can make a costume by adding some amusing detail. If you can't think of anything, come to the desk and we will be happy to give you some suggestions. Ah, the darling little turtle. Aren't you *happy* you found it? Mr. Macklin is the nature man and he will *explain* it to you."

She went on her way. Brush said, "I think I can do something."

"And don't tell. You won't tell, will you?"

"N-no, not if I can help it."

Brush turned back towards the main hall. On the veranda a large red-faced man was making himself loudly agreeable to some embarrassed children.

"How do you do, Judge Corey!" said Brush.

"Stop right there!" cried the judge. "I know your name as well as I know my own. Don't tell me!"

"My name's George Brush. I've come to see you about putting some of Caulkins' textbooks on the recommended lists for your schools."

"Good. Fine. Always glad to do the people's business. We'll have a little talk about that after dinner."

Brush began talking at once about the excellence of his books, but the judge's mind began to wander.

"They sound fine, buddy. They certainly do. I don't want to miss any of that. Be sure you write me a letter about it."

"I've written you three letters, Judge."

"Good. My secretary's saving them for me. What states do you cover, buddy? Been down to Texas lately? How's Bill Winderstedt? D'you know Bill? Say, Brush, I want you to meet my wife and daughter." He peered about him. "Don't know where they've gone. My daughter Mississippi don't know many people here yet. Say, I got an idea. What table you sittin' at, young fella? Don't say a thing! I'll tell 'em to sit you at our table. They're throwing a novelty dinner tonight. You'll like it. They do things well at this camp. Yes, sir, they see everybody has a good time. Table M. Remember that—Table M."

"Thanks, Judge. I'd like to."

The judge drew nearer and assumed a confidential expression. "I got another idea. A coupla us fellas are going over to Morganville to the Depot Hotel about ten for a little game of poker. All right?"

"I don't play, Judge."

"Oh, you don't play?"

"No."

"Tell the truth, I get tired of it myself. It's harmless, y'know, but it takes up too much of a fella's time. See what I mean? There's my wife and girl now." The judge turned his back on his approaching family, as though he feared that they might read his lips, and whispered: "Say, sonny, if you're staying around the lot here you might keep an eye on my little girl. She don't know many people here. A little canoe ride y'know . . . no rough stuff . . . just a half-hour canoe ride, something like that."

Mrs. Corey was a tall, stiff woman with a frightened expression

on her face; her daughter greatly resembled her. The mother wore a pince-nez hung upon a long gold chain; Mississippi wore thick blurred spectacles.

"Girls," said the judge, "I want you to meet Jim Bush, one of the finest fellas you could hope to see. Jim, this is my wife. She's put up with me for thirty years and she's a prince. And *this* is Mississippi, the sweetest and snappiest little home-girl in Oklahoma, if I do say it."

"I didn't catch the name," said Mississippi, politely.

"Jim Bush! Jim Bush!" roared her father.

"Isn't that funny! I know so many boys named Jim!"

"Well, this Jim is sitting at our table," continued the judge, with a wink, "and I don't want to see any monkey business going on, like there was last week."

"Why, Leonidas!" cried Mrs. Corey, fingering the gold chain. "I don't know what Mr. Bush'll think."

"Well, if he thinks what I think, he'll think plenty," cried the judge.

"Papa, listen!" exclaimed Mississippi, coquettishly, flinging her elbows against her ears and burying her hands in the small of her back. "Listen, I know what let's do. Let's not eat here. Let's row across the lake, papa, and eat at that place above the water with the lanterns. Papa, do that for 'Sippy."

"Girlie, I'd do it if I could. I'd do it in a minute, but I can't. Y'see, Jim, I'm stockholder in this camp, and I've got to make an important announcement at dinner tonight."

"Tell him, papa; it's your idea. Listen, Mr. Bush."

"Yes, sir, about how everybody who mentions the depression must pay a fine of fifteen cents. D'you like it?"

"Yes," said Brush.

"But you young people run across the lake and try it. You try it and tell me how it is."

"Now don't stay too late, Mississippi. You know how I worry," said her mother.

"I can't go tonight, Mrs. Corey," said Brush. "I've been asked to sing at the camp fire at eight o'clock." Back of his words lay his astonishment that anyone could propose paying for a meal in one place when the meal had already been paid for at another.

"Why, it's only six o'clock! Seems like you could be over and back in that time," said Mrs. Corey, and in a sudden burst of noise the Coreys settled the matter.

The judge then pretended to have misgivings. "I don't know if we can trust our girlie to a big six-footer like Jim here," he said, striking Brush sharply on the back.

Brush went down to the waterfront and prepared the canoe, and ten minutes later the couple were sitting down at the Venice Inn, prepared to consume the seventy-five-cent chicken dinner. Mississippi talked without pause, and as she talked she continually fingered, for coquetry, the hair at the back of her head and the folds of her dress over her lean clavicles. She declared an increasing admiration for Brush. "Now when can you come to Okey City, 'cause I want to give a big, big party for you. My father loves for me to give parties, and I know our crowd would be crazy about you. Really, our crowd has the *best* time. We're not foolish, you know what I mean; we're just friends together. When can you come, Mr. Bush?"

"I don't go to parties very much," said Brush, slowly, "but I'll call you up some day and I'd like to have a talk."

Mississippi swallowed and said, with affected casualness: "Of course, I don't know whether you're married or not, Mr. Bush, but I don't think it matters much when one's just friends. Do you?"

Brush kept his eyes on the plate. "I'm practically engaged," he said. "I'm about married."

This announcement led Mississippi to share with him her ideas on love and marriage. Brush became fascinated by the spectacle of so many disadvantages heaped upon one person. From sheer distress his mind began to wander and he only caught fragments of her remarks. "You know," she said, "I don't care how poor a man is, honest I don't, but he must have high ideals. My girl friends say I'm foolish; but I'm funny that way. I couldn't bring myself to marry a man that didn't have good ideals." When, however, Mississippi began boasting about her adventures with gin, and when she began smoking a cigarette, Brush could contain himself no longer. Suddenly his lips spoke without his knowing it.

"You shouldn't talk baby talk," he said.

Both were shocked. "Why, James Bush," said Mississippi, "I didn't think you were rude. I don't talk baby talk. A person can't help how she talks."

"I . . . I beg your pardon. I didn't know what I was saying," said Brush, rising and turning very red. "I never did a thing like that before, Miss Corey. I apologize."

"But I don't . . . do I? Do I talk baby talk? If there's anything about me you don't like, I want you to tell me so, honest. I'm not conceited. I like people to tell me my faults. Honest, Mr. Bush, I'm not sore."

"My name's Brush, George Brush. Your father got it all wrong. George Brush."

"Really, I want to be told my faults. I don't think I'm perfect; honest, I don't."

Brush sat down again. He leaned forward, his elbows on his knees, and stared into her distorting spectacles. "Miss Corey, I've made a great study of girls. Everywhere I go I study them and watch them. I think they're about the most wonderful thing in the world. And I've been studying you, too. May I ask you to take off your glasses a minute?"

Mississippi turned pale. With a trembling hand she removed her spectacles. A frightened, pinched face looked uncertainly into his.

"Thank you," he said, gravely. He rose and took a few steps about the table. "You can put them on again."

There was a silence. Then he returned to his former position before her, and lowering his head, began with great earnestness: "Now, out of all my study I've drawn up a few rules for girls. Can I tell them to you? You might get to be a really nice girl if you worked on these rules." Her hand fluttered to her mouth, a gesture which he took for consent. "In the first place, always be simple in everything you do. Never laugh loud, for instance, and never make unnecessary movements with your hands and eyes. A lot of girls never get married because they have no friend to tell them that. In the second place, of course, never drink liquor or smoke. When girls do that, it's hard to recognize them for girls. And third and most important . . ."

At this point Mississippi Corey had hysterics. Brush was never to forget those ten minutes. There was weeping and laughing and gasping for breath; there was choking over a

glass of water; there was lying down on a hammock and falling off a hammock. When at last the girl's sobs were under control, she was leaning on the parapet above the water, clutching Brush's hand and exclaiming: "Aren't I *terrible* to act like that in public! I think I'm terrible! But, honest, I'm not mad. I like to be told my faults. Goodness! I don't know what you'll think of me!"

Brush carried her down the steps to the dock and placed her in the canoe. For a time they paddled about the middle of the lake in silence. Mississippi washed her face. She seemed to regard herself as permanently dependent upon Brush's guidance. When he finally deposited her upon the shore, the campers were already beginning to seat themselves under the trees about the fire, and were singing of their own accord. "Working on the Railroad" was trying to drown out an upstart "Indian Love Call." Some boys were trying to amuse the company by throwing lighted flashlights from hand to hand. Brush excused himself and withdrew to clear his throat and gargle. He had asked to be first on the program, because he liked leaving an audience in the midst of its applause, in order to take a walk and savor the strange excitement that never failed to invade him after he had sung in public. When the program began he announced his selection: " 'Oh, for the wings of a dove,' by Felix Mendelssohn-Bartholdy, 1809–1847."

This pedantry and the title of the song threatened to endanger its reception, but soon all was going well. Brush then sang " 'The Lost Chord,' by Sir Arthur Sullivan, 1842–1900." He then bowed twice and disappeared among the trees. The audience settled down to prolonged applause and, when their singer failed to reappear, began to clap rhythmically in triple beats crying "We—want—MORE! We—want—MORE." The entertainment director anxiously darted among the tents and trees, hunting for his singer, but Brush hid himself behind the canoeshed until he heard the announcement that the Reverend Mr. Kedworth would give a little philosophy talk on "Smiles," and then moved on. The squares and lanes of the camp were empty in the moonlight. He stopped before the shelf of books in the social-room, but there was no Encyclopædia Britannica, and he moved on. He looked in the window of the house marked "First Aid"; a doctor in a white coat was reading by a

lamp. He was tempted to enter and engage him in a professional conversation, but, feeling an unaccustomed lassitude, he turned away and went on up the hill. There he came upon the brightly lighted windows of the kitchen. An army of young men and women were still washing the dishes of the week-end crowd. These were college students working their way through the summer. This was a thing he knew all about. Filled with happy excitement, he entered and offered his services. He was given a dishcloth and assigned to wiping glasses at the side of a gray-eyed girl, who immediately made a great impression on him.

Chapter IV

Further good times at Camp Morgan. Important conversation with a girl named Jessie Mayhew. Dick Roberts' nightmares concluded. George Brush refuses some money.

A TOURNAMENT was taking place in the kitchen. The students were being made to sing the songs of the various colleges from which they came. The girls at the silverware-sink sang the song of Texas Wesleyan. Then a man and a girl at the cups and saucers table sang "Wisconsin, thy halls are ever fair." Then the gray-eyed girl who was working beside Brush was called upon for the song of McKenna College in Ohio. She made a speech first, saying that she had no ear and no voice, but that she would do what she could so as not to be an exception. She turned out to be a monotone, but her manner and her sportsmanship were so pleasing that she received an ovation. Then came a man from Georgia Tech. and a girl from Missoula. Then a Swedish cook, who had never been to college, but who had cooked for the students at Uppsala, sang one of their songs. Then a demand arose for a song from the superintendent. No one had liked her very much, but from this evening, when she had turned very red and did what she could with the Goucher College song, opinion turned in her favor. Then the newcomer, George Brush, was called upon. He sang his Alma Mater so beautifully that all the workers held their breaths; he, however, went on the while swiftly and silently polishing glasses. The workers crowded about him, dishcloths in hands, asking him how long he was staying in the camp. Presently the superintendent called for silence by beating on a dishpan. "It's nine o'clock," she said. "At this rate we'll never get done. Hurry, everybody; let's finish up as soon as possible." Whereupon there followed a last ten minutes of concentrated work.

Brush whispered to the gray-eyed girl, "Can I call on you now?"

"What did you say?"

"Can I pay a call on you as soon as we're through?"

"Why . . ." she began, hesitatingly, . . . "why, yes."

"I'd like very much to talk to you."

They worked on in silence. At the signal for release there was a wild rush for the door on the part of those who wished to claim the canoes reserved for the workers. The superintendent crossed the room and, holding herself very straight, said to Brush: "I have a place vacant, if you'd like to stay and work in the dining-room."

"Thank you. I must leave tomorrow noon," he said, his eyes anxiously fixed on the back of the gray-eyed girl, who was going out of the door.

When he caught up with the girl he said, "Would you like to sit on the bench at the end of the pier?"

She did not answer. He saw that she had changed her mind and was hunting for the words with which to excuse herself. He said, abruptly and with unexpected intensity: "I know you must be pretty tired after all this extra work at the week-end, but I wish you'd make an exception for me. I'd rather call on you tomorrow, only I must leave before noon, and I guess we both have a good deal to do in the morning. So as a great favor would you let me call on you now?"

She looked at him. "We can sit in the clubroom," she said, briefly, and led the way to the farmhouse that had been set aside as a dormitory for the waitresses. The house, as they approached it, was in a state of bedlam. Girls' voices could be heard calling from room to room. "Louise, lend me your sandals." "You won't need a sweater; you'll die in it." Several young men were waiting at the steps. A girl appeared at a window on the second floor and called out, "Where's Jessie?"

"Here I am," said the gray-eyed girl, quietly.

"Jessie, honey, can I borrow your bandana?"

"Yes. Only, do be quiet when you come in, Hilda."

The parties went off in a shower of excited conversation, and the house promptly fell into a profound silence. Jessie led Brush into the clubroom on the first floor. It was fitted out with the cast-off furniture of the social rooms farther down the slope: a card-table one of whose legs was mended with adhesive tape, a dilapidated leather center, some kitchen chairs. It

was in great confusion. Jessie began mechanically putting it in order, gathering up the pillows, motion-picture magazines, ukuleles and tennis rackets. She sat down on the couch and began untying the ribbon that bound her hair.

"What's your name?" she asked.

"George Marvin Brush. I was born in Michigan. I'm a traveling salesman in school books. I came to this camp to see a man on business. This evening I asked if I could help in the kitchen, because I like to be where students are and where people are working. I've had to do that kind of work almost all my life."

Jessie leaned far back on the couch, slipped the ribbon off her hair, and shook her head from side to side. She listened to Brush with abstracted self-possession. "You have a fine voice," she said. "Everybody hoped you were going to stay on and work here."

"I wish I could."

"Won't you sit down?"

"Thank you."

Jessie rested her head on her elbows and looked at the ceiling. The pause that fell was so alarming to Brush that he broke it by moving his chair forward a few inches and beginning with gravity: "I live traveling around on trains all the time and I meet a lot of people, but almost everybody I meet depresses me really terribly. Why, just this afternoon and evening in this camp I've met the most depressing people and it was beginning to have a bad effect on me. And then I saw you and I knew at once that you were a very fine person, and I can't tell you what a difference it made. So this talk we're having is very important to me; and as we haven't much time, you being so tired and everything, I want you to forgive me if I seem to be pretty personal on so short an acquaintance. I want you to know who I am and what I'm like so that I can write letters to you."

Slowly and a little guardedly Jessie began to sit up straight. She now fixed her eyes on his, full of surprise, but without fear or repugnance.

"There's no one in the whole world that I get any pleasure writing letters to," he continued. "So when I meet a person as

fine as you, I don't want to lose the chance to know you better. And so that we can get to be . . . almost friends, I want to tell you who I am and what I'm interested in. Is that all right?"

Jessie blushed slightly. "Yes," she said.

"Well, as I said, my name is George Marvin Brush. I'm twenty-three years old. I graduated two years ago from the Shiloh Baptist College in Walling, South Dakota. I'm a Baptist and I'm pretty religious. I grew up on a farm in Michigan. . . . Can I ask you to tell me a few things like that about yourself?"

The girl drew in her chin abruptly, as though she were about to make a rude answer. She thought better of it, however, and said, with only a touch of curtness: "My name is Jessie Mayhew. I'm twenty-two years old. I'm a senior at McKenna College in Ohio. When I graduate I'm going to be a teacher. I'm Methodist."

The gray eyes looked coolly into the blue.

"Can I ask you . . . have you a father and mother?"

"No," said Jessie. After a pause she added, with assumed casualness: "I was brought up in an orphanage and then I was adopted by some people who died. I've supported myself since second year high school."

"I guess we're pretty much alike in some ways," said Brush. The ticking of the alarm clock on the mantel filled the room. "There isn't much more to tell about me. I grew up on the farm. I've got a father and mother and two brothers, both older. One of my brothers went away to be a sailor; the other's still on the farm. I go back and see them Christmas, but . . . you know, I feel like an orphan, too, almost. I love'm, of course, but always there is a kind of wall between them and me. You see, they didn't want me to go to college." He scanned her face to see the effect of this severe indictment. "So I worked my way through, just as you've been doing. You'd know that I'm not bragging when I tell you that I got the highest grades of anybody, and I was captain of track and basketball. I'd have been captain of football and baseball, too, only, working all the time, I didn't have time for practice and I had to drop them. I know without your telling me that you get high grades."

"Yes," said Jessie, reddening again, "I got all A's."

Brush smiled. He smiled very seldom. "Before I ask you to

let me write you letters," he continued, "it's only fair I tell you my faults. I think you ought to know that there are some things about me that are hard to like. What I mean is that people are always getting mad at me and . . . even disgusted. But before I tell you my faults, I want you to know that since my conversion I haven't done anything bad *intentionally.* Naturally I haven't told a lie, except one, when I told a man that I'd once been to New York City. The next day I went back to the town where he was and told him I hadn't. And my other faults, like saying things in a temper and being tight with money, I've always apologized for those pretty soon after."

"Why do people get disgusted with you?" asked Jessie.

"Because my ideas aren't the same as other people's. For instance, I was put in jail the other day because they didn't like my ideas about money." Whereupon he told the whole story of his arrest in Armina, adding to it accounts of his theories of voluntary poverty, pacifism, the punishment of criminals, and the story of his previous incarceration. "But even when I don't get taken to jail," he concluded, "I've always been called crazy. Do you see what I mean."

"Yes."

"Does that make you think I'm an . . . an inconvenient sort of person to know?"

"No."

"I don't mind my friends telling me once in a while that I'm crazy—as a joke, you know—but do you think . . . have you begun to feel like calling me crazy in earnest?"

"No," said Jessie. "I don't care anything what other people think. I like people to be different."

"Then I want to tell you about the three big secret disappointments in my life. They're getting to be less and less all the time, and when I can tell them to a person like you I see that they have no reason to be important at all. The first one is . . . is that at college the fellows never elected me to one of the three literary societies. I was the top student in the whole college and I was the captain of my teams, but they never elected me to Philomathian or Eunostia or to the Colville Society. I used to feel pretty badly about that; I used to wonder why they couldn't stand me. And the second disappointment, Jessie, was something that one of my teachers said to me. He was my

prof. in Religion A 6, and I admired him more than any other that was there. I used to take questions to him at his house and I thought he liked it. He used to get mad at me often, but just joking mad. You know how it'd be. But one time he got really mad. He said: 'You've got a closed mind, Brush, an obstinate, closed mind. It's not worth wasting time on you,' he said. 'I wash my hands of you,' he said; '*you'll never get anywhere!*' Imagine some one saying that! 'Now go away,' he said. 'Get away from me. Don't trouble me any more.' You know that was awful to me. Sometimes it comes back to me still, like it was the moment he said it, and the sweat—I mean the perspiration —comes out on my forehead. I don't want to live if I've got a closed mind and can't get anywhere—anywhere in *thinking*, I mean. But I don't believe what he said any more. I keep getting new good ideas all the time. I learn things as I go, at least that's the way it seems to me. As to the third disappointment, I don't want to tell you that just yet, but I'll tell you some day. But, Jessie, I don't want to give you the impression that I'm miserable or anything; because, really, at bottom, I'm the happiest man I've ever met. Sometimes it looks like everyone's unhappy except me. Just today in this camp I met such a mess of unhappy people that it began to get me; and then I saw you and I felt better right away." There was a pause, at the end of which he added, lamely: "So . . . I guess . . . that's how it stands."

Jessie said, without sharpness and with the beginning of a smile, "You do talk a lot."

"I know," he agreed, eagerly, "but I had to talk fast for lots of reasons." He gazed enthusiastically at her face a moment, then rose and said: "Will you let me give you a present to remember me by? This wrist watch is brand new and it's the best one I've ever had."

Jessie moved off the couch quickly. "No, no," she said, "I never like to have presents from people. I never like to. It doesn't mean I don't like people . . . but I don't like to take presents from them. Thank you just the same, though. Now, Mr. Brush, we're not old friends, and I don't like you to pretend we are. I'm interested in what you're saying about yourself," she added, seeing how crestfallen Brush had become. "I

didn't say what I said in order to send you away, because I like what you've been saying."

"Will you tell me a few things about how you grew up?" asked Brush, sadly returning the watch to his own wrist.

Jessie remained standing. She began to walk back and forth, as though to mark the casualness of what she chose to say. "Well, as I told you, I'm an orphan. I was found in a field. First I lived in an orphanage. That was near Cleveland, Ohio. Some people think I look Slovak. I don't know and I don't think it matters. When I was ten I was adopted by an old German shoemaker and his wife. They both died and ever since second year at high school I've supported myself by working in a hotel. I'm majoring in Biology and some day I'll either teach Biology or maybe I'll try to be a doctor."

"You don't believe," began Brush, fearfully—"you don't believe in all that about evolution, do you?"

"Why, yes, of course I do."

Brush almost whispered: "You don't think the Bible'd tell a lie, do you? Do you mean you can't see there's a difference as big as the whole world between a human being with a soul and a monkey jumping around in a tree?"

There was an awful silence. Then Brush put another fateful question: "You don't believe in women smoking cigarettes, do you?"

Jessie stopped and looked at him. "Do you think such things are important?"

"Yes, I do—terribly important."

"Well, I don't. I hardly smoke any, myself, but I like to see women doing things that show they can be taken just as seriously as men are." Her eyes remained on him. She saw how crushed he was. "I'm surprised that you're the kind of person that still thinks such things are important. I was just beginning to think you were the only young man I ever met who wasn't silly."

Brush continued to look at the floor. He said: "My vacation comes in November. Can I come to McKenna College and see you then?"

Jessie began walking up and down again. "You can do what you like, I guess," she said. "It wouldn't do any good, though.

There wouldn't be anything to talk about, if you have ideas like that. Besides . . . I live by myself. For these years, anyway, I'm *enough*, just myself. Besides, I haven't really got time for any new friends. Ever since sophomore year I've been head waiter in the dining-hall, and the rest of the time I study."

"But can I come?"

"Yes, you can come, like anybody else."

"I mean . . . would you go for a walk with me? Or have dinner or something?"

"Yes."

"Well, good-by," said Brush, putting out his hand.

"Good-by. I don't know why you're acting so serious. I've only known you an hour and a half. You look as though you'd lost your last friend."

"All I want to do now is think, so I'll say good-by."

"Good-by."

He went out into the hall, full of thought. Then he turned with sudden energy and said through the door: "Will you promise to think about it, at least? I don't see how a fine girl like you can believe that the Bible tells lies and that we come from monkeys, and that it's all right for girls to smoke cigarettes. What becomes of the world if we let all those ideas into it? What good is living in the world if we become like the foolish city people that believe things like that? Why . . . why you'd just be an ordinary person if you had ideas like that!"

"I'll think about it," said Jessie, wearily and a little bitterly, as she went back to the task of straightening the room. When that was done she went up to her room and sat down. She laid her arms firmly along the arms of the chair and stared at the wall in front of her. From time to time she muttered, "He's crazy." Then realizing that there was no sleep for her, she changed her shoes and walked around the lake.

Brush returned to the tent "Felix" and went to bed. He had hardly fallen asleep, however, when he became aware of a great tumult. He awoke with a start. Dick Roberts was thrashing about on his cot. In a choked voice that increased every moment in volume he was crying out: "I can't . . . I can't . . ." In the vague light that entered the tent from the moonlight outside, Brush could see the other occupants who had raised themselves on their elbows and were angrily turned towards

Roberts' cot. "What the hell's going on here?" they were saying.
"Who's throwing a fit, for God's sake?" Dick Roberts' son was
wailing, "Papa, papa . . ."

Brush jumped out of bed and, seizing Roberts' hand, began
to pump it up and down. "Hey, Roberts! Hey, Dick Roberts!"
he called, adding to the others: "It's nothing, fellas. Just a night-
mare. It's all right. . . . Hey, Roberts, y'all right?"

Roberts sat up and wiped his forehead. Then somberly and
in silence he leaned over and began putting on his shoes.
Brush hastily put on his shoes and trousers.

"Golly! what a row!" grumbled one of their tentmates.

"Sorry," said Roberts, and picking up his bathrobe started
to leave the tent.

"Papa, where y' goin'?" asked his son, in terror.

" 'Sh! Go to sleep, George."

"Papa! I wanta come."

"No, no. You go back to sleep."

Brush picked up a blanket and followed Roberts out of the
tent. He caught up with him in the dusty road that led
through the camp. Roberts was standing with lowered eyes in
the moonlight; he was perfectly still and seemed to be thinking
of something remote and profound. Brush stood and waited.

"You go on back," said Roberts, in a whisper, still without
raising his eyes. "I'll find somewhere to sleep down by the
shore here."

"Don't you think you'd better get your pants on? We'll go
for a walk."

"I wouldn't go back to that tent for a million dollars."

"It doesn't hurt what those fellas say. What does it matter
what people say?"

"I want to be alone," said Roberts, turning abruptly. He
continued down the hill. Arriving at the water's edge, he took
a paddle off the rack and pushed a canoe into the water. Brush
did the same. Roberts whispered, savagely: "Beat it! Get out of
here! I want to be alone, I said!"

"I must go wherever you go," said Brush.

Roberts started to direct his canoe toward the center of the
lake. He beat the water first on one side, then on the other. The
canoe wheeled in circles. Roberts became distraught with rage
and began shoveling the lake furiously. Brush's canoe glided

out like a seal. He pointed it in another direction, tactfully, as though he had come out for a meditative hour in the moonlight. Roberts lost his paddle. Brush drew near. "I'll get it for you," he said.

"No! No! Get out!" cried Roberts in hoarse whispers. "What the hell is this, anyway? I'm not crazy yet. I don't need a guard to follow me around. I'm not crazy."

"Mr. Roberts, I'll be quiet. I won't trouble you. I just want to make sure you're all right."

Roberts stared at him a moment, then began plowing the lake again. His canoe turned over and in a moment he was noisily swimming towards shore.

"This is getting complicated," muttered Brush, shepherding canoe, paddle, and swimmer. When he reached land, Roberts was trying to dry his pajamas by shaking himself and by wringing out the folds. Brush replaced the canoes and the paddles. "Wait a minute," he said. "I'll get you a towel." The bathhouse was locked, but Brush vaulted the board fence. He found some sour and blackened towels on the floor and threw them over the partition. When he vaulted back he found an old and nervous night watchman waiting for him with a flashlight.

"That's all right, boys," mumbled the watchman. "Have your fun, only don't make any noise."

"Borrow his flashlight," said Brush, "and go back to the tent and get your clothes on."

Roberts seized the flashlight, but before he started off he breathed, hoarsely, at Brush: "Go away! Get out! I want to be alone, I tell you!"

"I can't. I promised I'd follow you everywhere."

The night watchman shuffled along behind them: "Have all the good times you want, boys, only quiet," he said.

When Roberts emerged from the tent he was dressed. He held his automobile key in one hand and, running and stumbling, he started for the large field where scores of automobiles were drawn up in ranks. Brush ran along beside him. "If you don't take me along," he said, breathlessly, "I'll have to get some other people to help me."

Roberts was trembling so he could scarcely fit the key into the lock. Brush jumped upon the running-board, pleading

with him. The motor started and Roberts savagely turned the handle that closed the window where Brush's hand was resting. Brush ran to the First Aid house and burst in upon the doctor. "Doc," he cried, "lend me your car, quick! There's a man here who I think may be trying to commit suicide."

"What? Wait a minute. I must get some one to take my place."

"I can't wait. I may lose him. Give me your car key."

They hurried out together. "What's the matter with him?" asked the doctor.

"He's . . . well, he's just not happy," explained Brush.

Roberts had taken some time in extricating his car from the ranks, and Brush started out eagerly after the dim red tail-light speeding through the lanes of the forest. Morgan's Wood was a vast checkerboard of roads. Rustic benches and tables had been set at intervals among the scrawny trees, and occasionally cement fireplaces had been built. Towers of scaffolding, roughened with carved initials of thousands of visitors, rose above the tree-tops, furnishing lookouts for sight-seers and fire wardens. Occasionally a boarded-up refreshment stand stood beside the road, like a vast piano-box in the moonlight. As Brush overtook Roberts, the latter gave him a glance and stepped on the accelerator. They drove abreast for a time, shouting at one another, their cars lurching from side to side. They suddenly emerged into the main street of Morganville. Roberts was in need of gas and drove up to the still lighted garage. Brush, avoiding Roberts' sudden turn, swerved to one side and struck a hitching-post in front of the Depot Hotel. There was terrific din of shaken metal and shattered glass, and in the silence that followed it one wheel slowly and drunkenly crossed the street, looked about for a bed, and lay down.

Some white-clad figures appeared on the second-story porch of the hotel. Judge Corey's voice called out, "Who's dying down there, folks?"

"Judge, this is George Brush. Can I see you a minute?"

"Are you all right, boy?"

"Yes."

"Side door's open, Jim. Come up and have a drink."

"I don't drink."

"Come up, anyway, Jim. It's a great big free country."

Brush dashed up the stairs and burst into the room. "Judge," he said, breathlessly. "I want you to lend me your car . . ."

"Jim boy, you just had one."

"I know, but we gotta save a man from killing himself."

"Where is he?" asked the Judge, looking alertly into the hall. "Say, buddy, we can't have any of that around Camp Morgan. What's the matter with him, anyway?"

"I don't know, Judge. He's just not . . . happy."

"*Not happy?* Is he nuts?"

"No . . . it's . . . it's business, partly. It's the depression."

"Jim," said the Judge, angrily, "now don't you go mentioning the depression. That's what causes all this. Don't you say that word again. Where is the fella?"

"He's getting gas at the station next door."

"All right." The Judge turned and clapped his hands. "Folks, we're going for a ride in the woods. Say, Bush, Bough, Beach— By the way, what's your name, Jim?"

"Brush, George Brush."

"Brush, I want you meet these princes. This is Helma Solario, the best little trouper you could hope to know. Jeannie Socket, Bill Watkins, Mike Kusack. Girls, fellas, shake hands with Bush, friend of my daughter. By the way, Jim, you made a big impression."

"We must hurry, Judge. Really."

"My husband runs that garage," said Helma Solario, a plump black-eyed little woman, in an advanced stage of negligé and intoxication. "Mike, run down and tell him not to give the guy any gas." She went out on the porch and gave further instructions from there. "Bring the dope in here. We'll give him something to live for. Does he play poker? Ask him?"

"Come on, girls, we'd better go after him ourselves," cried the judge.

Brush descended the stairs, four at a time, and caught sight of Roberts driving off. The poker party followed in high spirits. They all climbed into the judge's car. Helma Solario sat on Brush's lap.

"This baby's alive, anyway," said Helma, tickling his ear. "Where do you come from, sweetness?"

"Michigan," replied Brush, peering anxiously into the forest at the right and the left of the road.

"All right, Michigan, when you find this guy tell him life's a big thrill. See? Tell him to stick around; we're going to have some more world wars. He'll love it. Tell him from me the depression's only begun. Next year's going to make this year look sky-high."

"You pay a fine for that," said the judge.

"Has he a family and kids?"

"Yes," said Brush.

"Sure he oughta wait around awhile until his kids grow up and call him an old boob. Why, he doesn't know the half of it yet. Old age is great, too, tell him."

"Now that's enough, Helma," said the judge.

"All right, tell him about the family life and old age of Judge Leonidas Corey. No one can ever say you aren't happy, can they, Leon? Just one damned million after another."

Brush saw Roberts' car drawn up in the undergrowth. "Stop the car, Judge. I've found him. Listen. I can do this alone from now on. Thanks a lot for bringing me here. I won't need you now."

"I want to talk to the fellow," said the judge.

"That'd be the last straw," said Helma. "God! Leave it to Michigan here. Good-by, baby. Tell him life's a big thrill."

The party drove off, leaving Brush still carrying his blanket, to peer about the woods for his friend. The car was empty. The surroundings lay in deep shadow. Brush listened carefully and heard nothing. Finally raising his eyes, he saw Roberts standing on the highest platform of one of the watch-towers. He went over to the foot of the tower and stood looking up.

"Damn it," said Roberts, "there you are again! Go away! Go on home!"

Brush did not answer. He waited for half an hour. Finally Roberts laboriously and awkwardly climbed down the ladder.

"It's getting chilly," muttered Brush. "You might want this blanket."

Roberts stared at him a moment, then started towards his car.

"I'm not going to let you get in the car," said Brush. "I'm stronger than you are."

Roberts began walking through the bushes, with Brush six feet behind him. This journey went on for over an hour. At times they found themselves at the lake's edge. Once they suddenly entered Morganville, where Roberts sat down for ten minutes on some one's front steps while Brush stood out in the middle of the street, tactfully gazing into the distance. Then plunging back into the forest again, they roamed through the clearings. Coming upon one of the picnic havens, Brush cleared his throat and said:

"Why don't you lie down here and get some sleep?"

"I tell you I never do sleep. How do I know I'll ever be able to sleep again?"

"It's two o'clock. I think you'll be able to sleep. I'll build a fire."

Roberts turned and again began stumbling through the trees. Brush caught up with him and seized his arm firmly. "You're not going any farther," he said, in a loud voice. "And you're not going to think any more about these things. I know what you're thinking all the time, and you've got to stop it. The world isn't as bad as you think it is . . . even if it looks bad. Now you lie down on that bench or table, wherever you like. I'm going to make a fire and sit here till morning. If you can't sleep, never mind; just look up through the trees. I shouldn't have let you tramp around with your head full of thoughts like that."

He laid the blanket on one of the benches. Roberts stretched himself on it and turned his contorted face away. After collecting several piles of dry sticks, Brush laid a fire according to the rules that had once gained him a badge in Ludington, Michigan. He sat down and looked into it. He asked, in a low voice: "Can I sing? Do you mind if I sing?" There was no answer. He began to sing softly. He tried "Far above Cayuga's Waters" and "The wings of a dove." He sang "Lie down, little croppies, lie down," and "Cowboy, go back to the hills." From there he went on to almost everything he knew. Finally he must have nodded, for he awoke with a start to find that day was breaking. The birds were beginning to make interrogative noises in the trees. He saw with surprise that an apparently cloudless sky could suddenly reveal itself as covered with soft pink clouds. As Roberts was snoring, Brush nodded off again. When he

awoke, Roberts was looking at him. Without saying a word, Roberts picked up the blanket and started off. He was pale and embarrassed. They returned to the camp in silence and went to bed in the tent "Felix."

Brush was a little late for breakfast at table M. He found Judge Corey alone.

"Jim, how did it go?" asked the judge.

"He's all right today, Judge."

"You're a prince, Jim. We couldn't have a thing like that happen at Camp Morgan. The doctor came and told me about it. Don't you worry about the car."

Jessie Mayhew stood by Brush. "How do you like your eggs?" she asked.

"Jessie," said the judge, "you give the fella the best of everything the camp's got. Nothing's too good for Jim. . . . My wife and daughter tell me you have a fine voice, too. Jim, young fella, lean your ear over here. I want to ask you something: When are you leaving camp?"

"Sometime this morning."

The judge paused, then began in a cordial and confidential tone: "Jim, young fella, you made a big hit with my daughter, a big hit. I know that little girl and it's not every man that interests her, no, sir. Now listen. I want to give you a little tip. Just between you and I, see? . . . just man to man. That girl ought to have a nice home of her own. See what I mean? You might say she ain't really happy up at our house. Jim, thirty-five thousand dollars goes with that girl. Yes, sir, if she can find a good home, thirty-five thousand dollars goes with her. Depression year, too. Think it over. Yes, and what's more, I'm in a position to settle a young man in some good job around the Capitol, too. Well, that's just between you and I. . . . How does it appeal to you, eh?"

Brush turned scarlet. Jessie Mayhew had been placing his cereal and coffee before him. He glanced at her face. "I . . . I hope she finds a good home, Judge," he said.

"Yeah, yeah. Well, think it over, boy, and in the meantime I'll see your school books get a high place. Yes, sir."

Chapter V

Kansas City. Queenie's boarding-house. First word of Father Pasziewski. George Brush drunk and disorderly.

BRUSH no longer regarded the farmhouse in Michigan as his home; he had no home, and for that reason when his itinerary brought him to a town or city where he had already made friends, he looked forward to the visit with a more than usual expectancy. Kansas City contained one of these substitute homes. Queenie's—Miss Craven's—boarding-house was a high, narrow, blackened edifice, standing amid the similarly blackened hulks of former mansions near where Eighth Street crosses Pennsylvania and Jefferson Avenues. Here a colony of rooming-houses barely maintains its existence, though near the center of the city, holding out, its broken windows patched with newspaper, its yards full of weeds and overturned bathtubs, against the last invasion of negro gamblers, cats, and the night quartering of tramps. Queenie's back windows overlooked a cliff strewn with bottles and automobile tires descending to a waste of railroad tracks and the sluggish soot-covered river.

Brush ran up the steps and rang the bell. Queenie came to the door with a mop in her hand.

"Hello, Queenie!"

"Why, Mr. Brush! I'm glad to see you."

"Are any of the fellows home, Queenie?"

"Seems like I heard'm all go out. You can go up and see. Will you be staying here tonight?"

"Yes, Queenie, I'll be here three nights."

"Well, I'll come right up and make your bed. Looks even worse'n usual up there, Mr. Brush, but you know how it is. They say they'll kill me if I clean up any, beyond just making the beds. I wish you'd persuade'm to let me come up and clean around."

"I'll try. Is there any news?"

"Let me think. Mr. Morris got his pay cut over to the hospital; yes, and Mr. Callahan got reduced, too."

Brush descended a few steps: "Has Herb been drinking bad, Queenie?"

"Well, you know I never know what goes on, but I think he's been drinking some. I don't know how it happened, Mr. Brush, but the whole banister come off the staircase the other day. And Mrs. Kubinsky—lives next door—said she saw somebody hanging by their finger nails to the gutter on the roof one night, only he was pulled back at the last minute. 'T's a wonder they're still alive after five years, Mr. Brush, if you ask me, because they're at death's door once a week; that's no zaggeration."

"I know," said Brush, with concern. They looked at one another. Brush added: "We've just got to work on them slowly, Queenie. Never say die. How's Father Pasziewski, Queenie?"

"He's pretty good. He's back on the job again. He takes the seven and nine."

"The kidney trouble just blew over?"

"They think now it was gall stones. Mrs. Kramer gave him some water from the River Jordan and he put it in his tea every day and it melted 'm down. I was over to the St. Veronica Guild, serving, and Mrs. Delehanty said that with him, if it wasn't one thing it'd be another, she said. He's not long for this world, she says."

Brush climbed the stairs to the top floor, which his four friends had rented from Queenie in perpetuity. Most of the doors had long been smashed, and after lying about as boards had finally disappeared in smaller and smaller fragments. Several partitions between the rooms contained holes, opened up in some historic rough-house, and now offering the testimony of their splintering edges and crumbling plaster. A smell floated about, made up of foul clothes, antiseptic soap, gin, and lemon-peel. Brush sat down on one of the beds and looked sadly about him. Here lived Herb and Morrie, two newspaper men; Bat, a mechanic in sound pictures; and Louie, a hospital chemist who in hard times had been obliged to descend to the duties of an orderly.

Brush's friendship with these tenants reposed upon a complicated treaty. On his part, Brush promised not to harangue them, unless invited, on religion, temperance, chastity, and tobacco; and they in turn promised to remain within reasonable limits of decency in conversation and in the invention of practical jokes.

The cement of this precarious friendship lay in the fact that Brush carried a wonderful second tenor and that the practice of singing in parts constituted their chief pleasure. Brush could do things in the refrain of "Wasting in despair" that threw his companions into an ecstasy that was almost anguish. On the first note at the close of the refrain "If she be not fair to me-ee," he would rise an octave in soft portamento and, holding the note, pass from a whispered falsetto to a golden fortissimo, then, as the three other singers, pale and shaken, moved on to the second note, he would stride majestically down the chord into the bass register. He could phrase "Far above Cayuga's Waters" so that it seemed to allude to some infinitely sad leave-taking, years ago, probably in the depths of a forest, with discouraged horns blowing in the distance. It required all this proficiency, however, to hold the group together. The treaty was drawn up abruptly on the night of Brush's first visit to the boarding-house. He had knelt down beside his bed to say his prayers.

"Either you drop that or you keep out of here forever," they said.

"Well, if I don't do it," he replied, darkly, "remember it's not because I'm a moral coward."

"Oh, get out of here!" cried Louie. "Get out and stay out! Go to hell!"

But the thought of "All through the night" intoned *mezzo-voce* returned to them; they swallowed their anger and the treaty was drawn up.

Brush now sat on the bed and sadly reviewed the problem presented by the room before him. Queenie entered with the linen.

"If I clean up now, will you protect me against them, Mr. Brush?" she asked, doubtfully.

"Can you do it tomorrow, Queenie. I don't feel awfully well. I'm going to take a nap."

"You don't *feel* well? Where do you feel bad?"

"It's not anything special. I'm just sick of hotels and trains. I'm sick of lots of things."

Queenie respected dejection. She moved quickly about the bed-making. At last she said: "I've got a coffee-pot on the stove, Mr. Brush. It might peck you up a bit."

"No, thanks," he answered, gazing at the ceiling. He was

suddenly surprised to hear himself saying, "Did you ever wish you were dead, Queenie?"

Queenie was immediately aroused. "Now don't you say that! Why, I'm ashamed to hear you say things like that, Mr. Brush. I once said something like that in confession in Spokane, Washington, and Father Lyons almost bit my head off. It's not like you, either."

Brush smiled, abashed. "I was only joking, Queenie. It just jumped out."

"A healthy young man like you, with a fine tenor voice."

Queenie stood by with further reassurances until she noticed that Brush had fallen asleep. She took a step forward, looked at him narrowly a moment, and tiptoed downstairs. As she entered the front hall the door was noisily flung open and Louie rushed in.

"Hello, Queenie!" he cried. "Hitch up your pants, Queenie; the depression's over. They've found a plan to make the ocean fresh water. You'll love it."

"Now don't you go making any noise. Mr. Brush is up in your room, asleep. He's kinda sick, he says."

"What? Jesus sick? Well, well! Say no more. I know how to cure him."

Louie dashed upstairs and had a look at the patient. Brush woke up.

"How the hell did you catch it?" asked Louie, drawing up a chair before him.

"Catch what?"

"You've got it. Fever B-17. Let me feel your pulse."

"I'm all right."

"There's no doubt about it. B-17. Percipient influenza. Where could you have picked it up?"

"Oh, let me alone!"

"Take your choice, immediate recovery or two weeks in bed —and not in this house, either, by God!"

"Aw, just leave me alone, Louie! What's the remedy like?"

"Get over on your own bed—polluting my pillow! You're a stink-hole of germs. I ought to report you."

"What's the remedy like?"

"When did you begin to feel funny?"

"I don't know. Today, yesterday."

"Had any lunch?"

"No."

"Lie down; lie down. I'm going back to the hospital to get the medicine. Queenie'll bring you up a big lunch. Eat as much as possible. You're not supposed to take this medicine on an empty stomach."

"I don't think I've got anything the matter with me."

"What do you know about it? I don't spend my life in hospitals for nothing. Here I am trying to do you a favor, and you go yipping around that you're all right. You're a sick man."

Louie fell down the stairs to the telephone. He was very excited and began calling joyously in all directions. He shared his plans with Herb and Morrie and Bat, and then tore over to the hospital. The idea grew and flowered. By three o'clock several doctors in white coats had climbed Queenie's stairs and held long conversations in German and Latin. A temperature chart had been hung on the wall. Sputum and urine had been put through precipitates. At half-past three the patient, awed and flushed, was sitting up in bed, eating T-bone steaks and creamed potatoes. From time to time he was told to hold his nose and take a swallow of the medicine which stood beside him in a large jar.

"You fellows are princes to go to all this trouble," he said, grinning shyly; then catching sight of Queenie, who was peering anxiously into the room from the landing, he called out: "That's all right, Queenie. I'm better already."

"Now hold your nose again, and drink a lot," commanded Louie. "Dr. Schnickenschnauzer, of Berlin, says you should drink it slow, but the Vienna fellas say you should drink it fast. How do you like it?"

"I guess it's all right."

"Now lie down a minute before you finish it."

"Will I sweat much?"

"Sweat? Baby, your very toe nails'll sweat. You'll steam like a lake in the morning."

"That's good, because I think I'm full of poisons. Up to a month ago I never had a sick day in my life, but lately I haven't been right. It's doing me good already, Queenie."

"I hope so, I'm sure, Mr. Brush."

Queenie had been forbidden to enter the room, but she now

managed to sidle in. She went to the medicine-jar and sniffed at it. She turned abruptly and cried out with indignation: "You boys ought to be ashamed of yourselves. I'm ashamed of you doing a thing like that. I suspected you was doing something all along."

"Queenie," said Herb, "you get outa here or we'll break every bone in your body."

"Don't you touch me! I'm ashamed of you all. I've a good mind to put you out of my house."

Herb and Louie picked her up in a sitting position and began to carry her to the stairs. Brush gave a roar and jumped out of bed. He seized hold of her and began to pull her back. For a moment Queenie was being bandied about like the star of an acrobatic troupe. Brush was blazing with energy and vigor. He hurled Louie into a corner and restored Queenie to her feet.

"I'll kill the first person that touches Queenie!" he cried. "Speak up, Queenie. What is it you want to say?"

"You don't know it, Mr. Brush, but just for a joke those boys . . . those boys have gone and made you drunk."

"What!"

"That's not medicine; that's just liquor. That's rum."

Brush let his breath out slowly in astonishment. He lowered his voice: "Am I drunk, Queenie?"

"You go put your head under the tap and it'll pass, most likely."

He sat down on the bed and tried to think. He glanced up somberly at his tormentors; "It's lucky for you I'm a pacifist. If I were a different kind of person I'd break every bone in your body. So this is being drunk. . . . When am I going to begin to do queer things? . . . Herb, you stand out here and tell me about it."

"Aw, George, it's nothing. You'll like it."

"When am I going to see things double? When am I going to start breaking things—banisters and things?"

"You're not going to break things, you poor fool! What d'ya mean? You're not drunk."

"Well, I'm something."

He rose and began striding about the room, shaking his head sharply. He stopped and stood looking at himself in the mirror, frowning. Then turning, he declared, in a loud voice:

"Anyway, I can't just stand here and be drunk. Now it's done it can't be helped. I'm even glad it happened, so long as it was accidental like this, because now I'll know what they're talking about all the time. So now let's go somewhere and do something." Here for the fun of it he began lifting tables and chairs with one hand, exclaiming: "Look't this. Look.—Herb, come on and try and throw me. I feel like a rough-house. I won't hurt you, any of you. I'm a pacifist, but I feel like a rough-house. I'm the strongest man ever tested in our gym back at college, and I can polish off any cigarette-smoker in ten minutes. Come on! Why don't one of you call me cuckoo? Tell me I'm crazy."

"Aw, dry up, dry up! Let's get the hell out of here. This guy makes me sick," said Bat.

"Let's go out and go places," said Brush. "Let's do something." Suddenly an idea struck him; he turned majestically to Queenie. "Queenie—Queenie Craven—here's five dollars. We are going out. While we are out you get Mrs. Kubinsky who resides next door, and you two clean these rooms like they were—was—offices in a bank. This place is going to be clean for once. You fellows live like hogs and it's gotta stop. You hear me? It's gotta stop! You're the most aimless, shiftless sons-a-bitches in the world. Drink, drink, drink, that's all you do. No wonder you get your salaries cut. Now get out and leave these rooms for a cleaning, because tomorrow you bastards are going to begin your lives all over again."

"Poops to you!" muttered Louie. "Herb, I'm clearing out."

"Stick around. He's only begun. . . . Queenie, if you do, I'll kill you."

Brush leaned forward and lifted Herb by the seat of his trousers. Herb fell on his face. Brush placed his heel on his shoulder blade and began turning it. "Take that back," he ordered. "Go on! Go on! You give the order to Queenie yourself."

Herb caught him by the ankle and threw him. The building shook. All five were in the whirlpool now, but Brush only blazed the more with strength and confidence. He worked his way to his feet and began tossing the tenants against one another, kneading the pile playfully.

Bat struck his funny bone against the floor and fainted. He was resuscitated in great pain. "Gee! I'm sorry," said Brush. "Honest, I apologize. I apologize for all those things I said, too. I didn't mean to hurt your feelings. I guess I'm . . . drunk, you know, or I wouldn't have. . . . Is it getting better?"

Bat lay down on the bed, holding his elbow.

"Let's sing to him," said Brush, and soon the quartet was leaning over the bed, their arms about one another's shoulders, closing in on some diminished sevenths.

"No more harmony for me," said Herb, "until I get some more of Dr. Schnickenschnauzer's in me."

"Then hurry," said Brush. "And I guess I'll have a little more, too. This is the only time in my life that I'll ever touch alcohol, so I'd better be sure I really touched it. I'm going to get it over with, once for all."

They had already had a good deal, but now they fell to for good measure.

"We'd better go down to Queenie's sitting-room, so as not to be in the way of the cleaning." For Queenie and Mrs. Kubinsky had entered with a battery of mops and pails and had begun stacking the furniture. The men gave three cheers each to Queenie and Anna Kubinsky, "the belles of Eighth Street," and went out.

Some sort of great journey took place that night. Rain came on and then the evening, but the party tramped up and down the hills of Kansas City, ran through the parks, and fell rattling over the cliffs. They climbed monuments. They entered newspaper offices and rebuked the press. They swept like crusaders through the lobbies of motion-picture houses. They defiled the City Hall.

The next morning Brush woke up and lay for a long time staring at the ceiling. He felt wonderfully well.

"Louis," he said to his roommate, "did I break anything yesterday?"

"No. Why?"

"Did I insult any passers-by—any women?"

"Not that I know of. Why?"

"I just wanted to know."

He got up and began to shave. It was his custom while shaving to prop up before him a ten-cent copy of *King Lear* for memorization. His teacher at college had once remarked that *King Lear* was the greatest work in English literature, and the Encyclopædia Britannica seemed to be of the same opinion. Brush had read the play ten times without discovering a trace of talent in it, and was greatly worried about the matter. He persevered, however, and was engaged in committing the whole work to memory. Now while shaving he boomed away at it.

Herb came in.

"What's the matter, big boy?"

"Herb, was I really tight last night?"

"You certainly were."

"Was I all those things? Was I stewed and boiled and pie-eyed?"

"Yeah. Why?"

Brush examined himself in the mirror, rubbing in the lather. "I've heard about them so much. I just wanted to know."

"Well, what did you think of it?"

Brush leaned against the wash basin and examined the floor. "I don't quite know yet," he said. "All I can say is, no wonder they made prohibition. I didn't know liquor was like that. You know, I felt I was the greatest preacher in the world and the greatest thinker in the world. It made me feel as though I was ready to be the greatest President of the United States. I forgot I had any faults in my character."

"Sure, that's the idea. Baby, you've only just begun. You'll have lots more yet."

"Mmm!"

"Well, listen, big boy. I've got a date for you. Yeah, just the kind of date you like."

"What do you mean?"

"You're always looking for a fine girl, aren't you? You know, to be the mother of your children?"

"You're just wasting your time, Herb. It doesn't get you anywhere to make fun of such things with me. Save your breath, Herb."

"I'm not kiddin' ya. I'm not kiddin' ya. What the hell are you so damned sensitive about?"

"I don't trust you when you try to be serious, Herb. Save your breath."

"Oh, all right, then. Here I come with a perfectly good invitation to go out to Sunday dinner in a nice home with a lot of beautiful girls in the house and you poop all over me. They've got money, too. The nicest girls in Kansas City."

"How'd you meet'm, Herb?"

"Insult me, will ya? Insult me."

"I didn't mean that as an insult. I just asked you."

"You don't know me, George. I've reformed. I'm a serious fella. In fact, if you must know, I'm courting one of these girls. I want to marry and settle down."

Brush kept his eyes on Herb's reflection in the mirror and went on shaving. "Where do they live?"

"MacKenzie Boulevard. Swell mansion. They've got money. Louie and Bat and I got asked to Sunday dinner today, and I told'm about you and they said bring'm along. It's Sunday dinner, big boy, and there'll be lots of eats. . . . Well, make up your mind. It's twelve o'clock now and I gotta phone Mrs. Crofut how many's coming."

Brush watched him in the mirror. "Herb, do you promise before God that there's no catch in this?"

"Oh, you give me a pain. Stay home; stay home! Go and eat at the wagon. I hope it chokes ya. I told Mrs. Crofut we'd sing for them. Stay home and spoil the quartet if you like."

"I'll come," said Brush, and returned to his *Lear.* "*When thou clovest thy crown i' the middle, and gavest away both parts,*" he cried, "*thou borest thine ass on thy own back o'er the dirt.*"

"What?" asked Herb. "What's that?"

"I wasn't talking to you. *Thou hadst little wit in thy bald crown when thou gavest thy golden one away.*"

A few minutes later Herb returned. "Well, since you made me promise, George, perhaps I ought to tell you there's a little catch in this . . . just a harmless joker, see? . . . I told'm you were a famous singer, see? They're all excited about it. They think you're a famous singer, like on the radio. A concert singer, and famous."

Brush's answer was composure itself. "That's not a lie," he said. "There must be five thousand people in this country who've been thrilled by my singing at one time or other. That's

not a lie." Herb fled from the room, but Brush followed him to the door, razor in hand, and shouted after him: "Why, just the other night at Camp Morgan they were spellbound. I didn't know the human hand could clap so long. I don't say that because I'm conceited, because a fine voice is just a gift. Tell Mrs. Crofut I'll be glad to come."

Chapter VI

Kansas City. Sunday dinner at Ma Crofut's. More news of Father Pasziewski. A moment of dejection in a Kansas City Hospital.

M RS. CROFUT certainly lived in a very fine house. If it had any faults at all, it was that the paint lacked freshness and that it was too closely hemmed in by a business college on one side and an undertaking establishment on the other. But apart from that, Brush agreed, it was a very fine home. It rose above the street in a mass of towers and gables and bays and porches. It had not always belonged to Mrs. Crofut—though the Crofuts were a very old family—because the horse-block on the curb said Adams. For some reason a dilapidated electric signboard lay half hidden in the rhododendron bushes; it said: "The Riviera. Cuisine Française." The boys entered without ringing the bell, and Brush found himself in a dark hall. He was curious about everything and, pushing aside some reed por-tières at the left, he saw a large room filled with small tables, as though it had once been a restaurant.

"Well, boys, how are you?" said a large, honest voice emerging from the back of the hall. "This is fine."

"Mrs. Crofut," said Herb, "I want you to shake hands with George Brush, the singer."

"It's a pleasure; and let me tell you we've been looking for-ward to it a lot. I declare, my daughters have been dolling up for hours. Let's go and sit in the day parlor until my girls come down," she said, alluding to a whispering and twittering of joy-ous young voices upstairs. Brush glanced up the great stair-case, past the stained-glass window, and saw a laughing face peering down between the posts of the balustrade. "Come in here and tell me what you've all been doing with yourselves."

Mrs. Crofut sat down with casual elegance in a huge rattan chair and beckoned them to seats about her. She had a fine large red face surmounted by a carefully built up head of yellow hair. A row of small yellow curls crossed her forehead. She wore a black silk shirtwaist covered with jet beads, and a gold watch

was pinned over her lungs. She was an enormous woman, but her waist was remarkably small and she carried her vast bulk with a constant attention to grace. Brush liked her at once and could scarcely take his eyes off her. She was joined a few minutes later by a tall thin girl, likewise with yellow hair.

"This is my girl Lily. . . . Aren't you the bold one! . . . This is Lily, Mr. Brush."

Lily stood squirming and giggling by her mother's chair, staring at Brush.

"Lily's the musical one," continued Mrs. Crofut. "Very sweet voice."

Serious conversation was interrupted by the entrance of a military parade of five more young ladies. They were all of about the same age, sixteen to eighteen, and were very shy and modest. One was a tall dark girl of foreign origin. All of them had one trait in common, a certain vagueness in the eyes, as though it were difficult to focus the glance on a single object. Introductions were not easily gotten over with. There was much staring and blushing and suppressed giggling.

"You have a lot of daughters, Mrs. Crofut, I'll say," said Brush.

"Lord! have I! And this isn't all, by any means, is it, Herbert? The fact is the older girls are eating by themselves upstairs; this is just what I call my kindergarten. You see, Mr. Brush," she said, with intimate complicity, "perhaps they aren't *all* my daughters; some of them merely make their home with me for the time being. Dolores there is a Cuban girl. Dinner's ready now, so let's go in. Go in, go in, girls. What's the matter with you today? They're as nervous as witches about meeting you, Mr. Brush, that's a fact. They're not themselves."

The company passed through several sitting-rooms and came to a large dining-room at the back of the house. Mrs. Crofut stood behind her chair and directed matters in a large way. "There are thirteen of us," she said, "so May has to sit at a table by herself. We drew lots and May's the goat." May, blushing with confusion and pleasure, seated herself in the bay window and took a drink of water. "Now, Mr. Brush, by rights, you ought to sit by me, but I'm just an old woman and I'm going to set you down among my girls. The girls all want to sit by

you and I'm not going to show any favoritism, so suit yourself.
I see Herb's going to sit by Gladys, as usual."

Brush did not stop to pick and choose. He found himself
between the Cuban girl and a girl called Ruth. Ruth was a soft-
eyed girl with brown hair. She wore a simple white dress and
scarcely dared raise her eyes from her plate. A number of awk-
ward silences fell during the soup. There was a good deal of
unabashed staring. Brush felt he had never seen so many beau-
tiful, quiet girls in one place before. Mrs. Crofut drank her soup
with great refinement; with one bejeweled hand she pressed a
corner of her napkin to her bosom. From time to time she
sipped from a tumbler containing a tonic. As the plates were
being removed, anticipation could no longer contain itself and
the quartet was called upon for a number. They linked their
arms about one another's necks, cleared their throats, frowning,
and entered upon "How can I bear to leave thee?" The recep-
tion was all that vanity could desire. They followed it with
"Wasting in despair," leading up to the famous specialty ca-
dence. The hostesses were lost in admiration and were greatly
solemnized. There was no giggling after that. The quartet sat
down, itself filled with awe, and the girls almost shuddered to
find themselves seated next so much achievement. Mrs. Crofut
collected herself first:

"Have you lived long in these parts, Mr. Brush?" she asked.

"No. My home is in Michigan."

"You don't say! I had a friend . . . Did you ever know a
Mr. Pasternak there? He was engaged in the lumber business.
He was very well off, really very well off."

"I . . . I don't remember him now."

"You don't? Well, he was a perfect gentleman and I believe,
as I say, very well off. It was lumber, I remember now. His
name was Jules,—Jules Pasternak." Whereupon she leaned far
back in her chair and laughed long and heartily. "Oh," she con-
cluded, wiping her eyes, "I hadn't thought of him for years."

No further information was offered about Mr. Pasternak, but
his warming image had passed through the room and hence-
forth there were no more alarming silences at the table. Lily
was sent to push back the curtains at the window.

"Very lovely girl, isn't she?" said Mrs. Crofut.

"Yes indeed," said Brush.

"Lovely girl. She was on the stage for a while."

"Was she?" asked Brush, looking at her with even greater interest. "Was she ever in anything by Shakespeare?"

Lily looked timidly at Mrs. Crofut. "Speak up, dearie. Were you?"

The answer was almost inaudible, but it was "No."

"I guess Mayme would know more about that," continued Mrs. Crofut. "Mayme's a great reader. Nose always in a book. Mayme's our red-head."

Mayme's red head was turned by this praise; she was suddenly seized by a desire to show off. In a high voice rendered hoarse by nervousness she screamed, "I read a story by him just the other day."

"Really," said Brush. "Did he write other things besides theater plays?"

"Shakespeare?" cried Mrs. Crofut, eager to support her daughter. "Why, he wrote every kind of thing. We've got one of his upstairs. Gladys, you're by the door. Run upstairs and get the books."

Her glance rested on Gladys' back as she left the table. "I like that type, don't you? Very pretty girl."

"Yes, indeed," said Brush.

"Lovely girl," repeated Mrs. Crofut.

Gladys returned with the books and went back for another that had fallen on the stairs. Their title pages were anxiously consulted. Everyone laughed at the thought that Shakespeare could have had a hand in "The Care and Feeding of Infants" or a bound volume of *Ainslee's Magazine* for 1903. *September Morn at Atlantic City* gave no author's name and *Barriers Burned Away* was attributed to E. P. Roe.

"There!" cried Mrs. Crofut, tapping the back of the novel with a jeweled forefinger. "I could have sworn that was by Shakespeare. I don't know how we could have come to make a mistake like that." Whereupon she went into gales of laughter, politely flinging her napkin over her face while she laughed. The girls laughed softly, proud to see their mother thus at her best; their doe's eyes passed softly from face to face, making sure that everyone was appreciating it.

"Well," she said, finally, "I guess we all like a good play. Mr.

Shore, did you ever see Lillian Russell? . . . Sit up straight, Pearl."

"No," said Brush, as soon as he realized that he was being addressed, "I don't think I ever did."

"Oh, she was fine! *Beautiful* girl."

Lily's voice was raised in a sudden scream. "Ma looks just like her." The other girls burst out into shrill corroboration. Lily continued: "Her room's-covered-with-pictures-of-her. Ma-tells-us-all-about-her. Ma-looks-just-like-her."

Mrs. Crofut lowered her eyes. "Well, people did use to say . . . but, of course, it was just foolishness. But let me tell you she was a very fine actress, and I may say, a very fine woman." Then lowering her voice and looking solemnly into Brush's eyes, she added, in a tone implying that only he would understand all the implications of her remark, "I never heard a word, not a word, against her reputation."

"That's fine," said Brush, deeply impressed.

Mrs. Crofut made a rapid transition to the conversational tone. "Herb," she said, "you haven't been around to see me lately. Where've you been keeping yourself?"

"It's the depression," said Herb. "Now I have to go to George Washington Park."

Mrs. Crofut threw up her chin loftily. "Well, be common if you want to. It's none of my business."

Herb made an answer that Brush did not understand.

"Now, boys, none of that," replied the hostess. "Eat your dinner. Just good clean fun today. We're having a good time. Just eat your dinner."

This was the first of a number of strange things that began to happen. Brush became more and more confused, but pinning his faith on Mrs. Crofut, whom he liked with increasing force, he bore up as best he could. A policeman sauntered into the room without removing his hat. He was greeted by cries of, "Hello, Jimmy." He took a certain liberty with one of the young ladies sitting near him.

"Now don't go behaving like that, Jimmy," said Mrs. Crofut. "There's a surprise package for you in the kitchen."

"You don't say," said Jimmy, and disappeared from the scene.

The next unexpected thing was caused by Dolores. Brush

had tried to engage her in conversation several times. On each occasion she had raised sullen eyes to his face for a moment, muttered a few words, and returned to her meal. The third time, however, she rose abruptly to her feet, overturning the chair behind her, and slapped him smartly across the face. She then ran to the door, turned, hissed and spat in his direction, and ran down the perspective of drawing-rooms.

Mrs. Crofut was horrified. She rose and followed Dolores through the room, screaming: "Go upstairs, Dolores. Go upstairs, you slut. You're a nasty slut. I'll give you something to learn you a lesson!" Then returning breathless to her place, she said: "Why, Mr. Shore, I'm so ashamed I don't know what to say. Imagine a thing like that! Here we were, having a nice home-like Sunday dinner, and that girl has to behave like that! However, don't give it another thought. These things will happen. Now we'll forget all about it. Tchk-tchk! You see, Mr. Shore, I have my troubles, like every one else."

"Yes," said Brush. "But you have what they call a silver lining. I never saw a home with so many nice and good-looking girls in it."

"Thank you," said Mrs. Crofut, sitting up very straight and getting a little more ruddy. "That's a real compliment coming from a great singer like you. I do think they're pretty nice girls, if I do say so myself."

"Wow!" cried Morrie, and bent his head to the floor, coughing and choking.

Mrs. Crofut rose, trembling with rage. "Now you behave yourself, young man. I don't care what you think and I don't like the way you're laughing. I don't care *what* you think. Answer me! Do I, or do I not, keep a careful eye on my girls? Do I, girls?"

"Yes, ma," said six tinkly voices.

"Answer me, Morrie!"

"Aw, ma, you get me wrong," said Morrie. "I wasn't laughing at you. I was laughing at Brush here."

"Well, if you had the gentlemanliness that he has, you wouldn't be making a fool of yourself in public places. Here we are, all friends, eating together and . . . and you have to bring in ideas like that. It doesn't give a very good idea of the home you come from, I must say."

"Mrs. Crofut," said Brush, "I'm sure he didn't mean to hurt your feelings. He's a very fine fellow, and I don't mind if he laughs at me."

Mrs. Crofut sat down slowly, still glaring at Morrie. A shocked silence fell upon the group. The girls sat with lowered eyes; one of them cried for a moment and then hurriedly brushed away her tears. But the affair had not blown over. Mrs. Crofut rose again and, pointing emotionally at Morrie, said:

"Come, tell me! What did you mean by that laugh? I won't have things like that said about me. I won't have it. Either I'm like a mother to these girls, or I'm not. Do I keep an eye on them, or don't I?"

Suddenly Herb's voice, flat and contemptuous, said: "Quit the high horse, ma. Who do you think you are?"

Now Brush stood up in his place, white with rage: "Herb, if you try that kind of thing I'll take you right out and turn the hose on you. I didn't know you were so crude. You've got a long way to go before you're fit to associate with people that live in homes.—Excuse me, Mrs. Crofut, and I apologize for *him*, too."

"That's all right, Mr. Shore," said Mrs. Crofut, who had sunk back into her chair and was sniveling into her tonic. "I don't expect any decency from a fellow like that, I'm sure."

"Come on," said Herb, "come on and fight it out, you goddam simp, you. Come on outdoors and fight it out."

"There's no use your fighting with me, Herb. You're as weak as water. Your cigarettes have done for you. You saw that last night."

Bat went over to Herb. "Sit down, Herb. Sit down. We'll tell him later. It's all right. We'll tell him later."

This altercation was followed with the liveliest interest by the young ladies. It brought the colored cook to the door, where she stood meditatively picking her teeth. When it blew over there was a general air of disappointment in the room.

Brush said, gravely: "I guess the best of friends quarrel every now and then. It doesn't mean that they're any the worse persons; it only means that human nature isn't raised up yet to what we hope it's going to be. I'm really very fond of Herb and I'm sorry I spoke to him that way. Sometime the day's

coming when there aren't going to be any quarrels, because in
my opinion the world's getting better and better. And in spite
of this little thing that's happened, today has been an example
of it. I want to thank you very much for taking me into your
home this way. Most of my life is spent on trains and in hotels
and I appreciate it; so I want to do something for you in re-
turn. Generally, I don't believe in going to the theater, and es-
pecially not on Sundays. But I think I know when to make an
exception, and can see when nobody's really harmed by it. I
want to invite you all as my guests to the movie around the
corner that opens at four o'clock."

"Well, now," said Mrs. Crofut, "that's real nice of you.
Girls, would you like to go to the movies with Mr.——"

"Brush."

"With Mr. Brush?"

There were squeals of enthusiasm.

"Now, Mr. Brush, I can't go myself, but my girls accept with
pleasure. Let me whisper in your ear a minute. Mr. Brush, I don't
want the girls to be any expense to you. I'll give them each
some pocket money and they'll pay their own. You can pay for
one, if you like."

"But, Mrs. Crofut, I *asked* them. I *want* to pay for them."

"No, no. I know better. All boys your age have quite a time
making two ends meet. You save your money."

Brush submitted to this arrangement and presently he was
proceeding down the street in a twitter of young feminine
voices. His companions walked with an exaggerated primness,
waving their hips delicately from side to side. They all talked at
once, each trying to get his agreement to any thought that oc-
curred to her.

Everything interested them. They followed closely an edu-
cational reel depicting the Vale of Cashmere, and another that
showed a Boy Scout congress and a train wreck. The President
of the country spoke a few words and they all agreed he was a
very nice man. The principal picture on the program was pa-
thetic, and they all cried happily and generously. Brush's hand-
kerchief passed back and forth among them. It was about a
beautiful girl threatened by the dangers that lurk in great
cities. It was full of suspense. The girls sitting beside Brush in-
sisted on clinging to him; he found himself holding two hot

convulsed hands on his knees. When Brush returned the girls to their home each one in turn flung her arms about his neck and printed rouge on his cheeks. Each declared she had enjoyed it very much and would be waiting for him to come again. She'd be waiting.

Brush was so dizzy with well-being that he was obliged to take a long walk to calm himself. "It just goes to show my favorite theory that the world's full of wonderful people," he said to himself, "if you know where to look." When he returned to Queenie's it was almost nine o'clock. The disarray on the scrubbed top floor had begun again. The rooms were billowing with Sunday papers. The tenants sat about with their heels above the level of their heads. They were in a sour humor.

"Well, baby," said Herb, "you had a great time, eh?"

"I certainly did."

Herb asked an obscene question. It was taken up and furthered by the others.

Brush stared at them in consternation: "You fellows promised not to pull that kind of thing."

"All promises are off," said Herb.

Brush stood still for a moment, then dragged his suitcase out of the cupboard and began packing.

"You've had a pretty good two days," said Herb, "all told. Pretty good for you. You got so cock-eyed drunk on Saturday that you puked on the War Memorial, and on Sunday you raped a whole cat-house. Pretty fast, kid, pretty fast."

Brush raised his eyes and looked at him, but said nothing. Herb let him have it again.

"That's not true," said Brush.

"Not true? What do you know about it? Gad! you're the simplest galoot in the world. You're so simple, you stink."

Kneeling by his suitcase, Brush scarcely raised his eyes. "Were those . . . fallen women?"

"Fallen? You couldn't get'm more fallen."

"Herb, you promised there was no catch in it!"

"All promises went out with daylight-saving time," said Herb, dryly. He flung out the pages of his newspaper and went on reading. The room was silent. Brush began to cry. He jumped up with sudden passion: "It can't be true. They weren't. You fellows don't know what you're talking about. I

324 HEAVEN'S MY DESTINATION

say they're perfectly all right and that's the kind of thing I don't make any mistake about. You fellows can't say things like that to me, just because you . . . Listen, Herb, it can't be true."

"It's gotta be true," said Herb, coldly scanning the headlines.

Brush marched wildly up and down the room. Suddenly, with a shout, he picked up a chair and, pointing the four legs horizontally before him, crashed them through the windowpane.

Louie whistled. "Tz-tz-tz! Naughty!" he said.

Brush stood by the window, looking out over the housetops. "You fellows pretend you don't know what it's all about, but you know. You're just pretending. You spend your whole life pretending it's not serious. . . . I wish I were there talking to them now. . . . I'm glad I went. I thank you very much."

Herb arose and, hitching up his pants, took his place in the middle of the room. "Take off your coat," he said. "I've got an account to settle with you. Come on, take off your coat and fight it out."

"I don't fight, Herb. Hit me, if you like."

"You'll fight. You'll fight, all right," said Herb, advancing.

Brush raised his arms passively to defend himself. The others joined in. They threw him down and stamped on him. In a paroxysm of hatred they kicked him and threw him downstairs and left him on the pavement. Louie curtly telephoned his hospital, and the ambulance took him away, unconscious.

The next morning Queenie called on him in his ward. She entered, ill at ease in hat and gloves, and casting alarmed glances about her. Catching sight of Brush's head, almost entirely bound with bandages, she crossed herself, then sat down and gazed at him. Brush smiled at her, sadly.

"Here's your suitcase and purse, Mr. Brush. It musta fallen out of your pocket some way. They told me to bring it to you."

"Thanks, Queenie."

"Are you in any pain, Mr. Brush?"

"No."

"Why, you look all knocked about. What did you do to'm to make'm all set on you like that? I knew they were wild boys, but I didn't think they'd try to break your bones, Mr. Brush."

Brush did not answer.

Queenie began to cry. "I told'm to pack up their things and go. I told'm I didn't want no hoodlums like that in my house. I told'm to get right out."

"No, no, Queenie. You let them stay. I'll explain to you some day." There was a pause. "Are they packing, Queenie?"

"I told'm to, but I guess they aren't packing very fast. They just told me to shut up and get out. But I'll let 'em stay if you say so, Mr. Brush. With these hard times I don'o' who I'd find. Mrs. Kubinsky—lives next door—'s had four rooms empty ever since August."

Queenie's tears were drying already. A giggle began to appear. "I declare you look funny with that rabbit's ear on your head, Mr. Brush. I'm glad you're in no pain."

"This is the hospital Louie works in, isn't it?"

"Yes. I saw'm in the hall when I come in. I declare he didn't look natural in white pants and coat."

"What did he say to you?"

"Oh . . . mostly hello."

"When you go out I wish you'd tell him to come and see me for a minute."

There was a pause.

"How's Father Pasziewski, Queenie?"

"I told you, Mr. Brush. He seems pretty well again. Funny, your asking about him so much, because he always asks about you, too."

Brush almost sat up. "Does he? . . . How?"

"Yes, I told him a lot about you once and he's very interested in you."

Brush lay back and looked at the ceiling. "The kidney trouble just got better of itself?" he asked, softly.

"They think now it was gall stones and they were melted down by drinking tea with some drops of the River Jordan in it. Mrs. Kramer was saving it for the christening of her grandchildren, but we think now maybe there aren't going to be any grandchildren, so Father Pasziewski got the benefit of it."

"Some day . . . tell Father Pasziewski I . . . I think of him a lot."

"Yes, I will. Can I write a card for you to somebody, Mr. Brush?"

"No, Queenie . . . there's nobody."

Queenie went out. Later in the day Louie passed through the ward. Brush whistled to him.

Louie drew up beside the bed and whispered in his ear: "You give me the belches. Hurry up. What do you want?"

"Louie, sit down a minute. I want to ask you a question."

"Well, hurry up about it. I've gotta go and get some arms and legs."

"Louie, tell me what's the matter with me?"

"You've no brains, that's all. God didn't give you any brains."

"I know." After a breath or two he looked at Louie. "What ought I to do about it?"

"Sure. Snap out of it. Get awake. Get wise to yourself."

"Sure, I want to. I don't know how to go about it, that's all. . . . There must be something serious the matter with me, because that's the third time people have suddenly hated me. . . . I must have some kind of brains, though, because I just got a raise, even in a panic year . . . and my grades were good at school; they were the best."

Louie put his face close to Brush's ear. "You'll learn in time. I guess you'll find your place in time, see? Only don't come around us any more. We got our own ideas and our own lives all arranged, see? and we don't like to be interrupted."

"Did the fellows say that?"

"Yes. Yes."

"All right. . . . So I suppose this is good-by. Only, listen. If ever you fellows change your minds and want to sing some more, drop me a line, will you?—Caulkins and Company."

"Listen, George. You asked me what you could do. All right, listen. Get to be one of the fellas. Learn to drink, like anybody else. And leave other people's lives alone. Live and let live. Live and let live. Everybody likes to be let alone. And run around with the women. You're healthy, aintya? Enjoy life, see? You're going to be dead a long time, *believe* me."

Louie had not noticed that Brush was slowly rising to a sitting position. Brush's voice now rose in an answer that grew to a shout in the full open ward:

"You can get away and stay away," he cried. "If I ever became like you fellows I'd expect to be dead a long time. I may be cuckoo, perhaps I am; but I'd rather be crazy all alone than be

sensible like you fellows are sensible. I'm glad I'm nuts. I don't want to be different. Tell the fellows I'll never change——"

"All right. Pipe down!"

"And if they want to have me back, they must have me as I am, only worse."

By this time the nurse had run up with a hypodermic. "This is a mental case," she exclaimed. "Help me, Louie. He ought to be in the annex. Hold his arm, Louie."

"I'll take it quietly, nurse. I'm sorry I lost my temper."

"You've gone and upset all the patients. Look at them staring at you!"

"I want to say just one more thing, nurse," he said, and shouted after the departing Louie: "And if you must know, I'm not crazy. It's the world that's crazy. Everybody's crazy except me; that's what's the matter. The whole world's nuts."

Chapter VII

*Three adventures of varying educational importance:
the evangelist; the medium; first steps in* ahimsa.

O N being discharged from the hospital Brush set out again
on that long swing of the pendulum between Kansas City
and Abilene, Texas, that was his work. At Abilene he waited his
turn in the halls of Simmons University, McMurray College,
and Abilene Christian College. He visited Austin College at
Sherman, Baylor College at Belton, and Baylor University at
Waco. He visited Daniel Baker College and Howard Payne
College at Brownwood; he visited the Texas Teachers College
at Denton, Rice Institute at Houston, Southwestern Univer-
sity at Georgetown, and Trinity University at Waxahachie. He
looked in at Delhart and Amarillo. He went down to San An-
tonio to see Our Lady of the Lake and to Austin to place an
algebra at St. Edward's University. Returning through Okla-
homa, he visited the state university at Norman, the Baptist
University at Shawnee, the college at Chickasha, the Agricul-
tural and Mechanical College at Stillwater. He digressed into
Louisiana and called at Pineville and Ruston; he spent a soli-
tary Christmas in Baton Rouge. Arkansas tempted him to Arka-
delphia and Clarksville and Onachita. And everywhere on his
journeys he selected certain high schools in strategic positions
where the employment of his textbooks could serve as influen-
tial examples for smaller schools in the neighborhood.

Many unusual adventures befell him during these weeks. Of
the great number we select three that illustrate certain stages
in his education.

On the train that carried him from Waco to Dallas he occupied
himself with reading a second-year algebra that had recently
been placed upon the market by a rival publishing-house. Such
reading held for Brush an element of suspense. He lived in fear
lest some other firm bring out a better series of textbooks than
those issued by Caulkins and Company, a contingency that
would greatly impair the energy and serenity of his sales talk. He

knew that his books were the best books obtainable, because he had himself read them, done all the problems, verified the answers, translated the sentences, and compared the methods with the methods employed by all the rival books in good standing. At this moment he was discovering with considerable relief that Dr. Ryker of the Worcester, Massachusetts, high schools was fumbling badly with the problem of rendering negative fractions comprehensible to fifteen-year-old boys and girls; that Dr. Ryker had no skill in contriving attractive and stimulating problems about racing airplanes and the hands of clocks; and that Dr. Ryker had all too clearly helped himself to the superior inspirations of Dr. Caulkins. Brush was deep in these matters when he heard a voice say:

"Young man, have you ever thought seriously about the great facts of life and death?"

He looked up to see leaning over him a tall unshaven man of fifty, wearing a soiled linen suit. A handkerchief was stuffed into the band of his collar and his cuffs were protected by black cotton guards. He had a white-and-yellow waterfall mustache and black steely eyes.

"Yes," said Brush.

The man removed a newspaper from beside Brush and sat down. "Are you right with God—this very minute?" he asked, putting his arm along the back of the seat in front of him and his nose very close to Brush's face.

"Yes," said Brush, beginning to blush violently, "I try to be."

"Oh, my boy," said the other, with a strong vibrato and an odor of decaying teeth, "you can't answer that question as quickly as that. No one can. Being saved,—oh, my boy!—isn't as easy as being vaccinated. It means wrestling. It means fighting. It means going down on your knees." He took hold of the lapel of Brush's suit and fingered it disparagingly. "I can see that you're still entangled with the world's snares and shows. Boy, do you touch liquor?"

"No."

"Do you use filthy tobacco?"

"No."

The man lowered his voice. "Do you frequent loose women?"

"No," said Brush, expelling the poisoned air from his nose.

"Do you indulge in lascivious thoughts?"

Brush coughed.

"Yes, sir," cried the man. " 'Let him who thinketh he stand, beware lest he fall.' The trouble with you is you're puffed-up. You're stiff-necked. Do you know the Good Book?"

"I study it."

"What's Romans five one?"

" 'Therefore, being justified through faith, we have peace with God, through——' "

"No. No, it's not."

"I . . . I think it is."

"No. By faith. . . . Therefore, being justified *by* faith. . . ."

"Yes, I guess it is."

"You *guess* it is," said the other, producing a Bible and striking Brush sharply on the knee with it. "Is that the way to talk about God's word? You *guess* it is?—Philippians three thirteen?"

" 'Brethren, I count not myself to have apprehended: but this one thing I do . . .' "

"Yes, go on."

" 'Forgetting the things which are behind . . .' "

" '*Those* things.' "

" 'And reaching forth to those things which are before, I press toward the mark . . .' "

"I didn't ask for the fourteenth verse. Brother, you don't know it. You think you know it. You *guess* you know it. The trouble with you is you're shallow. You haven't even *begun* yet. Oh, brother, I've had great experience with suffering, sinning men and women, and I want to tell you it's not enough to say that you've been saved."

Brush's eyes began guardedly to look about him for another seat. The man raised his voice and waved his arms about:

"I've been in the vineyard twenty-five years, wrestling with the devil. Yes, the world's full of suffering, sinning brothers and sisters. But there's a way to peace and mercy. Why don't you take it? Why don't you stretch out your hand and take it, instead of sitting around in city clothes like a Pharisee . . ."

The man had now risen and was addressing the car. Brush started to edge out by his knees. "Running away from con-

science, eh? Can't face it, eh? You'd rather sit there and pass for perfect, I know."

Voices from the back of the car broke in on him. "Aw, shut up! Go to sleep!"

"Brethren, fire and sword can't frighten me as long as I have a message."

Brush took another seat and opened the algebra. He was blushing and his heart was beating quickly. The evangelist, under a gathering storm of resentment from his fellow passengers, continued to harangue the car, using Brush as an example of moral cowardice. He began striding up and down the aisle, retorting to the jeers of his listeners. Brush, furiously biting the inner sides of his cheeks, finally rose and, taking the evangelist's arm, firmly directed him to a seat.

"You don't do any good making them mad," he said, and sitting down by the aisle, penned the other in beside the window. The evangelist continued with fiery eyes to fling some charges over his shoulder, but the controversy died down and he fell to muttering and grumbling to himself.

At last Brush said, "May I ask you some questions?"

"Brother, I'm here to help you."

"Have you a church somewhere?"

"No, brother, I'm a wandering witness for the Lord."

"Do you set up a tent?"

"No. I help my laboring brothers out. I use their churches. I take services for them."

"What do you—what do you live on?"

The other turned and peered at him with great displeasure. "What kind of a question is that? Brother, that's none of your business."

Brush stared gravely back at him.

"However," continued the other, "I'll tell you. The Lord doesn't neglect his workers. No, sir-reee, no, sir. He touches the hearts of people here and there, sometimes one place, sometimes another. Money? What's money? Brother, I don't believe in money. Matthew six twenty-five. This minute, boy, I have one dollar between me and the birds of the air," he said, emptying his pockets and producing two dollar bills, a clergyman's railroad pass, and a soiled letter addressed to the Reverend James

Bigelow. "Two dollars between me and the fowls of the air. But am I afraid? No. I live by faith and prayer. Psalms thirty-seven twenty-five."

"Have you a family?"

"Yes, boy, I have a noble wife and six fine children."

It seemed, however, that Dr. Bigelow's wife had found it best to take a place as laundress in a Dallas hotel. At first it appeared that the six children were doing well in school. But gradually it came out that the oldest two boys had run away, another had joined the navy, and that one daughter was bedridden; that left two children doing well in school.

Dr. Bigelow's assurance was considerably diminished under Brush's questioning. When they arrived at Dallas, Brush gave him ten dollars and, with lowered eyes, shook hands with him and took his leave.

Another adventure of this order took place at Fort Worth. Brush was taking an evening stroll through the residential section of the city, preparatory to settling down at the Public Library over the Encyclopædia Britannica, when he noticed a sign in the window of a faded brick apartment-house: "Spiritualistic Readings. Mrs. Ella McManus, medium. Tuesday and Friday evenings or by appointment. Fifty cents." It was a Friday evening. Brush wandered about the house for a time, hesitating. Around the corner, in another window of what appeared to be the same apartment, he saw a card that read: "Varicose Veins Reduced: Consultation Free." Finally he decided to go in. He was ushered into an overfurnished parlor in which a number of women were already seated. Mrs. McManus introduced herself; she was a short, stout woman with an air of importance and bad temper. After a prolonged conversation about the weather the company adjourned to the dining-room and sat down about the table, holding hands. The lights were turned off and a gramophone played "The Rosary." Presently Mrs. McManus began to shudder violently, and an Indian chief named Standing Corn addressed the company through her lips. He gave a stirring description of the next world, following it with some words to earth-bound spirits exhorting them to courage and patience. He rapped on the table at command, threw a tambourine across the room and caused a picture to fall from the wall. He then offered to answer any questions put

to him. Mrs. McManus had already secured the names and birthdays of the visitors, and now required to hold in her hand some object belonging to each of the questioners. She took the wrist watch of the woman at Brush's right, a Mrs. Caufman, and clutching it passionately to her bosom, gave her messages of the most convincing nature, referring by name to a host of departed relatives, giving the hiding-places of lost objects, and offering advice on intimate matters. The next interview was of a more general nature. A widow wished for a few words from her husband. The message was comforting in the extreme, but the widow wept the whole time so heartbrokenly that she was scarcely able to muster sufficient voice to return thanks to Chief Standing Corn and Mrs. McManus.

Brush sat with lowered head and furrowed brow.

Mrs. McManus asked: "Have you a question to put tonight, Mr. Brush, across the veil that separates but for a time the living and the dead?"

Brush hesitated. Then he said, "I'd like to speak to Dwight L. Moody."

There was a long pause. It was broken by Mrs. McManus intermittently assuming a voice even farther in the bass than that employed by Chief Standing Corn. Mr. Moody said that he was happy. " 'Oh, so happy. Where I am all is peace. Peace like the world cannot give.' What would you like to ask Mr. Moody?"

Brush gazed darkly before him and did not answer.

"I have another message from Mr. Moody for you. He says: 'Take care of your health.' And he seems to wish to send you a word about some one you love . . . I think it's a woman. . . . Yes, it is, and her name begins with an M—an M, I think. Do you know who that would be?"

"No."

"Well, perhaps it's an R. It will come more clearly directly. He says do nothing hasty just now. Especially in the money way. Save, or put away in very conservative investments, he says. And wait. He says—I know our other friends here won't mind my repeating this personal word—there's a certain woman that's come into your life lately . . . rather on the blond side, I should say. . . . You should find out slowly whether she's a *true* friend or not. He says to be cautious in all letters you write. Now he's gone. No! he says to keep up your courage.

He's waiting for you up yonder. It won't be long, he says, because up there fifty years is like a minit."

"If that was anybody," said Brush, somberly, "it wasn't the Moody I meant. I meant Dwight L. Moody."

"I hope Chief Standing Corn didn't make an error," said Mrs. McManus, a little sharply. "Of course, there are thousands of the dead by the name of Moody."

The telephone rang in the parlor.

"Will you answer the phone, Mrs. Caufman," said Mrs. McManus, dreamily, "and ask the party to call later?"

"Mrs. McManus is in the spirit world," reported Mrs. Caufman, "and asks that you call later." Then after a pause, in a lowered voice: "Not now! Anyway, not now! Don't y'understand? . . . First lukewarm, then cold. Yes. And massage downward, not up; *down*. Yes. Yes." Then returning to her chair, Mrs. Caufman said, deferentially, "The gentleman says he will call later, Mrs. McManus."

Brush sat up straight.

At the close of the meeting the others brought out their half-dollars and were emotionally thanking Mrs. McManus, when Brush said:

"I can't pay you for this evening, Mrs. McManus."

"What do you mean you can't pay me?" asked Mrs. McManus, turning very red and marching toward him.

"I mean: I have the money and everything, but I can't pay you for something you haven't earned. If you tell me the name of some church you go to, I'll send the money to that church, but I can't give it to you."

"Now wait a minute," she replied, going to the door, shutting it firmly, and standing with her back to it. "Girls, I want you to wait a minute and hear this with me."

"I can't pay you for a fraud, Mrs. McManus. It wouldn't be fair."

"Did you say I was a fraud?"

"Well, Mrs. McManus . . . you know you are. I couldn't help hearing Mrs. Caufman at the telephone. That showed she was an old friend of yours. And all that about Dwight L. Moody. I couldn't pay you for that."

Mrs. McManus turned coldly to Mrs. Caufman. "Cora," she said, "phone for the police. Mr. Brush, if you try to leave the

room I'll scream so the whole house'll be in here. . . . One minute, Cora. I'll phone, myself. It's too late to get out of it now, young man. I'll sue you. I'll sue you for everything you've got. I *thought* you were phoney, sitting there with that . . . that pie face of yours. I thought it was funny, a man of your type coming to a meeting like this, instead of tending to your own business. The minute you came in that door, I said to myself you were phoney. You and your Moodys! Well, it's the last time you'll insult me."

"I want you to call the police, Mrs. McManus," said Brush, "so they can warn other people against being given wrong ideas."

Mrs. McManus flung open the door majestically. "Now go!" she cried, "and never put your silly head in my door again. Girls, I want you to look at this man closely. If ever you see him again interfering with anybody, I don't care who it is, I want you to have him arrested. Look at him well! Do you see him?"

"Yes," said the terrified girls.

"Here I am doing a good work . . . as best I can, to the limit of my abilities . . . and that doubter, that atheist,—for that's what he is, an atheist. . . ."

Still Brush did not go. He stood in the doorway, lost in deep thought, his eyes resting on Mrs. McManus. At last he slowly put his hand in his pocket and drew out half a dollar.

"I guess I'd better give you this, after all," he said, slowly, "since I stayed. But I don't see how you can do it, Mrs. McManus. What I don't see is, what goes on in your head while you're making up these things. I mean, I don't understand how people *can* tell lies for long at a time. . . . I guess it's just human . . ."

"I don't want your money!" screamed Mrs. McManus.

Brush laid the money on the table and continued talking, half to himself, "I've got a lot to learn yet, I see."

He said good night to each of the ladies by name and took a long walk through the suburbs of Fort Worth, thinking the matter over.

The third adventure took place in a small town in Arkansas, Pekin. Brush called in the evening on a family, the Greggs, whom he had met on a previous trip. He arrived just as the younger

members of the family were setting out to attend a church so-
cial. He accepted their cordial invitation to go with them, and
he and Louise Gregg started off, stopping on the way to pick
up a former English teacher of Louise's in the grade schools, a
Miss Simmons. Miss Simmons turned out to be a vivacious
elderly lady, given to more affectations than Brush could have
wished. Their destination lay on the other side of the railroad
tracks, and crossing the waste of rails, they could see the
brightly lighted windows and wide-open door of the Sunday-
school rooms. It was a bright moonlight night and the three of
them stopped among the switches to admire the red and green
signal lights in the near and far distance and to catch the sound
of some singing voices that were approaching along the ties.

"Let's go along," said Miss Simmons. "It's those Cronin
boys."

The Cronin boys recognized their former teacher and began
inserting into their song a muffled version of an obscene nick-
name that had been attached to her for thirty years.

"Good evening, Bill. Good evening, Fred and Jarvis," said
Miss Simmons.

They returned a mock deferential "Good evening, Miss
Simmons," but, suddenly aware of their recent release from
the long and hated years of schooling, they grew bolder and
began in falsetto to address one another as Miss Simmons,
with the epithet, and with the invention of new material.

Brush walked over to them and in a changed voice said,
"You fellows have got to apologize for that."

"Who says so?" asked Bill Cronin, putting his hand in his belt.

Miss Simmons called: "Oh, Mr. Brush! Oh, Mr. Brush!
D-don't speak to them. The Cronin boys have always been
impolite, rude boys."

"I do," said Brush. "You apologize to Miss Simmons right
now."

Bill Cronin made a further remark, and Brush with a wide
sweep of his arm struck him behind his left ear and knocked
him down. The other two drew back a few steps and stared at
their brother. Bill groaned and twisted on the tracks. Then
rose on all fours.

"Apologize to Miss Simmons, all three of you," said Brush.

Bill Cronin mumbled an apology and the other two joined in.

Brush rejoined his companions. "I'm sorry about that," he said.

Miss Simmons was hysterical. "I think they're *terrible*. They always were terrible. . . . I think I must sit down."

Whereupon she sat down on the tracks. Brush fanned her with his hat. Over his shoulder he looked at the Cronins.

Bill was sitting on the ground. His brothers were leaning over him, whispering. Finally they lifted him up, and supporting him between them they guided him unsteadily toward the town.

"I'm all right now," said Miss Simmons.

"Are you sure?" asked Brush.

"Oh yes, I'm all right now."

"Then if you'll excuse me, I'll . . . be back in a few minutes," said Brush.

He caught up with the Cronins, who had sat down to rest on the platform of the freight station.

"How do you feel?" he asked. "I didn't mean to hurt you bad."

They were silent, avoiding his earnest glance.

"I don't believe in hitting people," he continued. "Do you think you're hurt any? . . . Did it give you a headache?"

There was another silence. Bill Cronin grunted and put his feet on the ground; the other two put their shoulders under his arms and the three began hobbling off.

"After all," continued Brush, "that was a pretty dirty thing you said about Miss . . . Miss What's-her-name. You know you oughtn't to do that. Won't you shake hands, Cronin?"

Bill Cronin, with bent head, mumbled something, and the march continued.

Brush called out: "If there's any doctor bills, I'd like to pay them. You can get my address from Louise Gregg."

When Brush entered the Sunday-school rooms he was met with great acclaim. Miss Simmons had fainted away on her arrival and the whole story had been retold many times. Everyone was talking at once: "It's time some one gave those boys a lesson. . . . They're just the biggest rowdies in town. . . . He's been sent to the penitentiary once already and now he ought to go again."

Brush accepted the tributes in silence. His face had turned

very red. The minister could not put the chivalrous act out of his mind. An hour later, during the refreshments, he made a speech, calling attention to the qualities in George Brush of a "true gentleman." He concluded by saying:

"Mr. Brush, won't you say a few words to us?"

Brush, deeply troubled, stood up and fixed his gaze on a light at the end of the room. He was thinking so hard that he seemed to forget where he was. At last he said:

"If I can help it, I don't like to contradict anything that a minister says . . . but I've been thinking about what happened out on the tracks, and I ought to say to you all that I'm sorry I did it. I'm really a pacifist and I don't believe in striking anybody. In the first place, it's too easy. And now that I hear that the Cronin boy has been to the penitentiary, I feel still worse about it."

"But—but, Mr. Brush! The man was rude to Miss Simmons. I understand that what he said was almost an insult."

Brush kept his eye on the light and said, slowly: "It's a hard thing to think clearly about. . . . I guess we ought to have let him insult her. You see, Mr. Forrest, the theory is this: if bad people are treated kindly by the people they insult, why, then they start thinking about it and then they become ashamed. . . . That's the theory. That's Gandhi's theory."

Mr. Forrest said, sharply: "When a lady's insulted, Mr. Brush, it's no time for a gentleman to talk about theories. You know what we think of Southern womanhood down here. We don't agree with you."

Brush brought his eyes back from the distance and fixed them on the minister.

"Well, I think the world's in such a bad way that we've all got to start thinking all over again," he said, with mounting force. "I think all the ideas that are going around now are wrong. I'm trying to begin all over again at the beginning." He turned to Louise Gregg, and said: "I've hit somebody today and I'm not fit to be here, so I'll say good-bye, Louise. I guess I'd better go."

He took his hat off the rack in the hall, and crossing to the middle of the railroad tracks, he stood for a long while at the scene of the crime, thinking.

Chapter VIII

Kansas City: The Courting of Roberta Weyerhauser.
Herb's Legacies.

D URING the days following his discharge from the hospital
in Kansas City Brush had given much thought to the
problem of finding Roberta. One day his eye had fallen on the
advertisement of a private detective agency. He called upon
the manager and laid most of the facts before him. Now after
many forwardings a letter from the agency reached him. It
gave the address of the farmhouse and added that one of the
daughters in the home, a Miss Roberta Weyerhauser, had left
the farm over a year ago, coming to Kansas City and had found
employment as a waitress at the Rising Sun Chop Suey Palace.

On the first noon following his return to the city, Brush hur-
ried to the restaurant for lunch. He climbed a narrow staircase,
and on the second floor entered a large room hung with Chi-
nese lanterns. The floor rose in gradually ascending levels about
a central space reserved for dancing. On each tier there was a
ring of tables for the diners. Brush seated himself at one of the
tables on the highest level and looked about him. There were
five waitresses standing about, and looking at them closely, he
decided that any one of them might be Roberta Weyerhauser.
They were dressed in a vaguely Chinese costume that included
red satin trousers. A disc of rouge had been drawn on each
cheek and their eyebrows had been painted in an upward curve
at the outer edges. The waitress who came forward to take
Brush's order was a tall bony girl with a mass of disheveled yel-
low hair and a sullen expression.

"What'll you have?" she asked.

Brush scanned the card. "What's specially good?" he asked,
slowly.

"'T's all wonderful."

"Is there anything here that's a favorite of yours?"

"I like'm all. I'm crazy about'm all," replied the girl, coolly,
scratching her head with the pencil. "Everyone of'm'll give you
a great big thrill you'll never forget."

Brush looked up. "Might I ask you your name?" he said.

"Sure. You can know everything. My name's Whosis. I live with my mother and we don't keep a phone. I get out at four o'clock, but I only let my boy-friend see me home. I don't like to dance and the pictures hurt my eyes; so what else would you like to know?"

Brush turned red. "I didn't mean anything like that," he said, in a low voice. "All I wanted to know was, was there one of the waitresses here named Roberta Weyerhauser."

"What is this, anyway?" she replied, angrily. "What's it *to* you? Who are you?"

"I . . . I'm just a friend of Miss Weyerhauser's."

"Say, who are you? Did somebody send you?"

"Are *you* Roberta Weyerhauser?"

"No, I'm not. My name's Lily Wilson, if you must know. And looka here: you tend to your business and I'll tend to mine. That way we'll get on better. See?"

Brush looked at her earnestly. "I asked you a question, that's all," he said.

"Hurry up. What'll you have?"

Without looking at him she took down his order, then cast a contemptuous glance at him and started to go. She had scarcely taken ten steps when she was suddenly struck with recognition of who he was. She gave an exclamation of astonishment and hatred and turned to look at him once more. He had been following her with his eyes and their glances met. She hurried off and his dishes were brought to him by another waitress.

He returned that evening for dinner. Dancing was going on. Most of the tables were filled and he was unable to find a place in Roberta's territory.

At lunch the next day he was back at his former table. Suddenly she was saying angrily in his ear:

"If you keep coming around here any more, I'll tell the manager and he'll tell the police. Now that's the truth."

"Roberta . . ."

"Don't you call me that!"

"Won't you give me ten minutes to talk to you?"

"I never want to see you again. I don't *ever* want to."

"Roberta, I have a right to talk to you."

"No, you haven't."

"Listen, for months and months I looked for your father's house. I tried every road. I didn't know how to find you."

"I'm glad you didn't. Hurry and give me your order and then never come back again. Now I mean it."

Brush gave an order.

When she laid the dishes before him, he said: "I'll have to keep coming back here until you set a place where I can meet you for a short talk."

"Well, I won't. I'll leave this job and I'll change my room and I'll go somewhere where you can't find me. I hate you more than I hate anybody in the world. I never want to see you again and I don't want to talk to you again. What happened was *terrible* and I never want to *think* about it again. Now that's all."

The Chinese manager of the restaurant seemed to have become aware of these conversations. He strolled about in the neighborhood with affected indifference. Roberta saw him approaching and fled. He stopped at Brush's table and asked:

"Is everything all right?"

"Oh yes," said Brush, hastily, "fine. Everything's fine."

When Roberta returned with the dessert, Brush whispered, "I want you to marry me, Roberta."

"You're crazy."

"Anyway, we're married already."

"You're crazy as a coot," repeated Roberta, crying as she punched his check. She hurried away. Brush put thirty dollars into an envelope, solemnly licked the flap and wrote his name, address, and telephone number on the cover.

At a few minutes after four his landlady called him to the telephone.

"I don't want your money," said Roberta, "and I won't take it."

"Can I see you somewhere?"

There was a short pause. Then, "If you promise not to come to the restaurant any more, I'll see you for a minute."

"Now? Can I see you now?"

"I have to go back to work at six."

"Where are you?"

"I'm in a drug store, center of town."

"Can you be by the steps of the Public Library in about twenty minutes?"

"I guess so. Where's it at?"

"Why," said Brush, "it's still at Ninth and Locust."

"If I come," said Roberta, "you've got to promise it's the last time. You've got to promise to leave me alone."

"Roberta, I can't promise that. But I promise to do everything I can not to trouble you."

There was a silence, then both furtively hung up.

Roberta was already waiting at the corner when Brush arrived. It was growing colder and a strong wind had risen. She was holding her hat with one hand: the other held Brush's envelope. She kept her eyes on the distance.

"Hello, Roberta!" he said.

She held out the envelope. "Here—I won't take it," she said.

"I won't take it, either," he replied. "I owe you money all my life. I'm going to support you until you die."

She threw the envelope upon the ground. Brush picked it up.

Still looking into the distance, she began speaking in low, angry tones: "I know you think you have me in a corner. Well, you haven't."

"Oh, Roberta, you don't understand!"

"Then what *is* it? What do you *want*?"

"Don't you see? I can't bear to have you be my enemy. I can't bear living on in life while there are things in the past that haven't been put right and fixed up—fixed up with friendship. Roberta—don't you see that? So that if you'll only let me call on you now and then, I think you'll get to know my character better and I think you'll get to like me. Because the most important thing in my life is that you and I be friends."

"All right! All right! I haven't anything against you. Call it friends, if you like, only don't ever come to the restaurant again. Don't keep hunting me all the time this way."

Brush was silent a moment. Then he said, solemnly:

"Nothing can change the fact that you and I are married already."

"There you go again. That's *awful* to say a thing like that. You're crazy."

"Roberta, can I go and talk to your father about it?"

At this she became distraught. "Now that's enough," she cried. "If you do that, I'll kill myself. I'm not joking—I tell you plainly I'll kill myself."

"Sh! Roberta, I promise I won't do anything you don't want me to."

"Oh, you won't?"

"No, of course not. Now listen and don't get mad at what I am going to say: I have to be in and near Kansas City for about a week and a half. Will you let me come and see you once a day, or once every other day? just for a talk or a meal or even a movie?"

"What good is talk if all you do is to get back to that . . . that crazy idea of yours?" There was another pause. Roberta shivered. "I'll be catching cold here," she said. "I'm not supposed to stand out in the cold this way. . . . I'll tell you what you *can* do. My sister Lottie is coming to Kansas City next Sunday to see me. You can talk to *her*."

"Will you be there, too?"

"Yes. Yes."

"Where?"

"We'll meet you here on this corner at four o'clock."

"Today's only Tuesday."

"I don't care. I can't see you before Sunday or I'll go crazy, too."

"Can I write you letters?"

"Yes, only don't come to the restaurant. Now I'm going."

"Roberta, will you . . . accept this present from me?"

He took from his pocket a mass of tissue paper and unwrapped the wristwatch which had last been offered to Jessie Mayhew. Roberta looked at it, then burst into tears and cried: "Don't you realize I don't want to have anything to do with you? Don't you see that my life's all arranged and I don't want anything new coming into it and that I don't want to think about anything that took place a long while ago? Don't you *understand* that?"

"No," said Brush, sadly.

"Well, I've got to go now," she said, and went down the street.

Left alone, Brush went into the Library and settled down to

read the article on Confucius in the Encyclopædia Britannica. His mind wandered from the subject, however, and presently he took a piece of paper from his pocket and began the first of his daily letters to the woman he meant to marry.

That evening he walked by Queenie's boarding-house, staring at the lighted windows on the top floor. The lights went out and a few minutes later Bat tore down the front steps and hurried away along the street. Brush rang the bell.

"Hello, Queenie! How are you?"

"I'm fine, Mr. Brush. How are you?"

"Can we go in here and talk where they won't see us? How are they, Queenie?"

"Didn't you know? Mr. Martin's terrible sick."

"Herb?"

"Yes. He isn't here any more. He's out to a hospital ten, fifteen miles in the country. . . . Yes. Mr. Baker says the doctors say he's going to die soon. Course, I don't know."

"Have you seen him there?"

"Yes. I went out with some laundry that come back late. The car fare's twenty cents each way."

"Queenie, will you go there with me tomorrow?"

"Well, . . ."

"You can go in and see him first, and when you've finished visiting, ask him if I can come up and see him. I won't say anything to make him mad, I promise. Will you do that?"

"I suppose I could go in the morning—I suppose I could. Mrs. Kubinsky's daughter—lives next door—could come in and answer the bell."

The next morning Brush appeared with a bunch of carnations and they started off.

"It's a nice ride," said Queenie. "There's nothing I like more than a good long street-car ride in the country."

"How's Father Pasziewski, Queenie?"

"Well, you know he was sick, and hardly had he got better than he began doing everything again. He went on hikes with the Knights of St. Ludowick and he took Mary's Flowers to the Zoo, like he used to do in the old days. He did all those things and the gall stones come back. Yes, sir, sure as you live."

"Did they?"

"Yes. You know, I don't think he'll ever get well. He's awful disappointed, Mr. Brush. Way down deep, he's an awful disappointed man."

"What about?"

"About the way his young people have turned out. You know all those Knights of St. Ludowick he took so much trouble with two years ago? Well, they've turned out to be practically gangsters. Yes, sir, they hold people up in the park and they steal automobiles and everything. And a lot of Mary's Flowers have become taxi-dancers."

"M-m-m! What's a taxi-dancer, Queenie?"

"Well, now you ask me, I don't quite know, myself. Only when at a dance a man hasn't got a girl himself, he pays other girls to dance with him. Something like that. Father Pasziewski says he might as well hold the meetings of Mary's Flowers at Billy Kohn's Roseland Glades."

"It's not immoral to be a taxi-dancer, is it, Queenie?"

"No, I guess not; but it's not as good as a trip to the Zoo. He just don't know what to do about it. They want to make a little money on the side, what with the depression and everything. Another thing: none of those Polish workmen that used to do bowling in the basement—none of them have jobs any more. They all live on cabbage; that's all they live on. Let's talk about something else, Mr. Brush. I declare I can't talk about the depression for very long at a time. I get dizzy."

Brush shyly glanced sideways at Queenie: "Does Father Pasziewski . . . does he still ever say anything about me?"

"I told you—Didn't I tell you?—he prays for you."

Brush turned pale. His heart stopped beating.

Queenie added: "You're on the Friday list. I'm on the Tuesday list; that was yesterday."

After a pause Brush asked, in a low voice: "You didn't just say that to be nice, did you, Queenie? Is that true?"

"Why, of course it's true! I thought I told you before."

At the end of an hour's ride they reached the hospital. It was one of a number of institutions set in a great park. Brush waited downstairs while Queenie, bearing the carnations, went into the wards. When she returned she said:

"He says you can come up. I'll wait for you here. . . . And,

Mr. Brush, he says . . . he was kinda violent, Mr. Brush . . .
he says, you're not to preach to him. He feels so strong about
it I guess you'd better not."

"Oh, I won't. Honest, I won't. I've learned not to. That's
one of the things I've learned. Is he in pain, Queenie?"

"I don't know, but he looks terrible. I want you to be ready
for it; he don't look at all well to me."

Brush entered the ward on tiptoe and looked about. He saw
Herb's eyes resting on him sardonically. He sat down by the
bed, appalled.

"Hello, nuts! How are you?" said Herb.

"I'm all right."

"I know. You're perfect. You're always perfect. It's great."

Brush kept his eyes on him, but made no answer.

"Well, since you've come here, I've got something to say to
you," continued Herb. "I didn't send for you. You came all by
yourself. See? And I'm going to do the talking. If there's any
talking going on I'm going to do it. Do you get that?"

"Yes."

"Well, in the first place, you might as well know that I'm on
the point of croaking, and I don't care if I do. And since that's
settled, I'm going to ask you to do me a favor. All you've got
to do is to say yes or no."

"Of course, I will, Herb."

"Wait 'til you hear what it is, damn you. . . . That's all, just
yes or no. It's all one to me, if you can't do it. Yes or no, and
then quits. Oh, don't sit there like a cock-eyed idiot with your
mouth open. Shut your mouth, anyway; you never can tell
what'll fly in. . . . It's not even a favor I'm asking you; it's
just a proposition. I'm not going to thank you, either. It's just
one of those things; take it or leave it."

A nurse who was leaning over an adjacent bed turned and
said: "You mustn't get excited, Fifty-seven, or I'll have to send
your caller away. Just a few minutes, that's all."

Herb groaned: "Oh, go to hell. . . . God! I hate hospi-
tals! . . . Now, listen, Jesus, it's this way. . . . Hell, what *is*
your name?"

"Brush—George Brush."

"Brush, then. I've got two hundred and forty dollars in the
bank and I'm going to leave them to you so that you can do

something for me. Now, I'm going to make this story short and snappy, see? I don't know whether you knew about it, but I had a wife and kid. I lived at Queenie's, and she lived with some friends of hers. We hadn't quarreled or anything . . . we weren't separated . . . it was just that way, that's all. I didn't see the point of living in the same house with her. I didn't see myself coming home to eat at regular hours, and wheeling baby-carriages about the streets and all that tripe—I'm not that kind of fella, that's all. Well, one day she beat it. She's never been seen since, so I guess it was with somebody that was passing through town. And she left the kid behind. The people she was staying with were awful sore, so I took the kid and parked it in another house where I knew some people. I pay them three dollars a week for it. So I'm going to leave you this money and, if you want to, you can see they get their three dollars a week. I couldn't give them the money in a lump or God knows what they'd do with it. Do you get the idea?"

He paused for breath. Brush started to say something, when Herb called out in anguish: "Now don't say anything. You always make a fool of yourself when you say something. If you go into that soft stuff of yours I'll kill you."

"I won't, Herb, I won't. I want to ask if I can adopt the kid . . . I mean, forever."

"Oh, I don't give a goddam."

"What's its name, Herb? How old is it?"

"I don't know its name. . . . Oh, I guess it's called Elizabeth. It's four or five years old."

"Herb, can I have it for my own, legally?"

"Oh, I wish I hadn't brought the thing up! Drop it! Drop it! Forget it!"

"Well, say yes or no, Herb. I could bring a lawyer . . ."

"You don't need a lawyer. Just take it."

"That's fine, Herb. There's nothing I'd like more."

"Poops! Well, don't say I saddled you with anything. It's just a proposition. It's all one to me."

Herb began fumbling under his pillow. He brought out a bankbook and some blank checks.

"Herb, I don't need the money," said Brush, hastily. "I've got more now than I know what to do with."

"Shut up! Write what I tell you!"

Brush made out two checks, one for twenty dollars to Herbert Martin; one to himself for the remainder. With great difficulty Herb signed them. "In the back pages here," he added, "you'll find the kid's address. Mrs. Barton, something Dresser Street. Get that?"

"Yes."

"And underneath it 's my mother's address. I give her four dollars a week. She hasn't been getting any for these last few weeks since the time when I was taken cuckoo, so I don't know what she's doing. She don't know, either, she's so full of gin. Some day when you think of it you might slip her twenty, thirty dollars, see? I don't care, though. They can all go to hell, for all I care. I'm glad I'm clearing out."

There was a long pause during which he glared angrily at the tops of the windows. Brush sat stiffly beside the bed.

Herb's eyes slid toward Brush. He said, "I see that the tricks the fellows played on you didn't do you any harm."

"No, no," said Brush quickly. "I was all right next day."

"They oughtn't to put the window-curtains up so high. They don't know how to run a hospital, that's all. You'd better go now before you say something wrong, Brush. You'd better not say anything, but just go. Only, leave your address, and if I think of anything else I'll have them write it to you."

Brush went. He turned at the door and looked back. Herb had covered his face with the sheet. Brush rejoined Queenie without speaking. They walked through the grounds in silence and stood by a marked telephone pole, waiting for the street car. Suddenly Brush flung himself face downward on the grass.

"Why, Mr. Brush, what's the matter?"

"I don't want to go on living, Queenie. I don't want to go on living in a world where things like that can happen. Something's the matter with the world, through and through."

At first, Queenie did not answer. She pressed her knuckles against her mouth. Then she said, "Mr. Brush, I'm ashamed of your talking that way."

"I believe there's a God, all right; but why's he so slow in changing the world? Why does he deliberately disappoint people like Father Pasziewski, and why does he let fine fellows like Herb get so mixed up?"

"Mr. Brush, it's awful to think things like that. I won't listen to you."

"But isn't there an explanation?"

"I won't listen to you."

Queenie covered her ears with her hands. Suddenly Brush rose and, taking hold of Queenie's wrists, firmly peered into her eyes. He said, softly, as though to himself, "Queenie, wouldn't it be terrible *if I lost my faith?*"

Queenie had no protests left in her. She stared back at him. He continued, slowly: "Even . . . then . . . I'd go on . . . just as I am, I guess . . . wouldn't I? . . . Only, I wouldn't get any pleasure out of it. The world isn't worth living in for its own sake. Anyway, I haven't lost my faith, but now I know it's not so easy as I thought it was. . . . Queenie, here's your twenty cents. I can't go back with you. I've got to walk back and think these things over."

The street car was hurtling toward them. Queenie screamed out: "You're not going to walk all that way!"

"Oh yes, I am."

Queenie was already on the step when another thought occurred to him: "Queenie, have you ever had anything to do with babies?"

"Yes."

"I'm bringing you one tonight."

"What?"

"I say that——"

"Step lively," said the conductor.

"I'm bringing you a baby about three o'clock. Herb's."

"Conductor," said Queenie, sharply, "will you hold this car a minute. . . . You'd better come and ride on this car, Mr. Brush. You're not well."

"I'm bringing an old lady, too—Herb's mother."

The conductor rang his bell. "Get on or off, lady," he said. "This car's gotta go places."

The car bore off an anxious Queenie, but not before she had leaned out of the window and called, "Now take care of yourself."

Brush walked to Kansas City. Gradually the exhilaration of the exercise and the interest of making plans for his new

dependents drove away his dejection. He called on the Bartons and carried Elizabeth off to her new home. Herb's mother refused to put her foot out of her room, or to permit Brush to enter it, but she listened through a crack to the arrangements he was making with her landlady. He then sent a telegram of reassurance to Herb and sat down to tell Elizabeth the story of the Flood.

Chapter IX

Ozarksville, Missouri. Rhoda May Gruber. Mrs.
Efrim's Hold-up Man. George Brush's Criminal
Record: Incarceration No. 3.

I N spite of the absorbing occupation that entered his life
with the appearance of Elizabeth and the problems of her
education, George Brush's mind was filled with the coming in-
terview on Sunday. In order to quiet his anticipation he de-
cided to fill in the time with work. There were a number of
professional calls in the vicinity waiting to be made, but first he
decided to journey some distance and confer with a certain
mathematics teacher and high-school principal at Ozarksville in
lower Missouri. Arriving at the town, he discovered that he had
more than a day's free time on his hands—the man he had come
to see was away on a tour of inspection in the rural districts—
and he decided to put into practice a plan that had long ap-
pealed to him. He resolved to pass a day in silence, following
the example of his master, Gandhi. From four o'clock on
Thursday until four o'clock on Friday not a word would pass
his lips; and to mark the occasion still more solemnly he de-
cided that not a particle of food would enter them.

He now communicated with the outside world by means of
paper and pencil. The staff of the Baker Hotel was astonished
to discover that its guest had been visited by so sudden an at-
tack of laryngitis. On Thursday night, Mr. Baker, staring at the
sky from the railing of his veranda, asked Brush whether he
thought it was going to snow. Brush drew out his pad and
gravely wrote the word, "No." He was mistaken. The next
morning he woke up to find that it had been snowing during
the night; it grew warmer, however; the snow changed to rain
and presently cleared to a mild winter day. He spent the
morning in his room, light-headed from hunger, but rendered
strangely happy by what he took to be the spiritual benefits of
the experiment. Soon after two o'clock he started out for a
walk, having put some apples in his pocket in anticipation of
the stroke of four. He was strolling down a street looking at

the houses to right and left when his glance fell upon an arresting sight. A little girl was sitting on the front steps of a house a few yards from the sidewalk; around her neck was a placard which read, "I AM A LIAR." Brush stared at the little girl and the little girl, pursing up her mouth importantly, stared at him. He hesitated only a moment, however. He walked up the path to the house and, drawing out his pencil and pad, wrote:

"What is your name?"

The little girl took his writing materials from him and wrote, "Rhoda May Gruber."

"You can talk?" wrote Brush.

Rhoda May insisted on being given the pencil and paper again. She wrote, "Yes."

"How long have you been here?"

"Ten years."

"Talk. You can talk," wrote Brush.

"Yes," wrote Rhoda May, "only I cannot talk now because I have been noty."

"Are your father and mother home?"

"Yes."

Brush hesitated, but it was too late. The Grubers had become aware of the unusual conversation on their front steps. They came out upon the porch.

"What's goin' on here?" asked Mr. Gruber, darkly.

Brush smiled reassuringly up at him.

Mrs. Gruber said, shrilly: "Rhoda May, git up off that step. Come here to me."

Mr. Gruber followed her with his eyes. "Take that thing off your neck," he said. "What did this man say to you?"

Mrs. Gruber gave Rhoda May a sharp pull and clutched her to her skirts. Rhoda May began to cry. Mr. Gruber turned back to Brush.

"What do you want? Eh? What is it you want?"

Brush began writing on his pad.

"You're deef-'n'-dumb, is that it?"

Brush shook his head, still smiling.

"You're not deef-'n'-dumb? Then what is it? . . . Rhoda May, what did this man say to you? . . . There's something funny about this," he said, raising his eyebrows significantly.

"You'd better run over to the Jones' telephone and call Mr. Warren or the sheriff." Then he turned back to Brush. "What is it you want? Are you selling something?"

Brush raised his head from his work, shook it, pointed at Rhoda May, then at the placard, and went back to his writing.

Rhoda May's wails rose louder. Her father slapped her smartly and roared: "Git in the house. Git in there. . . . You git in there, too, Mary. I'll tend to this."

Mrs. Gruber put out one trembling hand. "Now do be careful, Herman."

Brush now presented his statement: "I will be back later to talk to you about that punishment. I think you'll see what I mean."

Whereupon, walking down the path backwards, with gestures of cordiality, he returned to the sidewalk.

"You show up here again," called Gruber, "and I'll lick the hide off you, d'ya hear? I'll get the police on you, d'ya hear?"

Brush nodded, making gestures of pacification with his hands.

"You come around here and I'll knock your teeth out!" bellowed Gruber, and went into the house, slamming the door on Rhoda May's howls.

Four o'clock found Brush several miles from town, stumbling about in the mud of the road. As he looked at his watch and found that the vow was accomplished, he was filled with a satisfaction that was almost ecstasy. He turned back toward the town and did a quarter of an hour's running, then slowed down and ate an apple. He gazed with affection at the squatters' frame cabins, at the hound dogs that hesitantly approached the gates in the wire fences, at the chickens that had ventured out in the pale wintry sunshine. The path amid the dried weeds at the side of the road gave way to a sidewalk of planks. In the distance he could see a few rusty automobiles drawn up before the long arcade made by the projecting fronts of the stores beside the post-office.

At the edge of the town he came upon a store, or rather two stores thrown into one, that bore a sign: "N. Efrim, Dry Goods and Notions." One door had been boarded up. In the windows lay a disordered mass of such objects as dress patterns, slates, kites, and licorice whips. It occurred to Brush that

he might buy some milk chocolate here, and seeing a row of dolls in the window, that he might take one of them as a peace-offering to the Grubers.

Mrs. Efrim was sitting by the window, knitting, when Brush entered the store. She was a wrinkled old woman with the head of an intelligent and dolorous monkey. Over a thick woolen dress she was wearing a frayed sweater, and over the sweater a short greenish-black cape trimmed with rusty braid. She pushed her spectacles farther down her nose and looked over them at Brush.

"I'd . . . I'd like a doll, please," said Brush.

Mrs. Efrim laid aside her knitting and, putting her hands on her knees, painfully rose to her feet. They inspected the dolls together.

"It's for a girl ten years old," said Brush. "I guess you may know her. Her name's Rhoda May Gruber."

Mrs. Efrim nodded. Brush told her about the placard.

"Ain't that terrible, now!" said Mrs. Efrim.

They looked at one another and became great friends. Both were pining for conversation. They agreed that that was no way to bring up children. Brush, a little mysteriously, alluded to the fact that the bringing up of little girls had recently become a problem in his life. Mrs. Efrim had six children and Brush was glad to hear about their good and bad traits. He suddenly remembered that he was hungry, and offered Mrs. Efrim an apple, adding that he had eaten nothing for twenty-four hours, but that he felt fine. When he came to pay for the doll and the milk chocolate he laid a ten-dollar bill on the counter. Mrs. Efrim, making change, had a moment's hesitation before the cash register.

"I'll go and change it at the drug store," said Brush.

"No, no. I have it. You'll see. I have it fine, only it's hid."

"Hid?"

Mrs. Efrim looked at him and nodded mysteriously. "It don't do to have money in the till these days. No, sir. It don't hurt *your* knowing where it's kep'. Look!" Whereupon she put her hand behind a bolt of cloth and drew out a packet of one dollar bills and pushing aside some spools of ribbon came upon a store of fives. "That's the way we do it."

"I see."

The purchase was completed, but Brush lingered on, looking about the shop enviously.

"Young man," said Mrs. Efrim, who had again seated herself by the window, "do you know how to thread a needle?"

"I certainly do, Mrs. Efrim. I can sew pretty well, too."

"Well, my eyes aren't as good as they used to be. My children—every morning before they go off to school and to work—every morning they thread me up five or six needles, but sometimes they give out. Now, if you could thread me two or three needles . . ."

"I'd like to."

So it was that when the hold-up man entered Mrs. Efrim's store he came upon Brush standing by the window, threading needles.

"Stick up your hands," he roared. "Stick'm up, you two!"

"*Ach Gott!*" cried Mrs. Efrim.

"Stand where you are and keep your mouths shut. One peep out of you and you're dead. Do you speak English?—Eh? Spika Inglis?"

"Yes," replied Brush and Mrs. Efrim.

"All right, then. Now stay where you are."

This burglar was a nervous young man, new to the work and considerably hampered by the fact that the bandana handkerchief which he had tied about his nose was continually slipping and falling about his shoulders. He was given to crouching and glaring, and what he lacked in terrifying appearance he tried to make up for by shouting and by pointing his revolver squarely at the noses of his victims. He slowly crept over to the counter, keeping his eyes and his aim on Brush, opened the cash register and swept the silver change out of the drawer. Then he began uncertainly looking about for objects of value. Brush and Mrs. Efrim stood side by side with arms upraised. Brush's face shone with happy excitement. He glanced downward, trying to meet Mrs. Efrim's eyes in an exchange of intimate amusement.

"What are you laughing at, you big hyena," said the burglar. "Wipe that smile off your face or I'll plug you."

Brush assumed a grave expression, and the burglar continued his search. There was a long pause, filled only by the rumblings in Brush's famished stomach.

At last the burglar turned and said: "I didn't come in here

for two dollars and a quarter, you two. There's some more money somewhere here and I'm going to get it." He addressed Brush: "Take off your coat and throw it on the floor,—here by me. One extra move from you and you get it in the belly. Do you hear?"

"Yes," said Brush.

The burglar rested the revolver on the counter, retied the bandana about his face, and carefully went through Brush's pockets. He found two apples, a purse containing two dollars, a nail file, copies of *King Lear* and other classics, some newspaper clippings about India and an application for a marriage license.

"Can I say something?" asked Brush.

"What the hell's the matter with you—can you say something? What is it?"

"There's hardly any money in that coat, but I know where you can find some. . . . I'll pay you back, Mrs. Efrim, when it's all over."

The burglar stared at Brush, pointing the revolver at his eyes. "Well, where is it?"

"I won't say anything if you point that gun at me like that," said Brush. "You ought to know better than that."

"What's the matter with you?"

"You don't really mean to kill us, but you might kill us by accident."

"I don't, eh?"

"No, of course not. Not *kill*. Never point a gun at a person. That's a rule everybody ought to know."

"Well, I *do* mean to shoot you, so keep your face shut. Now where's this money you were talking about?"

"I *want* to tell you about it, but I won't tell you until you point that gun at the window."

The burglar turned the barrel a fraction to the left and shouted, "All right now, spit it out."

"You'll find some money on the shelf behind the cash register," said Brush, calmly, "behind that roll of blue cloth."

"*Gott—enu!*" cried Mrs. Efrim. "How can you tell him that! You're crazy! Telling him that!"

The man was looking at the bolt of cloth suspiciously: "So you say! So you say! What's the trick, eh?"

Brush said in a low, urgent whisper to Mrs. Efrim: "I'll pay you back, Mrs. Efrim. He needs it a lot more than we do. I swear to you you won't lose a cent." Then he continued to the burglar, "And there's some more in five-dollar bills behind those spools of ribbon."

Mrs. Efrim wailed still more loudly than before. Brush entered into an earnest debate with her. The hold-up man, still distrustful of the hiding-places, tried to follow the argument.

"You see, Mrs. Efrim, this is very interesting to me, because I have a theory about thieves and robbers. I'll explain it to you afterwards. Really, I'll pay you it all back."

"I don't want your money. I want my own," said Mrs. Efrim.

The hold-up man finally outshouted them: "Say, shut up, you two. What's the idea? Who do you think I am, anyway? I'm not fooling. I'm serious. Now what's all this about money over here?"

Brush repeated the directions. The man extracted the money from its hiding-places.

"All right, now. Where's some more. Out with it."

"That's all I know about over there," said Brush, "but if you'll let me put my hand down I'll get you some I have here."

"Where?"

"In my . . . my watch pocket, here."

"Say, what is this?" cried the man, as though in pain. "You keep your hands up or I'll shoot you."

"Well, I'd like to give you twenty dollars I have here."

"Keep your hands up! Say, are you yellow or cuckoo, or what? Keep your hands up. Where's this money?"

Brush motioned with his chin toward the pocket.

There was silence for a moment while they stared at one another.

Brush said, quietly: "You want money, don't you? That's what you came for. Well, I want to give you some. You need it a lot more than I do. Only you won't let me put my hand down to get it."

At that moment a gust of wind flung open the warped door of Mrs. Efrim's shop and then slammed it shut with a tremendous detonation. The current of air rushed through the room,

tossing the window curtains toward the ceiling and flinging a shower of the exposed objects over the floor. The burglar was so alarmed that the gun went off in his hand and the bullet shattered the window pane. Mrs. Efrim wailed louder than ever. The burglar let fall the revolver, jumped across the counter, and sank on one knee, still crying: "What is this, anyway? What's going on here?"

Brush picked up the gun and planted himself in the middle of the room. With furrowed brow, he pointed the barrel towards a corner of the ceiling.

"Now *you* hold up your hands," he said. "I don't believe in weapons of any kind, but I want you to stay there while I say something."

The hold-up man, swearing softly, stooped so that only his eyes appeared above the counter. Mrs. Efrim began pulling at Brush's sleeve. "Now, you make him give back that money before you do another thing."

"No, Mrs. Efrim, no! Don't you understand? This is a kind of experiment. We're going to give this man a new start in life, don't you *see*? I'll pay you back every cent that he's taken."

"I don't want your money. I want my own money. That's all I want. And I'm going to phone Mr. Warren this minute."

"No, Mrs. Efrim."

"Yes, I will."

"Mrs. Efrim," said Brush severely, "you move over there and put up your hands."

"*Ach, g'rechter Gott!*"

"Put up your hands, Mrs. Efrim. I'm sorry, but I know what I'm doing. Burglar," continued Brush, quietly, "what's your name?"

There was no answer.

"Do you know a trade of any kind?"

More silence.

"Have you been holding up people long?"

"Oh, shoot me and get this over with," muttered the burglar, contemptuously, but remained in hiding behind the counter. Brush was not abashed. He continued:

"I'm going to see that you leave this store with about fifty dollars in all. That'll give you room and board for a while. You

go somewhere where you can think things over. Now listen. Even I can see that you'll never be a very good hold-up man."

Brush was entering into a discourse on the rewards of honesty when an unfortunate interruption occurred. A customer opened the door of the shop, an old woman who promptly put her hand over her mouth and screamed through it:

"Why, Mrs. Efrim, what's the trouble?"

"I don't know, Mrs. Robinson," replied Mrs. Efrim, sullenly. "I don't know at all."

Brush turned his head a fraction and said, curtly: "You can't come in now because we're busy here. Come back in half an hour."

"Mrs. Efrim," gasped Mrs. Robinson, "I'll call Mr. Warren," and disappeared.

"That woman's coming in here has spoiled everything," said Brush, lowering his gun with an impatient sigh. "I guess we'll have to hurry.— Mrs. Efrim, there's a way he can escape through the back of the house, isn't there?"

"Don't ask me no questions," replied Mrs. Efrim. "I'm not going to tell you a thing."

Brush walked up to the counter and laid some bills on it. "Here's your money," he said to the burglar. "The price of the gun's in it, too. Now you can go. You'd better go out through there."

The man snatched up the money and, sidling about the room, filled up his cheeks with air, made an explosive sound, and dashed out of the door.

Brush put down the gun carefully. "That was awfully interesting, wasn't it?" he said, with a constrained laugh. "Now I want to pay you what I owe you."

Mrs. Efrim did not answer. She crossed the room and closed the till with a bang.

"Mrs. Efrim, don't be mad at me. I had to act that way to live up to my ideals."

"You're crazy."

"No, I'm not."

"You are. You're crazy. Whoever heard of anybody going out of their way to give money to a burglar. Yes, and letting him go free, too. No, I won't take your money. Look at all

that's been took from you already. Now go away before the police come and arrest you."

"I'm not afraid of the police."

"Now you mind what I say—go away."

"Mrs. Efrim, if I'd done anything wrong I'd apologize. I owe you about thirty-five dollars . . ."

Mr. Warren, the town constable, appeared at the door, followed by some men and by Mrs. Robinson.

"Now come out quiet," commanded Mr. Warren. "Hold up your hands and come quiet."

Brush said to Mrs. Efrim, smiling: "He thinks I did it! . . . Here I am, Officer." Mr. Warren handcuffed him. "Oh—oh, Mr. Warren," said Brush. "I hope I can eat with those things on, because I haven't eaten anything but an apple for twenty-four hours and I'm very hungry."

"Lock up your store and come with us, Mrs. Efrim," said Mr. Warren. "We'll want your story of what's been going on."

"There's nothing to tell," said Mrs. Efrim, shrilly. "It was just foolishness. No, I'm not going to leave this store. No, I'm not."

The officer insisted, however, and presently the procession was making its way down Main Street. As luck would have it Mr. and Mrs. Gruber were standing under the arcade.

"Look! Herman, look!" cried Mrs. Gruber, catching her husband's arm. "That's the man!—The kidnapper!"

"Charley Warren," said Mr. Gruber, "I charge that man with attempting to kidnap my daughter Rhoda May."

"Follow in behind, Herman," said Warren.

When they reached the jail, Brush was shown into a cell. He ate another apple, sighed heavily, and went to sleep.

Chapter X

Ozarksville, Missouri. George Brush meets a great man and learns something of importance about himself. The trial.

Aᴏꜰᴛᴇʀ breakfast the next morning the jailer opened the door of Brush's cell and said:

"You can go out into the yard if you want to. Judge Carberry can't see you till this afternoon. He's out fishing."

It was mild and sunny in the open air. The yard was surrounded on three sides by the jail and on the fourth by a high wire fence on the other side of which was the jailer's house and back yard. Beside the gravel path in the jail yard stood a number of rough benches. On one of these a man lay stretched on his back, wrapped in his overcoat, sunning himself. He turned his head and examined Brush. He had a thin, sardonic face and long silky mustaches.

"Well, well," he said, "another?" and sat up.

Brush went up to him and shook his hand. "My name is George M. Brush. I come from Michigan and I sell textbooks for Caulkins and Company."

"Any birth marks?"

"What?"

The man lay down again. "My name is Zoroaster Eels. I lie on benches for a living."

Brush looked at him in surprise, but Eels turned his back on him, so Brush continued his inspection of the yard. On the other side of the fence an enormous buff-colored cat was picking its way fastidiously among the weeds. Brush made a number of ingratiating sounds, but the cat ignored him and began washing its forepaws. A woman who was hanging clothes on the line called, "Here, Bitty! Here, Bitty!" stared at Brush with revulsion, and went into the house. Brush's thought turned to physical exercise. He strode energetically about the yard and did some hygienic bending. His fellow-prisoner turned and opened one eye. He yawned and sat up: "Relax, oh, relax," he said.

Brush went over to him. "Yes, I believe in relaxation, too," he said, "but the best relaxation comes after some kind of exertion."

Brush sat down. There was a silence; then he said, "They're real good to you in this jail."

"Wonderful," said Eels, and spat. "Wonderful."

Brush realized he had made an unconsidered remark. He blushed slightly and added: "The ham and eggs, I mean, and the use of the garden."

"They aim to please," said the other.

"They don't take your fingerprints here, though."

"I guess they would for you, if you asked them to. They can see you have the right spirit. You appreciate'm. You're the kind of prisoner they like to have." Whereupon Eels lay down and shut his eyes. "They'll be sorry when you go."

"Oh, I see," said Brush, laughing. "Everything you say is a joke. I couldn't understand you at first."

The other opened his eyes and regarded Brush narrowly, then closed them again. Brush, cut off from conversation, wandered forlornly about the yard, picking up rubbish and making a neat pile of it in one corner. Presently the other rose from the bench and with an altered manner came toward him.

"Why should we quarrel?" he said. "My name is Burkin, George Burkin. Shake hands, Brush, shake hands. I'm from New York City. I'm at present unemployed, but my profession is that of a motion-picture director. Come and sit down and let's discuss our shame. I've been stuck in here for a peeping Tom. What are you here for?"

"I'm here for two reasons. First they think I was trying to kidnap a little girl, and then they think I was trying to hold up a store, or at least help a hold-up man to escape."

"I see. It was all a misunderstanding, though?"

"Yes. Except the second one, but even then I knew what I was doing all the time. Would you like to hear about it?"

"Just a minute. Have you got a cigarette?"

"No, I don't smoke."

"You don't smoke?"

"No."

"Well, let's hear about it."

So Brush told him the whole story from the vow of silence to his arrival at the jail. He then added the account of his arrest at Armina, his theory of voluntary poverty, and his theory of robbers. After he had finished there was a long pause. Finally Burkin arose and, putting his thumbs in his belt, gazed, squinting meditatively, into the sun.

"Well," he said, "I've been hunting for some one like you for a long time. To think I had to go to jail to find you."

"For some one like me?"

"Yes. Do you know what you are? You're the perfectly logical man."

Brush, for delight, could scarcely believe his ears. "I? I'm *logical?*"

"The most logical man I ever met."

"Well . . . naturally I always claimed I was logical . . . but almost everybody I meet says I'm crazy." Then he added, hesitantly, "Is it a good thing to be logical?"

Burkin strolled away a few steps without answering. When he came back he said, "Well, at least, it's no fun."

"Oh yes, it is," said Brush, hastily. "I'm the happiest man I ever met."

"Have it your own way," said Burkin.

Brush hesitated again. "Will you tell me how . . . how the misunderstanding came up that made them put you in here?"

"Sure, I will," said Burkin. He stood with one foot on the bench in a pose of nonchalance, but his words emerged with increasing violence and a nervous twitch of the left side of his face which Brush had noticed earlier became more and more pronounced. "I was standing on the lawn of a house looking in the window. The people in the next house phoned for the police and I was stuck in here. That's all." There was a pause, then he broke out: "I never explain anything. I never regret anything. I don't care a goddam what they think. If they think I've been prowling around their streets, trying to catch their hags undressing, let'm think so. Let them keep me in jail here as long as they like. I don't care. I never explain. I never try to put idiots out of their misery. See? I am what I am."

Brush held his breath. Burkin leaned over him and shouted into his face: "Listen, now listen. The day'll come when they'll

be glad for me to so much as mention their goddam town. I'm
a movie-director. See? I'm the best that ever was or will be.
I'm the greatest artist America ever had in any line. See? I'm a
movie-director. It's my business to know everything. I knock
about the whole country in a Ford, just looking. That's all. One
night I'm in Ozarksville, Missouri. What of it? I'm walking
down the street and I see a lighted window. What of it? A man
and his wife and kid are eating supper. Now when you're
looking through a window at people who don't know they're
being looked at, you see a lot more than you see any other
way. Can you understand that?"

"Yes," said Brush, in a low voice.

"It's terrible how much you see. You see their very souls.
Can you understand that?"

"Yes."

"I stayed there for hours until the police took me away.
That's all. Do you like it?"

Brush said, quietly: "All you have to do is to tell them—like
that. They'd believe you."

Burkin shouted, "I tell you I never explain."

"I'm going to tell the judge myself," said Brush. Then
slowly raising his eyes with a smile, he added, "It's a pleasure
to believe you."

"Who the hell are you, anyway?" said Burkin, and walked
away as though in anger. When he came back he said: "Be-
sides, don't you know that the judge in this place is a tight old
bird? He's had the town in his pocket for forty years. He
doesn't even go through the forms of the law, let alone listen
to anything that's said to him. You haven't got any more chance
than I have. What are you looking so damned pleased about?"

"I don't know," said Brush, in a low voice. "I guess it's
because I like to have things happen to me."

"You're crazy," said Burkin.

"I know," he said, smiling, "but you said I was logical."

"Have you got anything to read in your baggage?"

"Yes, I have several things in the cell there. This is all I have
on me," and Brush produced a New Testament, his paper copy
of *King Lear* and a pamphlet on colonic irrigation.

Burkin took the *Lear* and gave the other two back. "You
mustn't separate those two," he said.

Brush stood with lowered eyes, thinking this over. "I don't like you to say things like that," he said.

"It's a big free country," replied Burkin, airily, and lying down again read *King Lear* from beginning to end.

George Brush had already become a legend of terror in the town, and by two o'clock the courtroom was filled with spectators sitting in a churchgoing silence. When Brush entered and took his place the silence became even more profound; the room held its breath. Brush's lips were pressed tightly together and he was paler than usual, but he looked about him with an unabashed glance. Judge Carberry had been for thirty-five years the best-known citizen in town, but when he entered all eyes rested upon him as though for the first time. He looked about him wearily, blew his nose, and sat down. He was a bald old man with small black eyes and a pointed nose set in a myriad of wrinkles that read kindliness, disillusion, and boredom. He was vexed by the unaccustomed throng and today pushed even farther than usual his habitual contempt for the procedure of the law. He grunted a few instructions to the clerk, who began to expedite matters furiously. While the charges were being read he artfully adjusted the screen of books—a vast bulwark of Blackstone—behind which it was his custom to read during sessions. He was hurrying through George Eliot and looked forward to a review of *Waverly* in the spring.

". . . attempted kidnapping," mumbled the clerk, ". . . aiding and abetting larceny . . . pleads not guilty . . . undertakes his own defense . . ."

Mr. Warren was called. "Wa-all, I got this here phone call from Mrs. Robinson that there was this hold-up goin' on over to Mrs. Efrim's store; so I . . ."

The judge stole a paragraph or two of *Adam Bede*, then raised his head. "Both these charges against the same person?" he asked, dryly.

"Yes, Your Honor."

"Same day?"

"Yes, Your Honor."

The judge let his eyes fall on Brush in a cool, contemptuous glance. Brush returned his gaze without flinching. There was a silence. Brush raised his hand. "May I speak, Your Honor?" he asked.

For a moment it seemed as though the judge had not heard him. "What do you wish to say?"

"Your Honor, I think you ought to know there is no case here at all."

"Indeed?"

"Yes, it's all a misunderstanding. And if you'll let me tell my account of it right now we can all be out of the court building in fifteen minutes. Also, Your Honor, I can explain the case of Mr. Burkin, who you're going to see after me, and that's just a misunderstanding, too."

"Have you ever been brought before a court before?"

"No, Your Honor." Then he added, with some difficulty. "But I've been arrested before."

"Oh, you have?"

"Yes, but they were misunderstandings, too. I was let go in an hour."

"Would you feel able to tell the court what you were arrested for, and where?"

"I'd be glad to, Your Honor."

"We should be glad to hear it."

"The first time was in Baton Rouge, Louisiana. I was arrested for riding in a Jim Crow car. I believe in the equality of races, Your Honor, in the brotherhood of man, and I rode in the Jim Crow car to show that I believed in it. They arrested me. The second time——"

Judge Carberry stopped him with a gesture of the hand. The judge looked slowly and a little dazedly over the spellbound audience, then turned toward the court stenographer as though to make sure that this testimony was being recorded. He then looked at the tops of the windows as though he were debating as to whether he should issue orders for new sashes. Finally his gaze returned to Brush. He blew his nose and said, politely, "Kindly continue."

"The second time was about a month ago in Armina, Oklahoma. I was drawing out my savings from a savings-bank and I told the president of the bank that in my opinion savings-banks are practically immoral. They arrested me for that."

"Had you any reason to think that the bank was unsound?"

"I didn't mean that, Your Honor. I meant that all banks like

that are due to fear and breed fear in the people. It's a theory of mine and it takes quite a while to explain."

"I see," said the judge. "Your ideas aren't the same as most people's, are they?"

"No," said Brush. "I didn't put myself through college for four years and go through a difficult religious conversion in order to have the same ideas as other people have."

Again the judge allowed his astonished gaze to wander about the room. He saw Mrs. Efrim, sitting in the midst of her six children, all dressed in their best clothes and staring up at him with awe-struck eyes. He saw the Grubers and Rhoda May scrubbed to startling pinkness and wearing a starched white party dress. "You may be seated," he said to Brush, then mumbling a few words to the clerk, he left the room. He went to the telephone and called up his wife. He talked slowly, with many pauses and with an affected indifference.

"Oh, Emma," he said, looking down his nose and scratching his cheek. ". . . euh . . . euh . . . better get your sewing and come down to the courthouse."

"What do you mean, Darwin?"

"Well . . . well . . . you might be interested in something that's going on here."

"Now, Darwin, if it's something improper, you know I don't like such things."

The judge slowly passed his tongue over his front teeth. "No . . . oh, no . . . perfectly proper."

"Well, what is it, Darwin?"

". . . There's a type here . . . little out of the ordinary. Better come down. Bring your sewing."

"Now, Darwin, I won't have you tormenting some poor prisoner. I know you. I know you and I won't have it."

The judge's shoulders shook. "Prisoner's tormenting me, Emma . . . seems like. We're putting on a little show today. Call up Fred and see if he's free. You can bring Lucile, too."

Fred Hart had been mayor of Ozarksville for twenty years. Lucile was his wife. The Harts and the Carberrys had played bridge together three nights a week for a longer time than that.

"Well, if I come down I want you to behave, Darwin. I've told you a thousand times I don't like you when you're sarcastic."

The judge returned to the bench. He gave the prisoner an awe-inspiring glance. He saw to it that the court marked time until the arrival of his wife. Mr. Gruber was sworn in and told his story of indignant virtue . . . only and treasured child. He dwelt upon the peekyuliar behavior of the accused, his pretense of being unable to speak. The whole court could see for itself that the accused could speak as well as anyone else. Brush raised his hand, but the judge sharply ordered him to lower it. Gruber droned on and the judge caught half a chapter of *Adam Bede*. Mrs. Gruber was called and gave a flighty, incoherent account of the affair. At last the judge saw his wife and the Harts slipping into the last row of seats. He put a bookmark into his volume and laid it to one side. Mrs. Gruber was dismissed and Brush was called upon.

"What's your business, young man, and what are you doing in Ozarksville?"

"I travel for Caulkins and Company, publishers of textbooks for school and college. I came to town to call on Superintendent MacPherson."

"I see. Have you ever had an impediment in your speech?"

"No, Your Honor."

"Did you have laryngitis yesterday?"

"No, Your Honor."

"Can you explain why you pretended to be incapable of speech yesterday?"

"Yes, Your Honor, easily."

"I should like to hear it."

"Your Honor," began Brush, "I am very interested in Gandhi."

The judge laid down his pencil sharply and said, in a loud voice: "Young man, you will please give me the answers to my questions and nothing else."

Brush squared his shoulders. "I am, Your Honor. It's the only way I can answer them. I . . . I've been studying Gandhi's ideas lately and——"

Judge Carberry threw an ecstatic glance at his wife, then drawing his hand down his face he roared: "Stop that! Stop it right now! I will not be made a fool of in my own courtroom. Young man, this is no time for desultory conversation. Do you

realize that you're standing here under two very serious charges? Do you?"

"Yes," said Brush, his jaws set.

The judge lowered his eyes and said, more quietly: "Now continue and let's have no nonsense."

Brush remained silent. There was a long pause.

The judge looked up. "Do you wish to add contempt of court to your other charges? Do you— Very well. Young man, perhaps you do not understand your position here. You have been charged with two offenses, either of which might send you to state prison for a very long time. You have been in Ozarksville for a little less than two days and already you have drawn across it a trail—a trail, I say—of suspicion and confusion such as it has not seen in fifteen years. And yet you conduct yourself before me *frivolously*, yes, *frivolously* in open court."

Brush turned even paler, but remained firm. "I'm not afraid of anything or anybody, Your Honor," he said. "All I want to do is to tell the truth, and you keep misunderstanding me."

"Well, begin again, then. And if you bring up the name of Gandhi again I shall put you in jail for a few days, where you can cool off."

Brush wiped his forehead. "The reason I didn't talk to anybody yesterday until four o'clock was that I had taken a vow of silence," he said.

The judge suddenly grasped the connection. When he reappeared, still panting, from behind his barrier of books, he glanced at his wife. Mrs. Carberry shook her fist at him.

"I see. Go on," he said.

"That vow of silence," continued Brush, "was in imitation of a certain leader in India. Soon after two o'clock I went out for a walk. I saw that girl sitting on the steps of her house. She had a sign around her neck that said 'I am a liar.'"

"What?" asked the judge.

"'I am a liar.'"

When this confusion was cleared up, everyone took a deep breath and the judge took a drink of water. He asked, "What was your purpose in approaching the child?"

"I didn't think that was any way to punish a child. I think

lying's a bad thing, but I don't think that's the way to punish a child that does lying."

"I see. Are you a father, may I ask?"

Brush was silent a moment. "No," he said, in a low voice. "I don't think I am."

"I *beg your pardon?*" asked the judge, leaning forward.

"Not that I know of," said Brush.

Judge Carberry shuffled the papers on his desk. "Well, we won't go into that now," he said. He then asked, loudly, "Is this little girl in court?"

Rhoda May was led to the witness stand. She was given laborious instructions about the oath and the Bible, but she entered into the proceedings with perfect assurance and unbounded enjoyment.

"Will you tell us what happened, Rhoda?" asked the judge.

Rhoda May turned and faced the audience. She kept her eyes proudly fixed on her mother's face. For a moment she turned back to the judge. "My name's Rhoda May," she said. "I was sitting at my house and that man came up the walk to my house and I knew he was a bad man right away."

"Why were you sitting on the steps, Rhoda May?"

"Because I'd been bad."

"Yes, and what did this man do?"

"He said for me to go away to a bad place, and I said no, because I love papa and mamma best."

"He asked you to go away with him?"

"Yes, but I didn't go, because I love papa and mamma best."

"Rhoda May, be careful. You must tell the truth. Did he *say* this with his mouth, or did he write it down?"

"He wrote it down, Judge Car-Berry. But I knew he was a bad man kidnapper right off. He looked at me like *this* and then I gave him a good kick. I gave him a good kick. And he began to run away and I ran after him and gave him another good kick in the face, and——"

"Mr. Gruber!" roared the judge.

"Yes, Judge Carberry."

"Take your daughter home. We will now proceed to the second charge."

A shocked silence ensued while the Grubers with lowered heads passed down the aisle.

The judge then said in a courteous tone: "Mrs. Efrim, will you be so good as to give us an account of the events that took place in your store yesterday afternoon?"

Mrs. Efrim, rustling in a voluminous black silk dress, edged her way past her children's knees and took her place on the stand. The judge paid her a deference that touched on gallantry. Her hand was scarcely lowered from the oath when she broke out:

"Judge Carberry, I can't tell you how terrible I feel to be in court this way. I've lived in this town forty years—my husband and I, may his soul be at rest!—without ever coming in this building, beyond paying our taxes in the basement, Judge Carberry."

"But, Mrs. Efrim, there's no reflection on yourself. I assure you——"

"You can say what you like, Judge Carberry," she said, hugging her elbows woefully, "and it's very kind of you, but it don't change the facts."

"Now, now, Mrs. Efrim," said the judge, leaning forward, "The Court considers it an honor that you should be kind enough to appear here today. Yourself and my friend Nathan Efrim have been among the most respected citizens in this town for many years and the Court holds it a privilege to have you among us today."

Mrs. Efrim cast a mighty glance at her six open-mouthed children and started to tell her story.

"Really, Judge Carberry . . . Your Honor . . . I have no charges to make against that young man. I guess he's just different from the rest of us, that's all. Even to this minute I don't know what happened. At first I thought he was a nice young man." Here she looked at him a moment. "I don't know what to think, Your Honor."

"Thank you, Mrs. Efrim, will you simply tell us what took place."

"Well, he came in. I was sitting by the window, knitting, when he came in . . . and he hadn't been there two minutes when it seemed like he began—I don't know how else to say it, Your Honor—he began *winding* himself into my confidence."

"You don't say?"

"I don't know what else I can say, Your Honor, Judge

Carberry. There's nothing he didn't do. He tried to give me an apple; he threaded me needles——"

"I beg your pardon?"

"He threaded me three-four needles. He asked me my children's names. He . . . he bought a doll. Yes, sir. He asked me to eat an apple and he said himself he hadn't eaten a thing for twenty-four hours. And then he . . . and then he got me to show him where my money was hid."

"Why, Mrs. Efrim, I never heard such a story in my life."

"Well, it was funny, Your Honor. There's nothing he didn't do, but I must say I liked him until he began acting queer when the hold-up man came in."

"Will you tell us about that, please?"

Mrs. Efrim, however, was unable to tell it. From her confused narrative Judge Carberry received the impression that there were three or more hold-ups, a storm, broken window panes, and some very curious exchanges of money. He thanked her elaborately, however, and she resumed her place among her children, who scarcely so much as dared to look at her sideways after her excursion into the important world. Mrs. Robinson was called. Her testimony was to the effect that there was no hold-up man with a handkerchief about his face—no one beyond the accused standing in the middle of the store with a revolver in his hand terrorizing Mrs. Efrim. This testimony was confirmed by Mr. Warren.

Finally Brush was called.

"Young man, did you obtain from Mrs. Efrim the secret of the hiding-places of her money?"

"Yes. She . . ."

"Did you tell the hold-up man where her money was hid?"

"Yes, Your Honor, but I meant to pay her back."

"Did you take the gun yourself and hold up Mrs. Efrim?"

"Yes, but I never meant——"

"Don't tell me what you meant or what you didn't mean. All I want is the facts, and the facts speak for themselves, don't they? Did you allow the hold-up man to escape when you knew the deputy sheriff was coming?"

Brush was silent.

"Are you going to answer that question?"

Brush continued looking stonily before him. The judge waited. Finally he began speaking in a low, penetrating voice:

"You've gone into another vow of silence, I suppose? And no wonder! There *is* nothing to say. The facts speak for themselves. You were going to tell me this is all a misunderstanding. You were sure we were going to be out of this courtroom in a quarter of an hour. . . . Put your hand down! . . . You wound your way into Mrs. Efrim's confidence, did you? You threaded needles for her! You even went so far as to buy a doll, did you? No wonder you found out where she had hidden her money."

Here the judge was so overcome with pleasure at his own wit that he descended behind the barrier of books and had a fit of coughing. When he emerged he discovered that Brush was descending the steps into the auditorium and apparently intended to leave the building.

"Where are you going *now*?" shouted the judge.

"I won't be talked to like that, Judge Carberry," said Brush.

"You're under arrest; Officer, restrain that man."

Brush said, "You won't let me speak!"

"Come back here. You're under arrest. So you've changed your mind? Now you want to talk, do you?—*Where are you going?*"

"Oh, I'm going to the jail, all right. I'd rather sit in jail and make rope than be treated like you're treating me, Judge Carberry. You haven't heard my explanations yet."

At this moment, to the great excitement of the already dazzled audience, Mrs. Carberry, very red in the face, advanced down the aisle of the auditorium.

"Darwin, you behave yourself," she said. Then turning to Brush, she added: "Young man, don't you mind what he says. You tell your story. That's just his way. He doesn't mean it. You go back and tell your story."

"Order! Order!" cried the judge. "Go back to your seat, ma'am, and leave the running of this court to me. . . . Now, Mr. Brush, I'll give you another chance." But the judge could not resist the addition of one further embellishment to his afternoon, and called after his retreating wife: "Ma'am, if you attend properly to the running of your home, I shall try to

attend to the running of my court." Whereupon he disap-
peared behind the bulwark of his Blackstones, from which he
presently appeared, much shaken, wiping his eyes. "Mr.
Brush," he said, grandly, "have you an explanation for your as-
tonishing conduct yesterday afternoon?"

"Yes, sir, I have."

"We are ready to hear it. And kindly remember you are under
oath. . . . One minute!" He took a deep drink of water,
mopped his face, and bade the stenographer look sharp.

Brush gave a clear and detailed account of the events in Mrs.
Efrim's store. When he had finished, the judge sat in silence a
moment, looking at his wife. He took off his glasses, breathed
on them, and slowly polished them. The audience followed his
movements in silence. He then turned to Mrs. Efrim:

"Mrs. Efrim, have you anything to add or correct in that
story?"

"No, Judge Carberry. Everything he said really happened."

"Well, now at least we have an idea of what this is all about.
Now, Mr. Brush, can you explain to the court your reasons for
giving Mrs. Efrim's money to the hold-up man?"

"Yes . . . it's all based on a theory of mine. I mean on two
theories of mine."

"What!"

"Yes, and a lot of it I owe to Gandhi."

"There's Gandhi again!" said the judge, resignedly.

"It's all based on *ahimsa*, Your Honor, but before I get to
ahimsa I have to tell you what I think about money."

So Brush told the court about voluntary poverty.

"And do you live by voluntary poverty?" asked the judge.

"Yes, Your Honor. And the point of that is this: a *poor* person
—even if he's a millionaire—is a person whose head's always
full of anxious thoughts about money; and a rich person is a per-
son whose head's not full of anxious thoughts about money."

"Thank you, Mr. Brush," said the judge, dryly, "I'm sure
we're all the better today for that thought."

"And the poorest persons in the world, therefore, are beg-
gars and robbers. Now you'll see what I mean when I say that
a robber is a beggar that doesn't know he's a beggar."

"And now, Mr. Brush, I'm going to ask you what good it does
to give your money away to these robber-beggars of yours?"

"It's easy to see that. When you give money to a robber you do two things: you show him that he's really a beggar at heart, and you make a certain strong impression on his mind that——"

"Yes, you do. You give him the impression that you're a coward or fool."

Brush smiled and shook his head. "I think I can explain this idea in another way. It's my favorite idea in the world and I've spent a lot of time on it. Your Honor, I'm a pacifist. If they put me in a battle I wouldn't shoot anybody. Now suppose that I was in a shell-hole and I met an enemy who was about to shoot me, and suppose I tore the gun out of his hands. Naturally he'd expect me to shoot him, but of course I wouldn't. That would make an impression on his mind, wouldn't it?"

"Yes, it would."

"Well, and if I pointed out some hidden money to a burglar that was trying to steal some money from me, that would make an impression on his mind, too."

"Yes, it would: I say again they'd think you were a fool."

"Judge, that might be what they'd call it, but at the back of their minds they would be taught something."

"Have you finished?"

"Yes, Your Honor."

"So you gave forty or fifty dollars to a burglar in order to make an impression on his mind?"

"Yes."

"Suppose that the man in the shell-hole shot you. What becomes of your lesson to him then?"

"Well, Judge, *ahimsa* would have been in my mind. That's Gandhi's word for it, Your Honor. And if somebody has *ahimsa* in his mind, I believe it has a chance of jumping from mind to mind."

"What becomes of *ahimsa*, Mr. Brush, if you suddenly come upon a man who's attacking your sister?"

"Yes, I've heard that before. Everybody brings up that argument about your sister being attacked, and I get angry about it. What if a thousand sisters are attacked. Let them be attacked. If the attackers are met with *ahimsa* the attackers will learn about it. That's the way the idea will spread. Somebody's sisters—millions of them—are being attacked all the time, and

things aren't getting any better; so it's time to try a new way to cure it. Let some of your sisters be attacked. Before the new idea can jump around the world from one person's mind to another's there will have to be a lot of people attacked."

"I see. I see. And you want us to go about releasing murderers and thieves, on the chance that this impression is made on their minds. Do you advise the Department of Justice to collect as many thieves as possible and give them each a hundred-dollar bill? Is that it?"

"Well, look how things are now in your system. People go on committing crimes, and the government goes on committing crimes to punish them."

"Oh, it does!"

"Yes, sir. It's a crime to kill, and the government does that, and it's a crime to lock somebody up in a room for years on end, and the government does that by the thousands. The government commits thousands of crimes in a year. And every crime makes more crimes. The only way out of this mess of crimes is to try this other way."

The judge was silent, stroking his face. The silence was filled by the anxious scribbling of the stenographer and the sounds of automobile horns from the street. He glanced at the audience which sat watching him with fallen jaw.

"And where did you get that idea?" he asked.

"It's mine and Tolstoi's."

While the judge spelled out the name for the stenographer, Brush drew from his pocket a little blue pamphlet, *Sayings of Leo Tolstoi*, and passed it up.

"Have you any other sources upon your person, Mr. Brush?"

Whereupon Brush began to draw similar little pamphlets from all his pockets. They were gravely passed up to the bench —Epictetus, *Thoughts from Edmund Burke*, *Sayings of Great Statesmen*, *Sayings of Great Philosophers*, *Stories from Famous After-dinner Speakers*. The judge passed the books to the stenographer. He then collected himself and said, dryly:

"Well, it's all sort of poetical and sentimental, Mr. Brush; but it's all very unlike the facts of life. And it seems to be based upon a profound misunderstanding of the criminal's mind."

"I don't know what you mean by the criminal's mind, Your Honor. All I mean is, a criminal is a human being who thinks

that the whole universe hates him. I think that awful things must go on in your mind when you think that the whole universe hates you. And the certain impression that we try to make on their minds is the impression that they are not hated."

Again the judge paused. Then he said, "And you expect the United States to——"

Brush interrupted him: "Judge Carberry, people like me, who believe in *ahimsa*—it's not our business to worry as to whether other people do or not. It's our business to do it ourselves and to take every chance, like this, to talk about it to other people. It's the truth and so it'll spread about the world of its own accord."

"Mrs. Efrim, do you feel that this explains what this young man did with your money?"

Mrs. Efrim rose hesitantly. "Judge Carberry . . . I guess he means what he says."

"Court is dismissed," said the judge.

The clerk said, quickly: "There's this other man, Your Honor—Burkin, charged with——"

"Court is dismissed," repeated the judge.

The clerk was required to repeat the announcement a number of times in addition, for the audience remained motionless in its seats, unwilling to quit so bewildering a display, but finally the Carberrys and the Harts took Brush in the mayor's car to the jail to call on Burkin.

"Let me explain about Burkin," said Brush. "He's a——"

"No. Wait 'til we get there," said the judge.

Burkin sat in his cell, rereading *King Lear*. He was brought into the office.

"What's it all about?" asked the judge.

Burkin was pale and contemptuous. "You wouldn't understand," he said. "You wouldn't understand. Go and give me your twenty days. I've got some letters to write."

The judge was silent, listening to him gravely.

Burkin continued: "Only leave me Little Rollo here. Big kidnapper and hold-up man. Big public enemy.—The law's a farce and you know it."

"Come on," said the judge. "What is it? Looking in windows?"

Burkin began to tremble and snap his fingers with excitement. "I tell you you wouldn't understand. Go tell the goddam mayor there never was anybody in Ozarksville who ever understood anything and there never will be."

Brush was suffering acutely. "Let me explain?" he asked, in a whisper.

"All right, Brush. What's the matter with your friend?"

Brush explained.

The judge turned to Burkin. "Even I can understand that, Burkin," he said. "Gentlemen, would you rather have your supper here in the jail or would you rather find it somewhere else? Have either of you got a car?"

"Yes."

"Well, I don't want to hurry you, gentlemen, but it would be less embarrassing for us if you decided to eat in some other town."

The prisoners gathered their things together and went down the hall.

Judge Carberry put his hand on Brush's shoulder and stopped him. Brush stood still and looked at the ground. The judge spoke with effort:

"Well, boy . . . I'm an old fool, you know . . . in the routine, in the routine. . . . Go slow; go slow. See what I mean? I don't like to think of you getting into any unnecessary trouble. . . . The human race is pretty stupid. . . . Doesn't do any good to insult'm. Go gradual. See what I mean?"

"No," said Brush, looking up quickly, puzzled.

"Most people don't like ideas. Well," he added, clearing his throat, "if you do get into any trouble, send me a telegram, see? Let me see what I can do."

Brush didn't understand any of this. "I don't know what you mean by trouble," he said. "But thanks a lot, Judge."

They shook hands and Brush climbed into the car beside Burkin. Burkin bent over the wheel with a black expression on his face, but Brush waved back at the judge, the mayor and the warden and disappeared down the street.

Chapter XI

A road in Missouri. Chiefly conversation, including the account of a religious conversion. George Brush again sins against ahimsa.

WHEN they had reached the edge of the town, Burkin asked, "Where do you want to go?"

"Kansas City, if it's all right with you," said Brush. "You see . . . I expect to get married Monday or Tuesday and I want to get there Sunday so as to talk it over."

"You don't say!"

"Yes, it's a long story and I'd rather not tell it just yet."

"That's all right with me, but there are some other things I'd like to know. How did it happen the judge and the mayor had to come to the jail to see us off? What was all that diddling about? Are they all crazy in that town or did you infect'm?"

Brush gave him a detailed account of the trial.

"Well, well," said Burkin, shaking his head, "such goings-on! You'd better look out, Brush. You can't go about long with upsetting ideas like that and get away with it. One of these days you'll be teasing the bourgeoisie one too many and they'll crack down on you."

Brush looked at him inquiringly, but said nothing. They decided to postpone their supper indefinitely and drove on for a time in silence over the plain. In the distance an occasional silo rose among some farm buildings. The first stars began to appear above a spiritless sunset.

"Stop!" cried Brush as they passed a man beside the road, his thumb extended for a hitch. "Stop for him!"

"Not in your life!"

"Stop, I say!" cried Brush, putting his hand on the wheel.

"You can't do that in this country," said Burkin. "It's not safe."

Brush pulled back the brake. "What are you afraid of everything for?" he said.

"He might be another hold-up man, y'fool! He'd take our car off us."

"I'll buy you another car," said Brush. "Always stop for hitch-hikers. Always do it, if you've got room."

Burkin gave in and began backing the car. He said: "Oh, you're rich enough for anything, aren't you? All right. He's your responsibility."

The man came running up.

"Get in, Pete," said Burkin. "The car's yours."

Not until the newcomer had been bestowed in the back seat among the suitcases, and the car had gathered speed, did Brush recognize who it was. "It's Mrs. Efrim's hold-up man," he said.

The man leaped for the door, but dared not jump out. "I gotta get outa here," he cried in a throaty voice. "Lemme out."

"Shut up and settle down," said Burkin. "We won't hand you over. Brush here saved you from the law once already, didn't he? So pipe down and take a snooze. And as for you, Brush, don't you lecture him. The poor geezer's suffered enough from you already."

"I don't wanna stick around with you guys. Go on, lemme out," the man repeated, but receiving no answer, he relapsed into a brooding silence.

Brush said into Burkin's ear: "I wish I knew what he was thinking. It would be very important to know. I think it's one of the most important things in the world to know what goes on in a person's mind when he's been treated with *ahimsa*."

"Nothing goes on in his mind," said Burkin. "All he's got is a few visceral reactions. He lives like a fox at the edge of a chicken farm."

"You're wrong," said Brush. "He's got a soul, a complicated soul like anybody else."

"Lemme out, you guys. All I wanna do is get out and walk."

"What's your name?" asked Burkin.

"Hawkins."

"Where do you want to go, Hawkins?" The man remained silent. Burkin continued: "What do you do? What's your trade? Come on, tell us your story. We've got two or three hours ahead of us. Come on, out with it. How did it all happen?"

Hawkins refused to answer.

Brush said, in a low voice: "You see, he's pretty uncomfortable, and that's what I expected. It's this way: The Bible says

that if a man does something bad to you, you ought to give him the chance to do more bad to you, like giving him your other cheek to slap. That's in the Sermon on the Mount. But I always thought that ought to be changed a little. If you do pure good to a man that's harmed you that shames him too much. No man is so bad that you ought to shame him that way. Do you see? You ought to do just a little bit of bad in return, so he can keep his self-respect. Do you see what I mean?"

"Pretty subtle for me," said Burkin.

Hawkins became violent. "If you don't lemme outa here I'll break every window in this car," he cried, and smashed one of the side windows.

Brush leaned over the back of the seat and gave Hawkins a cuff on the side of the head. "Sit down there quiet, Hawkins," he said.

"Brush, I don't like that," said Burkin. "Looks like you're reneging on *ahimsa* for us."

"I didn't really hurt him," whispered Brush. "I'm experimenting."

There was silence for a time, when Brush felt a sudden blow on the back of his head.

"Hawkins, you mustn't do that," he said. To Burkin he said, confidentially: "Isn't this interesting? You see what it means? It means that bad people can't bear to be benefited by anyone. Now I'll punish him a little so as to restore his self-respect."

Brush turned and, kneeling on the cushions of the front seat, grasped Hawkins' shoulders and shook him violently.

The car was entering a village. Burkin said over his shoulder, "Have some eats with us, Hawkins?"

"No."

"Aw, keep your chin up, Hawkins! What the hell's the matter with you? Have some eats. We'll pay for it."

They stopped the car before a lunchroom. Hawkins leaped out and darted up an alley.

Brush smiled after him. "I think that proves everything," he said.

Burkin did not answer. They sat down on the high stools and had a series of hamburger sandwiches, pouring scalding coffee down on top of them. At last Burkin said:

"How did they take that about voluntary poverty?"

"All right, I guess. They listened."

"Did you ever gain any converts with it, Brush?"

"You never know. I think it works in people's minds and perhaps they begin to practice long after."

They ordered some pie, and Brush resumed:

"For instance, I once talked to some millionaires about it."

"My God!"

"They were the only millionaires I ever met and naturally I was very interested in them. When I'm on a train I talk to everybody, and once on a train I fell into conversation with a young couple and somehow the conversation got around to voluntary poverty."

Here Burkin began laughing and choking so that he had to be beaten on the back.

"I was telling you about this couple," continued Brush. "It seems she'd been a schoolteacher in a small Oklahoma town and she'd married the baggage agent down to the depot. He still had a red neck and red wrists, as though he ought to have been in overalls still, but he was a good serious fellow; and she was a serious girl, too. She had on a brown dress and she was pretty and serious, and I liked them both. And I told them all about voluntary poverty. Well, after they had been out to lunch in the dining-car they came back to see me and by that time they were pretty excited. They had been talking it over, and so they told me their story. They both talked at once, almost, and while they were talking she kept her hand on his hand. It seems that oil had been found on their land and they were worth almost three million dollars and they didn't know what to do about it."

"I can't wait for the end of this story," said Burkin. "Tell me, how much did they give you?"

"Naturally, I wouldn't take it," said Brush.

"All right, go on."

"They didn't know what to do with it. They'd already given a hospital and a park to their home town, and they began by giving baskets of groceries to all the poor people, but soon they saw that was foolish, just to give hundreds of baskets of groceries every week."

"Well, what did you tell them to do?"

"You know what I told them? I told them they'd never be

happy as long as they had it. I told them to go back to the schoolhouse and the baggage depot."

"That's great. Don't you know that the townspeople would hate them?"

"The townspeople hated them already when they stopped giving groceries. But this couple didn't want to live in any other town."

"Tell them to go abroad for a while."

"They did go abroad. They expected it would cost them a good deal of money, but when they got back it had only cost them two thousand dollars. They said they hadn't missed a thing, either, but that they didn't like doing foolish things that cost money."

"What did they say when you tried to drive them back to poverty?"

"The girl cried."

"So they tried to palm the money off on you?"

"You see, the reason they came back from the dining-car was because they wanted me to give away some of the money for them. They were Methodists and they had read the Bible and they believed you should give away one-tenth of your earnings every year. Only they couldn't think of any real good ways of doing it. It was a kind of funny situation, because they were getting off at the next station and had to talk fast. There he sat with his fountain pen out, trying to write me a check up to two thousand dollars."

"Didn't you take it?"

"No, I couldn't take it. Don't you see that giving is a thing you can never do for anybody else? That's a theory of mine. If you give without feeling your gift with every inch of your-self——"

"That's all right. All I want's the facts. You can keep the theories to yourself. So you sent the little millionaires off like that?"

"Yes."

"Is the story over?"

"Yes."

"Let's get back to the car." When they reached the pavement, Burkin added, "God! you're a fool!"

They drove on in silence. Brush felt Burkin's soured resentment. Finally Burkin said, in an even, leaden voice:

"It's a good thing you haven't got more stuff. Yep, you might cause a lot of harm, fooling around with people's lives. You might start a new religion or something."

"What do you mean, stuff?"

"Brains. Brains. Personality. Stuff."

Brush was silent a moment. Then he said, "It's not very nice to say things like that."

"Take it or leave it."

They drove on farther in silence. When they approached the lights of the next town, Brush began leaning over the back seat where the luggage was. "I think I'll get out here," he said, pulling at his suitcase.

"What's the matter? Hell! What's the matter with you?"

"I don't want to ride with you if you think that way about me."

Burkin was all amazement. "What did I say?"

"What you said back there—that I hadn't any . . . brains or personality. I don't like what you said back in the jail-yard about the New Testament, either. And I don't like the jokes you keep making about . . . well, about women. So I think I'd better get out here, if you'll stop the car, please."

"God damn it! get out and stay out!" cried Burkin, violently. "I'm not going to twa-twa like a sewing-circle for anybody. Get out before I kick you out. You're the damnedest prig I ever saw. You're a bag of wind. Get out of here."

Brush was still leaning over the back of the seat, extracting his suitcase from Burkin's extraordinary collection of goods. His confusion was increased by his need to fumble for a handkerchief.

Burkin stared at him sharply, then exclaimed: "Oh, you cry, too, do you?" Suddenly he burst out laughing. "You weep and blush and everything, don't you? Brush, you're wonderful! Say, put the suitcase back, put it back. I apologize. I won't do it any more. I apologize for everything." And again he went off into a violent fit of laughter.

Brush hesitated. "I can't stay here . . . if you don't take me seriously," he said.

"Of course I do! What are you saying! You're all right. Stick around. I wouldn't dump you out in a forsaken hole like this for anything. I apologize, and of course I take you seriously. I

don't agree with you always . . . but, oh! I take you seri-
ously, all right!"

"Well," said Brush, relenting, "I'd have been sorry to have
left you in the middle of a quarrel like that. It's happened too
often lately, just when I had begun to be friends with some-
body. That's why I did what you called 'cry.'"

So Brush dried his eyes and the journey was resumed. From
time to time Burkin was shaken by after-reflections of his fit of
laughter. This made Brush uncomfortable, but finally he smiled
a little sheepishly himself. At last he said in a low voice:

"I think I know what you meant by saying I was a prig—and
you aren't the first person that's said it, either—but I don't
mean to be one. That's the only way I can be and still hold on
to my main ideas about life. Do you see what I mean?"

"All right. Let's not talk about it," said Burkin.

It was now a cold starlit night. The road ran smoothly over the
prairie. Brush was commanded to talk in order to prevent the
driver from falling asleep at the wheel, so he explained the busi-
ness of selling textbooks. From there he went on to relate some
of the adventures of the road—of how he had called on the great
singer, Madame de Conti, at the Iowa City Musical Festival and
of how she had taken a great fancy to him, even inscribing her
picture "To my good friend, the true American George Busch,
child of Walt Witmann's hopes"; of how he had been offered
thirty-five thousand dollars to marry Mississippi Corey; of how
he had gone four days without food in order to experience what
Russian students had suffered, and to share some of the trial of
the Mahatma; of how he had taken a bus from Abilene, Texas,
to Los Angeles in order to look at an ocean.

Burkin listened with an even level of attention that finally
had something ominous in it. After a pause he asked:

"How did all this start, anyway? Where'd you catch the reli-
gious bug in the first place? At home?"

"Oh no! My people don't believe anything. They just live
on from day to day. I didn't use to think about such things,
either. Through the first years in college I just lived on that way,
too. I was only interested in athletic scores and collecting
stamps. Then suddenly I was converted in the middle of my
sophomore year at college."

"What college was that?"

"Shiloh Baptist College, at Wallingkee, South Dakota, a very good college. I was president of the class, and I was very interested in politics, too—school politics, I mean. One day I saw a poster that a girl evangelist had come to town. She had set up a tent down by the railroad tracks and was holding meetings twice a day. Her name was Marian Truby. Her photograph was on the poster and it seemed like maybe her face was beautiful, so I went the first night just to look at her. Well, it turned out that she was not only a very beautiful girl, but a very wonderful speaker, too. I was converted that first night and I went forward to testify to it, and my life has been changed ever since. I went to every one of her meetings and after that I took every religion course there was in the college. Then the next most important thing in my life was when I began to read about Gandhi. I got hold of the life that he wrote of himself, and that gave me a lot more ideas——"

"Hold on here! Did you ever talk to the girl evangelist?"

"Only a minute or two," said Brush, reluctantly.

"What happened?"

"I didn't want to tell you about it . . . but since you've asked me . . . The last night of the meetings I went around to the back of the tent to tell her what a lot she'd done for me. She must have been pretty tired after preaching two sermons a day for a week and leading the hymns . . . and besides that she used to walk up and down the aisles and talk to people who were hesitating. . . . I don't like to tell you this because you might not understand it like I do. . . . I waited until the rest of the people had gone so that I could make it a little more personal. There was no door to knock on so I went right in. She was sitting in a sort of dressing-room and she was sort of moaning——"

"Did you say moaning?"

"Yes, moaning and groaning. And an older woman was standing over her, sticking a hypodermic syringe into her arm."

"You don't say!"

"Now that I know more about life I know what that was. But even that doesn't change my idea about all the good she did to me and hundreds of other people."

"Did you speak to her?"

"Yes, but she didn't look up. The older woman was mad and drove me right away."

"Have you ever seen her since?"

"No. I wrote her a letter, but she never answered it. If you put on the flashlight I'll show you her picture." Brush took from his purse a discolored newspaper clipping with a picture of Marian Truby. "I ask about her everywhere," he continued, "but I think she must have retired. Maybe she's sick somewhere. If I find that's so, I mean to support her for the rest of her life. You see, it says she was born in 1911 in Waco, Texas. I wrote the postmaster there, but he said there were no more Trubys there now."

"So your big ideas about life were fed you by a sixteen-year-old girl while she was hopped up with drugs?"

Brush made no answer.

Burkin continued in a low tone, edged with contempt: "Think it over. It all goes together—voluntary poverty and Christmas baskets for burglars. It all goes together. You've got the gaseous ideas of a sick girl. It has nothing to do with life. You live in a foggy, unreal, narcotic dream. Think it over. Listen, benny, can't you see that what you call religion is just the shiverings of the cowardly? It's just what people tell themselves because they haven't got the guts to look the facts of life and death in the face. If you'd gone to a respectable college you'd have had the chance to get wise to these things. You've lived all your life among the half-baked. You've probably never been exposed once in your whole life to anybody who really had any practice in thinking."

"You'd better stop the car," said Brush. "I'm going to get out." Then he added, shouting: "I suppose you think nobody with brains ever felt any religion."

"I could talk to you. I could show you things. But in two minutes you'd be squealing holy-murder and starting to jump out of the car. You don't want to grow up, that's the trouble with you. You haven't read anything. You haven't seen anything, except through the eyes of a girl in hysteria and some old dodo in Shiloh Baptist College. All right. Let's talk about something else."

Brush remained silent. At last he said, in a low voice, "Nothing that you could say would change my mind."

"It's now half-past eleven," said Burkin, decisively. "Will you let me talk to you for one half-hour, without your interrupting me?"

Brush was staring darkly before him. "Where did you go to college?" he asked.

Burkin named an Eastern university, adding: "But that wouldn't mean anything, except that I added a whole batch more education to it. I've worked on these things. I hung around the University of Berlin for a year. I lived half a year in Paris. I didn't stick in the smoking-cars of Texas and read cheap paper pamphlets from a mail-order house. Give me half an hour."

"I have a hard enough time with my own doubts without adding somebody else's to them," said Brush, in a low voice.

"What are you so afraid of doubts for? There's one thing worse than doubts, and that's evasions. You're full of evasions. You don't even want to look around. You don't give a goddam for the truth."

"I have the truth."

"All right, if you have the truth, why not listen to my error for half an hour?"

Brush was very unhappy. He glanced sideways at Burkin's face, then brought his wrist watch close to the dashboard light. "Go ahead," he said.

Burkin plunged into primitive man and the jungle; he came down through the nature myths; he hung the earth in astronomical time. He then exposed the pretentions of subjective religious experience; the absurdity of conflicting prayers, man's egotistic terror before extinction. At last he said: "If you'd read more I could show you the absurdity of the scholastic proofs of the existence of God and I could show you how the dependency complex begins. Is the half-hour up?"

Brush said, slowly: "When you began I thought you were going to say things that would stick in my mind and trouble me. You've talked three-quarters of an hour and you've only said one thing that had any point to it." His voice rose and presently he was shouting: "I guess we'd better change the subject, because you haven't thought enough about these things to make it worth my while. Why, can't you see that you don't know anything about religion until you start to live it?"

"Stop yelling, anyway."

"All you've done is *think* about it as though it were . . . as though it were a *fish* a long ways off. Even your doubts aren't the right doubts to have."

"I'm not deaf, I tell you. Shut up and sit down."

"You——"

"Oh, shut up!"

They drove in silence awhile. Finally they entered a village. All lights were out, save in a lunch-wagon by the railroad tracks.

"I'm getting out here," said Brush.

Burkin stopped the car. The nervous twitch on the left side of his face had returned. Brush put his suitcase on the curb.

"I owe you about three dollars for that broken window," he said, "and another dollar for gas."

"Yes, you do."

"Here it is."

"Good-by," said Brush, extending his hand.

Burkin drove off without answering.

Chapter XII

Kansas City. Serious conversation in a park. A Wedding. Practically an American home.

BRUSH returned to Kansas City by train. It was the first time in his life he had traveled by train on a Sunday. Even so, he was almost late for his appointment in front of the Public Library. He barely had time to rush back to his room at Mrs. Kubinsky's, change into his best suit, and run next door to take a look at Elizabeth. Elizabeth had entered Queenie's house a big-eyed pale child that smelled bad; already, however, she had taken on color, and Queenie gave a good account of her disposition.

The girls were already at the Library steps when Brush came running up the hill. They pretended to be deep in conversation.

"I'm only one minute late," he said. "I just got in from out of town an hour ago."

"This is my sister Lottie," said Roberta.

"Yes," said Brush, smiling. "I remember you from that night I was at your farm."

Lottie threw a quick glance at him and did not answer. She was not so tall as her sister; she had brown eyes and hair and gave the impression of being matter-of-fact.

"Would you like an ice-cream soda?" asked Brush. "Let's go to the drug store and have one first."

Making conversation was not easy. The girls sat on the high stools, earnestly engaged with the straws in their mouths.

"Is it too cold to go out to the park on the bluffs?" asked Brush.

"No, I guess not," said Lottie; so they all climbed on to a street car. The car was almost full and Roberta took a seat some distance from them.

"What are you interested in?" asked Brush.

"I?" asked Lottie. "Oh, nothing. Anything. Pigs and chickens, I guess, mostly. You see, Mr. Brush," she added, dryly, looking into his eyes, yet giving the impression that she did not see him, "I'm just a farmer's daughter—I don't go in for big ideas."

"I see," said Brush, uncomfortably.

Lottie turned her head and looked out of the window, as though she were sitting beside a stranger.

Brush cleared his throat several times, then said: "When we get to the park I want to show you some marks left by the ice-cap."

"I beg your pardon?"

"You see, the North Pole ice used to come all the way down to here. It stopped at Kansas City; that's what made the rivers. The ice was two thousand feet thick right where we are now. It was so heavy that it crushed the earth out of shape as far as . . . as far as Pennsylvania and Oklahoma."

"Well!"

"Naturally it carried some big rocks along with it, and those rocks ground down the big rocks under them and it's the marks of that grinding that I'm going to show you in the park."

"That'll be fine," said Lottie, without expression. She turned about and glanced at Roberta, who was sitting five seats behind her. She asked Brush, "When did all this happen?"

"About eight hundred thousand years ago."

Lottie gazed at him with cold irony, then turned her head away. Another silence ensued. Brush broke it by saying, urgently:

"Lottie, I want you to help me in persuading Roberta. I think it's tremendously important."

"Well, it was all an awful mess," said Lottie, just as quickly, "and I think the less we see of you the better."

"When I've done wrong," said Brush, in a low voice, "I can't wait until I've done everything I can to make it all right."

"You both did wrong. But at least it's all over now and there's nothing more that *can* be done about it," replied Lottie, decisively; then added, "Anyway, let's get to the park before we talk about it."

Brush glanced at her sideways. "Can I say one more thing before we change the subject?" he asked.

"I suppose so. What is it?"

"Try not to have a prejudice against me before you know me. I'm not the usual kind of traveling salesman."

Lottie looked at him with a faint smile. "I think I understand that," she said, and thereafter things went a little better.

Descending from the street car, Lottie gave Roberta a sharp pinch on the elbow.

When they reached the park they sat down on a bench overlooking the river. Lottie sat in the middle tracing designs on the ground with the tip of her umbrella. Brush waited a moment and then plunged into the heart of the matter:

"Don't you see, Lottie, that all serious-minded people would agree that I'm really her husband already?"

"No."

"Don't you see that we can never marry anyone else, unless one of us two is dead? There's . . . there's one of the Ten Commandments about that."

Lottie bit her upper lip and looked at the ground. Brush tried another approach:

"Lottie, what does Roberta want? Does she want to stay in that restaurant? I think it's an awful place. I can't let her do that. I owe her a living for the rest of her life and I can afford it easily. I've got more money than I know what to do with. Can't you tell me what she wants?"

"Well, to tell the truth, Mr. Brush, she . . ."

"You must call me George, Lottie. Don't you realize you're practically my sister?"

"All right. All right. George—to tell the truth, there's only one thing in the world that Roberta wants, and that is . . ." She glanced sideways at Roberta. Roberta was sobbing. Lottie paused, then stood up and whispered into her sister's ear: "Roberta, do go off for a few minutes' walk while I talk to him. Will you, honey?"

Roberta nodded, rose, and sat down on the next bench.

Lottie continued: "She wants papa to like her again." Brush stared at her. "She wants papa to have a good opinion of her; that's all. She was papa's favorite girl of the three of us. It's been terrible for him, really it has."

Brush whispered: "But you see I don't know anything about it. I don't know anything about what happened."

"Well . . ." began Lottie, then rejected her impulse to recount the past, and resumed her former thought: "What I think is, if perhaps—when she knows you better, and all that— if perhaps you married Roberta, then some day you could call on papa and show him you're not an ordinary traveling sales-

man . . . and you could talk to him about the Bible and things like that . . . and then he'd forgive Roberta."

"Then that's fine, Lottie. That's all I ask to do."

"But, George, don't you *see*? What good is it you two being married, if you don't love each other? What I thought was——"

Brush leaned over her earnestly and said: "I'll love her pretty well. I'll love her almost perfectly, you'll see. She'll never notice the difference. I'll tell you, confidentially, that there's only one other girl in the world I love more."

Lottie looked at him long and a little sadly. Then she smiled and put a hand on his arm. "George, you're kind of crazy," she said.

"Yes," he answered, hastily, "I know what you mean, but if you notice carefully, you'll see that I'm very logical."

There was a pause. Then Brush leaned forward and, looking at his shoes, asked, "Lottie . . . why did your father send Roberta away."

"Why . . . because . . . because . . ."

Brush raised his chin and looked at her.

"She was very sick and. . . . I thought you knew."

"No, I didn't know."

"Of course. You couldn't have known."

"No, I never knew," breathed Brush.

"Well, on the farm . . . we all went through quite a time . . . papa and . . . mamma . . . and Roberta . . . and I."

They gazed into one another's eyes for a moment.

"Lottie, I think you're fine," said Brush. "I hope I know you all my life."

Lottie became confused and looked away. "I guess you will," she said, almost inaudibly. But she had something else to say. It was such a difficult thing to say that she fell into a false casualness and for a moment her gestures became affected and contradictory: "I was thinking that . . . you might marry Roberta just to please papa . . . then separate right away . . . and after a while get a divorce."

Brush also turned red. "No," he said. "You see, there are two things against that. One thing is that I never believe in divorce, and if anybody stops to think about it they can see why. And the other thing is that I never believe in doing anything just for show. I . . . I don't believe in that. . . . Oh, Lottie,

don't you see that everything's all right? That we're going to have a fine American home?"

"Well, I've said all I'm going to say. You two'll have to decide it for yourselves from now on."

"Are you going to advise her to get married to me, though?"

"George, unless people love each other I don't think———"

"Lottie, when you have a hard decision to make, you know what you should do? You should go back to the first principles of the matter. You shouldn't ask what you want to do. You should look at it as though it were somebody else and not yourself. And, that's all very clear in this case. Lottie, I'll take the responsibility. I know I'm right. I know I'll love and protect Roberta until I die."

"All right," said Lottie.

"Will you go and ask her to come here? And, Lottie, listen: we'll have a nice home somewhere and you can come in all the time for Sunday dinner, and the whole family can come in from the farm, too. We'll have some fine times, you'll see. For instance, I have a very good tenor voice and people are always asking me to sing for them. . . . Oh, Lottie, all this that began so badly will end up all right; it'll end up all the better. Now do you see how important it is?"

Lottie, a little dizzy in the conflict of ideas, went over to where Roberta was sitting. They had a long whispered conversation.

"But he's crazy," said Roberta.

"Yes," said Lottie, "I know. But he's crazy in a sort of nice way." She began laughing. "I'd marry him in a minute, myself."

"You would, Lottie?"

"Yes, I think I would; only, he hasn't asked me."

Whereupon they both began laughing into their damp handkerchiefs. "One more ice-cream soda and I'd do it," said Lottie.

"But, Lottie, he's *terrible*!"

"I know. But I've decided I prefer him that way. Compare him, I mean, with Gus Brubacker, back home, or Oscy Deschauer. Besides, he told me to tell you he had a fine tenor voice."

"What'll we talk about?"

"What?"

"What'll we talk about? What'll we talk about when we're married?"

"Oh, he's full of conversation. Didn't you hear him telling me all about the ice that used to be over Kansas City? Besides, he's so rich that you can have a radio."

"Is he *rich*?"

"He talks that way. Hurry, Berta, and make up your mind. He's waiting and he'll think we're laughing at him."

"Lottie, help me! Shall I?"

"Don't ask me! Don't you like him?"

Roberta shook her head, her face suddenly somber. "You know why I could never like him."

"Listen, Berta, he'll never drag that up, never. I know. There's nothing mean about him. He's kind of stupid, but he's good as gold. If you ask me, I say you ought to marry him. Then take him to see papa."

"All right, I will," said Roberta, rising.

"Wait till I blow my nose," said Lottie.

While this was going on Brush sat on the bench, thinking. He had taken Lottie's umbrella and was abstractedly tracing initials on the gravel: a large R for Roberta, then an A for Adele, the widow to whom he had proposed marriage on his twenty-first birthday; and F for Frances, Miss Smith, his chemistry teacher in the Ludington High School; at a distance from these initials an M. U. for Marian Utley; whereupon, in a flood of reminiscence, he wrote a J for Jessie Mayhew, a V, an S, a C; then erased them all and traced a large R and sat looking at it. Roberta and Lottie were laughing?—laughing or crying?

Finally they came toward him hand in hand. He rose and said: "Before I ask you to marry me again, there's something else I ought to tell you. I forgot to tell you before that I . . . I own a little girl. A friend of mine died and left me his little girl. She's the brightest little girl that you could find anywhere, and I know you'll like her."

This seemed to make no change in the situation and Roberta accepted his proposal.

He took her hand and said: "It's going to be fine, Roberta. You'll see. What you'll want to do will always be the first thing in my mind. At first, though, I'll have to be away a good deal

on the road, but I'll write you a letter every day. Later I think
I can get the firm to give me the Illinois and Ohio territory.
We're going to have a wonderful life together . . . you'll see.
There'll be lots of times when we'll be laughing a lot . . .
while we're washing the dishes, and so on . . . and soon we'll
have a little house of our own. I'm very good at fixing things,
like electric lights and furnaces. And I'm good at carpentering,
too. I'll build you an arbor in the back yard where you can sit
and sew. And Lottie can come and stay with us as long as she
wants to. We could never find a better friend than Lottie. . . .
Don't you think it sounds . . . like it'll be fine?"

Roberta, standing with lowered eyes, said, "Yes."

"I know I'm kind of funny in some ways," he added, smiling,
"but that's only these earlier years when I'm trying to think
things out. By the time I'm thirty all that kind of thing will be
clearer to me, and . . . and it'll all be settled."

They were married on Wednesday and had their photograph
taken—Queenie, Elizabeth, Lottie, Roberta, and Brush. Brush
received a three-weeks vacation from his firm and they moved
into a four-room apartment over a drug store. The first install-
ment was paid on a second-hand edition of the Encyclopedia
Britannica. On the first Sunday after the wedding the Weyer-
hauser family came into town from the farm to go to church
with them and to stay to Sunday dinner. Brush sat at the end
of the pew, his arm lightly but proudly lying along the back of
it. During the sermon Elizabeth put her head on his lap and
went to sleep, and his eyes made a guarded journey about the
congregation to ascertain how other fathers met this situation.
After church the three younger women busied themselves in
the kitchen. Mrs. Weyerhauser had the shock of hearing herself
called Grandma—for, Herb having died, Brush and Roberta
were now Papa and Ma. The manners of the host and his father-
in-law towards one another were still somewhat stately, but they
gave promise of becoming more easy with time.

Apparently all was well with the new household, but only
apparently, for some flaws began very gradually to reveal them-
selves. Roberta had been correct in her doubt as to what they
would talk about when they were married. For some reason
Brush, who had never in his life been at a loss for things to talk

about, now found himself hard put to it to fill the long
evenings with interesting matter. He took to taking notes
during the day on subjects that would serve, and when
Roberta called him to dinner he would take out his purse and
run his eyes over the topics he had collected. He tried putting
forth some of the theories that never ceased fermenting in his
mind, and though Roberta listened with lowered eyes (their
eyes never met at any time) he found that his eagerness to pro-
pound them had somehow left him in this company. He dis-
covered that there was one subject that never failed to arouse
Roberta's interest—the lives and appearance of motion-picture
actors—and he took to culling from the papers such items on
these subjects as were suitable for retelling in a Christian home.

Another flaw appeared when Brush became aware that he
and Roberta were engaged in a furtive, unceasing, game of
strategy to obtain the first place in Elizabeth's affection. The
worst of it for Brush lay in the fact that Elizabeth all too often
showed a marked preference for himself. This filled him with a
satisfaction of which he was soon ashamed. He tried time after
time to give the advantage to Roberta, only to be filled with
ignoble pleasure when the effort did not succeed.

On the last night before he set out on his long three-months
trip (the firm of Caulkins assured him that his approach suited
the southern territory more than the northern and refused to
consider his application for a change) Lottie came into Kansas
City for the farewell dinner. She had a long, earnest conversa-
tion with Roberta in the afternoon, and during dinner Brush
noted that they had both been crying. He looked at them in
surprise, but made no comment. That was left to Elizabeth.

"Mamma cried," said Elizabeth.

"Eat prettily now!" said Roberta, hastily.

Brush was about to inquire further, when he caught sight of
Lottie's raised eyebrows sending him a signal.

Brush had a theory that children should be permitted to see
the stars. The custom that put them to bed at dusk seemed to
him to overlook the fact that a frequent view of the stars was
an important element in the spiritual education of mankind.
For this evening he had obtained permission to delay Elizabeth's
retirement until after dark. Roberta dressed her for the open
air and Brush carried her up the ladder to the trap door that

opened upon the roof. He moved a soap-box across the floor of tar paper and gravel to the chimney and, seating himself on it, held Elizabeth in his arms and waited for the benefits to show themselves. The child lay humming contentedly to herself, and looking down at her, Brush seemed to observe a strange indifference to the sky. She smiled up at him, a smile that seemed to allude to their wickedness in evading her mother's rules on an early departure to bed.

They were silent for a time. Then Brush put her to her nightly test.

"What's your name?"

"Elizabeth Martin Brush."

"What do you do if you're lost?"

"Policeman."

"Where do you live?"

"Twelve twelve Brinkley Street."

"What do you do?"

"Tell the trufe . . ."

"Yes."

". . . love God . . ."

"Yes."

". . . and brush my teef."

"That's right."

She was able to tell what country she belonged to; she counted to twenty, and repeated a portion of the alphabet. She was then allowed to relax. After a long silence he looked down to see that her wide eyes were gazing tranquilly at the stars.

The trap door was raised. "She ought to go to bed now, dear," said Roberta.

"All right. We're coming."

Roberta waited, holding the trap door open. As he took it he said in a low voice: "Roberta, is something the matter?"

She made no answer. While Elizabeth was being put to bed, Brush sat by Lottie, having another cup of coffee. Lottie's face was thoughtful. She played with the spoon in her saucer.

"George," she said, "there's no need to keep up this apartment while you're gone so long. Why can't Roberta come back to the farm? There's plenty for her to do there and it would be much better for the baby, especially when the hot weather comes."

"But, Lottie, this is our *home*. I think it's very important that a married couple has a separate home of their own, even if the husband has to be away some of the time."

"George, are you very happy with Roberta?"

"Why, yes, of course! I'm the happiest man in town. It's not like you, Lottie, to ask things like that."

"Roberta wants to go back to the farm."

There was silence for a minute, then Brush said: "I'll give up the business. I'll get a job in town here somewhere . . . because my home's more important to me than my business is."

"No, that wouldn't help. George, I don't want to hurt you or anything. . . . We're both tremendously fond of you, George, you know that. But . . ."

"What *is* it? What are you trying to say?"

"George, don't you see? Roberta wants to live alone."

Brush turned white, but did not raise his eyes. Then he rose and said: "I think I'd better take a walk."

Lottie went to him and put her arm around his shoulder and said: "George, don't be mad at me. I'm only trying to help you see what's best."

Brush muttered: "But that's terrible. I don't see how you can say a thing like that."

"George, you're both awfully nice people, but you know as well as I do that you don't really suit each other. Everything's fine now; you've been married and that awful thing in the past is all settled and forgotten. Don't you think——?"

But by now Brush was standing by the door with blazing eyes. He said: "Are you going to be one of those city people, too, with ideas like that? I'm ashamed of you, Lottie. Don't you know about God's laws? Roberta and I have been married and we'll be married until we die. The only reason you can say a thing like that is because you've never been married and don't know what an important thing it is. Roberta and I are one person, don't you understand that? I'm going for a walk. I've got to get some air."

Roberta had come into the room. "All I want is to live by myself, George," she said. "I like you very much, George, but . . . we're different, you know we are." Whereupon she rushed into the kitchen, shutting the door behind her.

Brush said: "Isn't this just what all married people go through? . . . and then they come out of it?"

"George!" said Lottie, sadly.

Brush put on his hat and coat. Then he said: "Why don't you say it right out? You want me to get a divorce like all those people in the newspapers, and so go on smoking and . . . giggling and drinking to the cemetery. That's what you want. You want us to lead lives like . . . like senseless, silly people that have no ideas and no religion and no thoughts about the human race. It's not important if Roberta and I are different, as she calls it. It's not important if we don't get on like some couples do. We're married, and it's for the good of society and morals that we stay together until we die."

"George," said Lottie, in a level voice, "go into the kitchen and tell Roberta you love her more than anyone in the world. More than anybody ever loved anybody else. Go on. Go on, do it. That's what a marriage promise is."

They looked at one another darkly.

"Let her have Elizabeth," continued Lottie. "She'll be perfectly happy with her; but don't make her stay in this apartment for three months, pretending that she's waiting for the——"

Brush's train left at midnight. His suitcases stood ready beside the door. He picked them up, then suddenly in wild emotion hurled them against the wall.

"I don't want to go on!" he cried. "What good does it do to go to work if I haven't got a home to work for?" He put his hands over his face. "I don't want to live," he said. "Everything goes wrong."

Lottie went over to him. She tried to pull one of his hands down from his face, but he would not let it go.

"George, don't act so," she said, quietly. "You're the finest person I ever knew . . . but this is an entirely different kind of thing. Be frank, look at things simply. See? Be kind to Roberta; this is the way to be kind to Roberta."

He put his hands down and looked at her. "Isn't the principle of a thing more important than the people that live under the principle?" he asked.

"Nobody's strong enough to live up to the rules," said Lottie, with the beginning of a smile in her gravity. "I guess we're

all allowed an exception once in a while. . . . Say a nice good-by to Roberta."

Roberta had silently come into the room. He kissed them both good-by and, although it was only nine o'clock, went to the station. He walked around the station feverishly, then went up to one of the shops.

"Do you sell pipes?" he asked.

"Yes."

"I'll take one . . . that one. What's the best kind of pipe tobacco that you've got?"

With his new possessions he went into the smoking-room and tried to look matters over in a new light.

Chapter XIII

George Brush loses something. Last news of Father Pasziewski. Thoughts on arriving at the age of twenty-four.

AGAIN George Brush set out on the long swing of the pendulum to Abilene, Texas, resuming the life in trains, buses, street cars and blank hotel bedrooms, his evenings spent in public libraries, and the long walks at night encircling the towns he was visiting. He refused to recognize the profound dejection that filled him; he pretended that he was enjoying his work, his Sundays, and his reading. There were two things that now somewhat mitigated his depression; one was his pipe, the other was his study of the German language. Caulkins and Company had decided to put out a First and Second German Reader, and as usual Brush felt himself called upon to make a personal experience of their superiority. He memorized the paradigms and wrote out all the exercises. He found three misprints. He learned by heart "Du bist wie eine Blume" and "The Lorelei." He began talking to himself and thinking in hog-German. He no longer lived by voluntary poverty, and with the addition of Herb's money he grew incredibly wealthy; he had over eight hundred dollars. Out of this superfluity he bought himself a portable gramophone, and while he was dressing he played himself the German instruction records. He became very enthusiastic about the German classics and prolonged all his conversations with the German teachers he called upon; Caulkins' Readers sold in great numbers.

But these consolations were more apparent than real. They could not conceal the stab of physical pain that went through him when, on the evening walks, he glimpsed through half-drawn blinds the felicities of an American home, or when in church he discovered that the old-fashioned hymns no longer had the power to render him inexplicably happy. From time to time whole nights passed without his being able to sleep; occasionally he sat down to a meal, only to discover that he had no appetite whatever.

One day he arose to discover, quite simply, that he had lost his faith. It was as though in some painless way he had lost his arms and legs. At first his only emotion was astonishment. He looked about him; he had mislaid something that would turn up presently. But it did not turn up and the astonishment was followed by a mood of cynical exhilaration. When he went to bed he would find himself falling on his knees as usual, but he would spring up at once, a little guiltily, and, getting into bed, would lie there, smiling grimly at the ceiling. "Es ist nichts da," he would mutter aloud to the sky, "gar nichts."

For a while this gave his life and his business interviews a new energy. Now he laughed and talked more in the chance encounters on trains and in hotels. He spent his evenings at the movies, laughing long and loudly at the least pretext. He began to take advantage of his expense account recklessly; he chose the dollar dinner, with steak, rather than the sixty-cent dinner, vegetable plate, or sausage and potatoes.

By the time he reached Texas something was happening to his health, and finally at Trowbridge, in western Texas, he went to the hospital. The doctor was puzzled and then alarmed. Apparently Brush had a little of everything. There was a touch of amœbic dysentery and a suggestion of sinus; there was something of rheumatism and more than a hint of jaundice. His respiratory organs weren't right, a kind of asthma, and his heart had a murmur. The whole machine had run down and he grew worse daily. He lay in the hospital for weeks, his face turned to the wall. His few remarks were quotations from *King Lear* translated into bad German. He knew what was the matter with him and on one occasion tried to explain to the doctor his theory of sickness, but he soon gave it up with the words: "Ich sterbe, du stirbst, er stirbt, sie und es stirbt; wir sterben, ihr sterbet, sie sterben, sie sterben." When he first arrived at the hospital he had filled out a card, giving his name, age, and business address, and the hospital office had written to Caulkins and Company about his condition. A number of letters from the firm and forwarded by the firm had come to him, but Brush left them unopened on the table by his bed.

Brush had had very little to do with hospitals, but he had a theory that trained nurses were the true priestesses of our time. Whenever he saw or met one he gazed upon her with

profound admiration and reverence. Miss Colloquer, who was assigned to him, was faultless in the performance of her duties, but she seemed to have no inkling of the higher qualities that Brush expected of her.

One day she put her head around the edge of the screen that protected him. "Asleepums?" she asked, softly.

"No."

"Here's a nice, *nice* caller to see you," she said, straightening the sheets into a long line across his chest. "It's Dr. Bowie. He's my minister at the First Methodist. You want to see him, don't you?"

Brush shook his head.

"Oh yes, you do. He's a werry, werry nice man. Now let me make you booful a minute," she said, straightening the part in his hair. "There! Oo's a perfect lamb, yes, you are. As good as gold. Come in Dr. Bowie."

Dr. Bowie was an elderly, bearded man, wearing a frayed frock coat; a black string tie was tied about the collar of his blue flannel shirt. He came from a long talk with the director of the hospital.

Brush with both hands held his pillow over his eyes. He lowered it for a moment, glanced at his visitor, and replaced it on his forehead.

"What's this? What's this, my dear boy?" asked Dr. Bowie, drawing up his chair by Brush's bed. Brush did not answer. Dr. Bowie lowered his voice: "Now, isn't there anything you want to tell me?" Brush still did not answer. Dr. Bowie was slightly antagonized, but he controlled himself. "The doctor tells me that you're a sick man, a pretty sick man, my boy. We must think of that, yes, sir." He brought out a questionnaire blank and laid it surreptitiously on his knees, and drew out a pencil. "Are your dear parents living, Mr. Brush?"

The pillow moved up and down.

"Now don't you think we'd better telegraph them that you're sick? Don't you think that you'd get well right off if your father or your dear mother were here?"

"No," said Brush.

"What are their names and address?"

Brush gave the answer and Dr. Bowie licked his pencil and wrote it down. It turned out that Brush was a married man

also, and Roberta's address was recorded, with the date of the marriage.

Dr. Bowie consulted the next question and murmured "Mm—no children——?"

"Two," said Brush. "One that's alive and one that's dead. The live one is Elizabeth Martin Brush. She's four. And the dead one's name is . . . is . . ." He consulted the ceiling, then added with decision . . . "is named David."

Dr. Bowie's eyebrows rose, but he recorded the facts. "Now isn't there some message you'd like to give me for your family, Mr. Brush?"

"No."

Dr. Bowie laid aside his paper a moment. "I want you to think seriously for a moment, my dear boy. I certainly hope that God will restore you soon to a life of Christian usefulness; but God's will is not always our will. He calls us when He wants us. Have you any church affiliation, may I ask?"

Brush took the pillow away from his forehead. "No," he said, clearly. "None."

Dr. Bowie drew in his chin and cleared his throat. "Now a great many people, a *great* many, have found it a comfort— what a comfort!—to ask forgiveness of God in the presence of his minister—oh, my boy!—for the things they've done wrong in this life. It lightens the load, my brother."

Brush's mouth straightened out. "I've broken all the Ten Commandments, except two," he answered. "I never killed anybody and I never made any graven images. Many's the time I almost killed myself, though, and I'm not joking. I never was tempted by idols, but I guess that would have come along any day. I don't say these things to you because I'm sorry, but because I don't like your tone of voice. I'm glad I did these things and I wish I'd done them more. I made the mistake all my life of thinking that you could get better and better until you were perfect."

There was a long pause. Dr. Bowie swallowed his soft palate several times; then said, in a feeble voice: "In spite of that, Mr. Brush, it has always been my custom at the bedside of patients . . . in a critical condition . . . to say a few . . . words of prayer."

Brush raised his head a moment and looked at him fiercely. "Don't!" he said.

"My boy, my boy!" replied the other, his hands fluttering in midair.

"If there were a God he wouldn't like it," cried Brush, with unexpected force. "Don't you know that you're not supposed to ask for . . . for *facts?*"

"Mr. Brush!"

"You're only supposed to ask for things like being good or having faith or something like that."

"Very well . . . ah . . . !"

"But it doesn't get you anywhere. Look at me. The more I asked the worse I got. Everything I did was wrong. Everybody I knew got to hate me. So that proves it. When you were young I guess you asked to be all those things; and yet look at you; you're pretty stupid, if I must say so, and dry and . . . I'll bet you even believe in war."

Dr. Bowie had risen in horror and was nervously gathering together his questionnaire, hat, raincoat, cane, and Bible. Brush continued: "The second thing that shows that there is no God is that he allows such foolish people to be ministers. I've secretly thought that for a long time, and now I'm glad to be able to say it. All ministers are stupid—do you hear me?— *all.* . . . I mean: all except one."

Dr. Bowie's anger had so risen that his horror was gone. He leaned over Brush. "Young man," he said, distinctly, "are those the words and thoughts you're going to die with?"

They stared at one another. Brush greatly weakened by his outburst, closed his eyes. "No," he said. ". . . I'm sorry."

"I realize you're a sick man. I hope you'll think over the foolish proud things you've said. I'll come and see you again." He stood looking at Brush's closed eyes a moment. Then he said: "There seems to be a good deal of mail for you here. Would you like me to read it to you?"

"No. There's not a letter in the world that would interest me at all."

Miss Colloquer had come in, smiling. "Dr. Bowie, do open that little package that's come. Perhaps it's a present for Mr. Brush. You'll let *him* open it, won't you, Mr. Brush? It's from Kansas City."

Brush nodded wearily.

Dr. Bowie opened it. In the tissue paper lay an ordinary silver-plated spoon.

Miss Colloquer loved a mystery and would not let the matter rest until they had found the letter that accompanied the present. It was from a Marcella L. Craven. It said that she hoped Mr. Brush was well and enjoying his work. The boys on the top floor were all well and still had jobs. Roberta and Lottie and Elizabeth had paid a call on her one day and they were in fine health. The writer hoped Mr. Brush would come back soon because Elizabeth wanted more lessons. "She couldn't be fonder of you if you were her own father, Mr. Brush, that's the truth. I forget if I told you that Father Pasziewski died. I will tell you the details about it when you come. Mrs. Kandinsky and I called on him a few days before he died. And it seemed he knew he was going to die and he wanted to give us something to remember him by. So he sent Anna into the dining-room and he gave us each a spoon. And he asked me to give you a spoon from him, too. He said it was a sort of foolish thing to give, but that perhaps you could use a spoon some way. I told him you liked to hear about him, Mr. Brush, and he seemed to have a special feeling about you. It's a terrible pity you never met."

"Don't read any more," said Brush. "Thank you," and holding the spoon in his hand he turned his face to the wall. Then looking back a minute, he asked: "What day is it today, Miss Colloquer—what day of the week?"

"Why, today's Friday."

"Thank you."

From that day he began to get well. At first he was silent and thoughtful, but gradually the talkativeness began to reappear, and finally he was able to resume his itinerary. He so arranged his appointments that he was able to revisit Wellington, Oklahoma, on his twenty-fourth birthday. He returned to the path through the deep weeds and came to the pond near the deserted brick factory. Again there were turtles on the log; again the bird-calls foretold a hot day. He lay flat on his face and finally fell asleep, but not before he had passed an earnest hour. A few days later in Killam, a man heard him sing at a community-chest bazaar and offered him a good deal of money to

sing on the radio in Chicago. Brush said he'd like to do it, but that his route didn't pass through Chicago. The man doubled his offer; Brush replied that he'd do it free of charge, but that his route didn't pass through Chicago. The next day in Lockburn, Missouri, Brush came upon a very pretty waitress reading Darwin's *The Cruise of the "Beagle"* in her spare time. He arranged to put her through college. The next week, the manager and guests of Bishop's Hotel at Tohoki, in the same state, were astonished to discover that one of their number, a tall solidly built young man, had suddenly lost the use of his voice and was communicating with the outside world by means of pencil and paper. Several days later, in Dakins, Kansas, the same traveler was arrested and confined for a few hours in the jail. The charge was later found to have been based on a misunderstanding. He was released and continued on his journey.

THE IDES OF MARCH

"Das Schaudern ist der Menschheit bestes Teil;
Wie auch die Welt ihm das Gefühl verteure. . . ."
Goethe: FAUST, *Part Two*

"The shudder of awe is humanity's highest faculty,
Even though this world is forever altering its values. . . ."

Gloss: Out of man's recognition in fear and awe that there is an Unknowable comes all that is best in the explorations of his mind,—even though that recognition is often misled into superstition, enslavement, and overconfidence.

Historical reconstruction is not among the primary aims of this work. It may be called a fantasia on certain events and persons of the last days of the Roman republic.

The principal liberty taken is that of transferring an event which took place in 62 B.C.—the profanation of the Mysteries of the Bona Dea by Clodia Pulcher and her brother—to the celebration of the same rites seventeen years later on December 11, 45.

By 45 many of my characters would have long been dead: Clodius, murdered by bullies on a country road; Catullus, though we have only St. Jerome's word for it that he died at the age of thirty; the younger Cato, a few months earlier in this very year, in Africa, resisting Caesar's absolute power; Caesar's aunt, widow of the great Marius, had died even before 62. Moreover by 45, Caesar's second wife Pompeia had long been replaced by his third wife Calpurnia.

A number of the elements in this work which may most seem to have been of my contriving are indeed historical: Cleopatra arrived in Rome in 46, was installed by Caesar in his villa across the river; she remained there until his assassination when she fled back to her own country. The possibility that Junius Marcus Brutus was Caesar's son is weighed and generally rejected by almost every historian who has given extended consideration to Caesar's private life. Caesar's gift to Servilia of a pearl of unprecedented value is historical. The conspiratorial chain-letters directed against Caesar were suggested by the events of our own times. They were circulated in Italy against the Fascist regime by Lauro de Bosis, reportedly on the advice of Bernard Shaw.

The attention of the reader is called to the form in which the material is presented:

Within each of the four books the documents are given in approximately chronological order. Those in Book One cover September, 45 B.C. Book Two, which contains material relevant

to Caesar's inquiry concerning the nature of love, begins earlier and traverses the whole of September and October. Book Three, mainly occupied with religion, begins earlier still and runs through the autumn, concluding with the ceremonies of the Good Goddess in December. Book Four, resuming all the aspects of Caesar's inquiry, particularly those dealing with himself as possibly filling a role as an instrument of "destiny," begins with the earliest document in the volume and concludes with his assassination.

All the documents in this work are from the author's imagination with the exception of the poems of Catullus and the closing entry which is from Suetonius's *Lives of the Caesars.*

Source material dealing with Cicero is copious; with Cleopatra, meager; with Caesar, rich but often enigmatic and distorted by political bias. This is a suppositional reconstruction provoked by the inequalities in those records.

THORNTON WILDER

BOOK ONE

I The Master of the College of Augurs to Caius Julius Caesar, Supreme Pontiff and Dictator of the Roman People.

> (Copies to the Priest of Capitoline Jupiter, etc.; to Madam President of the College of the Vestal Virgins, etc., etc.)
>
> [*September 1, 45* B.C.]

To the most reverend Supreme Pontiff:

Sixth report of this date.

Readings of the noon sacrifice:

A goose: maculations of the heart and liver. Herniation of the diaphragm.

Second goose and a cock: Nothing to remark.

A pigeon: ominous condition, kidney displaced, liver enlarged and yellow in color. Pink quartz in crop. Further detailed study has been ordered.

Second pigeon: Nothing to remark.

Observed flights: an eagle from three miles north of Mt. Soracte to limit of vision over Tivoli. The bird showed some uncertainty as to direction in its approach toward the city.

Thunder: No thunder has been heard since that last reported twelve days ago.

Health and long life to the Supreme Pontiff.

I-A Notation by Caesar, confidential, for his ecclesiastical secretary.

Item I. Inform the Master of the College that it is not necessary to send me ten to fifteen of these reports a day. A single summary report of the previous day's observations is sufficient.

Item II. Select from the reports of the last four days three signally favorable and three unfavorable auspices. I may require them in the Senate today.

Item III. Draw up and distribute a notification to the following effect:

With the establishment of the new calendar the Commem-

oration of the Founding of the City on the seventeenth day of each month will now be elevated to a rite of the highest civic importance.

The Supreme Pontiff, if resident in the City, will be present on each occasion.

The entire ritual will be observed with the following additions and corrections:

Two hundred soldiers will be present and will deliver the Invocation to Mars as is customary on military posts.

The Adoration of Rhea will be rendered by the Vestal Virgins. The President of the College will herself be held responsible for this attendance, for the excellence of the rendition, and for the decorum of the participants. The abuses which have crept into the ritual will be corrected at once; these celebrants will remain invisible until the final procession, and no resort will be made to the mixolydian mode.

The Testament of Romulus will be directed toward the seats reserved for the aristocracy.

The priests exchanging the responses with the Supreme Pontiff will be letter perfect. Priests failing in any particular will be given thirty days' training and sent to serve in the new temples in Africa and Britain.

I-B Caesar's Journal-Letter to Lucius Mamilius Turrinus on the Island of Capri.

> [*For a description of this journal-letter see the opening of Document III.*]

968. [*On religious rites*]

I enclose in this week's packet a half-dozen of the innumerable reports which, as Supreme Pontiff, I receive from the Augurs, Soothsayers, Sky Watchers, and Chicken Nurses.

I enclose also the directions I have issued for the monthly Commemoration of the Founding of the City.

What's to be done?

I have inherited this burden of superstition and nonsense. I govern innumerable men but must acknowledge that I am governed by birds and thunderclaps.

All this frequently obstructs the operation of the State; it closes the doors of the Senate and the Courts for days and

weeks at a time. It employs several thousands of persons. Everyone who has anything to do with it, including the Supreme Pontiff, manipulates it to his own interest.

One afternoon, in the Rhine Valley, the augurs of our headquarters forbade me to join battle with the enemy. It seems that our sacred chickens were eating fastidiously. Mesdames Partlet were crossing their feet as they walked; they were frequently inspecting the sky and looking back over their shoulders, and with good reason. I too on entering the valley had been discouraged to observe that it was the haunt of eagles. We generals are reduced to viewing the sky with a chicken's eyes. I acceded for one day, though in my capability of surprising the enemy lay one of my few advantages, and I feared that I would be similarly impeded in the morning. That evening, however, Asinius Pollio and I took a walk in the woods; we gathered a dozen grubs; we minced them into fine pieces with our knives and strewed them about the sacred feeding pen. The next morning the entire army waited in suspense to hear the will of the Gods. The fateful birds were put out to feed. They first surveyed the sky emitting that chirp of alarm which is sufficient to arrest ten thousand men; then they turned their gaze upon their meal. By Hercules, their eyes protruded; they uttered cries of ravished gluttony; they flew to their repast, and I was permitted to win the Battle of Cologne.

Most of all, however, these observances attack and undermine the very spirit of life within the minds of men. They afford to our Romans, from the street sweepers to the consuls, a vague sense of confidence where no confidence is and at the same time a pervasive fear, a fear which neither arouses to action nor calls forth ingenuity, but which paralyzes. They remove from men's shoulders the unremitting obligation to create, moment by moment, their own Rome. They come to us sanctioned by the usage of our ancestors and breathing the security of our childhood; they flatter passivity and console inadequacy.

I can cope with the other enemies of order: the planless trouble making and violence of a Clodius; the grumbling discontents of a Cicero and a Brutus, born of envy and fed on the fine-spun theorizing of old Greek texts; the crimes and greed of my proconsuls and appointees; but what can I do against the apathy that is glad to wrap itself under the cloak of piety,

that tells me that Rome will be saved by overwatching Gods or is resigned to the fact that Rome will come to ruin because the Gods are maleficent?

I am not given to brooding, but often I find myself brooding over this matter.

What to do?

At times, at midnight, I try to imagine what would happen if I abolished all this; if, Dictator and Supreme Pontiff, I abolished all observation of lucky and unlucky days, of the entrails and flights of birds, of thunder and lightning; if I closed all temples except those of Capitoline Jove.

And what of Jove?

You will hear more of this.

Prepare your thoughts for my guidance.

The next night.

[*The letter continues in Greek.*]

Again it is midnight, my dear friend. I sit before my window, wishing that it overhung the sleeping city and not the Trasteverine gardens of the rich. The mites dance about my lamp. The river barely reflects a diffused starlight. On the farther bank some drunken citizens are arguing in a wine shop and from time to time my name is borne to me on the air. I have left my wife sleeping and have tried to quiet my thoughts by reading in Lucretius.

Every day I feel more pressure upon me, arising from the position I occupy. I become more and more aware of what it enables me to accomplish, of what it summons me to accomplish.

But what is it saying to me? What does it require of me?

I have pacified the world; I have extended the benefits of Roman law to innumerable men and women; against great opposition, I am extending to them also the rights of citizenship. I have reformed the calendar and our days are regulated by a serviceable accommodation of the movements of the sun and the moon. I am arranging that the world be fed equably; my laws and my fleets will adjust the intermittence of harvests and surplus to the public need. Next month torture will be removed from the penal code.

But these are not enough. These measures have been merely the work of a general and of an administrator. In them I am to

the world what a mayor is to a village. Now some other work is to be done, but what? I feel as though now, and only now, I am ready to *begin*. The song which is on everyone's lips calls me: father.

For the first time in my public life I am unsure. My actions have hitherto conformed to a principle which I may call a superstition: I do not experiment. I do not initiate an action in order to be instructed by its results. In the art of war and in the operations of politics I do nothing without an extremely precise intention. If an obstacle arises I promptly create a new plan, every potential consequence of which is clear to me. From the moment I saw that Pompey left a small portion of every venture to *chance*, I knew that I was to be the master of the world.

The projects which now visit me, however, involve elements about which I am not certain that I am certain. To put them into effect I must be clear in my mind as to what are the aims in life of the average man and what are the capabilities of the human being.

Man—what is that? What do we know of him? His Gods, liberty, mind, love, destiny, death—what do these mean? You remember how you and I as boys in Athens, and later before our tents in Gaul, used to turn these things over endlessly. I am an adolescent again, philosophizing. As Plato, the dangerous beguiler, said: the best philosophers in the world are boys with their beards new on their chins; I am a boy again.

But look what I have done in the meantime in regard to this matter of the State religion. I have bolstered it by re-establishing the monthly Commemoration of the Founding of the City.

I did it, perhaps, to explore in myself what last vestiges of such piety as I can discover there. It flatters me also to know that I am of all Romans the most learned in old religious lore, as my mother was before me. I confess that as I declaim the uncouth collects and move about in the complicated ritual, I am filled with a real emotion; but the emotion has no relation to the supernatural world: I am remembering myself when at nineteen, as Priest of Jupiter, I ascended the Capitol with my Cornelia at my side, the unborn Julia beneath her girdle. What moment has life since offered to equal that?

Hush! There has just been a change of guard at my door. The sentries have clashed their swords and exchanged the password. The password for tonight is CAESAR WATCHES.

II The Lady Clodia Pulcher, from her villa at Baiae on the Bay of Naples, to the Steward of her Household in Rome.
 [*September 3, 45* B.C.]

My brother and I are giving a dinner on the last day of the month. If any mistakes occur this time I shall replace you and offer you for sale.

Invitations have been sent to the Dictator, and to his wife and aunt; to Cicero; to Asinius Pollio; and to Gaius Valerius Catullus. The entire dinner will be conducted in the old mode, that is to say, the women will be present only in the second part of the dinner and will not recline.

If the Dictator accepts this invitation, the strictest protocol will be observed. Start rehearsing the servants now: the reception before the door, the carrying of the chair, the tour of the house, and the leave-taking. Make arrangements to hire twelve trumpeters. Inform the priests of our temple that they are to perform the ceremony suitable for the reception of the Supreme Pontiff.

Not only you, but my brother also, will taste the Dictator's dishes in his presence, as was done in the old days.

The menu will depend upon the new amendments to the sumptuary laws. If they are passed by the day of the dinner only one entree may be served to the entire company. It will be the Egyptian ragout of sea food which the Dictator once described to you. I don't know anything about it; go at once to his chef and find out how it is prepared. When you are sure of the recipe, make it at least three times to insure that it will be perfect on the night of the dinner.

If the new laws have not been passed, we will have a variety of dishes.

The Dictator, my brother, and I will have the ragout. Cicero will have lamb on the spit in the Greek manner. The Dictator's wife will have the sheep's head with roast apples which she praised so highly. Did you send her the recipe as she asked you to? If so, change the preparation slightly; I suggest that you

add three or four peaches soaked in Albanian spirits. The Lady Julia Marcia and Valerius Catullus will be offered their choice among these dishes. Asinius Pollio will probably eat nothing as usual, but have ready some heated goat's milk and some Lombardy porridge. I leave the matter of the wines entirely in your hands; watch the laws about it.

I am having twenty to thirty dozen oysters dragged under water in nets to Ostia. Some of them can be brought up to Rome on the day of the dinner.

Go at once to Eros, the Greek mime, and engage him for the evening. He will probably make his accustomed difficulties; you may hint to him the quality of the guests I am expecting. When you have closed the interview you may tell him that in addition to his usual fee I will give him Cleopatra's mirror. Tell him I wish him, with his troupe, to perform "Aphrodite and Hephaestus" and Herondas's "The Procession of Osiris." Alone, I wish him to declaim Sappho's "Garland-Weaver's Cycle."

I am leaving Naples tomorrow. I shall stop a week with the family of Quintus Lentulus Spinther at Capua. I shall expect a letter from you there telling me how my brother is occupying himself. You may expect me in Rome about the 10th.

I wish to have a report from you on the matter of cleaning up all scribbling about our family in public places. I want this to be very thorough.

> [*What Clodia meant by this last paragraph is best illustrated by a passage in one of Cicero's letters and by some selected graffitti:*]

II-A Cicero, in Rome, to Atticus, in Greece.
 [*Written in the spring of this year.*]

Second only to the master of us all, Clodia has become the most discussed person in Rome. Verses of unbounded obscenity are scribbled about her over the walls and pavements of all the baths and urinals in Rome. I am told there is an extended satire dedicated to her in the cooling-off hall of the Baths of Pompey; seventeen poets have already put their hands to it; it receives additions daily. I am told that it turns in large part upon the fact that she is widow, daughter, niece, granddaughter, and

great-granddaughter of consuls and that her ancestor Appius first laid down the road upon which she now seeks consolatory if not remunerative companionship.

The lady, it is reported, has heard of these tributes. Three cleaning men are engaged nightly in surreptitious erasure. They are overworked; they cannot keep up with their task.

Our Dominie [*Caesar*] does not have to engage workmen to efface calumny. There are scurrilous verses enough; but for every decrier he has three advocates. His veterans have re-armed themselves with sponges.

Poetry has become a fever in our city. I am told that the verses of this new-come Catullus—verses also addressed to Clodia, though in a different vein—are likewise scrawled upon our public buildings. The Syrian pie vendors have got them by heart. What do you say to that? Under the absolute power of one man our occupations are taken from us, or lose their savor. We are not citizens but slaves and poetry is the resource of an enforced idleness.

II-B Graffitti scrawled on the walls and pavements of Rome.
. . . .

Clodius Pulcher in the Senate says to Cicero:
My sister wouldn't budge; she wouldn't give me a foot, he says.
Oh, says Cicero, we thought she was more genrus.
We thought she give you above the knee, he says.
. . . .

Her ancestors laid down the Appian Way. Caesar
Took up this Appia and laid it down in another way.
Haw, haw, haw.
. . . .

The Fourpenny Girl is a millionaire, but avaricious and no idler;
How proudly she brings in her fifty pennies at dawn.
. . . .

Monthly, Caesar commemorates the Founding of the City.
Hourly, the dissolution of the Republic.
. . . .

[*The following popular song, with variants, was found scrawled in public places throughout the world.*]

The world is Rome's and the Gods gave it to Caesar;
Caesar is the descendant of the Gods, and a God.
He who never lost a battle is to every soldier a father.
He has planted his heel on the mouth of the rich man,
But to the poor he is a friend and a consoler.
By this you know that the Gods love Rome:
They have given it to Caesar, their descendant and a God.

. . . .

[*The following lines of Catullus appear to have been adopted by the general public at once; within a year they had reached the remotest parts of the Republic as an anonymous proverbial aphorism:*]

Suns set and are able to rise again;
But once our brief light has set
Night is f'rever and must be slep' out.

III Caesar's Journal-Letter to Lucius Mamilius Turrinus on the Island of Capri.

[*Probably from August 20 to September 4.*]

[*This journal-letter was maintained from the time that the recipient was captured and maimed by the Belgians in 51 to the Dictator's death. The entries offer a wide variety in form; some are written on the backs of discarded letters and documents; some have been written in haste, others with great care; some have been dictated and are in the hand of a secretary. Though they have been numbered serially they are only occasionally dated.*]

958. [*On the possible etymology of three obsolete words in the Testament of Romulus.*]

959–963. [*On some trends and events in current politics.*]

964. [*He gives his low opinion of Cicero's employment of metrical devices in his orations.*]

965–967. [*On politics.*]

968. [*On Roman religion. This entry has already appeared in this volume as Section I-B.*]

969. [*On Clodia Pulcher and her upbringing.*] Clodia and her brother have invited us to dinner. I seem to have discussed the situation of this couple sufficiently in my letters to you,

but, like the rest of Rome, I find myself returning to the subject.

I am no longer immediately filled with compassion when I encounter one of those innumerable persons who trail behind them a shipwrecked life. Least of all do I try to find excuses for them when I see that they have found them for themselves, when I see them sitting on the throne of their own minds, excused, acquitted, and hurling indictments against the mysterious Destiny which has wronged them and exhibiting themselves as pure victim. Such a one is Clodia.

That is not the role she performs before her numerous acquaintance; for them she affects to be the happiest of women. It is the role, however, which she plays in her own eyes and before me, for I am, I think, the only person living who knows of a certain circumstance of which she was perhaps a victim and on which she has for over twenty-five years based her claims to being, each day again, a fresh victim.

Another excuse could be found for her and for those other women of her generation whose disorders are similarly calling attention to them. They were born into the great houses of wealth and privilege and were brought up in that atmosphere of noble sentiments and unceasing moralizing which we are now calling "the Old Roman way." The mothers of these girls were in many cases great women, but they had developed a series of qualities they could not transmit. Maternal love, pride of family, and wealth had combined to make hypocrites of them and their daughters were reared in a sheltered world of bland untruths and evasion. The conversation in their homes became too full of loud silences, that is of subjects which we do not discuss. Their daughters, the more intelligent ones, on growing older became aware of this; they felt they had been lied to and they promptly flung themselves into a public demonstration of their liberation from hypocrisy. Imprisonment of the body is bitter; imprisonment of the mind is worse. The thoughts and actions of those who awaken to the fact that they have been duped are painful to themselves and dangerous to others. Clodia was the most intelligent, as her behavior is now the most flagrant. All of these girls acquired or assumed a passion for being seen in low company and the ostentation of vulgarity has become a political factor with which I must deal. The plebeian

world is ameliorable in itself, but what can I do with a plebeian aristocracy?

Even the young women whose conduct is irreproachable— like Clodia's sister, like my wife—exhibit the resentment of the awakened dupe. They had been brought up to think that the domestic virtues were self-evident and universal; they had been starved of the knowledge that most attracts the young mind: that the crown of life is the exercise of choice.

In her conduct I see reflected also a matter which I have frequently discussed with you, perhaps too often—the fact that the usage and very structure of our language exhibits and inculcates the belief that we are passive in the presence of life, bound, committed, and helpless. Our language tells us that we are *given* such and such qualifications at birth. That is to say: there is a Great Giver who gave Clodia beauty, health, wealth, high birth, and conspicuous intelligence and to another slavery, disease, and stupidity. She has often heard it said that she was endowed with beauty (by what endower?) and that another was cursed with a sharp tongue—did God curse? Even if we assume the existence of a God who, as Homer says, pours out from his urns his good and evil gifts, I am amazed at the pious who insult their God by failing to see that as this world is run there is a field of circumstance that is not commensurate with God's providence and that God must have so intended it.

But to return to our Clodia: the Clodias under such a dispensation never receive enough; they are poisoned by resentment against this niggardly Giver who has only given them beauty, health, wealth, birth, and intelligence, who is holding back a million gifts, namely, perfect felicity in every moment of every day. There is no rapacity equal to that of the privileged who feel that their advantages have been conferred upon them by some Intelligence and no bitterness equal to that of the ill-conditioned who feel that they have been specifically passed over.

Oh, my friend, my friend, what better thing could I do for Rome than to put the birds back into the world of birds, thunder back into the phenomena of the atmosphere and the Gods back into the memories of infancy?

I need hardly say we are not attending Clodia's dinner.

IV The Lady Julia Marcia, widow of the great Marius, from her farm in the Alban Hills, to her nephew Caius Julius Caesar in Rome.

[*September 4.*]

Clodius Pulcher and his sister have invited me to dinner on the last day of the month; they tell me, my dear boy, that you will be there. I had not intended coming into town until December when I must take up my duties in connection with the Mysteries [*of the Good Goddess*]. Naturally, I would not think of going to that house without the assurance that you and your dear wife would be there also. Will you return one word by this messenger as to whether you will really be present or not?

I must confess that I am not a little curious to see—after all these years of rustication—how that Palatine Hill society lives. The scandalized letters I receive from Sempronia Metella and Servilia and Aemilia Cimber and Fulvia Manso are not of much help. They are so busy calling attention to their own virtue that I cannot make out whether the daily round at the top of the world is brilliant or trivial.

I have another reason for seeing Clodia Pulcher, also. It may be that, sooner or later, I shall be obliged to have a very serious conversation with her—for her mother's and grandmother's sakes, dear friends of my youth and middle years. Can you divine what I mean? [*As will be seen, Caesar did not grasp this intimation. His aunt was on the Governing Board of the Mysteries of the Good Goddess. If the proposal arose that Clodia be disbarred from participation in the Mysteries, the decision would rest largely with the lay committee and not with the representatives from the College of the Vestal Virgins. The final responsibility would devolve, however, upon Julius Caesar himself, as Supreme Pontiff.*]

We country bumpkins are prepared to obey precisely all your laws against luxury. Our little communities love you and give thanks to the Gods daily that you are guiding our great State. There are six of your veterans on my farm. The diligence and cheerfulness and loyalty which they show to me are a reflection, I know, of their worship of you. I try not to disappoint them.

Give my love to Pompeia.

[*Second letter in the same packet.*]

My dear Nephew, this is the next morning.

Forgive my presumption in taking the time of the master of the world, but may I ask you a second question to be answered by this messenger?

Is Lucius Mamilius Turrinus still living? Can he receive letters? Can you give me an address for him?

I have put these questions to a number of my friends, but no one seems to be able to answer them with certainty. We know that he was gravely wounded fighting beside you in Gaul. Some say he is living in complete seclusion in the lake country, in Crete, or in Sicily. Others say that he has been dead for a number of years.

I had a dream the other night—you will pardon an old woman—in which I seemed to be standing by the pool of our villa at Tarentum, with my dear brigand of a husband beside me. Two boys were swimming in the pool—yourself and Lucius. You came up out of the water, and putting his hands on your shoulders my husband looked deep into my eyes and said smiling: "Saplings of our great Roman oak."

How often you both came to our house. You spent the whole day hunting. And what enormous dinners you ate. And do you remember how, at the age of twelve, you used to declaim Homer to me, your eyes flashing. And then you and Lucius went off to Greece together to study, and you wrote me long letters about philosophy and poetry. And Lucius, who had no mother, wrote to your mother.

Oh, the past, the past, Caius.

I woke from that dream weeping, weeping for those lost presences, my husband, your mother, Clodia's father and mother, and for Lucius.

Oh, dear, I am wasting your time.

Two answers: Clodia's dinner: and Lucius's address, if he lives.

IV-A Caesar's reply to Julia Marcia, by return messenger.
 [*The first two paragraphs are in the handwriting of a
 secretary.*]

I have no intention, my dear Aunt, of going to Clodia's din-
ner. If I thought there were anything of real interest for you
there, I would of course oblige you by going. Pompeia, how-
ever, joins me in urging you to come to us on that evening. It
may be that Clodia has had the effrontery to invite Cicero and
he may have had the weakness to accept; if so, I shall steal him
from her party and offer him up to you. I think you will like to
see him again; he is even wittier than he used to be and he can
tell you all about the society on the Palatine Hill. Moreover,
do not take the trouble to open your house; the pavilion in our
garden is at your disposal and Al-Nara will be delighted to wait
on you. While you are in the pavilion, my dear lady, I shall di-
rect that during the night watches the sentrymen refrain from
clashing their swords; they shall exchange their passwords in a
whisper.

You will see enough of Clodia when you come to town for
the Ceremonies. Contemplating Clodia I find scarcely a drop
in my heart of that compassion which Epicurus enjoins us to
extend toward the erring. I hope you will have those serious
talks with her, of which you speak, and I hope you will show
me how I may find my way to some sympathy toward her. I
am rendered uncomfortable by the dryness within my heart
toward one to whom I have been bound by so wide a variety
of associations.

 [*Here Caesar continues the letter in his own hand:*]

You talk of the past.

I do not let my thoughts dwell on it for long. All of it, all of
it, seems of a beauty that I shall not see again. Those presences,
how can I think of them? At the memory of one whisper, one
pair of eyes, the pen falls from my hand, the interview in which
I am engaged turns to stone. Rome and her business become a
clerk's task, arid and tedious, with which I fill my days until
death relieves me of it. Am I peculiar in this? I do not know.
Can other men weave past joy into their thoughts in the pres-
ent and their plans for the future? Perhaps only the poets can;
they alone use all of themselves in every moment of their work.

I think that such a one has come among us to replace our Lucretius. I am enclosing a sheaf of his verses. I want you to tell me what you think of them. This mastership of the world which you ascribe to me is more worth administering since I have seen these examples of what our Latin tongue can do. I am not enclosing the verses which have reference to myself; this Catullus is as eloquent in hatred as in love.

There is a present awaiting you in Rome—though my share in it will cost me some of that application to my present duties which, as I have said, follows upon any return I may make to the past. [*Into the monthly Commemoration of the Founding of the City Caesar introduced a salutation rendered by Rome to the spirit of her husband Marius.*]

As to your second question, my dear Aunt, I am not in a position to answer it.

Pompeia sends her love. We await your coming with much joy.

V The Lady Sempronia Metella, in Rome, to the Lady Julia Marcia on her farm in the Alban Hills.
 [*September 6.*]

I can't tell you how delighted I am, my dearest Julia, to hear that you are coming to the City. Don't trouble to open your house. You must stay with me. Zosima, who adores the ground you walk on, will wait on you; I can get on very well with Rhodope who is turning out to be a treasure.

Now make yourself comfortable, dear, because I'm afraid this is going to be a very long chat.

First, do listen to an old old friend's advice: don't go to that woman's house. One can go on saying for years that one doesn't listen to gossip, that the absent cannot defend themselves from slander, etc., etc.; but, after all, isn't the provocation of so much gossip an offense in itself? I personally don't believe that she poisoned her husband or that she has had improper relations with her brothers, but thousands do believe it. My grandson tells me that songs about her are sung in all the garrisons and taverns and verses about her are scribbled over all the Baths. There's a nickname for her in everyone's mouth which I won't venture to put down here.

Really, the worst thing one *knows* about her is the influence she has over that whole Palatine set. It was she who began this business of dressing up as one of the people and mingling with the lowest elements of the city. She takes her friends out to the gladiators' taverns and drinks all night with them, and dances for them, and I leave the rest to your imagination. She makes up picnic parties, Julia, and goes to the taverns out in the country among the herdsmen and the military posts out there. These are *facts*. One of the results of this anyone can see: it's the effect on the language; it's now smart to talk pure *pleb*. And there's no doubt that she and she alone is responsible. Her position in society, her birth, her wealth, her beauty, and—for one must confess it—her fascination and intelligence have led society right down into the mud.

But at last she is frightened. And she has asked you to dinner because she is frightened.

Now listen: a very serious thing is brewing and one which will finally fall upon your shoulders for a decision.

> [*In the following paragraphs a number of substitute expressions are employed:* The Ox-eyed *(in Greek) is Clodia;* The Wild Boar *is her brother, Clodius Pulcher;* The Quail *(a soubriquet conferred upon her by the ladies long before her marriage) is Pompeia, Caesar's wife;* The Thessalian *(short for the Witch of Thessaly) is Servilia, the mother of Marcus Junius Brutus; and* The Tapestry Class *is both the Mysteries of the Good Goddess and the committee that directed their celebration.* The Weathermaker *is, of course, Caesar.*]

Abandoned though this woman is, I don't believe in debarring her from *certain reunions*; but there's no doubt that her disbarment is going to be proposed. She and *The Quail* were present at the last meeting of the Executive Council which took place just before she went south to Baiae. They asked the Chair—*The Thessalian* was sitting in your chair—to excuse them and they left early; and the minute they were gone groups all over the hall began talking about her. Aemilia Cimber said that if *The Ox-eyed* stood anywhere near her during *The Tapestry Class* she would strike her in the face. Fulvia Manso said that she would not strike her during the rites, but that she would leave at once and submit a complaint to the Supreme Pontiff.

And *The Thessalian*, who being in the Chair should not have given any opinion at all, said that the first thing to do was to lay the matter before you and the President of the College of the Vestal Virgins. *Her* indignant tone, I must say, struck me as slightly comical, for we all know that she has not always been as dignified as she now pretends to be.

So there you are! I don't think that you or your nephew would ever let her be disbarred, but what an idea! And what a scandal! You know, I don't think even these older women realize any more what a *scandal* is. Last night I suddenly realized that within my memory there have been only three disbarments and in each case the woman immediately killed herself.

And yet, on the other hand, it is a frightful thing to think that *The Tapestry Class*, which is the most beautiful and sacred and wonderful thing, should include a creature like *The Ox-eyed*. Julia, I have never forgotten what your great husband said about it: "Those twenty hours during which our women draw together are like a column upholding Rome."

It's a great puzzle to all of us: why does *The Weathermaker* (I mean no disrespect, dear, as you know) allow *The Quail* to see so much of her? We are all so surprised by that. Because seeing *The Ox-eyed* inevitably entails seeing *The Wild Boar*, and no woman of principles could ever possibly want to see *The Wild Boar*.

But let us change the subject.

I received a great honor yesterday which I must tell you about. *He* singled me out to talk to me.

I went, of course, with all Rome to call on Cato on the day commemorating his great ancestor. Thousands filled the streets near the house, trumpeters, flute players, priests. Inside the house the Dictator's chair had been set up and, of course, everyone was agog. At last he came. And you know, my dear, how unpredictable he is! As my nephew says: he's formal when you expect him to be informal, and informal when you expect him to be formal. He came walking through the Forum and up the hill without the sign of a retinue, just strolling between Marc Antony and Octavius. I tremble for him because it *is* dangerous; but that's one of the things that the people really worship him for; that's *Old Rome*, and you must have been able to hear the shouting from your own farm! He came into the

house, bowing and smiling, and went right up to Cato and his family. Now you could hear an ant walk. Well, it's no news to you that your nephew is a perfection. We could hear every word he said. First the gravity and the deference; even Cato was weeping and held his head very low. Then Caesar gradually became more informal; he included the family, and then he became very playful and *very funny* and soon the whole hall was laughing.

Cato answered well, but very briefly. All the agonizing political differences seem to have been forgotten. Caesar accepted one of the cakes that were being passed around and then began addressing one bystander and then another. He refused to sit in the Dictator's chair, but everything he does is so charming that it didn't seem to be a slight on the house. And then, my dear, he espied *me*, and asking a servant for a chair he sat down beside me. You can *imagine* my state.

Has he ever forgotten a fact or a name? He remembered having spent four days with us at Anzio twenty years ago, all my relatives and all the guests. He very delicately warned me about my grandson's political activities (but *what*, my dear, can I do about that!). Then he began asking me my opinion of the monthly Commemoration of the Founding of the City. Apparently he had remarked my presence—think of it, at half a mile distance and while he was marching up and down in that complicated ritual! What portions did I find most impressive, which passages were too long or too obscure for the people? Then he got onto religion itself, the auspices and the lucky and unlucky days.

Dear, he is the most charming man in the world, but also—I have to say it—isn't he *frightening*? He listens with such total attention to every little thing one struggles to say. And those great eyes are so flattering, flattering and frightening. They seem to say: "You and I are the only really sincere people here; we say what we really mean; we tell the truth." I hope I wasn't a complete goose; but I wish someone had warned me that the Supreme Pontiff was going to ask me how, what, where, and when I think about religion, because that is what it finally came to. At last he took his leave and we could all go home. And I went straight to bed.

I ask you in a whisper, Julia: what *must* it be like to be his wife?

You asked me about Lucius Mamilius Turrinus.

Like you, I suddenly realized that I didn't know a thing about him. I assumed that he had died or that he had sufficiently recovered to hold some post in the remoter parts of the Republic. Now in search of information of this kind I have found out that the best thing to do is to ask one of our old trusted servants. They constitute a sort of secret society; they know everything about us; and they're proud of all they know. So I consulted our old freedman Rufus Tela, and, sure enough, here are the facts:

In the second battle with the Belgians, at the time that Caesar was almost caught, the enemy captured Turrinus. He had been gone thirty hours before Caesar realized that he was missing. Then, my dear, your nephew hurled a regiment at the enemy's encampment. The regiment was almost annihilated, but it brought back Turrinus *in a pitiable state*. The enemy, in order to extract information from him, was progressively cutting off his limbs and depriving him of his senses. They had cut off an arm and a leg, perhaps more, put out his eyes, cropped his ears, and were about to burst his eardrums. Caesar saw that he received all possible care and since then he has been surrounded, by his own wish, with all possible secrecy. Rufus seems to know, though, that he lives in a beautiful villa on Capri, absolutely walled off. Of course, he's still very rich and has a large household of secretaries, attendants, and all that.

Isn't that a simply *heart-rending* story? Can't life be simply *horrifying*? I remember him so well—handsome, rich, capable, obviously destined for the highest places in the state, and so charming. He almost married my Aurunculeia, but his father and all those Mamiliuses were too conservative for me, to say nothing of my husband. Apparently, he is still interested in politics and history and literature. He has an agent here in Rome who sends him all the news and books and gossip, but no one knows who the agent is. He seems to wish to be forgotten by all except a few close friends. Of course, I asked Rufus who goes to see him. Rufus said that he receives almost no one; that the actress Cytheris occasionally goes and reads to

him, and that once a year, in the spring, the Dictator goes and stays a few days, but apparently never mentions his visits to anyone.

Rufus, who is pure gold, begged me not to repeat any of this to anyone but you. He's a very remarkable old African and seems to respect something in the invalid's wish to be forgotten. I'm going to do as he wishes and I know you will. I'm *horrified* by the length of this letter.

Come as soon as you can.

VI Clodia, at Capua, to her brother Publius Clodius Pulcher in Rome.

> [*September 8.*]
> [*From the villa of Quintus Lentulus Spinther and his wife Cassia.*]

Brainless:

S. T. E. Q. V. M. E. [*Clodia ironically employs an epistolary convention of the day meaning "If you and your army are enjoying good health, it is well"; by changing two letters she says "If you and your riffraff are well, it is bad."*]

Plucked again. [*Caesar's secret police had again gained access to a letter passing between them. The brother and sister arranged, however, that innocuous letters were carried in superficial concealment by their messengers as a screen for their real letters which were more thoroughly concealed.*]

Your letter was insane nonsense. You say: *They will not live forever.* How do you know? Neither he nor you nor anyone else knows how long he will live. You should make your plans as though he were to die tomorrow or live thirty years more. Only children, political orators, and poets talk of the future as though it were a thing one could know; fortunately for us we know nothing about it. You say: *There have been convulsions weekly.* [*Caesar's attacks of epilepsy.*] I tell you you are wrong and you know my source of information. [*Caesar's wife's maid, Abra, had been recommended to that position by Clodia and was paid by Clodia to keep her informed of all that passed in Caesar's house.*] You say: *Under this Cyclops there is nothing we can do.* Listen, you are no longer a boy. You are forty. When will you learn not to wait for chance but to build on what you have and to use

each day to consolidate your position? Why have you never been anything more than Tribune? *Because your plans always begin with next month.* The gulf between today and next month you always try to overleap by the use of violence and your troops of bullies. *Ship's-Snout* [*in Greek: this is Caesar*] rules the world and will continue to rule it for one day or for thirty years. You have no career, you are nothing, unless you accept that fact and work in and around it. And I tell you solemnly, any attempt to work *against it* would lead to your destruction.

You must regain your old favor with him. Never let him forget that you were once of powerful assistance to him. I know you hate him; that is of no importance. Hate and love have nothing to do with anything, as he knows well. Where would he have got, if he had *hated* Pompey?

Watch him, Brainless. You could learn a great deal.

You know his weak side: that indifference, that *absence* which people call his magnanimity. I'll wager that he really likes you, because he likes what is spontaneous and uncomplicated, and that he's practically forgotten that you were an idiotic trouble maker. And I'll wager that he was secretly amused that for twenty years you kept Cicero trembling like a field mouse.

Watch him. You might begin by imitating his diligence. I believe it when they tell me that he writes seventy letters and documents a day. They fall over Italy like snow, every day—what am I saying, they fall over the world from Britain to Lebanon. Even at the Senate, even at dinner parties there's a secretary behind him; the very second that the idea of a letter occurs to him he turns and dictates it in a whisper. One moment he's telling a village in Belgium that it can change its name to his and he sends them a flute for the town band, the next moment he's thought out a way of harmonizing the Jewish dowry laws with Roman usage. He gave a water clock to a city in Algeria and wrote a fascinating letter *in the Arab mode.* Work, Publius, work.

And remember: this is the year we conform.

All I ask of you is one year.

I'm going to be the most conservative woman in Rome. By next summer I mean to be an Honorary Votary of Vesta and a Directress of the Mysteries of the Good Goddess.

You can get a province.

From now on we spell our name Claudius. Grandfather cur-
ried a few votes by adopting the Plebeian spelling. Tiresome.

Our dinner's a failure. *Ship's Snout* and the *Little Lentil*
[*again in Greek; this is Caesar's wife*] have refused. *Hecuba* has
not replied. When he hears this, Cicero will probably send a
last-minute refusal. Asinius Pollio will be there and I'll fill up
the table somehow.

Catullus. I want you to behave nicely to him. I'm gradually
getting rid of that. Let me do it in my own way. You wouldn't
believe it: what goes on! I have as high an opinion of myself as
the next woman, but I never pretended to be all the goddesses
rolled in one, nor Penelope, to boot. I'm not afraid of any-
thing, Publius, except those horrifying epigrams. Look at those
he's hurled at Caesar; everyone's repeating them; they remain
on him, like personal disfigurements. I don't want any of those,
so let me manage this in my own way.

Do you realize, then, that our dinner's a failure? Put that in
your head. No one will come to our house but your Green
Mustaches and the roe of Catiline. Yet we are what we are.
Our family laid down the pavements of this city and I don't in-
tend that anyone shall forget it.

One more thing, Brainless.

The *Little Lentil* is not for you. I forbid it. Put it out of your
mind. I forbid it. There is where you and I have always made
our greatest mistakes. Think of what I'm saying. [*Clodia is al-
luding to her brother's seduction of a Vestal Virgin; and perhaps
to her unseemly pursuit through the law courts of the brilliant
Caelius, a former lover whom she charged with having stolen her
jewelry. He was successfully defended by Cicero in an oration which
ransacked the lives of both brother and sister and rendered them
notorious and ridiculous in the eyes of the Roman populace.*]

So keep saying to yourself: respectable for one year.

I, your Ox-eyed, adore you. Send me some thoughts on this
by return messenger. I shall be staying here four or five days,
though on my arriving this afternoon, one look at Quintus and
Cassia made me want to hurry north. I shall agitate their com-
placency, have no fear. Verus and Mela are with me. Catullus
will join me here the day after tomorrow.

Send me an answer by this messenger.

VI-A Clodius to Clodia.
 [*For answer, the messenger was carefully rehearsed in an obscene expletive.*]

VII Clodia, at Capua, to Caesar's Wife, in Rome.
 [*September 8.*]

Darling:

Your husband is a very great man, but he is a very rude man too. He has sent me a very short word that he cannot come to my dinner. I know that you can persuade him to come. Do not be discouraged if he refuses the first three or four times.

Asinius Pollio is coming and that new poet Gaius Valerius Catullus. Remind the Dictator that I sent him every scrap I had of the young man's verses and that he has neither returned the originals nor sent me copies of them.

You ask me, darling, what I think of the cult of Isis and Osiris. I'll tell you all about it when I see you. Of course, it's very beautiful to the eye, but it's really all nonsense. It's for servant girls and porters. I'm sorry I started taking people of our kind to it. Baiae's so boring that going to the Egyptian cults was just one of those things one does to pass the time. If I were you, I wouldn't urge your husband to let you attend them; it will only vex him and make you both unhappy.

I have a present for you. At Sorrento I found the most wonderful weaver. He makes a gauze so light that you can blow yards of it up to the ceiling and then grow old waiting for it to drift down again. And it's not made of fishes' gills like that shiny material the dancing girls wear. You and I will wear it at my dinner; we'll dress as twins! I've made a design and Mopsa can start work on it the moment I arrive in town.

Do send me a word back by this messenger.

And do drag the ungracious man to my dinner.

I kiss you squarely at the corners of each of your beautiful eyes. Twins! Though you are so much younger than I am!

VII-A Caesar's wife to Clodia, by return messenger.

Dearest Mousie:

I cannot wait to see you. I am wretched. I cannot go on living

as I am. You must advise me. He says we cannot come to your
dinner. Every request I put to him he refuses. I cannot go to
Baiae. I cannot go to the theater. I cannot go to the Temple of
Isis and Osiris.

I want to have a long long talk with you. How can I get a
little more freedom? Every morning we quarrel and every
night he apologizes; but I never make the least real progress,
and I never get what I want.

Of course, I love him very very much, because he's my hus-
band; but, oh dear, I wish I could get some pleasure out of life
some time. I weep so much that I have grown very ugly and
you will hate me.

Of course, I shall keep asking him to come to your dinner,
but oh!—I know him. The gauze sounds marvelous. Hurry.

VIII Caesar's Journal-Letter to Lucius Mamilius Turrinus.
 [*Probably between September 4 and 20.*]

970. [*On the laws of primogeniture and a passage in
Herodotus.*]
971. [*On the poetry of Catullus.*] Many thanks for the six
comedies of Menander. I have not been able to read them yet.
I am having them copied and shall return the originals and
perhaps some comments of my own before long.

You must, indeed, have a rich library. Are there some gaps
that I could help you fill? I am ransacking the world now for a
correct text of Aeschylus's *Lycurgeia*. It took me six years to
put my hand on *The Banqueters* and *The Babylonians* of Aris-
tophanes, which I sent you last spring. The latter as you noticed
was a poor copy; some customs-house clerks in Alexandria had
covered it with the inventories of cargoes.

I am putting into this week's packet a sheaf of poems. Old
masterpieces disappear; new ones, under Apollo, arrive to take
their place. These are by a young man, Gaius Valerius Catullus,
son of an old acquaintance of mine who lives near Verona. On
the way north in [*50*] I spent the night at their house and re-
member the sons and the daughter. In fact, I remember ap-
praising the poet's brother—who has since died—more highly!

You will be astonished to know that the woman addressed in
the poems under the name of Lesbia is no other than Clodia

Pulcher to whom you and I have written poems in our day. Clodia Pulcher! By what strange chain of significances has it come about that this woman who has lost intelligible meaning to herself and lives only to impress the chaos of her soul on all that surrounds her should now live in the mind of a poet as an object of adoration and should draw from him such radiant songs? I say to you in all gravity that one of the things in this world that I most envy is the endowment from which springs great poetry. To the great poets I ascribe the power to gaze fixedly at the whole of life and bring into harmony that which is within and that which is without them. This Catullus may well be of that company. Are these sovereign beings then subject to the deceptions of the lesser humanity? What disturbs me now is not his hatred of me but his love of Clodia. I cannot believe he is addressing merely her beauty, and that the beauty of the body is sufficient to evoke such triumphs in the ordering of language and idea. Is he able to see in her excellences which are hidden from us? Or does he see the greatness that undoubtedly was within her before she wrought on herself the havoc which now arouses detestation and laughter throughout the city?

For me these questions are connected with the first questions which one puts to life itself. I shall continue to inquire into them and shall report my findings to you.

972. [*On politics and appointments.*]

973. [*Concerning certain reforms introduced into the Mysteries of the Good Goddess. See Document XLII-B.*]

974. [*On some casks of Greek wine Caesar is sending as a present.*]

975. [*On Cleopatra's request that when she is in Rome she be permitted to attend the Mysteries of the Good Goddess. See Document XLIII-A.*]

976. [*Recommendation of a servant.*]

977. [*On the enmity felt toward him by Cato, Brutus, and Catullus.*] I called on Cato on the day commemorating his great ancestor's services.

As I have told you before, writing to you has a strange effect on me; I find myself examining matters which I do not otherwise consider. The thought that came to my pen that moment and which I was about to reject is this:

Of the four men whom I most respect in Rome three regard me with mortal enmity. I mean Marcus Junius Brutus, Cato, and Catullus. It is very likely that Cicero would also be pleased to miss me. There is no doubt about all this; many letters reach me which were not intended for my eyes.

I am accustomed to being hated. Already in early youth I discovered that I did not require the good opinion of other men, even of the best, to confirm me in my actions. I think there is only one solitude greater than that of the military com-mander and of the head of the state and that is the poet's—for who can advise him in that unbroken succession of choices which is a poem? It is in this sense that responsibility is liberty; the more decisions that you are forced to make alone, the more you are aware of your freedom to choose. I hold that we cannot be said to be aware of our minds save under responsi-bility and that no greater danger could befall mine than that it should reflect an effort to incur the approval of any man, be it a Brutus or a Cato. I must arrive at my decisions as though they were not subject to the comment of other men, as though no one were watching.

And yet I am a politician: I must play the comedy of extreme deference to the opinion of others. A politician is one who pre-tends that he is subject to the universal hunger for esteem; but he cannot successfully pretend this unless he is free of it. This is the basic hypocrisy of politics and the final triumph of the leader comes with the awe that is aroused in men when they suspect, but never know for certain, that their leader is indif-ferent to their approval, indifferent and a hypocrite. What?— they say to themselves—: what? can it be that there is absent from this man that serpent's nest which is lodged within us all and which is at once our torture and our delight—the thirst for praise, the necessity of self-justification, the assertion of one's self, cruelty, and envy? My days and nights are spent amid the hissing of those serpents. I once heard them in my own vitals. How I silenced them there I do not know, though the answer to that question, as put to a Socrates, exceeds all other ques-tions in interest.

It is not by reason of such serpents' nests, I think, that I am hated by a Marcus Brutus, a Cato, and by this poet. It is in-deed from their minds that they hate me and from their views

of government and freedom. Even if I brought them up to the place I hold and showed them the world stretched out as one can only see it from here; even if I could split open my skull and show them the experience of my lifetime, so many hundredfold closer to men and government than theirs has been; even if I could read with them, line by line, the texts of the philosophers to whom they cling, and the histories of the countries from which they draw their examples; even then I could not hope to clear their eyes. The first and last school-master of life is living and committing oneself unreservedly and dangerously to living; to men who know this an Aristotle and a Plato have much to say; but those who have imposed cautions on themselves and petrified themselves in a system of ideas, them the masters themselves will lead into error. Brutus and Cato repeat liberty, liberty, and live to impose on others a liberty they have not accorded to themselves—stern, joyless men, crying to their neighbors: be joyful as we are joyful; be free as we are free.

Cato is not educable. Brutus I have sent to Hither Gaul as governor, to school. Octavius is beside me, seeing all the traffic of state; I shall soon send him out into the arena.

But why should Catullus hate me? Can great poets generate indignations out of sentiments acquired in old textbooks? Are great poets stupid in everything except poetry? Can they form their opinions from the table conversation of the Aemilian Draughts and Swimming Club?

I confess, my dear friend, that I am astonished by a weakness that I feel awakening in me, a delirious weakness: oh, to be understood by such a one as Catullus and to be celebrated by his hand in verses that would not soon be forgotten.

978. [*On a principle of banking.*]

979. [*On some conspiratorial activities in Italy agitating for his assassination. See our LXI.*]

980. Do you remember where Redhead Scaevola asked us to go hunting with him the summer we returned from Greece? The second wheat there promises very well. [*This is a financial tip, obliquely stated in order not to alert their several secretaries.*]

981. [*On the poverty of adjectives which discriminate color in the Greek language.*]

982. [*On a possible abolition of all religious observances.*]

Last night, my noble friend, I did something which I have not done for many years: I wrote an edict; reread it; and tore it up. I indulged an uncertainty.

These last few days I have been receiving unprecedentedly absurd reports from the disembowelers of birds and the auditors on thunder. Moreover, the Courts and the Senate have been closed for two days because an eagle let fall an untidy mess within an arrow's flight of the Capitol. My patience was drawing short. I refused to perform myself the ceremonial of propitiation, to mime the frightened self-abasement. My wife and my very servants looked at me askance. Cicero deigned to advise me that I should comply with the expectations of popular superstition.

Last night I sat down and wrote the edict abolishing the College of Augurs and declared that henceforward no days were to be regarded as unlucky. I wrote on, giving to my people the reasons for this action. When have I been happier? What pleasures are greater than those of honesty? I wrote on and the constellations glided before my window. I disbanded the College of Vestal Virgins; I married the daughters of our first houses and they gave sons and daughters to Rome. I closed the doors of the temples, of all our temples except those of Jupiter. I tumbled the gods back into the gulf of ignorance and fear from which they came and into that treacherous half-world where the fancy invents consolatory lies. And finally the moment came when I pushed aside what I had done and started to begin again with the announcement that Jupiter himself had never existed; that man was alone in a world in which no voices were heard than his own, a world neither friendly nor unfriendly save as he made it so.

And having reread what I wrote I destroyed it.

I destroyed it not for Cicero's reasons—not because the absence of a state religion would drive superstition into clandestine forms and still baser practices (that is already taking place); not because so sweeping a measure would disrupt the social order and leave the people in despair and dismay like sheep in a snowstorm. In certain orders of reform, the dislocations caused by gradual change are almost as great as those caused by a total and drastic alteration. No, it was not the possible

repercussions of the move which arrested my hand and will; it was something in and of my self.

In myself I was not certain that I was certain.

Am I sure that there is no mind behind our existence and no mystery anywhere in the universe? I think I am. What joy, what relief there would be, if we could declare so with complete conviction. If that were so I could wish to live forever. How terrifying and glorious the role of man if, indeed, without guidance and without consolation he must create from his own vitals the meaning for his existence and write the rules whereby he lives.

You and I long since decided that the Gods do not exist. Do you remember the day that with finality we agreed upon that decision and resolved to explore all its consequences—sitting on the cliff in Crete, throwing pebbles into the sea, counting porpoises? We took a vow never to allow our minds to offer entrance to any doubt upon this matter. With what boyish light-heartedness we concluded that the soul was extinguished at death. [*The English language cannot reproduce the force of this phrase in Caesar's Latin where the very cadence expresses a poignancy of renunciation and regret. The recipient of the letter understood that Caesar was referring to the death of his daughter Julia, the wife of Pompey, the overwhelming loss of his life. Mamilius Turrinus was with him when the news of her death reached Caesar's headquarters in Brittany.*]

I thought I had not relapsed from all the strictness of these assertions. There is only one way, however, to know what one knows and that is to risk one's convictions in an act, to commit them in a responsibility. In drawing up the edict last night and in foreseeing the consequences that would ensue, I was driven to examine myself most strictly. All the consequences I would most gladly face, certain that the truth would ultimately fortify the world and all that are in it, but only if I were certain that I was certain.

Some last hesitation arrests my hand.

I must be certain that in no corner of my being there lingers the recognition that there is a possibility of a mind in and behind the universe which influences our minds and shapes our actions. If I acknowledge the possibility of one such mystery,

all the other mysteries come flooding back: there are the Gods who have taught us what is excellent and who are watching us; there are our souls which are infused in us at birth and which outlive our death; there are the rewards and punishments which furnish a meaning to our slightest action.

Yes, my friend, I am not accustomed to irresolution and I am irresolute. You know how little I am given to reflection; whatever judgments I arrive at I arrive at I know not how, but instantaneously; I am not adept at speculation, and since the age of sixteen I have regarded philosophy with impatience, as a tempting but fruitless exercise of the mind and as a flight from the obligations of immediate living.

It seems to me that there are four realms in which, with dread, I see in my life and in the life about me, the possibility of this mystery:

The erotic—have we not explained away too easily all that accompanies the fires that populate the world? Lucretius may be right and our jesting world wrong. I seem to have known all my life, but to have refused to acknowledge that all, all love is one, and that the very mind with which I ask these questions is awakened, sustained, and instructed only by love.

Great poetry—poetry is indeed the principal channel by which all that most weakens man has entered the world; there he finds his facile consolations and the lies that reconcile him to ignorance and inertia; I count myself second to no man in my hatred of all poetry save the best—but great poetry, is that merely the topmost achievement of the man's powers or is that a voice from beyond man?

Thirdly, a moment that accompanies my illness and whose intimation of greater knowledge and happiness I cannot hastily dismiss. [*This sentence is evidence of the unbounded confidence that Caesar felt in his correspondent. Caesar never permitted any reference to be made to his attacks of epilepsy.*]

And finally, I cannot deny that at times I am aware that my life and my services to Rome seem to have been shaped by a power beyond myself. It may well be, my friend, that I am the most irresponsible of irresponsible men, capable long since of bringing upon Rome all the ills that a state can suffer, but for the fact that I was the instrument of a higher wisdom that selected me for my limitations and not for my strength. I do not

reflect, and it may be that that instantaneous operation of my judgment is no other than the presence of the *daimon* within me, which is a stranger to me, and which is the love which the Gods bear to Rome and which my soldiers worship and the people pray to in the morning.

A number of days ago I wrote you in arrogance; I said that, respecting no man's good opinion, I was not interested in any man's advice. I come to you for counsel. Think over these things and give me all your thought when I see you in April.

In the meantime I scan all that passes without and within me, and particularly love, poetry, and destiny. I now see that I have been putting these questions all my life, but one does not know what one knows, or even what one wishes to know, until one is challenged and must lay down a stake. I am challenged; Rome is requiring some new enlargement of me. My time grows short.

IX Cassia, wife of Quintus Lentulus Spinther, from her villa at Capua, to the Reverend Maid, Domitilla Appia, Clodia's cousin, a Vestal Virgin.
 [*September 10.*]

For the sake of our long friendship, my dear Domitilla, I feel I must write you at once about a decision I have taken. I intend to ask for the disbarment of Claudilla [*Clodia Pulcher*] from the Mysteries of the Good Goddess.

I realize all the gravity of what I shall do.

Claudilla has just stayed at my house for three days on her journey from Baiae to Rome and some events have taken place which I feel I must recount to you in detail.

On arriving she showered us with endearments. She has always pretended that she loved me, my husband, and my children; she has assumed that we love her; but I have long known that she has never loved any woman, not even her mother, nor any man either.

As you know, to receive Claudilla as a house guest is like receiving a proconsul returning from his province. She arrives with three friends, ten servants, and a dozen outriders.

Now my husband and I have long known that any view of another's happiness is repugnant to your cousin. In her presence

we may not exchange understanding glances; we may not ca-
ress our children; we may not point out improvements to the
villa; we may not take pleasure in the works of art which my
husband has collected. The immortal Gods, however, have
given us much happiness and we are not clever at dissembling,
even when the laws of hospitality enjoin us to appear con-
tentious and discontented.

Claudilla is always at her best at beginnings. The first day she
was gracious to all. Even my husband conceded that she talked
brilliantly. After dinner we played "portraits" and she did, he
said, the best portrait of the Dictator that could conceivably be
made.

Now the things I am going to tell you may not seem as de-
cisive to you as they do to me, several of them may even seem
to you to be trifles.

The second day she decided to create havoc about her. That
she insulted me I pass over; that she made my husband un-
happy fills me again this moment with rage. My husband takes
a great interest in genealogy and great pride in the achieve-
ment of the Lentulus-Spinther family. She began making fun
of them: "Oh, my dear Quintus, you can't really, etc. . . . a
few mayors up in the Etruscan country . . . but no one actu-
ally believes they were even noticed by Ancus Martius . . . a
respectable family, of course, Quintus." I don't know anything
about such things; of course, she has everybody's cousin's name
right back to the Trojan War. She knew she was lying and she
just did it to *poison* my husband, which it did.

Without telling us, she had invited the poet Gaius Valerius
Catullus to join her here. We were glad to see him, particularly
my children, though we would much have preferred to see him
alone. When she's around he's either in the heavens or in hell.
This time he was in hell, and soon we all were.

Now, Domitilla, I do not stay awake to find out what visits
my guests may be paying in one another's rooms; but I do not
like to feel that my house has been selected to be the scene of
a cruel indignity. Since your cousin invited Valerius Catullus to
join her here I was ready to assume that she looked favorably
on a love which has been sufficiently widely celebrated in his
verses which I think are very beautiful. But apparently not: she
chose my home in which not only to bar the door to him but

to bar herself in with another man—that wretched little poet
Verus. My husband was awakened during the night by noises
in the stable and there was the poet borrowing a horse in order
to depart at once for Rome. He was beside himself with rage;
he tried to apologize, he stammered, he sobbed. Finally my hus-
band took him to our old villa across the road and watched
over him until morning. Even a Vestal, dear Domitilla, can
understand how shameful, how derogatory to our whole sex,
her behavior was—how contemptible. The next morning I
spoke to her about it. She looked at me coldly and said: "It is
quite simple, Cassia. I will not permit any man, any man, to
think he has any rights over me whatever. I am a completely free
woman. Catullus insists he has a claim on me. I had to show
him quickly that I did not recognize any such claim. That is all."

I could think of no answer then, but I have thought of a
thousand since. I should have trusted to my impulse and have
asked her to leave the house at once.

As we were finishing dinner that afternoon my children
came into the court with their tutor, visiting the altars for their
sunset prayers. You know how devout my husband is and all
our household. Claudilla, in their hearing, began scoffing at
the salt ceremony and the libations. I could endure it no longer.
I stood up and asked everyone else to leave the court. When
we were alone I told her to take her party and go. There is an
inn four miles up the road. I told her that I would apply for
her disbarment from the Mysteries.

She looked at me a long time in silence.

I said: "I see you do not even see wherein you have been offen-
sive. You may leave in the morning, if you prefer," and I left her.

In the morning she was most correct. She even apologized
to my husband for any words which may have appeared un-
suitable. But I have not changed my mind.

X Clodia, on the road to Rome, to Caesar.
 [*From the Inn at the 20th Milepost, south of Rome.*]
 [*September 10.*]
 [*This letter is in Greek.*]

Son of Romulus, descendant of Aphrodite:
I have received the expression of your contempt and of your

profound regret that you cannot be present at my brother's dinner. It appears that you are engaged on that afternoon with the Spanish Commission. This you tell to me who know—who better?—that Caesar does what he wishes and that what he wishes is accepted without demur by the Spanish Commission and by the trembling proconsuls.

You have long since made it clear to me that I may never see you alone and that I may never come to your house.

You despise me.

I understand that.

But you have a responsibility toward me. You made me what I am. I am your creature. You, a monster, have made me a monster.

My claim has nothing to do with love. Beyond love, far beyond love, I am your creature. In order not to importune you with this thing they call love I have done what I have done: I have brutified myself. You who understand everything (for all your pretense at being noble and blank) you understand that. Or does your public and ostentatious stupidity forbid you to know the things that you know?

Tiger! Monster! Hyrcanian Tiger!

You have a responsibility toward me.

You have a responsibility toward me.

You taught me all that I know; but you stopped short. You withheld the essential. You taught me that the world has no mind. When I said—*that* you remember and why I said it—that life was horrible, you said no, that life was neither horrible nor beautiful. That living had no character at all and had no meaning. You said that *the universe did not know that men were living in it.*

You do not believe that. I know, I know that there is one thing more that you have to tell me. Anyone can see that you behave as though something for you holds reason, holds meaning. What is it?

I could endure my life if I knew that you were wretched also; but I see that you are not so and that means that you have one more thing to tell me—that you *must* tell me.

Why do you live? Why do you work? Why do you smile? A friend—if I can be said to have friends—has described to me your behavior at the house of Cato. It seems that you were gra-

cious, that you charmed the company, that you set it laughing, that you talked interminably with—who can believe it?—Sempronia Metella. Can it be possible that you live by vanity? Is it enough for you that you hear the City now and—beyond the City—your future biographers describing you as magnanimous or charming? Your life did not use to be a series of postures before a mirror.

Caius, Caius, tell me what to do. Tell me what I must know. Once, let me talk to you, let me listen to you.

> Later.

No, I will not be unjust to you, though you are unjust to me.

It was not you alone who made me what I am now, though you completed the work.

It was that monstrous thing that life did to me. You are the only person living that knows my story—that is a responsibility. Such another thing life did to you also.

X-A Caesar to Clodia.
 [*Not by return messenger, but some four days later.*]

My wife, my aunt, and I are coming to your dinner; do not speak of it until you receive my formal acceptance.

You write me of things I told you. Either you are deceiving yourself or me, or your memory is faulty. I hope that arising from the conversation of your guests—who include, I am told, Cicero and Catullus—some matters will be touched on that you have known, but have forgotten.

The degree of my admiration for what you were is known to you. Its restoration, like so much else, is in your power. I have always found it difficult to be indulgent to those who despise or condemn themselves.

XI Caesar to Pompeia.
 [*September 13. From his offices, at eight in the morning.*]

I hope, my dear wife, that you have thought over the injustice of your charges against me this morning. I ask your pardon for having left the house this morning without answering your last question.

It makes me very unhappy to refuse you anything. It makes

me doubly unhappy to refuse you the same request over and over again, refurnishing reasons which on earlier occasions you have told me you understood, you agreed with, and you accepted. Since it is these repetitions which try my patience and do an injustice to your intelligence, let me put some of them down in writing.

I can do nothing for your cousin. The record of his cruelty and corruption on the Island of Corsica becomes more widely known every day. It may develop into an enormous public scandal; my enemies may finally render me responsible and it may take a great deal of time which I should be giving to other things. As I told you, I can give him any post, within reason, in the Army; I will not appoint him within five years to any administrative position.

I repeat that it is most unsuitable that you attend the ceremonies at the Temple of Serapis. I know that many remarkable things take place there for which it is not easy to furnish an explanation, and I know that the Egyptian rites arouse strong emotion and send the votaries away in states of mind which they and you describe as "happier" and "better." Believe me, my dear wife, I have studied them closely. Those Egyptian cults offer particular dangers to our Roman natures. We are active; we believe that even the smaller decisions of the daily life have a moral importance; that our relation to the Gods is strictly related to our conduct. I have known women of your position in Egypt. From time to time they visit their temples in order to prepare their souls for immortality after death; they roll on the floor and howl; they take long imagined journeys during which they are "washing their souls" and passing from stage to stage of divinity. The next day they return to their homes and are again cruel to their servants, deceitful to their husbands, avaricious, noisy and quarrelsome, self-indulgent, and totally indifferent to the misery in which the mass of the people of their country live. We Romans know that our souls are engaged in this life, and the journeys they make and the washing we give them are nothing more than our duties, our friendships, and our sufferings if we have them.

As to Clodia's dinner I ask you to trust my judgment. In these other matters I am willing to furnish arguments; I could do it

in this case also, but this letter is already long and we both have more profitable things to do than to rehearse the history of that couple. They might have become outstanding friends of the Roman good, as their ancestors were, instead of laughing-stocks to the people and a consternation to patriots. This they know well. They do not expect us to accept their invitations.

You tell me that my appointees are everywhere enriching themselves at the expense of the State. I was surprised this morning to hear you say this. I do not think, my dear Pompeia, that it is a wife's business to taunt her husband with inefficiency or reprehensible neglect on the basis of rumors she has picked up in general conversation. It is more suitable that she ask him for an explanation of charges which affect her honor as much as they affect his. If you lay before me an example of such profiteering I shall give you an answer. It could not be a short one, for I would have to open your eyes to the difficulties inherent in administering a world, the extent to which one must compromise with the greed of capable men, to the antagonism always present in one's subordinates, to the differences that distinguish conquered lands from those long incorporated in the Republic, and to the methods one employs in assisting headstrong men to plunge to their own ruin.

Your frequent charge that I do not love you cannot be repeatedly answered without humiliating us both. No amount of protestation could assure you of my love, if you were not aware of it in every moment of our life. I return to you daily from my work with the most affectionate expectation; I pass with you all the time that is not devoted to my official duties; the very refusal of your requests is evidence of my concern for your dignity and greater happiness.

Finally, you ask me, my dear Pompeia: *Are we to have no enjoyment in our life?* I beg you not to ask me that question lightly. All wives inevitably marry also the situation in which their husbands find themselves. Mine does not admit of the leisure and freedom that many enjoy; yet your position is one which many women envy. I shall do what I can to afford you a greater diversity of recreation; but the situation is not easily alterable.

XII Cornelius Nepos: Commonplace Book.
 [*The great historian and biographer appears to have kept
 an account of the events of his own time, information
 gathered from the most varied sources, as material
 toward some future work.*]

¶ The sister of Caius Oppius tells my wife that at dinner
Caesar discussed with Balbus, Hirtius, and Oppius the possible
transfer of government to Byzantium or Troy. Rome: inade-
quate port, floods, extremes of climate, disease from the now
uncorrectable overcrowding. Possibility of campaign into
India?

¶ Dinner again with Catullus at the Aemilian Draughts and
Swimming Club. Very pleasant company, young noblemen,
representatives of the most illustrious houses of Rome. My
chagrin in questioning them about their ancestors—their ig-
norance concerning them and, I must add, their indifference.

They have elected Catullus to be their honorary secretary, I
think out of tactful consideration for his poverty. Thus he is
provided with an attractive apartment overhanging the river.

He seems to be their adviser and confidant. They bring him
their quarrels with their fathers, their mistresses, and their
money lenders. Three times during dinner the clubhouse door
was flung open and a distraught member rushed in shouting
"Where's Sirmio?" (this nickname seems to be derived from
his summer lodge on Lake Garda) and the two retired to a cor-
ner for a whispered consultation. His popularity does not ap-
pear to be based, however, on any indulgence toward them; he
is as severe as their fathers and, although extremely licentious
in conversation, is little short of austere in his life and attempts
to inculcate "the Old Roman Way" in them also. Curious.

He seems to have chosen his best friends among the less
cultivated members or, as he calls them to their faces, the Bar-
barians. One of these members told me that he never talks lit-
erature, except when drunk.

He appears to be both stronger than he looks, and more
frail. On the one hand he can outdo almost any member of the
Club in those feats of strength and balance that arise so natu-
rally toward the end of drinking parties—crossing the ceiling
by swinging from rafter to rafter, or swimming the Tiber with

a cat upheld in one hand, the cat howling but dry. It was he who stole the golden porpoise from the roof of the Tiburtine Rowing Club which figures so largely in the song he wrote for his own fraternity. On the other hand his health is undoubtedly frail. He seems to suffer from some weakness of the spleen or bowels.

His love affair with Clodia Pulcher. Surprise to all. Inquire into it.

¶ Marina, a sister of our second cook, is a servant at the Dictator's house. She talked freely to me. There have been no attacks of the Sacred Malady for some time. The Dictator spends every evening at home with his wife. He often rises in the middle of the night and goes into his study overhanging the cliff and works. He has an army pallet there and often falls asleep in the open air.

Marina denies he has fits of temper. "Everybody says he has rages, sir, but it must be in the Senate and the Courts. I've only seen him in a rage three times in all five years, and never at servants, even when they make enormous mistakes. My mistress is often in a temper and wants us whipped, but he only laughs. We all tremble like mice in his presence, sir, but I don't know why because he is the kindest master in the world. I think it's because he looks at us all the time and really sees us. Mostly his eyes are smiling as though he knew what a servant's life is and what we talk about in the kitchen. We all understand very well that cook who killed himself when the stove caught fire. There were important guests and the Housemaster did not want to tell the Dictator so he made the cook go in and tell him. So the cook went in and told him the dinner was spoiled and the Dictator only laughed and said 'have we some dates and salad?' and the cook went and killed himself with the vegetable knife in the garden. He was angry, oh, it was terrible, when he discovered that Philemon who was his most favorite amanuensis and had been with him years, tried to poison him. It wasn't like anger it was like weight, sir, just weight. You remember he wouldn't let him be tortured, but directed that he be killed quickly. And the Chief of Police was very angry because he wanted to torture him to find out who was behind it. But what he did was worse than torture, I think. He called us all into the room, about thirty of us, and for a long time he looked at

Philemon in silence and you could hear an ant walk. And then he talked about how we are all in the world together and how bits of trust begin to grow up between people, between husband and wife, and general and soldier, and master and servant; and I think it was the worst rebuke anybody ever got in the world, and while it was going on two girls fainted. It was like as though there were a God in the room, and afterwards my mistress vomited.

"Octavius is home from school at Appolonium. He's a very silent boy and never talks to anybody.

"The secretary from Crete was heard saying to the secretary from Rimini that maybe the Queen of Egypt is coming to Rome, that's Cleopatra the witch.

"My mistress can do anything with him. Whenever she weeps, he becomes like a distraught person. We cannot understand that, because he is always right and she is always wrong."

Cicero to dinner. Much coquetry: his life is over; the ingratitude of the public, et cetera. On Caesar: "Caesar is not a philosophical man. His life has been one long flight from reflection. At least he is clever enough not to expose the poverty of his general ideas; he never permits the conversation to move toward philosophical principles. Men of his type so dread all deliberation that they glory in the practice of the instantaneous decision. They think they are saving themselves from irresolution; in reality they are sparing themselves the contemplation of all the consequences of their acts. Moreover, in this way they can rejoice in the illusion of never having made a mistake; for act follows so swiftly on act that it is impossible to reconstruct the past and say that an alternative decision would have been better. They can pretend that every act was forced on them under emergency and that every decision was mothered by necessity. This is the vice of military leaders for whom every defeat is a triumph and every triumph almost a defeat.

"Caesar has cultivated this immediacy in everything that he does. He seeks to eliminate any intermediary stage between impulse and execution. He carries a secretary with him wherever he goes and dictates letters, edicts, laws, at the moment they occur to him. Similarly he obeys any impulse of nature at the moment he is aware of it. He eats when he is hungry and he

sleeps when he is sleepy. Time after time in the weightiest councils and in the presence of the consuls and the proconsuls who have crossed the world to confer with him he has left the meeting with a smiling apology and withdrawn briefly into the next room; but which of the calls of nature it was we could not know, perhaps it was to fall asleep, to eat a stew, or to embrace one of the three child-mistresses he keeps always at hand. I will say on his behalf that he accords these liberties to others as well as to himself. I shall never forget his consternation at one such reunion when he learned that an ambassador had fore-gone his dinner and was hungry. And yet—for there is no end to that man—in the siege of Dyrrhachium he starved with his soldiers, refusing the rations that had been reserved for the commanders. His unusual cruelty against the enemy when the siege was lifted was, I think, merely the delayed irritation of his hunger. He elevates these practices into a theory and declares that to deny that one is an animal is to reduce oneself to half a man."

Cicero does not enjoy discussing Caesar for long at a time; but he is not averse to retouching a portrait of himself with materials from that of Caesar. I was able to bring him back to the subject once more.

"Every man must have an audience: our ancestors felt that the Gods were watching them; our fathers lived to be admired of men; for Caesar there are no Gods and he is indifferent to the opinion of his fellow men. He lives for the opinion of after-time; you biographers, Cornelius, are his audience. You are the mainspring of his life. Caesar is trying to live a great book; he has not even enough of the artist in him to see that living and literary composition cannot furnish analogies to one another." Here Cicero began to shake with laughter. "He has gone so far as to introduce into life that practice inseparable from art which is erasure. He has erased his youth. Oh, yes, he has. His youth as he thinks it was, as everyone thinks it was, is a pure creation of his later years. And now he is beginning to erase the Gallic and the Civil Wars. I once reviewed five pages of the *Commentaries* in minute detail with my brother, Quintus, who was in closest association with Caesar during the events he is describing. There is not a single untruth, no—but after ten lines Truth shrieks, she runs distraught and disheveled through her

temple's corridors; she does not know herself. 'I can endure lies,' she cries. 'I cannot survive this stifling verisimilitude.'"

> [*Here follows the passage in which Cicero discusses the possibility that Marcus Junius Brutus may be Caesar's son. It is given in the document which opens Book IV.*]

. . . .

". . . Never forget that throughout the twenty most critical years of his life Caesar was penniless. Caesar and money! Caesar and money! Who will ever write that story? In all the myths of the Greeks there is no story to equal it, however fantastic—spendthrift without income and lavish with another's gold. There is no time to go into that now, but to put it in a word: Caesar could never conceive of money as money when it was *at rest*. He could never think of it as a safeguard against the future, or as a thing of ostentation, as an evidence of one's dignity, or power, or influence. For Caesar, money is only money at the moment of its doing something. Caesar felt that money is for those who know what to do with it. Now it is obvious that multimillionaires do not know what to do with their money except to hug it or to brandish it; Caesar, indifferent to money—an attitude which is of course most impressive and bewildering and even frightening to the rich—could always find plenty to do with money. He could always activate another's gold. He could sing gold out of the strong-boxes of his friends.

"But doesn't his attitude go deeper than indifference? Doesn't it mean that he is not afraid, not afraid of this world about us, not afraid of the future, not afraid of that Potential Predicament in the shadow of which so many people live? Now isn't a large part of fear the memory of past fright and of past predicament? To a young child who has never seen his guardian frightened by thunder and lightning, it does not occur to be frightened by them. Caesar's mother and aunt were very remarkable women. Greater terrors than thunder and lightning could not discompose their features. I can imagine that through all the terrors of the proscriptions and massacres—with flights by night through a burning countryside, hiding in caves—they never allowed the growing boy to see anything in them but a confident serenity. Could that be it, or does it go farther and deeper still? Does he believe himself to be a God, descendant of the Julian clan, born of Venus?—and hence

beyond the reach of this world's evil as he is beyond receiving any satisfaction from this world's gifts?

"At all events, he lived all those years without money of his own, in that little house down among the working people, with Cornelia and his little daughter; and yet the patrician of all patricians, wearing as wide a purple band as Lucullus's, contradicting Crassus, contradicting me—oh, there's no end to him!

"But—and there is a subtle point here—Caesar is delighted to enrich others. The chief charge laid against him now by his enemies is that he permits his intimates to amass unconscionable fortunes, and the majority of his intimates are scoundrels. Yet isn't that a sign that he despises them, for he identifies the possession and accumulation of money with weakness—what am I saying?—with *fright*?"

¶ Asinius Pollio to dinner. He talked of Catullus and the poet's bitter epigrams against the Dictator. "Strangest thing in the world. In conversation the poet defends Caesar against the constant contempt of his fellow club members; yet in his work releases that unbounded virulence. To observe: Catullus, most licentious in his verses, is astonishingly strict in his life and in his judgments on the lives of others. He apparently regards his relations with Clodia Pulcher—relations which he never mentions in conversation—as a pure and lofty love which no one could confuse with the ephemeral loves in which his friends are continuously involved. His epigrams against the Dictator though superficially political are uniformly couched in terms of obscenity. His hatred of Caesar seems to spring from two sources—his disapproval of the Dictator's notorious immorality and his disapproval of the type of men with whom the Dictator surrounds himself and whom he permits to enrich themselves at the public expense. Again it is possible that he fears the Dictator as a rival for the affection of Clodia Pulcher or feels for him a jealousy, as it were retrospectively."

XIII Catullus to Clodia.
 [*September 14.*]
 [*Catullus on the 11th and 13th wrote two drafts for this letter. They were never sent to Clodia, but were read by Caesar among papers found in Catullus's room and*

*transcribed for the Dictator by his secret police. These
drafts can be found in Book II as Document XXVIII.*]

I do not wish to be spared any knowledge that this world is
a place of night and horror.

The door you closed on me at Capua had that to say.

You and your Caesar came into it to teach us this: You, that
love and beauty of form are a deception; he, that in the far-
thest reaches of the mind one finds only the lust of the self.

I have always known that you were drowning. You have told
me so. Your arms and your face still struggle above the surface
of the water. I cannot drown with you. The very door you
closed upon me was a last appeal, for cruelty is the only cry
that is left you to utter.

I cannot drown with you, because I have one thing left to
do. I can still insult this universe which insults us. I can insult
it by making a beautiful thing. That I shall do; and then put an
end to the long crucifixion of the mind.

Claudilla, Claudilla, you are drowning. Oh that I were deaf;
oh that I were not here to know that struggle, to hear those
cries.

XIII-A Clodia to Catullus.
 [*By return messenger, the same day.*]
 [*In Greek.*]

Little-Stag—true, all true—how can I do other than be
cruel to you?—Endure it, suffer it, but do not leave me.

I will tell you all—it is my last resource—Prepare yourself for
this horror: my uncle violated me at the age of twelve—on what,
on whom can I avenge that? *That?* In an orchard, at noon.
Under a blazing sun. Now I have told you all.

Nothing can help me. I do not ask help. I ask companion-
ship in hatred. I could not endure it in you that you did not
hate *enough.*

Come to me. Come to me, Little-Stag.

But what is there to say?

Come.

XIII-B Catullus.

> Odi et amo. Quare id faciam, fortasse requiris.
> Nescio, sed fieri sentio et excrucior.

> "I hate and I love. Perhaps you ask how that is possible.
> I do not know; but that is what I feel and I hang upon a
> cross."

XIV Asinius Pollio, at Naples, to Caesar in Rome.
 [*September 18.*]
 [*Asinius Pollio, traveling as Caesar's confidential agent,
 answers twenty questions forwarded to him by the Dic-
 tator.*]

My General:
 [*Here follow several thousand words concerning certain
 highly technical procedures employed by the great banking
 houses situated near Naples; an equally long reply con-
 cerning some administrative problems in Mauretania;
 then some information about the wild beasts that were
 being shipped from Africa to take part in the festival
 games at Rome.*]
Question 20: The reason for Gaius Valerius Catullus's ill-will
against the Dictator and an account of the poet's love affair
with the Lady Clodia Pulcher.
 I have attempted many times, my General, to obtain from
the poet a clear statement of his antagonism against you. My
General should know that Valerius is an extremely complicated
and contradictory nature. For the most part he is judicious,
patient, and even-tempered. Although he is only slightly older
than the majority of the members of our [Aemilian Draughts
and Swimming] Club, he has long held the position there of
being councilor and peace maker. He is, as we say, "head of the
table." Nevertheless, there are three subjects which he cannot
discuss or hear discussed without being thrown into a violent
rage. He changes color; his voice alters, and his eyes flash. I have
frequently observed him to be trembling. These subjects are
bad poets, loose behavior in women, and yourself and certain
of your associates. I have had occasion to tell my General

already that the majority of the members of that Club affect the Republicans. This is even more true of the two other clubs whose membership is restricted to the young patricians, the Tiburtine Rowing Club, and the Red Sails. It is not true of the Forty Steps which remains exceedingly proud of having been founded by my General. The Republican opinions held by the former clubs, however, do not pass beyond the degree of table talk. The young men are extremely ill-informed on affairs of state, and they are not sufficiently interested to listen to an extended discussion of them; nor will Valerius. His objections veer from position to position; at one moment he is inveighing against the private character of certain officials, the next he is invoking certain principles of political theory, the next he is rendering you responsible for some burglaries that were reported in the suburbs.

I cannot help feeling that his irrational irritability on these three subjects is a reflection of the unhappy situation he is in respecting Clodia Pulcher. It is extremely unfortunate that of all the women in Rome he should have fallen in love with her. When he first came to the city eight years ago she was already the laughingstock of the Club, though at that time her husband was still living. She was the laughingstock not because of the number of her lovers, but because of the unvarying course followed by any amatory relationship with her. She exerts her fascination over a man in order to learn his weaknesses and in order finally to insult him with the greatest possible thoroughness and precision. Unfortunately for her, she does not do this very well. She is in such haste to arrive at the phase wherein she is to humiliate her lover that the fascination is quickly dispelled. Certain Club members who had promised themselves at least six months of enchantment have returned to the Club in the middle of the first night and without their cloaks.

That Valerius should love this woman with such intensity and for so long a time has caused consternation in all who know him. My brother—who is a much closer friend of the poet than I can claim to be—says that when he talks of her he seems to be talking of someone we have never known. It is generally conceded that, next to Volumnia, she is the handsomest woman on the Hill, that she is easily the wittiest and the most intelligent, and that the diversions, country parties, and dinners which she

gives are not equaled by any others in Rome; but Valerius tells my brother of her wisdom, her kindness to the unfortunate, the delicacy of her sympathy, her greatness of soul. I have known her for many years; I enjoy her company; but I am never un-aware that she hates the air she breathes and everything and everyone about her. It is generally thought that there is one ex-ception, her brother Publius. Cornelius Nepos laid before me his theory that her campaign of vengeance against men is possi-bly a consequence of the incestuous relations she may have had with her brother. It may be, though I do not think so. Her atti-tude to him is that of an exasperated and relatively indifferent mother. Passion or the revulsion from passion would have ren-dered it more exasperated and more possessive.

My admiration—indeed, my love—for the poet is very great. Few things could make me happier than to see him recover from the infatuation which is torturing him and to see him shed the childish and incoherent prejudices which he holds against my General.

The Lady Clodia Pulcher has invited me to a dinner to which she tells me she has invited both my General and that poet. At first the prospect seemed to me unpleasing, but on second thought it seems to offer a peculiarly fitting occasion for dis-pelling certain misunderstandings. I could well understand that my General would not wish to attend that dinner, how-ever; in that case, I hope that I may be permitted to arrange a meeting with the poet at a later time.

XIV-A Cornelius Nepos: Commonplace Book

¶ Met Asinius Pollio in the Baths. As we sat in the steam we discussed again the reasons for Catullus's hatred of our master.

"There is no doubt about it," he said. "It has to do with Clodia Pulcher. Now to my knowledge Caesar has never shown any interest in her. Do you know of any?"

I replied that I knew of none, but was not likely to know.

"I think there has been none. She was a mere child in the years when he was fluttering the boudoirs. There has certainly been nothing between them; but for some reason, Catullus (I feel certain of it) associates them. The epigrams against the Dictator are violent, are savage, but they have very little point.

Have you remarked that they are all, without exception, couched in obscene terms? To denounce Caesar for immorality and for enriching a few high officials, believe me, that is like —throwing sand against a strong wind. There is something childish about them; the only thing that is not childish about them is that they are unforgettable."

Here he brought his mouth close to my ear: "You know my admiration for our master. Nevertheless, I say to you: a man who cannot formulate a more pointed, a more piquant case against him has not yet begun to reflect. . . . No, no, I think there is no doubt about it: Catullus has conjured up some grounds for sexual jealousy."

Here he waved his hands in the air: "Catullus is both a man and a child. It must be seen to be believed. You heard what Cicero said when he first read the love poems? No? 'This Catullus is the only man in Rome who takes passion seriously; he will probably be the last.'"

XV Catullus to Clodia.
 [*September 20.*]

My soul, soul of my soul, life of my life, I have slept all day.

Oh, to be able to sleep until [*Friday*]. It is torture to be awake and not beside you; it is starvation to be asleep and not beside you. At dark I went out with Attius—another torture, to be thinking only of you and yet not to talk of you. It is midnight. I have written and written and torn up what I have written. Oh, the sweetness, the wildness of love, what tongue can tell it? Why must I attempt it; why was I born to be hunted by demons to tell of it?

Forget, oh forget the cutting things we have said to one another. The passion which is our joy is also our furious enemy. It is the vengeance of the Gods that we cannot be forever *one* and totally *one*. It is the rage of the soul that there is a body and the rage of the body that there is a soul. But oh! let us succeed where so few have succeeded. Let us burn the two into one; and oh, Claudillina, let us efface whatever the past held; let us stamp it out. Believe me, it no longer exists. Be proud;

refuse to remember it; it is within your power to ignore it. Resolve every morning to be each morning's new Claudilla.

I kiss you to hide my eyes from you. I hold you. I kiss you. I kiss you. I kiss you.

XVI Pompeia to Clodia.
 [*September 21.*]

Here's a letter from him to you. It's a perfectly horrible letter and I'm ashamed to forward it.

Anyway! So you see I *can* come. But don't thank *me*. Why didn't you tell him from the beginning that that poet would be there? Sometimes I think that all my husband thinks about is poetry. Almost every night he reads it aloud to me in bed. Last night it was Lucretius. All about atoms, atoms, atoms. He doesn't read it; he knows it by heart. Oh, dear, he's such a strange man. This week I simply adore him, but he's such a strange man. Clodiola, I've just heard Cicero's nickname for him. Isn't that simply *death-defying!* I've never laughed so in my life. [*It is hard to know which of Cicero's soubriquets for Caesar so convulsed the Dictator's wife. It may have been simply* The Dominie, *or it may have been one of several complicated compound Greek epithets:* The Autophidias, *or* The Man who lived as though he were shaping his own honorific sepulchral monument; the Benevolent Strangler—*which reflects his contemporaries' bewilderment at Caesar's wholesale pardon of his enemies and his deeply disturbing failure to display the least resentment against them; or* "Nobody-here-but-smoke," *a phrase from Aristophanes's* The Wasps, *where a man imprisoned in his house by his son gives this answer when he is discovered trying to escape by the chimney.*]

I tried on the dress. It's marvelous. I'm going to wear the Etruscan tiara and I'm having gold beads sewn on the skirt, very thick at the bottom and gradually thinning out until there are none at the waist. I don't know whether the sumptuary laws permit it and I'm not going to ask.

Did you see me give you the sign during the Foundation Day *ballet*? When I pull the lobe of my right ear that's a message to you. Of course, I don't dare turn my head to right or

left. Even though he's two miles away, doing all that marching up and down and shouting gibberish I know that he's got his eyes glued on me.

I'm learning my piece for the you-know-what [*the Mysteries of the Good Goddess*]. Darling, I have simply no memory. All that old-fashioned language. *He* helps me with it. Madam President said that since he's Supreme Pontiff he's allowed to know *certain parts* of it. The awful parts, of course not; do you suppose any wife has ever told her husband about *them*? I suppose not.

I hear that Aunt Julia's coming to your dinner, too. She's going to stay with us. This time I'll make her tell me about the days of those earlier civil wars when they had to eat snakes and toads and when she and my grandmother killed lots of men. It must be a very *odd* feeling to *kill* a man!

Hugs.

XVI-A [*Enclosure*] Caesar to Clodia.

The Dictator's respects to the Most Noble Lady. The Dictator has deferred the engagement that prevented his presence and accepts the invitation of the Most Noble Publius Claudius Pulcher and the Most Noble Lady. He also requests their permission to invite the Spanish Commissioner and the Deputation of Twelve to her house following the dinner.

The Dictator understands that the Greek mime Eros is performing before the Most Noble Lady's guests. The performance of this mime is of the highest artistry. It is reported, however, that it is accompanied by a considerable degree of obscenity, particularly in the composition called "Aphrodite and Hephaestus." It is unsuitable that the generals and administrators from Spain and the remoter districts of the Republic carry back to their posts the impression that the diversions of the capital are of such a character. The Dictator requests that the Most Noble Lady call the attention of the artist to this observation of the Dictator.

The Dictator sends his thanks to the Most Noble Lady and requests that during the earlier part of the evening she waive the protocol which it is customary to observe in his presence.

XVII Cicero from his villa at Tusculum to Atticus in Greece.
 [*September 26.*]

Only the Muses, my Pomponius, can console us for the loss
of all the things we have valued. We have become slaves, but
even a slave can sing. I have reversed the procedure of Odys-
seus: to save himself and his associates from destruction he
deafened his ears to the sirens; I, however, have given all my
attention to the Muses in order to drown out the death rattle
of the Republic and the expiring groans of liberty.

I do not agree with you: I lay the general suffocation to the
charge of one man.

The patient at the point of death called in this doctor who
restored in him every faculty but the will and promptly bound
him to himself as his personal slave. I entertained for a time the
hope that the doctor would rejoice in his patient's restoration
and release him to the full exercise of his independence. That
hope has dwindled.

So let us cultivate the muses; that is one freedom no man
can take from us.

The doctor himself takes an interest in the melodies that
arise from this universal jail. He has sent me a sheaf of verses by
this Catullus you speak of. I have known the young man for some
time and am even addressed in one of the poems. I have known
this poem for a year, but by the Gods, I am not certain as to
whether it is addressed to me in admiration or in derision. I
am sufficiently grateful that he does not call me pander nor
pickpocket—playful attributions which few of his friends
escape.

I do not share Caesar's unbounded enthusiasm. For some of
these poems I have not so much an admiration as a weakness.
Those which are based upon Greek models we may call the
most brilliant translations we have yet seen; when they depart
from Greek prototypes we are confronted with some strange
matter.

These poems are in Latin but they are not Roman. Catullus
comes from over the border and prepares us for that adulter-
ation of our language and our forms of thought which must
inevitably overwhelm us. The poems to Clodia, and particu-
larly those commemorating the death of her sparrow, are not

without grace, but they have their comical side. I am told that they are already scrawled across the walls of the Baths and that there is no Syrian sausage vendor who has not committed them to memory. The sparrow! We are told that it often perched in Clodia's bosom—a much-traveled thoroughfare, only occasionally available to birds. Well, let us have Anacreontic threnodies on this bird and impassioned exhortations to kisses beyond counting—but what do I find? A rapid transition, or rather no transition, and we are talking about death; and by Hercules, the commonplaces of stoic philosophy are richly marshaled.

> Soles occidere et redire possunt;
> Nobis cum semel brevis lux occisus est
> Nox est perpetua et una dormienda.
> [*A translation is given in II-B.*]

That is high and mournful music. I am having it cut into the wall of the pergola that looks toward the setting sun;—but where is the sparrow and where are the kisses? An indefensible disproportion joins the beginnings and the ends of those poems. That is neither Greek nor Roman. A secret train of thought, an association of ideas beneath the surface of the lines, is operating in the poet's mind. It is Clodia's death, it is his own, that is figured in that of the sparrow.

If we are to be condemned to a poetry based on buried trains of thought, my dear Pomponius, we shall soon be at the mercy of the unintelligible parading about among us as a superior mode of sensibility. It is true that our minds are a market place in which the slave brushes against the sage, or an untended garden where the weed springs beside the rose. At any moment a trivial thought may leap and associate itself with the sublime which in turn may be illustrated or interrupted by the homeliest detail of daily life. This is incoherence; this is the barbarian within us all and from which Homer and the great writers of six hundred years have worked to free us.

I am to meet this poet at a dinner which Clodia is giving in a few days. Caesar will be there. I intend so to direct the conversation that this truth will be made clear to them. The maintenance of categories is the health not only of literature, but of the State.

XVIII Report from the Dictator's Secret Police: concerning
Gaius Valerius Catullus.

> [*September 22.*]
>
> [*These reports were submitted daily. They included inter-
> cepted letters, conversations engaged in or overheard, and
> accounts of persons or the activities of persons whose names
> were often forwarded to the police by the Dictator.*]
>
>

Subject 642: Gaius Valerius Catullus, son of Gaius, grand-
son of Titus; gentleman from the region of Verona. Age: 29.
Resides at the Aemilian Draughts and Swimming Club. Fre-
quents: Ficinius Mela; the brothers Pollio; Cornelius Nepos;
Lucius Calco; Mamilius Torquatus; Horbatius Cinna; the Lady
Clodia Pulcher.

The papers in this subject's rooms have been examined.
They include family and personal letters and in large quantity
material of poetry.

Subject shows no political interests and it is assumed that in-
quiries in regard to him may be dropped.

> [*Notation by the Dicator*: "Reports on subject 642 will
> be continued. A transcript of all documents found in
> Subject's lodgings will be forwarded as soon as possible."
> *The following papers were then placed before the Dictator.*]

XVIII-A Catullus's Mother to Catullus.

Your father has taken on many new duties in the town. He is
busy from morning to night. The crops have not been what
was expected. This is due to the many storms. Ipsitha had a
very bad cold but is better. Your dogs are well. Victor is pretty
old now. He sleeps by the fire most of the time now at my feet.

We heard from Cecinnius's agent that you had not been
well. You do not tell us such things in your letters. Your father
is distressed. You know what a good doctor we have here and
what care would be devoted to you. We beg you to come to us.

All Verona knows your poems by heart. Why do you never
send them to us? Cecinnius's wife brought over twenty of them
to us. It is strange that we must receive from a neighbor's hand
the one you wrote about your dear brother's death. Your father

carries it with him wherever he goes. It is hard to speak of it. It is very beautiful.

I pray daily that the Immortal Gods may protect you. I am well. Write us when you can. August 12.

XVIII-B Clodia to Catullus.
 [*The preceding spring.*]

It is too boring to have to deal with an hysterical child.
Never try to see me again.
I will not be spoken to in such a fashion. I have broken no promises, for I made none.
I shall live as I choose.

XVIII-C Allius to Catullus.

Here's the key. No one will disturb you. My uncle uses the rooms sometime, but he has gone to Ravenna. "Oh, Love, ruler of Gods and men."

XIX Anonymous Letter [written by Clodius Pulcher, but in a woman's hand] to Caesar's wife.

It has been reported to me, great and noble lady, that you have accepted an invitation to dine at the house of Clodius Pulcher tomorrow night. I would not take up the time of one who fills with such distinction so lofty a place did I not have information to impart to you which you could not obtain elsewhere.

This is a letter of warning for which I think you will not be ungrateful. I know to my great sorrow that Clodius Pulcher bears toward you a sentiment which has long passed the bounds of admiration. He who hitherto has never known what it is to love, who—alas!—has caused more suffering than joy to our sex has at last been humbled by that God who spares no one. It is not likely that he will ever declare his passion to you; the respect he bears to your immortal husband will and must prevent that; but it may be that what he feels may break even the restraints of duty and honor.

Do not attempt to ascertain who I am. One of my motives in

writing to you I cannot hope to conceal: it is jealousy—jealousy
that you hold undisputed sway in a heart where once I thought
myself beloved. Soon after writing this letter I shall put an end
to an existence which has lost its reason for being. Let my dying
words warn you that even your noble nature would not be able
to reform one who has dissipated his golden promise in thought-
less disorder; even you cannot recall him from the influence of
that most wicked woman, his sister; even you cannot avenge
the wrongs he has done to our sex. He believes that you could
reclaim him to virtue and to public usefulness. He is deceived;
even you, great lady, could not do that.

XX Abra, Caesar's wife's Maid, to Clodia.
 [*September 30.*]

 Our party will start for your dinner at three. My mistress
and the Old Lady in litters, himself walking.
 Himself cheerful. Herself in tears. He made me take all the
gold beads off the gown. Sumptuary laws.
 Heard an important conversation. Forgive me, my lady. Old
Lady had long talk with her. Said that maybe you will be for-
bidden [*underneath, half-erased:* disbarred] from ceremonies.
My mistress very angry, shouted that himself would prevent.
Old Lady said maybe yes, maybe no. My mistress tears; begs
that Old Lady will prevent it. My mistress goes to himself,
begs that that will not happen. Himself calm and cheerful, says
he knows nothing about it and unnecessary to get alarmed.
 Am about to do my mistress's hair. Will take an hour.
 My mistress asks questions about your brother.
 My respectful obedience to your ladyship.

XX-A Caesar's wife to Clodia.

 TERRIBLE THING HAS HAPPENED. ON THE WAY TO YOUR
DINNER THREE MEN JUMPED OVER WALL AND TRIED TO KILL
MY HUSBAND. DO NOT KNOW HOW BADLY HE IS WOUNDED.
WE HAVE ALL GONE HOME. DO NOT KNOW WHAT WE ARE
GOING TO DO. WRETCHED AT MISSING YOUR DINNER. HUGS.

XX-B Head of the Official Police to Head of the Secret Police.

We have rounded up two hundred and twenty-four persons found near the scene of the attack. Have begun the questioning. Six men highly suspect. We have begun the torture. One killed himself before questioning.

Crowds have collected before the house of Publius Clodius Pulcher. The rumor has spread that the Dictator was on his way to dine there and the attempted assassination is imputed to Clodius's agents. The crowd has begun throwing stones at the house and is talking of setting fire to it.

A number of the house servants attempted to leave by a gate on the Trivulcian Lane and were beaten by the crowd.

Later.

Crowds before the house increasingly threatening.

Marcus Tullius Cicero was in the house, wearing insignia as former consul. Was escorted to his home by military detachment. Crowds spat at him and some stones were thrown.

In the house remain Clodia Pulcher, a young man who gave his name as Gaius Valerius Catullus and one servant.

Asinius Pollio was also a guest, but left immediately on hearing of the attempt and went to the Dictator's house. As he was in uniform he was allowed to pass by the crowd and was applauded.

Publius Clodius Pulcher escaped before we could detain him.

Later.

The Dictator suddenly arrived at the door of the house, accompanied by Asinius Pollio and six guards.

He received loud acclamation. He addressed the crowd; bade them return to their homes and give thanks to the Gods for his safety. He assured them that he knew no reason why the residents of this house should be suspected of participation in the attempt on his life.

In the hearing of all, he directed that none of the suspects be tortured until he had seen and questioned them.

He directed me to make every effort to put my hand on Clodius Pulcher, but to treat him respectfully.

XXI Asinius Pollio to Vergil and Horace.
 [*This letter was written some fifteen years after the Preceding.*]

Gout and a bad conscience, my friends, are enemies of sleep; both held me long awake last night.

Some ten days ago, at our master's table [*i.e., that of the Emperor Caesar Augustus*] I was abruptly called upon to recount the curious events connected with the interrupted dinner given by Clodia Pulcher to Catullus the poet, to Cicero, and to the Divine Caesar during the last year of his life. Fortunately for me, the Emperor was called away soon after I had begun my narration. Even in the brief portion which I had recounted, you must have been aware that I was stumbling. Our Emperor is a large-minded man, but he is master of the world, a God, and the nephew of a God. As his divine uncle used to say: Dictators must know the truth, but must never permit themselves to be told it. Unprepared, I was hastily trimming my story to fit an Emperor's ears. You two should know the truth, however, and tonight I shall hope, in dictating the story, to forget and to appease my two discomforts.

We had been awaiting for some time the arrival of the Dictator and his party. Outside the house, Clodia had lined the streets with priests and musicians and a large crowd had gathered to watch him pass. We were the last to learn that an attempt had been made upon his life. From the first (and to this day) the people of Rome have believed that it was Clodius Pulcher's hired bullies who attempted to assassinate his guest. As we waited stones began falling in the court and bundles of burning straw were flung over the walls and fell at our feet. Finally some terrified servants told us the news. I received permission from Clodia to go to Caesar's house. As I was in uniform I passed through the crowd without difficulty. I learned later that Cicero had addressed the mob from the door of the house, reminding them of his services to the Republic and bidding them return to their homes; that the crowd had been unimpressed and even insolent, and that he had hurried home barely escaping with his life; and that a number of servants, attempting to leave by the garden gate, had been clubbed to death.

On my way across the Palatine Hill I picked up the trail of Caesar's blood. I found him sitting in the courtyard of his house being treated for his wounds. The faces of his servants were white; his wife was distraught; only he and his aunt were calm. The assassins' knives had made two deep cuts in his right side, reaching from his throat to his waist. The physician was washing and binding these with sea moss. Caesar sat jesting impatiently. As I approached him I saw in his eyes an expression which I had only seen there during the moments of greatest danger in the wars, a look of expectant happiness. He called me to him and asked me in a whisper how things were at Clodia's house. I told him.

"Good physician," he said. "Make haste, make haste, make haste."

From time to time members of his secret police entered bringing reports of the search for his attackers.

Finally the surgeon drew back and said: "Sire, I now resign the healing to nature herself. She asks of you immobility and sleep. Will the Dictator graciously drink this opiate."

Caesar rose and took several turns about the court, attentive to his condition, his eyes resting smilingly on me. "Good physician," he said at last, "I shall obey you in two hours; but first I have an errand I must perform."

"Sire! Sire!" cried the physician.

His wife flung herself at his knees, wailing like Cytheris in a tragedy. He raised her up, embraced her, and beckoned me sharply to the door. There he collected a few guards, bade his litter follow him, and we sped across the Palatine. At one point he was forced to stop by pain or weakness. He leaned against the wall in silence; his hand directed me to be silent. For a few moments he breathed deeply; then we continued on our way. As we drew near to Clodia's house we could see that the police were having difficulty in their attempt to disperse the crowds. All Rome was streaming up the hill. When the people recognized the Dictator a great cry went up and space was cleared for him to pass. He walked slowly, smiling from right to left and touching the shoulders of those beside him. Before Clodia's door he turned, raised his hand, and waited for silence.

"Romans," he said, "may the Gods bless Rome and all who

love her. May the Gods preserve Rome and all who love her. Your enemies have attempted to take my life—"

Here he opened his dress and showed the bindings on his side. There was a horror-struck silence followed by a roar of grief and rage. He continued calmly:

"—but I am still among you, capable, and earnest to serve your welfare. Those who attacked me have been caught. When we have examined the matter to the bottom a report will be made to you of all that has happened. Return to your homes; draw your wives and your children about you and give thanks to the Gods; then sleep well. A measure of wheat shall be given to every father of a family that he and his may rejoice with me and mine over this happy issue. Go quietly to your homes, my friends, without lingering; for the rejoicing of a child is noisy, but the rejoicing of a man is silent and contained."

He stayed a moment while many came forward to press their foreheads on his hands.

We went into the house. In the courtyard Clodia stood ready to receive him, at the point where her brother should have been standing. A few steps behind her Catullus was holding himself, erect and sullen. Caesar greeted them formally and apologized for the absence of his wife and aunt. In a low voice Clodia apologized for the absence of her brother.

"We will make the tour of the altars," he said. This he did with that incomparable mixture of serenity and gravity which he brought to the performance of all ritual. After giving a smiling glance toward Catullus he added the Collect for the Setting Sun which is customary in households north of the Po. He then suddenly became extraordinarily lighthearted. He had found one servant crouching behind an altar. He took her playfully by one ear and led her to the kitchen. "Surely, the dinner is not all spoiled. You can make us one dish; and while you are making it we will begin with our drinking. Asinius, you will fill our cups. I see, Clodia, that you have prepared a dinner in the Greek manner. We shall have a feast of talk, for the company is well chosen and there is no lack of subjects for our discussion." Here he put the garland on his head saying: "I shall be [*in Greek*] *King of the Banquet.* I shall select the subject, reward the discreet, and impose the penalties upon the stupid."

I attempted to fall in with his mood, but Clodia could not find her tongue and for a time remained pale and shaken. Catullus reclined with lowered eyes until he had drunk several cups of wine. Caesar continued talking, however, with animation; to Clodia about the sumptuary laws, and to Catullus about his plans for controlling the floods on the Po. Finally, when the tables were withdrawn, Caesar rose, poured the libation, and announced the subject of our symposium: whether great poetry is the work of men's minds only, or whether it is, as many have claimed, the prompting of the Gods. "Before we begin," he said, "let us each recite some verses that we may be reminded of the matter before us." He nodded toward me. I recited the "Oh, love, ruler of Gods and men" [*from Euripides' play, now lost, the* Andromeda]; Clodia spoke Sappho's "Invocation to the Morning Star" [*also lost*]; Catullus spoke very slowly the opening of Lucretius's poem. There was a prolonged silence while we waited for Caesar to take his turn and I knew that he was struggling against the tears which so frequently overcame him. After he had drunk deep he recited, as though negligently, some verses of Anacreon.

The first speech fell to me. As you know, I am more at home in the countinghouse and in the councils of war than in these academies. I was glad to remember the lessons of my pedagogue and I repeated the commonplaces of the schools, that poetry, like love, indeed proceeded from the Gods and that both were accompanied by a state of possession that had universally been conceded to be more than human; that the perdurance of great verses was itself a sign of a more than human source, for all the works that a man makes are destroyed by overwhelming time but that the verses of Homer outlive the monuments they describe and like the Gods who inspired them are eternal. I said many foolish things, but none which had not already been said many thousand times.

When I had finished, Clodia rose, drew the folds of her gown about her and saluted the *King*. My opinion of Clodia had never been as harsh as that held by the majority of our community. I had known her for many years, though I had never been among those of whom Cicero had said that "only her dearest friends are in a position truly to detest her." Never, however, did I have occasion to admire her more than on that

evening. Her house was in disorder; she had good reason to believe that her brother had been killed and that she herself lay under suspicion of having planned or at least foreknown, the attempt on the Dictator's life. At that moment the behavior of Caesar must have seemed inexplicable to her. She was pale, but composed; her famous beauty seemed to have been enhanced by the dangers through which she had passed; and the speech that she made was so ordered and of such cogency that at its termination I was more than half-swayed to her opinion. She began by saying that she accepted in advance whatever penalties the *King* would impose upon her, for she knew that the things she had to say would be unfavorably received in this company.

"If it be true, Oh King," she began, "that poetry comes among us at the prompting of the Gods, then indeed we are twice miserable—once because we are men, and twice because we would know this much of the Gods, that they wish us to remain as children ignorant and as slaves deceived. For it is poetry that puts a fairer face on life than life can claim to; it is the most seductive of lies and the most treacherous of counselors.

"Neither the sun nor the situation of man permit themselves to be gazed at fixedly; the first we must view through gems, the second through poetry. Without poetry men would go into battle, brides would enter into marriage, wives would become mothers, men would bury their dead and themselves die; but drunk on poetry, all these men and women rush toward these occasions with I know not what unbounded expectations. The soldiers acquire glory, the brides call themselves Penelope, the mothers bear heroes to the state, and the dead sink into the arms of their mother the Earth that bore them, living forever in the memory of those they leave behind. It is by poets that all men are told that we press forward to a Golden Age and they endure the ills they know in the hope that a happier world will arrive to rejoice their descendants. Now it is very certain that there will be no Golden Age and that no government can ever be created which will give to every man that which makes him happy, for discord is at the heart of the world and is present in each of its parts. It is very certain that every man hates those who have been placed over him; that men will

as easily relinquish the property they have as lions will permit their food to be torn away from between their teeth; that all that a man wishes to accomplish he must complete in this life, for there is no other; and that this love—of which poets make so fine a show—is nothing but the desire to be loved and the necessity in the wastes of life to be the fixed center of another's attention; and that justice is the restraint of conflicting greeds. But these are things which no man says. Our very state is governed in the language of poetry. Among themselves our leaders rightly call the citizens a dangerous beast and a many-headed monster; but from the hustings, well surrounded by armed guards, in what terms do they address the turbulent voters? Are the voters then not 'lovers of the Republic,' 'worthy descendants of their noble fathers'? Office in Rome is won by bribes in one hand, threats in the other; and in the mouth, quotations from Ennius.

"Many will say that this is the great virtue of poetry that it civilizes men and sets the patterns by which they may aspire to live, and that thereby the Gods are handing down laws to Their children. It is most evident, however, that this is not so, for poetry has upon men the action which all flattery has: it puts to sleep the springs of action; it robs men of the desire to deserve such commendation. At first glance it seems to be merely a childishness, an aid to weakness and a consolation to misery, but no! it is an evil. It weakens weakness and redoubles misery.

"Who are the poets who have added these new discontents to the eternal discontents of men? It is a small company, renewed generation after generation. Popular observation has long since made the portrait of a poet: they are inept in all practical matters; their absentmindedness renders them frequently ridiculous; they are impatient, easily exasperated, subject to excessive passions of all sorts. Pericles's sneer on Sophocles as a governor of the city is but the other half of the story of Menander passing through the market with one foot sandaled and one foot bare. These traits, which are known to all, are interpreted by some as indicating that poets are occupied with truths that lie behind appearance and that their contemplation of these truths is like a madness or a God-given wisdom. For me, however, there is another explanation. I

believe that all poets in childhood have received some deep wound or mortification from life which renders them forever fearful of all the situations of our human existence. In their hatred and distrust they are driven to build in imagination another world. The world of poets is the creation not of deeper insights but of more urgent longings. Poetry is a separate language within the language contrived for describing an existence that never has been and never will be, and so seductive are their images that all men are led to share them and to see themselves other than they are. I take it to be confirmation of this that even when the poets write verses which pour scorn on life, describing it in all its evident absurdity, they do it in such a way that their readers are uplifted by it, for the terms of the poets' condemnation presuppose a nobler and fairer order by which we are judged and to which it is possible to attain.

"These then are the men whom some say are the mouthpieces of the Gods. I say that if the Gods exist I can imagine them to be cruel or indifferent or incomprehensible, to be inattentive to men or beneficent; but I cannot imagine them to be occupied in the childish game of deluding men as to their state through the agency of poets. Poets are men like ourselves, but they are ill and suffering. They are in possession of one consolation which is their feverish dreams. But it is not from a dreaming life but from a waking life that we must learn to live in a waking world."

When Clodia had finished, she again saluted *The King* and passing the garland to Catullus sat down. Caesar praised her speech in large terms and without the irony which Socrates employed in similar occasions. His sense of delight at the occasion seemed to have increased; he bade me fill the cups again and when we had drunk he called on Catullus. Throughout the earlier part of Clodia's speech, the poet had continued sitting with lowered eyes, but gradually his aspect had changed and from the moment he arose and placed the garland on his head all were aware that he was deeply engaged, either through anger or through interest in the matter discussed.

> [*There are many versions extant of the so-called* "Alcestiad of Catullus." *That which Caesar sent as Entry 996 of his journal-letter to Lucius Mamilius Turrinus is substituted here for Asinius Pollio's briefer account.*]

Every child knows, Oh King, that Alcestis, the wife of Admetus, King of Thessaly, was the golden pattern of all wives. As a girl, however, marriage was the last thing she wanted. She was tormented by just such a question as has been placed before us today. She wished before her life ended to have acquired some certain answers to the most important questions which can be asked. She wished complete assurance that the Gods existed and that They were attentive to her; that the promptings of her heart were guided by Them and that the good things and the ill that might befall her were known to Them and, as it were, designed by Them for purposes of Their own. She looked about her and saw that there was little likelihood of her learning these things if she were to pass her life as Queen, wife, and mother. Her heart was filled with one ambition: to become a priestess of Apollo at Delphi. There she had heard one lived in the very presence of the God; there messages were received from Him daily; there one could be certain. It is reported of her that she said of wives and mothers that there were many; that to them there was nothing more important than the good or ill-will of their husbands; that the sun rose only for their children to whom they were bound by that furious love that tigresses feel for their cubs; that their years passed, filled with the innumerable duties of ordering a household, as their minds were filled with the fears and prides and joys of their possessions; and that finally they were laid to rest, knowing no more of why they lived and suffered than the animals of the hills. She felt that there was more to be obtained from life than being the instrument of its forces and that that *more* could be obtained at Delphi. The priestesses of Apollo, however, are called by the God; and for her, in spite of all her prayers and sacrifices, no call came. Her days were spent in waiting for a message and in trying to read the will of the God in signs and portents.

Now Alcestis was the wisest and the most beautiful of the daughters of King Pelias. All the heroes of Greece sought her hand in marriage; but the King, wishing to keep her beside him, imposed upon these suitors an all but impossible task. He declared that Alcestis would be given as a bride only to that man who, harnessing together a lion and a boar, could drive them once around his city's walls. Year followed year and suitor

after suitor failed in the attempt. Peleus, who was to be the father of Achilles, failed and the sagacious Nestor; Laërtes, the father of Ulysses, failed and Jason the mighty leader of the Argonauts. Lions and boars fell upon one another in fury and the drivers barely escaped with their lives. And the King laughed and was well pleased and the Princess interpreted their failures as a sign from the God that she was destined to remain a virgin and to serve Him at Delphi.

Finally, as is well known, Admetus, King of Thessaly, came down from his mountains. He drove the lion and boar like mild oxen about the city and won the hand of the Princess Alcestis. With love and rejoicing he carried her off to his palace at Pherai and great were the preparations for the wedding.

Alcestis was not yet ready, however, to become wife and mother. Daily, with a sort of fear, she felt herself coming to love Admetus more and more, but she continued to await the call of Apollo and with one pretext after another she deferred the day of the wedding.

Admetus for a time was patient throughout these delays, but finally he could contain his ardor no longer. He besought her to give him an explanation of this reluctance and in reply she told him all that was in her mind. Now Admetus was a pious and devout man, but he had long ceased to look outside himself for any aid or consolation from the Gods. On one occasion in his life, however, he had felt Their closeness to his interests and this he now reported to her eagerly:

"Alcestis," he said, "look no further for a sign from Apollo concerning your marriage, for that sign has clearly come. It is He alone who has brought you here, as you will see from my story.

"Before I returned to Iolcos to attempt the trial, I fell ill, as well I might, for my great love was at war with my despair lest I fail to harness the lion and the boar. For three days and nights I lay at the point of death. I was tended by Aglaia who had been my nurse and my father's before me. It is she who tells me that in my delirium during the third night she was aware that Apollo was present in my mind and was teaching me how to yoke together a lion and a boar. Aglaia is here now; you have but to ask her."

"Admetus," said Alcestis, "there is no lack of reports about

the Gods from the delirium of young men and the tales of old nurses. It is just such stories which have increased the confusion in which all men live. No! Admetus, let me go to Delphi! Even though I have not been chosen to be priestess there, I can be a servant. I can serve His servants and clean the steps and pavements of His house."

Admetus did not understand her difficulty, but he was sadly giving her his permission when their conversation was interrupted. Word was brought them that a visitor had arrived at the palace, an old blind man who turned out to be Tiresias the priest of Apollo at Delphi. In amazement, Admetus and Alcestis went to the courtyard to receive him. When they drew near he called out in a loud voice:

"I bring a message to the house of Admetus, King of Thessaly. I am in haste to deliver it and to return whence I came. It is the will of Jupiter that Apollo live on earth as a man among men for the space of a year. And Apollo has chosen to live here as a herdsman of Admetus. I have given my message."

Admetus took a step forward and asked: "Do you mean, noble Tiresias, that Apollo will be here, daily, daily,—?"

"Outside the gate," shouted Tiresias, "are five herdsmen. One of them is Apollo. Do not seek to know which one is He. Assign them their duties; do justly; and ask me no more questions, for I have no answers."

With these words and without any sign of reverence, he called the herdsmen to come into the court and himself went on his way. The five herdsmen that slowly came into the courtyard were like any herdsmen; they were covered with dust after their long journey and greatly abashed by the intense gaze that was fixed upon them. King Admetus could scarcely find his voice, but finally he welcomed them and directed they be given their lodging and their dinner. For the rest of the day a silence fell upon all the people in Pherai. They knew that some great honor had come to their country, but it is difficult to be at once happy and puzzled.

Toward the end of that day, when the first stars were appearing, Alcestis slipped out of the palace and went to where the herdsmen were sitting about a fire. She stood at the edge of the firelight and besought Apollo to speak to her in His own person, to emerge from that hiding in which the Gods delight,

and to give her an answer to the questions that were her very life. Her prayer was not short. The bewildered shepherds were at first quiet and respectful; then they began passing the wineskin from hand to hand, grunting; one fell asleep and snored. Finally, the shortest one dried his mouth with the back of his hand and said:

"Princess, if there be a God here, I do not know which it is. For thirty days we five have walked across Greece. We have drunk from the same wineskin, have put our hand in the same dish, and slept by the same fire. If there were a God among us, would I not know it? Yet, lady, this I shall say: these are no ordinary herdsmen. That fellow that's asleep—there's no illness he can't cure, snake bite or broken bones. When I fell into a quarry five days ago I was most certainly a dead one, but that fellow leaned over me and said some abracadabra and look at me now. Yet I know well that he's no God, Princess. Why, in one town, Princess, there was a child with a stopped-up throat, Princess; she'd turned purple and it would have cut your heart to see her. This fellow wanted to sleep. He wouldn't cross the road to see her. Is that a God? And that fellow beside him, that one—can't you stop drinking while the Princess is looking at you?—he never loses his way. In the darkest night he knows his north from his south. But I know well that he's not the God of the Sun. Now the redhaired one, he's no ordinary herdsman, either. He performs miracles and wonders. He reverses the order of nature. He is an inventor."

With these words the herdsman walked over to his redhaired companion and began kicking him awake. "Wake up. Wake up. Show the Princess some wonders." The sleeping man stirred and groaned. Suddenly from the upper air and from the distant hills voices could be heard calling "Alcestis! Alcestis!" Whereupon the man turned over and fell asleep. Again he was kicked awake. "Do some more. Do the waterfall from the treetops. Do the balls of fire." The man swore gruffly. Balls of fire began racing across the ground. They slid up the trees and burst; they climbed onto his companions' heads; they played with one another drolly like animals. Finally the glade fell into darkness. "Those are indeed things which no other man can do, but I would take my oath, Princess, that he is no God. One of the reasons is that none of his wonders mean anything. We

are astonished and after astonishment comes disappointment. During the first days of our journey we asked for more and more wonders, for they diverted us; but finally we were tired of them and to tell the truth, we were ashamed of them and he was ashamed of them, for his tricks had no relation to anything outside themselves. Would a God be ashamed of his wonders? Would He ask Himself what they meant?

"So, you see, Princess!" he concluded, stretching out his arms as though he had finished his reply to her prayer. But Alcestis would not be put off so easily. She pointed to the fourth herdsman.

"That man? He is no ordinary herdsman, either. He is our singer. Believe me, when he plays his lyre and sings, lions hang suspended in their leap. It is true that at times I have said to myself, 'Surely, this is a God.' He can fill us to the brim with joy or sorrow at times when we have no reason to rejoice or grieve. He can make the memory of love more tender than love itself. His wonders are greater than those of our healer, our nightwalker, and our miracle worker; but I have watched him, —Princess, his wonders have more effect upon us than upon him. He soon rejects the song he has made. Us it can transport each time, but not him. He loses joy in the thing he has made and is in labor to fashion another. That is enough to assure me that he is not a God, nor even a messenger of the Gods, for the Gods cannot be thought of as despising their handiwork.

"And I? What do I do? What I am doing now. My interest is to inquire into the nature of the Gods—whether they exist and in what ways we may find Them. You may well imagine—"

> [*Here the narrative was interrupted, and we return to Asinius Pollio's letter.*]

At this moment the Dictator arose and murmuring, "Continue, my friend," began to cross the room. Catullus repeated, "You may well imagine," but had scarcely said the words when Caesar fell to the floor in a convulsion of the Sacred Malady. In his writhing he tore the bandages from his side and the floor was soon streaked with his blood. I had been present before at these seizures. I made a ball of the folds of his robe and placed it between his teeth. I directed Catullus to help me straighten his body and Clodia to bring all the robes she could find to warm him. Soon his babbling ceased and he fell into a deep

sleep. We watched beside him for a time, then placed him in his litter and the poet and I accompanied him to his home.

Such were the events of Clodia's twice-interrupted dinner. Both my friends were to die within the year. The poet who had seen that greatness humbled in insanity wrote no more stinging epigrams against him. My master never alluded to his illness, but on several occasions he reminded me of the "happy occasion" when we dined with Clodia and Catullus.

Dawn has come as I have dictated these words. My pain has been forgotten or has abated, and I have acquitted myself of a debt which I have been owing my friends.

BOOK TWO

The reader is reminded that the documents in each Book begin at an earlier date than those in the preceding Book, traverse the time already covered, and continue on to a later date.

XXII Anonymous Letter [*written by Servilia, mother of M. Junius Brutus*] to Caesar's wife.
 [*August 17.*]

Madam, it is not likely that the Dictator has yet informed you that the Queen of Egypt will soon arrive in Rome for an extended visit. Should you wish confirmation of this fact you have only to visit your villa on the Janiculan Hill. On the farther slope you will find workmen engaged in constructing an Egyptian temple and in elevating obelisks.

It is important that your attention be called to this visit and to its political dangers, for it is the subject of laughter around the world that you are completely inadequate to the high place you occupy and that your understanding of the political situation of Rome is no better than that of a child.

Cleopatra, madam, is the mother of a son by your husband. The boy's name is Caesarion. The Queen has kept him hidden from the eyes of her court, but continually spreads about the rumor that he is of divine intelligence and great beauty. The truth on very good authority, however, is that he is an idiot and that although he has passed his third birthday he is unable to talk and is scarcely able to walk.

The Queen's sole aim in coming to Rome is to legitimize her son and to establish his succession to the mastery of the world. The plan is preposterous, but there are no limits to the ambition of Cleopatra. Her skill at intrigue and her ruthlessness—which did not stop short of the assassination of her uncle and of her brother-husband—and her ascendancy over your husband's lust are sufficient to bring confusion to the world even though she cannot dominate it.

This is not the first time that you have been publicly insulted

by your husband's ostentatious adulteries. That his infatuation should blind him to the danger this woman brings to the public order is but another evidence of the senility which has begun to be apparent in his administration.

There is little you can do, madam, either to safeguard the State or to defend the dignity of your position. You should be informed, however, that the women of the aristocracy of Rome will refuse to be presented to this Egyptian criminal and will make no appearance at her court. Should you show a similar firmness you will be making some first steps in regaining the respect of the City which you have lost through your selection of friends and through the thoughtlessness of your conversation —a thoughtlessness which even your extreme youth cannot excuse.

XXIII Caesar's Journal-Letter to Lucius Mamilius Turrinus on the Island of Capri.
 [*About August 18.*]

 942. [*On Cleopatra and her visit to Rome.*]
Last year the Queen of Egypt began requesting permission to pay a visit to Rome. I finally granted it and have offered her for residence my villa across the river. She will stay at least a year in Italy. The whole matter is still a secret and will not be announced to the City until the very eve of her arrival. She is now approaching Carthage and should be here in about a month.

 I confess that I look forward to this visit with much pleasure and not only for the reason which first leaps to the mind. She was a remarkable girl. Even at twenty she knew the loading capacity of each of the major wharves of the Nile; she could receive a deputation from Ethiopia and refuse all of its requests and make the refusals appear to be benefits. I have heard her scream at her ministers' stupidity during a discussion of the royal tax on ivory and she was not only right, but right with a wealth of detailed and ordered information. Indeed, she is one of the few persons I have known who have a genius for administration. She will have become a still more remarkable woman. Conversation, conversation will be a pleasure again. I shall be flattered, understood and flattered, in a realm where few are capable of understanding my achievements. What questions

she asks! There are few pleasures equal to that of imparting to a voracious learner the knowledge that one has grown old and weary in acquiring. Conversation will be a pleasure again. Oh, oh, oh, I have sat holding that catlike bundle on my lap, drumming my fingers on ten brown toes and heard a soft voice from my shoulder asking me how to prevent banking houses from discouraging the industry of the people and what are the just wages of a chief of police relative to those of the governor of a city. Everyone in our world, my Lucius, everyone is lazy in mind except you, Cleopatra, this Catullus, and myself.

And yet she is lying, intriguing, intemperate, indifferent to the essential well-being of her people, and a lighthearted murderess. I have been receiving a series of anonymous letters warning me of her propensity to murder. I have no doubt that the lady is not long separated from a beautifully wrought cabinet of poisons; but I know also that at her table I need no taster. The prime object of her every thought is Egypt and I am its first security. If I should die, her country would fall a prey to my successors—patriots without practical judgment or administrators without imagination—and this she knows well. Egypt will never recover its greatness; but Egypt, for what it is, lives by me. I am a better ruler over Egypt than Cleopatra; but she shall learn much. During her stay in Rome I shall open her eyes to things that no Egyptian ruler has ever conceived of.

946. [*Again, on Cleopatra and her visit to Rome.*]

Cleopatra can never do a thing without pomp. She asked to be permitted to bring a court of two hundred and a household of a thousand, including a large royal guard. I have cut down these numbers to a court of thirty and a retinue of two hundred, and have told her that the Republic will undertake the responsibility of guarding her person and her party. I have directed, also, that outside of her palace grounds—my villa has already been renamed the Palace of Amenhotep—she may not employ the insignia of royalty except on the two occasions of her official welcome on the Capitoline Hill and of her official leave-taking.

She informed me that I was to appoint twenty ladies of the highest birth, headed by my wife and my aunt, to constitute for her a company of honor for the illustration of her court. I

replied that the women of Rome are free to enter into whatever engagements of this kind they may wish to and I sent her a form of invitation which she might forward to them.

This did not please her. She replied that the extent of her domains, which are more than six times as large as Italy, her divine descent—which she now traces back, in the greatest detail through two thousand years to the Sun—entitle her to such a court and that it is unbecoming that she *request* the ladies of Rome to attend her receptions and routs. The matter rests there.

I have had a part in the formation of these swelling claims. When I first met her, she was proud to state that there was not one drop of Egyptian blood in her veins. This was obviously untrue; descent in the royal house to which she belongs had always been confused by substitutions and adoptions; the effects of consanguineous marriage having been fortunately mitigated by impotence on the part of the Kings and gallantry on the part of the Queens, and by the fact that the beauty of Egyptian women far surpassed that of the descendants of the Macedonian mountain brigands. Moreover, Cleopatra at that time, apart from participation in a limited number of traditional functions, had not deigned to interest herself in the customs of the ancient country over which she ruled. She had never seen the pyramids, nor such temples on the Nile as were farther removed than an afternoon's journey from her palace at Alexandria. I advised her to make public the fact that her mother's mother was not only an Egyptian but the true heir of the Pharaohs. I persuaded her to wear Egyptian costume at least half of the time and I took her on a journey to view the monuments of a civilization that dwarfed, by Hercules, the woven huts of her Macedonian ancestors. My instructions succeeded beyond my reckoning. She is now the true Pharaoh and the living incorporation of the Goddess Isis. All the documents of her court are in hieroglyphs to which she appends, in condescension, a Greek or Latin translation.

All this is as it should be. The adherence of a people is not acquired merely by governing them to their best interests. We rulers must spend a large part of our time capturing their imaginations. In the minds of the people, Fate is an ever-watching force, operating by magic and always malevolent. To counter its action we rulers must be not only wise but supernatural, for

in their eyes human wisdom is helpless before magic. We must be at once the father they knew in their infancy who guarded them against evil men and the priest who guarded them against evil spirits.

Perhaps I have forgotten to tell you also that I directed that she may bring in her train no child under five years, neither hers nor one belonging to any member of her company.

XXIV Cleopatra, in Alexandria, to her Ambassador at Rome. [*August 20.*]

Cleopatra, the Everliving Isis, Child of the Sun, Chosen of Ptah, Queen of Egypt, Cyrenaica, and Arabia, Empress of the Upper and Lower Nile, Queen of Ethiopia, etc., etc., to her Faithful Minister.

Benediction and Favor

The Queen departs from Alexandria on the morrow for Carthage.

On this journey she will present herself to her subjects at Parastonium and Cyrene. She will rest at Carthage awaiting your word as to the most suitable time for her arrival in Rome.

You are directed to send to her at Carthage the following information:

A list of the Lay Directresses of the Mysteries of the Good Goddess, and

A list of the votaries of Hesta—both lists with notes as to their family relationships, earlier marriages, etc.

A list of the personal associates of the Dictator, men and women, particularly those whom he visits or who are visitors to his house for other than official reasons.

A list of the confidential servants in the Dictator's house, with their length of service, previous employment, and such details concerning their private lives as you can discover. This study is to be continued by you at all times and the Queen wishes to see further information when she arrives in Italy.

A list of the children, living or dead, who at any time have been attributed to the Dictator, together with their supposed mothers and all relevant information.

An account of the previous visits of all Queens to Rome, to-

gether with precedents of etiquette, ceremonial, official recep-
tions, gifts, etc.

The Queen trusts that you have not been negligent in in-
suring that her apartments will be sufficiently warmed.

XXV Pompeia to Clodia at Baiae.
 [*August 24.*]

Dearest Mousie:

The invitation to dinner has just arrived and I'm saving it
until my husband comes home at dark. I am writing this letter
in haste to return by your messenger.

What I have to say is very *very confidential* and I hope you'll
destroy it the minute you've read it.

This is the secret: a *person* from the banks of the Nile is
going to spend a long visit in the City. There are certain aspects
of that visit that I do not *deign* to consider or discuss, particu-
larly as the *political* aspects are of far greater importance and
danger than the personal ones. I hope it will never be said of
me that I regarded my *personal* life as of the slightest impor-
tance compared to the world-wide considerations which are
inextricably bound up with the situation I occupy. I am not
sure whether you know that this person has a son whom she
claims to be of very high Roman blood indeed. On that claim
she bases hopes and ambitions for the future greatness of her
country which are, of course, preposterous.

A Certain Person is, for *reasons*, completely blind to these
dangers, and I have no choice but to be doubly clear-sighted.
It may be that on two official occasions I must permit this
Egyptian criminal to be presented to me. I shall indicate by my
manner that I consider her presence an impertinence and I
shall be watchful for an opportunity to humiliate her publicly
and if possible to force her to return to her own country. I shall,
of course, refuse to put my foot into the residence which has
been loaned to her.

Do write me your thoughts on this matter. My cousin will be
returning here from Naples soon after you receive this. Please
send word by him.

Postscript: Everybody knows that she killed her uncle and

her husband, and that her brother was her husband which is an Egyptian custom and is an example of what we may expect.

XXV-A Clodia to Caesar's Wife.
 [*From Capua, September 8.*]

Many thanks, my good, good friend, for entrusting the secret to me.

Your letter is very like you. How wise you are to look at the matter from all sides, and to see all the dangers that lie concealed behind the event you foretell. And how right and noble of you it is not to fly off into passionate indignation as so many other women would do.

May I make one small suggestion, however, and one which I would only make to you because only you *could* put it into effect? You might consider approaching this annoying visitor in another way. It occurs to me that if you conducted yourself —as only you can—with all the graciousness compatible with your dignity, how surprised she would be! In that way you could insinuate yourself into this visitor's circle; you could keep your eye on what is going on; and you could prevent the Other Person in the Case from completely forgetting himself.

I would not recommend this course to anyone but you, for it requires great skill. You could do it. Do think this over.

I long to talk to you about it—which will be very soon. In the meantime I send you my admiration and affection and this bottle of Sicilian perfume.

XXVI Clodia, at Baiae, to Catullus in Rome.
 [*August 25.*]

My sister tells me I should write you a letter. A number of other people have appointed themselves to be your advocate and have told me that I should write you a letter.

Here, then is a letter. You and I long since agreed that letters are nothing. Yours tell me what I knew already or could well imagine, and they frequently depart from the rule which we had laid down that a letter should consist principally of facts.

Here are my facts:

The weather has been incomparable. There have been many

parties on sea and on land. I leave all reunions which have
been abandoned to conversation only and for which the host
has made no plans for entertainment. It is not necessary to say
that conversation is more than usually insupportable in the en-
vironment of Baiae.

I studied astronomy with Sosigenes and am henceforth the
enemy of all poets who enlarge upon their own idiotic senti-
ments in the presence of the stars. I took up the study of the
Egyptian language. When I discovered that it sounded like the
babbling of infants and that its grammatical structures were at
a level with its sounds I gave it up. We did a great deal of ama-
teur theatricals in Greek and Latin. I worked many days with
Cytheris. She refused all payment and returned a present I had
sent to her. When I insisted that she receive some mark of my
indebtedness she asked for a poem of yours in your handwriting.
I gave her "The Wedding of Peleus and Thetis." She refused
to take part in any plays, but she declaimed that poem most re-
markably, and during my lessons with her she frequently ren-
dered portions of the tragedies. My style is very different from
hers but she is absolute mistress of her style. Marc Antony
often joined us at the end of my lessons. There is only one
pleasing thing about him, his laughter; he laughs all the time
and yet it is not tiresome. When she is not talking about her
art, Cytheris is tiresome. She has the apathy of happy women.
I discovered, though not from her, that she is one of the few
persons who are permitted to visit Lucius Mamilius Turrinus
on Capri. [*Clodia wrote to Turrinus, asking permission to visit
him; she was courteously denied.*] I know a number of men whom
I could love very much, if they were mutilated and blind. I
went over Verus's new book of verses with him.

I made a number of new enemies. You know that I never lie
and that I do not permit people to lie in my presence. I was, as
you call it, "unfaithful to you" on a number of occasions. As I
am unable to sleep at night, I sometimes arrange companion-
ship for those hours.

Those are the facts concerning my life this summer and
those are the answers to the questions contained in your ex-
tremely monotonous letters. On rereading them I find that
you have given me very few facts. You have not been writing to
me but to that image of me lodged in your head whom I have

no wish to confront. The facts about you I have learned from my sister and your other advocates. You have paid visits to my sister and to Manilius and Livia [*Torquatus*]. You have taught their children how to swim and how to sail. You have taught their children how to train dogs. You have written reams of verses for children, and another poem for a wedding. I tell you again you will lose your poetic gift, if you abuse it. Such verses can only increase the blemish that already mars so much of your work, that resort to colloquial terms and provincial expressions. Many people are already denying that you are even a Roman poet. You and I are agreed that Verus has not the basic talent which you have, but both in his manners and in his verses he has a uniform elegance and taste; while you continue to cultivate a *northern* uncouthness.

This letter, like all letters, is totally unnecessary. However, I have two more things to say: on the last day of September, my brother and I are giving a dinner and I hope you will be present. I have asked the Dictator and his wife. (Incidentally, I am told that you have been spitting some more epigrams; why do you not acknowledge that you know nothing and care nothing about politics? What possible satisfaction can you derive from making vulgar little noises in the shadow of that great man?) I have also asked his aunt, Cicero, and Asinius Pollio.

I am starting north on the eighth. I am bringing a number of friends with me, including Mela and Verus. We shall stop a number of days with Quintus Lentulus Spinther and Cassia at Capua. I suggest that you join us there on the ninth and return with us to the city a few days later.

Should you decide to come to Capua I beg of you to entertain no expectation of sharing my insomnia. For the tenth time I ask you to consider the nature of friendship, to learn its advantages and to abide within its limits. It makes no claims; it establishes no possession; it is not competitive. I have made some plans for my life during the coming year. It will differ widely from that of the year just passed. The dinner to which I have invited you will give you an idea of its character.

XXVI-A Catullus:

> Miser Catulle, desinas ineptire
> Et quod vides perisse perditum ducas.
> Fulsere quondam candidi tibi soles,
> Cum ventitabis quo puella ducebat,
> Amata nobis quantum amabitur nulla.
> Ibi illa multa tum jocosa fiebant;
> Quae tu volebas nec puella nolebat.
> Fulsere vere candidi tibi soles.
> Nunc iam illa non volt; tu quoque inpotens, noli,
> Nec quae fugit sectare, nec miser vive;
> Sed obstinata mente perfer, obdura.
> · · · ·
> At tu, Catulle, destinatus obdura.

> "Wretched Catullus, put an end to your raving
> And that which you see to be lost, count it truly lost.
> Radiant were the days that formerly shone upon you
> When you hastened whither the girl led the way—
> She who was loved by you and me as no woman will ever be
> loved.
> Many then were the delights;
> What you wished for she wished no differently.
> Radiant indeed were the days that shone upon you.
> Now she is of a different mind; you, being helpless, give up
> your longing;
> Cease to pursue the fleeing and to live in wretchedness;
> But endure with affirmed heart; hold fast.
> · · · ·
> You, Catullus, since these things are so, hold fast."

XXVI-B The Commonplace Book of Cornelius Nepos.
 [*This entry is of a later date.*]

"Do you not find it extraordinary," I asked, "that Catullus should let these poems pass from hand to hand? I can think of no precedent for so candid a revelation."

"Everything there is extraordinary," replied Cicero, raising his eyebrows and lowering his voice as though we were being

overheard. "Have you remarked that he is constantly holding a dialogue with himself? Whose is this other voice that is so often addressing him—this voice that urges him to 'bear up' and to 'pull himself together'? Is that his genius? Is that some other-self? Oh, my friend, I resist this poetry as long as I can. There is something indecorous about it. Either it is the raw experience of life which has not yet sufficiently made its transmutation into poetry or it is a new kind of sensibility. His grandmother, I am told, was from the North Country; perhaps these are the first airs blowing on our literature from the Alps. They are not Roman. Before these verses a Roman does not know where to rest his glance; a Roman blushes. Nor is it Greek. Poets before now have told us of their sufferings, but their sufferings are already half-healed by song. But these!—there is no mitigation. This man is not afraid to acknowledge that he suffers. Perhaps that is because he shares it in dialogue with his genius. But what is this other-self? Have you one? Have I one?"

XXVII Caesar in Rome to Cleopatra in Carthage.
 [*The following letter, in the Dictator's hand, accompanied a formal greeting on the Queen's approach to Rome.*]
 [*September 3.*]

 August Queen, it gives me no pleasure to add to this most sincere message of welcome the following injunctions: I must remind you that I place much importance on the conditions you agreed to when this visit to Rome was planned. I refer to the number of persons in your retinue, the regulations concerning the arboring of royal insignia, and to the requirement that there shall be no child under five years of age in your company. Should you fail to observe this agreement I shall be obliged to distress myself and to distress you by taking action derogatory to your dignity and inconsonant with the esteem I bear you. Should there be any children now in your company you will either leave them at Carthage or return them to Egypt.
 Do not allow the severity of my words, however, to mislead you as to the great satisfaction with which I look forward to your stay in Rome. Rome gains heightened interest for me when I think that I shall be soon showing it to the Queen of Egypt, the Rome that is here now and the Rome that I am planning.

The world holds but a few rulers, and among them but a small number who have any inkling of what it is to direct the fortunes of nations. The Queen of Egypt is great in genius as she is great in position.

The condition of leadership adds new degrees of solitariness to the basic solitude of mankind. Every order that we issue increases the extent to which we are alone, and every show of deference which is extended to us separates us from our fellows. In looking forward to the Queen's visit I promise myself a mitigation of the solitude in which I live and work.

I have this morning made a visit to the palace which is being prepared for the Queen. Nothing is being left undone which would minister to her comfort.

XXVII-A First Reply to the Above Letter. Cleopatra to Caesar.
 [*In hieroglyphs, preceded by the Queen's titles, descent, etc., on an enormous sheet of papyrus, followed by the Latin translation; sent through the Roman administration's messenger service in advance of the royal progress.*]
 [*September 2.*]

The Queen of Egypt has directed me, her unworthy chamberlain, to acknowledge the reception of the Dictator's letter and presents.

The Queen of Egypt thanks the Dictator for the presents she has received.

XXVII-B Second Reply. Cleopatra to Caesar.
 [*Sent from the royal ship on its arrival at Ostia, October 1.*]

The Dictator has sent the Queen of Egypt a letter on the difficulties of being a monarch.

There are others.

A Queen, great Caesar, may be a mother. Her royal position renders her more, not less, subject to those loving anxieties which all mothers feel, particularly if their children are of delicate health and affectionate disposition. You have told me that you were, in your time, a loving parent. I believed you. You defended yourself to me against the charge that you permitted reasons of state to force you to deal unfeelingly with your

daughter. [*Apparently at the instigation of her father, Julia broke her engagement to one man in order to marry Pompey. She died before the Civil War arose between Caesar and Pompey, but the marriage was a completely happy one.*]

Unfeelingly you have dealt with me, and not only with me but with a child who is no ordinary child, being the son of the greatest man in the world. He has returned to Egypt.

You have described to me the solitude of a ruler. A ruler has reason to feel that most of the approaches made to him are colored with self-interest. Is it not the danger of rulers to increase this solitude by ascribing to others that motivation alone? I can imagine a ruler turned to stone by such a view of his fellow men and turning to stone all those who approach him.

As I approach the city I wish to say to its master that I am the Queen and the servant of Egypt and that my country's fortunes are never absent from my mind, but that I would feel myself less than royal did I not recognize also that I am a mother and a woman.

To return to you your own words: *Do not allow the severity of my tone, in the words I have just written, to mislead you as to the satisfaction with which I look forward to my stay in Rome.*

I ascribe the ungentleness of your conduct to the fact that you have, indeed, created for yourself a solitude that is excessive even for the ruler of a world. You have said that it may be possible that I might lighten that burden.

XXVIII Catullus to Clodia, in Rome.
 [*The following two letters, probably written on Sept. 11 or 12, were never sent. They are the drafts for the letter already given as Document XIII. Catullus did not destroy them at once, for two weeks later they were discovered in the poet's rooms by Caesar's secret police and copies of them were forwarded to the Dictator.*]

Kill me outright—since that is what you desire—I cannot kill myself—it is as though my eyes were bound on some play, as though I were watching breathlessly—to see what new horror you would devise. I cannot kill myself until I have seen the last terrifying exposure of what you are—what are you?—

murderess—torturer—mountain of lies—laughter—mask—
traitor—traitor of our whole human race.

Must I hang on this cross and not die—watching you for
eternities?

To whom can I turn? To whom can I cry? Do the Gods ex-
ist? Have you shrieked them from the skies?

Immortal Gods, did you then send this monster to the earth
to teach us something? That beauty of form is but a sack of
evils? That love is a hatred in disguise?

No—no—that lesson I will not take from you—the opposite
is true—I shall never know love; but by you I know that love
exists.

You came into the world—a monster and an assassin—to kill
the Loving—you laid a treacherous ambush and with laughter
and a howl you raised the ax to kill the part in me that lives and
loves—the immortal Gods will aid me to recover from my
horror—that you in the disguise of the Lovable are moving
about among men, waiting for occasion to inspire love and to
slay it—it was me you selected for this assassination—me who
has one life to live and one love to love and who shall never
love again.

But know—exhalation of Hell—that though you have killed
the one love I have to give, you have not killed my belief in
love. By that belief I know you for what you are.

There is no need for me to curse you—the murderer sur-
vives the victim only to learn that it was himself that he longed
to be rid of. Hatred is self-hatred. Clodia is locked with Clodia
in eternal loathing.

XXVIII-A Catullus to Clodia.

I know, I know that you never promised to be constant.

How often—with the ostentatious honesty of the dishonest
—you broke a kiss to affirm your independence of all engage-
ment. You swore you loved me, and laughed and warned me
that you would not love me forever.

I did not hear you. You were speaking in a language I did
not understand. Never, never, can I conceive of a love which is
able to foresee its own termination. Love *is* its own eternity.

Love is in every moment of its being: all time. It is the only glimpse we are permitted of what eternity is. So I did not hear you. The words were nonsense. You laughed and I laughed too. We were pretending that we were not to love forever. We were laughing at all those millions in the world who are Pretenders to Love, who know well that their love will have a termination.

Before I put you forever out of my mind I think of you once more:

What will become of you?

What woman in the world walked in such love as I gave to you?

Insane one, do you know what you have thrown away?

While the God of Love gazed at you through my eyes age could not touch your beauty. While we spoke to you, your ears could not hear the tongues of the world, envy and detraction and all the gusts that are blown about in the malignant air of our human state; while we loved you you could not know the solitude of the soul—does that mean nothing to you? Insane one, do you know what you have thrown away?

But that is not all. Your state is a thousand times worse. Now you are revealed; your secret is out. Since I know it, you can no longer hide it from yourself: you are the eternal assassin of life and love. But how terrifying to you must be the knowledge of your failure, for you have made clear the greatness and the majesty of your enemy, love.

All, all that Plato said was true.

It was not I, I in myself, who loved you. When I looked at you the God Eros descended upon me. I was more than myself. The God lived in me, looked through my eyes and spoke through my lips. I was more than myself and when your soul was aware that the God was in me, gazing at you, for a time you too were filled with the God. Have you not told me so? In what hours, in what whispers have you not told me so.

But you could not long endure this presence, for you came into the world, a monster and an assassin, to kill all that lives and loves. You wear the disguise of the Lovable and you live only to prepare one treacherous ambush after another; you live only for the moment when with laughter and a shriek you may lift the ax and slay the promise of life and the promise of love.

I am no longer breathless with horror. I have ceased trembling. I can muse with wonder, asking myself where you obtained the passionate hatred of life and why the Gods permit this enemy of the world to move about among us. I will never feel pity for you, this horror has no room for pity. Some great intention for the world's enlightenment stirred in you and was poisoned at the source.

I loved you and I shall never be the same again, but what is my state compared to yours?

XXVIII-B Catullus.

> O dei, si vestrum est misereri, aut si quibus unquam
> Extremam iam ipsa in morte tulisti opem,
> Me miserum aspicite et, si vitam puriter egi
> Eripite hanc pestem perniciemque mihi,
> Quae mihi subrupens imos ut torpor in artus
> Expulit ex omni pectore laetitias.
> Non iam illud quaero, contra ut me diligut illa,
> Aut, quod non potis est, esse pudica velit;
> Ipse valere opto et taetrum hunc deponere morbem.
> O dei, reddite mi hoc pro pietate mea.

"Oh, immortal Gods, if pity be among your attributes,
Or if ever you have brought supreme aid to one already at the
 point of death,
Turn your eyes upon me, a most wretched man, and if I have
 lived a pure life,
Tear out from my heart this plague, this pestilence
Which, stealing like a lethargy throughout my deepest fibers
Has driven all joy from my breast.
I no longer ask that this woman return my love
Nor—for that is impossible—that she be chaste;
All I aspire to is that I be healed and that this black malady be
 removed.
Oh, immortal Gods—grant this in return for my devotion."

XXIX Caesar to Cornelius Nepos.
 [*September 23.*]

This letter is confidential.

I have been informed that you are a friend of the poet Gaius Valerius Catullus.

Word has reached me in a very indirect way that the poet has been ill or at least in extreme distress of mind.

I have been a friend of his father for many years and although I have had few occasions of meeting the poet himself I follow his work with much interest and admiration. I wish that you would call upon him and send me word as to his condition. In addition, I should feel very indebted to you if you would report to me, at any time and at any hour, that you find him ill or in any kind of distress.

The esteem in which I hold you and your work leads me to add that I should feel it to be an unkindness did you or your family not keep me informed of any ill-fortune (which the immortal Gods avert) that might befall you or yours. At a very early age I was convinced that the true poets and historians are the highest ornaments of a country; this conviction has only increased with time.

XXIX-A Cornelius Nepos to Caesar.

It is a satisfaction to know that the great leader of the Roman people feels concern for the health of my friend and fellow countryman Catullus and has expressed himself in friendly terms toward me and my household.

It is true that some ten days ago a member of the Aemilian Draughts and Swimming Club, where the poet resides, called on me in the middle of the night saying that Catullus's condition was causing alarm to his friends. I hurried to his rooms and found him in pain and in delirium. A doctor Sosthenes, the Greek, was administering emetics and then calmatives. My friend did not recognize me. We sat with him through the night. In the morning he was much improved. Gathering himself together with resolution he thanked us for our attentions and assured us that his illness was at an end and requested us to leave him. I returned later in the afternoon and found him in un-

troubled sleep. He was awakened soon after by a clumsy mes-
senger bringing a letter from that woman who plays no small
part in the troubles we had been witnessing—as his delirium
had attested. In my presence he read the letter and remained a
long time silent in deep thought. He made no reference to what
he had read but against all persuasion dressed in formal attire
and left the Club.

I have given the Dictator these details in order that he may
make his own observations.

XXX Caesar's Journal-Letter to Lucius Mamilius Turrinus
on the Island of Capri.

991. [*On Cleopatra and her visit to Rome.*]
The Queen of Egypt is approaching. Missy Crocodile is
being fanned across the straits.

My correspondence with Majesty has been as spirited as
could be expected. Her Latin is broken, but I notice that she
manages to achieve precision when an occasion requires it.

I do not expect a literal obedience to the regulations that I
have laid down governing her visit here. The Queen is incapable
of complying precisely with any direction that may be given
her. Even when she believes herself to be obeying implicitly, she
manages to admit a deviation or two. I must expect this. I con-
fess that I am charmed by this invariable variation, though I
have been obliged before now to show her a stern face on it. It
is prompted by her unfathomable pride and by the independ-
ence of a woman who is herself accustomed to punish any slight-
est disobedience by death.

Her letters—even in one conjuncture, her silence—have de-
lighted me. She is indeed a woman now and a most queenly one.
At moments I find myself dreaming that she is more woman
than queen and must arrest my thoughts.

Cleopatra is Egypt. No word she lets fall and no caress she
dispenses is without a political implication. Each conversation
is a treaty and every kiss a pact. I could wish that association
with her did not require so constant a vigilance and that her
favors had more abandon and less art.

It is many years, many years, however, since I have known a
disinterested friendship on the part of anyone except yourself,

my aunt, and my soldiers. Even in my home I seem to be playing a perpetual game of draughts. I lose a "man"; I am menaced from the flank; I rally to a sortie; I capture a "horseman." My good wife seems to derive some pleasure from this skirmishing, though it is not conducted without tears.

Nay more, it is many years since I have felt directed toward me a disinterested hatred. Day by day I scan my enemies looking with eager hope for the man who hates me "for myself" or even "for Rome." I am much condemned for surrounding myself with unscrupulous adventurers who enrich themselves from the appointments I accord them. Yes, I sometimes think that it is the candor of their greed that pleases me; they do not pretend to love me for myself. I shall go so far as to say that I have occasionally been moved to pleasure when one or other of them lets fall an expression of his contempt for me—in that ocean of flattery in which I live and move.

It is difficult, my dear Lucius, to escape becoming the person which others believe one to be. A slave is twice enslaved, once by his chains and once again by the glances that fall upon him and say "thou slave." A dictator is believed to be niggardly of benefits, incalculable in displeasure, jealous of capable men, athirst for flattery, and not ten but twenty times a day I feel myself drifting toward those qualities and must draw back sharply. And ten times a day, as I await the arrival of the Queen of Egypt, I find myself dreaming of the possibility that she, now grown a woman, can see that all that I can give to her and to her country I give outright; that she need not contrive to obtain it; that all the devices within her power cannot obtain what it is unsuitable to accord her; and that these things being understood, we may move in a realm that is . . . but I am drifting beyond the possible.

XXXI Cicero, in Rome, to Atticus in Greece.
 [*This letter aroused much merriment and derision in an-*
 tiquity and in the Middle Ages. It is perhaps apocryphal.
 We know that Cicero wrote Atticus a letter concerning
 marriage and that in the two succeeding letters he im-
 plored his friend to destroy it—which Atticus would cer-
 tainly have done. On the other hand, there have come
 down to us over a dozen versions of what might well have

been the letter in question. All these differ widely among themselves and all are larded with obviously burlesque interpolations. We here select the passages which the majority of the versions have in common, our theory being that a secretary of Atticus probably made a copy of the original letter before its destruction and that this copy began circulating surreptitiously throughout the Roman world.

[*It should be remembered that Cicero not only divorced his universally respected wife Terentia after many years of increasingly contentious marriage, but that he promptly married and divorced his rich young ward Publilia; that Cicero's brother Quintus had long been stormily married to Atticus's sister Pomponia whom he had recently divorced; and that Cicero's beloved daughter Tullia had been none too happily married to the husband Dolabella, an ambitious and dissolute friend of Caesar whom her father had selected for her.*]

One marriage in a hundred is happy, my friend. This is one of those things which everyone knows and which no one says. No wonder that the exceptional marriage is widely celebrated for it is the exceptional which makes news. But it is a part of the folly of our human race that we are forever tempted to elevate the exception into the norm. We are attracted to the exception, for every man thinks himself exceptional and destined for the exceptional; and our young men and women advance into marriage under the assumption that ninety-nine are happy and one unhappy, or that they are marked for the exceptional happiness.

Given the nature of women and the nature of the passion which draws men and women together, what chance has marriage of being happier than the combined torments of Sisyphus and Tantalus?

By marriage we place into the hands of women the governance of our household which they promptly extend, as far as they are able, to an interest over all our goods. They rear our children and thereby acquire a share in the disposition of the children's affairs when they have reached maturity. In all these matters they pursue ends totally opposed to those a man envisages. Women wish only the warmth of a hearth and the shelter

of a roof. They live in fear of catastrophe and no security is sufficiently secure for them and in their eyes the future is not only unknown but catastrophic. To forfend those unknown evils there is no deception to which they will not resort, no rapacity they will not exert, and no other pleasure or enlightenment they will not combat. Had civilization been left in the hands of women we should still be housed in the caves of mountains and man's invention would have ceased with the domestication of fire. All they ask of a cave beyond its shelter is that it be a degree more ostentatious than that of a neighbor's wife; and all they ask for their children's happiness is that they be secure in a cave similar to their own.

Marriage inevitably commits us to extended examples of our wives' conversation. Now the conversation of women within the married relationship—I do not now speak of that other crucifixion, their conversation at social gatherings—behind all the disguises of guile and incoherence treats of only these two subjects: conservation and ostentation.

It shares a characteristic of the conversation of slaves, and logically so, for the position of women in our world has much in common with that of slaves. This may be regrettable but I would not be among those who would apply themselves to altering it. The conversation of slaves and women is directed by ruse. Guile and violence are the sole resorts available to the dispossessed; and violence on the part of slaves can only be resorted to through close consolidation with their fellow unfortunates. Against such consolidation the state rightly maintains a constant vigilance and the slave is driven to seek his ends by guile. The recourse to violence is likewise closed to women because they are incapable of consolidation; they distrust one another like Greeks and with good reason. Hence, they, too, resort to ruse. How often in visiting my villas and conferring all day with my foremen and laborers I have retired to bed as exhausted as though I had wrestled with each, body and mind at the alert lest I be crippled or robbed. The slave introduces the aims he has in mind from every direction and by every indirection; there is no trap for concession that he does not employ, no flattery, no show of logic, no pressure on fear or avarice; and all this to avoid building a pergola, to eliminate an inferior, to enlarge his cottage, or to obtain a new coat.

Such too is the conversation of woman; but how much more diverse her aims, how much wider her resources of attack, and how much more deeply rooted her passion to attain her ends.

For the most part, a slave merely desires conveniences; but behind a woman's wishes lie forces which are for her the very nature of life itself: the conservation of property; the esteem in which she is held by those matrons of her acquaintance whom she despises and dreads; the claustration of a daughter, whom she wishes to be ignorant, joyless, and brutified. So deeply rooted are a woman's aims that they have to her the character of self-evident truth and unshakable wisdom. Hence, she can feel only contempt for any opinion that opposes her own. Reason is unnecessary and trifling to one so endowed; she is deaf in advance. A man may have saved the State, directed the affairs of a world, and acquired an undying fame for wisdom, but to his wife he is a witless fool.

> [*Here follows a paragraph about the sexual relationship. It has been so distorted by the glee and invention of copyists and transmitters that it is impossible to determine the original text.*]

. . . .

These things are not often said, though occasionally the poets reveal them—those same poets who are primarily responsible for the delusion that marriage is a heaven and who betray us into seeking the Perilous Exception. Euripides left no word of it untold in the *Medea*. Little wonder that the Athenians drove him from Athens with imprecations for telling such truths. The mob was led by Aristophanes who has shown that he knew these things—though with less candor; he stifled his knowledge in order to hound from the city a greater poet. And Sophocles! What husband has not smiled grimly to himself before the scene where Jocasta heaps lies on lies, putting a fair face on a calamitous situation. Notable example of that so-called conjugal love that will conceal any fact from a husband in order to maintain an ostensible contentment; bold illustration that for mentality a wife can barely distinguish a husband from a son.

Oh, my friend, let us console ourselves with philosophy. There is a realm where they have never entered; indeed, in which they never have taken the faintest interest. Let us welcome that

old age which frees us from that desire for their embraces—
embraces which must be paid for at the cost of all order in our
lives and any tranquility in our minds.

XXXII Abra, Pompeia's Maid, to Clodia.
 [*October 1.*]

I have been in great anxiety, honored Madam, concerning
yourself and your house and concerning our Master after the
attempt on his life. Madam, all has been in great dismay here;
the house always full of visitors and police and my mistress at
her wits' end. Himself, praise the Immortal Gods, woke up at
noon and seemed none the worse; in fact, very merry which
made my mistress most angry. He was very hungry and ate and
ate and the doctor protested and my mistress got down on her
knees and begged him not to eat. But he made such jokes that
we had all we could do to keep straight faces.

I heard him say to everybody standing around, Madam, that
he never enjoyed a dinner more than the one he enjoyed at your
house. The General Marc Antony said why and he said because
the company was so good. And, begging your pardon, Marc
Antony said you mean Claudilla and himself said Claudilla is
an extraordinary woman. I hope I am correct in telling things
like this to Madam.

Now I should tell Madam that he announced to all who
came in during the day that Cleopatra, she that is queen of
Egypt, will arrive today or tomorrow.
 [*October 6.*]
The Master was not home last night, the first time in a very
long time and everybody has their ideas.

The Queen has sent my mistress the most wonderful pres-
ents, especially one the most wonderful thing ever seen. Some
workmen came yesterday in great secrecy and set it up and put
it in motion. It is an Egyptian palace, Madam, no higher than
one's knee. And when you take off the front wall you can see
all the people inside and there is a barnyard and a royal proces-
sion and in the most beautiful clothes and colors. But that is
not all. When you start water running, this is hard to explain,
Madam, the little people all move, the Queen and all her court
walk into the house, *up the stairs, yes,* and through the house

and the animals go and drink in the Nile and a crocodile swims *against the water*, and the women weave and fishers fish and, Immortal Gods, I cannot tell all that they do. One could look at it forever. My mistress was very delighted and had lights brought and we thought she would never go to bed. Everybody says how clever it was of the Queen, because my mistress forgot everything when she was watching this palace and she forgot that her husband was not at home.

[*October 8.*]

Yesterday the Queen came to visit my mistress. We thought she would wear very fine clothes, but she just wore a blue dress and not a single jewel, so she must know the law about them. Her hair was not dressed at all, madam, just anyhow and I had taken two hours with mistress's. My mistress thanked her for the toy palace and then the whole time was taken up in explaining it. The Queen is very simple. She even knew my name and explained things to me. But as my mistress's secretary said you can see that she's thinking all the time. When the Master he came home, he asked how did it go and my mistress very dignified said why very well, what did you think? Oh, Madam, you should see my Master these days. It is like having ten boys in the house. He is always teasing my mistress and pinching her.

XXXIII Cornelius Nepos: Commonplace Book.

[*October 3.*]

The Queen of Egypt has arrived. She was received at Ostia by a deputation from the City and the Senate but refused to disembark because the Dictator's insignia was not present among the welcoming guidons. This was reported to Caesar who hastily dispatched Asinius Pollio to the port bearing his trophies. She then came to Rome, traveling by night.

· · · ·

The Queen has received no one and is reported to be indisposed. She has, however, sent magnificent presents to some thirty persons of note.

· · · ·

[*October 5.*]

The Queen was received at the Capitoline today. The magnificence of her train exceeded anything ever seen in the City.

To me at a distance she seemed very beautiful; Alina [*his wife*], having a view of better advantage [*probably sitting among the votaresses of Hestia*] and being a woman, reports that she is decidedly plain, having cheeks so plump that they are condemned as "jowls." Gossips report that there was a fierce struggle with the Dictator in regard to her costume. The Queens of Egypt, in dress of ceremony, apparently through identification with the Goddess Isis, wear no garments above the girdle. Caesar insisted that she cover her bosom according to the Roman usage, and it was done though lightly. She made a short speech in broken Latin, a longer one in Egyptian. The Dictator replied in Egyptian and Latin. The omens at the sacrifice were extremely favorable.

XXXIII-A Cicero in Rome to his Brother.
 [*October 8.*]

The words "Queen of Egypt" cast a deep spell, my friend, but not upon me.

I have corresponded for a number of years with this Queen; I have done innumerable services for her chancellery. It can be presumed that she knows my interests and my disposition and my services to this Republic. Arriving in this city she distributes presents to every clerk in the backstairs of government, gifts of a splendor that are suitable only from one royalty to another. To me she sent another such gift. It could feed Sicily for a year; but what have I to do with jeweled headdresses and emerald cats. By the Immortal Gods, I let her steward, the blockhead Hammonios, know that I am not a drunken actor and that I am a man who more values a gift by its appropriateness than by its expense. "Has the library at Alexandria no manuscripts?" I asked him.

The spell cast by this Queen is greatly diminished by the closer view. I indulge a theory that each of us has one age in life toward which we are directed as iron filings are directed toward the north. Marc Antony is forever sixteen and the discrepancy between that age and his present years makes for an increasingly sorry view. My good friend Brutus has been a deliberative and judicious fifty since the age of twelve. Caesar is at forty—a Janus

looking toward youth and age, irresolute. By this law, young though she is, Cleopatra is a woman of forty-five, which renders what youthful charms she possesses embarrassing. Her plumpness is the plumpness of a woman who has had eight children. Her walk and port is much admired but not by me. She is twenty-four; her walk is the walk of a woman trying to give the impression that she is twenty-four.

One must be on the alert to recognize these things, however. The prestige of her title; the magnificence of her dress; the effect of her two signal advantages—namely, her fine eyes and the beauty of her speaking voice—subdue the unwary.

XXXIV Letter and Questionnaire: Cleopatra to Caesar.
 [*October 9.*]

My *Deedja*, *Deedja*, *Deedja*—*Crocodeedja* is very unhappy-happy, very happy-unhappy. Happy that she is to see her *Deedja* on the night of the twelfth, all the night of the twelfth, and unhappy that the night of the twelfth is a thousand years away. When I am not with my *Deedja* I sit weeping. I tear my robe to pieces, I wonder why I am here, why I am not in Egypt, what I am doing in Rome. Everybody hates me; everybody sends me letters wishing me dead. Cannot my *Deedja* come before the twelfth? Oh, *Deedja*, life is short, love is short; why cannot we see one another? All day and night other people are seeing my *Deedja*. Do they love him more than I do? Does he love them more than he loves me? No, no, there is nothing in the world that I love more than my *Deedja*, my *Deedja* in my arms, my *Deedja* happy, happy, happy in my arms. Separation is cruel, separation is waste, separation is meaningless.

But if my *Deedja* wishes it so I weep; I do not understand, but I weep and wait for the twelfth. But I must write a letter every day. And oh my *Deedja*, write me a letter every day. I cannot sleep when night comes after a day when I have had no real letter from you. Every day there are your presents with five words. I kiss them; I hold them long; but when there is no real letter with the presents I cannot love them.

I must write a letter every day to tell my *Deedja* that I love only him, and think only of him. But there are other tiresome

little things I must ask him, too. Things I must know so that I
will be a dignified guest worthy of his protection. Forgive
Crocodeedja these little tiresome questions.

1. At my party, at my rout, I go to the lowest step of my
throne to welcome my *Deedja's* wife. Do I also go to the low-
est step to meet my *Deedja's* aunt? What do I do to welcome
the consuls and the consuls' wives?

> [*Caesar's answer*: Hitherto all queens have come to the
> lowest step. I am changing all that. My wife and my aunt
> will be with me. You will meet us at the arch. Your throne
> will not be raised by eight steps, but by one. All other
> guests you will greet standing before your throne. This
> arrangement may seem to rob you of the dignity of
> eight steps, but eight steps are not a dignity for those
> who must descend them and you would have to descend
> them to welcome the consuls who are or have been
> sovereigns. Think this over and you will see that *Deedja*
> is right.]

2. The Lady Servilia has not replied to my invitation. *Deedja*,
you understand that I cannot suffer that. I know ways to en-
force her attendance and I must use them.

> [*Caesar's answer:* I do not understand you. The Lady
> Servilia will be present.]

3. If it's a cold night, I shall not move an inch from my bra-
ziers or I shall perish. But where can I get enough braziers for
my guests at the water-ballet?

> [*Caesar's answer:* Furnish the ladies of your court with
> braziers. We Italians are accustomed to the cold and we
> dress to warm ourselves.]

4. In Egypt royalty does not receive dancers and theater
people. I am told I should invite the actress Cytheris, that she
is received by many patricians, and that your nephew or cousin
Marc Antony goes nowhere without her. Must I invite her?
Indeed, must I invite *him*?—he comes every day to my court;
he has very impudent eyes; I am not accustomed to being
laughed at.

> [*Caesar's answer:* Yes, and more than invite her: learn to
> know her. She is the daughter of a carter but there is no
> woman of the highest aristocracy who could not learn
> from her what dignity, charm, and deportment are.

You will soon discover all the reasons for my admiration of her. In addition I am indebted to her for a personal reason: her long association with my relative Marc Antony has given me, in him, a friend. We men are for the most part what you women make us—and women too; for men cannot remake a woman who is herself ill-made. Marc Antony was and always will be the best athlete and the best-liked athlete in a provincial school. Ten years ago a few moments of sober conversation exhausted him and he would be fretting to balance three tables on his chin. Wars themselves employed but a fraction of his thoughtless energy. Rome lived under the menace of practical jokes which did not stop short of setting fires to entire blocks, to loosing all the boats on the riverside, and to stealing the garments of a Senate. He had no malice; but he had no judgment. All this Cytheris has remade; she has taken nothing away, but has rearranged the elements in a different order. I am surrounded by and hate those reformers who can only establish an order by laws which repress the subject and drain him of his joy and aggression. The Cato and the Brutus envision a state of industrious mice; and in the poverty of their imaginations they charge me with the same thing. Happy would I be if it could be said of me that like Cytheris I could train the unbroken horse without robbing him of the fire in his eye and the delight in his speed. And has not Cytheris had a fair reward? He will go no place without her, and with reason, for he will find no better company.

But I must close. A deputation from Lusitania has been waiting this half hour to protest against my cruelty and injustice. Tell Charmian to put all in readiness for a visitor tonight. He will enter, dressed as a night guard, through the Alexandrian port. Tell Charmian that it will be nearer sunrise than sunset; but as soon as ardor at war with prudence can effect it. Let the great Queen of Egypt, the phoenix of women, sleep; she will be awakened by no ungentle hand. Yes, life is short; separation is insane.]

XXXIV-A Cytheris, the actress, at Baiae, to Cicero, at his villa
near Tusculum.

> [*This letter, written the previous year, is appended here to
> illustrate further the subject treated in Question 4 of the
> preceding questionnaire.*]

The Lady Cytheris presents her profound respects to the
greatest advocate and orator which the world has seen and to
the savior of the Roman republic.

As you know, honored sir, the Dictator has directed that a
collection of your witticisms be prepared for publication. Word
has reached me that the collection contains an account of the
table conversation carried on at the dinner which Marc Antony
gave in your honor some three years ago and includes some re-
marks of mine which now appear to be disrespectful of the
Dictator.

I implore you, encouraged by the generous words which you
have so frequently and graciously bestowed on me, to remove
any such expressions as may be ascribed to me at that time.

It is true that during the Civil Wars I felt differently toward
the Dictator. My two brothers and my husband fought against
him and my husband lost his life. Since then the Dictator, how-
ever, has pardoned my brothers, with the clemency that dis-
tinguishes him; he has given them lands, he has introduced
reforms into our troubled state; he has won our hearts and our
loyalties.

Next year I am retiring from the stage. My retirement and my
old age would be rendered a misery by the thought that these
impatient words of mine were in circulation, and in the wide cir-
culation destined for any work that bears your illustrious name.

This misery you alone could spare me. As a token of my
gratitude and my admiration, kindly accept the manuscript
which I enclose. It is the prologue which Menander wrote for
his "The Shipwrecked Girl" and is in his own hand.

XXXV Caesar to Clodia.
> [*October 10.*]

It is with regret that I see that appeals will be lodged with
me urging that you be excluded from a reunion which includes

all the respected women in Rome. No reports have yet reached my attention that would justify your exclusion.

There is, however, another matter I must lay before you. I read many letters which were never intended for my eyes and whose writers and recipients are not aware of my knowledge.

No blame attaches to a woman who being loved is unable to love in return. In such a situation, however, a woman knows well the ways in which she may intensify or mitigate the sufferings of her suitor. I am referring to the poet Catullus, whose gifts to Rome are not of less consequence than those of her rulers and whose composure of mind I feel to be among my responsibilities.

Threats constitute a weapon all too easily placed at the hand of a man in power. I employ them seldom. Yet there arise cases when those in authority are aware that neither the persuasion of reason nor the appeal to mercy can alter the mistaken conduct of a child or of a wrong doer. When threats are of no avail, punishment must follow.

You may judge that the right action requires your retiring from the City for a time.

XXXV-A Clodia to Caesar.

The Lady Clodia Pulcher has received the letter of the Dictator, not without surprise. The Lady Clodia Pulcher requests permission of the Dictator to remain in Rome until the day following the reception of Cleopatra, Queen of Egypt; thereafter she will retire to her villa in the country until December.

XXXVI Caesar to Cleopatra: From the daily letters.
 [*Second half of October.*]

 [*In Egyptian. Many of the words of this letter are unknown today and are here supplied by conjecture. They are probably in the* argot *of the Alexandrian waterfront taverns and were acquired by Caesar during the riotous excursions made into that underworld during Caesar's stay there a few years before.*]

Tell Charmian to open this package carefully.

I stole it. I haven't stolen anything since the age of nine and

have been experiencing all the sensations of the housebreaker and the snatcher of purses. I see that I am now setting out upon that road of prevarication and play acting which is the criminal's part. [*It has been suggested that Caesar may have robbed his wife's dressing table of a bottle of perfume.*]

But what would I not do for the great Queen of Egypt? I have not only become a thief; I have become an idiot. I can think only of her. I blunder in my work. I forget names; I mislay papers. My secretaries are in a consternation; I can hear them whispering behind my back. I make visitors wait; I postpone tasks—all this that I may hold long conversations with the everliving Isis, with the Goddess, with the witch who has stolen my mind away. There is no drunkenness equal to that of remembering whispered words in the night. There is nothing in the world that can compare with the great Queen of Egypt.

. . . .

[*In Latin.*]

Where is my wise *Deedja*, my good *Deedja*, my most intelligent *Deedja*?—Why is she so unwise, so obstinate, so cruel to herself and to me?

My pearl, my lotus, if our Roman wheat paste disagrees with you *why will you eat it?*

It disagrees with all Easterners. It disagreed with your father. It disagreed with Queen Anes'ta. We Romans are brutish. We can eat anything. I pray of you, I implore you: be wise. I pray that you are not suffering; but I am, I am. My messenger will wait until Charmian sends me back some report about you. Oh, star and phoenix, take good care of yourself; be wise.

You turned my doctor away from your door. Could you not let him see you? Could you not talk to him for *one moment?* You tell me your Egyptian medical knowledge is ten thousand years old and that we Romans are children. Yes, yes, but—I must speak severely with you—your doctors are ten thousand years old in nonsense. Think, think for a moment about medicine. Doctors are mostly impostors. The older a doctor is and the more venerated he is, the more he must pretend to know everything. Of course, they grow worse with time. Always look for a doctor who is hated by the best doctors. Always seek out a bright young doctor before he comes down with nonsense. *Deedja*, tell me you will see my Sosthenes.

I am helpless. Take care of yourself. I love you.

. . . .

Oh, yes. I obey the Queen of Egypt. I do everything she tells me to do.

The top of my head has been purple all day.

Visitor after visitor has looked at me with horror, but no one has asked me what was the matter with me. That is what it is to be a Dictator: no one asks him a question about himself. I could hop on one foot from here to Ostia and back and no one would mention it—*to me*.

At last a cleaning woman came in to wash the floor. *She* said: "Oh, divine Caesar, what is the matter with your head?"

"Little mother," I said, "the greatest woman in the world, the most beautiful woman in the world, the wisest woman in the world said that baldness is cured by rubbing the head with a salve made of honey, juniper berries, and wormwood. She ordered me to apply it and I obey her in everything."

"Divine Caesar," she replied, "I am not great nor beautiful nor wise, but this one thing I know: a man can have either hair or brains, but he can't have both. You're quite beautiful enough as you are, sir; and since the Immortal Gods gave you good sense, I think they didn't mean for you to have curls."

I am thinking of making that woman a Senator.

. . . .

Never have I felt so helpless, great Queen. I would resign all my other powers in exchange for this one, but I cannot; I cannot control the weather. I rage at these cold rains as I have not raged at anything for many years. I am become a sort of farmer: my clerks glance at one another with raised eyebrows; they see me continually going to the door to examine the sky. During the night I rise and go to my balcony; I estimate the wind; I look for the stars. I send you herewith another blanket of fur; wrap yourself well. I am told that these cruel rains will last two days more. All through the winter we shall have occasional days of sunlight. A friend of mine has a villa at Salerno, shielded from the north. You will go there in January and I shall join you. Be patient; occupy yourself. Send me word.

XXXVII Catullus to Clodia.
 [*October 20.*]

 Soul of my soul, when your word came this morning I wept.
 You have forgiven us. You understand that we meant no of-
fense, no offense, Claudilla. I ask myself what I said that could
have made you so angry. But we will think of it no longer. You
have forgiven us and it is forgotten.
 But oh, great Claudilla, incomparable Claudilla, be ready to
forgive us again. We do not know when we are about to stum-
ble into your displeasure. Be assured now and forever that we
never, oh NEVER, intend to cause you pain. Let this declaration
stand for all time. What meaning or offense could you have
found in—but there! it is forgotten.
 But Claudilla, I must add that you also must try not to
wound me. When you said in front of *him*: "Valerius has never
quite made a poem which is equally successful throughout."
Claudilla, don't you know that just that is the terror of a poet?
A few verses come right; the rest he must contrive. What, have
I never made an entire poem? And in front of *him*!
 In the matter of the Queen's reception, I shall, of course,
obey you. I had no particular interest in going. Many members
of our Club are going in a body and they have been urging me
to write an Ode for it. I have a few strophes down; but it is not
going very well and I shall be glad to give it up. All that I hear
about her leads me to believe that she is insupportable—par-
ticularly, the immodesty of her dress.
 No, I have not been ill.
 Later.
 I was about to send this letter off when I heard by chance
that *you are going to the country for several months*. Why? WHY?
Is it true? Immortal Gods, it cannot be true. You would have
told me. WHY? You have never been away in the winter. What
does it mean? I do not know what to think. You have never
been away in the winter.
 If it is true, Claudilla, Claudilla, you will send for me. We
shall read. We shall walk by the sea. You will point out the stars
to me. No one has ever talked about the stars as you talk about
them. I worship you always, but then you are all Goddess. Yes,

go to the country, my brightest star, my treasure, and let me join you there.

But the more I think of it, the more unhappy I become. What does it mean?

I know that I must ask for nothing. I must make no claim. But a love like mine must speak; it must cry out a little. Great and terrible Claudia, listen to me this once. Do not go into the country—I mean: if you must go into the country, GO ALONE. I dare not ask again that it be with me; but, at least, alone.

Yes, I will say it: I have been ill. Since love first came among men, despised lovers have pretended they were ill; but this was no pretense. Do you wish to kill me? Is that your aim? I do not wish to die. I swear to you I shall fight it to my last breath. I do not know how much longer I can endure. Something that is stronger than I is lying in wait for me. It is in the corner of my room all night, watching me while I sleep. I awake suddenly and seem to feel it above my bed.

I tell you now that if you go into the country with him I shall surely die. You call me a weakling. I am not. I could hold your friend in the air for an hour and then hurl him against a wall, and remain untired. You know that I am not a weakling and that only a powerful force could kill me.

I do not mean these words to sound angry. If it is true that you are going to your villa, promise me that you will be alone. And then if you do not wish me to join you there, I will do what you have so often urged: I shall go to my home in the north until you return to the city.

Send me word about this. And oh, Claudia, Claudilla, ask me to do something—something that I can do. Do not ask me to forget you or to be indifferent to you. Do not ask me to have no interest in how you pass your time. But if we are separated, set me a task, something that will be a daily link with you. Great queen, greater than all the queens of Egypt, wise and good, learned and gracious, with one word you can make me well. With one smile, you can make me, make us, the happiest poet that ever praised the Immortal Gods.

XXXVII-A Clodia to Catullus.
 [*By return messenger.*]

Yes, it is true, dear Gaius. I am going into the country and alone, entirely alone. That is, only with Sosigenes the astronomer. The life of the city has become tiresome. I shall write you frequently. I shall think of you with affection. I am unhappy to hear that you have been ill. I think it would be wise for you to go to your home. I am sending presents for you to give to your mother and your sisters.

You ask me to assign you a task. What task could I assign you that your genius has not already whispered in your ear? Forget all that I have ever said about your verses and remember only this: you and Lucretius alone have made Rome a new Greece. You once said that the writing of tragedies was not your work. At another time you said that you might be able to write a "Helena." Any verses you write would give me happiness; if you also wrote a "Helena," we could play it when I return from the country. I shall leave on the morning after the Queen's reception and shall return a few days before the festival [*of the Good Goddess*].

Take every care of your health. Do not forget your "Ox-eyed."

XXXVIII Caesar's Journal-Letter to Lucius Mamilius Turrinus on the Island of Capri.

 1008. [*Of Cleopatra's admiration for the wine of Capri.*]
 1009. [*Apology for tardiness in sending off the packet.*]
 1010. [*Of love poetry.*] We are all vulnerable to the songs of the country people and of the market place. There have been times when I have gone about tormented for days by some song heard over the garden wall or sung by my soldiers around their campfires. "*Don't say no, no, no, little Belgian,*" or "*Tell me, moon, where is Chloe now?*" But when the verses are of a sovereign hand, it is no torment, but—Hercules!—an enlargement. My stride is doubled and I am twice my height.

Today I can hardly refrain from blurting out to the faces of all my callers some lines—no need to cite the verses of Greece

for, by the Immortal Gods, we now fashion our own songs in
Rome.

> Ille mi par esse deo videtur,
> Ille, si fas est, superare divos,
> Qui sedens adversus itentidem te
> Spectat et audit
> Dulce ridentem. . . .
> *[That man to me seems equal to a God,*
> *That man surpasses the Gods—if such*
> *a thought be allowed—*
> *Who sitting before you*
> *Gazes and hears you*
> *Sweetly laughing. . . .]*

Those are the words of Catullus, written in what were for
him happier times. I have reason to suspect that he is now the
unhappiest of men. He captured his noontime in song; I am
now at high noon and he has heightened its blaze for me.

XXXIX Notes from Clodia to Marc Antony.
 [Toward the end of October.]

Court was very brilliant today. The oldest portions of the
Roman wall have fallen before the invader: Servilia; Fulvia
Manso; Sempronia Metella.

Your absence was noted. Majesty deigned to speak gra-
ciously of you, but I know her now and that pinched expres-
sion about her mouth.

Tell my dear Incomparable [*Cytheris*] that the Queen has
been inquiring about her. She said that the Dictator has spo-
ken of her, the Incomparable, with great admiration.

 · · · ·

After you left the Nile was overflowing its banks with ill-
contained rage. She muttered to me that there was an Egyptian
proverb that said: "All the braggart's wounds are on his back."
I protested and was taken into the boudoir and given some pas-
tries. I told of your bravery at Pharsalia; your bravery against
Aristobulus. I have no doubt you were very brave in Spain,
too, but I knew no details so I invented a towering exploit for

you before Cordova. It is now history. She abruptly, too abruptly, changed the subject.

[*October 27.*]

All is ready.

Egypt is certainly yours, if you do exactly what I tell you. And when I tell you. All depends on the when.

Arrive early at the reception and pay little attention to her.

The Master of the Citadel will certainly be going home early with his wife and aunt.

I shall arrive late. I shall tell her that you are going to propose to show her the greatest feat of daring ever exhibited in Rome and I shall urge her not, oh not, not to consent to see it. And is not that what it will be?—the greatest feat of daring ever seen in Rome?

Do not forget your promise, however. You are not to fall in love with her. If there is any danger of that, I refuse to help you and all wagers are off.

Destroy this note, or rather give it to my messenger so that I may destroy it.

XL The Lady Julia Marcia to Lucius Mamilius Turrinus on the Island of Capri.

[*October 28.*]

With what joy, my dear boy, I received your letter and learned that I may write to you. And that I may visit you. Let me come soon after the new year. All my thoughts are bent now on the Ceremonies [*of the Good Goddess*]; then I must return to my farm, put the year's accounts in order, and supervise the Saturnalia in our hill village. That done I shall come to the South—with what joy!

You say that you have time to read long letters and I generally have all too much time to write them. This will not be a long letter, I trust; it is just a word to acknowledge yours and to tell you of the events of last night which I think will interest you. You assure me that you have channels whereby you learn the externals of what passes in Rome and I shall try to restrict my account to such matters as I observe personally and as are not likely to have reached you by other hands.

Last night took place the reception at which the Queen of Egypt opened her palace to Rome. You will be told by others, no doubt, of the magnificence of the appointments, the lakes, the shows, the games, the tumult, the food, and the music.

I have made a new friend where least I expected to acquire one. There are perhaps reasons why the Queen should go to considerable lengths to ingratiate herself with me, but I think I am not easily deceived and I can say that the interest we took in one another was not feigned. Each was an object of curiosity to the other, each of an extreme difference; such contrasts with a touch of distrust may turn to contempt and ridicule, with a touch of good will to delighted friendship.

I arrived by boat with my nephew and his wife; we were greeted by the Queen at the gate which had been built as a reproduction of the Temple of Philae on the Nile. Our Tiber was all Egyptian and of new beauty; and such was the Queen. There are those who deny it; surely their eyes are askew with prejudice. Her skin is the color of the finest Greek marble and as smooth; her eyes are brown, large and most living. From them and from her low but ever-varying voice proceeds an unbroken message of happiness, well-being, amusement, intelligence, and assurance. Our Roman beauties were there in number and I became aware that Volumnia and Livia Dolabella and Clodia Pulcher were stiff, ill at ease, and as it were haunted by an imminent irritability.

The Queen was dressed, I am told, as the Goddess Isis. The jewels she wore and the embroidery on her gown were of blue and green. She led us first through the gardens, directing her remarks chiefly to Pompeia who seemed struck with fright and could find no answers, I am sorry to say. The Queen's manner is completely simple and should be able to banish constraint from all who address her; so it did with me. She led us to her throne and presented to us the nobles and ladies of her court. She then turned to greet the long lines of guests who had been waiting while her attention was given to the Dictator.

I had intended to return early to bed, but lingered viewing the countless diversions with friends of my generation and tasting the extraordinary dainties (much to the fright of Sempronia Metella who assured me that they had been poisoned). Suddenly I felt a hand brush my arm. It was the Queen asking

me if I would sit down with her. She led me to a sort of bower, warmed by braziers, and seating me beside her on a couch smiled at me for a moment in silence.

"Noble Lady," she said, "it is the custom in my country when one woman meets another to ask certain questions . . ."

"I am delighted, great Queen," I said, "to find myself in Egypt, and to observe the customs of that country."

"We ask one another," she replied, "how many children we have had and whether the confinements were difficult."

At this we both burst out laughing. "That is not a Roman custom," I said, thinking of Sempronia Metella, "but I think it very sensible." And I told her my history as a mother and she told me hers. She drew from a cabinet beside her some admirable paintings of her two children and showed them to me. "All else," she whispered, "is like a mirage of our deserts. I adore my children. I could wish to have a hundred. What is there in the world to equal one of those darling heads, those darling fragrant heads? But I am a Queen," she said, looking at me with tears in her eyes, "I must go on journeys. I must be busy with a hundred other things. Have you grandchildren?" she asked.

"No," I said. "None."

"Do you understand what I mean?" she asked.

"Yes, Majesty, I do."

And we sat silent. My dear boy, that is not the conversation I expected to have with the Witch of the Nile.

We were interrupted by my nephew bringing forward Marc Antony and the actress Cytheris. They were indeed taken aback to see the two of us sitting in tears amid the loud orchestras and the high torches.

"We were talking of life and death," said the Queen, rising and passing her hand across her cheeks. "My party is the happier for it."

She appeared to ignore my great-nephew, but she addressed Cytheris: "Gracious lady," she said, "I have been told—and by no mean judge—that no one speaks the Latin language, nor the Greek, more beautifully than you do."

This letter is already too long. I shall be writing you again before I see you. Your last request I shall indeed comply with explicitly. Your letter and the prospect of my visit have made me very happy.

XLI Cytheris, the Actress, to Lucius Mamilius Turrinus on the Island of Capri.
 [*October 28.*]

I have been looking forward with happy expectation, my dear friend, to my visit to you in December. We shall talk and we shall read and again I shall climb all the heights and descend to all the coves. No cold and no storm will discourage me.

Something took place last night which renders this voyage doubly grateful. A long and dear association of my life came to an end; a bell rang; a music ceased. You are the only person who will ever hear any word of it from me. You, who have heard so much of its progress, will hear its ending. The life that I have lived with Marc Antony for fifteen years has come to an end.

Since long before the arrival of the Queen of Egypt, Marc Antony had been engaged in mocking her reputation for fascination and astuteness. He boasted to me of how he had been able to irritate the Dictator by representing himself as superior to any meretricious charms that Cleopatra might cast over natures less firmly rooted than his own. Few can have been in the position that I have been to observe the unbelievable patience with which the Dictator has supported the thoughtlessness of his nephew, a patience which has borne provocations of greater consequence than the one I am describing—though they could scarcely have been more exasperating.

Since the Queen's arrival, Marc Antony has attended her court frequently, and reports have reached me that there he has harassed her with an ironic gallantry. The Queen, apparently, did not counter this impertinence with playful superiority as she could well have done; but on several occasions in full presence she rebuffed him with undisguised anger. Rome began talking.

Last night we attended together her great reception. My friend was in the highest spirits. On the way I noticed for the first time that his remarks about her betrayed true admiration and a sort of amazed delight. I knew then that, still unknown to himself, he was the victim of passion.

When I see you I shall describe to you the magnificence of the palace and of the entertainment offered to us. I do not know how such receptions are conducted in Alexandria, but I

suspect that the Queen was amazed to see how ill we Romans behave at large gatherings.

As usual the women withdrew into constrained groups, standing or sitting by themselves. In other portions of the grounds the younger men, drinking heavily, became boisterous and engaged in those inevitable contests of daring and strength which are their only pastime. You may well imagine that Marc Antony was in the forefront. They built first one and then another bonfire and forming in long lines raced across the gardens to jump them. I have learned to turn my back to these hazards; but I was soon aware that my friend was climbing trees and leaping from bough to roof followed by those whom he had challenged. Accidents occurred; heads and limbs were broken, but the tumultuous drunken singing only rose the higher. The exquisite pageants which the Queen had prepared were left to be viewed by a few women and a few grandfathers.

By midnight the men began to tire of these sports; many lay in drunken sleep among the bushes; the bonfires died down. A ballet was staged amid many-colored torches on an island and the artificial lake was filled with swimming girls.

The Dictator came upon me watching this show and did me the honor of sitting beside me. His wife had not enjoyed the evening and was pressing him to take his leave. I am now convinced that what then took place had been contrived by Clodia Pulcher, though she had worked with material all too ready to her hand. Clodia, like Marc Antony, had been attending the Queen's court almost daily. Rightly or wrongly, she had come to regard herself as the Queen's intimate and principal confidante in Rome. I had had occasion to witness Clodia's arrival at the party. She came late, accompanied by her brother and a sprinkling of gallants from the Aemilian Draughts and Swimming Club. The Queen had long since left her station before the throne and was mingling with the guests. Throughout the greater part of the evening the Dictator had remained by his wife's side and had merely paid the Queen the most objective deference; but at this moment they were advancing side by side toward the avenue, returning from a fight between lions and tigers which had taken place in the stockade for wild beasts. Clodia saw before her a situation in which she could never participate: a woman who envied no one in the world; a Dictator

twenty years younger; and a happiness that was then expressing itself in a laughter that meant ill-will to no one. I have known Clodia for many years; I could divine the pain that this spectacle cost her.

When the water-ballet was ended, Caesar's party rose to go in search of the Queen in order to take our leave. She was not at the lake. She was not in the palace. At the left of the avenue a stage had been constructed. Earlier in the evening it had served as the scene for a musical drama based on Egyptian history, but it now lay deserted and fitfully lighted by the torches from the court of honor near by. I cannot now remember what guided our steps in that direction. The scene represented a glade by the banks of the Nile, a grove of palm trees, bushes, and a thicket of reeds. To be brief, we surprised the Queen struggling and protesting in the embrace of a very drunken and ardent Marc Antony. There is no doubt that she was protesting, but there are degrees of protest and one could gather that this protest had been continuing for some time in a situation where escape was not difficult. In the half-dark we could not be sure what we saw.

Appearances were saved. Charmian, the Queen's attendant, appeared at that moment from behind the scene, bearing the brazier without which Cleopatra cannot support our cold weather. The Queen berated Marc Antony for clumsiness. The Dictator berated him for drunkenness. The moment was apparently passed off in laughter. No explanation was made, however, of why they had found themselves in so deserted a spot. I, from whom Marc Antony can keep no secret, knew that he was experiencing what he had experienced for me fifteen years before and had not known elsewhere in all his vagaries. What it meant for the Queen I could not know save as it was reflected in the great man beside me; no actor can equal Caesar and only an actor could divine that he was struck to the heart. No one else, I think, observed this. Pompeia had lingered behind us on the path.

We took our leave. In the litter, Marc Antony laid his head against my ear sobbing and repeating my name a hundred times. There could be no clearer farewell.

I knew that sooner or later this hour would come. The lover had become a son. I shall not pretend to a lightheartedness

I do not feel; but I shall not exaggerate a suffering which, without my realizing it, had already been half-transmuted into resignation. I come to Capri with a higher recognition of friendship—that friendship which I could never know with Marc Antony, for friendship flowers from minds which are akin. Wonderful are its resources; but I am a woman. Only to you, whose wisdom and patience have no end, can I cry out for the last time that friendship—even yours—is and must be second to the love I have lost. It filled my days with radiance as it filled my nights with unbearable sweetness. For fifteen years I have found no reason to ask myself why one lives or why one suffers. I must now learn to live without the loving glances from those eyes on which I have dreamed my life away.

XLI-A Cleopatra to Caesar.
 [*Midnight, October 27.*]

Deedja, Deedja, believe me, believe me, *what could I do?* He led me there, pretending that he and his companions were to show me the greatest feat of strength ever seen in Rome. He was both drunk and very sly. I am in a maze. I do not know how that could have taken place. I am certain that creature Clodia Pulcher was somehow a part of it. She had goaded or challenged him to it. She had shown him the plan first. I am sure of it.

Deedja, I am innocent. I shall not sleep until you send me word that you understand it all; that you trust me and love me. I am mad with horror and grief.

Send me, I pray you, word by this messenger.

XLI-B Caesar to Cleopatra.
 [*From the house of Cornelius Nepos, whither Cleopatra's messenger had traced Caesar and where he found him sitting beside the sick bed of G. Valerius Catullus.*]

Sleep, sleep well.

Now it is you who are doubting me. I know my nephew well. I understood what had taken place at once. Do not doubt your *Deedja's* understanding.

Sleep well, great Queen.

BOOK THREE

XLII Caesar, Supreme Pontiff, to Madam, the President of the College of the Vestal Virgins.
[*August 9.*]

Reverend Maid:

This letter is for your eyes alone.

Last spring the Lady Julia Marcia repeated to me some admirable words which you had let fall in a conversation with her. She is unaware of the importance your words were to have for me and she knows nothing of the letter I am now writing you.

She remembered your saying that you regretted that there were occasional elements of grossness in the sublime rituals of our Roman religion. Those words recalled a similar expression of my mother, the Lady Aurelia Julia. You may remember that when I was previously elected to the office of Supreme Pontiff in the year [*61*] the ceremonies of the Good Goddess, being held in my house, my mother was Lay Directress. The Lady Aurelia was a woman of exemplary piety and deeply versed in the religious traditions of Rome. As Supreme Pontiff I gave her every assistance in the celebration of the rites at that time, but you may be assured that I was told no more of what takes place during them than was fitting for a man holding that high office to hear. She did tell me, however, that she energetically deplored certain passages of ancient and barbarous coarseness that inhered in the ritual and which, she said, were not essential to the greatness of the action arising from it. You may also remember that in that year (this much I was permitted to know) she took upon herself the responsibility of substituting serpents of clay for living serpents—an innovation which was adopted without opposition and which, if I am not mistaken, has persisted to this day.

I am aware, revered Madam, that it is the custom that the Vestal Virgins retire from the ceremonies at midnight, that is prior to the concluding ceremonial. I think I am not wrong in concluding from this that certain symbolic actions take place

after that hour which might be repugnant to the sensibilities of the dedicated and the chaste. A reflection of such a repugnance I have not failed to notice throughout my life in the attitude of the women of my household. To a far greater extent I have been aware, however, of their joy in those rites, and of the deep devotion they brought to them. The great Marius said of them, "They are like a column upholding Rome." I could wish that it be said of them and of the body of our Roman ceremonies what Pindar said of the Eleusinian mysteries: *that they held the world together from falling into chaos.*

Permit me to urge you, noble maid, to meditate upon the subject I have brought to your attention. Should you think it advisable you may send this letter to the Lady Julia Marcia. I feel it to be within the power of you two, mutually aiding one another, to perform a signal service in the highest interests of our people. It is not without fear and awe that one would venture to alter one word or gesture in such ancient and hallowed exercises. It is my opinion, however, that it is the law of life that all things grow and change, casting aside the husks that protected their origins and emerging into fairer and nobler forms. It is so that the Immortal Gods have ordained it.

XLII-A Caesar to the Lady Julia Marcia on her farm in the Alban Hills.
 [*August 11.*]

I enclose the copy of a letter which I have just written to the President of the College of the Vestal Virgins. I hope I have expressed correctly the idea which you had in mind.

A great deal of resistance to any innovations in these matters is to be expected. Women, for good and for ill, are impassioned conservators. Men have long since eliminated the grosser elements in their rituals—the rites of the Arval Brethren and others. Perhaps I should say, they have dethroned them and set them to one side; they remain as vestiges, marginal to the ceremonies, some harmless clowning which takes place before and after the principal rites.

It is with mortification that I survey the roster of our first families, seeking several women of good sense who would be of assistance and support to you in this necessary work. In the

preceding generation it would not have been difficult to have named a score. Now I see only those who will attempt to place obstacles in your way: Sempronia Metella and Fulvia Manso, from unthinking conservatism; Servilia, from resentment that she was not the initiator of the project; Clodia Pulcher, from the spirit of contradiction. I would not be surprised if Pompeia also attempted to voice an opinion contrary to our intentions.

My dear aunt, I gave myself yesterday some not inconsiderable pleasure. As you know I am founding some colonies on the Black Sea. My map shows me an admirable location whose conformity suggests that it furnish the site of two adjacent towns. I am naming them after your great husband and yourself; they will be called Marius City and Julimarcia. I am told that the place is salubrious and of great beauty, and I am sending to it the most highly recommended of the families who have applied for transportation.

XLII-B Caesar's Journal-Letter to Lucius Mamilius Turrinus on the Island of Capri.
[*About September 6.*]

973. [*Concerning reforms introduced into the Mysteries of the Good Goddess.*] As an anonymous letter has recently informed me, a dictatorship is a powerful incitement to the composition of anonymous letters. I have never known a time when so many were in circulation. They are continually arriving at my door. Inspired by passion and enjoying the irresponsibility of their orphaned condition, they nevertheless have one great advantage over legitimate correspondence: they expose their ideas to their ultimate conclusion; they empty the sack.

I have stirred up a hornet's nest of them by attempting to remove certain primitive crudities which I know—though none too clearly—are incorporated in the celebration of the Mysteries of the Good Goddess. My shrouded correspondents are, of course, women. They do not suspect that I am at the bottom of this effort at reform; they merely appeal to me as Supreme Pontiff and ultimate arbiter.

What takes place during those twenty hours must make a powerful impression on the votaries, an effect so great that the majority of the celebrants, elevated to a pitch of ecstasy and

supplication, are scarcely aware of the obscenity. The obscenity is for them an intensification of the truth and of the magic efficacy of the rites.

The Mysteries, I take it, avert sterility and prevent monstrous or catastrophic births. They harmonize and, as it were, sanctify that woman's life about which even the most skilled doctors tell me they know very little. In doing this I can well understand that it does not stop there; it affirms life itself, all mankind, and the creation. Little wonder that our women return to us like beings from another world and move about us for a time like radiant strangers. They have been told that they keep the stars in their courses and that they maintain in place the very paving stones of Rome. When after a time they give themselves to us it is with a pride not unmixed with contempt, as though we men were but the accidental instruments of their mighty task.

Now far be it from me to rob these ceremonies of one jot of their power and consolation. I ask only to increase their influence. I have observed, however, that these good effects do not endure beyond a few days. Were our women able to remain for a longer time in their elevated state I would willingly concede that they rule the stars in the sky and support the pavements of Rome. I am beyond any man I have ever met the admirer of the essential feminine; beyond any man I have ever met I am least censorious of their failings and least exasperated by their vagaries. But then!—what advantages I have had! I ask myself in amazement: "What opinion must that man hold of womankind who has not had the advantage of living in the proximity of great women?" What arrogance he must acquire from the mere fact that he is a man! What easy honors he must obtain from brutalizing over the women of his association! My eye travels over many men every day; it is not difficult to single out those who are what they are because of their proximity at some time to an exceptional woman. I have done more for the status and independence of women than any ruler that has ever lived. In these matters Pericles was obtuse and Alexander a stripling. I have been widely charged with light behavior toward them. That is nonsense. Among the women whom I have frequented I have left but one enemy behind me, and she, before I met her, had chosen to become the enemy of all men. Her I almost

won from her self-hatred and almost saved from her damnation, but that only a God could do.

I have no hesitation in ascribing the brevity of that festival's good effects to the fact that it is overstrained; the celebrants are stretched to a pitch of excitement that obliterates the mind, and this degree of excess is a result of the obscene elements. I have grounds for believing that these aspects are more in evidence in the concluding session which begins at midnight. At that hour it is the custom that the Vestal Virgins, unmarried women, and pregnant mothers retire to their homes; and I now understand why my loved Cornelia and Aurelia used to feign illness at midnight and withdraw to their apartments, even when they had responsibilities in the ceremonial, leaving the governance to Servilia who must indeed have conducted herself like a maenad.

You may well say that I am working in the darkness of ignorance in attempting to alter the balance of good and evil in this matter. But when have I ever done anything else but work in darkness? Particularly these last months, each step I take seems to me like that of a man blindfolded. He hopes that there is no precipice before him. I write my will and make Octavius my heir—is that a step into the darkness? I appoint Marcus Brutus to be Praetor of the City and close to me—is that a sure step?

—I have just reread these lines, two days after having written them. I am astonished to see that I have not drawn from them the consequence that is uppermost.

Who is this Good Goddess?

No man has ever been told her name; no woman is permitted to utter it; perhaps themselves do not know it.

Where is she? In Rome? Present at the confinements of our wives? Preventing the births of wolf-children? Presumably she was present at my birth, ripped by the doctor from my mother's side.

Why, it is very certain she does not exist, apart from the imaginations of these votaries. That is also an existence and, as we have seen, a useful one.

But if our minds can make such Gods and if from the Gods we have made there flows such power, which is no more than a power resident within us, why cannot we employ that power

directly? These women are employing but a small part of their strength, because they are ignorant that that strength is their own. They regard themselves as helpless, as victims of malevolent forces and as beneficiaries of this Goddess whom they must implore and propitiate. Little wonder that their exaltation soon subsides, that they again descend into that incessant occupation with details where every detail is of equal power to enthrall or to distress them, that unremitting activity which so resembles a despair—a despair which does not know it is despairing, or an application to duties so intense that it can drown out despair.

Let each woman find out in herself her own Goddess—that should be the meaning of these rites.

At least, the first steps toward that end shall be the elimination of obscenity. Let us at least say of religion that it means that every part of the body is infused with mind, not that the mind is overwhelmed and drowned in body. For the principal attribute of the Gods, without or within us, is mind.

XLIII Cleopatra, in Egypt, to Caesar.
 [*August 17.*]

Cleopatra, the Everliving Isis, Child of the Sun. Chosen of Ptah, Queen of Egypt, Cyrenaica, and Arabia, Empress of the Upper and Lower Nile, Queen of Ethiopia etc., etc. To Caius Julius Caesar, Dictator of the Roman Republic and Supreme Pontiff.

Herewith the Queen of Egypt submits her application for inclusion among those in Rome who are permitted to attend the Rites in Celebration of the Good Goddess.

XLIII-A Caesar's Journal-Letter to Lucius Mamilius Turrinus on the Island of Capri.

975. It was from you that I obtained an idea which is now so self-evident to me that I am in danger of forgetting that you gave it to me: the importance for administration of encouraging an identification of the Gods of other countries with those of our own. In some regions this has been difficult; in others, astonishingly easy. In most northern Gaul the God of the oak

tree and the storms (no Roman has ever been able to pro-
nounce his name—Hodan, Quotan) has long since coalesced
with Jupiter; He smiles daily on the marriages of our soldiers
and clerks with the golden-haired daughters of those forests.
The Temples of my ancestress [*Venus; the Julian family traced
its descent from Julus, son of Aeneas, son of Aphrodite*] in the
East are one with those of Astarte and Ashtoreth. If I live long
enough, or if my successors also see the importance of this
unity among the cults, all the men and women in the world
will call themselves brother and sisters, children of Jupiter.

This world-wide unification has recently produced a slightly
ridiculous consequence, some illustrations of which I am en-
closing in this packet. Her Pyramidal Majesty, the queen of
Egypt, has applied for admission to the mysteries of our very
Roman Good Goddess. You have always had a taste for both
genealogy and theology, but even you would not wish to ex-
plore the immense documentation with which she supports
her claims. Cleopatra does nothing by halves; my anteroom is
filled with the bales of this documentation.

Her application rests on two counts: her descent from the
Goddess Qu'eb and her descent from the Goddess Cybele.

A little of this makes one dizzy, but I shall digest for you some
three hundred pages as though they were in her own words,
though I have not the texts before me:

"The Greek theologians authorized the identification of
Qu'eb and Cybele over two hundred years ago (see attached
two hundred pages). On the occasion of the visit of Queen
Dicoris of Littoral Armenia to Rome in [*89*] the Master of
Rites ruled an 'identity of emanation' between Cybele and the
Good Goddess (see attached bundles X and XI).

"The Supreme Pontiff will remember that when the Queen
of Egypt laid the charts of her ancestry before him in Alexan-
dria (fiddlesticks)—although at that time she had not made
public her Egyptian lineage (indeed, she hadn't)—she was pre-
paring to announce her claim to Tyre and Sidon by reason of
her great-grandfather's marriage (her great-grandfather was no
stronger lying down than standing up) to Queen Aholibah. I
am therefore through Queens Jezebel and Athaliah, descen-
dant and hereditary archpriestess of Ashtoreth. Through this
relationship, Queen Jezebel having been cousin-german to

Dido, Queen of Carthage (notice the threat—my grandfather wronged her great-aunt) and so on and so on." It is all quite true. The Eastern potentates are each ones their own cousin many times. I have written her that after suitable instruction she will be admitted to the earlier portion of the rites; that the permission is not accorded to her through any claim on her part to be descended from the Good Goddess or from any other divinity, but merely that the Goddess rejoices receiving—during the earlier part of the evening—all women who wish to bow before her.

I wish to add that the above rigmarole tends to present an unjust picture of the Queen of Egypt. It happens to reflect the only aspect of her mind on which she is not exceptionally sensible.

I should add that the Queen failed to include an extremely curious fact among the arguments supporting her request. Perhaps she does not know of it. The votaries of the Good Goddess during the rites wear a headdress which is certainly neither Greek nor Roman and which is known among them as the "Egyptian Turban." How it came to be there no one has ever explained. But who can explain the symbols, the influences, and the expressions of that universal mixture of joy and terror which is religion?

XLIV The Lady Julia Marcia from Caesar's House in Rome, to Clodia.
 [*September 30.*]

This letter is confidential.

Julia Marcia sends regard to Clodia Pulcher, daughter and granddaughter of her most dear friends.

I am looking forward to being present at your dinner tomorrow night, to meeting there for the first time your brother, to renewing an old friendship with Marcus Tullius Cicero, and to seeing you.

I returned to the City three days ago in order to attend a meeting of the Directresses of a religious festival venerated for its antiquity and held in grateful awe by its votaries. At this meeting eight petitions were laid before me that you be excluded from this year's festival. I have read these petitions with regret, even with great sorrow, but I do not find the charges

sufficiently grave or definite to justify the measure they re-
quest. That these petitions exist, however, is a matter which
myself and the other women responsible for the devotion and
harmony of the rites cannot ignore.

The procedure I am about to propose is one of compromise.
I feel certain that I can insure its acceptance, always granting
that no further petitions are submitted which contain incon-
trovertible evidence that your disbarment be advisable. In pro-
posing this compromise I do not wish to be understood as
taking lightly the many protests which rightly or wrongly your
actions have aroused. My motive is to avoid unjustifiable scan-
dal in an institution which was so greatly loved by those who
greatly loved you.

I inform you in great confidence that Cleopatra, Queen of
Egypt, will be in Rome before long and that she has submitted
a petition that she be admitted to the ceremonies we are dis-
cussing. This application, accompanied by much argumenta-
tion and many precedents and analogies, has been laid before
the Directresses and before the Supreme Pontiff. The decision
will probably be that the Queen will be permitted to attend
the rites before midnight when it is customary that the Vestal
Virgins, unmarried women, pregnant women, and [*here follows
a technical term meaning not belonging to the tribes into which
citizens of Rome were divided*] withdraw. I am going to propose
that you be appointed Instructress of the Queen of Egypt and
that therefore you will be obliged to accompany her to her palace
at midnight. Your enemies will be satisfied, I feel sure, by the
knowledge that you will not return to the rites after you have
retired from them with your guest.

You will think my proposal over, Clodia, and I hope that to-
morrow night you will find occasion to convey to me your
compliance. The only alternative is that you challenge the pe-
titions brought against you and face your accusers in a plenary
session of our committees. If we were dealing with secular
matters I should certainly advise you to do so; these charges and
their defense are, however, matters of decorum, dignity, and
reputation. To discuss them openly is to admit that these at-
tributes are damaged.

The Supreme Pontiff is not aware of these discussions and I
need hardly say that I shall make every effort to prevent their

reaching his attention save in the final disposition which I have
proposed for your decision.

XLIV-A Caesar's Journal-Letter to Lucius Mamilius Turri-
nus on the Island of Capri.
 [*About October 8.*]

 1002. [*On Clodia and a mime of Pactinus*] I am more fre-
quently discomfited by little things than by big. I have just
found myself obliged to forbid the performance of a play on the
stage. I enclose a copy of the play in question, a mime by Pac-
tinus called *The Prize of Virtue*. You are probably aware, though
I forgot to tell you, that I instituted the practice of giving
twenty prizes of varying amounts of money to girls of the
working class who receive the highest commendation from
their neighbors for good manners, faithful attendance on their
parents and masters, and so on. I think this has had some good
effect. It has incidentally provoked as great a plague of witti-
cisms and satire as any action in which I have ever engaged. It
has added enormously to the merriment of Rome; every street
cleaner discovers himself to be a wit and you may well imagine
that I am not spared.
 One result has been the overwhelming success of the at-
tached farce. You will observe that the fourth episode treats of
Clodia and her brother. The audience was not slow to perceive
the application. It was reported to me that at the close of that
scene, on each occasion, the audience rose in a tumult of
applause, derision, and savage glee. Strangers embraced one
another, shouting; they leaped up and down and on two occa-
sions tore down the handrails of the aisles.
 After eight representations I ordered that the play be with-
drawn. After the second Clodius Pulcher appeared in my offices
to protest. I sent word that I was busy on African matters and
could not see him. I wished the famous couple to drink for a
time the bitter brew of their own concocting. Finally, he reap-
peared in sufficiently humble suppliance and I complied with
his request.
 It vexed me to close it. It is without literary merit, but hith-
erto I have never curbed the freedom of expression of the citi-
zens nor punished opinion however outrageous. Moreover, I

wince to think that many will suppose that I suppressed it because it contained many shafts directed at myself.

The audience at a theater is the most moral of congregations. The fact that all those Romans are seated shoulder to shoulder seems to instill into them an elevation of judgment which they are not found to exercise anywhere else. They have no hesitation in deciding whether the behavior of the characters in a play is good or bad and they demand of them an ethical standard which they are far from requiring of themselves. Pandarus in an audience trembles with virtuous indignation before the pander on the stage. Twelve prostitutes side by side at a play are more prudish than one Vestal Virgin. I have often remarked that the moral and ethical attitudes of a theater audience are some thirty years out of date; in a mass, men reflect the views they received as children from their parents and guardians. And so at this farce the audience was whipped up into an ecstasy of denunciation of our Clodia. Each spectator felt himself or herself to be irreproachably virtuous.

That lofty emotion may well have lasted an hour. Oh, that we had an Aristophanes among us. He could both pillory Clodia and Caesar, and then turn the laughter on the audience's laughter. Oh, Aristophanes!

XLIV-B From *The Prize of Virtue*, a mime by Pactinus.
 [*A judge of the contest, obviously intended to be Caesar, sits in his office interviewing applicants for the prize. He is represented as a sly and lecherous old man. He is attended by a clerk.*
 The play is in verse.
 This is the fourth episode.]

Clerk: There is a pretty girl waiting to see Your Honor. [*Latin pulcher: pretty.*]
Judge: What? Is there to be no pretty boy? [*This is one of those innumerable imputations to Caesar of pederasty with which the literature abounds.*]
Clerk: This is his sister, Your Honor.
Judge: Well, get on with it. You know I'm not particular.
Clerk: She's weeping, Your Honor.
Judge: Of course, she's weeping, if she's virtuous, blockhead.

Virtuous women weep the first half of their lives, and women without virtue weep the second half of their lives, and so the Tiber never runs dry. Show her in.

(Enter a Young Girl, dressed in rags.)

Come nearer, little girl. I don't seem to see anything clearly any more—except villas at Tivoli. [*Where Caesar had confiscated the estates of two noblemen of Pompey's party who had been particular favorites of the Roman populace.*] So you want a prize for virtue, do you—you little darling?

The Young Girl: Yes, Your Honor. You won't find a more virtuous girl in the whole city.

Judge: (caressing her): Are you sure you haven't come to the wrong office, my little pigeon? Hm . . . let me see, let me see. This is, ahem, not your first youth, is it?

The Young Girl: Oh, no, sir. The first youth was under the consulship of Cornelius and Mummius [*i.e. 146* B.C.].

The Judge: I can well believe it. Tell me, little rose, is your father living?

The Young Girl: (weeping): Oh, sir, it's not kind to bring that up against me now.

The Judge: Then, perhaps you'll tell me if your husband's living?

The Young Girl: Your Honor, I didn't come here to be accused of this and that in the most insulting way.

The Judge: Sh. Sh. I just thought I saw a snowflake in your hand. [*Murderers were popularly believed to suffer from a scrofulous flaking of the skin in the palm of the hand.*] Tell me, my dear, did you always take tender care of your father and mother?

The Young Girl: Oh, I did, I did. I helped them to their last breath.

The Judge: A loving daughter. And have you been kind to your pretty brothers?

The Young Girl: Your Honor, I've refused them nothing.

The Judge: You haven't gone beyond the bounds of modesty, I hope. [*Modesty was a village and temple ten miles north of Rome.*]

The Young Girl: On, no, sir! Not beyond the city gates. We kept it all in the home.

The Judge: A paragon! A paragon! Now tell me, little sweetness, why are you dressed in rags?

The Young Girl: You may well ask, kind gentleman. There's no more money circulating in Rome. I think Mammurra has taken it all up to Lower Gaul. [*In a previous episode, Mammurra, dressed as a wise woman of Gaul, received a prize of virtue for "sweeping the house clean."*] My older brother brings no money in, of course, because he's a pensioner of the Veined Nose [*i.e. Caesar. The frugality of Caesar's domestic life had long led to the charge that he was parsimonious*]. My second brother brings in no money, because all his holdings were *beetled* into The Tiber. [*Caesar had recently straightened the course of the Tiber by digging away portions of its banks under the Vatican and Janiculan hills. The Roman populace had been particularly fascinated by this operation, because of a new excavating device or machine which had been employed. This machine, invented by Caesar during his military campaigns, was promptly labeled a "beetle." The region sacrificed to the river had contained the lowest resorts of the city.*]

The Judge: And you, little butterfly? Haven't I heard that you pick up many a fourpenny bit?

[*And so on.*]

XLV Abra, Pompeia's maid, to the Headwaiter at the Taverns of Cossutius (an agent of Cleopatra's Information Service).
[*October 17.*]

Like you say first I will answer your questions by number.

I. I worked for the lady Clodia Pulcher for five years. During the war we left Rome and lived in her house in Baiae. I will be free in two years. I have worked here two years. I am thirty-eight years old. I have no children.

II. This month I am not allowed to leave the house. None of the servants are. They have found that somebody is stealing things. That's what they say, but I do not think it is that. We all think that it is the secretary, the one from Crete, that they are watching.

III. My husband is allowed to visit me every five days. He is searched when he goes out. No peddlers can come in. They come to the garden door and we buy there.

IV. Yes, I send letters to the Lady Clodia Pulcher every

time that Hagia, the midwife, comes. [*It is presumed that the midwife was attending a servant in Caesar's household.*] She is not searched. The things I write the Lady Clodia Pulcher are like this: how the Queen of Egypt came to call on my Mistress; when my Master is away from the house all night; sometimes things that the wine butler says they are talking about at table; when the Master has the falling sickness. The Lady Clodia Pulcher does not pay me money. She has made a tavern for my husband on the Appian Way by the Tomb of Mops. If my letters are satisfactory to you, my husband and I would like a cow.

V. No, I am sure, nothing definite. But I think my Master does not like me. Six months ago they had a big quarrel about me, and a bigger quarrel two days ago. But my Mistress would never let him send me away she would cry so. She is never tired of talking about jewels, clothes, hair, et cetera, and there is nobody but me to talk to. That's how it is.

VI. About my Mistress's letters. Last year my Master told the Porter that all letters for my Mistress should be put with his. When they arrived during the day they were kept in the Porter's room until they were sent to the Master's offices. But several times a day my mistress went to the Porter and said are there any letters for me and he would give them to her. She made a big quarrel and cried and now all letters come to her. Only he said all anonymous letters must be destroyed without being read. Most are. There are many. Some are exciting. Some not.

Here begins my letter:

My Master is very kind to my mistress. From the time he comes home from the offices he spends almost all the time with her. When he has visitors on business he talks to them in the next room and keeps the door open and makes the visits as short as possible. When she goes to bed, he has friends come to see him for an hour or two because he does not like to sleep much, I mean does not need to sleep much. As these friends, like Hirtius, Mammurra, Oppius, drink much and laugh loud, they go to the Master's workroom on the cliff over the river. As it takes my Mistress almost two hours to get ready to go to bed, she is often still awake when he comes back. Often while she is getting ready, he leaves his friends and sits by us and talks to her while I am combing her hair, etc. Now what I mean to say is this: she almost always finds something to quarrel about.

She almost always cries. Many times he sends me from the room while they talk about something. She quarrels about the sumptuary laws, about the leopard cub which the Queen of Egypt gave her, about the Lady Clodia Pulcher not being invited to come to the house, about what days we go to the villa at Lake Nemi, about going to the theater.

Now there has been a great quarrel two days ago. When my Mistress left the room for a moment I think my Master quickly pushed his hand around among all the jars and bottles on her toilet table and he found an anonymous letter that came to her many weeks ago. I think he read it and put it back where it was. When she came back he pretended to find it all over again. That's what I think happened. It was a letter saying that Clodius Pulcher, the man that burned Cicero's house and that threatened to kill all the Senators, that man, that he loved my mistress like madness, and that she must be warned against him because maybe he could not control his love. My Master was very calm, but I know him he was also white with rage. He said that the letter was obviously written by Clodius Pulcher himself and that only a man who really despised a woman and wished to make a fool of her would write a letter like that. My Mistress said she hated Clodius Pulcher, but that it was obvious that he did not write that letter. Then I was made to leave the room. When I came back she had cried and she began to cry again and she kept saying that life was impossible, simply not to be endured.

My Master sent for me and said that I had brought the letter in. I swore by a terrible oath that he gave me that I had known nothing about the letter; but I think he knows. I do not think, however, that he will send me away.

Do you want me to write to you what nights my Master stays away from the house all night?

The wine butler says that he heard the Master talking to Balbus and Brutus—Decimus Brutus, that is, not the good-looking one—about moving Rome to Troy. Troy is in Egypt, I think.

The secretary, the one from Sicily, says that he has changed his mind, there will be no war against the Parthians. The Cretan secretary said you fool, of course, there will. That's all I know about that.

There's going to be an edict about no carts coming into the center of town after ten o'clock and they can only stay an hour.

I forgot to say that Clodius Pulcher rode up on his horse while my Mistress was in her litter going to Lake Nemi and began talking to her until Affius came up and said he had orders no one was to speak to our party. Affius is head of the farm and in charge of our journeys. He was with the Master in the wars and has only one arm.

Now I will stop.

I wish to say this that I do not like it here, I am uncomfortable. I have asked the Lady Clodia Pulcher to take me back, but she says I must stay here. I know a way that I could leave here. If this letter to you is what you want I will stay and write a few more.

The cow we would like is a tawny spotted one.

XLVI Caesar's Journal-Letter to Lucius Mamilius Turrinus on Capri.
 [*About October 13.*]

1012. The Queen of Egypt and I have been quarreling. It is not the quarrel habitual in boudoirs, though it frequently arrives at a termination which cannot be said to be new.

Cleopatra declares that I am a God. She is shocked to discover that I have not long since come to acknowledge that I am a God. Cleopatra is very certain that she is a Goddess and the worship of her people confirms her daily in this belief. She assures me that the divinity which lives in her has endowed her with unusual perspicuity in recognizing divinity. Through that endowment she is in a position to assure me that I am one also.

All this makes for conversation of a very flattering sort, interrupted by droll byplay. I pinch the Goddess and the Goddess squeals. I put my hand over the Goddess's eyes and, by the Immortal Gods, she is unable to see a thing. She has answers for all these sophistries. It is the one subject, however, on which the great Queen is not accessible to reason and on which I have learned not to permit our conversations to take a serious turn. On that subject alone she is, perhaps, oriental.

Nothing seems to me to be more dangerous—not only for

us rulers, but for those who gaze upon us with varying degrees of adoration—than this ascription of divine attributes. It is not difficult to understand that many persons will feel at times as though they were inflated by unusual powers or caught up into currents of some inexplicable rightness. I had this feeling frequently when I was younger; I now shudder at it and with horror. How often I have had it thrown back at me, generally by flatterers, that I said to the timid boatman in the storm: "Have no fear; you bear Caesar." What nonsense! I have had no more exemption from the ills of life than any other man.

But that is not all. The history of nations shows how deeply rooted is our propensity to impute a more than human condition to those remarkable for gifts or to those merely situated in conspicuous position. I have little doubt that the demigods and even the Gods of antiquity are nothing more than ancestors about whom these venerations have been fostered. All this has been fruitful; it expands the imagination of the growing boy and it furnishes sanctions for good manners and public institutions. It must be outgrown, however—outgrown and discarded. Every man that has ever lived has been but a man and his achievements should be viewed as extensions of the human state, not interruptions in it.

There is no one but you with whom I can talk of this. Every year this discomfiting deification increases about me. I remember with shame that there was a time when I endeavored, for administrative reasons, to fan it: sufficient evidence that I am a man and a most fallible one, for there is no human weakness equal to that of trying to inculcate the notion that one is a God. I had a dream one night that Alexander appeared at the door of my tent with sword lifted, about to slay me. I said to him: "But you are no God," and he vanished.

The older I grow, dear Lucius, the more I rejoice in being a man—mortal, mistaken, and unabashed. Today my secretaries timidly brought me a succession of documents on which I had made various kinds of errors (to myself I call them Cleopatra-errors so obsessive is that enchantress). I corrected them one after one another, laughing. My secretaries frowned. They could not understand that Caesar would be delighted at his mistakes. Secretaries are not exhilarating companions.

The words "divinity" and "God" have been in use among us for some time. They have a thousand meanings and for any one person a score.

The other night I found my wife under strong emotion imploring the Gods to send a sunny day for her trip to Lake Nemi. My aunt Julia is a farmer and she does not believe that they will alter the weather for her convenience, but she is certain that they are watching over Rome and have placed me here as governor. Cicero does not believe that they would hesitate to let Rome glide into ruin (he would not wish to share with them the honor of having saved the state from Catiline), but he has no doubt that they placed the conception of justice in men's hearts. Catullus probably believes that men have developed an idea of justice from quarreling with one another over property and over boundary lines, but he is certain that love is the only manifestation of the divine and that it is from love, even when it is traduced and insulted, that we can learn the nature of our existence. Cleopatra holds that love is the most agreeable of activities and that her attachment to her children is the most compelling emotion she has ever experienced, but that these are certainly not divine—divinity for her resides in the force of one's will and the energy of one's personality. And none of these meanings are meanings for me, though at various times in my life I have held all of them. With the loss of each of them I have been filled with an increased strength. I feel that if I can rid myself of the wrong ones, I shall be coming closer to the right one.

But I am an aging man. Time presses.

XLVI-A From the Commonplace Book of Cornelius Nepos.

The Dictator has issued an edict that no more towns may change their names to a form of his own. The reason for this is, I think, that he has discovered that he is being more literally worshipped than he cares to be. He has ceased sending presents to townships and regimental headquarters; they are invariably placed in shrines and become centers of pilgrimage for healing and supplication.

There is no doubt that this is taking place, and not only in

the barbarous outposts of the Republic and in the mountains of Italy, but here in the City.

It is said that his servants are continually being bribed to steal his garments, the parings of his nails, the refuse of his shaving, and his very urine—all of these are said to possess magical properties and are preserved for adoration.

Fanatics occasionally are able to penetrate into his house where they are mistaken for assassins. One of these prowlers, dagger in hand, was surprised one night near to where Caesar was sleeping. A summary trial was held on the spot and Caesar himself conducted the interrogation. The man was all but incoherent, but not with fear. As the interview proceeded he lay on the floor gazing ecstatically at the Dictator's face and babbling that all he wanted was "one drop of Caesar's blood with which to sanctify himself." Caesar, to the consternation of the guards and servants who had collected, asked him many questions and finally extracted from him the whole story of his life. This close interest, which many a consul has not been able to arouse, raised the poor man's veneration to a still more delirious state and at the end he was imploring Caesar to kill him with his own hand.

Turning to the bystanders, Caesar is reported to have said with a smile: "It is often difficult to distinguish hate from love."

Caesar's physician Sosthenes to dinner.

He was talking about the effect of Caesar on others.

"Of what other men have such stories been told and believed?

"Until recently scores of ill persons were placed nightly by their families to sleep against the wall which surrounds his house. They have been driven away; now you will see them, row by row, lying under and around his statues. On his journeys farmers beseech him to plant his foot on their less productive fields.

"And the stories! You hear them in the soldiers' songs; you see them in verses and drawings scrawled in public places. It is said that he was conceived by his mother of a bolt of lightning; that he was born through her mouth or ear; that he came into the world without organs of generation and that those he ultimately possessed were grafted onto him from a mysterious

stranger he met among the oak trees of the Temple of Zeus at Dodona whom he slew for that purpose; or that they came from a statue of Zeus by Phidias. There is no abnormality that has not been charged against him and it is believed that, like Jupiter, he has predilections within the animal kingdom. It is widely held that he is literally the father of his country and that he has left hundreds of children in Spain, Britain, Gaul, and Africa.

"And yet superstition and popular belief do not shrink from inconsistency. It is said, on the other hand, that he guards so austere a continence that the unchaste feel intolerable pain when he passes near them.

"What man, what mere man, has fired the imaginations of the people to so luxuriant a body of legend? And now that Cleopatra has come to town, what do we not hear?—Cleopatra, the rich mud of the Nile. Go to the taverns, go to the barracks—the heads of the Roman people are swimming at the thought of those embraces. We are celebrating the nuptials of the Unconquered Sun and the Fecund Earth.

"I am his physician. I have tended that body through convulsions and have bound its wounds. Yes, it is mortal; but we physicians learn to listen to our patients' bodies as musicians listen to the various lyres which are placed in their hands. His is bald, aging, and covered with the wounds received from many wars; but every portion is informed by mind. Its powers of self-repair are extraordinary. Illness is discouragement. The illness from which Caesar suffers is the one illness which denotes overreaching enthusiasm. It is related to the character of his mind.

"The mind of Caesar. It is the reverse of most men's. It rejoices in committing itself. To us arrive each day a score of challenges; we must say yes or no to decisions that will set off chains of consequences. Some of us deliberate; some of us refuse the decision, which is itself a decision; some of us leap giddily into the decision, setting our jaws and closing our eyes, which is a sort of decision of despair. Caesar embraces decision. It is as though he felt his mind to be operating only when it is interlocking itself with significant consequences. Caesar shrinks from no responsibility. He heaps more and more upon his shoulders.

"It may be that he lacks some forms of imagination. It is

very certain that he gives little thought to the past and does not attempt to envisage the future clearly. He does not cultivate remorse and does not indulge in aspiration.

"From time to time he permits me to put him through certain tests. I ask him to exercise strenuously, then lie in repose while I engage in various observations, and so on. During one of these enforced immobilities he asked me, 'If I were to escape assassination and live into old age, of what organ's weakness would I die?' 'Sire,' I said, 'of an apoplexy.' He seemed very pleased. I knew what was in his mind. There are two things he dreads: physical pain, to which he is most unusually sensitive, and indecorousness.

"At another time he asked me whether there were any pressure or action whereby a man might put an end to his life quickly and without bloodshed. I showed him three and I have no doubt that since that day he has regarded me with particular affection and gratitude.

"I, in turn, have learned much from him. I used to think that eating, sleeping, and the satisfaction of the sexual appetite were best regulated by the formation of habits. I now believe with him that they are best served by responding to them at the first prompting. I have thereby not only lengthened my day, but liberated my spirit.

"Oh, it is an extraordinary man. These legends have, in their way, a just base; but with one difference. Caesar does not love, nor does he inspire love. He diffuses an equable glow of ordered good will, a passionless energy that creates without fever, and which expends itself without self-examination or self-doubt.

"Let me whisper to you: I could not love him and I never leave his presence without relief."

XLVI-B From a Report of Caesar's Secret Police.

Subject 496: Artemisia Baccina, midwife, healer, and fortune-teller, resident in the suburb of the Goat. Under interrogation, Subject 496 confessed to having been present at rites celebrated by the Confraternity of the Buried Sun. Said there were ten or twelve chapters in Rome. (See Subjects 371 and 391.) Finally under intensive interrogation said the Confraternity was headed by Amasius Lenter (Subject 297, executed August 12.)

Rites open with slow torture and death of a black pig, black cock, etcetera, and concluded with veneration of a vial of blood, said to be the blood of the Dictator. Subject is being deported to Sicily and placed under vigilance of the police there.

XLVI-C From Notes left by Pliny the Younger.
 [*Written about a century later.*]

Curious. My gardener reported that the following belief is widely held by the common people. On my walks I have questioned vine dressers, hucksters, and others and find this report confirmed.

They believe that the body of Julius Caesar was not burned after his assassination (though we have no doubt of that), but that an organization or mystery cult seized it and dividing it into many pieces, buried each piece under one of the wards of Rome. They declare that Caesar knew of an old prophecy which affirmed that the survival and greatness of Rome was dependent on his murder and dismemberment.

XLVII Announcement by the Queen of Egypt.
 [*October 26.*]

Cleopatra, Queen of Egypt, [*etcetera, etcetera*] regrets that the Reverend College of the Vestal Virgins will be unable to attend her reception tomorrow evening.

Arrangements have been made, however, to receive the Reverend College at three o'clock on that day.

With the concordance of the Supreme Pontiff and the Reverend President of the College a performance will be given at that time of

> The great Coming-Forth of Horus,
> The beauty of Osiris,
> The attack upon the Neshmet Boat,
> The Lord of Abydos comes to his Palace.

The portions of these ceremonies which are unsuitable for presentation in the evening will be rendered in all their solemnity before the dedicated guests in the afternoon.

The Queen of Egypt will graciously receive the Reverend Maids at that time.

XLVIII Caesar to Cleopatra.
 [*October 29.*]

All Rome talks of the magnificence of the Queen's reception; the more discriminating return repeatedly to speak of her royal deportment, of her arts as a hostess, of her discretion, and of the spell of her beauty.

I am permitted to speak of my love and admiration which will never grow less.

My visits to the great Queen will be less frequent in the days that lie ahead, but I adjure her never to doubt my love nor my unceasing attention to the welfare of her country.

It would give me great pleasure to receive the Queen more frequently in my home. I am requesting the actress Cytheris to give lessons to my wife in the declamation and gestures that are required of her at the Mysteries of the Good Goddess. As you are to be present at that reunion also, I think you would derive much interest from these lessons—though far be it from me to imply that the Queen has anything to learn in beauty of speech or in dignity of port.

At the close of the lessons I feel certain that Cytheris will not refuse any wish you may express to hear her declaim passages from the Greek and Roman tragedies—a privilege which our descendants will envy us.

The Lady Clodia Pulcher is retiring to her villa in the country for a time. I think it is fitting that you should know that I indicated this move to her some time ago, though she asked permission to remain in the City until the day following your reception. The reason for this withdrawal springs from a matter which I shall recount to you at some time, if you wish to hear it.

The happiness which the Queen's visit has brought me has occasionally drawn my thoughts away from my work. Were I a younger man this happiness would become one with the work and would furnish new incentives to its prosecution. My lengthening days remind me, however, that I have not that apparently unlimited time for project and execution which I once possessed.

Allow me to combine my work with happiness by calling on the Queen on [*Saturday*] to show her the plans which I have drawn up for colonial settlements in North Africa. If the

weather is favorable then, I should like to take the Queen to
Ostia by boat, pointing out to her the measures we have taken
for the control of flood and the deceleration of the current. At
Ostia we shall be able to see the progress made on the harbor
works, concerning which the Queen has already given me such
invaluable advice.

There is one more thing I wish to say to the great Queen. I
hope she will remain in Italy for an even longer visit than she
had first planned. To encourage this decision, may I suggest that
she send to Alexandria for her children? I shall place one of my
newly finished galleys, which have already proved themselves to
be the swiftest on the sea, at the Queen's disposal for this er-
rand and shall look forward to sharing her joy at their arrival.

XLVIII-A Cleopatra to Caesar.
 [*By return messenger.*]

A misunderstanding, great Caesar, has arisen between us.

I realize that no protests of mine can clear away the misap-
prehension under which you are laboring. In my suffering I
can only hope that time and events will convince you of my de-
votion and loyalty.

Once more I must say, however, that the situation in which
I found myself—with an astonishment no less than yours—was
contrived by malicious persons.

Marc Antony had persuaded me to accompany him to that
portion of the gardens to see what he called "the greatest feat
of daring ever seen in Rome." He assured me that it would be
undertaken by himself in association with some five or six of
his companions. As the moment had come for me to make an-
other tour of the grounds I acceded to his request, taking
Charmian with me. The rest you know.

I shall not rest until I have obtained proofs of the complicity
of others in what then took place. I know that proofs will not
convince you of my innocence unless I can also furnish you ev-
idence of my tireless concern with all that has to do with you
and your interest and with your happiness. This ambition alone
leads me to accept your invitation to prolong my stay in the
City. I gratefully accept also your invitation to attend the ses-
sions directed by Cytheris in your home.

I do not wish at this time, however, to send for my dear children, though I thank you for the opportunity you have extended.

Great friend, great Caesar, my lover, the thing which is uppermost in my mind is that you have unjustly been made to suffer. I cry out in anguish against those forces of destiny which by an infernal device that no mere humans could compound have made me an instrument for your disappointment. Oh, do not believe it. Do not permit yourself to be the victim of so transparent a mischance. Remember my love. Do not now begin to doubt the glance in my eyes and the joy in my surrender. I am still a young woman; I do not know what form a more experienced woman would give to the protestations of innocence. Should I be indignant that you distrust me? Should I be proud and angry? I do not know; I can only be candid, even at the expense of modesty. Never have I loved, never shall I love, as I have loved you. Who can have known what I have known—a delight that was not separable from gratitude, a passion that was none the less for being all homage? Such was the love suitable to the difference between our ages; it need fear no comparison with any other. Oh, remember, remember! Trust! Do not now separate me as by a curtain from that divinity within you. Blackest of curtains that is made up of a belief in my treachery. I treacherous! I unloving!

These words are not royal. They are sincere. I have expressed myself in this manner for the last time, until you permit me to resume it. I now adopt that of a visitor of state, for conformity with your wishes is the rule of my love.

XLIX Alma, wife of Cornelius Nepos, to her sister Postumia, wife of Publius Ceccinius of Verona.
 [*October 30.*]

You will have seen all the letters we sent concerning this matter by the Dictator's courier to you and to the poet's family. Here are a few details I shall add for your eyes alone. My husband is grieving as though he had lost a son (avert the omen! our boys are very well, thanks be to the Gods). I loved Gaius [*Catullus*], also, and have loved him since we all played together as children. But affection should not blind our eyes—I

can speak frankly to you—to the lessons of this deplorable mistaken life. I did not like his friends; of course, I did not like that wicked woman; I did not like the verses he wrote during these last years; and I shall never like nor praise the Dictator who has been in and out of our house these days as though he were an old family friend.

We had often asked Gaius to stay with us, but you know his brusque independence. So when he appeared at our door one morning, followed by old Fusco carrying his bedding, and asked to live in our garden house, then I knew he was really ill. My husband reported this move at once to the Dictator. The Dictator promptly sent over his physician, a Greek named Sosthenes, the most conceited pig-headed young man I have ever met. I have no hesitation in saying that I am an excellent physician myself. I think it's a gift which the Immortal Gods confer on all mothers, but this Sosthenes kept brushing away remedies which have *proved* their efficacy since time immemorial. But that's a long story.

Now, Postumia, there's not the slightest doubt that *that woman* killed him. After leading him through every avenue of hell for three years, she suddenly became all kindness and that's how she killed him. She never appeared herself, but every day came letters, gifts of food—and what food!—Greek manuscripts, and messages of inquiry twice a day. All this made Gaius very happy, but there are all kinds of happiness; this was that puzzled bodiless happiness which, I suppose, deceived husbands feel when their wives are suddenly very kind to them. As the days went by and she did not appear herself we could see that he was resigning all hope of health and letting himself drift into death. At about three o'clock on the afternoon of the twenty-seventh his servant Fusco—you remember him; he used to tend boats on Lake Garda—came running to the house. He said that his master was delirious and was dressing himself to go to the Queen of Egypt's reception. I hurried out to the garden house and found him lying unconscious in a great pool of bile which he had vomited up. My husband sent at once for Sosthenes who came and sat with Gaius until his death an hour before dawn. I was not permitted entrance to the sickroom, but who should appear at about ten o'clock but the Dictator himself. He was splendidly dressed and must have slipped away

from the Queen's reception which, after all, was less than a mile away. All night we could hear the orchestras and see the sky lit up by her bonfires. I overheard Fusco telling my husband that when the Dictator first came into the room, Gaius raised himself on one elbow and shouted to him wildly to go away. He called him "thief of liberty," "monster of greed," "murderer of the Republic" and many more names, all of which are, of course, *absolutely true*. My husband joined them at about that time—he had been away hunting for our old balsam-burner. He tells me that the Dictator was receiving all this in silence, but that he was as white as a ghost. It had probably been some time since Caesar had been ordered to leave a room, but he left.

He returned at about two hours after midnight, having changed from his fine clothes. Gaius was sleeping; when he awoke he seemed to be reconciled to his visitor. My husband said he even smiled and said, "What, no fringes, great Caesar?" Well, as you know, my husband worships the man. (For the most part we've arranged in our house simply not to discuss him.) Cornelius says that Caesar was quite wonderful from then on, wonderful in his silences and in his replies. He says that, of course, Caesar had been present at more deathbeds than anyone else. You know all those stories about Gaul, of how the wounded soldiers used to refuse to die until their General had made his nightly rounds. Oh, I confess, Postumia, that—wicked ruler though he is—there is something very impressive and yet unforced about his presence. My husband says that he himself stayed in one corner of the room with Sosthenes and that he could hear very little of what the two were saying. Apparently at one point, Gaius, the tears streaming down his face, almost flung himself out of bed crying that he had wasted his life and his song for the favors of a harlot. I would not have known how to answer that, but it seems that the Dictator could. My husband says that he talked in even lower tones, but he gathered that Caesar was praising Clodia Pulcher as though she were some Goddess. Gaius was not in pain, but he was growing weaker. He lay with his eyes on the ceiling, listening to Caesar's words. From time to time Caesar fell silent, but when the silence had lasted too long for him, Gaius touched his wrist with his fingers, as though to say "go on, go on." And all Caesar

was doing was talking about Sophocles! Gaius died to a chorus from *Oedipus at Coloneus.* Caesar placed the coins on his eyes, embraced Cornelius and the wretched physician, and went home, without guards, through the first light of dawn.

You may wish to repeat some of this to his mother and father, though it seems to me that it would only distress them further. I should feel no small responsibility if either of my boys were to succumb to such an infatuation as we have witnessed here. I think I may say that their *upbringing* will have spared them that!

> [*The letter continues with the discussion of the sale of some real estate.*]

XLIX-A Caesar's Journal-Letter to Lucius Mamilius Turrinus on the Island of Capri.
> [*Night of October 27–28.*]

1013. [*On the death of Catullus.*] I am watching beside the bed of a dying friend, the poet Catullus. From time to time he falls asleep; I then take to my pen, as always, perhaps to avoid reflection. (Though I should have learned by now that to write to you is to invoke from the depths of my mind those questions which I have spent my life evading.)

He just opened his eyes, gave the names of six of the Pleiades, and asked me that of the seventh.

Even as a young man, Lucius, you possessed an unerring eye for the Inevitable Occasion and the Inevitable Consequence. You wasted no time in wishing that things were otherwise. From you I learned, but slowly, that there are large fields of experience which our longing cannot alter and which our fears cannot forfend. I clung for years to a host of self-delusions, to the belief that burning intensity in the mind can bring a message from an indifferent loved one and that sheer indignation can halt the triumphs of an enemy. The universe goes its mighty way and there is very little we can do to modify it. You remember how shocked I was when you let fall so lightly the words: "Hope has never changed tomorrow's weather." Adulation is continually assuring me that I have "accomplished the

impossible" and "reversed the order of nature"; I receive these tributes with a grave inclination of the head, but not without a wish that the best of my friends were present to share with me the derision they deserve.

I not only bow to the inevitable; I am fortified by it. The achievements of men are more remarkable when one contemplates the limitations under which they labor.

The type of the Inevitable is death. I remember well that in my youth I believed that I was certainly exempt from its operation. First when my daughter died, next when you were wounded, I knew that I was mortal; and now I regard those years as wasted, as unproductive, in which I was not aware that my death was certain, nay, momently possible. I can now appraise at a glance those who have not yet foreseen their death. I know them for the children they are. They think that by evading its contemplation they are enhancing the savor of life. The reverse is true: only those who have grasped their nonbeing are capable of praising the sunlight. I will have no part in the doctrine of the stoics that the contemplation of death teaches us the vanity of human endeavor and the insubstantiality of life's joys. Each year I say farewell to the spring with a more intense passion and every day I am more bent on harnessing the course of the Tiber, even though my successors may permit it to expend itself senselessly in the sea.

He has opened his eyes again. We have had a paroxysm of grief. Clodia! Every moment as I watch this I understand more clearly her ruined greatness.

Oh, there are laws operating in the world whose import we can scarcely guess. How often we have seen a lofty greatness set off a train of evil, and virtue engendered by wickedness. Clodia is no ordinary woman and colliding with her Catullus has struck off poems which are not ordinary. At the closer range we say *good* and *evil*, but what the world profits by is intensity. There is a law hidden in this, but we are not present long enough to glimpse more than two links in the chain. There lies the regret at the brevity of life.

He is sleeping.

Another hour has gone by. We talked. I am no stranger to deathbeds. To those in pain one talks about themselves; to those of clear mind one praises the world that they are quitting.

There is no dignity in leaving a despicable world and the dying are often fearful lest life was not worth the efforts it had cost them. I am never short of subjects to praise.

During this last hour I have paid an old debt. Many times during the ten years of my campaigns I was visited by a recurrent waking dream. I have walked to and fro before my tent at night improvising a speech. I imagined that I had collected before me an audience of chosen men and women, particularly the young, to whom I wished to communicate all that I owed —boy and man, soldier and administrator, lover, father, son, sufferer and rejoicer—to Sophocles. Once before I died I wished to empty my heart—so promptly refilled—of that thanks and praise.

Oh, yes, he was a man and that was a man's work. An old question is answered. It is not that the Gods refused to help him, though it is certain They gave him no help. That is not Their way. If They were not hidden he would not so have peered to find Them. I too have journeyed through the highest Alps when I could not see a foot before me, but never with his composure. It was enough for him to live *as though the Alps were there.*

And now Catullus, too, is dead.

L Caesar to Cytheris.
 [*November 1.*]

You may well imagine, gracious lady, that one in my position hesitates to submit requests to those for whom he holds the highest regard, lest the request seem to carry a weight that he does not intend to put upon it. Assume that I am in no other situation than that when I first had the pleasure of making your acquaintance and when you first aroused an admiration which has only increased with the passing of time.

My wife has been learning the responses which fall to her in certain ceremonies which will take place in December. I have been permitted to instruct her in these, but only to that limited extent which their secrecy admits. Could I request you to accord a few hours to instructing her in the delivery of these responses and in the deportment consonant with their solemnity?

As the Queen of Egypt is to be present at a portion of the ceremonial I should be particularly gratified if she were permitted to share whatever hours of instruction you felt able to give my wife.

It was with great happiness that I learned by accident a few days ago that you were a cherished friend of Lucius Mamilius Turrinus and that you occasionally visited him on the Island of Capri. It is his wish that as little reference be made to him as possible and even these lines confer upon this letter a character of secrecy. My happiness is not only that you enjoy his friendship and he yours, but that through you (and I hope, madam, through me) his genius may—if I may use the expression—operate in the world, even though we are not permitted to use his name. It would be remarkable enough that any man should have passed through the desperate situation that he did and be enduring its consequences and yet remain unshaken in soul; but that this should have befallen him who was already superior to all men in wisdom as he was superior to them in those attributes of soul which we call beauty is a subject of wonder, the limits of which I have never reached. The Island of Capri is surrounded for me by an air which I can only call awe. That I am not the sole reflector of that genius is not only a happiness to me, but a relief. Many things remain unspoken between my friend and myself. Among them is the regulation that I receive no letters from him and that I may visit him but once a year. I am occasionally saddened by these restrictions, but with the passing of time I come to see that they too are marked by that almost otherworldly wisdom that he never fails to impart.

Since we are talking of great men, I enclose transcripts of the last verses written by Gaius Valerius Catullus who died five nights ago.

LI The Queen of Egypt: Memorandum for her Secretary of State.
 [*November 6.*]

The Queen of Egypt has received with satisfaction the information you have submitted to her. Her commendation has particular reference to your reports of October 29 and November 3, together with their attached documents.

The Queen has taken notice of your appraisal of the centers of discontent.

> [*Here follow Cleopatra's comments on twelve individuals or groups from among whom attempts to overturn the state or assassinate the Dictator might be expected. The potential conspirators do not include the Cascas, Cassius, or Brutus. Material from this section is reflected in our Book Four.*]

In addition, the Queen calls your attention to the following matters:

1. The reports from Source 14 [*Abra*] are worthless. Her simplicity is feigned. It should not be difficult to increase their value by threats of exposure and by other pressures.

2. Are you convinced that you have explored all the significance of the Dictator's disappearance during my reception on the 27th? His attendance at the sickbed of a scurrilous versifier does not appear to afford a sufficient explanation.

3. Every effort should be made to place an agent in the household of Marc Antony. The evidence you have collected of his disloyalty to the Dictator in [*46*] is herewith returned. It should be deposited among the documents which you are safeguarding against any possible theft or confiscation. I am retaining the other material you found in his home.

4. The dressmaker Mopsa. Obtain for me as soon as possible a complete account of her life, parentage, associates, and so on. Also a schedule of her engagements during this month. She is coming to me on the 17th to make my robe for the Ceremonies of the Good Goddess.

5. Your work for this week is to be an intensive study of the situation of the Lady Clodia Pulcher and her brother. What interpretations are being made of her retirement to the country? When is she returning to the City? The report of Sosigenes [*the Egyptian astronomer*] was unsatisfactory. I wish you to instruct him in what to observe.

I agree with you that Clodius Pulcher is attempting to seduce the Dictator's wife. I wish you to follow this with the closest attention. There is little doubt that communications are passing between them through Source 14. Report to me any suggestions you have for taking advantage of this situation.

In acknowledgement of the diligence and skill you have

shown in the difficult tasks laid before you, it is with pleasure that I assign to you and to your descendants forever the Oasis of Sesseben, together with its revenues and imposts, limited only by the regulations laid down under the 44th and 47th edicts of my reign [*limitations imposed on the levies which regional officials and landowners may assess against farmers, and limitation on the charge for the watering of camels at springs and waterways*].

LII Pompeia to Clodia.
 [*November 12.*]

I miss you all the time, dearest Mousie. Nobody can understand why you have to go off into the country now when so much is going on in the city. I asked my husband what interest you could possibly take in mathematics and he said that you were very good at such things and that you knew all about the stars and what they did.

I give you ten guesses about who comes to our house all the time, at least every other day, and we have the most unusual times. Cleopatra! And not only Cleopatra, but Cytheris, the actress. And my husband arranged it all. Isn't that strange?

First Cytheris came to teach me you-know-what. Then Cleopatra started coming to learn some of that, too. At the end of the lesson the Queen asks Cytheris to recite, and oh, such things, my blood runs cold. Cassandra going mad and Medea planning to murder her babies, and everybody dying. And then my husband comes home early and it's jabber, jabber, jabber about Greek plays. And he gets up and he's Agamemnon and Cytheris is Clytemnestra and Cleopatra is Cassandra and Octavius and I have to be chorus, and then we all have supper. Oh, my dear Claudilla, you should be here because I have no one to laugh with; they are all so serious about these things. For me it is very very funny when my husband starts roaring and when Cleopatra goes mad.

Really, I rather like the Queen. Of course, she's not like you and me. I used to think she was quite ugly but sometimes she is almost beautiful. But, really, I am not the least bit jealous. My husband doesn't behave to her any differently than he behaves to Aunt Julia.

Yesterday, the Queen of Egypt asked my husband when you were coming back. She said that she hoped you would come back soon, as you are her instructress for the rites. My husband said he did not know what your plans were, but that he assumed you would be back by December first.

Dearest, I saw your brother, the younger one I mean; he came up to me on his horse while I was on the road to Lake Nemi. He looks so like you that I am always astonished. People say that he is a bad man, and even you say so, but I know he is not. You must not take that attitude to him, Claudilla, dear. Anyone would be bad, if you told them all the time that they were bad.

From this letter you must think that I am very happy, but I am not. I almost never go out of the house and no one I wish to see ever comes into it. I went to the Queen of Egypt's once; I went to pay a confinement call on Porcia, Brutus's wife. Sometimes I just sit and wish I were dead. What I think is that if one doesn't live when one's young, when do you live? I adore my husband and he adores me, but I like *people* and he doesn't.

I've just heard that my call on Porcia was simply wasted; word has just come that she's had a miscarriage, so I needn't have gone at all.

LIII Cytheris to Lucius Mamilius Turrinus, on the Island of Capri.
 [*November 25.*]

The air of Rome, my dear friend, is uneasy and fretful; its tongues are growing sharp and satirical, without laughter; one hears stories daily of behavior and crimes that are not so much passionate as erratic and illogical. For a time I thought that this malaise lay only within myself, but now all are remarking it. Our Master is busier than ever; edicts fall about us daily. Regulations are laid down for usury and every man must clean the street in front of his door; a great map of the world has been set into the pavement before the law courts, picked out in golden eagles which denote the location of new cities. Young husbands stand before it, stroking their chins, trying to decide whether they shall set up a new home in ice and sleet or under a burning sun.

I was about to accept your invitation to come to Capri at once, when this Master requested that I come to his house to instruct his wife and his royal guest in the ceremonial that will be required of them in early December. We have had eight sessions, frequently concluded by readings from the tragedies in which we all take part, including Caesar himself. I find myself moving in a tragedy within a tragedy.

I am coming to understand that mystery, Caesar's marriage. I see that it is not based on any morbid inclination toward very young girls, as so many sneering tongues have held. Caesar is a teacher; it is a sort of fury in him. He can only love where he can instruct; the return he asks is progress and enlightenment. Of these young girls he asks only what Pygmalion asked of marble. I gather that he has been three times rewarded—by Cornelia, by his daughter, and by the Queen of Egypt; and many times resisted. The resistance he is now meeting is enormous and crushing. Pompeia is not an unintelligent girl, but his method toward her is so unintelligent that he is frightening and starving whatever intelligence she has. Love as education is one of the great powers of the world, but it hangs in a delicate suspension; it achieves its harmony as seldom as does love by the senses. Frustrated, it creates even greater havoc, for like all love it is a madness. On the one hand he loves her as a delicate growing thing and as a woman (and Caesar's glance resting on a woman is like no other man's), and on the other hand he loves her for the potentiality she may possess to be an Aurelia, a Julia Marcia. In his mind Rome is a woman; he married Pompeia to shape her into one more of those living statues of the great Roman matron.

Cleopatra has disappointed him also. One can only guess how intoxicatingly she must first have filled the requirements of a beloved pupil. She still is. I worship this colossus, but I am an old woman; I am no longer educable. Yet I understand well the eager rapture with which she receives every word that falls from his lips. He discovered, however, that he could teach her nothing essential, for the essence of what he has to teach is moral, is responsibility; and Cleopatra has not the dimmest sense of what is right and wrong. Caesar does not know that he has this passion for teaching; all that has for him the invisibility of things which are self-evident. Hence he is a very bad

teacher. He assumes that all men are both teachers and vora-
cious learners; that everyone is vibrant with moral life. Women
are more subtle teachers than men.

I shall never cease to be moved by the view we occasionally
have of great men trying to make a marriage where no mar-
riage can be, continuing to expend a defeated tenderness on
ill-compounded wives. The patience they acquire is a very dif-
ferent thing from the patience that wives exhibit toward hus-
bands; that is in the natural order of things and should no
more be singled out for praise than the honesty of the honest.
One has seen these insulted husbands finally withdrawing into
themselves; they have learned the basic solitude of man as their
happier brothers will never know it.

Such a husband is Caesar. His other bride is Rome. To both
he is a bad husband, but from an excess of conjugal love.

Let me go on a moment more.

I have only recently come to understand some words that
you let fall years ago, that "wickedness may be the exploration
of one's liberty"—have I got that right?—and that "it can be
the search for a limit that one can respect." How stupid I am not
to have digested that before, my dear prince; I could have played
it into my Medea and into my Clytemnestra. Yes, in the light
of that thought, can't we say that a great deal of what we call
"wickedness" is the very principle of virtue exploring the laws
of its own nature? Isn't that what Antigone, my Antigone, our
Antigone, meant when she said: [*In Sophocles's play, in reply to
Creon's assertion that her slain "good" brother would not wish
her wicked brother to receive an honorable burial*] "Who can say
but that in the underworld his [*wicked*] deeds may seem to be
blameless?" Yes, there lies the interpretation of Clodia's dis-
orders and unless Caesar is watchful, Pompeia will journey out
in search of a limitation to her curiosities. Nature affords them
to our senses: fire burns our fingers and the action of our hearts
prevents our running up mountainsides; but only the Gods
have put a veto on the adventures of our minds. If They do not
choose to intervene, we are condemned to fashion our own
laws or to wander in fright through the pathless wastes of our
terrifying liberty, seeking even the reassurance of a barred gate,
of a forbidding wall. It is a recurrent joke among writers of

farces that wives rejoice in being beaten by their husbands. It reflects, however, an eternal truth—that there is a great comfort in knowing that those who love you love you enough to take the responsibility for marking out the permissible. Husbands often err—but in both directions. Caesar is a tyrant—both as husband and as ruler. It is not that, like other tyrants, he is chary of according liberty to others; it is that, loftily free himself, he has lost all touch with the way freedom operates and is developed in others; always mistaken, he accords too little or he accords too much.

LIV Clodia to her brother.
 [*From Nettuno.*]
 [*Selections from almost daily letters throughout November.*]

Don't come here, Brainless. I don't wish to see anyone.

I am completely happy as I am. Cicero is next door, repining and writing those doleful insincerities he calls philosophy. We met several times, but are now reduced to sending each other gifts of fruit or pastry. He could not interest me in philosophy and I could not interest him in mathematics. He's a very witty man, but for some reason he's never witty to me. I dry him up.

I do nothing all day and would be very bad company for you. I study numbers and can forget anything else for days at a time. There are properties in the study of infinity that no one has ever dreamed of. I have frightened Sosigenes with them. He says they are dangerous.

I am very angry with you for appealing to old Eagle-beak to close that play. Any mortification only begins for us from the moment we take any notice of such things. When will you learn that the enjoyment of the malicious is doubled when they learn that we have been wounded by their remarks?

As you say, it is vexatious to be charged with a thousand crimes that one never got around to committing. I certainly left my dear parents as soon as I could, but I never lifted a hand to annoy them. Not only did I not kill my poor husband, but I got down on my knees and begged him not to kill himself with overeating. I have never felt a tremor of passion for you or for

Dodo; in fact, I have too often gazed with astonishment at the starved water rats that committed themselves to finding you attractive.

As to this last matter [*the death of Catullus?*], I don't wish you ever to mention it again. It is all so complicated; no one else will ever understand it. I don't wish to hear it mentioned.

The worst of being charged with crimes, however, is that it makes one restless to deserve all that censure. But, of course, only something enormous would do. Something to darken the sun.

Of course, I am angry that people should be saying that *he* directed me to go into the country. Although it's utter nonsense, it's more exasperating than all the other lies put together. But I shall not come into town merely to refute it.

[*November 27.*]

Come to Nettuno, Publius. I cannot endure this any longer, but I am not yet ready to come into town.

For the sake of heaven, come and don't bring anyone with you.

The worst about inactivity is that it sets one brooding about the passing of time. And it has set me to remembering, as though I were an old woman. Last night I could not sleep; I got up and burned all my mathematical notebooks; then I threw in all the letters I have received for ten years. Sosigenes danced around like an old moth trying to restrain me.

Start the minute you receive this letter. I have an idea. Marc Antony failed to complete "the most daring feat ever seen in Rome." Well, I know another.

Mopsa is here making me a new robe and turban for the Lalalala games.

[*November 28.*]

I hope this letter fails to reach you and that you are already on your way. If not, start at once.

I have just received a letter from the Dictator requesting me to return to Rome to take up my instruction for the Queen of Egypt. He has asked me to dinner on the second.

LV Cleopatra to Caesar.
 [*December 5.*]

 I send you the following information, great Caesar, know-ing well that my motives may be misunderstood by you. A month and a half ago I would have told it to you at once; that thought has decided me now.

 The Lady Clodia Pulcher has had two robes and turbans made for the ceremonies on the night of December 11th. She intends to dress her brother in one of them and introduce him into your house. Your wife is aware of this, as a letter from her, now in my possession, shows.

LV-A Caesar to Cleopatra.
 [*By return messenger.*]

 I thank you, great Queen. I am indebted to you for many things. I regret that this sorry matter to which you have called my attention should be among them.

LVI Alina, wife of Cornelius Nepos, to her sister Postumia, wife of Publius Ceccinius of Verona.
 [*December 13.*]

 Just a word in haste, dearest Postumia. Rome is standing on its head. There has never been such an uproar. Public offices have been closed and most of the shopkeepers don't even open the shops. Word must have reached you before this: that Clo-dia Pulcher introduced her brother dressed as a votary into the Ceremonies of the Good Goddess. I was standing a few feet from him when he was discovered. They say it was the Lady Julia Marcia who called attention to it. Our singing had been going on for an hour, and the responses. Some women flew at him and tore off the turban and the bands. Such screaming you never heard. Soon women were striking him from all sides as hard as they could; others dashed about covering up the sa-cred things. Of course, there wasn't any other man within shouting distance; but presently some guards came and picked him up, bleeding and groaning, and dragged him off.

 This is the end; really, I don't know what to say. Everybody says, This is the end. People are even saying, Now let Caesar

move Rome to Byzantium. In a moment I must hurry down to the trial. Cicero made a terrible and wonderful speech against Clodius and Clodia yesterday. All sorts of people are being called to testify and rumors are flying about. Some think that the Queen of Egypt had a hand in it, because Clodia served as her instructress; but the Queen was indisposed and did not even go to the rites.

The strangest thing of all is the behavior of Caesar. As Supreme Pontiff he should be directing the inquiry. But from the beginning he's refused to have anything to do with it. There's no doubt that his wife is as guilty as they are. Isn't it awful, awful, awful?

My husband has just come in. He says that Pompeia's family —twenty of them—went to Caesar last night to urge him to speak in her defense. It seems that he was very quiet and listened to them for an hour. Then he rose and said he had no intention of appearing at the trial; that it was possible that Pompeia was not implicated in this matter, but that it was not difficult for a woman in her position so to conduct her life that such a suspicion would never fall upon her; that the suspicion was damaging enough, and that he was divorcing her the very next day—that is today.

I'm hurrying to the trial, dear. I may have to give evidence. It is a strange feeling to be hurrying through the streets of this city! It's as though the city itself were in disgrace and that we all ought to move out of it.

BOOK FOUR

LVII Servilia in Rome to her son Marcus Junius Brutus.
 [*August 8. This letter reached Brutus at Marseilles as he
 was about to return to Rome concluding his governorship
 of Hither Gaul.*]

Return, Marcus, return to the city which is bending all its
eyes upon you.

The hero whose name you bear [*Junius Brutus who expelled
the Tarquins*] lives in you, by spirit if not by blood, and his task
is on your shoulders.

Return to the city whose health is your own health and whose
freedom is your own freedom. Romans are again calling on the
name of Brutus and all eyes are bent on you.

The man against whom Rome's rage is directed is no little
man. The man who now stifles Rome is great in all things and
greatest in error. The murderer must be of equal stature with
the murdered or Rome is twice enslaved. There is only one
Roman at that height and all eyes are bent on you. The hand
that strikes him down must be passionless as justice. The tyran-
nicide's task is a holy task; it is remembered with grateful tears
by generations unborn.

Come look on him; give him the honor that is his due; look
on him as a great son looks on a great father, and with the blow
not of one man but of ten thousand thousands—slay him.

Thinking of the child soon to be born to you, raise up your
hand and strike.

LVII-A Brutus to Servilia.
 [*Returning the letter to her.*]

This letter is yours. That I have read it does not make it mine.

The words with which you direct me to murder a friend and
benefactor are clear enough. The words with which you call
my parentage in question are not clear.

By the age of twenty, madam, every man should be suffi-
ciently his own father. His father by the body is of large, though

lesser, importance. Those who call that parentage in question, however, should do so only under oath and under the most solemn oath and with the most absolute clearness.

This you have not done. Thereby I have lost, in two ways, a measure of the respect I am bound to owe you.

LVII-B Cornelius Nepos: Commonplace Book.
[*Notes on Cicero's conversation.*]

I thought the moment propitious for asking the question which all Rome had wished to put to him for thirty years. "Tell me, my friend, what is your opinion—is Marcus Junius Brutus the son of Julius Caesar?"

He sobered at once.

"Cornelius," he said, "we must be careful how we use the word 'opinion.' With much evidence I venture to say that I know a thing; with a more limited amount I venture to say that I have an opinion on it; with less still I venture a conjecture. In a matter of this kind I have not sufficient even for a conjecture. Suppose, however, that I felt I had a conjecture— should I give it to *you*, you who will undoubtedly put it in a book? In a book, conjectures have a way of looming larger than facts. Facts can be controverted; a gloss can nullify them; but conjectures are not easily dismissed. The histories we read are little more than processions of conjectures pretending they are facts.

"Is Marcus Junius Brutus the son of Caesar? Put it this way: do I know, or have I any opinion as to whether this relationship is believed to exist by Brutus, by Caesar, or by Servilia?

"Brutus is among my best friends. Caesar is . . . Caesar is the man whom I have observed most attentively for thirty, for forty, years. Servilia—well, overtures were once made that I should marry Servilia. Let us weigh this matter.

"I have seen the first two together many, many times and I can affirm to you that I have never seen any faintest sign pass between them that could be interpreted as an acknowledgement of such a relationship. Caesar holds Brutus in high regard. He has for him the affection, the tacit affection, of an older man for a younger man of notable capability. Perhaps I should say grudging affection—that is to say, something like a

fear of him, or at least a . . . come now, Cornelius, do we seniors always rejoice in the knowledge that there will be brilliant historians and orators in the generations that follow us? Do we not feel that it is the duty of our successors to be inferior? Moreover, Caesar has always maintained his distance from all men of incorruptible independence—from all twelve of them, from all six of them. It cannot be said too often that Caesar is unhappy in the society of capable men—or, rather, of men who are possessed of both ability and high character. Oh, yes, he is; oh, yes, he is. He likes ability if it's unscrupulous, and he likes high character if it's impractical, but he cannot endure both in one man. He's surrounded himself with scoundrels; he likes the talk of scoundrels; he likes their jokes—Oppius, Mammurra, Milo—scoundrels all of them. When he works, he works with people like Asinius Pollio, honest, loyal, and a mediocrity.

"Now Brutus's deportment to Caesar differs at no point from his deportment to any of us seniors. Brutus feels affection for no one, never has, and never will—except, of course, for his wife, and perhaps because of her, a little for his father-in-law. You know that impassive and handsome face, that deliberate utterance, that austere courtesy. If he thought that Caesar were, or even might be, his father—no, I cannot believe it! I have seen him thank Caesar for favors; I have seen him disagree with Caesar; why, I have seen him present his wife to Caesar. Caesar is all actor and we shall never know what he thinks, but Brutus is no part an actor and I would take my oath that he has never even considered this possibility.

"There remains our conjecture as to what Servilia thinks.

"But before I come to that, there is one thing more that should be said: thirty years ago this relationship was firmly believed by many to be an undoubted fact. The dates, as one might say, support this paternity. At that time Caesar was consolidating his political advancement by a calculated succession of double adulteries. Women then played a far greater part in the life of the Republic and Servilia had one of the most brilliant political heads, male or female, in the entire aristocracy. She could sway the policies of twenty stupid and wavering multimillionaires; all she had to do was to tell them *what to be afraid of next*. Do not judge the Servilia of those years by the Servilia

of today. Today she is merely a frantic intriguing woman, floundering amid preposterous and conflicting principles and flooding the city with anonymous but transparent letters. The weather of Rome has deteriorated for women. Do not even judge the Clodia of ten years ago by the Clodia of today. Rome twenty and thirty years ago was an arena of forceful women— think of Caesar's mother, Pompey's mother, and Caesar's aunt. They thought of little else than politics and did not permit their husbands, lovers, guests, and children to think of anything else. People affect now to be shocked by the fact that their mothers and grandmothers appear to have been repeatedly married and divorced simply for reasons of political expediency. They forget that this was not only because these brides brought with them wealth and family connections—everyone knew that the bride was in herself a political general. Why, as the struggle between Sulla and Marius came to a head, poisoning was so frequent an occurrence that one thought twice before dining at the home of one's own sister.

"You can imagine what art it required of Caesar to glide in and out of the beds of these warring Clytemnestras! The story has never been told. The prodigy of it lies in the fact that each of his successive paramours worships him to this day. How often, finding myself in the company of one or other of our aging matrons, I have turned the conversation to praise of this man, only to discover that I am being listened to by a breathless and half-swooning girl, convinced that she was the only inspiratrix of that parded career."

Here Cicero fell to laughing and choking again and had to be beaten encouragingly on the back.

"Now, notice," he continued, "Caesar who in wedlock has only been able to achieve one child, outside wedlock went far toward justifying his appellation of 'the Father of his Country.' I think there is little doubt that he made every effort to bind these influential paramours to him by the bond of a child. Furthermore, it was often observed that when the woman of his attentions announced to him that she was pregnant . . . are you following me? . . . and when he was convinced that he was indeed the father of this . . . this expectation, he invariably made a very handsome return; he presented the lady with a gift, and with no mean gift.

"During the years we are speaking of, however, never forget that Caesar was penniless. Yes, throughout the twenty most critical years of his career, Caesar was . . . spendthrift without income and lavish with another's gold.

[*He follows Cicero's digression on Caesar and money, already given in Document XII.*]

At all events, Caesar rescued from inactivity enough of his friends' money to present Volumnia with the "Andromache" of Apelles (fit subject for an adulteress), the greatest painting in the world, though a fading relic of its former self. Can you doubt that her twin daughters are the daughters of Caesar? Isn't that the *nose*—the nose, twice? And to Servilia he gave the rose-colored pearl that she wears so religiously at every celebration of the Founding of the City. That is the first pearl in the world and at the time it was the most talked-of object in Rome. The unappetizing bosom on which it now reposes, my friend (in defiance of the sumptuary laws) was once as beautiful as itself. Is it the reward for bearing Marcus Junius Brutus? We shall never know, we shall never know."

LVIII Caesar, in Rome, to Brutus, at Marseilles.
[*August 17.*]
[*By private courier.*]

I do not have to tell you with what satisfaction I have received reports from many sources of the exemplary manner in which you have fulfilled your high office. I trust that my commendation is a satisfaction to you for two reasons; the lesser reason is that it comes from a friend who takes pride and pleasure in all you do; the greater reason is that I, too, am a servant of the Roman state and suffer when she is injured and rejoice when she is nobly served. By the immortal Gods I would that from all the provinces I heard news of such justice, such tireless concern for all her subjects, and such energy in the execution of her laws. To thousands awaking from the sleep of barbarism you have made Rome loved and honored; you have made her feared only so far as equity should be feared by us all.

Return, my dear young man, to the country which asks increasingly greater labors of you.

The letter I now write you is for your eyes alone and I direct

you to destroy it when it has been read. Take what time you wish to write me a reply; my courier will await your convenience.

I do not believe that in a republic it is among the responsibilities of a leader to indicate or appoint his successor. Similarly, I do not believe that the head of a republic should be invested with dictatorial powers. Yet I am Dictator, and I am convinced that the powers I have been obliged to assume are necessary for the State and I am convinced that only my appointment of a successor can save that State from another long and exhausting civil war. You and I have had many long conversations concerning the nature of government and the degree to which our Roman citizens at this time can be left to govern themselves. We have not always been in agreement as to the extent to which they are capable of governing themselves. I appointed you to the post which you are now leaving in order that you might learn through the daily exercise of administration the enormous extent to which the rank and file of men are dependent on those placed over them. I now wish you to hold a similar position in the capital and to discover for yourself a similar truth concerning our citizens in Italy.

I wish you to serve as Praetor. I am appointing your brother-in-law [*Cassius*] to serve with you. I wish you to be Praetor of the City; of the two offices it is the more difficult, the one more exposed to the public view, and the one closer to my self.

As I have said above, I believe that, given the disposition of our citizens and the political situation in the Peninsula, it is my duty to appoint my successor. It is true that a man in my position can only appoint a successor; he cannot confirm him. There is one thing of which all men are equally ignorant and that is the future. A successor must confirm himself. There are ways, however, in which, living and dead, I may still render aid to the man who follows me. One such aid is to introduce him to the methods by which the world is administered and to share with him information and experience which is not elsewhere obtainable. As Praetor of the City these would be at your disposal.

I am made aware daily that my life may be cut short at any time. I do not choose to employ those safeguards against my enemies which might secure my bodily safety at the cost of encumbering my movements and alarming my mind. There are

many hours during the day when it would not be difficult for an assassin to destroy me. The recognition of these dangers has impelled me to give thought to my succession. In dying I shall leave no sons behind me. Even though I had sons I do not believe that leadership is transmitted by paternity. Leadership is for those who love the public good and are endowed and trained to administer it. I believe that you possess that love and are so endowed; the training I have been in a position to secure for you. The decision as to whether you wish to assume the supreme command is open to you.

I ask you to send me your thoughts on this matter.

LVIII-A Brutus to Caesar.
 [*By immediate return.*]

I thank you for your commendation. I thank you for the assistance you gave to me throughout the duration of my office. I accept the Praetorship of the City and shall hope to fill it in a manner that will retain the good opinion which moved you to confer it upon me.

The further office which you designate I do not wish to consider. My reasons for refusing it are contained in your own letter. Permit me to cite your words: I do not believe that in a republic it is among the responsibilities of a leader to indicate or appoint his successor. Caesar's position only a Caesar can fill; should it fall vacant, that office and that concentration of power must necessarily come to an end. May the Immortal Gods long preserve you to direct the state in the manner that you alone can perform; when you depart from that office may They preserve us from civil war.

My further reasons for refusing this office are private to myself. With each succeeding year I feel myself more and more drawn to the study of philosophy. When I have served you and the State for a time as Praetor of the City I shall call upon you to release me in order that I may devote myself exclusively to such studies. In them I hope to leave behind me a monument not unworthy of our Roman spirit and of your good opinion.

LIX Caesar to Porcia, wife of M. Junius Brutus, in Rome.
 [*August 18.*]

I cannot deny myself the pleasure of telling you that some
days ago I recalled your husband to this City. It was not with-
out regret, Madam, that I recalled him, for those who love
Rome could well wish him to remain forever in Hither Gaul,
continuing the notable services that he is there rendering Her.
Permit me to repeat to you the words which I have recently
written to him:

"By the immortal Gods, I would that from all the provinces
I heard news of such justice, such tireless concern for all her
subjects, and such energy in the execution of her laws."

Allow me to say that there is nothing which touches your
house which does not affect me also. No differences of opin-
ion have shaken the profound respect which I bear to those most
closely associated with you. [*Porcia was the daughter of the
Younger Cato.*] The word has reached me that you are awaiting
the birth of a child. Not you alone, Madam, but all Rome awaits
the child of so noble a heritage. I rejoice to think that the child's
father will be present in that auspicious hour.

LIX-A Porcia to Caesar.
 [*August 19.*]

Porcia, wife of Marcus Junius Brutus, sends many thanks to
Caius Julius Caesar, Dictator, for the kindness of his letter and
for his part in the most welcome news which it contains.

LIX-B Caesar's Journal-Letter to Lucius Mamilius Turrinus
on Capri.
 [*About August 21.*]

947. No man is free of envy. I harbor three envious im-
pulses, if that name can be given to three subjects of admiring
meditation. I envy you your soul, Catullus his song, and Bru-
tus his new wife. Of the first two I have spoken to you at some
length, though not for the last time.

The third is not a new arrival to my thoughts. Even while
she was the wife of my vainglorious and incompetent friend

[*M. Calpurnius*] Bibulus I had remarked her. How extraordinarily silence becomes a woman, not a silence which is an absence and vacancy—though that is uncommon enough—but a silence which is all attention. Such graced my Cornelia whom I called "my speaking silence"; and such my Julia, long silent and silent even in my dreams; such Cato's Porcia.

And yet when they were moved to speak, what eloquence or wit could rival it? They could speak of the smallest things in the ordering of the household and Cicero in full Senate could not so enthrall the ears. My envious meditations have instructed me why. The trivial is only unendurable from the lips of those who put an importance upon it. Yet our lives are immersed in the trivial; the significant comes to us enwrapped in multitudinous details of the trivial; the trivial has this dignity that it exists and is omnipresent. By their very nature women are the custodians of an immense amount of such consequential insignificance. To a man the rearing of children appears to be a servitude more harassing than the rearing of animals and more exasperating than bivouacking among the gnats of the Egyptian desert. A silent woman is one who has distinguished in her mind the detail which must fly to oblivion and the detail which merits a second attention.

Envy of another man's wife is not generally thought to have this pacific character; but such has been mine. While Bibulus was alive, I was often in the house and saw and envied him his return in the evening to that judicious tranquility. When Bibulus died I took to long thoughts, but a move seemed out of the question. Long thoughts had Brutus also, no doubt; he was much censured for divorcing Claudia [*daughter of Appius Claudius, a distant cousin of Clodia*] after so long a married life; but I could understand it and all Rome is aware of a happiness that even the grimmest stoic must envy, and even the watchful dictator condone. [*The marriage reinforced the only party of opposition among the aristocrats which could be said to have the wide support of popular opinion. Brutus married his cousin, his mother Servilia being the sister of Porcia's father, the younger Cato; Cassius and Lepidus were married to half-sisters of Brutus, daughters of Servilia by her earlier marriage to the Consul Silenus; both were women of extremely bad reputation.*] Is she on a par with your mother and mine and with my aunt?—I do

not know. It may be that her virtues have that inflexibility that mars those of her husband and her father, joyless men. One cannot but deplore an austerity which came into being through revulsion against a flagrant environment; it is not slow to adopt censoriousness and complacency. I take some pleasure in remembering that my young friend Brutus was not always so marble a philosopher. He languished for a time beside the Incomparable [*Cytheris the actress*] and he made his fortune by grinding the faces of the Cappadocians and the Cyprians; I, being Consul that year, barely saved him from a clamorous trial for extortion.

Yes, these moralists are virtuous by revulsion, hence their rigidity. May this "speaking silence" have a beneficent effect on the noble and handsome Brutus. [*This is a play on words, for* brutus *means both brutish and ugly.*]

LX The Broadsides of Conspiracy.
 [*The following broadside or chain letter was circulated throughout the Peninsula by the thousands during the first weeks of September 45. This first one appeared in Rome September 1.*]

The Council of Twenty to every Roman worthy of his ancestors: Prepare to shake off the Tyranny under which our Republic groans. Our fathers died to acquire those liberties of which One Man now is robbing us. A Council of Twenty has been formed; it has taken oaths before the altars; it has received assurance from the Gods that its course is just and will succeed. Every Roman who receives this bulletin is enjoined to make five copies of it. With all secrecy, see that these copies reach the hands of five men, Romans likely to be of this opinion or to be so persuaded; they in turn are enjoined to make further copies.

Other bulletins will follow. By degrees their measures will become more definite.

Death to Caesar. For our country and our Gods. Silence and Resolution.
 The Council of Twenty

LX-A Asinius Pollio to Caesar.
 [*This is the conclusion of Pollio's report to Caesar from
 Naples on September 18, given as our Document XIV.*]

I forward to my General the thirteen copies of the broadside
which were sent to me during the last six days—three at my
lodgings in Posilipo, ten here. My General will notice that five
of them appear to have been written by the same hand which
has, however, attempted to disguise itself. Quintus Cotta re-
ceived 16; Lucius Mela, 10.

A corresponding movement has been set in motion in these
parts for the common people, that is for those who cannot read
and write. Pebbles and shells are being circulated on which are
written: XX/C/M/ [*for Death*]. My orderly has collected a
number of these. He assures me that they cause more indigna-
tion than enthusiasm and provoked the circulation of other
stones marked XX/M. Both inscriptions can be found scrawled
on the pavements, walls, etc.

I do not venture to submit suggestions to my General as to
measures calculated to counteract this activity. I give, however,
the results of a discussion on the matter held in our offices by
Cotta, Mela, Annius Turbatius and myself.

1. The movement started in Rome. Its first appearance here
was fifteen days later.

2. Three slaves were apprehended while delivering these
letters. They were subjected to torture. Two declared that they
had found the broadsides, addressed to us, in public places (an
old woman found one on the tray of figs she was selling) and
then delivered them in the hope of attaining a reward. The
whole circulation depends on the custom of giving fees to the
bringers of messages. The third slave said that the letter, ad-
dressed to me, had been given him for delivery with a fee by a
veiled woman on the waterfront.

3. The initiators of this activity do not appear to be the
Clodius Pulcher group, as lacking the astuteness and patience,
nor the Cassius-Casca malcontents, who would think only in
terms of a small group. The desire to enlist wide adherence,
the relative absence of incitation to violence, together with the
claims to religious approval suggest a studious and perhaps

elderly group. We do not exclude the possibility of a Cicero or Cato arriving at this type of measure.

4. It is difficult to see how a chain letter movement could transfer itself from negative to positive action. We are agreed, however, that the movement could achieve results detrimental to good government and await whatever instructions may be issued to counteract it.

LX-B Second Broadside.
 [*This broadside achieved even wider circulation through-
 out the entire Peninsula. Copies first appeared in Rome
 on September 17.*]

The Council of Twenty to every Roman worthy of his an-cestors: second bulletin. Every Roman who receives this bul-letin is enjoined to make five copies of it and with all secrecy to see that they reach the hands of the five men to whom they forwarded the preceding one.

Herewith is our directive:

Beginning on the sixteenth of this month September, every Roman as far as possible will see that himself and his house-hold will make their purchases in the city, present themselves before the Courts, and engage in all activities of public life on the even days of the month only.

In addition, those in Rome will render themselves ostenta-tiously assiduous in acclaiming the appearances of the Dictator and in accompanying his train at all public appearances. In conversation they will declare themselves enthusiastically in favor of all projects which he entertains, particularly the trans-ference of the capital to the East, a military campaign to India, and a restoration of the Kingdom.

Our next bulletin will contain still more definite measures.

Death to Caesar. For our country and our Gods. Silence and Resolution.

 The Council of Twenty

LX-C The Commonplace Book of Cornelius Nepos.
 [*This entry was written after Caesar's Death.*]

Throughout the Fall of 45, the principal subjects of conver-

sation were so-called chain letters and the visit of Cleopatra. In fact, the initiation of the chain letters was ascribed by many to the Queen of Egypt, as they were thought to have a devious oriental cast, such as would not have occurred to a Roman. The injunction to perform one's public business on the even days of the month was watched by the public with breathless interest. At first it was noticed that a preponderance of activity was taking place on the uneven days. This gradually relaxed and the reverse became apparent.

LXI Caesar's Journal-Letter to Lucius Mamilius Turrinus.
 [*Enclosing a copy of the first broadsides of the conspiracy.*]
 [*September 8–20.*]

979. Someone has thought up a new way to prepare the people for an overturn of the State and for my death by assassination.

I enclose a copy of one of these public notices. They are circulating throughout Italy by the thousands.

Scarcely a day has passed during the last year when I have not received new detailed evidence of one or other of these conspiratorial movements. I am brought lists of names and accounts of their reunions. I intercept letters. The majority of such groups are unbelievably maladept. Their membership generally includes one who is eager to sell his information for money or favor.

Each new conspiracy awakens in me a great interest—I was going to say "a happy interest," soon disappointed.

In the first place, I have little doubt that, soon or late, I shall die by the hand of a tyrannicide. I have not chosen to encumber my life with the constant protection of armed guards nor my mind with the practice of vigilant anxiety. I could wish that it were the dagger of a patriot that strikes me down, but I am equally exposed to those of the madman and the envious. In the meantime, by incarceration, exile, admonition, and exposure, I have arrested such plots as have come to my notice.

As I say, I have followed them with interest. It is always possible that among those who plan my death I shall find the man who is right in the matters where I am wrong. There are many better men in the world than I am, but I have not yet seen the

man who could be a better ruler of our State. If he exists I think he would now be planning my death. Rome as I have shaped it, as I have had to shape it, is not a comfortable place for a man whose genius is the genius for ruling at the top: if I were not Caesar now, I would be Caesar's assassin. (That thought had not occurred to me until this moment, but I see it is true; it is one of the many discoveries that come to me from the practice of writing letters to you.)

But there is an even profounder reason why I should wish to know something about the man who slays me, even though that knowledge is mine only during the last moment of my life. This brings me back to that inquiry which, as you know, occupies me increasingly: Is there a Mind in or above the universe which is watching us?

I am often called "Destiny's favorite." If the Gods exist they placed me where I am. They placed every man where he is, but the man who fills my seat is among the more conspicuous of Their appointments—as, in his way, the poet Catullus is; as you are; as Pompey was. The man who slays me would perhaps afford us some light upon Their nature—Their selected instrument. But even as I write this my pen falls from my hand. I shall probably die by the dagger of a madman. The Gods hide themselves even in their choice of instrument. We are all at the mercy of a falling tile. We are left with the picture of Jupiter going about dislodging tiles which fall upon a lemonade vendor or upon Caesar. The jury that condemned Socrates to death were not august instruments; nor were the eagle and the tortoise that slew Aeschylus. It is probable that my last moment of consciousness will be filled with the last of many confirmations that the affairs of the world proceed with that senselessness with which a stream carries leaves upon its tide.

There is another element in the eagerness with which I inquire into each new conspiracy. Would it not be a wonderful discovery to find that I am hated to the death by a man whose hatred is disinterested? It is rare enough to find a disinterested love; so far among those that hate me I have uncovered nothing beyond the promptings of envy, of self-advancing ambition, or of self-consoling destructiveness. It may be that in that last moment I may be permitted to look into the face of a

man whose only thought is Rome and whose only thought is that I am the enemy of Rome.

980–982. [*Already given in Document VIII.*]

983. [*On the weather.*]

984. [*On the increasing divergence between written and spoken Latin and the decay of case endings and the subjunctive in popular speech.*]

985. [*Again, on primogeniture and the inheritance of property.*]

986. [*Accompanying the second broadside.*]

I enclose the second public notice of the Committee of Twenty. I have not yet learned who are the initiators of this series. It smacks of some new kind of malcontent.

Since childhood I have been attentive to the attitude which men bear to those who have been placed over them and who are in a position to restrict their movements. What deference and loyalty masking what contempt and hatred! The deference and loyalty proceeds from a man's gratitude that his superior relieves him of responsibility and from the terrors of weighty decision; the contempt and hatred from his resentment against the man who limits his freedom. During a part of every day and night even the mildest man is, however obscurely, the murderer of those who can command his obedience. In my youth I was often filled with consternation to discover that, waking or sleeping, I was prone to dream the death of my father, my tutors, and my governors toward whom I often bore a real, if intermittent, love. It was, therefore, with a kind of pleasure that I used to listen to the songs which my soldiers sang about their campfires; for every four songs that elevated me to the Gods there was a fifth that diminished me to idiocy, senile vice, and decay. These last they sang loudest and the woods rang with glee at my death. I found in myself no anger, but only a little laughter and a few accelerated steps toward old age when I discovered that even Marc Antony and Dolabella had for a time joined with a group which was plotting my death; for a time the master they loved had merged with all the masters they had hated. It is only dogs that never bite their masters.

This combination of impulses is a part of the movement of the world and is not for us to approve or disapprove, for like all

the fundamental impulses it produces both good and ill. And from it I draw confirmation of my conviction that the central movement of the mind is the desire for unrestricted liberty and that this movement is invariably accompanied by its opposite, a dread of the consequences of liberty.

LXII Notes by Catullus, found by Caesar's Secret Police.
 [*These reached the Dictator on September 27.*]
 [*These rough drafts were on the reverse of leaves containing fragments of poetry or on slates. In both cases they had been negligently erased.*]

 A Committee of Ten has been formed. . . .
 This Committee of Twenty, having taken oaths before the altars of the Gods . . .
 beginning on the twelfth of next month, September . . .
 . . . on the uneven days of the month will refrain from all . . .
 assiduous attendance at the public appearance of the Dictator . . . acclamations of profuse flattery . . .

LXII-A Caesar to Catullus.
 [*September 27.*]

It has been brought to my attention that certain friends of yours have initiated a series of documents designed to overturn the government of this Republic.

I regard these measures as childish and mistaken rather than criminal. Your friends will have observed the means I have already taken to render them harmless and ridiculous. Pressure is being brought upon me, however, to inflict public punishment on their perpetrators.

I find it difficult to believe that you had any hand in so inept an excursion into public affairs; but there is evidence to show that you were at least aware of it.

For the sake of my long friendship with your father I am willing to deal leniently with these mistaken young men. I place their fortunes in your hands. If you are able to inform me

that their part in the circulation of these letters will cease, I shall regard the matter as closed.

I do not wish to hear any defense of their action. An affirmative word from you will be sufficient. That word you can give me day after tomorrow when I shall meet you, I am told, at the dinner being given by C. Publius Clodius and the Lady Clodia Pulcher.

LXII-B Catullus to Caesar.
 [*September 28.*]

The letters of which you speak were planned by me alone and the first copies of them were sent out by me alone. There is no Committee of Twenty.

The means I have employed to remind Romans of their shrinking liberties may well seem inept to a Dictator. His powers are unlimited, as is his jealousy of any liberty other than his own. His powers extend to ransacking the private papers of the citizens.

The composition of these letters by me has already ceased, since their efficacy is at an end.

LXII-C Third Broadside of Conspiracy, written by Julius Caesar.

> [*By* "their efficacy is at an end" *Catullus meant that the country was now so flooded by letters written in imitation of his own that the movement was soon dissipated in the bewilderment and flagging interest of the citizens. This Third Broadside which appeared a few days after the Second received the widest circulation of all of them.*]

The Council of Twenty to every Roman worthy of his ancestors, this third bulletin.

The Council of Twenty now feels that these letters have received a sufficiently wide circulation. Hundreds of thousands have been aroused to a patriotic hatred of the oppressor and to an eager expectation of his death.

In the meantime you are instructed to prepare the people for this happy event. Hence, lose no opportunity to ridicule the so-called achievements of the tyrant.

Belittle his conquests. Remember that the territory was con-
quered by the Generals working under him to whom he de-
nied all merit. He is called Unconquered, but it is well known
that he suffered many costly defeats which were concealed from
the Roman people. Spread about many stories of his personal
cowardice before the enemy.

Remember the Civil Wars; remember Pompey. Remind the
people of the brilliance of his circuses.

The distribution of lands: enlarge upon the injustice done to
the large landholders. Intimate that the veterans received only
stony or marshy land.

The Council of Twenty has drawn up detailed plans for the
control of public order and finance. The senile edicts of the
Dictator will be revoked at once: the sumptuary laws, the re-
form in the calendar, the new currency, the ten-head system of
distributing grain, the senseless expenditure of public funds on
irrigation and the control of waterways. Prosperity and plenty
will reign.

Death to Caesar. For our country and our Gods. Silence and
resolution.

> The Council of Twenty

LXIII Caius Cassius at Palestrina to his mother-in-law,
Servilia, in Rome.

> [*November 3.*]
> [*Reading between the lines, the following letter discusses
> opportunities for assassinating Caesar and means of in-
> ducing Brutus to join the conspiracy.*]

The company which is seeking to do honor to our friend is
increasing daily. There are many whose names we do not
know. Our efforts to learn those of the admirers last month
[*Query: Those who attacked Caesar on September 27?*] have been
unavailing.

It is difficult to find an occasion when an honor of this sort
may be conferred, for it must both come as a surprise to the
recipient and at the same time make as strong and agreeable an
impression as possible upon the bystanders. Plans were well
advanced to effect this at the conclusion of the Queen of Egypt's
reception. Our guest of honor mysteriously disappeared from

the assembly, however, and it was thought that he had received some intimation of the ovation that was to be accorded him.

I am increasingly of the opinion that this gratifying event should be delayed until at least one more of our friend's closest associates be included among those conferring this honor. We are deeply indebted to you for your efforts toward this end. The person I have in mind has avoided my company and has even sent excuses that he is unable to see me in his home.

We understand all the weight, honored Madam, of your arguments urging haste. We also are alarmed at the possibility that others may forestall us in this laudable enterprise, and with results that could only be disastrous. I hope to call upon you when next I come to the City.

Long life and health to the Dictator.

LXIV Porcia, wife of M. Junius Brutus, to her aunt and mother-in-law, Servilia.
 [*November 26.*]

It is with respect but firmness, Madam, that I must ask you to cease to pay visits to this house. My husband has not concealed from me the reluctance he has to receive you and the relief that he feels at your departure. You will not have failed to remark that he never calls upon you in your home; you may infer from that that he receives you here only from a sense of filial duty. His agitated behavior and his troubled sleep following your visits have led me to take this action. I might well have taken it earlier, for I feel it unsuitable that I, as his wife, should be sent out of the room at each of your interviews.

You have known me for many years. You know that I am not a contentious woman and that I have previously acknowledged many an indebtedness to you. That my sisters have also been obliged to take this same action does not render it easier for me [*i.e. her sisters-in-law; apparently the wives of Cassius and Lentulus had also closed their doors to their mother*].

My husband does not know that I am writing this letter to you. I am not averse to his knowing it, if you wish to tell him so.

I thank you for your letter of sympathy on my great loss [*her miscarriage*]. I would have been more sensible of your expressions of affection and esteem, had you elsewhere shown me

that I was sufficiently a member of this household to be included in your agitating interviews with my husband.

LXIV-A Inscription.

> [*The following words were inscribed on a tablet of gold which, among other similar memorial tablets, were set into the wall behind the household altars of the Porcian and Junian families where they remained until the destruction of Rome.*]

Porcia, daughter of Marcus Porcius Cato of Utica, being married to Marcus Junius Brutus the tyrannicide, was aware that her husband was concealing from her the plans that he was then revolving for the liberation of the Roman people. On a night she plunged a dagger deep into her thigh. For many hours she gave no groan nor any sign of the great pain that consumed her. In the morning she showed her husband this wound, saying: If I have kept silent about this thing, can I not be trusted to keep the counsels of my lord? Thereupon her husband embraced her weeping and communicated all the thoughts that he had kept hidden in his soul.

LXV The Lady Julia Marcia from the Dictator's House in Rome to Lucius Mamilius Turrinus on the Island of Capri.
 [*December 20.*]

We have been going through a distressing time, my dear boy. You will forgive me, if I do not go into it at length. This terrible event [*the profanation of the rites of the Good Goddess*] has stricken us all. We leave the house as seldom as we can. We look into one another's faces, like ghosts. We are expecting some punishment—I was about to say: we wish for some punishment. But, of course, we are punished already. As you can imagine it has robbed Rome of all joy in the Feast of Saturn [*the Saturnalia began on December 17*] and my bailiff writes me that a shadow has even fallen across our hill villages. I grieve particularly for the children and the slaves, for whom this season has always been the crown of the year.

The latest news fills me with no less alarm than the scandal itself. The wicked couple has been acquitted. There is no doubt

that the judges were bribed with enormous sums by Clodius. What is there to say? We must live in a city where public opinion is overridden by money. They tell me that crowds gather all day before the houses of the judges and stand spitting against the walls and doorposts. I had a few words with Cicero this morning. He is overwhelmed with despair. His speech at the trial was the greatest he has ever made. I told him so, but he only waved his hands in the air and the tears streamed down his face.

My nephew's refusal to prosecute the matter is understandable, though I regret it profoundly. What he shrank from doing as a husband, he was not absolved of doing as the Supreme Pontiff. There is one detail about all this that I feel I must tell, though in great confidence. My nephew knew in advance that that dreadful man was coming to the rites. He could have had him seized at the door, but Caesar wished that the matter be exposed in the way it was done.

How I wish you were here, my dear Lucius. He is not himself. He has asked me to stay with him for a while. At my urging we have remained in the Public House. [*A Supreme Pontiff generally lived in the Public House on the Sacred Way, placed at his disposal by the State. Caesar, following on his wife's implication in the scandal, would have preferred to move to his house on the Palatine Hill.*] He has plunged even more deeply into work. It seems certain now that we are to go to war with the Parthians. The Isthmus of Corinth is to be pierced with a canal. The Field of Mars is to be transferred to the region at the foot of the Vatican Hill and the present Field is to contain a vast housing project. Libraries for the people are to be opened, six of them in various parts of the City. This is our tabletalk at dinner, but these are not the subjects weighing on his heart. Oh, that he had some friend here with whom he could be at ease. He does not invite his convivial companions. From time to time we are joined by Decimus Brutus and the other Brutus, but the evenings are not successful. Our friend can only extend friendship to those who first extend it warmly to him. As my husband used to say of certain people: "bold-in-love is shy-in-friendship."

Let me share another secret with you. Advance warning of Clodius's sacrilegious effrontery came to us from—of all

persons—the Queen of Egypt. It is widely believed in the City that he will marry her. That possibility would furnish ample motivation for her exposure of the dreadful plan. You have my complete assurance, however, that there is no truth in that rumor. Something happened between them; I do not know what it was. I think it plays a large part in his present dejection; I know that she is suffering. It is generally believed that we older women are very clever at divining the sentimental histories that are being lived in our vicinity. Not I. All I can say is that some stupid impediment arose to interrupt a most happy conversation. I observe that my great-nephew [*Marc Antony*] has made a journey to the east coast.

It is absurd that Caesar live here alone. We have been talking it over. The season of pretty young girls has passed. Who would be more suitable as a wife for him than our good Calpurnia, whom we have all known so long and who has carried herself with such quiet dignity through so many difficult circumstances? I think you will soon hear that she has moved into this house after the quietest of weddings.

The dogs are barking. He has just returned. I hear him greeting the household. Only one who loves him deeply can know that the good cheer in his voice is assumed. I am astonished at myself: I have loved and lost many in my long life, but never have I felt so great a helplessness before another's suffering. I do not even know its spring—or of its many possible springs, the principal one.

The next day.

This is written in haste, my dear Lucius. To whom can I speak but to you?

Strange things are happening. He too could not contain himself and spoke of it to me, with a feigned lightness. He was speaking of the many conspiracies that are continually being uncovered, plots to overturn the State and to assassinate him. He was folding and unfolding some papers in his hand. "Last year it was Marc Antony," he said. "Now it appears that Junius Brutus is thinking of these things." I drew back with horror. He leaned over me and said with a strange smile: "He cannot wait until these old bones are quiet."

Oh, that you were with us here.

LXVI Cleopatra to the Lady Julia Marcia, on her farm in the
Alban Hills.
 [*January 13.*]

Your assurance to me that you are completely recovered of
your indisposition has given me great joy. I trust that the mes-
sengers I sent daily to your door did not become a burden to
those who were attending you.

I have waited for your restoration to health to lay before you
a most urgent question. I am surrounded by a wall of enemies;
I am fortunate in this, however, that you are not only the sole
person to whom I can turn, but that you are the person best
fitted to advise me.

Gracious lady, I came to Rome in order to further the inter-
ests of the great country over which I rule. I came here as a
stranger ignorant of the customs, of the Romans and exposed
to the danger of making errors which might jeopardize my en-
tire mission. To protect myself I organized a system of ob-
servers whereby I might be kept informed of much that was
passing in the City. At no time have I used the information
which I have received in any way that might disturb the best
interests of the citizens; on a number of occasions I have been
able to serve the public order.

Through diligence and good fortune I am in a position to
follow most closely the plans of a group which designs to over-
turn the State and assassinate the Dictator. The group I speak
of is not the first that has been brought to my attention; it is
the most determined. It is not advisable that I include the
names of these conspirators in this letter.

Most gracious lady, it would be difficult for me to lay my in-
formation before the Dictator at this time. In the first place, he
might well be vexed that for a second time a woman and a for-
eigner should be informing him of a matter that so closely con-
cerns him. In the second place, a grievous mischance has
separated me from his trust and confidence. My only consola-
tion is that he knows that my loyalty to his position in the
Roman Republic is unshaken and unshakable.

The conspiratorial group to which I refer planned to murder
the Dictator as he returned at midnight on January 6 from
supervising the elections of the aldermen. Their plan was to lie

in wait about and under the bridge that crosses the rivulet by the shrine of Tebetta. On that occasion I sent anonymous letters to four of their members telling them that Caesar was aware of their intentions. They now plan to attack him as he leaves the games on 28th of January. You can understand that it would be unwise for me again to write to the conspirators and I have promised my informant who is enrolled in their number that I shall not do so.

I most urgently ask your advice on this matter, noble lady. The most obvious recourse, I realize, would be to submit this information to the head of the Dictator's confidential police. That I cannot do, however. I am only too well aware of the incompetence of that organization. It submits reports to the Dictator wherein misrepresentation masks negligence and private prejudice is set forth as assertion, important information is withheld, and trifles are enlarged.

Let me hear from you.

LXVI-A The Lady Julia Marcia to Cleopatra.
 [*By return messenger.*]

I thank you, great Queen, for your letters and again for the many marks of your concern for me during my illness.

Of this last letter: my nephew is aware in general terms of the group that you speak of. That it is the same organization and that he knows their names I am assured by the fact that he discussed the ambush at the bridge. I have no doubt, however, that your information is more detailed than his and that it is of the greatest importance. It has been a constant anxiety with me, great Queen, that he does not bring to the suppression of such conspiracies the energy and attention which he devotes to the dangers to the State.

I shall see that he learns of the plans drawn up for an attack on his life to be made on the 28th. When a suitable moment presents itself I shall let him know that we are indebted to you for this warning.

The season we are going through has been filled with so many reasons for distress and confusion that the happy hour I spent with you seems to have taken place many years ago. May

the Immortal Gods soon restore to Rome a measure of tran-
quility and may they avert from us Their just anger.

LXVII Caesar's Journal-Letter to Lucius Mamilius Turrinus
on the Island of Capri.
 [*The following entries appear to have been written
 throughout January and February.*]

 1017. [*Arguments for and against constructing a canal
across the Isthmus of Corinth.*]
 1018. [*On the increasing demand for Roman luxuries in the
cities of Gaul.*]
 1019. [*Request for volumes to stock the new public libraries.*]
 1020. You once asked me, laughing, whether I had ever
experienced the dream of the void. I told you I had, and I have
dreamed it since.

 It is perhaps occasioned by a chance posture of the sleeping
body or by some indigestion or derangement within us, but
the terror in the mind is no less real for that. It is not, as I once
thought, the image of death and the grin of the skull. It is the
state in which one divines the end of all things. This nothing-
ness, however, does not present itself to us as a blank and a
quiet, but as a total evil unmasked. It is at once laughter and
menace. It turns into ridicule all delights and sears and shrivels
all endeavor. This dream is the counterpart of that other vision
which comes to me in the paroxysm of my illness. Then I seem
to grasp the fair harmony of the world. I am filled with un-
speakable happiness and confidence. I wish to cry out to all the
living and all the dead that there is no part of the universe that
is untouched by bliss.
 [*The entry continues in Greek.*]
 Both states arise from vapors in the body, yet of both of them
the mind says: henceforth this I know. They cannot be dis-
missed as illusions. To each our memory brings many a radiant
and many a woeful corroboration. We cannot disown the one
without disowning the other, nor would I—like a village peace-
maker reconciling the differences of two contending parties—
accord to each a shrunken measure of the right.
 These last weeks, not my dream, but my waking state has

been the contemplation of futility and the collapse of all belief. Oh, worse than that: my dead call to me in mockery from their grave clothes and generations still unborn cry out, asking to be spared the clownish parade of a mortal life. Yet even in my last bitterness I cannot disavow the memory of bliss.

Life, life has this mystery that we dare not say the last word about it, that it is good or bad, that it is senseless, or that it is ordered. That all these things have been said of it is evidence only that all these things are in us. This "life" in which we move has no color and it gives no sign. As you once said: the universe is not aware that we are here.

Let me then banish from my mind the childish thought that it is among my duties to find some last answer concerning the nature of life. Let me distrust all impulses within me to say at any moment that it is cruel or kind, for it is no less ignoble from a situation of misery to pronounce life evil than from one of happiness to call it good. Let me not be the dupe of well-being or content, but welcome all experience that reminds me of the myriad cries of execration and of delight that have been wrung from men in every time.

From whom better than from you could I have learnt this? Who ever so constantly invoked the extremest ranges of yea and nay—who, but Sophocles, known throughout his ninety years as the happiest man in Greece, and yet from whom no dark secrets were hid?

Life has no meaning save that which we may confer upon it. It neither supports man nor humiliates him. Agony of mind and uttermost joy we cannot escape, but those states have, of themselves, nothing to say to us; those heavens and hells await the sense we give to them, as all living things awaited, incult and abashed, the names that Deucalion and Pyrrha pronounced over them. With this thought I dare at last to gather about me those blessed shades of my past whom hitherto I had thought of as victims of life's incoherence. I dare to ask that from my good Calpurnia a child may arise to say: On the Meaningless I choose to press a meaning and in the wastes of the Unknowable I choose to be known.

The Rome upon which I have built my life does not exist in itself save as an agglomeration of structures larger or less large than another, of citizens more or less industrious than those of

another city. Flood or folly, fire or madness may destroy it at any time. I thought myself to be attached to it by inheritance and upbringing, but such attachments have no more meaning than the beard that I shave from my face. I was called to its defense by the Senate and the Consuls; so Vercingetorix defended Gaul. No, Rome became a city for me only when I chose, as did many before me, to give it a sense and for me Rome can exist only in so far as I have shaped it to my idea. I now see that for years I childishly believed that I loved Rome and that it was my duty to love Rome because I was a Roman—as though it were possible or worthy of respect to love accumulations of stones and throngs of men and women. We are not in relationship to anything until we have enwrapped it in a meaning, nor do we know for certainty what that meaning is until we have costingly labored to impress it upon the object.

1021. [*On the rebuilding of Carthage and the construction of a mole in the Bay of Tunis.*]

1022. I was told today that a woman was waiting to see me. She entered my offices entirely veiled and not until I had dismissed my secretaries was I permitted to know that this was Clodia Pulcher.

She came to warn me that there was a conspiracy afoot to take my life and to assure me that neither herself nor her brother had any part in it. She then began to give me the names of these agitators and to tell me the days that were being selected for their attempts.

By the immortal Gods, these conspirators failed to take into account that I am the darling of women. No day goes by without new aid from these fair informers.

I was on the point of telling my visitor that I knew all this already, but I held my tongue. I saw her as an old woman sitting by the fire and remembering that she had saved the State.

There was one new fact that she was able to impart to me: these men are meditating the assassination of Marc Antony also. If that is true, they are even more inept than I had thought.

From day to day I postpone measures to frighten these tyrannicides, nor can I make up my mind what should be done with them. It has been my practice hitherto to encourage all nuisance to come to a head; it is the deed itself and not the punishment that is instructive to the public. I know not what to do.

Our friends have chosen an ill-judged moment to raise their hands against me. The City is already filling up with my veterans [*re-enlisting for the Parthian War*]. They follow me about the streets with shouts. They cup their hands before their mouths and joyously call out the names of battles we won, as though they had been carefree foot races. I ordered them into every danger and I drove them mercilessly.

These conspirators I have only overwhelmed with kindness. The majority of them I have already pardoned once. They crept back to me from the skirts of Pompey and kissed my hand in gratitude for their lives. Gratitude sours in the belly of a small man and he must puke it up. By the rivers of hell, I know not what to do with them, and I do not care. They gaze piously at the images of Harmodius and Aristogiton [*the "classic" tyrannicides of Greek history*]—but I am wasting your time.

LXVIII Inscriptions in Public Places.
 [*Cards bearing the following words were found attached to the statue of Junius Brutus, the Elder.*]

Oh, that thou wert with us now, Brutus!

Oh, that Brutus were alive!
 [*The following were found propped against the chair reserved for Brutus as Praetor of the City.*]
Brutus! Are you sleeping?

You are no Brutus!

LXVIII-A The Commonplace Book of Cornelius Nepos.
 [*From December forward Nepos entered all matters, even those dealing with early Roman history, in cypher.*]

Fr. An agitated visit. He says that he has been approached by Longshanks [*Trebonius? Decimus Brutus?*]. It was impossible to discuss the basic madness of the project. I limited myself to giving him a sound drubbing and to turning the conspiracy to ridicule. I pointed out to him that there was not a name among the agitators that was not known to my wife and to her friends; that any conspiracy which sought his adherence was bound to

fail, for he was known to be a man who could not hold his tongue; that his visit to *me* was evidence that he had not sufficient conviction in the aims of such an uprising to have any part in it; that he had nothing to contribute to it but his wealth and that a conspiracy that required wealth was a failure in advance, for money has never yet bought secrecy, courage, nor fidelity; that should this conspiracy succeed his fortune would be wiped out in five days; that there was little doubt that Caesar was in possession of the most detailed particulars and that we may expect to hear momently that the hotheads will be dragged from their homes and locked up in the caves under the Aventine Hill; and that the great man whom they are attempting to remove will probably not deign to execute them, but will send them to the shores of the Black Sea, where they can lie awake nights remembering the tumult of high noon on the Appian Way and the smell of roasting chestnuts on the steps of the Capitol. Yes, and the look on the face of the man they thought they could replace, as he mounts the steps to the platform and turns to address the guardians of Rome.

· · · ·

The City held its breath. The seventeenth [*of February*] has passed without event.

· · · ·

Every public event is now read in one light. The people are again paying the closest attention to the daily omens. Cicero is back in the City. He was seen to speak rudely to Longshanks and to pass the Blacksmith without greeting.

Since Caesar's remarriage the Queen of Egypt is suddenly very popular. Odes to her are displayed in public places. Her departure has been announced, but deputations of the citizens present themselves at her door, urging her to prolong her visit.

· · · ·

The tide of rumors has abated. A new chief and a stricter discipline? The influx of veterans?

LXIX Caesar's Journal-Letter to Lucius Mamilius Turrinus on the Island of Capri.

1023. By the immortal Gods, I am angry and I shall take pleasure in my anger.

The charge that I am the enemy of liberty was never brought against me while I commanded the armies of Rome, though, by Hercules, I so limited their movements that they could not walk a mile from their tents. They rose in the morning when I told them to and they lay down to sleep at my direction; and no one protested. The word freedom is in everyone's mouth, though in the sense that it is being used no one has ever been free or ever will be free.

In the eyes of my enemies I sit clothed in the liberties which I have stolen from others. I am a tyrant and they liken me to the potentates and satraps of the East. They cannot say that I have robbed any man of money, of land, or of occupation. I have robbed them of liberty. I have not robbed them of their voice and their opinion. I am not oriental and have not kept the people in ignorance of what they should know, nor have I lied to them. The wits of Rome declare that the people are weary of the information with which I flood the country. Cicero calls me the Schoolmaster, but he has not charged me with distorting my lessons. They are not in the slavery of ignorance nor under the tyranny of deception. I have robbed them of their liberty.

But there is no liberty save in responsibility. That I cannot rob them of because they have not got it. I have never ceased from placing before them the opportunity to assume it, but as my predecessors learned before me, they know not where to grasp it. I rejoice at the extent to which the outposts of Gaul have shouldered the burdensome freedom which I have accorded them. It is Rome which has been corrupted. The Romans have become skilled in the subtle resources for avoiding the commitment and the price of political freedom. They have become parasites upon that freedom which I gladly exercise— my willingness to arrive at a decision and to sustain it—and which I am willing to share with every man who will assume its burden. I have been watching my Praetors [*Cassius and Brutus*]. They fulfill their duties with clerklike diligence; they mutter "freedom, freedom," but not once have they raised their eyes and voices toward a greater Rome. On the contrary, they have laid before me sheaves of suggestions that would at the same time reinforce their little dignity and diminish Her greatness. Cassius wishes me to silence the enthusiasts who day by day in

public places rail against me and our edicts. Brutus wishes to safeguard the purity of our Roman blood by limiting the right to citizenship. By the immersions of Castor and Pollux, his African doorman knows better than that. That is the refusal of freedom, for it is by taking a leap into the unknown that we know we are free. The unmistakable sign of those who have refused their freedom is envy; it is the jaundice of the eye that cannot rest until it has ascribed base motives to those who do not receive but who make their freedom.

But I have reminded myself that the mind is free and my anger has passed. The mind is easily wearied and easily frightened; but there is no limit to the pictures it makes; and toward those pictures we stumble. I have often remarked that whereas men say there is a limit beyond which a man may not run or swim, may not raise a tower or dig a pit, I have never heard it said that there is a limit to wisdom. The way is open to better poets than Homer and to better rulers than Caesar. No bounds have been conceived for crime and folly. In this also I rejoice and I call it a mystery. This also prevents me from reaching any summary conclusion concerning our human condition. Where there is an unknowable there is a promise.

LXX Caesar to Brutus: Memorandum.
 [*March 7.*]
 [*In a secretary's hand.*]

The following dates are now established:

I shall leave on the seventeenth [*for the Parthian War*].

I shall return to Rome for three days on the twenty-second, should it appear advisable, to address the Senate on the electoral reform.

Billeting: the numbers [*of recruits and veterans joining up*] are exceeding my expectations. The eight temples [*assigned to them for lodging, in addition to the facilities afforded by the barracks*] may not be sufficient. Tomorrow we are moving from the Public House to the Palatine. The Public House should contain at least two hundred.

 [*Caesar continues in his own hand.*]

Calpurnia and I hope that you and Porcia will dine with

us, on the Hill, on the afternoon of the fifteenth, for my
leave-taking. We are asking Cicero, the two Marcuses [*Antony
and Lepidus*], Cassius, Decimus, Trebonius, and their wives, that
have them. The Queen of Egypt will be with us after dinner.

So great is the pleasure that I take in your company, and in
that of Porcia, that I could wish that you alone were our guests
at that time. Since there will be others present, let me avail my-
self of this opportunity to lay upon you an injunction justified
by our long friendship and by the kind offers of service which
you have frequently made to me.

The separation from my dear wife will be hard for me; it will
be hard for her. I shall rejoin her for a short time next autumn
in Dalmatia or—without public notice—at Capri. In the mean-
time, I could know no greater consolation than to be assured
that you and Porcia were holding her in your loves. To Porcia
she has been bound by a close friendship since childhood; to
you she bears the esteem which your character and your loyalty
to me deserve. There is no second home that she could fre-
quent with more profit and none to which my thoughts would
more frequently have preceded her.

LXX-A Brutus to Caesar.
 [*March 8.*]
 [*The following is the unfinished draft of a letter which
 was not sent.*]

I have taken note of the arrangements you have reported
to me.

It is with regret that I must say that I shall not be able to be
among your guests on the fifteenth. It has more and more
become my practice to devote to study the few hours remaining
to me at the close of the day.

I shall indeed, during your absence, seek to be useful to
Calpurnia Piso in every way that I can. I think it well, however,
that you consign her to the particular attention of others than
myself, more active in the social life and less preoccupied by
public business.

Your letter speaks, great Caesar, of my loyalty to you. I am
glad you have done so, for it makes clear to me that you accord
to loyalty the same meaning that I do. You will not have for-

gotten that I took up arms against you and received your pardon and that you have permitted me on many occasions to express opinions contrary to your own. From this I assume that you accept the loyalty of those who are first loyal to themselves and that you recognize that such loyalties may often come into conflict.

Your letter speaks, great Caesar, of my loyalty to you. That you have done so is——

It is with regret that I must reply to you that my wife's ill-health will prevent our——

. . . before your departure, to express a measure of the gratitude I bear to you. That indebtedness I cannot repay. Since earliest childhood I have received——

I have taken note of the arrangements you have reported to me.

INGRATITUDE BASEST OF ALL THOUGHTS AND AC

[*The following phrases are in early Latin. They appear to be an oath used in courts of law.*]

"Oh, Jupiter, unseen and all-seeing, who readest the hearts of men, witness now that what I declare is true, and if there be any fault in it, may . . ."

Three yards of wool, medium weight, finished in the manner of Corinth; one stylus, trimmed fine; three broad lamp wicks.

My wife and I shall, indeed, with pleasure, that so great an oak, not forgetting him on whom shall rest the last glance of those great eyes, not without surprise and never to be forgotten so.

LXX-B Brutus to Caesar.
 [*As sent.*]

I have taken note of the arrangements you have reported to me.

Porcia and I shall come to you with pleasure on the fif-
teenth.

Rest assured, great Caesar, that for her own sake and for
yours, we love Calpurnia no less than ourselves and that we shall
not be happy until she looks upon our home as her own.

LXXI Caesar's Journal-Letter to Lucius Mamilius Turrinus
on the Island of Capri.

1023. I have been remiss in writing to you. The days have
been filled with preparations for my departure.

I am impatient to be off. My absence will constitute no in-
considerable gift to the City which is as harassed as I am by the
continual rumors of sedition. It is ironical, is it not, that in my
absence these men are powerless to alter the government and
that when I have passed the Caspian Sea they have no choice
but to return to their proper duties.

Their number appears to include some fifty members of the
Senate, many of them holding the highest positions in the
City. I have given that fact the grave consideration it deserves
and I remain unshaken.

The Athenians passed a vote of censure on Pericles. Aristides
and Themistocles were driven by them into exile.

In the meantime, I guard myself, within reason, and I con-
tinue my occupations.

My son [*i.e., his nephew Octavius, formally adopted in his will
which was written in September but not yet made public*] returns
to Rome soon after my departure. He is an excellent young
man. I particularly rejoice that he has written me of his high
regard for Calpurnia. I have told her that he will afford her the
companionship of an older brother, nay, of an uncle. Octavius
traversed his youth in a year and is now well advanced into his
middle age. His letters are not less sententious than those in *The
Correspondence of Telemachus* [*a "model letter writer" widely
used in schools*].

Th great Queen of Egypt is returning to her country, having
learned more about us than many who have spent a lifetime
here. To what uses she will put that knowledge, to what uses she
will put her ever-astonishing self it would be hard to say. There
is a gulf between men and animals; I have always thought it to

be narrower than many suppose. She possesses the rarest endowments of the animal and the rarest endowments of the human being; but of that quality that separates us from the swiftest horse, the proudest lion, and the shrewdest serpent she has no inkling: she knows not what to do with what she has. Too wise to be gratified by vanity; too strong to be content with ruling; too large for wife. With one greatness she is in perfect harmony and on that score I did her a great injustice. I should have permitted her to bring her children here. She does not know it yet to the full; she is that figure which all countries have elevated to the highest honor and awe: she is the mother as goddess. Hence those wonderful traits that I was so long in explaining to myself—her lack of malice, and her lack of that fretful unease to which we are so wearisomely accustomed in beautiful women.

I bring my precious Calpurnia to you next autumn.

LXXII Calpurnia to her sister Lucia.
 [*March 15.*]

Each day, before this departure, grows more precious. I am ashamed that I had not realized before more clearly the fortitude that is required of a soldier's wife.

Yesterday afternoon we dined with Lepidus and Sextilia. Cicero was there and the company was very merry. Later my husband said he had never felt such friendship for Cicero, or from him; and this in spite of the fact that they baited one another with such sharpness that Lepidus did not know where to rest his eyes. My husband gave an account of the revolution of Catiline as though it had been a rebellion of mice against a worried cat called Cicero. He rose from the table and darted about the room peering into the wrong corners. Sextilia was laughing so that she got a stitch in her side. I find a new husband every day.

We came away early and before dark. My husband asked if I would let him show me some places that he loved. I was anxious to be off the streets, as you may well imagine, but I have learned not to urge caution on him. I know that he is well aware of the danger and chooses these risks in all consciousness. He walked beside my litter, followed by a few guards. I

called his attention to an enormous Ethiopian who seemed also to be following us. He explained that he had once promised the Queen of Egypt that he would never object to the presence of this attendant who has since appeared and disappeared mysteriously, sometimes standing all night before our house and sometimes following him about for three days at a time. He is, indeed, a terrifying figure, but my husband appears to be very fond of him and was continually addressing remarks to him.

The high wind was rising that was soon to turn to storm. We went down the hill and into the Forum, stopping, dear Lucia, at this and that while he recalled a moment in history and in his own life. How he rests his hands on what he loves and how he gazes into my eyes to make sure that I am sharing his memory! We went into little dark streets and he put his hand against the house where he had lived for ten years as a young man. We stood at the foot of the Capitol. Even when the storm broke and the passersby fled by us like leaves, he would not hasten his steps. He made me drink from the spring of Rhea [*reputed to insure fecundity*]. How is it that I can be the happiest of women, and yet so filled with foreboding?

Our little trip was all unwise. We both passed a most disturbed night. I dreamed that the pediment of the house had been lifted in the storm and dashed upon the pavement. I awoke to find him groaning beside me. He awoke and flung his arms about me and I could feel the loud beating of his heart.

Oh, may the Immortal Gods watch over us.

This morning he is not well. He was fully dressed and ready to set out for the Senate when he changed his mind. He returned to his desk for a moment and has fallen asleep there, which his secretaries tell me has never happened before.

Now he has awakened and gone off, after all. I must hurry and prepare for the guests this evening. I am ashamed of this letter, so womanish.

Suetonius: The Lives of the Caesars: Book One.
[*Probably written some seventy-five years later.*]

When he sat down, the conspirators thronged about him and Tillius Cimber, who had put himself at the head of them, came close to him as though he were about to ask a question. When Caesar with a gesture tried to hold him at a distance, Cimber seized hold of his toga at both shoulders. As Caesar exclaimed: "Then this is violence!" one of the Cascas, standing at his side, plunged a dagger into him, just below the throat. Caesar caught hold of Casca's arm and ran his pen through it; but as he tried to rise to his feet he was held down by another stab. When he saw that he was surrounded on all sides by drawn daggers, he wrapped his head in his robe at the same time drawing its folds about his feet with his left hand so that when he fell the lower part of his body would be decorously covered.

In this manner then he was stabbed twenty-three times. He said no word, merely groaned at the first stroke, though certain writers have said that when Marcus Brutus fell upon him he said in Greek, "You, too, my son!"

All the conspirators took themselves off and left him lying there dead for some time. Finally three common slaves put him on a litter and carried him home, one arm hanging down over the side.

Antistius the physician said that of all those wounds only the second one in the breast would have proved fatal.

EARLY STORIES

The Marriage of Zabett

IN the days when Martinus Scheihoffen was pursuing the
Devil with forty armed men about the yellow lakes, there
lived in the village of Kaage a woman named Zabett der Derken.
Her father, Peder, the merchant, was a rich man, and it was on
his gold pieces that the family enjoyed a merry life made up of
guests and drinking. On the feast days, Zabett loved to go to
church and muse with closed eyes on the sufferings of the saints.
At such times she regretted her idle life, but when she left the
church and stopped in the sunlight, laughing and mocking
with the women, she wondered if anything were ever better
than gossiping on the church porch. Zabett was past the age
when most girls marry, and, although she was beautiful and
sought-after and enjoyed most the laughter and talk with the
men, she remembered how when a man tried to catch hold of
her hands, the touch set her a-trembling, and thereafter she lay
shuddering the whole night through. This she could not ex-
plain, and it made her afraid.

One day her father gave her a string of pearls—pear-shaped
—of which every alternate pearl was rose-colored; this, he said,
was sent to her from his new partner in Lubeck. Her father
said nothing more about it until, a month later, he gave her a
stuckle for her dress, of cloth-of-gold, with the three towers of
Lubeck embroidered on it in black thread; this, he said, was
sent her by Jans Ketterlingen, his new partner in Lubeck. From
then on, Zabett thought often of the stranger, whose portrait,
dark-smiling, and holding in his hand astronomical instru-
ments, hung in her father's counting-house. At last the day
came when her father stopped her, lifting her hands from the
organum on which she was playing, and told her that his part-
ner at Lubeck, one Jans Ketterlingen, had heard often of her
beauty and high spirits and would come in a month to Kaage
to ask for her in marriage. This intention he must declare to
her before his visit, since his stay in the village must not exceed
two or three days. Zabett smiled shyly up at her father as he put
into her hands an inlaid box from the Turks, a gift from Myn-
heer Ketterlingen of Lubeck,—and she forgot, foolish girl,

how when some man stole a kiss from her in the dance, she turned pale and sickened and shuddered.

After that when she went to church and pondered upon the exhaustion and sufferings of the holy men and women who had hungered and gone naked and bled and died for the love of God, she mentioned in her prayers to them a new name, and in her mind were the delicate hands and black beard of Ketterlingen, her betrothed. The thought of him induced a new mood in her, and after the congregation had left the church and the old stableman was blowing out the lamps, she went up to the altar and wonderingly put her hands upon the wounded feet of the statue, and looked musingly into the suffering eyes, remembering the whole of His story. And the time drew on when Mynheer was daily expected.

On the very afternoon of Jans' arrival, the two walked through the fields together, and he spoke to her of the cause of his coming and the brevity of his visit; then he fell silent, waiting for her to speak. Zabett suddenly felt the grain quiver, and terror of the man slid into her heart as water rushes into the lungs of a drowning man. But she could not answer him, no, for about her neck rested the pearls of two colors; on her shoulders floated his scarf and at home her mother was kneading the wedding breads. Moreover, that evening she did not cry out when, seated by the fire, he took her in his arms and kissed her, albeit she suffered the fire of fires, such as burns for heretics.

That night the wretched woman left the house, ran through the cold, wet streets, and kneeling in the church porch, cast herself with a sudden surrender into the wisdom of God. Then was the whole porch illuminated with a pulsing light, and the door of the church was opened by a hand unseen. She went in, and flinging herself upon the pavement, rehearsed before a great and mystical company the history of her stony heart; how that a lifelong blindness had prevented her seeing that the warning of her body was a result of the jealous care of her heavenly husband, to whom she had been betrothed since the hills were made. And a voice answered her: "Go back, Zabett, delay thy marriage with the merchant of Lubeck. Live a little longer as a child of the world, until the sign of thy release be shown in a sudden hour. Let no one mark a change in thee." And Zabett arose and returned home.

Oh, to tell of the torments of a life unaltered about an altered spirit. What groanings she suppressed as she went about her daily life, laughing and chattering in the church porch with the women of Kaage. She persuaded Jans to put off the date of the marriage, but his caresses she could not put off, and often she would hide from him, trembling, behind doors and hangings. She talked long to her father and mother, but in her heart she strained away from the increasing discussion of gold and wedding-feasts and respectable guests, to listen to the attributes of God and the lengths to which a soul may approach unto them. So she waited for the miraculous intimation of her release.

But none came. At last she could delay the wedding no longer, nor did it seem that she could any longer feign merriment and gaiety; the strange struggle had left strange wounds. Ah, Zabett, distracted wert thou on the eve of thy wedding; thou lookedst for signs on earth and in the sky and in the flights of birds. No archangel burned against the sunset; no virgin mother smiled from among the first stars; the moon arose not out of due season; no trees were visited by unconsuming flame; no visitor with unmistakable eyes knocked at thy door. Nay, saintly lady, but in thy last and frantic hour, as thou satst yearning at the window, three white and delicate feathers floated against thy face and cooled thy eyelids and thy wan brow. And a voice distant and tremulous said: "Take nothing with thee. Go. Found for me an order of women, bound by vows to expect my return daily." Then Zabett arose with a glad heart, and taking in her hand a penny for bread in the morning, she stole forth into the dusk. But as she ran, she lost her way thrice, and thrice came into a street that ended in a stone wall, where a voice said: "Trust in God." The third time she understood, and threw away the penny which she carried; straightway the stone wall disappeared, and she went on rejoicing.

This was the St. Zabett of Kaage who founded the great convent wherein I write these words; me and many another she spared from that exile of a woman's soul from Heaven, the marriage of the body. She is our intervention; without her we should be dead, slain by the caresses of our husbands.

1917

"Spiritus Valet"

"THE record of Sebastian Torr's life is the meagrest we have of any great poet's life since antiquity. It is full of strange silent periods during which the poet seems to have entirely disappeared, and among these perhaps the most conspicuous is the hiatus that bridges the century, that between 1896 and 1902. From out of this dark age the only evidence of the poet's continued existence issued in the shape of the seven short but matchless lyrics to 'the golden-haired lady.' The present biographer does not despair of some day identifying this lady and obtaining from her many facts, letters, and perhaps poems. Until then we can only marvel at the complete obscurity in which the world so often allows its greatest geniuses to remain."

This paragraph was lightly marked in Mrs. Manners' copy of Frederick Burton's Life of Sebastian Torr. In fact many paragraphs were marked, for Mrs. Manners was one of the few people who had known the poet *as* the poet. Many, no doubt had known him as a man—many thousand one might say, remembering his travels—but that without ever remotely suspecting that the dark magnetic gracious listener was the great self-concealing poet, the eternal incognito. But he had left a clew with Mrs. Manners by which, a little time after his departure, she was able to know that her reticent acquaintance had been her favorite poet. She has always been glad to tell the little she remembered of the great man; how he rented in 1895 her mother's cottage in Brookline for a few spring months, and how when he went away, never to be heard from directly in this connection, he left her (as though from a delicate gratefulness for the enjoyment he had received from the gardens, an enjoyment for which "paying the rent" fell ludicrously short of making amends) a sheaf of poems on the tree and flower life he had found there. She received them under the name he was at that time availing himself of, and it was only when she saw them published as his in the magazine that she realized her privilege, and that the quiet-voiced abstracted tenant was Sebastian Torr.

Her account of this acquaintance with the great man she made as casual and detached as was fitting, especially during

the lifetime of her husband to whom the few slender anecdotes that made up her little contribution to the Torr cult became a weariness. At the time of the poet's death, when the interest in his life and work rose to so tremendous a height, she was called on daily for the memoir by enthusiastic friends, and she herself grew to be weary of the little set piece to which her originally spontaneous recital had degenerated.

She seemed to herself to be growing weary of many more things than this daily. It frightened her a little that she was indifferent to her friends, to the arts and to every form of social recreation. Her mind was full of the refrain that she must soon be saying farewell to her admired golden hair, and to her voice and to her lustrous young distinction. In a sense she was willing to give them up since the flood of ennui had born away her vanity with her other enthusiasms; but in another sense she wanted them a little longer; until, say, she could make one big stroke with them before she resigned them. Her desire was to enter middle age and the forties with some really great gesture. Without that she would feel she had never been really young: "without some stunning termination to it," she told herself— "youth will have seemed to have had about it always something of middle age; every period of life should mark itself off from its succeeding time, or life will seem to have been one long old age."

These wan thoughts had been much in her mind the day that Mr. Frederick Burton called, but only after he had been many moments gone did she realize that in the object of his visit lay the opportunity she waited for. He had called on her many years before, when he was at work on his biography of Torr, and taken down the little set piece which in due time came to fill a page and a half in the "life." She had given him the manuscript of the Garden Verses to preserve in the safe of the New York Sebastian Torr Society. He came to her now from the hall without formalities and, with a kind of fierceness, plunged into the object of his visit immediately. He demanded of her all the letters and verses she had received at any time from Sebastian Torr and she which had so subtly concealed.

"But, Mr. Burton, I never received a letter from him," she replied in a daze.

He laughed incredulously. "How successful you have been.

And how you have been smiling at us all these years. Of course you are 'the golden-haired lady.' By making your telling of the story so indifferent, you felt sure you put our observation to sleep."

"No, you are entirely mistaken, Mr. Burton. You must find some other golden-haired lady. My acquaintance with Torr was just as I have related it, no more, no less."

"Your reticence does you a certain credit, Mrs. Manners, and I assure you we expected it. These poems about you were written in the 'lost interval' just succeeding his meeting with you in '95. Your husband was alive at the time, and the secrecy with which he wrapped himself about in the years that followed, is due to his honorable desire to shield you from any possible imputation. You see, Mrs. Manners, denial is no longer possible; the case is perfectly clear."

Mrs. Manners had been too long starved of just this sort of excitement to realize that this speech constituted an insult to her. The only thing she recognized in it was a soothing flattery. "You will have to believe me. I have no letters; I have no secrets."

"I realize, Mrs. Manners," he replied in a lower voice, ignoring her protest, "that such letters as you possess must be of an intimate nature. We do not ask you to make public any passages in them that might place you in a difficult position. I want you to feel that I am a friend and fellow-enthusiast with whom you may discuss the matter with perfect confidence. The lives of both of us have centered about the same man." It was in this vein that he pleaded with her for little less than half an hour, against the steady increase of her disclaimer. At the end of that time she asked him a little brusquely to leave her, since he would not believe her statement. He retreated slowly, calling on the ceiling to witness that he would return again and again until he had shown Mrs. Manners that any slight sacrifice she could make of her selfish reticence would bring all the lovers of literature in the world with thank-offerings to her door.

From behind her window-curtains she saw his silk-hat stoop as he entered his limousine. "Could it be possible," she asked herself, "that he is paying a series of calls on a number of golden-haired ladies, of whom perhaps *I* am the least likely? Or does he really believe me to to have been the Beatricé of modern time? Perhaps already he has spread his assurance that I am the

subject of Torr's greatest work." And then after she had mused
a while she started suddenly. "What harm would it do if I en-
couraged the rumor a little, if without saying yes I could sigh
and grow pale and change the subject?" She played with the
idea a while. "And then sometime burst out into a momentary
blaze of anger, asking them never to mention that name to me
again, and so return the next day humbly begging their par-
don! Why, that would be Romance. I might even, if I dared,
write the letters myself."

This terrible thought held her rigid for a moment. A strange
warning tremor passed over her mind, like a chill wind that
rises before dawn above the lowlands. "Why not?" she asked her-
self, in a defiant mood. "He is dead; it cannot harm him—I
shall start them tonight!" Suddenly an exhausting turmoil
swept her mind as though the wind on the lowlands had
reached the sea and was struggling with it. She felt it only as
some force in her nature that was combating her intention,
and to this force she cried almost aloud that *she would do it.*

II

"Dearest Judith, I have been struggling alone in this dark
boarding-house ever since Saturday morning. Tell me what I
am to do. I cannot live unless I see you every day. I cry aloud
(my arms feel unreal for lack of thee), and like Sappho, I am as
pale as the grass under the snow. My only comfort is my re-
solve that I too shall 'write of you such things as have never been
written of any woman,' and it is because of this promise that I
am asking you to let me meet you once more. I have written a
little poem about you as it is, but I will not send it to you; you
must come and take it from me."

It was very late, but she wrote on in a kind of adventurous
fever. She was closing up the chapter of her youth with as fine
a flourish as any woman had ever achieved. But still from time to
time that warning sensation would return, a mental suffering
so acute that it passed into the physical as naturally as water
passes into ice.

"I will expect a telegram from you any minute, my terrible
flower, telling me when you are coming. You must send a
telegram or I will be expecting you to come in the door every

moment, and *that* would be terrible. Oh, the agony of thinking that every time a door opens it is you, and that every footstep on the stair is yours, knowing all the while that you may never come at all. So do not leave me to expect a surprise visit from you, or you will find me dead."

There was a knock on the door. Mrs. Manners quickly hid her writing materials and opened it. Mrs. Drury, her housekeeper, stood in the hall with her hands crossed below her throat. She gazed at Mrs. Manners with speechless terror in her eyes.

"Well, what is it? What is it you want?"

Mrs. Drury was still trying to regain the control of her voice. The sight of the warm room and shaded lamp had begun to dispel her fear, and embarrassment was adding to her difficulty.

"Has something happened to you, Mary? Why are you staring at me so. Can you speak?"

"Are you alone, Mrs. Manners?" she at length brought out, peering into the room.

"Of course, I'm alone. Can you tell me, Mary, what has happened to you?" Mrs. Manners began to feel very exactly what was the matter with her housekeeper, but she did not stoop to the artifice of asking her if the house was on fire or the silver stolen. She was shaken by that vehement force within her, that she came to know so well, the force that was set against her writing the great letters. "Come in and sit down, if you wish to, Mary."

"No, thank you. I seemed suddenly taken with a great sorrow at something and a great fright, Mrs. Manners. You will forgive my interrupting you. When our moods are greater than our wills we can do nothing. I had a feeling as though there were a great sorrow and wrong on the stairs. It brought back to my mind all that I have been through. . . . I have felt that way on the seashore. . . . Goodnight."

Mrs. Manners had found nothing to say. She was herself struggling with uneasiness and amazement. She turned back to her table, murmuring and moving her lips: "I shall finish these letters in spite of you!" As she opened the drawer the sheaf of manuscript seemed to rise, as with a flurry of wind and floating into the air, fell about her chair with a soft and piteous motion. The determination in her words had led her to opening the drawer suddenly; the release of the air-current was due to that,

she explained to herself. Oh, this thing that she had to fight, this thing that she had to fight, she had learned now how to torment it. She had to write a passage like this to fairly feel it groan or grow malignant or frozen with suffering:

"My dear Judith, all the oceans will be too shallow for my drowning if you do not come away with me. You must pity me because my love is so full of hate, but is so true that I become strong in saying it to you. What bond have you with your husband that you must keep me always outside of your life. You have made me a dweller of the shadow, one who must always wait around the corner, and I call myself the night-brother of the street-lamps. I sat in Washington Square half the night looking upon your window, when for a few moments you could so easily have stolen out to me. All the oceans of the world will be too shallow for my drowning if you do not come away with me soon. Your torn Sebastian."

She penned this letter with an intentional cruelty. She had long since personified to herself this attendant warning. She told herself that it was the remnant of her conscience in the matter, protesting against her literary deception. She loved to see it wring its hands, or stagger back as though struck when she penned some more than usually audacious line. And during this letter she was keeping one triumphant eye on its suffering. She was only half ready for it, therefore, when it sprang at her, mentally or physically, she could not tell. She remained unconscious a long time, fallen upon the floor; and when she rose she found the ink-bottle spilled upon the page. In the cold dawn and with terror at her heart she wondered whether it was her own arm that had struck the ink-bottle in falling or whether it was this Thing that had at last definitely passed through into the physical world. She resolved that she was only partly beaten, that although she would write no more letters she would carry such as she had to Mr. Burton that very day.

She spent the morning in the sunlight of her breakfast-room copying the letters into an old diary, using diluted ink. Since she could not hope to imitate Torr's handwriting her only chance lay in pretending that she had carefully copied the letters as they came, into a very private diary, and then had destroyed the originals. She, therefore, interspersed her record with such items as this, borrowed from old letters to herself: "My mother

arrived in town today in a critical state. We pray that it is not a return of the old trouble." or: "To the Opera this evening. Nordica very fine indeed. John has begun to talk again of our going to Europe. I can not sleep for worrying over the wretched boy, from whom I received the following two letters today. If we go to Europe I suppose he will kill himself. I feel quite sure that he was watching my return from the Opera, although I did not see him on any of the nearer park benches. Something seems to tell me when he is watching me. What shall I do, what shall I do?"

She finished copying about noon. In the sunlight the Thing had been unable to even make her aware of its presence; of the eight different ink-bottles she used in the diary, not one had spilt. But she felt that over herself the effect of the previous night's experience lay heavily. It seemed that the lustre of her hair had begun then to fade. She had no time to lose; if the festival she had planned to close her youth with did not take place soon she would have to go to it as though to the obsequies of youth themselves. And it was from humorous fear of such an event that she ordered her car for three that afternoon, and climbed into it, clutching the manuscript, with a kind of undue haste.

She had made her appointment to meet Mr. Burton at the rooms of the Torr Society at three-thirty and suddenly she felt a little ashamed of her anticipation of the hour. She resolved to keep him waiting a while and told the chauffeur to follow the length of the Drive as fast as he wished since there were very few cars out, the day being overcast. She sat in the shadow, not gazing out, still holding the diary tightly. As the first great drops of rain began to fall the impulse came to her to read what she had written. She turned the pages at random:

"Judith Radiant-Head, I have been made happy all day by a chance word you let fall Friday morning. I wonder if you remember, before I tell you, what it is. You said that the thought of me had been clinging about you all day like the Queen of Night's aria from *The Magic Flute*. It was love that prompted you to that remark, and it is my literary sense that tells me this time that you are in love with me; I enjoy an evidence, you see, that other people cannot so confidently summon. I too shall en-

deavor to give my life up to saying such authentic things of my love for you that people will say: 'this man loved,' before they say: 'this poet wrote.' That too is why I am so strangely happy today—Sebastian."

Suddenly, by hallucination, she saw the poet sitting beside her, searching her face, and with hand outstretched for the diary. She was never to be in doubt for a moment as to whether she had seen a "spirit" or merely a projection of her too long brooding fancy; this was an evocation of her own mind. But the Thing was present too, and the battle was to take place on the obdurate field of her mind once more. She thrust the book into her coat, crying out: "I am resolved. This is to be my new life." A grateful unconsciousness again fell upon her.

III

Mrs. Manners had been obliged to dismiss her secretary. Very likely the girl was on the point of asking for release as it was. It would only be another indication—but of what? Of a sudden change of attitude to her, of course. But why? Why, after receiving from twenty to fifty invitations and social notes in every day's mail, why had the number sunk to five or six timid ventures? The sales of her booklet were still mounting; the play which was supposed to have been based on her story, as seen in the tragic letters, was still drawing crowds; all the greater evidences of her supreme distinction were still hung high over the world of culture, but she herself was being so suddenly left to her bewilderment. Surely society had not taken offence suddenly at the passionate character of the letters addressed to her, or at the controlled response that the letters implied as her part in the relationship. These aspects had been generously condoned by the reviewers with a kind of gallant haste. Mr. Burton's preface had drawn a picture of himself as literally wresting the letters from the tearfully reluctant lady after long hours of argument. No, the attitude of New York to her now had no resemblance to that of a group merely shocked or scandalized. And as she would sit and ask herself these questions for the thousandth time a chill fear would creep over her heart, a chill she had grown so used to that it seemed to her to be

nothing more than one of the many human weaknesses of mind that man is burdened with, as though this consciousness of fate threatened even the happiest of us.

It had come to her first (as though to replace the choking sensations she had had to endure during the writing of the letters) the moment after she had read the request from the Torr Society that she speak to them at their annual banquet. It had come to her tremendously at the banquet itself. And oh, how many times since in the very midst of those great worldly receptions that had been given for her, after the publication of the diary. Above the music, the conversation, and the laughter on the stairs, she could hear the approach of a reversal, a sudden knife-thrust through the silk.

She tried to examine again the direction that the world's attitude to her had taken. Was it indifference, or was it revulsion? Indifference does not fall so suddenly on a favorite, not even in New York. Then if it was revulsion, was it because of something in her story in the past, something in her present personality, or something that had been murmured about against her? All three must have contributed to it, she told herself sadly, and perhaps this was the fate she had so long felt to be poised above her. Then there would be a compensation in its fall, if it was no worse than this. She could retire to a New England village—but how little she felt like retiring after this taste of real power!—and enter upon her middle age as a great lady of almost legendary character, albeit the legend dark and forbidding (since New York would have it so).

The door-bell rang. So there was still some one in town with the courage to call upon her? Someone to whom perhaps she could put this question of importance. The butler announced a lady who would not give her name. This deviation from convention was enough to arouse Mrs. Manners' alarm to unreached heights; she turned to the door as though to defend herself. She felt herself to be shaking with her fears. After a pause there faced her a quietly dressed middle-aged lady of severely lovely aspect. Her face was modeled by a carefully guarded serenity, as though serenity itself was the earnest of spiritual treasure. Her eyes had a slow regard that was of the essence of control. No expression could have been more likely to break

through the barrier of Mrs. Manner's making, built as it was of her fears, her unsound "clutch" on distinction, her inexperience (the result of her long egotistical happy solitude) and her timorous antagonism. The visitor did not show any intention of shaking hands with Mrs. Manners.

"I have read the book of the letters," she said calmly. "I know that they are a pure invention of your own."

Mrs. Manners was able to muster a little presence of mind. "Who are you?" she asked with considerable spirit.

"I am the real 'golden-haired lady,'" she replied as the smile left her face. "I have the letters, I have the material, and after my death the book is to appear. Until then you may live in this dishonorable dishonor. You have committed the great offense. You have dealt with another's personality irreverently. It is as great an offense against the dead as against the living."

"Then if your book is coming out after your death to refute me. . . ."

"Why do I come to you now? To charge you with deception, merely because it gives me pleasure?"

"I suppose that is it." Mrs. Manners was gradually gathering herself together.

"No," replied her visitor. "I was sent."

"*He* sent you. I see now. He came to me first. . . . You know that he came to me first?"

"And when he found that he could not persuade you to abandon your intention, he tried to reach our physical means of restraining you. . . . But they cannot make use of them. They cannot steal or strike. . . . But they have agents of their own, spiritual agents, intuition and subtle perceptions. And it is to the lowest of these that he has stooped, in order to discredit the effect of the injury you have done him. He has made use of Rumor. You are now given over to Rumor. I have heard you discussed on the street and in the papers. You are helpless against the whispers of a city."

"All this cannot frighten me. I ask nothing better than a long retirement. I have always been company enough for myself." Mrs. Manners spoke with false assurance. There are ways, she was telling herself, of climbing out of such difficulties as she was now in; she might reveal her own deception, for in-

stance, claiming it to have been a literary *tour-de-force*, such *jeux* are common enough in France. "How did you receive your messages from this man?" she asked.

"We are not separated," she answered, turning to go. Mrs. Manners did not detain her. But watching from behind her window-curtains she saw her joined by a companion, a tall reticent thoughtful young man.

1918

Eddy Greater

THE fall of 190- I spent in London collecting material for my *Life and Works of Sebastian Torr* for the English Sebastian Torr Society. This task, I soon found, could merely end in my serving cold my predecessor's data as to this strange, obscure poet of the previous generation. I could only annotate super-abundantly the thin book of verse that was his, retell the handful of anecdotes, and deduce lamely from them the shadowy career of a poet. It was in a fit of despondency following this discovery, that I endeavored to beguile a rainy afternoon by visiting the gift shops of the city, tentatively searching for a wedding present. The marriage was still afar off, so under the removed urgency I wandered from shop to shop, marvelling at length over their servile adherence to type. Mrs. Creighley's, ultimately arrived at, concentrated the elements. It was dark and narrow; very few *objets d'art* were exposed to the visitor: here and there under glass lay objects of hand-hammered silver, necklaces meandering among the folds of claret velvet; a few examples of Chinese pottery, consummately cracked and holding rock lilies whose bulbs had been scoured for their high lights; little trays of uncut jewels, carelessly displayed—tourmaline, aquamarine, stones prized for their negative watery tints. Mrs. Creighley likewise represented a type. She was handsome in a business way; she wore draperies rather than gowns, yet gave an impression of efficiency and shrewdness. A portion of her stock-in-trade had found its way to her person, a gun-metal chain on an odd enamel ring. Her appreciation of her "little things" was too readily ecstatic and her voice low but over-rich. In her Commerce was flattering Art by imitation, to the embarrassment of Art.

This excellent woman was engaged, upon my entrance, with two ladies who were spreading bits of brocade critically upon their knees, and matching jewels with them. Her quick welcoming smile, however, urged me to take my liberty of the shop, which I did, arriving at last in the further corner upon a pile of what appeared to be framed texts. I found them to be autographed letters: Whistler inviting a lady to dinner; Dégas

making an appointment with a model; the menu card of a din-
ner given by the brothers Goncourt, signed by all the guests
with much too lively maxims and nicknames. The name these
documents enjoyed in common was the familiar Eddy Greater,
the soubrette of the seventies, who was in the height of her fame
during the years of Sebastian Torr's last illness. The reading I had
done for a study of his period was full of her engaging figure.
The successive light operas of Offenbach were then enjoying
tremendous runs in Paris and London, culminating in "La
Bôite au Lait" and "Madame Favart," bright theatrical things,
full of gay tunes and famous women. The musical actresses of
the seventies, who remembers them now? Mildred Palmer,
with the face of a sheep and her mass of copper-colored hair,
maintained by the son of a famous Scotch peer until the arrival
of her dropsical millionaire from India. Little Manina Shayer,
who is reported to have sung *A Soldier's Maid* eight thousand
times. They all drove their carriages in Hyde Park, made flam-
boyant descents on Paris, and drove the organized society of
modest ladies of fashion to a jealous distraction. Eddy Greater
was not as magnificent in manner as Mildred Palmer, nor did
she command as socially distinguished a clientele; she was not
as pretty as Manina Shayer, nor as good a singer; nor was she
the clever actress that was Rosalie Barlow. But she was the most
intelligent and the most versatile of all the great lights-of-love.
The men of letters of the time, such as were unmarried and
unprincipled, flocked to her dinners and even galloped beside
her in the park, if they were in society, or sent verses to her if
they were not.

One often wondered what became of them as time went on.
In the first place, that type of musical play went out, under the
press of Gilbert and Sullivan; newer prima donnas, more in-
genuous and better chaperoned, took their places. The old fel-
lows in the club used to say that Mildred Palmer followed her
millionaire to India and now looked very much like a rajah's
lady; and that Manina Shayer, whose mixed blood became
more and more evident with time, retired to a plantation in
the West Indias with a quadroon. Well, what became of Eddy
Greater, a part of whose correspondence I was discovering,
framed and passe-partouted?

"Ah, you've the autographs!" murmured Mrs. Creighley,

suddenly appearing at my elbow and lighting a discreet lamp. "Of course I can't show them to everyone."

"They're of the greatest interest. Where did you get them?" I asked.

"Oh, they've belonged to a cousin of mine, a very interesting woman. She used to sing on the stage when she was a girl, and these were addressed to her. A Mrs. Clarke."

"Oh, she was . . . Mrs. Clarke was . . . the . . . ?"

"Yes. She bore the absurd name of Eddy Greater. Fancy calling yourself Eddy! She enjoyed a certain fame in her day. You wouldn't have remembered her very likely. But look at the correspondence! Whistler, Zola, Manet. . . . I'm asking three-for-a-pound, though I'm really quite frightened to show them to some people—some people, that is, mightn't understand!"

"She might have some really interesting—"

"Oh, yes. There's a great deal more than this. But she won't part with it. She has all sorts of manuscripts and little sketches. She only allows me to sell these, because—well, to tell the truth —I believe her resources are very low. I like to help her, of course!"

"Is she in London?"

"Yes, indeed, she is. She's in the shop."

I looked about me vaguely.

"She's in my office in back! She's having a cup of tea with me. I fancy she's brought some more things to sell me, but— it's a *real* struggle for her, you know. To give them up, I mean."

"Could you present me to her, Mrs. Creighley? My card, here. I've been engaged in studying the lives of many of these men—"

"Oh, she wouldn't open her mouth to you. She sits there, so—for hours. But sometimes she's lively enough, Heaven knows. I don't mind your trying though. Can you come in now?"

Mrs. Creighley then led me into her inner office, an apartment that proved to be better lighted than the shop, but no less ranged about with objects of display. Mrs. Creighley's desk —one saw her sitting at it, urging up the price of the heirlooms as they came to her—was scarcely mercenary enough to break in upon the impression the room gave of being half drawing-room and half private gallery. As I entered it I was

beaten back by the light of the setting sun that poured across the roofs and chimneypots in a stream, red and vindictive, through Mrs. Creighley's high windows onto Mrs. Creighley's deep carpets. It played on a tea urn, and on a brass tray laden with cups; it burnished the mahogany, and it plated the white ceiling with a caked and imperial gold; but it had nothing to do with the lady who sat with her back to it, over the tea urn. In the midst of this tumult sat a figure, grey, composed, abstracted. A woman of middle-age, one would say, robed in faded purples and wasted reds, hung about with relics and amulets; some queen-mother, superceded, unattended and forgotten, having about her still the twilight of royalty and old processional honors. Her face—though in the darkness—had the texture of an old glove, touched with pink. She remained for a time unaware of our entrance, but sat gazing at some mote in the air, incomputably distant, her nose lifted, as though balancing a difficult pince-nez.

The interview proved Mrs. Creighley to have been right. This Mrs. Clarke, Eddy Greater, refused to be drawn out, and while her cousin and I eked out her unresponsiveness with a highly artificial conversation of our own, her hand rose and fell, carrying the teacup to her lips. Even to direct questions as to these notable friends of hers, she made monotonous disclaimers. Her voice was low and curiously hoarse, and the few phrases she permitted herself: "I don't know," "I can't remember" and "I believe so," were only too obviously protective measures set up by one who could, but would not, expatiate. Finally I thanked Mrs. Creighley, who said she would see me through the shop, and rose to go.

"Your material is of the greatest interest, Mrs. Clarke," I said. "Can I give you my card? Should you consider—ah—sharing anything further you may have, I hope you will let us know. The Sebastian Torr Society will be pleased to buy any documents of the period that—"

She had received my card spiritlessly on her lap, but now she looked up with arrested attention. One saw her thus as quite aged, and with a touch of eccentric madness in her thin, angular face and looped, variegated costume.

"Sebastian Torr? What do you know about him?" she asked

sharply, adding as she relapsed into her abstraction, "Drunkard!
—I have nothing but these few things you have seen. Goodbye."

Mrs. Creighley had preceded me into the shop. "You mustn't
mind," she said from the gloom, "she is strange with every-
one. I fancy she had quite a difficult time in her youth. Did I
tell you she was on the stage? You wouldn't have heard of her,
it was so long ago. Not that she wasn't all right, Mr. Caruthers!
But I imagine in these days the stage could be very difficult for
a girl of high principles."

The tone of my commiseration implied an unqualified ac-
ceptance of Eddy Greater's model life and consequently des-
perate struggle for advancement. I bought a little pile of
autographs and pushed out into the falling dusk.

In the days that followed I planned to return to the shop,
confident that it required only time to draw from the aged
singer further and more valuable mementos of her brilliant
epoch. Any such trying process was disposed of, however, by my
receipt of a pencilled note at my hotel. "Dear Mr. Caruthers," it
read, "I have more things for you to see. I am at 45 Queens-
chapel Road, every evening at seven, Mrs. Clarke." After a
great deal of inquiry, a hotel retainer was found who knew the
general direction of Queenschapel Road. This woman was led
out to my cab-driver, and after a prolonged discussion of land-
marks we set out. After hàlf-an-hour's driving we fell into the
habit of stopping at public-houses for reassurance. We were
penetrating into a suburb, all walls and hedges. The road
seemed prepared at any moment to resign its claim to city su-
pervision, and relapse into villagedom. There were suspicions
of orchards and lanes and even pastures. At last we drew up
before a large, ugly house, of what at first appeared to be a
highly solitary situation, beating two faded signs: "Altar Guild"
and "Sacristan, 3:00 to 5:00 P.M." Descending to the pave-
ment I looked about me and saw through the dark that had
fallen, the light smoking rain, and a vague screen of foliage,
that opposite the house of our intention stood a suburban cathe-
dral, a vast bumpy structure, uncompleted and infested with
side entrances, breaking into little gilded domes and leaning
before and behind upon ghostly scaffolding. I bade my driver
draw off towards a nearby gloom that I assumed to be a clump

of weeping willow trees, and started to ascend the stairs. The door before me suddenly opened and three ladies rushed out in a little flurry of screams and giggles. "We shall be so late!" one said. "Father Raglin will be very annoyed," said another. "The third time this week." Two were in nun's garb, and the third wore a discreet modification of it that resembled penury, widowhood and convent in one. They rushed off to the dripping church without seeing me and I continued my ascent.

The bell was answered immediately by an old woman who must have been sitting by the door. She nodded when she saw me, as though I were a frequent caller, and led me into the front room, clean, high and uncarpeted. There was a faint smell of incense about, and through folding-doors, came the sound of low impassioned Jesuitical murmuring. These doors creaked to admit Mrs. Clarke, who closed them behind her. Seen thus for the first time, in motion and facing the light, she appeared less impressive. I was seeing an elderly lady with a sharp, hunted face framed in hair that was still dark. Her lips were thin with acquisitiveness, and her eyes were wide and fixed, and bore the flag of a fixed idea. She wore the same costume that I had seen on the stairs, and in the new association I saw her to be a lay sister or a postulant, one too ignorant to be admitted, or too unspiritual, yet too devoted to reject. She swept and polished and embroidered, one saw; she dusted the woodwork in the choir and mended the vestments in the press; and passed a piece of chamois over the altar vessels.

She sat down immediately at the table and said in her guttural voice: "Now! I have a diary of Sebastian Torr's. For three years. How much will you give me? It's full of poems he wrote me. I used to know him. There are photographs of us two, standing together. Now!"

"Let me see it," I said.

"Yes, yes. You shall. There is most of a long poem, too. And the story of his illness, when he was getting worse. How much will you give me?"

"Mrs. Clarke, I must see it first. If it contains all this you say I may be able to give a hundred and fifty pounds."

"A hundred and fifty pounds! Do you hear, I will not *show* it to you for that."

"You must be reasonable, Mrs. Clarke. I can make no prom-

ises without seeing the manuscript," I replied, and my firmness exerted a quieting effect on the old woman, whose excitable haggling had acquired a touch of hysteria. She dabbed her eyes and suddenly drew open a drawer of the table, where lay three worn note-books. My eyes at once caught the handwriting I had been studying for so many months, Sebastian Torr's, indubitably. I saw the indentations of daily entries; I saw with these eyes the lost poems, the legendary lost poems, the Imogen lyrics and the seven Primitive Rituals; I saw a half-dozen daguerreotypes—I hung over these things for several minutes while Mrs. Clarke stood up, translating my pleasure and awe into the terms of her own cupidity, increase for increase.

"I will give you four hundred pounds," I said finally.

Mrs. Clarke gave a second cry of dismay and repudiation, and for the first time I became aware of a touch of the histrionic in this pathetic funereal quasi-distinguished old woman. Suddenly the folding-doors, behind which the murmuring had ceased, opened to admit a small, precise priest. He bowed impersonally to me, and by the slightest of signals requested Mrs. Clarke to leave us alone. She closed the drawer of the table, locked it and left the room without a glance at us.

"Mrs. Clarke has told me of your interest in these old papers of hers, Mr. Caruthers," said the priest. "For the journal she showed you to-night she is willing to accept a thousand pounds."

"I can't pay it," I replied immediately. "You know such sums are not paid for small manuscripts like these—"

"I am aware of that. You must understand that we are not charging you a thousand pounds for the literary value of the journal. I have read it. It is the daily record of profligacy and degeneration. The poems may be fine; but they are blasphemous or licentious, or both. We could not but feel that we are contributing to the destructive forces about us by selling this journal. I suppose it would enjoy a certain sensation?" He waited until I nodded. "The verses would become a part of everyone's culture—very likely?" Again I nodded. "The responsibility on us becomes fairly great. But for a thousand pounds—"

I was listening to a popular preacher whose ears were charmed by his own stilted phrasing. The cool, delicate voice would go on forever, multiplying distinctions.

"Good-night." I said suddenly, rising. "Mrs. Clarke has my card. My offer of four hundred pounds rests with her."

I left the room in a rage, descended the stairs and aroused my driver without noticing that the rain had begun to fall more heavily, and that I was carrying my hat and coat in my hand. A thousand pounds was impossible. It was in the days before the great sales, besides which I could never persuade the society nor any of its rich enthusiasts to pay a thousand pounds for a manuscript that would be eventually published—such poems are never lost!—leaving an only incidental interest in their original handwriting. On the drive home I furiously cast away all interest in the journal. Let them keep it; I should never penetrate into their strange retreat again. But during the days that followed my eagerness to possess it took an almost physical form; I fell ill of disappointment and frustration, and had about resolved to journey out to Queenschapel Road, when another pencilled note was left at my hotel making an appointment with me at one of Mrs. Crooke's tea-rooms situated in the center of the city.

The organizing genius that has given the name of Mrs. Crooke to the world as a household word built a chain of untidy, identical shops throughout London, choosing for the most part the more important bus transfer stations. The trade-mark displays a Japanese girl tilting an umbrella, but the firm is more closely associated with the rubber-plants in the windows and the embarrassing turn-stile in the door. Our appointment was for three, but arriving early I saw through the stile and rubber-plants that Mrs. Clarke was already waiting for me. It was early and we were the only customers. In the distance a tall waitress was sewing on an apron-string and conversing with the cashier in her little pagoda. We sat in silence a moment while Mrs. Clarke seemed to be hurriedly preparing the line of argument, into which she finally launched herself, with more than her usual hoarseness.

"I will sell you the journals for four hundred pounds. But you must not publish them. Not for five years at least. They must not know, Father Xavier and Father Lara. They would never let me be a nun; I would be washing dishes forever. Do you see now?" I nodded greedily. "I will pretend to them that I have burned the manuscripts, or thrown them into the lake."

Wonder as to what she would do with the money, and how she could conceal its expense from her confessors crossed my mind, and I asked her, only to find that my question had tapped the fixed idea that was burning in her eyes.

"No one will ever know. I shall build a chapel in my cathedral in Paris. For my friends, for all of us, Manina Shayer, Fanny Bonner and the rest—eight of us. I owe it them, they are telling me that all the time. I am the last and I owe it them."

During the shaken silence that followed this feverish confession the waitress at the end of the room bit off her thread, shook out her apron-string, licked her fingers and descended on us. I gave the order, adding that we would like a fire lighted in the grate beside us. The waitress looked at the grate as though she had never seen it before, stuck one forefinger into the hollow of her cheek skeptically, and went away. Presently a boy appeared with sugar on his face, lit the kindling, made a tremendous racket with a coal scuttle, and returned to his interrupted tea. Throughout these incongruous proceedings Mrs. Clarke and I had sat shielding, as it were, our religious and literary passions from the vulgarity and horse-play about us. When tea had been placed before us, I attempted to lead her into conversation on her old acquaintances, but she cut me short, saying she never thought of them, and I saw something of the abhorrence of the convert for the days before the change. I arranged to meet her at the same place the next day, with the money, when a shadow suddenly fell across the table. Mrs. Clarke was in the act of extending to me "on account" the first *cahier* of the diaries which she brought with her. She looked up and a change came across her face, more of resignation than fear. "Father Lara!" she said, half rising. The priest with exquisite manners was beside us.

"Veronica, have I your permission to burn these books?" he asked, almost with deference.

"Yes, Father Lara," she said, her chin trembling strangely, and her eyes returning to their myopic fixity.

"These have come between us again. First you clung to them because they represented the life you have put behind you. The second time they caused you to fall into avarice. Now they have led you into disobedience against our authority. Veronica, have I your permission to destroy them?"

She sighed her admission again. He took the journals, and with a sudden movement threw them into the burning coals.

"I could have given your damned authority a thousand pounds for those papers," I cried.

Father Lara without looking at me remarked gently: "The obedience of the least of our postulants is worth more than ten thousand pounds to us. Come, Veronica, you will be late for the class."

Without another glance at me they went out, Mrs. Clarke buttoning her cheap cotton gloves with a sort of tearful dignity. Perhaps I could still have extracted a page or two from behind the moulded iron grate, but a strange lassitude had fallen upon me, from which I was aroused by the tall girl.

"The man with the collar's been lookin' in over the rubber-trees ever since you came," she said. I paid the account, and went out thinking of the two cherished ambitions that would never be fulfilled—that strange chapel of dead actresses and my edition of Sebastian Torr.

1920

Précautions Inutiles

THERE was only one ruler in the world who had more power than the Queen Bei Chu, and that was the Emperor of the East. He was incredibly powerful, but in the West only a few old statesmen ever realized his existence; he lived at such a distance and court life was so self-centered under the Queen Bei Chu. The combined domains of these two rulers constituted the whole voyageable world. Beyond them, to the East, lay a great stretch of curling water, barely poising itself on the shelf of creation; to the North, wastes of blue-shadowing snow, thinly inhabited by moss-eating animals; to the West and South, the mountains that could be seen from the Queen's windows and that no one ever crossed, for they were infested with intelligent storms that emerged from unmapped pockets to attack the adventurer.

Queen Bei Chu had ascended the throne upon the death of her father, in her thirteenth year. Her father's chief advisor, an old priest, had been appointed Regent, and his duties included the education of the Queen. Reading and writing one never ceases to learn, but education proper lasts six months and is very fatiguing. It includes declamation and ceremonial, and it was through ceremonial that the Queen first came to hear of the two experiences that awaited her next, Marriage and Love, or Love and Marriage. The old priest was brief and dull in his exposition; it was from her father's library that the Queen gained her real idea of these matters. The library contained six thousand romances, the diaries of four hundred favorites, and innumerable volumes of love poetry.

Love, she learned, was a state of frenzy in which black appeared white, and white, black; in which one was so tormented by the idea in one's head that eating and drinking lost their attraction; in which the whole matter of ceremonial became trivial, and one fell into grave errors in the ritual of congratulation and lost one's cleverness in ordering the folds of a robe. Many poets gave evidence of having suffered, describing vividly their flushed faces and wasted bodies.

"This is terrible," thought the Queen.

She read in a thousand passages that she could not escape falling in love. It strikes variously, through the eye generally. She would take pleasure from the view of some man, and live thereafter in a state of wretchedness. Nor did there seem to be any way of choosing one's beloved: camel-driver or prince, thief or priest, would some day wrest from her all interest save that which centered in him. The Queen shuddered with apprehension, nor did all the recounted felicities of love, the assurances of its divine origin and its practical results, relieve her. She, the Queen, who had never desired anything without obtaining it, and never desired anything inappropriate, would someday be sitting behind her lattice, possessed with longing perhaps for a groom of the stables or a preoccupied student. Pale with mortification and terror she rose from her bed and called her musicians: and throughout the long nights of a week the Queen's tears fell into her scented lap while the exquisite and melancholy complaint of the flute rose and fell on the balcony and the distant mountains dreamed in the moonlight. "Alas! Me, wretched!" cried the Queen.

She saw that being the first in the land she would be obliged to love someone lower than herself, to humiliate herself before a man whose duty it was to pay her the seven courtesies of acknowledgment. Suddenly, however, she realized that the earth held one man she might regard as her equal; she could love the Emperor of the East. From that moment her mind was filled with the one idea of preparing herself to love the Emperor of the East. Every care, of course, must be taken that one did not fall in love with someone else first. All men under fifty were removed from the palace enclosure. In her daily progress to the temple she kept her eyes fixed on her lap, in pain lest some accident should force her to look up. She read of a poet who had fallen in love with a portrait, and forthwith flower panels were substituted for figure-pieces throughout the palace; only the Emperor's portrait and her father's were found there. The rumor that the Emperor was projecting a western journey was becoming more of a certainty daily, and the Queen went on to the further preparations, not less important, those that would ensure the Emperor's falling in love with her. By classical reading she induced in herself an elevated and imperial temper; she moulded her face and harmonized her gesture by listening to

the best music; but being a woman she did not neglect less abstract precautions. She designed two hundred robes before she could evolve one in which modesty and seduction played equal parts. Her voice was trained to exhibit both natural magic and discreet self-possession. She committed to memory a thousand wise and witty things to say.

As the day of the Emperor's arrival approached, her advisors were thrown into a state of terror. They warned her a thousand times that his visit was but a preliminary to aggression, and that there were factions in her own city that were prepared to resist him. Bei Chu did not hear them, but sat dreamily gazing at the mountains and fingering the folds of her mantle. They went on to assure her that the Emperor expected her resistance (she smiled), but if he were received pacifically he meant to postpone his assault until the end of his visit.

When the imperial caravan approached the city, the Queen awaited the audience surrounded by her courtiers, each one looking at the long carpet of yellow brocade, one end of which lay at her feet, the other at the city gate. The caravan was sixteen miles long and so compact and orderly that when a camel at the head knelt down for a moment to shake a bee out of his ear, the last provision-cart was abruptly halted. The procession approached the walls, the Emperor's younger brother on a white mule trotting in advance. Suddenly a cloud of arrows, as swift and graceful as homing swallows, fell upon him from the left tower. The visitors had expected resistance, as they had surely planned aggression, and were prepared for it. Forthwith they drew themselves up in array, bringing forward some monstrous machines of war that had never been seen in the East, and that were presently dropping balls of fire into the complacent city. Before sunset the gates were beaten down, and the invaders rushing through the streets swinging their swords. In the palace all was at first confusion, and then silence. The Queen sat dreamily in a deserted hall, awaiting the felicitous encounter. When the palace caught fire, she strayed into the streets and was immediately torn hither and thither by her distracted subjects. She seemed hardly to have realized the state of the city, and sang softly under her breath, holding her exquisite hands decoratively before her. She wandered many hours, until, her gown in ribbons, her head-dress undone, the vermillion brushed

from her finger-tips, she sank down exhausted, one arm encircling a stone lion at her own gate. As she sat there, the Emperor rode up on horseback to view the latest of his palaces. In the shifting lights of the burning city he saw the Queen, and with that intuition for recognizing one another that is a secret of the aristocracy, and of all superior mortals, he immediately dismounted, and with such beautiful humility as only a superior can show to a dependant, he raised her up and placed her on his horse.

The affairs of the Queen's kingdom were none the worse for a change of government. The subjects protested at the loss of certain insignia, the substitution of a new language and the personal idiosyncrasies of their new overlords; but they had to acknowledge that the streets were cleaner, pestilences less frequent, justice more easily arrived at, and taxation more wisely distributed. The Queen, having found out that the beauty of her gowns and the cultivation of her mind played little part in her marriage, took her place as another Empress without illusions, and in due time devoted herself, as befitted her rank, to the composition of Memoirs, of which these pages are a respectful condensation.

1922–23?

A Diary: First and Last Entry

FORTY years ago, when I was eight, I was taken to an emi-
nent surgeon in regard to certain pains in my back. The great
man told my mother after ten minutes' examination that I could
not live a year. My mother assured me on the stairs that the
doctor had spoken hopefully of my condition and after a lemon-
ade we went home on the train. The flight of time proved that
my mother's falsehoods are truer than a doctor's affidavit, for
I passed several years without discomfort, reading in a bow-
window. At the end of the first year I think my mother—who had
ceased to be pretty on that day in the doctor's office—looked
at me narrowly from time to time, wondering if it were worth
while to have grown old suddenly in anticipation of a son's
death that remained indefinitely remote. In due time the pains
returned and I was led before a visiting German specialist who
promptly despaired of my life. My mother's face in the elevator
bore the same expression of encouraging solicitude, but there
was a faint gleam about the eyes that said that the expensive
lemonade might be deferred until an authority more unmis-
takable than a Viennese degree had announced my extremity. I
retired again to my window-seat, to emerge at intervals, and to
stand with my mother beneath the vacant mirrors of many con-
sulting rooms; from each interview my mother carried away
decisive assurance of my death.

This morning the scene was re-enacted, though the heroine
was far away. Bad as my French is, it at least served me in ex-
tracting from this filthy Neapolitan doctor the news that I have
but six months to live. The verb *mourir* is irregular, but I found
its future, and he solemnly nodded. Out of a complacency that
was not pity he was willing to promise me a year, but I held
him with my eyes (perhaps I had been drinking) until he gave
me what he really believed. This time I too believed, the cun-
ning little terrier; the wolf was not the less convincing for
having been cried a dozen times. So I have six months to live
and can start spending more freely the money I intended
should last me a year. And of these six months I am going to

keep a diary that I may examine with greater precision the curious life I am about to leave. If the world knew with what passionate appraisal I am observing it, it would not choose this time to be trivial.

The first thing I did with my increased allowance was to go to dinner at Bertolini's. There sat the same Americans, South Americans and Germans; I was annoyed with myself for not having dressed, for they were not dressed either. I had a *compôte* Metternich, and a *faisan* Souvaroff, stuffed with truffles, breathing Madeira, and buttressed with mashed chestnuts, *Salade Pierre Courtin* and what not, each with its wedded wine. Oh, wines in procession, oh, wine, the whole weight of Greek and Christian symbolism do not do thee more than justice. My defiance and rage fell from me like the garments that children have put on in play. He who has once been happy is forever out of time's grasp.

"Be still a moment and you can hear the world falling through space!" was the frequent injunction of a schoolteacher of mine. Captured by the phrase the class would listen breathlessly to a silence slightly stained by the shouts of distant trains rushing into St. Louis. Tonight the world is falling through space like a cannon-ball that some genial admiral lets fly in amusing salute to the austerer planets. I sit high in bed and can hear the slip of the world as it turns and turns, like a pullman taking a curve with a sigh. It is two o'clock in the morning and even the streets of Naples are quiet. Your Baptists have it that God, a round-shouldered old man in a white girdled robe after Blake, driven with concern for men, tirelessly follows their sleep and waking. They would picture him now going up all these little alleys, these filthy stairway-streets, counting families and making mental comments on the unaccountable inclinations of men. He has just passed through my walls. It is some credit to me that I do not take much of his time. He pats with amused indulgence the hillock of my feet. He likes me because I have broken myself of the habit of saying my prayers and no longer urge him to stop wars, and avert financial panics, and be gracious to my Aunt Cora, or endow me with this or another preposterous grace. He is warned that my importunity, made strong by long abstinence, may some day assault his peace and upset the economy of Heaven. We understand one another.

The intuition that is part of the primitive man in us keeps reminding me that there is a large body of water near, though I cannot hear a water-sound, hard as I try. This very minute about Procida the black water is lapping, and hollow and chiming sounds are filling the caves of Sorrento. Inside me my expensive dinner is making interrogative noises, finding new corridors to push along and falling from level to level. Thoughts of lantern-groping God, of the quinine-minded author of Mandragola, of the threading earth, and these sensations of repletion have all but left me unconscious of the sharp pains that have been rending my side. At all events he who has once been happy is forever out of time's grasp.

1924

The Warship

THE ship Trumpeter which left London for Australia in the early Eighteenth Century with a hundred convicts and their families on board never reached its destination and no report of any survivor nor of any identified object connected with it ever reached the world. The ship's company did not entirely perish, however. The captain and the greater part of the crew were drowned in the storm that wrecked the vessel; many of the passengers and most of the children died in the hardships of the first few weeks thereafter; but finally over a hundred persons reached an island on the west coast of Australia. These survivors settled down upon the island which they promptly christened "England", but which in a few generations of oral transmission became "Inglan". In time the ingenuity of the colonists had established an agreeable mode of living; a church, a school, a parliament and even a theatre had come into being, and within a hundred years the population had more than doubled. It was greatly reduced in 1870, however, by an obscure disease which attacked the community, probably through some disproportion in the ingredients of the islanders' diet. A few years later the population was again diminished by the loss of a dozen of the ablest men who ventured in a rough-hewn boat to visit an island which could be occasionally seen at sunrise on the northern horizon.

In 1880 a castaway reached the colony, a Finnish sailor, who had been drifting for many days in an open boat. It was several years before he learned sufficient English to tell the Inglaners about the outside world, a hazy account of the Napoleonic Wars, of an English queen, and detailed information about Baltic politics. This Finnish sailor never recovered from the ill-effects of his exposure and died in the sixth year of his life on the island. No other visitor ever reached Inglan; no ship was ever sighted in the distance; and presently the Inglaners lost interest in maintaining the distress signal on the peak that rose behind their settlement.

In the original company of the shipwrecked there had been only a few men and women who were able, even imperfectly,

to read, write and compute, and they were already aged by the
time the community came to feel a need for written records
and had devised a substitute for paper on which to inscribe
them. At the same time the colony was seized with a passion
for recovering the lore of the outside world and particularly for
anything connected with religion. Official scribes were ap-
pointed and all who could remember a passage or even a phrase
from the Bible or the hymns contributed their share. In this
way a brief anthology was committed to writing, including a
synopsis of the Pilgrim's Progress, some fragments from the
marriage and burial services and a number of English and
Scotch ballads. To this library the islanders went to school,
where they likewise were given accounts of such things as
animals, grains and utensils. Geography consisted of vague maps
of the world and the British Isles and detailed descriptions of
London, Plymouth, and Bristol. At the beginning of the Nine-
teenth Century a gifted musician arose who fashioned himself
some instruments and on the basis of the songs that had been
retained made some new ones. Soon after a poet declared him-
self and versified copiously. A young woman who had gazed
long at squares and triangles deduced the first books of Euclid
from them and a school of mathematicians flourished for half a
century.

Up to the time of the epidemic of 1870 the health of the com-
munity had been excellent, but thereafter it declined rapidly.
The uniformity of the diet and the increasing bonds of consan-
guinity had a part in this, but chiefly a psychological factor that
was an effect of the shut-in-ness of the island existence. The
colonists were not aware of any desire to leave Inglan and view
the outside world, yet they felt themselves lost, abandoned of
God, and aimless. Vigorous personalities arose from time to
time who found the opportunities and problems of even this
restricted existence sufficient to justify a human dignity, but
the majority relapsed into a fretful and listless submission to the
passing of time. A large proportion of the children died at birth
or grew up sickly, unsocial, eccentric and quarrelsome. A fer-
mented drink was brewed from the fruits on the island and in-
temperance became universal. But most strikingly of all, in spite
of the small size of the territory and in spite of the fact that
every colonist was many times the cousin of his neighbor, the

Inglaners divided themselves into factions and lived in an atmosphere of distrust that frequently came to a head in strife and bloodshed.

In 1910 there were only twelve adults living under civilization in Lunnon itself and they no longer made efforts to reclaim the few hermits who had withdrawn themselves to the remoter parts of the island. Jonh Weever, the Captain of Inglan, as he was called, tried strenuously to inspirit his community; he offered rewards for inventions, for writings, and for feats of skill. His eldest son, Roja, felt the incitement beyond the others and never tired of contriving improvements for the island; but at the same time he distressed his father by continued speculation as to the nature of the outside world. To Captain Jonh the existence of the outside world was a matter lost in myth, tradition and hearsay. Report said that hundreds, even thousands, of human beings lived there in dwellings of extraordinary size and beauty. Roja dreamed of finding a way to such a world, or of the possibility of such a world's coming to Inglan. Captain Jonh would sigh into his beard, shaking his head at such thoughts. "Whether that world be still there," he would say, "whether it be better than our own or worser; how far away it lies—these things we cannot know, neither be we like to know. The best thing for us to do, my son, is not to beat our heads about them, but to do our duty where we be." But Roja would not be put off. He stirred up the men of Lunnon to renew the huge distress signal on the peak. It was long and tedious work, but for a time the islanders were filled with an unaccustomed excitement. The storms of the next two rainy seasons, however, tore the great structure down, and even when Roja became Captain in his father's place he made no effort to rebuild it.

One night when he had put his sons and daughters to bed and made the rounds of Lunnon, Captain Roja descended to the water's edge and sat down, gazing across the sea. He turned over in his mind the destiny that had placed him there, the depleted colony, the rancorous spirit of his subjects, the difference that lay between today and the glorious days that his grandfather had described to him, and he thought of the days that lay ahead when his children would have survived him. And as he sat thinking a strange sight appeared before him. A great ship came around the headland, hung with lights, festooned

with two great rows of lights from stem to stern. Music came from it and the sound of shouting. Clouds of smoke hung in the quiet air behind it. Fore and aft two great skeleton turrets rose into the stars. For a moment Captain Roja thought of lighting a bonfire or setting fire to St. Paul's, but he paused. The vision was beautiful, but terrible. He knew that neither himself nor his companions could live in that world; all that power and energy was troubling and remote. He sat down again and watched the marvel pass into the distance, and the other shadowy forms that had gathered on the slope behind him gazed and trembled and went in silence to their homes.

1936

ESSAYS ON FICTION

On Reading the
Great Letter Writers

THE very nature of letter writing is such that when we get together to discuss it there should never be more than a dozen persons. The great letter sequences are full of passages that you and I were never meant to see. I grant that some of the letters that I shall discuss were written with one eye on a larger audience; but many a letter by even the most conscious artists in this literature was not intended for the Complete Edition. There are letters even of Horace Walpole, the virtuoso, that he did not label "*Confidential: Please burn*" because he assumed as a matter of course that they would not be wrapped in ribbons and returned to him with the rest. Moreover, until the last fifty years, letters had always been edited, and the letter writers who might have had a lurking suspicion that their pages might be published someday never doubted that the local passages or the humdrum passages or the intimate passages would be cut out. They did not foresee the type of attention that the twentieth century would bring to such work; "morbid" they would have called it.

Moreover, there is an extraordinary aspect about the letter writers' work whereby one understands that even the consciousness of other readers does not impair or undermine the sincerity and the singlemindedness of the letters they address to the friends they really love. In the old sense, there is a "mystery" here. It is related to the mystery behind all creative literature above a certain level. Art is confession; art is the secret told. Art itself is a letter written to an ideal mind, to a dreamed-of audience. The great letter-sequences are written to close friends. But even the closest friends cannot meet the requirements of the artist, and the work passes over their shoulder to that half-divine audience that artists presuppose. All of Mme. de Sévigné's life was built about those wonderful letters. On one plane they were written to regain her daughter's affection, to attract her daughter's admiration and love. But Mme. de Sévigné knew that her daughter merely brought an amused, an indulgent, a

faintly contemptuous appreciation. And time after time the letter rises beyond the understanding of the daughter and becomes an *aria* where the overloaded heart sings to itself for the sheer comfort of its felicity, sings perhaps to the daughter as she might have been. In such passages Mme. de Sévigné even defeated the purpose of the rest of the letter, even risked drawing upon herself her daughter's vexation and ill-humor. But sing she must. The audience of a work of art is never clear in a true artist's mind, but is made of souls that he has guessed at—old hero worships repersonified and loves transferred: as though the audiences at concerts and art galleries and the company of book-buyers were made up of Michelangelos and Platos and Violas and Imogens and Cardinal Newmans. Your letters and mine are messages to friends and we do them as well as we can to please the friends; but the great letters are letters to friends plus the most exacting spirits the mind can imagine.

But art is not only the desire to tell one's secret; it is the desire to tell it and to hide it at the same time. And the secret is nothing more than the whole drama of the inner life, the alternations between one's hope of self-improvement and one's self-reproach at one's failures. "Out of our quarrels with other people we make rhetoric," said William Butler Yeats; "out of our quarrels with ourselves we make literature." Self-reproach is the first and the continuing state of the soul. And it is the way we go about assuaging that reproach that makes us do anything valuable.

I have had to say all this in order to make clear what I am looking for in great letters. My friends: in literature, I am fond of grace and charm and suavity; but I am not *very* fond of it. But isn't that the quality that most of the great letter writers are praised for? Yes. But I confess that if Horace Walpole offered me nothing more than the brilliant picture of his times (and a very limited picture it is, as one discovers in reading that great and almost exactly contemporaneous document, Wesley's *Journal*); if he offered me nothing but his parliamentary news, and dowager tattle, I should not return to him as I do. And if William Cowper brought merely his charming news of eight persons, three Belgian hares, one dog, one cat, and one garden,

I doubt whether he would be so surely surviving into a world of railroads, aviation, and steel construction. And yet that is all that many critics and readers seem to mention. Every great letter writer in the world, save one, presents behind all the verbal felicity an infinitely more satisfying pleasure. They have all left signposts, footprints, clues of the life of their more-than-usual, their extraordinary hearts. All but one, and I wash my hands of Voltaire. His armor is complete. He was perfectly contented with his brains. In all those volumes he left no sign that he had ever found his superb mind unequal to face the impressiveness of nature, the complexity of human relationships, or the pain and loneliness in man's situation. Sometimes I think that in one novel, or rather novelette, *L'Ingénu*, he allowed instinctive emotion to claim itself to be richer than intelligence. But at least in all that immense correspondence, that dazzling correspondence, he preserves his *sang-froid*. But all the great letter writers except Voltaire offer much richer treasure than their literary skill, and the only reason that so many people approach them so lightly is this:

This great branch of literature has been betrayed into the hands of the anthologists. The whole aim of reading the great letter-sequences has been reduced to skipping toward the much-advertised *tours-de-force*. Even in St. Paul thousands of people regard I Corinthians 13 as a sort of wall motto, never caring to restore it to its place in that great curve of anxious exhortation that is presently to mount still more impressively (yet never losing the character of a letter) to climax after climax in the passages on the resurrection. Regarding the Epistle merely as literature, as technique, I have to find myself merely happily laughing with admiration at such a display.

The first rule in reading the great letter writers is this: *Read them in extent.*

What we get then through reading these letters in great length is this:

Gradually a face hovers between the words.

Gradually a personality (unmistakable for any other, just as you and I are unmistakable for any other) defines itself. When one has passed the hundredth letter not only the profile of the personality is becoming clear to us but that wonderful phenomenon takes place: we hear the voice of the writer in the very

word order. There is a William Cowper sentence cadence; there is an Edward FitzGerald sentence cadence (and very beautiful it is too); and this particular music is of course linking itself up with the portrait, with the traits, with the smile, I can almost say: with the glance from the author's eyes.

This particular joy you scarcely ever derive from novels. For the most part they are engaged on other business. But of course one receives it from Jane Austen. One receives it appallingly from Richardson, where it is identified with the heroine. I am told one receives it from Turgenev, though naturally it is untranslatable and has its home in the vowel-and-consonant accidents of the language. And there are times when it becomes so penetrating in Shakespeare that one swears that one has seen him.

But this isn't all. These letter writers have survived from hundreds and thousands of others who likewise had literary gifts just because they not only reported the world about them persuasively, but because they had this great talent for designing their own portrait in and between the lines. And if they are so gifted at talking about themselves, isn't it possible that every now and then they will let the cat out of the bag—that is, tell the secret of which I was speaking a few moments ago; bring us news from the furthest corners of their spirits, mark for us some of the road? After all, nothing is interesting for long save this, and there is a possibility that these writers with their special gift for writing themselves over will admit us to their happiness or suffering.

I am supposed to be speaking about English writers, but I want to say a few more words about the greatest of all letter writers, Mme. de Sévigné. Indeed, she has almost a place in English letters, since two of our greatest loved her with a special love. Horace Walpole read and reread the volumes of her correspondence that kept making their first appearance in his time; he called her "Notre Dame des Rochers," and when he finally received the manuscript of one of her letters he treasured it above everything else he possessed. And Edward FitzGerald went so far as to prepare a little atlas and biographical dictionary and practically a concordance of her letters for his own use. The anthologists have made havoc with her reception in France.

All students in that country, especially the girls, are obliged to study and imitate and comment upon a volume of her *Selected Letters*. And all the showpieces, all the stunt letters are there. But the way to enter the fair country that is her mind is to begin by not looking for the anecdotes of the court, or the flowerets of language, or the inimitable little jokes through which she sees life (for later "all these things shall be added unto you"), but to enter it as Marcel Proust said his grandmother did, by the door of the heart. For me the key to Mme. de Sévigné is an acquaintance with her grandmother. Her grandmother was Mère Marie de Chantal, the co-worker of St. François de Sales. Mère Chantal was canonized as a Saint of the Church almost during Mme. de Sévigné's lifetime. She was one of those saints like St. Teresa who found no difficulty in living two full life-times in one, a Mary and a Martha. Her writings are among the minor classics of the Church. They are full of an over-whelming fixed adoration of God, and one has only to read them for a few pages to realize that it is the same blinding in-tensity that has been inherited by the granddaughter and fixed by some tragic accident upon a human being. And Mme. de Sévigné knew it, and the anthologies do not include those bitter and heartbroken passages in which the cards are really laid on the table:

This is my destiny; and the sufferings which follow upon my love for you, being offered to God constitute my penitence for an attachment which should be only for him.

Do I exaggerate?
She writes her friend Guitant:

I still am in the dark as to whether my dear daughter is coming back to Paris or not. However, I am preparing her rooms in our Car-navalet and we shall see what Providence has decreed. I ceaselessly keep this idea of Providence, Providence in my mind. All my thoughts are resigned to this sovereign will. There is my devotion. There is my scapulary. There is my rosary. There are my vigils. And if I were wor-thy of believing that I had a spiritual rôle to play I should say that it lay in that. But I am not worthy: for what is one to do with a mind that sees clearly, but with a heart of ice?

One has to read thirty or forty letters to come upon such passages, but, having found them, all the rest glows with an

even greater beauty. For example, I have never seen quoted in any book or article on Mme. de Sévigné a short phrase that explains the miracle of the style, and perhaps of all style:

Farewell, my blessed child; now I can go on telling you that I love you without fear of boring you, since you are willing to endure it in favor of my style: you excuse the importunity of my heart through your approval of my intelligence, isn't it just that?

Nor this terrible word:

All that is hateful in me, my daughter, proceeds from my lifetime of devotion to you.

In one of my books I made literary use of this situation with distinct allusion to Mme. de Sévigné: and I keep receiving indignant letters from lovers of the Frenchwoman saying that I imagined it; that she, being the incarnation of grace and charm and the salon, was too sane to allow of such an interpretation.

Let us proceed now to some English letter writers and read them from this point of view: what I call *reading on three levels*: the surface level, that is the *literary exercise*; the second level, which I call the *profile of a personality*; and the third level, which is *news of the soul*.

Horace Walpole is continually being dismissed as a gossip. But the word "gossip" has many definitions good and bad and Horace Walpole succeeded in illustrating most of them. At times he certainly illustrated the lowest: gossip, I think, is the art of retelling someone else's tragedy as though it reflected credit on oneself. He certainly illustrated the middle ground of gossip: a preoccupation with other people's affairs in that effort we all make to persuade ourselves that our lives are eventful. We bring from childhood the passionate expectation that life will be colorful, but life is seldom ever as exciting as it was when we were five and six and seven years old. Some few people create a glamorous world by overpraising their neighbors and their friends, but most people by detracting from them. Horace Walpole did both. I no longer believe that this kind of thing is malice and the desire to undermine other people's practice of the pleasures our consciences forbid us. I think it is just disappointed hero worship. We discover that

even the nicest girls in the world are not so nice as Shakespeare's girls and the noblest men when we meet them fall short of Plutarch's. Well, Horace Walpole was always making even the vivid eighteenth century more vivid than it had any right to be. Harry Seymour Conway was not so wonderful as Harry thought; nor was the Duchess of Bedford so detestable; the eternal witticisms of George Selwyn were not so bright as he claims they were and I think Dr. Johnson was not so uninteresting. The funerals and coronations of the Georges were not so fascinating as he makes them. The gossip colors up life, to escape from the boredom of its monotony and expectedness. Walpole tells lies, like someone whistling in the dark to keep up his courage. But there is a third definition of gossip on this rising scale and that is an unquenchable curiosity about human traits and the springs of conduct; we have no English word for it and we borrow and debase the French word "*curiosité*." This is an interest in human beings so intense and so unremitting that it approaches and resembles love. It is impossible to people who despise human nature or believe it incapable of any very happy surprises. To the eyes of this curiosity nothing one discovers is really repugnant. It is this attitude we define when we say that the angels are never shocked by what they see among us. Psychoanalysis and the new half-truths from Vienna are widely decried because they are said to discover the disgusting in half the conduct of life. On the contrary, they supply this *curiosité* with new resources of charity and pity. They do not remove the responsibility for failure, but they distribute the blame over a wider number of elements.

Horace Walpole did not have, to please me, enough of this highest use of gossip; but it is there. Yet in his letters there is much material about himself where we may employ our *curiosité*. And none more striking than in the story of his failure to understand the aged Mme. du Deffand's frantic infatuation for him until, after her death, he himself found himself possessed by a frantic infatuation for one or both of the Miss Berrys. Two faintly embittered people, both intelligent as the serpent and the devil, had scoffed amusingly at love all their lives, to discover almost at the age of eighty that their lives were being laid waste because they wanted someone to say to them: You are the person I love most in the world. It is in that story that we

reach my third level of approach. And the soul in the last struggle of pride and suffering stares up at one from the page. The quality one derives from Walpole then is the range and the possibilities in curiosity.

From the letters of Cowper we receive the unremitting gift of his gentle and shadowed spirit. These pages gain all their richness from the fact that they are written against a background of despair. William Cowper lived an even more uneventful life than Edward FitzGerald. He seemed to be forever holding the wool yarn for elderly ladies. If a bee enters by the window it is quite an exciting event in the poet's life. A balloon ascension in the neighborhood takes up about as much space in Cowper's letters as all the wars and revolutions of Europe. A snake was caught under the kitchen door; an electioneering delegation intruded one evening into the parlor. These are the excitements of Olney. Most of the encyclopedists feel that the gentle, tolerant humor with which these are communicated to us is the reason for Cowper's fame.

But there are layers and layers beneath that surface which Scott has immortalized in the phrase "Cowper's divine chit-chat." If you take up the complete letters (and there is still no really complete *Letters*) and if you are patient and watchful you will see another plane that William Cowper did not intend you to see: some very subtle and gradual shifting of likes and dislikes and cautions and hesitations among the modest *dramatic personae*. The world in which these people live is so quiet that psychological shades become dramatic. We are in the wonderful world that Jane Austen ruled: Relativity is at work, and all the coloring of Carlyle's *French Revolution* is extracted from the exchanged visits of a few neighbors. When Dr. John Newton was a wandering preacher the gentle and high-strung poet came under his influence. Dr. John Newton applied the methods of an almost hysteric revivalism to the young man. He was converted. But at the age of forty he was informed from Heaven in a dream that he had committed the unpardonable sin and would never be saved. Now what is the attitude one takes to the revivalist who converts one to Eternal Life, even though one discovers soon after that the conversion was useful only to form the conviction that one is eternally damned? Love and respect, of course; love and respect, tempered, ladies and gentle-

men, by the most implacable dislike. One writes faithful and affectionate letters, but one's horror is betrayed every fifteen months by some shade. Another illustration: One lives side by side for years with a devoted, intelligent elderly lady. Business of reading aloud for years Captain Cook's voyages to the South Seas and the news sheets about the court of Poland and the perhaps justified restlessness of the American colonies. But other ladies all over fifty come to look at the flowers, come to have their skeins of worsted held and to listen to the first readings of "John Gilpin" and the new translation of Homer. All three, all four are united in politeness, congeniality, and affection. But the balance of affection in a group can never remain poised at an equation, and even those gentle hearts are capable of laying claims on one another. Suddenly one member of the group drops out of the letters as though she had never been. Years later there are allusions so deft, wrapped in their formal latinity, that you almost tell yourself that you imagine it. The editor informs us in a footnote what happened, but going back we see that we could have gathered it from the tiny overstatements, and from the not-so-tiny reticences.

But there is a layer even below this, and here lies the deep interest in Cowper. Cowper was convinced that he had committed The Unpardonable Sin. No one is quite sure what that sin is in the scripture and no one is quite sure what Cowper did that he called The Unpardonable Sin. He says that once in his boyhood he had had to improve upon some occasion from God. At all events he was quite convinced that there was heavenly grace for every repentant sinner in the world, except himself. And the smell of sulphur is never absent for long from the parlor and garden at Olney. His dearest friends (several of them are clergymen), knowing his impeccable life, his deeply religious mind, and even his sense of humor, try to argue with him, sometimes with some harshness. But he mildly holds his ground; he knows the Biblical texts about forgiveness and the limitless possibilities of divine love. All that is perfectly true—except for William Cowper.

Now are you prepared to be both impatient and even angry at the poet and yet to believe that he believes it? Or are you among those horsey people who in the presence of mental suffering stride about crying: "Just think of other things, my dear.

Get some good exercise, drink a lot of milk, and read P. G. Wodehouse"?

Again we are in a relative world. The reality of a person's sufferings to himself is what must concern us. The child that has been hurled across the room by a father temporarily drunk does not understand and make allowance for the effect of alcohol. The child's world goes dark. The despair of the heart is not any the less because of a lack in reasoning power or education.

Loving William Cowper then is a spiritual exercise. One must learn not to be exasperated by him. One must think of Mary Unwin, who had several times a day to flatter this spiritual vanity in him—this delusion in him that he was unique, the horrible exception to God's mercy—she had to protest even at breakfast that he must be mistaken, and yet not protest too hard. For I am sorry to have to tell you that William Cowper liked to mention his eternal damnation quite frequently. Mary Unwin had also to comfort him before and after his visits of insanity. And one day after years of faithful friendship she had to enter a room and discover him trying to hang himself from the ceiling. Again, because we know this profoundly moving background the divine chit-chat speaks to us with a quality beyond mere grace and humor.

But there remains one letter writer with whom this method does not carry us far. Edward FitzGerald's letters move in an atmosphere of high tragic implication, but he has buried the Key. Watch as carefully as you choose, and with all the practice you have acquired from the letters of Mme. de Sévigné, Cowper, Swift, Charles Lamb, St. François de Sales, Lady Mary, Jane Welsh Carlyle—for all these are full illustration of the three levels of interest. Even as St. Paul is, even as Cicero is.

With FitzGerald the surface is beautiful. I may say that it seems to me that Edward FitzGerald taught me how to read—his way of reading so closely and of finding importance in passages of Shakespeare and Milton and Cervantes that I had always thought were the mere business, or even padding, of masterpieces. He is the most beautiful illustration in all English literature of how to be bookish in the best sense, loving great books as though they were people. "Well, well," he says every year, "I hope to read *Don Quixote* once more before I die." The

second plane he conducts as well, in my opinion, as anyone else in English—even better than Charles Lamb, whose verbal fooling repels me a little, wonderful though he is. The profile of the personality of Edward FitzGerald is one of the great gifts of the time. I can't help but believe that it comes over even better in the letters than it did in life, a not uncommon phenomenon in people with the literary gifts. (Goldsmith is another illustration.) Carlyle and Tennyson and Thackeray loved him very dearly and left unshakable testimony, but always with a touch of Victorian didactic superiority in regard to his absence from the battlefields. As I say, we have no facts on the third level, but we have that atmosphere that has led to his being called the Hamlet of letter writers, the enigmatic FitzGerald. What was the matter? What was his soul suffering from? Wasn't it just the inadequacy of the view on life that he borrowed and modified from Omar Khayyám? Wasn't it just a refusal to cope with the dismaying look of experience and the longing for death? He had made a number of dear friends ("My friendships are more like loves," he would say) and they died or moved away and became wrapped up in their wives and children and wrote him perfunctory letters. And his own death delayed and delayed and delayed.

Novels I suppose are pure literature and diaries are pure life. Autobiographies are life, but life that has been adroitly re-arranged for the show window. The great books of confession, the Rousseau and the Augustine, are all too few. So that we come back to the great letter writers for the happiest mixture of both. When even fiction is not real enough, when even Dosto-evski and Stendhal, for all their inner truth, remind us that ac-tually on the planet the brothers Karamazov never lived—a childish test, but an eternally human objection against novels. And when on the side of real life we tire of biographies, because they happened all too palpably on the planet and repel us with that awful thought, What would Keats or Walt Whitman or Queen Victoria say if they read their biography? Wouldn't they cry out: But this is only one tenth of the truth; all that is really myself escaped?

Between these two discontents: between the fictional

character of fiction and the all-too-graphic character of bio-graphic work, there are letters. These people not only really lived as you and I are living, but they are reporting themselves faithfully. You may read them for their style, or for the ac-quaintance of their personality, or you may read them for the dark patterns in their life and for the courage they bring to it.

1928

James Joyce

1882–1941

During thirty-five years of self-imposed exile James Joyce never ceased from the contemplation of Dublin. From Trieste, from Rome, from Zürich, earning his living in the appalling treadmill of the Berlitz schools, night after night he relived the Dublin of 1900, its sights and sounds and smells and inhabitants—bound to Dublin in love and hate, parallel, irreconcilable, each emotion whipping on its contrary; a love that could only briefly make peace with the hatred through the operation of the comic spirit; a hatred that could only intermittently make peace with the love through the intensity of artistic creation. This unresolved love and hate recurred in every aspect of his life: it went out toward his youth, toward the religion in which he was brought up, toward the rôle of artist, toward the very phenomenon of language itself. It compelled him to destroy and to extol; to annihilate through analysis and to make live through passionate comprehension.

The price that must be paid for a love that cannot integrate its hate is sentimentality; the price that must be paid for a hate that cannot integrate its love is, variously, empty rhetoric, insecurity of taste, and the sterile refinements of an intellect bent on destruction.

Between these perils Joyce won some great triumphs.

Like Cervantes, he groped confusedly for his subject and his form. The history of a writer is his search for his own subject, his myth-theme, hidden from him, but prepared for him in every hour of his life, his *Gulliver's Travels*, his *Robinson Crusoe*. Like Cervantes, unsuccessfully, Joyce tried poetry and drama. Knowing the incomparable resources of his prose rhythms, one is astonished at these verses—a watery musicality, a pinched ventriloqual voice. Knowing the vital dialogues in *Dubliners* and that electrifying scene, the quarrel at the Christmas dinner-table, in *A Portrait of the Artist as a Young Man*, one is astonished at the woodenness of his play *Exiles*.

Like Cervantes, he turned with greater success to short

narratives, and, like him, found in the dimensions of the long
book his form and his theme.

Ulysses brought a new method into literature, the interior
monologue. The century-long advance of realism now con-
fronted this task: the realistic description of consciousness. To
realism, mind is a babbler, a stream of fleeting odds and ends of
image and association. Joyce achieved this method with a
mastery and fullness of illustration that effaces any question of
precursors. He alone has been able to suggest the apparent in-
coherence and triviality of this incessant woolgathering, and yet
to impose upon it a coordination beyond itself, in art. With what
consternation the Masters would have beheld this sight. Shake-
speare reserved divagation for Juliet's nurse, Jane Austen for
Miss Bates. Hamlet's interior monologue is based upon the
assumption that for a short time the human mind may pursue
its idea in purity. Yet all art is convention, even the inner
monologue. Joyce's discovery has the character of necessity, a
twentieth-century necessity, and again it was wrung from him
by the operation of his love and hate. There is destruction in
that it saps the dignity of the mind; there is profound sympa-
thy in the uses to which he put it for characterization. With it
he explores three souls, Stephen Dedalus and the Blooms; one
failure and two great triumphs.

Dedalus is confessedly autobiographical; how can unrecon-
ciled love and hate make a self-portrait? Here the price is paid,
sentimentality. Dedalus extends his bleeding heart, not with-
out complacency; he mocks himself for it, but even in the
mockery we surprise the sob of an Italian tenor. The miracle of
the book is Leopold Bloom, Joyce's anti-self, *l'homme moyen
sensuel*, and his wife, Marion—transcendent confirmations of
the method itself. If we could surprise the interior monologue
of any person—it seems to affirm—we would be obliged to en-
large the famous aphorism: to understand that much is not
only to forgive that much; it is to extend to another person that
suspension of objective judgment which we accord to our-
selves; a homage to the life-force itself in the play of conscious-
ness relegating all questions of approval or disapproval.

*

Ulysses exemplifies, as a technical problem, the mastery of the long book—where Proust and so many others have failed. This has been achieved, perilously, by a resort to curious architectural devices and by the play of the comic spirit—these Chinese boxes of complicated schematization: each chapter marked by one color; each chapter representing an organ in the human body; each under the sign of a theological virtue and its allied vice; each bearing a relation—partly as parody, partly for emotion—to a corresponding book of the *Odyssey*. At first glance how unlike the abounding creativity of the great books—of Rabelais, Cervantes, and Dante—are these devious ingenuities and buried cross-references; and yet Ulysses has the climate of the great books. It circulates in the resources of the style, equal to every mood and to every game; in the lofty requirement that the reader give his whole attention to every word; in the omnipresence of a surpassingly concrete Dublin; in the humanity of the characters; and in the earnestness of an element that one can only call "confessional."

After *Ulysses*, Joyce went through a period of disorganization: the search for the new subject; the increasing threat to his eyesight.

One day a friend sent him a postcard picturing the Bay of Dublin and Howth Head—that promontory in which Celt and Dane and Saxon have always seen the outline of a sleeper's head. Joyce resolved to write the thoughts of that sleeping man. For seventeen years he worked on *Finnegans Wake*, peering over the page with fading vision, elaborating its complexities, like some ancient illuminator fashioning the traceries of the *Book of Kells*. A book in sleep-language—the inner monologue unlocked to still greater possibilities of apparent incoherence and hence requiring a still more elaborate schematic scaffolding. Those who have deciphered even a small part of the work have glimpsed the grandeur of the plan: the sleeper reliving the history of mankind and identifying himself with the heroes and sinners of the world's myth literature; his thoughts influenced by the stars that pass over his head and couched in a language which reproduces the talking-on-two-levels characteristic of sleep; a language in which all the tongues of the world have

coalesced into a *pâté*, the barriers between them having become imperceptible at that level; the sleeper wrestling all night with the problem of original sin, with the sense of guilt acquired from offenses which his waking self knows nothing of. Toward dawn, his enemies mastered, identifying himself with Finn, the ancient Irish hero, he awakes to a new day in the eternal cyclic revolutions of lives and civilizations. Finn! Again wake!

We cannot know yet whether hate has buried this conception under the debris of language analyzed to dust or whether love through identification with human history, through the laughter of the comic genius, and through the incomparable musicality of its style, has won its greatest triumph of all.

Joyce recommended this work to the world as his greatest, and it may be that when we come to know it, our gratitude for so many excellences in the earlier books will be exceeded by all that we owe him for this one.

1941

Gertrude Stein's
Four in America

M ISS GERTRUDE STEIN, answering a question about her
line

> Rose is a rose is a rose is a rose,

once said with characteristic vehemence:

> Now listen! I'm no fool. I know that in daily life we don't go around
> saying "is a . . . is a . . . is a . . ."

She knew that she was a difficult and an idiosyncratic author.
She pursued her aims, however, with such conviction and in-
tensity that occasionally she forgot that the results could be
difficult to others. At such times the achievements she had made
in writing, in "telling what she knew" (her most frequent for-
mulization of the aim of writing), had to her the character of
self-evident beauty and clarity. A friend, to whom she showed
recently completed examples of her poetry, was frequently
driven to reply sadly: "But you forget that I don't understand
examples of your extremer styles." To this she would reply with
a mixture of bewilderment, distress, and exasperation:

> But what's the difficulty? Just read the words on the paper. They're in
> English. Just read them. Be simple and you'll understand these
> things.

Now let me quote the whole speech from which the open-
ing remark in this introduction has been extracted. A student
in her seminar at the University of Chicago had asked her for
an "explanation" of the famous line. She leaned forward, giving
all of herself to the questioner in that unforgettable way which
has endeared her to hundreds of students and to hundreds of
soldiers in two wars, trenchant, humorous, but above all ur-
gently concerned over the enlightenment of even the most ob-
tuse questioner:

> Now listen! Can't you see that when the language was new—as it
> was with Chaucer and Homer—the poet could use the name of a

thing and the thing was really there? He could say "O moon," "O sea," "O love" and the moon and the sea and love were really there. And can't you see that after hundreds of years had gone by and thousands of poems had been written, he could call on those words and find that they were just worn-out literary words? The excitingness of pure being had withdrawn from them; they were just rather stale literary words. Now the poet has to work in the excitingness of pure being; he has to get back that intensity into the language. We all know that it's hard to write poetry in a late age; and we know that you have to put some strangeness, something unexpected, into the structure of the sentence in order to bring back vitality to the noun. Now it's not enough to be bizarre; the strangeness in the sentence structure has to come from the poetic gift, too. That's why it's doubly hard to be a poet in a late age. Now you all have seen hundreds of poems about roses and you know in your bones that the rose is not there. All those songs that sopranos sing as encores about "I have a garden; oh, what a garden!" Now I don't want to put too much emphasis on that line, because it's just one line in a longer poem. But I notice that you all know it; you make fun of it, but you know it. Now listen! I'm no fool. I know that in daily life we don't go around saying "is a . . . is a . . . is a . . ." Yes, I'm no fool; but I think that in that line the rose is red for the first time in English poetry for a hundred years.

Four in America is full of that "strangeness which must come from the poetic gift" in order to restore intensity to images dusted over with accustomedness and routine. It is not required in poetry alone; for Miss Stein all intellectual activities—philosophical speculation, literary criticism, narration—had to be refreshed at the source.

There are certain of her idiosyncrasies which by this time should not require discussion—for example, her punctuation and her recourse to repetition. Readers who still balk at these should not attempt to read this volume, for it contains idiosyncrasies far more taxing to conventional taste. The majority of readers ask of literature the kind of pleasure they have always received; they want "more of the same"; they accept idiosyncrasy in author and period only when it has been consecrated by a long-accumulated prestige, as in the cases of the earliest and the latest of Shakespeare's styles, and in the poetry of Donne, Gerard Manley Hopkins, or Emily Dickinson. They arrogate to themselves a superiority in condemning the novels of Kafka

or of the later Joyce or the later Henry James, forgetting that they allow a no less astonishing individuality to Laurence Sterne and to Rabelais.

This work is for those who not only largely accord to others "another's way," but who rejoice in the diversity of minds and the tension of difference.

Miss Stein once said:

> Every masterpiece came into the world with a measure of ugliness in it. That ugliness is the sign of the creator's struggle to say a new thing in a new way, for an artist can never repeat yesterday's success. And after every great creator there follows a second man who shows how it can be done easily. Picasso struggled and made his new thing and then Braque came along and showed how it could be done without pain. The Sistine Madonna of Raphael is all over the world, on grocers' calendars and on Christmas cards; everybody thinks its an easy picture. It's our business as critics to stand in front of it and re-cover its ugliness.

This book is full of that kind of ugliness. It is perhaps enough to say: "Be simple and you will understand these things"; but it is necessary to say: "Relax your predilection for the accustomed, the received, and be ready to accept an extreme example of idiosyncratic writing."

Distributed throughout Miss Stein's books and in the *Lectures in America* can be found an account of her successive discoveries and aims as a writer. She did not admit that the word "experiments" be applied to them.

> Artists do not experiment. Experiment is what scientists do; they initiate an operation of unknown factors in order to be instructed by its results. An artist puts down what he knows and at every moment it is what he knows at that moment. If he is trying things out to see how they go he is a bad artist.

A brief recapitulation of the history of her aims will help us to understand her work.

Gertrude Stein left Radcliffe College with William James's warm endorsement, to study psychology at Johns Hopkins University. There, as a research problem, her professor gave her a study of automatic writing. For this work she called upon her fellow students—the number ran into the hundreds—to serve

as experimental subjects. Her interest, however, took an unex-
pected turn; she became more absorbed in the subjects' varying
approach to the experiments than in the experiments them-
selves. They entered the room with alarm, with docility, with
bravado, with gravity, with scorn, or with indifference. This
striking variation re-awoke within her an interest which had
obsessed her even in very early childhood—the conviction
that a description could be made of all the types of human char-
acter and that these types could be related to two basic types
(she called them independent-dependents and dependent-
independents). She left the university and, settling in Paris, ap-
plied herself to the problem. The result was the novel of one
thousand pages, *The Making of Americans,* which is at once an
account of a large family from the time of the grandparents'
coming to this country from Europe and a description of "every-
one who is, or has been, or will be." She then went on to give
in *A Long Gay Book* an account of all possible relations of two
persons. This book, however, broke down soon after it began.
Miss Stein had been invaded by another compelling problem:
How, in our time, do you describe anything? In the previous
centuries writers had managed pretty well by assembling a
number of adjectives and adjectival clauses side by side; the
reader "obeyed" by furnishing images and concepts in his mind
and the resultant "thing" in the reader's mind corresponded
fairly well with that in the writer's. Miss Stein felt that that
process did not work any more. Her painter friends were
showing clearly that the corresponding method of "descrip-
tion" had broken down in painting and she was sure that it
had broken down in writing.

 In the first place, words were no longer precise; they were
full of extraneous matter. They were full of "remembering"—
and describing a thing in front of us, an "objective thing," is
no time for remembering. Even vision (a particularly over-
charged word), even sight had been dulled by remembering.
The painters of the preceding generation, the Impressionists,
had shown that. Hitherto people had known that, close to, a
whitewashed wall had no purple in it; at a distance it might
have a great deal of purple, but many painters had not allowed
themselves to see purple in a distant whitewashed wall because
they remembered that close to it was uniformly white. The

Impressionists had shown us the red in green trees; the Post-Impressionists showed us that our entire sense of form, our very view of things, was all distorted and distorting and "educated" and adjusted by memory. Miss Stein felt that writing must accomplish a revolution whereby it could report things as they were in themselves before our minds had appropriated them and robbed them of their objectivity "in pure existing." To this end she went about her house describing the objects she found there in the series of short "poems" which make up the volume called *Tender Buttons*.

Here is one of these:

Red Roses
A cool red rose and a pink cut pink, a collapse
and a sold hole, a little less hot.

Miss Stein had now entered upon a period of excited discovery, intense concentration, and enormous productivity. She went on to writing portraits of her friends and of places. She revived an old interest in drama and wrote scores of plays, many of which are themselves portraits of friends and of places. Two of her lectures in *Lectures in America* describe her aims in these kinds of work. She meditated long on the nature of narration and wrote the novel *Lucy Church Amiably*. This novel is a description of a landscape near Bilignin, her summer home in the south of France. Its subtitle and epigraph are: "A Novel of Romantic Beauty and Nature and which Looks Like an Engraving . . . *'and with a nod she turned her head toward the falling water. Amiably.'*"

Those who had the opportunity of seeing Miss Stein in the daily life of her home will never forget an impressive realization of her practice of meditating. She set aside a certain part of every day for it. In Bilignin she would sit in her rocking chair facing the valley she has described so often, holding one or the other of her dogs on her lap. Following the practice of a lifetime, she would rigorously pursue some subject in thought, taking it up where she had left it on the previous day. Her conversation would reveal the current preoccupation: it would be the nature of "money," or "masterpieces," or "superstition," or "the Republican party." She had always been an omnivorous reader. As a small girl she had sat for days at a time in a window seat in

the Marine Institute Library in San Francisco, an endowed institution with few visitors, reading all Elizabethan literature, including its prose, reading all Swift, Burke, and Defoe. Later in life her reading remained as wide but was strangely non-selective. She read whatever books came her way. ("I have a great deal of inertia. I need things from outside to start me off.") The Church of England at Aix-les-Bains sold its Sunday-school library, the accumulation of seventy years, at a few francs for every ten volumes. They included some thirty minor English novels of the 'seventies, the stately lives of colonial governors, the lives of missionaries. She read them all. Any written thing had become sheer phenomenon; for the purposes of her reflections, absence of quality was as instructive as quality. Quality was sufficiently supplied by Shakespeare, whose works lay often at her hand. If there was any subject which drew her from her inertia and led her actually to seek out works, it was American history and particularly books about the Civil War.

And always with her great relish for human beings she was listening to people. She was listening with genial absorption to the matters in which they were involved.

Everybody's life is full of stories; your life is full of stories; my life is full of stories. They are very occupying, but they are not really interesting. What is interesting is the way everyone tells their stories.

And at the same time she was listening to the tellers' revelation of their "basic nature."

If you listen, really listen, you will hear people repeating themselves. You will hear their pleading nature or their attacking nature or their asserting nature. People who say that I repeat too much do not really listen; they cannot hear that every moment of life is full of repeating. There is only one repeating that is really dead and that is when a thing is taught.

She even listened intently to dog nature. The often-ridiculed statement is literally true that it was from listening to her French poodle Basket lapping water that she discovered the distinction between prose and poetry.

It can easily be understood that the questions she was asking concerning personality and the nature of language and concerning "how you tell a thing" would inevitably lead to the

formulization of a metaphysics. In fact, I think it can be said that the fundamental occupation of Miss Stein's life was not the work of art but the shaping of a theory of knowledge, a theory of time, and a theory of the passions. These theories finally converged on the master question: What are the various ways in which creativity works in everyone? That is the subject of this book. It is a subject which she was to develop more specifically in a book which of all her works is most closely related to this one: *The Geographical History of America or The Relation of Human Nature to the Human Mind*. It led also to a reconsideration of all literature, reflected in the beautiful lecture "What Are Masterpieces and Why Are There So Few of Them?"

Miss Stein held a doctrine which permeates this book, which informs her theory of creativity, which plays a large part in her demonstration of what an American is, and which helps to explain some of the great difficulty which we feel in reading her work. It is the Doctrine of Audience; its literary aspect is considered in the Theory of the Moment of Recognition. In *The Geographical History of America* it is made to illustrate a Theory of Identity.

Let me enter into the subject by again quoting from her words in a conversation:

Why is it that no preachers, no teachers, no orators, no parliamentary debaters ever have any ideas after the age of thirty-five? It is because when they talk they only hear what the audience is hearing. They get mixed up in their head and think that it is possible for one person to agree totally with another person; and when you think *that* you are lost and never have any ideas any more. Now what we know is formed in our head by thousands of small occasions in the daily life. By "what we know" I do not mean, of course, what we learn from books, because that is of no importance at all. I mean what we really know, like our assurance about how we know anything, and what we know about the validity of the sentiments, and things like that. All the thousands of occasions in the daily life go into our head to form our ideas about these things. Now if we write, we write; and these things we know flow down our arm and come out on the page. The moment before we wrote them we did not really know we knew them; if they are in our head in the shape of words then that is all wrong and they will come out dead; but if we did not know we knew them until the moment of writing, then they come to us with a shock of surprise. That is the Moment of Recognition. Like God on the Seventh Day

we look at it and say it is good. That is the moment that some people call inspiration, but I do not like the word inspiration, because it suggests that someone else is blowing that knowledge into you. It is not being blown into you; it is very much your own and was acquired by you in thousands of tiny occasions in your daily life. Now, of course, there is no audience at that moment. There is no one whom you are instructing, or fighting, or improving, or pleasing, or provoking. To others it may appear that you are doing all those things to them, but of course you are not. At that moment you are totally alone at this recognition of what you know. And of that thing which you have written you are the first and last audience. This thing which you have written is bought by other people and read by them. It goes through their eyes into their heads and they say they agree with it. But, of course, they cannot agree with it. The things they know have been built up by thousands of small occasions which are different from yours. They *say* they agree with you; what they mean is that they are aware that your pages have the vitality of a thing which sounds to them like someone else's knowing; it is consistent to its own world of what one person has really known. That is a great pleasure and the highest compliment they can pay it is to say that they agree with it.

Now these preachers and orators may have had such moments of recognition when they were young; they may even have had them when they are addressing an audience—though that is very rare. After they have faced a great many audiences they begin to think that the audiences are literally understanding, literally agreeing with them, instead of merely being present at the vitality of these moments of recognition, at their surprising themselves with their own discovery of what they know. Then they gradually slip in more of the kind of ideas that people can agree with, ideas which are not really ideas at all, which are soothing but not exciting—oh, yes, they may be exciting as oratory, but they are not exciting as creation—and after a while they dry up and then they do not have any real ideas any more.

A portion of the ideas expressed above is found in the "Henry James" section of the present book:

Mr. Owen Young made a mistake, he said the only thing he wished his son to have was the power of clearly expressing his ideas. Not at all. It is not clarity that is desirable but force.

Clarity is of no importance because nobody listens and nobody knows what you mean no matter what you mean, nor how clearly you mean what you mean. But if you have vitality enough of knowing enough of what you mean, somebody and sometime and sometimes a great many will have to realise that you know what you mean and so

they will agree that you mean what you know, what you know you mean, which is as near as anybody can come to understanding any one.

Miss Stein never claimed that these doctrines were new. She delighted in finding them in the great works of the past. She was never tired of saying that all real knowledge is common knowledge; it lies sleeping within us; it is awakened in us when we hear it expressed by a person who is speaking or writing in a state of recognition.

From consciousness of audience, then, come all the evils of thinking, writing, and creating. In *The Geographical History of America* she illustrates the idea by distinguishing between our human nature and our human mind. Our human nature is a serpents' nest, all directed to audience; from it proceed self-justification, jealousy, propaganda, individualism, moralizing, and edification. How comforting it is, and how ignobly pleased we are when we see it expressed in literature. The human mind, however, gazes at experience and without deflection by the insidious pressures from human nature tells what it sees and knows. Its subject matter is indeed human nature; to cite two of Miss Stein's favorites, *Hamlet* and *Pride and Prejudice* are about human nature, but not of it. The survival of masterpieces, and there are very few of them, is due to our astonishment that certain minds can occasionally report life without adulterating the report with the gratifying movements of their own self-assertion, their private quarrel with what it has been to be a human being.

Miss Stein pushed to its furthest extreme this position that at the moment of writing one rigorously excludes from the mind all thought of praise and blame, of persuasion or conciliation. In the early days she used to say: "I write for myself and strangers." Then she eliminated the strangers; then she had a great deal of trouble with the idea that one is an audience to oneself, which she solves in this book with the far-reaching concept: "I am not I when I see."

It has often seemed to me that Miss Stein was engaged in a series of spiritual exercises whose aim was to eliminate during the hours of writing all those whispers into the ear from the outside and inside world where audience dwells. She knew that she

was the object of derision to many and to some extent the knowledge fortified her. Yet it is very moving to learn that on one occasion when a friend asked her what a writer most wanted, she replied, throwing up her hands and laughing, "Oh, praise, praise, praise!" Some of the devices that most exasperate readers—such as the capricious headings of subdivisions in her work, such sequences as Book IV, Book VII, Book VIII, Volume I—though in part they are there to make fun of pompous heads who pretend to an organic development and have no development, are at bottom merely attempts to nip in the bud by a drastic intrusion of apparent incoherence any ambition she may have felt within herself to woo for acceptance as a "respectable" philosopher. It should be noted that another philosopher who wrestled with the problem of restating the mind of man in the terms of our times and who has emerged as perhaps the most disturbing and stimulating voice of the nineteenth century—Søren Kierkegaard—delayed his recognition and "put off" his readers by many a mystification and by an occasional resort to almost Aristophanic buffoonery.

There is another evidence of Miss Stein's struggle to keep her audience out of her mind. *Four in America* is not a book which is the end and summary of her thoughts about the subjects she has chosen; it is the record of her thoughts, from the beginning, as she "closes in" on them. It is *being written*—before our eyes; she does not, as other writers do, suppress and erase the hesitations, the recapitulations, the connectives, in order to give us the completed fine result of her meditations. She gives us the process. From time to time we hear her groping toward the next idea; we hear her cry of joy when she has found it; sometimes it seems to me that we hear her reiterating the already achieved idea and, as it were, pumping it in order to force out the next development that lies hidden within it. We hear her talking to herself about the book that is growing and glowing (to borrow her often irritating habit of rhyming) within her. Many readers will not like this, but at least it is evidence that she is ensuring the purity of her indifference as to whether her readers will like it or not. It is as though she were afraid that if she went back and weeded out all these signs of groping and shaping and reassembling, if she gave us only the completed thoughts in their last best order, the truth would

have slipped away like water through a sieve because such a final marshaling of her thoughts would have been directed toward audience. Her description of existence would be, like so many hundreds of thousands of descriptions of existence, like most literature—dead.

Another spiritual exercise she practices is no less disconcerting. She introduces what I like to call "the irruption of the daily life." If her two dogs are playing at her feet while she is writing she puts them into the text. She may suddenly introduce some phrases she has just heard over the garden wall. This resembles a practice that her friends the Post-Impressionist painters occasionally resorted to. They pasted a subway ticket to the surface of their painting. The reality of a work of art is one reality; the reality of a "thing" is another reality; the juxtaposition of the two kinds of reality gives a bracing shock. It also insults the reader; but the reader is not present, nor even imagined. It refreshes in the writer the sense that the writer is all alone, alone with his thoughts and his struggle and even with his relation to the outside world that lies about him.

The fourth section of this book, by far the most difficult, seems to me to be full of these voices and irruptions. Miss Stein is sitting on the terrace of her villa at Bilignin toward the end of the day. The subject of George Washington comes toward her from a distance:

Autumn scenery is warm if the fog has lifted.
And the moon has set in the day-time in what may be drifting clouds. . . .
George Washington was and is the father of his country. . . .
It should not be a disturbance if they can mistake a bird for a bat or a bat for a bird and find it friendly.

At first view the plan of this book appears to furnish little more than a witty diversion, a parlor game—What kind of novels would George Washington have written? What kind of military strategy would Henry James have devised? One soon discovers, however, that it is a very earnest game indeed. It asks about "how creativity works in any one," about the relations between personality and gifts, personality and genius. No less searchingly, it asks another question: What is an American and what makes him different from a citizen of any other country?

Soon after Miss Stein settled in France for an almost unbroken residence of over forty years a very unusual thing happened to her: she was really taken into a number of French homes. She was told their secrets, told their finances, and told their politics. That must seldom have happened to any American who was at once so loved, so tirelessly ready to listen to details, and who had so consuming a passion to reduce the multitudinous occasions of the daily life to psychological and philosophical laws.

In addition, she spent some time in England during the earlier part of the War of 1914–18. She spent a number of summers in Spain and related what she saw to the characters of her three close friends, the Spanish painters Picasso, Juan Gris, and Picabia. All the time, however, she was meeting and "listening" to Americans and the contacts with Europeans continued to sharpen her perception of specific American nature. When after thirty years' absence she returned to America and traveled it from coast to coast her delight was not only in the experience itself; it was also the delight of seeing her conclusions confirmed and extended.

The section on Ulysses S. Grant begins with a lively discussion of the relations between people and the Christian names they bear. Miss Stein relates it to superstition and to religion, as later she will relate it to the spell cast by novelists, the novelist Henry James and the hypothetical novelist George Washington.

She is tracking down certain irrational ways we have of knowing things, of believing things, and of being governed by these ways of believing. Even the strongest minds have been nonplussed and rendered angry by the extent to which they can be caught up into belief by imaginative narration. One remembers St. Augustine's anguished repudiation of the hold which theatrical performances had taken of him in Carthage. "Novels are true," says Miss Stein. Similarly, great minds have tried to revolt from the sway that superstition can exert over them—involuntarily downcast by omens, predictions, recurrences of certain numbers—just as lesser minds can be given courage by a palm-reading and can be crossed with fear by a broken mirror. There is no "truth" in these things, people say; but perhaps man knows nothing and will never know anything;

the important thing is that he behaves as though he knew something and the irrational ways of knowing which are found in religion and superstition and in submission to a novel are among the more powerful driving forces toward how he behaves.

Miss Stein is talking about religion throughout this section and she is furnishing analogies to the kind of "knowing" that goes to make up religious belief. One of them is the haunting sense that your name is the right name for you.

Religion, as Miss Stein uses the term, has very little to do with cults and dogma, particularly in America. She makes a score of attempts to define it, but the attempts result in fragmentary analogies, straining the syntax of the English language to express flashes of insight. Religion is what a person knows—knows beyond knowing, knows beyond anyone's power to teach him—about his relation to the existence in which he finds himself. It is the tacit assumption that governs his "doing anything that he does do," his creativity. "Religion is what is alright if they have to have their ups and downs." "Religion is not a surprise but it is exciting." "There is no advice in American religion." "American religion is what they could not compare with themselves." "Nobody in America need be careful to be alone, not in American religion. . . ."

To illustrate what American religion is, she first chooses the figure of a camp meeting. There is no leader, or, to put it more exactly, there is a leader but the people are not led. Here is the first striking difference from European religion. It is in the open; there is even some deliberation as to whether the trees have to be there. Just as we hear that Americans have no home, just because their whole country is their home, so their church really has no house. The fact is Americans do not localize anything, not even themselves, as the whole book constantly reiterates. Here again we are a long way from European religion. Moreover, American religion is thanking, not supplication. Americans do not even wish. We shall see the extent to which they do not "wait"; they are not "ready," except in limited contingencies, they do not "prepare"—so little does an American believe that one forces circumstances to one's will. It is at the very heart of American religion that the majority of Americans "like what they have," and readers of *The Geographical History of America* will see how this relative absence of resenting the

universe, despising the universe, trying to subjugate or reshape a "destiny" derives from the physical constitution of our country and the problems our pioneers met. Now, in a camp meeting some walk up and down, some stand, some sing, some kneel, some wail; there is a leader but they are not led; and a congregation of four hundred is not four hundred, but it is one and one and one and one . . . up to four hundred.

The foregoing does not mean that Americans are passive. The true passivity—that is, the true slavery and the true ineffectiveness—is to wish and to wait and to yearn and to conspire. Nor does the group that is one and one and one, and so on, mean that the American is an uncurbed individualist, for "they all go forward together." "They act as if they all go together one by one and so any one is not leading." "Go forward" has no moralizing sense; in Gertrude Stein it is hard to find a moralizing sense. Moralizing comes from that realm of belief which is acquired, learned, arrogated to oneself and promulgated; but which is not truly believed or lived by.

The passage to the effect that Americans cannot earn a living or be a success is likely to cause the bewildered astonishment that it first aroused in Miss Stein. ("Now, Lizzie, do you understand?") It is conceded that some Americans can make money, and that they can do what they have to do and that they can become "names which everyone knows," but that is not the same thing. Again Miss Stein is seeing Americans against her immense knowledge of French domestic life, compared to which the American relation to money is frivolous and the American relation to the whole practical side of life is without perseverance, foresight, or thorough application. The French would put it overwhelmingly that we are not "*sérieux.*" In conversation Miss Stein went even further; she said that "Americans are really only happy when they are failures," and laughing deeply she would furnish a wealth of illustration. Again the reader should be warned against interpreting this passage in moralizing terms; this is not the sentimental commonplace that life's failures are the true successes nor does it mean that Americans are unworldly knights-errant. An American's inability to make a living is not a consequence of his "values" but of the way his mind works in him.

The portrait of an American is then beginning to assemble

about the image of General Grant and his hypothetical alter ego, Hiram Grant, retired from the army and become very busily a failure in the harness store at Galena, Illinois. He did not wait for the great position that would someday fall to him, because Americans do not wait—that is, they do not live in the expectation that circumstance is coming toward them bearing gifts. There is no animism in American religion. The skies do not pity nor punish nor bring gifts. Nor does her American yearn, strain, or intrigue for the situations he may profit by; he is what he is, and what he *is*, not what he *wills*, is his expression. Some of the most exasperating of Miss Stein's phrases are employed to express this aspect of her subject. She seems to have a low opinion of the verb "sit," which to her expresses both the passivity and the expectancy which are not present in her Americans. Apparently, the word "there" and the verbs "come" and "go" all imply a degree of intention that is not in her Americans. So we get such upsetting combinations of these usages as: "Ulysses Simpson Grant was there as often as he came but he never came."

All this prepares us for the statement that Americans never die; they are killed or they go away, but they are not dead. This is in great contrast, of course, to the Europeans, who "wait for" their death, prepare, resist, foresee, bewail, or accept their death. This she puts down to the American sky, which is not really a sky but is just air; but it is obviously related to the other elements of the American religion, that all you have is in every moment of your consciousness (and that you like all that you have) and so self-contained is every moment of consciousness that there is nothing left over for expectation or memory. The American, then, who has lost that moment of consciousness is not that European thing called "dead"—so fraught with immemorial connotations—he has gone away. For this Miss Stein finds the striking image that every American is an only child—is *one*, has everything, and is the center of everything—is then naturally very solemn and cannot die.

This is followed by an apparently difficult passage which, however, yields us some light on a number of Miss Stein's most characteristic locutions. General Grant was not "one of two" or "one of three"; for relief or guidance or comfort or support he did not ally himself with anyone else and even when he came

to fill that high station for which he had not been waiting he was "not differently surrounded by himself"—surrounded, of course, he was, as we all are, but "surround does not mean surrender" (and surrender is here not the act of war but the loss of one's own knowing: "This is what I mean and this will I do").

So we begin to see what kind of a saint General Grant would have been if he had been a leader in religion. And now we see another reason why I went to some length to discuss Miss Stein's theory of Audience and her theory of the distinction between human nature and the human mind. It looks as though General Ulysses S. Grant and the saint he might have been had it in common that they did not listen to those seductive appeals from the Audience which keep crowding up from human nature. Neither Grant waited nor was anxious; neither came nor sat; both "knew what they knew at the moment of knowing it," a knowledge unsullied by expectation or memory. They did not let will or determination order them about; they did what they did, but they did not set about to do what they were to do.

One word hovers over the entire book and is never spoken. It is the word "abstract." American religion is presented as very abstract, and so are the mentalities of the Americans described here who are certainly prototypes of the generalized American. In *The Geographical History of America* Miss Stein goes on to explain that such minds are so formed by the physical character of the environment in which they live. "Everyone is as their land and water and sky are," and in America there is no sky— there is just air; there is just "up"; the majority of Americans, in addition, either know the straight line of the sea or the lake, or they know a land so devoid of natural features that "when they make the boundary of a State they have to make it with a straight line." In European geography there are no boundaries which are straight lines.

The section on Wilbur Wright begins with another teasing play with Christian names. The reader can now share Miss Stein's delighted consternation on receiving a letter from a man named Ulysses Lee. "And there is nothing more to be said is there. Names call to names as birds call to birds." We have learned what a "Ulysses" nature is; a nature of that degree of

abstraction could conceivably be born into a situation in which he would find himself called Ulysses Lee.

In driving through Le Mans Miss Stein once came upon the monument which the French had raised to Wilbur Wright. She tells us that she was struck with the "funny feeling" that Wilbur Wright was not there. France contains many monuments to its eminent dead and in a way she felt that their eminent dead were there. As she has told us, Americans do not die, they go away; but it was very clear that they do not go away to their monuments. This set her brooding again about American religion and American death and about Wilbur Wright and how he made what he made. Presently she found a relationship between aviation and painting and between painting and acting.

Now a writer is not confronted by his past books. They are not even there in his mind, staring at him. His past work is not an audience to him. He is not his work and he is not connected to his work, save at the moment of creation. All painters, however, and particularly European painters, are surrounded by their paintings, even if their paintings are distributed all over the world. They are "extended" to their paintings. They are not alone. And the paintings are not "left"—are not relegated to a place outside consciousness. We are repeatedly told that no painting can be "left."

This has something to do with seeing, and leads to a similar situation in actors and in Wilbur Wright. Actors in a profound sense see rather than hear what they say. (The words are but a small part of the creativity in their art and the words having been created in the "recognition" of the dramatist are resumed by the actor into his total creation, which is preponderantly visual. He "paints" a rôle employing the words of the dramatist as the raw material of his painting, just as his face, body, voice, and dress are raw material. It is in this sense that he "sees what he says.")

These creators who see their past work are eternally surrounded by it and are not alone. This is not urged as a reproach upon them; it is the character of their creativity; nor is their past work an audience to them in a bad sense, for they are their creativity, past and present. In the vocabulary of Miss Stein seeing always stands high. She enjoyed repeating that "seeing is believing." Readers will remark that among these thousands

of references to creativity there is no reference to music. "Music is for adolescents," she used to say. The eye is closer to the human mind, the ear to human nature. She had passed through a phase of her life as an impassioned and informed music-lover and had put it behind her. Only once have I heard her concede that music—it was after a hearing of Beethoven's "Archduke" Trio—can occasionally issue from the human mind.

A reader having reached the middle point in the Wilbur Wright section is presumably becoming accustomed to Miss Stein's disregard for the first or generally received meanings of words and to her powerful compressions. (They have a relationship by contrast with her repetitions: a repetition is a small degree of progression by alteration and emphasis; a compression is a sweeping summary or a violent leap into new matter.) A reader is ready for such a passage as the following (the punctuation is impertinently mine):

A painting is something seen after it has been done and—in this way —left alone; nobody can say: "he—or I—left it alone." No painting is left alone.

The airplane was that kind of creation and the man whose work it was to make the flying machine and to fly it saw himself moving; he was in his creation as a painter is in and of his painting.

There are many difficulties in this section for which I am not competent to furnish a gloss. The day will come when devoted readers of Miss Stein will furnish a lexicon of her locutions. There are hundreds of them which may strike a first reader as incoherent expressions thrown off at random; but they are found recurringly distributed throughout her work. The task of her future commentators will consist in tracing them to their earliest appearances embedded in a context which furnishes the meaning they held for her. Thereafter they became bricks in her building, implements in her meditation. To her their meaning is "self-evident"; she forgets that we have not participated in the systematic meditation which was her life.

I leave to the reader's contemplation also the spectacle of the extraordinary emotion which accumulates toward the end of each of these sections. Miss Stein loves, overwhelmingly loves, each of the heroes of this volume. "Who knows what

Grant did. I do." "It is Ulysses S. Grant that is interesting, very interesting." "I cannot think of Ulysses Simpson Grant without tears." "Wilbur Wright is fine." "East and West. George Washington is best."

The Henry James section begins with Miss Stein's account of how she came to make an important discovery concerning writing. It is a curious thing to me that in each of her retellings of this story she has omitted a fact that throws further light on it. This fact is that when she wrote the poems called *Before the Flowers of Friendship Faded Friendship Faded* she began writing them as translations of a group of poems in French by her friend Georges Hugnet. They are far from being literal translations, even in the beginning, but they take their point of departure from his poems, and they remained, as her discussion shows, "the poems he would have written if he had written them."

Hence, she was not writing "what she wrote, but what she intended to write." A sort of ventriloquism had introduced itself into the process of writing, and she became aware that the words had a sort of smoothness which they did not have in the poems which she wrote "from herself alone." Suddenly this smoothness reminded her of a smoothness she had long noticed in Shakespeare's *Sonnets*. She says (in the fourth lecture on *Narration*):

I concluded then that Shakespeare's sonnets were not written to express his own emotion I concluded that he put down what some one told him to do as their feeling which they definitely had each time for each sonnet as their feeling and that is the reason that the words in the sonnets come out with a smooth feeling with no vibration in them such as the words in all his plays have as they come out from them.

Many scholars have reached a similar conclusion as to Shakespeare's *Sonnets*, and not only in regard to the series written on the preposterous theme "Go, young man, and get married in order that you may leave a copy of your excellences to the afterworld."

Miss Stein was perhaps a little nettled to find also that the poems of *Before the Flowers of Friendship Faded* gave more pleasure to her friends than her earlier poems had given. This

discovery led her straight to the problem of audience. There are two kinds of writing: the kind in which the words mean what they say and the kind in which the "meaning has to be meant as something [that] has been learned"—it has been written to satisfy a preconceived notion as to what it will be like when it is finished, or to satisfy someone else's expectation of it. It is surprising that at this stage of drawing up this distinction she expresses so little disapproval of the second type of writing. She appears to be reconciled to it, it is the way in which the majority of all books have been written.

Henry James, it appears, wrote in a combination of the two ways of writing. In this he resembled a general whose activity consists in doing what he has to do in a situation that has already been prepared. In a general's work for a while "nothing happens together and then all of a sudden it all happens together." For a general and for Henry James "everything that could happen or not happen would have had a preparation."

This treatment of Henry James does indeed awaken a feeling which one had had about his work. It does not mean that other novelists like Fielding, Jane Austen, and Anthony Trollope— to name three for whom she had the highest admiration—did not likewise follow a design and know well in advance the pattern their book was to take. Henry James went further; he finished the book before he wrote it; he wrote the book to resemble a book which he had completely envisaged. Like a general he arrived on a scene which had already been prepared or, as we are repeatedly told, had "been begun." He was to an unprecedented degree an audience to his own composition. We could wish that Miss Stein had helped us through these subtle distinctions by an occasional specific illustration. One is indebted to her, however, for two exquisite characterizations of Henry James's quality. She is speaking of a woman who lived in a *château* near Belley:

She lived alone and in the country and so did Henry James. She was heavy set and seductive and so was Henry James. She was slow in movement and light in speech and could change her speech without changing her words so that at one time her speech was delicate and witty and at another time slow and troubling and so was that of Henry James.

And again:

> He had no fortune and misfortune and nevertheless he had no distress and no relief from any pang. . . . He had no failure and no success and he had no relief from any failure and he had no relief from any distress.

There is an extended portion of this section in which Miss Stein gradually changes into a different style. It is the style of the "Portraits." In fact, when she alludes to this book in one of her *Narration* lectures, she calls it a book of portraits. In her lecture "Portraits and Repetition" she says:

> And so I am trying to tell you what doing portraits meant to me, I had to find out what it was inside any one, and by any one I mean every one I had to find out inside every one what was in them that was intrinsically exciting and I had to find out not by what they said not by what they did not by how much or how little they resembled any other one but I had to find it out by the intensity of movement that there was inside in any one of them. . . .

In another place in the lecture she calls this work catching "the rhythm of personality." Opinions on this extreme style vary even among Miss Stein's greatest admirers. Some assure us that from the first reading they obtain a clear image of the personality so described; others acknowledge occasional flashes of insight but hold that Miss Stein was mistaken in thinking that she had been able to convey the "movement" of her sitters' personalities to anyone but herself. Readers who are indebted to her other writings for so wide a variety of pleasures—for the narrative brilliance of *The Autobiography of Alice B. Toklas*, the massive grasp of *The Making of Americans*, the critical insight and aphoristic skill of her lectures, the illumination and the trenchant thinking about fundamentals contained in the present book—such readers will return again and again to the most difficult pages not willingly conceding that these are forever closed to them.

The fourth section, "Scenery and George Washington," has the subtitle "A Novel or a Play." Its characters are "Scenery" and "George Washington." The section opens, as I have said, with an evocation of the valley below Miss Stein's villa at Bilignin toward which comes, as from a distance, the figure of

Washington and the inquiry as to what kind of novels he
would have written.

Now Miss Stein felt that the novel was threatened with ex-
tinction and she was much concerned with whether it could be
saved. Her fears concerning it were not based, as those of many
critics have been, on the fact that the assumption of omniscience
on the part of the storyteller is untenable in our time. Her ob-
jection was that what happens "from outside" is no longer im-
portant to us, that we are aware of so much happening that the
event is no longer exciting; and that we no longer feel that the se-
quence of events, the succession in time, is of much signifi-
cance. As she says in the second *Narration* lecture:

. . . there is at present not a sense of anything being successively
happening, moving is in every direction beginning and ending is not
really exciting, anything is anything, anything is happening. . . .
And this has come to be a natural thing in a perfectly natural way that
the narrative of today is not a narrative of succession as all the writing
for a good many hundreds of years has been.

And in the lecture "Portraits and Repetition" she says:

A thing you all know is that in the three novels written in this gen-
eration that are the important things written in this generation, there
is, in none of them a story. There is none in Proust in *The Making of
Americans* or in *Ulysses.*

Miss Stein interrupts her discussion to give samples of the
event novel, the succession novel, and she assures us that is not
the kind of novel George Washington wrote. What he wrote
was "the great American novel," an entirely new kind of novel
and a thing which, if we can know it, will throw invaluable light
on the American nature. With what she calls "Volume VI"
begins a flood of definitions—that is, analogical definitions of
what this novel is, just as the Grant section furnished a flood of
descriptions of what "American religion" is.

In the first place, it has to do with the American time-sense.
In the lecture "What Is English Literature" she shows how the
English, living for centuries their "daily island life," made their
literature out of it.

They relied on it so completely that they did not describe it they just
had it and told it. . . . In America . . . the daily everything was

not the daily living and generally speaking there is not a daily everything. They do not live every day . . . and so they do not have this as something that they are telling.

We are back at the abstractedness of the American mind. It does not draw its assurance of knowing anything from an intense localization in time and place. The endless procession of phenomena separate themselves from their specific contingency and reform themselves as a generalized knowing.

And so . . . Henry James just went on doing what American literature had always done, the form was always the form of the contemporary English one, but the disembodied way of disconnecting something from anything and anything from something was the American one. . . . Some say that it is repression, but no it is not repression it is a lack of connection, of there being no connection with living and daily living because there is none, that makes American writing what it always has been and what it will continue to become.

It should be unnecessary to say that this George Washington was not a novelist because he aesthetically composed his life or because he stood off at a distance and viewed his life. A novelist is sovereign over the elements of his imagined world; but they have also an objective life (derived from the "knowing" that he has acquired); he may not force or wrench them, nor make them report a fairer world than he has experienced. We seem to be told by Miss Stein that George Washington moved among events like a novelist among his characters at the moment of their creation.

(I am fond of talking about Napoleon but that has nothing to do with novel writing. Napoleon could not write a novel, not he. Washington could. And did.)

And because he was an American novelist, George Washington was disattached from the concrete and the specific. He could and did love concrete things. ("He was charmed with the dresses of the little baby"—how astonishing are Miss Stein's ways of enclosing the general in the specific! That is an example of the writing which she exalts in the Henry James section, where the "writing and the writer are alike," of a "sound heard by the eyes," and that "does not mean what it says because it just is"—that is, lands squarely on its truth and is only watered

down by "preparation" and explanation, as I have watered it down here.) George Washington's love of the concrete in our human life and his pleasure in baby dresses was of the American order; it tended to transmute its experiences from things of human nature to things of the human mind. The human mind cannot be consoled by things nor rendered proud; it does not preach nor despise; it merely sees and tells what it sees. Such a novel George Washington was writing every day.

The pages begin to bristle with Miss Stein's most idiosyncratic expressions and we are again in the "portrait" style. This introduction is already too long to permit of an attempt to wrestle with them. The solution of many of them, however, can be found elsewhere in Miss Stein's work. For example, the long passage on Washington's youth beginning with the disconcerting phrases:

He could just smile if he was born already. . . . And he was not born. Oh indeed no he was not born

has a history in her work. As early as *A Long Gay Book* Miss Stein was observing that many people are rendered uneasy, are even crippled, by the thought that they were once helpless babies, passed about and tended by others. The dignity of their human mind (which, of course, knows no age) is undermined by thoughts of themselves in infancy. It is this idea which grows into fuller statement in *The Geographical History of America* in the development of the astonishing question:

What is the use of being a little boy if you are going to grow up to be a man?

The word "tears" occurs frequently in this book. What things in our human lot seem to have moved Miss Stein to tears? It was not the misfortunes of our human nature, though she was a greatly sympathetic resource to her friends when their griefs were real. What moved her deeply was the struggle of the human mind in its work, which is to know. It was of Henry James's mind (and the phrase applies as beautifully to those great heroines of his last novels who live not to assert themselves but to understand) that she says "he had no relief from any pang."

She said to me once:

Everyone when they are young has a little bit of genius, that is they really do listen. They can listen and talk at the same time. Then they grow a little older and many of them get tired and they listen less and less. But some, a very few continue to listen. And finally they get very old and they do not listen any more. That is very sad; let us not talk about that.

This book is by an impassioned listener to life. Even up to her last years she listened to all comers, to "how their knowing came out of them." Hundreds of our soldiers, scoffing and incredulous but urged on by their companions, came up to Paris "to see the Eiffel Tower and Gertrude Stein." They called and found bent upon them those gay and challenging eyes and that attention that asked nothing less of them than their genius. Neither her company nor her books were for those who have grown tired of listening. It was an irony that she did her work in a world in which for many reasons and for many appalling reasons people have so tired.

1947

Joyce and
the Modern Novel

T HE subject I am going to treat tonight is the question we are so often asked: Why did Joyce have to write in so difficult a way? Why didn't he recount "simply" that Leopold Bloom identified Stephen Dedalus with a son he had lost? And why this impenetrable thicket of polyglot puns in *Finnegans Wake*? Why all these complicated things going on all the time? Readers turn to the various manuals on *Ulysses* and they find out each episode is controlled by an organ of the human body; each episode has a predominating color. Episode VII has reference to the lungs: its color is red-brown, and its art is rhetoric. In episode VI you attend a funeral; you must remember your *Odyssey* and the descent to Hell; the color of it is black and white, and its organ is the heart. Why must Joyce erect so many formal patterns?

There are a number of answers. In the first place, James Joyce was hunting for a style that would reveal the extent to which every individual—you and I, the millions of the people who walk this earth—is both sole and unique and also archetypical. To establish that each human being is archetypical, he had to draw on the human being whom he knew best: himself. So the book likewise is confession, and it is confession at a very deep and agonizing level. It is a wonderful experience to unburden the heart in confession, but it is a very difficult thing to do. The subject longs to tell his charged secret and longs not to tell it. So the complications are partly one step forward and two steps back and two steps forward and four steps back. *Finnegans Wake* is, in spite of all we know of its comic force and its lyric beauty, an agonized journey into the private life of James Joyce.

Another thing that complicates the book is the comic spirit, a constant flow of bitter or tender wit.

In addition, there is an obsessive compulsion toward the all-inclusive—what you might call the kitchen-stove complex. Joyce will get everything in there including the kitchen stove if he possibly can. It is a sort of need to make the catalogue ab-

solutely complete. Not a dozen, but every one of the Sutras of the Koran, every one of Tom Moore's *Melodies*, and, I suspect, every one of the Saints in the calendar. These, and many other series, he stuck into the book like plums into a vast plumcake.

How, as a literary method, does he render an individual archetypically? Joyce was fundamentally a great realistic writer. One of the greatest realistic writers that ever lived was Flaubert, and Joyce worshiped Flaubert. And *Madame Bovary* and *Un Coeur simple* are the greatest achievements of what we call the realistic method. People who open *Finnegans Wake* for the first time would say that certainly this was the least realistic book ever written. But the concrete world is there with a tremendous precision. For in order to pass to the general, one must retain a firm grasp on the particular. In order to see what Joyce accomplished, let us draw an illustration from the theater, making clear the limitations of the realistic theater and novel.

Let us pretend that we are attending a performance of *Romeo and Juliet* in 1910 or 1890. The curtain rises on the banquet scene in *Romeo and Juliet* where Romeo meets Juliet for the first time. What we see are real chandeliers, real rugs, tables laden with supposedly real food and drink, and it is all boxed in within a picture frame. So it was staged, not as Shakespeare intended, but as the nineteenth century staged it. The nineteenth century was a very bad century for the theater and a glorious century for the novel.

And what did it convey? It said that these events took place to one set of persons, at one moment in time, in one place. That is the theater of the Unique Occasion.

Now, you and I and everybody live a complete life under unique occasions. Every single moment of our life is unique in that sense. Every human being lives only unique occasions, just as we all die one death—our death and no one else's. Likewise, of the millions of times that "I love" has been said, each time it is really said just once. The participation in essential love or essential death is, as they now are saying, "existential"—totally individual.

The realistic novel is the art of these unique occasions. *Tess* and *Anna Karenina* and the novels of Jane Austen securely place their characters in one time and one place.

But I can hear you objecting that from all those books a true

"generalization" arises, to which Emma Bovary herself has given her name—the type of an outlook on life—*Bovaryisme*. And we all know the other Emma, too, Jane Austen's Emma, is the kind of woman who goes around bossing, ineptly bossing, the affairs of others. Yes, they participate in "type," but they are lodged in specific circumstances and their generalization follows from the weight laid on particularization.

The realistic method is the glory of the novel; few novels have transcended it, and it was Joyce's point of departure. He wanted not to tell how Mr. So-and-so met Miss So-and-so and how they got married in such-and-such a place. It was this kind of realization that led to a search for a new way of making it arresting to us. Let us approach the problem from another angle:

After I'd graduated from college I was sent to Europe to study archeology. One day our class in Rome was taken out into the country to dig up a bit of the Etruscan world, a street. Once thousands of persons had walked it. The rut was very deep. Those who have uncovered such a spot are never the same again.

Now in the twentieth century we all have something of the mind of an archeologist. The other centuries knew that many people had lived and died a long while ago, and they knew there were many people living on the earth. But the invention of the printing press (its consequences are still unfolding) had made these realizations far more actual. Now everybody knows them, not as something you learn in school and recite to one another, but "in their bones"—that millions and billions have lived and died, and that probably billions and billions (let us not despair of the human race) will live and die. The extent of this enlarged realization alters the whole view of life.

You have lost some husband, brother, or parent in the war. Your grief is very real to you. Yet now we know as never before that a great many died in this war and in the wars of Carthage and Troy and Ur, and in the Thirty Years War—what end is there to any human thing in which you are not also companion to billions? It does not diminish your grief, but it orients it to a larger field of reference.

This shift in outlook brings two results. We are less interested in the anecdote, in the "plot," Mr. So-and-so met the attractive Miss So-and-so. We wish them well; but the mere

account of their progress no longer arrests us in the same way. As Gertrude Stein said,

If you read any of the four greatest novels of the Twentieth Century for *what happens next*, you might as well throw the book away at the beginning: Proust, Joyce, *The Magic Mountain*, *The Making of Americans.*

Plot must be stated differently in order to arrest the attention. The railway stations will continue to sell all sorts of things, but we are talking about adequate reading for adults. The "anecdote" has lost its importance.

The second result is an urgent search for the validity of individual experience. Though I realize that my joy or my grief is but "one" in the ocean of human life, nevertheless it *has* its reality. I know that the existential thing pouring up in me, my joy or my fear, is a real thing and yet that the intensity with which I feel it can be called absurd. It is absurd to claim that "I," in the vast reaches of time and place and repetition, is worth an assertion. This problem drove man back into a journey of self-examination. What is my "I"? What is the reality of my "I"? That's where the New Psychology came in.

Now, Joyce is the great novelist of these two things. He is the novelist who has most succeeded in placing man in an immense field of reference, among all the people who have lived and died, in all the periods of time, all the geography of the world, all the races, all the catastrophes of history. And he is also the one who has most dramatically engaged in a search for the validity of the individual as an absolute.

To express his insights he was driven to fashion a new technique. It is interesting now to see that the search began early. He felt the need of burying beneath the narratives an almost compulsive network of cross-relations, categories, and systems. For a generation *Dubliners* appeared to be a collection of remarkable but loosely related stories. We now know that they fall into a series of interlocking, illustrative patterns.

Now, how would we "present" any individual, or ourselves —ourselves in this room—existing and somehow related to totality? How do we do it in such a way that we would be freed a little from the terror of shrinking to nullity?

First we would seek for our place in myths. Myths are the dreaming soul of the race, telling its story. Now, the dreaming soul of the race has told its story for centuries and centuries and centuries, and there have been billions of stories. They're still telling them. Every novel for sale in a railway station is the dreaming soul of the human race telling its story. But the myths are the survival of the fittest of the billions of stories most of which have been forgotten. No chance survival there. The retelling of them on every hand occurs because they whisper a validation—they isolate and confer a significance—Prometheus, Cassandra, Oedipus, Don Quixote, Faust.

Joyce not only drew on myth; he used history as though it were myth. He made a hero who was Everyman, and to describe him to us he played on the vast repertory of myth and history as upon a clavier. Then he added to his technique another procedure: the dream.

Every great writer has been interested in dreams. Think of how interested in dreams Shakespeare was. Joyce had read the classics of psychoanalysis—though he seems to make fun of them—and there he found what he wanted. There he found the use which our subconscious makes of the symbol—the symbol as clarification and aid, and the symbol substituted for the thing disavowed; there he found the pun and slip of the tongue as betrayal; there also he found the thing which Jung extended much further than Freud: the fact that all of us are motivated by an unconscious reliance on these myths and symbols which help us over difficulties. *Finnegans Wake* is overwhelmingly committed to a belief in the unconscious.

In *Ulysses* Joyce had explored the pressures of the unconscious on the conscious mind. He had gone further than anybody else in unmasking its apparent incoherences. There are no incoherences in the human mind, not even under insanity. Having done a book of the mind awake, he decided to show the mind asleep—to write a Night Book. For this he was driven to invent a technique—a night language. He was greatly helped by the discoveries of Freud.

Freud once said to me,

Oh, I don't think that writers will be able to use the tenets of psychoanalysis for two or three hundred years. Numbers of my friends—

Arnold Zweig and Stefan Zweig and Franz Werfel—have been using psychoanalysis in their novels; but it still comes out as clinical document, as schemata. Only in two or three hundred years will the *Dichter* have assimilated it at so deep a level that they'll know without knowing they know it. And it will come out as pure novel.

But already the greatest novelist or the twentieth century had digested it so deeply that he could play with it, turn it around, illustrate it; it was there as a deep visceral "knowing," a sort of sovereign and joyous possession.

The hero of *Finnegans Wake* is the most "generalized" character in all literature, but he is also completely a unique and individualized person. We overhear and oversee him in bed above his tavern at the edge of Dublin. His conscience is trying him for some obscure misdemeanors committed—or perhaps only partially envisaged—during the day. He is in disgrace. He identifies himself with Lucifer fallen from Heaven, Adam ejected from Paradise, Napoleon defeated at Waterloo, Finnegan of the old ballad laid out for his wake. It is the Book of Falls, and as the night advances he plunges deeper and relives all the crimes of which man is capable; he stands trial (the very constellations of the night sky are sitting in judgment). He submits his defense and extenuation. Finally dawn arrives; the sun climbs through the transom of the Earwickers' bedroom. The last chapter is a wonderful sunburst of Handelian rhetoric; all the resurrection myths of the world are recalled along with Pears' soap advertisements and the passing trains and the milkman. The phoenix is reborn; Everyman re-awakes.

The technique, then, had to ensure a constant oscillation between the homeliest particularizations and the vastest generalization. Joyce, with what I call his compulsion toward all-inclusiveness, had to make sure of including the red man, and the yellow man, and the black man, and the brown man, to include allusions to Australia and Africa and the other continents.

I am told that "twelve-tone series" composers have to touch every one of the notes of the scale before they are allowed to repeat any one of them. Joyce requires of himself a similar obligation. And not only man and his cultures: the physical universe is represented: the constellations of both hemispheres. Light and dark are there in the colors of the spectrum. The universe of sound is there in Guido d'Arezzo's scale—all

half-hidden polyglot puns. Also the elements of matter: gold, silver, copper, lead, carbon.

All these devices were necessary to "orient" the individual within the universe. To them one ingredient more has been added: Joyce was a great comic genius. The comic spirit is constantly relieving us of the burden of life's logical implications. Confront life logically and you might as well resign at once. Human beings cannot bear much wrong and cannot bear much logic and they cannot bear too much self-examination; and the comic spirit was given to us as reconciliation and as an alibi from drawing the last deductions. Push *Don Quixote* and *Le Misanthrope* just a little further and you find agonizing material; the comic spirit has saved them from the precipices over which they hang: defeat and despair. It is necessary to remember this book was written over just such a precipice. There's a limit to which the human heart can endure or sustain itself, even with the aid of the comic spirit. Joyce seems to have sustained himself with his humor, his exercise of confession, and his all but unimaginable industry. He submitted to eleven operations upon his eyes. Finally, he spent hours a day, with diminishing eyesight, fashioning these complicated verbal constructions, always guarding their relation to the heart of the book and bearing in mind their resemblance to the ornamentation of the *Book of Kells.*

Since man in the twentieth century is increasingly aware of the futility of the anecdote alone, and seeks an orientation to a larger universe, do all books henceforward have to be written like this?

I think we are going through a phase when books must reflect these preoccupations. Notice *The Magic Mountain*—Hans Castorp's education. It is about a man learning how to live and think in the twentieth century. Its "Anecdote" is negligible. It is as though for the time being we resigned from that excessive interest in that thing which has fascinated the world for so long: individual personality; the pendulum is now swinging and we are interested in the great types.

Many will say: "Do I have to read this? I'm a busy housewife. I have three children. I belong to the PTA. Do I have to read books like this?"

Did you ever read Rousseau's *Émile* or *La Nouvelle Héloïse*?

I never did—but I can pretty well believe that all of us, whether we know it or not, have been in large part formed by them. Every century has its underground books which have permeated thought. Often they have been transmitted through relatively few readers. I believe those two great books of Rousseau are shaping us still—though many of us will probably never read them. *Finnegans Wake* is going to be passed on through its ardent enthusiasts to generations still unborn. It will take its part in the emergence from parochialism and nationalism and the complacencies of "our system" and "our technological superiority."

The terrible thing is to live in our twentieth century with nineteenth-century mentality. To be "out of phase"—that's what is blighting. That's what starves and frightens and shipwrecks so many souls. The realizations of new dimensions and new obligations pour in on us from the world of science, but we would rather retreat into the accustomed and the soothing. Joyce and Pound and Eliot have advanced into the new territory; they have shown us how understanding can reduce fear. The difficulties they present to readers are the exact counterparts of the difficulties we experience in living at this time, and their triumphs are notification and guide to us as to where we may find clarification and strength.

1954

CHRONOLOGY

NOTE ON THE TEXTS

NOTES

Chronology

1897 Thornton Niven Wilder born April 17 in Madison, Wisconsin, second child of Amos Parker Wilder and Isabella Thornton Niven. (He is named after grandfather Thornton McNess Niven, Jr. [1836–1908], a Presbyterian minister who served as chaplain under General Thomas "Stonewall" Jackson during the Civil War, and great-grandfather Thornton McNess Niven [1806–1895], a Hudson Valley engineer and builder. Father, born 1862 in Calais, Maine, the grandson of a Revolutionary War veteran, graduated from Yale in 1884 and received a Ph.D. in political economy; he became a renowned public speaker, and edited and eventually owned the *Wisconsin State Journal.* Mother, born 1873 in Dobbs Ferry, New York, was the great-granddaughter of Arthur Tappan [1786–1865], co-founder with his brother Lewis of the American Antislavery Society; she did not attend college but acquired an excellent education in literature, languages, music, and art, wrote poetry, and translated from Italian and French. Parents married on December 3, 1894; their first child, Amos Niven, was born in 1895. Thornton's twin brother died at birth. Family legend had it that infant Thornton was so frail he was carried around on a pillow.)

1898 Sister Charlotte Elizabeth born.

1900 Sister Isabel born.

1905–7 Through his Yale friend William Howard Taft, then Secretary of War, Amos Wilder is appointed consul general in Hong Kong. Family arrives in China on May 7, 1906. Thornton briefly attends local German school. Returns to the United States in October 1906 with mother, brother, and sisters, living in Berkeley, California. Studies violin and piano, and sings in Episcopal church choir. Attends McKinley and Emerson public schools. Conducts home theatricals. Watches rehearsals and has walk-on parts in productions at the University of California's Greek Theater.

1909 Father is posted to Shanghai and has home leave to visit family in California.

1910 Sister Janet Frances born. Thornton travels to China with
 his mother and sisters Isabel and Charlotte in December.

1911–13 After a brief stay at a German school in Shanghai, attends
 British-run China Inland Mission School 450 miles away
 in Chefoo (Yantai), where Henry Luce is a fellow student.
 Early in 1911, because of her health and political instabil-
 ity in China, mother takes two youngest children to Italy,
 where they remain for two years. In 1912, Thornton re-
 turns to America and joins brother Amos at the Thacher
 School in Ojai, California, where he co-writes and directs
 his first play, *The Russian Princess*, playing the role of the
 villain, the Grand Duke Alexis. Father refuses to allow
 him to play Lady Bracknell in school production of *The
 Importance of Being Earnest*. Mother returns to Berkeley
 in spring 1913, reuniting the Wilder children under one
 roof; Thornton transfers to Berkeley High School, where
 he is active in the dramatic and vaudeville clubs and
 begins writing a series of three-minute plays. Is an indif-
 ferent student but a voracious reader: reads Shakespeare,
 Dickens, Henry James, Scott, and German classics. Sees
 Sarah Bernhardt, Sidney Howard, and Sir Johnston Forbes-
 Robertson perform. In summer 1913, goes to San Luis
 Obispo, where he spends first of several summers doing
 farm work.

1914–15 Father resigns from the Consular Service for medical rea-
 sons and relocates to New Haven, Connecticut, to as-
 sume post of General Secretary of the Yale-in-China
 program. Thornton graduates from Berkeley High School
 in June 1915. At father's insistence, enrolls in the fall at
 Oberlin College. Writes to a former teacher: "I have [my
 father's] promise in writing for one year only. Then Yale,
 and I hope Prof. [George Pierce] Baker's class for post-
 graduate at Harvard."

1916–17 Stays two years at Oberlin, where he befriends fellow stu-
 dent Robert Maynard Hutchins, studies the organ, con-
 tinues writing plays, and publishes in the *Oberlin Literary
 Magazine*; finds a mentor in English professor Charles
 H. A. Wager. During the summers, works on farms in
 Kentucky, Vermont, and Massachusetts. In September
 1917, enrolls at Yale (repeating sophomore year), where
 his contemporaries include Hutchins, Luce, Stephen Vin-
 cent Benét, Reginald Marsh, John Farrar, and Philip
 Barry. Important teachers are William Lyon Phelps and
 Chauncey Brewster Tinker.

1918–19 Wilder continues busily seeing plays, writing mostly drama, including several full-length plays, among them *The Trumpet Shall Sound*. In 1918, wins the John Hubbard Curtis Prize for his short story "'Spiritus Valet.'" Spends summer 1918 working as clerk in the War Industries Board in Washington, D.C. In September 1918, joins the Army's First Coast Artillery Corps stationed at Fort Adams, on Narragansett Bay outside Newport, Rhode Island; is discharged as a corporal and returns to Yale shortly after war's end. Reviews plays for *The Boston Transcript*, and is critical of conventional melodrama and frothy comedies; is active in Yale's Elizabethan Club. First three acts of four-act play *The Trumpet Shall Sound* are published in the *Yale Literary Magazine*.

1920 *The Trumpet Shall Sound* receives Yale's Bradford Brinton Award after its final act is published in the *Yale Literary Magazine*. Wilder graduates from Yale in June, and works on Connecticut farm during the summer. In the fall, begins an eight-month residency at the American Academy in Rome, informally studying archeology. (He later wrote: "For a while in Rome I lived among archeologists, and ever since I find myself occasionally looking at the things about me as an archeologist will look at them a thousand years hence.")

1921 Writes to his mother in April 1921: "I have found an Italian playwright whose plays I adore, the Sicilian Luigi Pirandello. Philosophical farces, actually,—strange contorted domestic situations illustrating some metaphysical proposition. . . ." Attends the first performance in Rome of Pirandello's *Six Characters in Search of an Author*. Is introduced to modern German expressionist drama. Meets Ezra Pound. Concludes his postgraduate year abroad with a six-week stay in Paris, where he begins writing "Memoirs of a Roman Student," which becomes his first novel, *The Cabala*. Reads Proust, Flaubert, and Madame de Sévigné. In June accepts offer, arranged by his father, to teach French at the Lawrenceville School, a preparatory school for boys near Princeton, New Jersey. Meets Stark Young on the return voyage.

1922–24 Establishes himself as a successful teacher and assistant dormitory master at Lawrenceville and as a speaker in local literary circles; reads extensively in seventeenth- and eighteenth-century French literature in the Princeton library; works on drama and *The Cabala* (he submits an

early version, under the title "The Trasteverine," to the Dial Press, which rejects it). Attends theater whenever possible in New York, Trenton, and Philadelphia, where, in 1923, he meets producer and director Max Reinhardt. Publishes pieces in the magazine *S4N*, and brief excerpts from *The Cabala* in *The Double Dealer*, a New Orleans literary journal. Continually writes plays. In 1924, makes the first of many stays at the MacDowell Colony in Peterborough, New Hampshire, where he meets Edwin Arlington Robinson and other authors, painters, and composers. Requests and is granted a two-year leave from Lawrenceville.

1925 Studies for a master's degree in French literature at Princeton and works to complete *The Cabala*, which is accepted for publication by Albert & Charles Boni in November. Covers Broadway for *Theatre Arts*.

1926 Writes to a friend in January: "I am full of plays that can't get written. I can't sleep. I am hateful." *The Cabala* is published to critical acclaim in England and America; in April *The New York Times* hails "the debut of a new American stylist" and calls it a "magnificent literary event." Starts work on *The Bridge of San Luis Rey* at the MacDowell Colony during the summer. In the fall, chaperones a young man around Europe; is introduced to Ernest Hemingway by Sylvia Beach in Paris. Is unable to attend December premiere of his revised version of *The Trumpet Shall Sound*, directed by Richard Boleslavsky, at the American Laboratory Theatre in New York, a production that is reviewed unfavorably.

1927 After living in Connecticut while working on *The Bridge of San Luis Rey*, returns to Lawrenceville in July as master of Davis House. Accepts a commission to translate novel *Paulina 1880* by Pierre-Jean Jouve for Longmans, Green (the translation, never published, may not have been completed; the manuscript is almost certainly lost). In November, *The Bridge of San Luis Rey* is published by Albert & Charles Boni to immediate acclaim on both sides of the Atlantic. (To a friend, he later wrote: "It seems to me that my books are about: what is the worst thing that the world can do to you, and what are the last resources one has to oppose it. In other words: when a human being is made to bear more than human beings can bear —what then? . . . *The Bridge* asked the question whether the intention that lies behind love was sufficient to justify

the desperation of living.") During Christmas holiday in Miami, meets boxer Gene Tunney and producer and director Jed Harris.

1928 Meets F. Scott Fitzgerald and Edmund Wilson at Fitzgerald's house in Delaware. Writes to Fitzgerald that he enjoys teaching at Lawrenceville and will probably remain there "for ages"; "a daily routine is necessary to me: I have no writing habits, am terribly lazy and write seldom." In May, delivers the Daniel S. Lamont Memorial Lecture at Yale, his first major public lecture, on "English Letters and Letter Writers." Rents a house for his mother and sisters Isabel and Janet for an extended stay in and around London. Travels to Europe, and studies the work and techniques of European dramatists and theater companies by attending performances in Germany, Austria, and Hungary. Is awarded the Pulitzer Prize for *The Bridge of San Luis Rey*. Hikes the Alps and motors through the south of France with Tunney; begins work on novel *The Woman of Andros*. In November, *The Angel That Troubled the Water and Other Plays* is published; some of the plays are published in periodicals.

1929 Wilder returns from Europe in January and, under lecturing contract with the Lee Keedick Agency, sets out on a two-month cross-country lecture tour. His royalties and related professional fees are now the main support of his parents and two youngest sisters, and in March he buys property on Deepwood Drive in Hamden, Connecticut, to build a house for the family, referring to it later as "The House *The Bridge* Built." Sister Isabel and lawyer J. Dwight Dana assume duties of caring for his business and domestic arrangements. Wilder travels to Europe with mother; sees Tunney and Hemingway. Film (mostly silent, with a segment in sound at the end) of *The Bridge of San Luis Rey*, directed by Charles Brabin, is released.

1930–31 Accepts invitation from his close friend Robert Maynard Hutchins, now president of the University of Chicago, to serve as a part-time visiting lecturer in classics and writing at the university for spring quarter of 1930; the appointment, during which he teaches no more than two quarters each year, extends through 1936. *The Woman of Andros* is published in February 1930 and becomes a best seller; in *The New Republic*, Marxist critic Michael Gold attacks it and Wilder's previous work for ignoring social issues. Develops close, lifelong friendships with Ruth

Gordon, Alexander Woollcott, and Sibyl Colefax. *The Long Christmas Dinner and Other Plays in One Act* is published in November 1931.

1932–33 Wilder is asked to translate from German and adapt *The Bride of Torozko*, a play about religious prejudice in a Hungarian town by Hungarian playwright Otto Indig, but project stumbles (play is staged on Broadway in 1934, and Wilder's version is not used). In summer 1932, begins to work intensively on novel *Heaven's My Destination.* Wilder's translation of André Obey's play *Le Viol de Lucrèce* opens late in 1932 in New York as *Lucrece*, starring Katharine Cornell and Brian Aherne and directed by Guthrie McClintic; it runs for 31 performances. *Lucrece* is published by Houghton Mifflin in 1933. Reads the European comedies of Nestroy, Raimund, Goldoni, and Lessing, "just to make sure," as he writes later to Ruth Gordon, "that I've expunged every lurking vestige of what Sam Behrman and George Kaufman think comedy is."

1934 Wilder goes to Hollywood to work on a film treatment of *Joan of Arc* for RKO studios, to star Katharine Hepburn and to be directed by George Cukor; film is never made. Also does writing jobs for Sam Goldwyn, including work on *We Live Again* (film based on Tolstoy's novel *Resurrection*), and *Dark Angel*. Turns down other major film assignments (as he will later do). Back at the University of Chicago, meets Gertrude Stein, who comes to lecture in November.

1935 *Heaven's My Destination* is brought out by his new publisher, Harper & Brothers, in January. Stein's *Narration: Four Lectures* is published with an introduction by Wilder. During a leave of absence from University of Chicago, he spends six months in Europe in the summer and fall, seeing Stein, Alice B. Toklas, Franz Werfel, Max Reinhardt, Pablo Picasso, and Sigmund Freud. Upon returning to America tells reporters that he intends to "abandon" the novel in favor of writing only plays, viewing the novel's omniscient voice as "out of gear with twentieth-century life" and drama "the new vehicle to succeed the narrative form." His journal notes include ideas for ten plays, among them "M Marries N" (an early working title for *Our Town)* and *The Merchant of Yonkers.*

1936 Father dies on July 2. Wilder resigns from University of Chicago. Begins work on *Our Town.* Stein's *Geographical*

History of America, with an introduction by Wilder, is published.

1937 Completes his Lee Keedick public-lecture contract, writing his brother: "The new life's begun. Taught my last class. Delivered my last lecture. The living is wonderful, and alarming; but I've plunged jubilantly into work and play no. #1 is almost done; plays no. #2 (on the Arabian Nights) and #3 ('Our Town' . . .) all planned out, as are several more." As a favor, works on a new "acting version" of Ibsen's *A Doll's House* for Jed Harris and Ruth Gordon. Works on plays at the MacDowell Colony in June. In July, travels to Paris as the first American delegate to the Institut de Coopération Intellectuel of the League of Nations, and delivers a lecture in French; sees E. M. Forster, Orson Welles, and Coco Chanel. Visits Stein and Toklas at their home in Bilignin, and attends Salzburg Festival. Retires for the fall to seclusion in Ruschlikon, near Zurich, to complete *Our Town*. Writes Sibyl Colefax in October: "Lord! What I got myself in for. A theologico-metaphisico transcription for the *Purgotorio* with panels of American rural genre-stuff." In December, after a successful tour, his version of *A Doll's House* opens on Broadway.

1938 After one performance in Princeton and a week's run in Boston, *Our Town* opens on Broadway on February 4 to mostly favorable reviews. Later that spring, Wilder is awarded his second Pulitzer Prize. Moves to a hotel in Tucson, Arizona, to complete *The Merchant of Yonkers*. Works on *The Alcestiad*. In September, takes over the role of the Stage Manager in *Our Town* for two weeks. *The Merchant of Yonkers* opens on Broadway on December 28, 1938, to a disappointing reception.

1939 Travels in Mexico and Texas, then goes to Europe in May and stays through the end of June; sees Jean Cocteau, Ruth Draper, Gertrude Stein, and Sibyl Colefax. Returns home and plays the Stage Manager in summer-stock productions of *Our Town* in Pennsylvania and Massachusetts. Describes his enthusiasm for James Joyce's *Finnegans Wake* as his "constant new companion." Devotes fall to nonfiction, except for an adaptation for Broadway of *The Beaux' Stratagem* for producer Cheryl Crawford, which he does not finish. Completes statement on the nature of theater ("Some Thoughts on Playwriting," published in

1941) and an introduction for an edition of *Oedipus Rex* (not published until 1955). Producer Sol Lesser appeals for his help in adapting *Our Town* for the screen, a task that involves meetings and continuous collaboration via letters and telegrams over several months.

1940 Stirred by news of events in Europe and inspired by ideas in Joyce, Wilder begins working on a play called *The Ends of the Worlds* that will become *The Skin of Our Teeth*. Attends May 22 premiere in Boston of film version of *Our Town*, directed by Sam Wood and starring William Holden and Martha Scott. Acts in summer-stock productions of *Our Town*. Goes to Quebec City for several weeks to work on *The Skin of Our Teeth*.

1941 Puts aside work on play to travel in late winter and spring to Columbia, Ecuador, and Peru at behest of the State Department's Bureau of Educational and Cultural Affairs, for which he studies Spanish intensively. Reads the letters of Simón Bolivar. Teaches a double load during the summer term at the University of Chicago. Travels to England with John Dos Passos as American representatives to the International Committee of PEN; meets with H. G. Wells, Edith Evans, E. M. Forster, and Cecil Beaton. Resumes work on *The Skin of Our Teeth* late in the year.

1942 Completes *The Skin of Our Teeth*. In May 1942, is accepted into the Army Air Intelligence and declares he would take "the khaki veil with an explosive cry of relief." Before reporting for duty, goes to Hollywood to write the screenplay for Alfred Hitchcock's *Shadow of a Doubt*, based on a scenario by Gordon McDonnell. On June 26, begins six weeks of basic training in Miami, then reports to Harrisburg, Pennsylvania, for Intelligence School, and is assigned as a captain to the headquarters of the 328th Fighter Group at Hamilton Field, California, and later to Washington, D.C. After previews in New Haven, Baltimore, and Philadelphia, *The Skin of Our Teeth* opens on Broadway on November 18. The next month, in *The Saturday Review of Literature*, Joseph Campbell and Henry Morton Robinson attack the play as stolen "in conception and detail" from James Joyce's *Finnegans Wake*, a charge Wilder chooses not to answer publicly, although he writes that "the ant-like industry of pedants, collecting isolated fragments, has mistaken the nature of literary influence since the first critics arose to regard books as a branch of merchandise instead of an expression of energy."

1943 In spring, Wilder is awarded his third Pulitzer Prize. Receives promotion to major on April 15, and is shipped overseas to the intelligence section of the Twelfth Air Force in Constantine, Algeria, and later to Algiers, where he is involved in planning operations. Is promoted to lieutenant colonel on August 27, 1944, and is posted to Caserta, Italy.

1944 Spends three days in Rome, his first visit since his American Academy residency. Directs all-military production of *Our Town* in Caserta. Second film adaptation of *The Bridge of San Luis Rey*, directed by Rowland V. Lee and starring Lynn Bari, Francis Lederer, and Alla Nazimova, is released. *The Skin of Our Teeth* and *Our Town* are produced in Switzerland; the latter, again directed by Jed Harris, has its first major New York revival.

1945 Wilder goes to Belgrade in February for performance of Serbo-Croatian version of *Our Town* staged by Tito's Partisans. During the Italian campaign, continues to prepare intelligence material and interrogate prisoners. Is awarded Bronze Star. Returns to America in May and is discharged from the Air Force in September. Because of poor health, cannot accept the post of cultural attaché at U.S. Embassy in Paris. Resumes work on *The Alcestiad* but puts it aside in November to start the novel *The Ides of March*. Reads Kierkegaard and avidly follows periodical literature on the new vogue of existentialism.

1946 In January at Yale, meets Jean-Paul Sartre, who asks him to translate his play *Morts sans sépulture*. Works on *The Ides of March*. Mother dies on June 29. Wilder writes short play in honor of the Century Club's centenary and records radio broadcast of *Our Town* for Theatre Guild on September 29. Receives Order of the British Empire (O.B.E.) for wartime service.

1947 Travels to the Yucatan Pennisula at the end of January, then on to Florida in April, working on *The Ides of March*. Writes in April to his agent: "I hate being alone. And I hate writing. But I can only write when I'm alone. So these working spells combine both my antipathies." Is awarded honorary doctorate by Yale in June. Completes introduction to Gertrude Stein's *Four in America* in July, and finishes *The Ides of March* in the fall.

1948 Travels to London in January to consult about Laurence Olivier's production of *The Skin of Our Teeth*. Meets T. S.

Eliot, V. S. Pritchett, Kenneth Tynan, and Peter Ustinov. Sees Sartre in Paris in February. *The Ides of March* is published on January 16. In an interview, he says: "Modern man has taken such pride in the exploration of his mind that he has forgotten there must be some laws governing that exploration. Whether it comes under religion or ethics or mere judgment, such laws must be found and respected. Otherwise the mind leads him straight to self-destruction. So my book is Caesar's groping in the open seas of his unlimited power for the first principles which should guide him." Plays Mr. Antrobus in summer-stock productions of *The Skin of Our Teeth* in Massachusetts, Connecticut, and Pennsylvania. By this time, has embarked on his voluminous scholarship on the career of Spanish dramatist Lope de Vega (1562–1635), a passion comparable to his long devotion to *Finnegans Wake*. In November, lectures for two weeks at the University of Frankfurt on "The American Character as Mirrored in Literature," and later at universities of Heidelberg and Marburg; spends two days in Berlin meeting students during the Berlin Airlift. Continues on to Switzerland, Italy, and Spain. His translation of Sartre's *Mort sans sépulture* is produced Off Broadway as *The Victors* in December to mixed reviews.

1949 Wilder returns to Hamden. Works on a new play, *The Emporium*. Visits Ezra Pound at St. Elizabeths Hospital. Is awarded honorary degrees by New York University and Kenyon College. Delivers lecture "World Literature and the Modern Mind" on the occasion of the Goethe Bicentennial at the Aspen Festival in June, where he also extemporaneously translates addresses by Albert Schweitzer and José Ortega y Gasset.

1950 Travels in Europe in spring; sees Max Beerbohm, Sacheverell Sitwell, and Noel Coward. Returns to the United States to accept honorary degree and perform in *Our Town* at the College of Wooster. Plays Stage Manager in *Our Town* at the Wellesley Summer Theatre, "the twelfth company I've played it with," he writes to Laurence Olivier and Vivien Leigh, adding "I advise every playwright to get somehow somewhere *that* side of the footlights." Accepts appointment as Harvard's 1950–51 Charles Eliot Norton Professor of Poetry, a position requiring six public lectures to be published by Harvard University Press. Moves into Dunster House in Septem-

ber; in addition to lecturing, agrees to teach large American literature class, and accepts scores of invitations to talk and meet with students and groups in Boston area. Lectures on Thoreau, Poe, Melville, Dickinson, and Whitman in a series entitled "The American Characteristics in Classic American Literature."

1951 Collapses from exhaustion March 9 and is hospitalized for several weeks. Resumes lighter schedule. Gives the 1951 Harvard Alumni Association's Commencement Address on June 21. Calls the Harvard experience the hardest year of his life. Receives honorary degrees from Harvard and from Northwestern University in June. That fall, travels to Europe to revise his Norton lectures for publication, a project that is ultimately never completed.

1952 Throughout the year, works on various projects: the Norton lectures, *The Emporium, The Alcestiad*, a possible screenplay for Vittorio De Sica, and a Christmas pageant play called *The Sandusky, Ohio, Mystery Play.* In May, is awarded the Gold Medal for Fiction by the American Academy of Arts and Letters. In June, receives honorary degree from Oberlin. Spends summer at MacDowell Colony. In September, heads the American delegation to a UNESCO congress in Venice. Travels to Paris to meet with Ruth Gordon and Tyrone Guthrie, who have asked him to consider revising *The Merchant of Yonkers.* Versions of three of his Harvard lectures are published in the *Atlantic Monthly.*

1953 Returns to America and resumes work on old projects. Is featured on cover of *Time*, June 12. Returns to MacDowell Colony late summer. Continues to work on *The Emporium*; finishes revisions of *The Merchant of Yonkers.*

1954 *The Merchant of Yonkers* opens successfully as *The Matchmaker* at the Edinburgh Festival in June, directed by Tyrone Guthrie and starring Ruth Gordon. "If I do finish *The Emporium* by July I'll be a very blithe fellow, indeed, and a public nuisance in Edinburgh. Of course, if I could finish the four-year-late Harvard lectures, too, all Europe would rock," he writes to Gordon. After a well-received tour, *The Matchmaker* opens a successful run in London. Wilder goes to the Berlin Festival in September, and travels on to Hamburg, Paris, and southern France to work on *The Alcestiad*, which he describes as "a humdinger—the true extension of the *Our Town–Skin* line."

1955–56 On August 22, 1955, *The Alcestiad*, retitled *A Life in the Sun*, opens at the Edinburgh Festival, directed by Guthrie and starring Irene Worth, to generally negative reviews. Wilder begins collaboration with composer Louise Talma on an opera based on *The Alcestiad*. In November *The Matchmaker* moves on to the United States where Wilder is initially involved in production details, but he is in Europe when the play opens on December 5, 1955, on Broadway, where it runs for 486 performances, Wilder's Broadway record. Works and travels in Europe; returns to the U.S. in February 1956. In June, drives to Mexico and back; as has been his lifelong habit, travels to different cities, different continents to work and "regenerate": "What do all of these long stays abroad mean, but my eternal effort to find a time and a place when I can follow an idea through," he writes in May.

1957 Along with *The Happy Journey to Trenton and Camden*, two new one-act plays, *Bernice* (starring Ethel Waters) and *The Wreck on the Five-Twenty-Five*, are performed at Congress Hall in West Berlin in September, with Wilder in the cast. Is inducted into the prestigious German society Orden Pour le Mérite für Wissenschaften und Künste. In October, is awarded the German Book Sellers Peace Prize in Frankfurt, the first American to receive this prize, delivering an address, "Culture in a Democracy," in German to audience of two thousand guests. Is awarded honorary degree by the Goethe University (Frankfurt) and receives Austria's Medal of Honor for Science and Fine Arts. Contributes preface to *Three Plays by Thornton Wilder: Our Town, The Skin of Our Teeth, The Matchmaker*.

1958 In Washington in February, receives a medal from the Peruvian government. Works on two cycles of one-act plays, "The Seven Ages of Man" and "The Seven Deadly Sins," intended to be performed on an arena stage. Works with Norman Bel Geddes on "epic film" called *The Melting Pot*, but project ends when Geddes dies in May. In August Paramount Pictures releases a film version of *The Matchmaker*, directed by Joseph Anthony and starring Shirley Booth, Anthony Perkins, and Shirley MacLaine.

1959 Travels in Europe. "It's not quite clear to me what I'm doing in Europe," he writes. "I seem to remember that I came here to work, and work went fine on the boat and then I got joined to various human communities. . . .

But, boy do I work! The lives—the life-stories that I've entered." Back in the U.S., he deals with business matters, works to finish his "Seven Deadly Sins" plays, and in August acts as the Stage Manager in *Our Town* at Williamstown, Massachusetts, his final appearance as an actor.

1960–61 Continues work on "Seven Deadly Sins" and "Seven Ages of Man" play cycles. Offers to help Katharine Hepburn and Spencer Tracy fashion a movie from *The Skin of Our Teeth*, but nothing comes of the project. Helps Jerome Kilty adapt *The Ides of March* for the stage. Adapts *The Long Christmas Dinner* for use as a one-act opera libretto set by composer Paul Hindemith; in German translation, the opera premieres in Mannheim, West Germany, on December 26, 1961.

1962–64 *Plays for Bleecker Street* (comprising three one-act plays: *Someone from Assisi, Infancy*, and *Childhood*) opens Off Broadway and enjoys a successful run. In German translation, the Wilder-Talma opera based on *The Alcestiad* opens in Frankfurt on March 1, 1962, to 20-minute ovation. Wilder presents "An Evening with Thornton Wilder" to President Kennedy's cabinet in Washington, D.C., on April 11. On May 20, 1962, departs for a long retreat in the Arizona desert; by late May is in Douglas, Arizona. Here he stays 20 months, initially in a hotel, and by the fall of 1962 in an efficiency apartment. By the end of the year has put aside work on his "Seven Deadly Sins" and "Seven Ages of Man" plays and begins working on a novel that becomes *The Eighth Day*. In March 1963, reveals this work for the first time to his family, describing his story as "*Little Women* being mulled over by Dostoevsky." Theatrical adaptation of *The Ides of March*, starring John Gielgud and Irene Worth, opens in London in June 1963 but soon closes. Wilder leaves Douglas in late November 1963 to accept the Presidential Medal of Freedom at the White House on December 6, announced the previous July by President Kennedy but conferred by President Johnson after Kennedy's assassination. *Hello, Dolly!*, a musical adaptation of *The Matchmaker*, opens on Broadway, on January 16, 1964; royalties provide Wilder financial security for the rest of his life.

1965–67 Wilder resumes extensive foreign and domestic travel, working almost exclusively on *The Eighth Day*. On May 4, 1965, Lady Bird Johnson awards him the National Book

Committee's first Medal for Literature at the White House. He completes *The Eighth Day* and reads proofs in Innsbruck, Austria, in November 1966. *The Eighth Day* is published on March 29, 1967; it is a critical and financial success, and receives the National Book Award for Fiction. In September 1967, Wilder buys second home at Katama Point on Martha's Vineyard with his sister Isabel.

1968–75 Travels often, with stops in Paris, Munich, Milan, Venice, Zurich, Cannes, Florida, New York, and Martha's Vineyard. Begins to suffer from circulatory problems; eye problems and hearing worsen. Writes to Gene Tunney in 1970: "Physical pain is the summit of aloneness, of solitude. I tried to catch glimpses of a companionship in Endurance." Toys with many writing ideas, but settles into writing a series of semi-autobiographical chapters. One of them, drawing on many affectionate visits to Newport, Rhode Island, grows into his novel *Theophilus North*, written between April 1972 and April 1973 and published in October 1973; critically praised, it becomes a best seller. To friends he writes: "The book is about the humane impulse to be useful, about compassion, and about non-demanding love." Continues to travel but is more and more confined to Hamden home. Begins work on sequel to *Theophilus North*. Spends summer of 1975 on Martha's Vineyard; is operated on in September for a cancerous prostate. Dies of an apparent heart attack at home in Hamden on December 7, 1975.

Note on the Texts

This volume contains five novels by Thornton Wilder: *The Cabala* (1926), *The Bridge of San Luis Rey* (1927), *The Woman of Andros* (1930), *Heaven's My Destination* (1935), and *The Ides of March* (1948), along with six stories and four essays.

The Cabala drew on Wilder's experiences as a resident at the American Academy in Rome in 1920–1921. He began writing the novel, which used working titles including "The Trasteverine" and "Memoirs of a Roman Student," during a six-week visit to Paris after his Academy residency had ended. An early version was rejected by Dial Press; a one-page excerpt, simply entitled "Sentences," was published in *The Double Dealer* in September 1922. *The Cabala* was accepted by Albert & Charles Boni in November 1925 and published the following April in New York and in England by Longmans, Green & Co. in 1926. Although Wilder read galley proofs, the Boni edition is riddled with errors, some of which were later corrected. When *The Cabala* was included in *A Thornton Wilder Trio* (New York: Criterion Books, 1956), many errors were corrected but new ones were introduced, and certain idiosyncrasies of Wilder's spelling and punctuation in the first edition were changed. The final edition published in Wilder's lifetime, *The Cabala & The Woman of Andros* (New York: Harper & Row, 1968), corrects the errors of the first edition but otherwise stays faithful to his original version; it contains the text printed here.

Not long after the publication of *The Cabala*, Albert & Charles Boni offered Wilder a $250 advance for his next novel, *The Bridge of San Luis Rey*. Wilder made steady progress on a draft while staying at the MacDowell Colony in Peterborough, New Hampshire, during the summer of 1926 and continued working on it while traveling in Europe later that year, mailing excerpts to his publisher in New York for subsequent revision. In mid-summer 1927 he submitted the final section of his manuscript to Albert & Charles Boni, which published the book in November of that year; the English edition, brought out by Longmans, Green & Co., appeared a few days before the American. The text printed here is taken from the 1927 Albert & Charles Boni edition of *The Bridge of San Luis Rey*.

Wilder compiled notes and sketched out chapters for *The Woman of Andros* in the latter months of 1928, after he had completed a hiking and motor tour of the Alps and the south of France with championship boxer Gene Tunney. The novel's first chapter was read to a

small audience in Vienna late that year. After Wilder's momentum on the book was interrupted by a demanding American lecture tour undertaken mostly in spring 1929, he was able to give it his full attention during a summer residency at the MacDowell Colony and on his return home from several weeks in Europe in October. "Is it drenched I ask myself with the wrong kind of pity?" Wilder reflected when the novel was nearly finished. "The perpetual harping on the supposition that people suffer within. Am I sufficiently realist?" He continued to make substantial revisions and, after recopying the manuscript, submitted it on October 29, 1929, to Albert & Charles Boni, which published it the following February. An English edition was also published in 1930 by Longmans, Green & Co. The present volume prints the text of the 1930 Albert & Charles Boni edition of *The Woman of Andros*.

In summer 1932, once again at the MacDowell Colony for a summer residency, Wilder started work on *Heaven's My Destination*, at first entitled "The Ideas and Adventures of Jethro Bentley." Completed in 1934, it was submitted to his new publisher, Harper & Bros., which published it in January 1935. As with *The Bridge of San Luis Rey*, the English edition, brought out by Longmans, Green & Co., appeared first and was published late in 1934. The 1935 Harper & Bros. edition of *Heaven's My Destination* contains the text printed here.

Wilder interrupted work on his play *The Alcestiad* in November 1945 to begin writing *The Ides of March*. He worked on the novel, at times fitfully, over the next two years, completing it in the early fall of 1947. It was published by Harper & Bros. in America and by Longmans, Green & Co. in 1948; the text printed here is taken from the 1948 Harper & Bros. edition.

The texts of the stories in this volume are taken from their first periodical publication or manuscript source:

"The Marriage of Zabett," *Oberlin Literary Magazine*, June 1917.

"'Spiritus Valet,'" *The Yale Courant*, May 1918.

"Eddy Greater," *Yale Literary Magazine*, June 1920.

"Précautions Inutiles," unpublished typescript, 1922–23, Thornton Wilder Papers, Yale Collection of American Literature, Beinecke Rare Book and Manuscript Library, Yale University.

"A Diary: First and Last Entry," *S4N*, February 1924.

"The Warship," *Yale Literary Magazine*, February 1936.

The texts of the essays "On Reading the Great Letter Writers," "James Joyce, 1882–1941," "Joyce and the Modern Novel," and "Gertrude Stein's *Four in America*" are taken from Donald Gallup

(ed.), *American Characteristics and Other Essays* (New York: Harper & Row, 1979).

This volume presents the texts of the original printings chosen for inclusion here, but it does not attempt to reproduce nontextual features of their typographic design. The texts are presented without change, except for the correction of typographical errors. Spelling, punctuation, and capitalization are often expressive features and are not altered, even when inconsistent or irregular. The following is a list of typographical errors corrected, cited by page and line number: 6.20, Cabala.; 14.40, troup; 15.24, marvelling he; 15.32, troup; 17.3, Rothchilds:; 28.22, not?; 45.34–35, I Promessi Sposi; 47.28–29, distintegration; 48.23, etherialized; 50.27, bailly; 53.20, Millamonts; 71.5, Orpheus; 76.24, vistors'; 92.28, eyes.; 106.15, *fachini*; 118.20, woman her; 127.12, señora; 127.28, *querarme*; 132.39, Perhaps; 148.5, heart,; 160.22, Victoria; 160.35, Alarçon; 168.28, likely) it; 173.37, magdelinism; 177.37, look; 179.13, farm,; 179.15, and children's; 182.26, shown; 188.16, Service; 189.24, *sacrementales*; 209.23 and 223.13, threshhold; 229.10, difficulty "I; 229.10, no,; 247.19, betwen; 252.24, heaviness "In; 289.19, Upsala; 298.24, Brush, and; 311.12, Schnickenschnauser's; 319.9, about her; 331.36, Matthews; 358.16, sleeve,; 365.25, clerk; 398.22, . . . and; 404.15, hair,; 419.34, moves; 424.28 home; 454.9, Octavious; 454.11, The; 454.14, My; 454.16, wrong.; 457.34, retrospectively.; 462.15, "This; 462.17, last."; 463.26, smoke"; 497.20, have; 547.8, weakness,; 559.8, *waterways.*; 559.26, its; 561.5, tradegies; 577.13, *Death.*; 607.16, lays; 608.15, Jan's; 611.20, it"; 613.25–26, "write . . . woman,"; 615.7, but it; 618.36, face saw; 622.39, passepartouted.; 632.27, one does; 633.24, arrow; 634.13, idiosyncracies.

Notes

In the notes below, the reference numbers denote page and line of this volume (the line count includes headings). No note is made for material included in standard desk-reference books. Biblical quotations are keyed to the King James Version. For more biographical information than is contained in the Chronology, see Robin G. Wilder & Jackson R. Bryer, *The Selected Letters of Thornton Wilder* (New York: HarperCollins, 2008) and Gilbert Harrison, *The Enthusiast* (New Haven, CT: Ticknor & Fields, 1983). Grateful acknowledgment is made to Jackson R. Bryer, Penelope Niven, Robin G. Wilder, and Tappan Wilder for their assistance with the Chronology.

THE CABALA

4.11 Fabre] Jean-Henri Fabre (1823–1915), French entomologist and author of the renowned 11-volume *Souvenirs entomologiques* (*Entomological Memoirs*, 1879–1907).

4.34 Santa Maria Maggiore] Catholic basilica in Rome, dating from the 5th century and dedicated to the Virgin Mary.

5.19 Tivoli] Town known in antiquity as Tibur, in the hills overlooking Rome.

5.37 Bourbons] Since the 16th century, members of the House of Bourbon have ruled at various times as kings of France, Spain, Luxembourg, Parma, Naples, and Sicily.

7.17 Via Cavour] Avenue in Rome named for Camillo Benso, Conte di Cavour (1810–1861), Italian politician and leading figure in the unification of his country.

7.19 Palestrina] Giovanni Pierluigi da Palestrina (1525?–1594), Italian composer and the master of Renaissance polyphony.

7.22 Jubilee] Roman Catholic celebration derived from an ancient Hebrew practice and held usually every 50 years, during which pious acts result in a plenary indulgence.

10.2–3 *animae periculum*] Latin: soul in peril (i.e., he had become a danger to her soul).

10.4 St. Januarius] Bishop of Naples, martyred around 350 CE, and the patron saint of Naples. It is said that capsules of his dried blood, kept in a

reliquary in the Cathedral of San Gennaro in Naples, liquefy every year on three celebratory occasions.

10.17–18 Mantegna's . . . Helen"] Fictitious painting by Italian Renaissance painter Andrea Mantegna (c.1431–1506).

11.40 Elizabeth and Frederick] I.e., Elizabeth I of England (1533–1603) and Frederick II of Prussia (1712–1786).

13.11 potboy] Menial in an alehouse or inn.

13.11–12 newspaper devil] Apprentice in a newspaper printing press, charged with fetching type or pouring ink.

13.38 Domenichino] Domenico Zampieri (1581–1641), Italian Baroque painter.

15.4 Medtner] Nikolai Medtner (1880–1951), Russian composer.

15.10 Grétry] André Grétry (1741–1813), Belgium-born French composer.

15.12 Harold Bauer] English-American pianist (1873–1951).

15.14 the Flonzaleys] Famed string quartet, formed in New York City by Éduard de Coppet in 1902 and disbanded in 1928.

15.15 pages of Loeffler] Most likely *Music for Four Stringed Instruments* (1917) by Charles Martin Loeffler (1861–1935), German-born American composer.

15.29–30 Taganrog] Coastal city in southern Russia.

15.31 d'Indy] Vincent d'Indy (1851–1931), French composer.

15.33 *Les Indes Galantes*] Opéra-ballet (1735) by Jean-Philippe Rameau (1638–1764).

16.4 Fortuny] Mariano Fotuny (1871–1949), Spanish fashion designer known especially for his pleated gowns.

16.20 *faisan Souvaroff*] Pheasant stuffed with foie gras.

16.31 *oeufs cardinal*] A dish of eggs cooked with herbs inside a half-tomato.

21.25 the Fountain of the Boat] La Fontana della Barcaccia, a fountain designed by Bernini on the Piazza di Spagna, near the Spanish Steps.

21.27 Piave] River in northern Italy that flows into the Adriatic Sea near Venice. It was the site of an 1809 battle during the Napoleonic Wars.

21.32 Moissi] Alexander Moissi (1879–1935), Albanian-born stage actor, was a famous Hamlet and Faust, and also a champion of works by Tolstoy, Strindberg, Chekhov, and Pirandello.

23.11 Pizzetti's sonata] Ildebrando Pizetti (1880–1968), Italian composer.

24.9–10 Here lies . . . water] Keats' epitaph, which he adapted from Beaumont and Fletcher's play *Philaster, or Love Lies A-Bleeding* (c. 1610): "All your better deeds / Shall be in water writ."

25.3 Colonna] Powerful noble family in medieval and Renaissance Rome.

31.12 pardi!] French: of course.

31.27 opus reticulatum] Latin: reticulated work, referring to a pattern of brickwork used in ancient Roman architecture.

31.32–34 ". . . domus . . . rivis."] From Horace's *Odes*, I.vii: "Albunea's echoing home and the tumbling Anio, Tiburnus's grove and the orchards watered by the running streams."

34.1–2 Sze-chuen] I.e., Sichuan, province in south-central China.

35.2 donation of Constantine] Forged document from around 750, allegedly by emperor Constantine the Great (c. 272–337), granting possessions and privileges to the pope.

36.34 Aqua Paola] The Fontana dell'Aqua Paolo, in Rome's Trastevere district, was built in the 17th century as the terminus for an aqueduct that brought drinking water to the area.

38.30 Tausig] Karl Tausig (1841–1871), Polish pianist and composer.

39.15 Freud's book on Leonardo] *Leonardo da Vinci and a Memory of His Childhood* (1910).

43.18 haughty Barberini] The massive Palazzo Barberini in central Rome was begun in 1625 by Maffeo Barberini (1568–1644), who had ascended to the papal throne as Urban VII.

43.20–21 francobollo shop] Store selling postage stamps.

45.16 Pope Sylvester Lefthand] Sylvester I was pope from 314 to 335, during the reign of Emperor Constantine, and is sometimes credited with writing the first Italian-form sonnets.

45.34–35 the comedies . . . *Sposi*] The many comedies of Carlo Goldoni (1707–1793), Venetian playwright and librettist, established a dramatic ideal. The classic Italian novel *I Promessi Sposi* (*The Betrothed*), by Alessandro Manzoni (1783–1873), was published in 1827.

51.17 *L'Abbesse de Jouarre*] Play (1886) by French historian, philosopher, and philologist Ernest Renan (1823–1892), best known for his *Life of Jesus* (1863).

53.20–21 Millemants . . . Célimènes] The heroines of William Congreve's *The Way of the World* (1700), Shakespeare's *As You Like It* (c. 1600), and Molière's *The Misanthrope* (1666), respectively.

53.25 Yvette Guilbert] French cabaret singer and actress (1865–1944).

54.2 Madame de Sévigné] Marie de Rabutin-Chantal, marquise de Sévigné (1626–1696), celebrated for her prolific correspondence with her daughter, first published in 1725.

54.2 *concetto*] Italian: idea.

57.32 *boudeur*] French: sulky.

61.8 *Salome* . . . *Petrushka*] Opera (1905) by German composer Richard Strauss (1864–1949); ballet (1911) by Russian composer Igor Stravinsky (1882–1971).

62.32 *La Villegiatura*] Trilogy of comedies by Carlo Goldoni (see note 45.34–35).

63.24 Gluck's *Armide*] Opera (1777) by German composer Christoph Willibald Gluck (1714–1787).

68.40 hymn . . . Newman's] "Lead, Kindly Light," words written in 1833 by John Henry Newman (1801–1890).

71.24–25 Alix aux Enfers] French: Alix in the Underworld, perhaps a play on the title of Jacques Offenbach's 1858 operetta *Ophée aux Enfers*.

72.5–6 Commendatore Boni] Giacomo Boni (1859–1925), Italian archeologist, director of excavations in the Roman Forum from 1899 to 1922.

72.7 Benedetto Croce] Benedetto Croce (1866–1952), Italian philosopher, historian, and liberal social critic (1866–1952).

72.9–10 stormy . . . *d'Autore*] *Six Characters in Search of an Author* (1921), the most celebrated work by Italian playwright and novelist Luigi Pirandello (1867–1936), begins with an acting company in rehearsal and the arrival of six strange people who disrupt everything. The play outraged many in its audience on its opening night in Rome and nearly caused a riot.

72.10–12 Casella's . . . Bossi] Alfredo Casella (1883–1947), Italian composer; Felix Mengelberg (1871–1951), Dutch conductor; Enrico Bossi (1861–1925), Italian organist and composer.

72.37 Duse . . . Besnard] Eleanora Duse (1858–1924), celebrated Italian actress, usually known simply by her last name; Albert Besnard (1849–1934), French painter.

75.21 *magister hieraticorum*] Latin: master of the mysteries.

75.23 Orzinda-Mazda] A garbled form of Ahura Mazda (Lord Wisdom), the principal Zoroastrian deity. (The god was later called Ormazd in Middle Persian, the language in which "zinda" means "living"; Wilder's incorrect rendering can be translated as "Or, the living wisdom.")

76.22 *nepote*] Italian: nephew.

80.15 Glazounov] Alexander Glazunov (1865–1936), Russian composer.

80.17 Reinhardt] Innovative Austrian-American director and author
Max Reinhardt (1873–1943), who later directed Wilder's *The Merchant of
Yonkers* (1938) on Broadway.

80.35 Moroni] Giovanni Battista Moroni (c. 1520–1578), Italian portrait
painter of the late Renaissance.

81.7 *fine*] French: brandy.

82.23 IHS] Greek monogram of the name of Jesus Christ.

83.31 the page of Augustine] See Augustine, *Confessions* IX.x.23–25.

85.12–13 Bosanquet] Bernard Bosanquet (1848–1923), English philoso-
pher and social reformer, an exponent of "Absolute Idealism."

86.3–4 the Imitation] Devotional work (c. 1427) attributed to Thomas à
Kempis (c. 1380–1471), a German monk.

88.7 *Appearance and Reality*] Treatise (1893) by Francis Herbert
Bradley (1846–1924), English philosopher.

88.7 Spengler] German historian Oswald Spengler (1880–1936), author
of *The Decline of the West* (1918–23).

88.7–8 *The Golden Bough*] Twelve-volume study (1890–1915) by the
British anthropologist James George Frazer (1854–1941).

88.13–14 *Eccolo . . . dico!*] Italian: "Look, this son of Whitman, of Poe,
of Wilson, of William James,—even of Emerson!"

89.2 *And the rich . . . away.*] Luke 1:53.

89.9–10 *Sicut . . . nostris.*] From the Latin version of the Lord's
Prayer: "As we forgive those who trespass against us."

89.38–39 Schweitzer's *Skizze*] The German-French theologian, musi-
cian, and physician Albert Schweitzer (1875–1965) published his *Das Messian-
itäts und Leidengeheimnis: Eine Skizze des Leben Jesu* (known in English as
The Quest of the Historical Jesus) in 1901.

91.15 *issimus*] Latin suffix indicating a superlative.

91.37 Thomist] I.e., influenced by the teachings of St. Thomas Aquinas
(c. 1225–1274).

97.9 *Es muss sein!*] German: "It must be!"— a phrase inscribed at the
start of the fast section of the last movement of Beethoven's String Quartet
No. 16 in F major, op. 135 (1826).

101.38 *insignis pietate*] Latin: the phrase "distinguished by his piety," in-
scribed as an ornate embellishment (*ornatissimus*) on his tomb.

106.15 *facchini*] Italian: porters.

107.38 *O . . . mantovana*] Italian: "O courteous Mantuan spirit," Beatrice's phrase for Virgil in Dante, *Inferno*, II.58.

109.2 came another] I.e., William Shakespeare.

THE BRIDGE OF SAN LUIS REY

111.1–2 THE BRIDGE . . . REY] Wilder borrowed the bridge's name from a California mission founded by the Spanish missionary Junipero Serra (1713–1784). It was named for St. Louis of France (King Louis IX, 1214–1270).

116.24–25 the gods . . . boys kill] See Shakespeare, *King Lear*, IV.i.1: "As flies to wanton boys are we to the gods, / They kill us for their sport."

116.26–27 very sparrows . . . God] See Luke 12:6–7: "Are not five sparrows sold for two farthings, and not one of them is forgotten before God? But even the very hairs of your head are all numbered. Fear not therefore: ye are of more value than many sparrows."

123.33 Moreto's *Trampa Adelante*] Agustín Moreto y Cabaña (1618–1669), Spanish playwright, was a contemporary of Lope de Vega. *Trampa adelante* ("On with the Trick") was published in 1654 and performed five years later in Lima.

125.8 *chicha*] Latin American fermented drink usually made from maize.

127.25–29 'Don Juan . . . seguros. . . .'] From *Trampa adelante* (see note 123.33): "Don Juan, if you appreciate my love, / And a sure faith is foolish, / Getting angry at my fears / Is not to believe me prudent. / Are you so sure. . . ."

127.31 the First Day] The play is divided into three "Jornadas" ("days" or acts).

127.32–33 saying to Gabriel . . . *child?*] See Luke 1:34.

130.15 Vatinian hate] Publius Vatinius, Roman statesman during the last decades of the Roman republic, was an often cruel and despised ruler who was scorned by Cicero and considered the most hated man of his time. See Catullus, *Carmina*, 14 and 53.

132.13 *Grignan*] Village in southeastern France, where Madame de Sévigné's daughter, Madame de Grignan, lived in a castle of the same name.

135.22 as Jupiter . . . Semele] In Greek mythology, Semele was the mother of Dionysus by Zeus; she was tricked by Hera into persuading Zeus to visit her in his real form and was killed by the power of his thunderbolts.

139.17–19 stories . . . Harlequin] Rodrigo Díaz de Vivar (c. 1043–1099), known as El Cid Campeador, Spanish hero famous for his military feats, especially the siege of Valencia in 1094. Judas Maccabeus, the second

century BCE Jewish leader Judah Maccabee, led a revolt against the repressive king Antiochus IV Epiphanes, the ruler of the Hellenistic Seleucid Empire. After Judah Maccabee's forces drove their enemies out of Jerusalem, the Jewish Temple in the city was rededicated in 165 BCE, an event commemorated by the festival of Chanukah. Harlequin, or Arlecchino, was a figure in Italian commedia dell'arte, a much-put-upon clown.

139.30 his precious burden] I.e, the Eucharist.

140.3 Morales and Vittoria] Cristóbal de Morales (c. 1500–1533), Spanish composer of elaborate masses and motets. Tomás Luis de Vittoria (1548–1611), known as "the Spanish Palestrina," brilliant and influential composer of sacred music.

142.27–29 the bitterest tongue . . . heard about it] See François, Duc de La Rochefoucauld (1613–1680), *Reflections* (1678), maxim 136: "Some people would never have fallen in love if they had never heard of love."

146.8 *cholo*] Spanish: half-breed.

147.19–20 *A sagitta volante in die*] Latin: from the arrow that flies by day. From Psalm 91.6: "Thou shalt not be afraid for the terror by night; nor for the arrow that flieth by day."

160.34–35 Tirso . . . Alarcón] Tirso de Molina (c.1571–1648), Spanish priest and playwright, author of hundreds of plays that demonstrate great range and wit. His *El Burlador de Sevilla* marks the first literary appearance of Don Juan. Juan Ruiz de Alarcón (c. 1581–1639), born to Spanish nobility in Mexico, dramatist of dark humor and invective.

163.37 virtú] Italian word for "virtue, excellence," used to refer to fine antique *objets d'art*.

164.36 Pygmalion] Mythological artist who fell in love with the statue of a woman he was carving, whom Aphrodite then brought to life as Galatea.

169.1 cafés-chantants] French: "singing cafes," usually an outdoor café with singers, especially popular in Paris during the Belle Époque.

169.38 *El Buen Retiro*] The royal palace in Madrid.

170.19 eleven thousand virgins of Cologne] St. Ursula, according to legend, began a pilgrimage from her native England to Rome accompanied by eleven thousand virgins. When they reached Cologne they were all massacred by Huns.

171.10 Brantôme . . . Aretino] Pierre de Bourdeille, seigneur de Brantôme (c. 1540–1616), French soldier and traveler whose *Mémoirs* (1666) offers a vivid and at times scandalous portrait of his era and its personalities. Pietro Aretino (1492–1556), Italian satirist, poet, and playwright famous for his scathing and sometimes salacious wit.

173.37 magdalenism] An old term for female prostitution, but here used
to indicate a reformed sinner.

174.2–3 Saint Gelasius . . . Pelagia] Gelasius (d. 496) was elected pope
in 492 and vigorously defended the papacy. The Roman comedian Genesius,
martyred around 300, is the patron saint of actors. The apocryphal saint Mar-
garet of Antioch, according to *The Golden Legend*, was swallowed by Satan in
the form of a dragon whom she killed with the crucifix she carried. Pelagia of
Antioch, according to an account by St. John Chrysostom, was a 15-year-old
virgin who fatally threw herself from the roof of her house rather than be dis-
honored by soldiers who had come for her.

174.17 Escurial] Sixteenth-century complex of buildings in Madrid, built
by Philip II.

176.36 the Old Comedy] Originally a term used for the earliest Greek
comedy, epitomized by Aristophanes, driven by political satire and buffoon-
ery. It became a generic term for such a style in later cultures.

177.1 *Belshazzar's Feast*] An imagined play depicting the events in
Daniel 1:1–31.

180.21 *piano*] Italian: softly. Such a marking in a musical score indicates
that the passage is to be played softly.

183.31 Monreale] A Norman-style cathedral completed in 1182 near
Palermo, Sicily.

184.5 *sub specie aeternitatis*] Latin: viewed as if from eternity.

187.16 the Empress of Austria] Marie of Spain (1528–1603), daughter of
the Holy Roman Emperor Charles V and wife of Maximilian II, also the Holy
Roman Emperor. For her funeral in 1603, Tomás Luis de Vittoria composed
a requiem mass.

188.19–20 *dies irae*] Latin: day of wrath: a 13th-century hymn describing
the day of the Last Judgment, used as part of the liturgy for the Roman
Catholic funeral mass.

189.23–24 *autos sacramentales*] Spanish: sacramental acts: allegorical
dramas similar to medieval morality plays in which the mysteries of virtue and
vice are enacted as popular entertainment. They were presented in Spain
from the 13th century onward, and dramatists as great as Lope de Vega and
Calderón wrote them.

THE WOMAN OF ANDROS

194.1–3 The first part . . . Menander] Publius Terentius Afer (c. 185–c.
159 BCE) was a Roman playwright, six of whose comedies are extant. *Andria*
(*The Woman of Andros*), thought to be his first play, was first produced c. 170
BCE and was based on a play of the same name by the Greek playwright

Menander (c. 342–c. 292 BCE). The title character, Chrysis, a kind and thoughtful woman, never appears on stage, having died before the action begins.

206.29–30 hetaira's] In ancient Greece, a cosmopolitan courtesan.

207.37 Tanagran] From the Boetian town of Tanagra, best known for its terra cotta figurines that usually depict women in everyday dress.

211.26–27 sempstress] Archaic term for seamstress.

213.6 *agnus castus*] Vitex agnus-castus, a fragrant Mediterranean plant with medicinal uses.

228.18 the *Ion* of Euripides] Eighteen plays of Greek tragedian Euripides (c. 480–406 BCE) have survived. *Ion*, thought to have been written c. 414 BCE, concerns an abandoned child, Ion, whose mother, Creusa, is unaware of their relationship. Xuthus thinks Ion is his son, and unwittingly Creusa tries to murder her own son, after which she takes refuge in a temple where Ion tries to find her and exact his revenge. There the truth is revealed, and Athena reconciles mother and son, who is destined to rule Athens.

232.14 palaestra] A section of ancient gymnasia devoted to wrestling.

248.28–29 its precious burden] I.e., the birth of Jesus.

HEAVEN'S MY DESTINATION

250.1–4 *George Brush . . . destination*] Wilder was devoted to the work of Irish novelist James Joyce (1882–1941); in Joyce's *A Portrait of the Artist as a Young Man* (1916), a classmate one night writes mockingly in Stephen Dedalus's geography text: "Stephen Dedalus is my name, / Ireland is my nation. / Clongowes is my dwelling place / And heaven my expectation."

250.8–9 Of all . . . age] See 211.35–36.

251.19 "Quarritch,"] Wilder may have named the Pullman car after the well-known London book dealer Bernard Quaritch (1819–1899).

254.27–28 "Thou, Lord, seest me."] Genesis 16:13.

263.37 bertillioned] Or bertilloned, measured (and often photographed) by the police for identification.

270.18 'The Lost Chord,'] An 1877 song by Sir Arthur Sullivan (1842–1900), set to an 1858 poem by Adelaide Anne Procter (1825–1864).

271.11 Elks'] The Benevolent and Protective Order of Elks is a large American fraternal and charitable organization founded in New York City in 1868.

271.16 caves of Kentucky] Mammoth Cave in the Green River valley of south-central Kentucky is the center of the world's longest cave system.

271.17 John McCormack] Famous Irish tenor (1884–1945).

276.15 Chautauqua] The Chautauqua community, founded in 1874 in Jamestown, New York, was designed to promote intellectual and spiritual development. Subsequently "Chautauqua" came to be used as a generic term for various troupes that traveled throughout the country presenting cultural entertainments.

278.12 "The Rivals"] Comedy of manners (1775) by Irish playwright Richard Brinsley Sheridan (1751–1816).

287.14–15 "Working on the Railroad"] "I've Been Working on the Railroad," an American folksong first published in 1894.

287.15–16 "Indian Love Call"] Song from the 1924 operetta *Rose Marie*, music by Rudolf Friml (1879–1972), lyrics by Oscar Hammerstein II (1895–1960) and Otto Harbach (1873–1963).

289.10 "Wisconsin . . . fair."] Perhaps a conflation of lines from the University of Wisconsin college songs "Hail, Wisconsin" and "Our Dear Old Alma Mater."

302.32 "Far above Cayuga's Waters"] School song of Cornell University, situated on the bank of the Cayuga River in Ithaca, New York. The lyrics were written by two classmates, Archibald Croswell Weeks and Wilmot Moses Smith, around 1870 and set to a popular ballad.

302.33–34 "Lie down . . . down,"] Anonymous 18th-century Irish Protestant folksong. "Croppies" refer to people with cropped hair.

306.4 "Wasting in despair"] Song by Robert Still (1910–1971), setting a poem by English poet George Wither (1588–1667).

306.6 "If she . . . me-ee,"] The refrain is actually "If she be not so to me."

306.24 "All through the night"] Welsh folksong first published in the late 18th century.

313.26–28 "*When thou clovest . . . dirt.*"] Spoken by The Fool in *King Lear*, I.iv.160–62.

317.16 "How can I bear to leave thee?"] Originally a German song by Johanna Kinkel (1810–1858), known in English as "Soldier's Farewell."

319.1 Lillian Russell] American stage star and famous beauty (1861–1922) whose vehicles included *The Grand Duchess* (1890) and, with the burlesque team Weber and Fields, *Fiddle-dee-dee* (1900) and *Whoop-dee-doo* (1903).

328.3 ahimsa] Sanskrit: avoidance of harm. The doctrine of non-violence has been especially identified with Hinduism and Buddhism.

332.33 "The Rosary."] Popular song by American composer Ethelbert Nevin (1862–1901).

356.37 *"Gott—enu!"*] German: heaven help us!

358.27 *"Ach, g'rechter Gott!"*] German: oh good God!

365.21–22 books . . . Blackstone] I.e., the monumental multi-volume study of common law, *Commentaries on the Laws of England* (1769), by English jurist Sir William Blackstone (1723–1780).

365.24 *Waverly*] *Waverley*, novel (1814) by Walter Scott (1771–1832).

365.31 *Adam Bede*] Novel (1859) by George Eliot, pen name of English writer Mary Ann Evans (1818–1890).

376.32 Epictetus, *Thoughts from Edmund Burke*] Greek Stoic philosopher Epictetus (c. 55–c. 135); Edmund Burke (1729–1797), Irish-born British author and member of Parliament.

380.40 The Bible says] See Matthew 5–7.

402.18–19 "Du . . . Lorelei."] Both poems are by German writer Heinrich Heine (1797–1856).

403.9–10 "Es . . . nichts."] German: it's nothing . . . nothing at all.

403.30–32 "Ich sterbe . . . sterben."] Conjugation of the German verb *sterben*, to die.

THE IDES OF MARCH

409.1 THE IDES OF MARCH] In *The World's Best* (New York: Dial Press, 1950), an anthology of excerpts from the work of 105 authors with their comments, edited by Whit Burnett, Wilder submitted a section from Caesar's journal (439.34–445.16) and contributed this note:

> During the nineteenth century the novelists seem never to have been troubled by the claim to omniscience which is at the base of their art. First signs of discomfort in regard to it appeared in Flaubert and Turgenev. It became acute in Henry James and now in some form or other undermines the self-confidence of all storytellers. Are readers believing that our stories are "true" and in what sense do we believe them ourselves?
>
> This is the crisis of the novel. Writers for the stage are not confronted by it.
>
> The assumption of omniscience is no less present in writing for the theatre, but once the action is passing upon the stage we are not aware of the narrator who is presenting it to us. A novel may be described as "everything pertinent to our understanding of an action or a series of actions" and throughout a novel we are aware that an all-knowing intelligence is recounting to us this pertinent matter. On the stage, how-

ever, it is always "now"; no intervening editorial voice is present; and in a very dramatic sense our seeing is believing.

In *The Ides of March* I tried to dispense with the fictional narrator. When one purports to recount the thoughts of a Caesar, a Cicero, and a Catullus, the claim to omniscience becomes doubly preposterous. All art is pretense but the pretense of the historical novel is particularly difficult to swallow. I therefore moved the pretense over to a different terrain: I pretended to have discovered a large collection of letters and documents written by these notable persons. I attempted to coerce belief by submitting a sort of apparatus of historical method and scholarship. It all "looks" more credible than if I had written a running narrative full of such phrases as "Caesar remembered their first meeting" and "Cleopatra concealed her anger." But more important from the point of view of credibility was the fact that I had approached the effect of the theatre. Each of the letters and documents is in the present tense; no narrator is heard describing the whole action as having taken place in the past. As on the stage each speech rises from the actor in an immediate spontaneity—as their "time" on the stage becomes our "time" in the audience—so in a novel-in-letters each document tends to give the impression of a speech, a cry, at which we are present.

I am far from pretending that this affords a solution to the problem of the novel. The novel-in-letters runs into other difficulties, difficulties so great that the form can only be the vehicle for a very limited type of story. Time is a sense in which I did not seriously attempt to cope with them, as Richardson did. I begged the question by surrounding my work with a veil of irony, offering it as a sort of parody of historical scholarship. I begged the question in that I not so much asked the reader to "believe" me as to "play this game" with me.

In a copy of the English edition of the novel that he gave to his friend, diplomat Terrance Catherman, Wilder added many marginal comments to the book, including these remarks he appended to his foreword:

So it's a kind of crossword puzzle. Many of the events we traverse four times. They're like a statue that you view from four sides.

Hence the book only begins to speak at its *second reading*.

But in this way I get (for my own interest, anyway) a sense of the density of life—its intermixedness, its surprises,—its mysteriousness.

The way of telling a story chronologically, from beginning to end, bored me—seemed too slick—not rich and complicated and true enough.

In life we often learn much later what really took place.

411.3 LAURO DE BOSIS] Italian intellectual and aviator (1901–1931) who died when his plane disappeared as he was dropping anti-fascist leaflets

over Rome. De Bosis had taught Italian at Harvard and Columbia, and had known Wilder at the American Academy in Rome in 1920. He later translated *The Bridge of San Luis Rey*. *The Ides of March* is dedicated to him, and to Edward Sheldon (1886–1946), mentor to Wilder and playwright whose career was stymied by a progressive crippling disease. Wilder further pays tribute to these men by partly embodying their characters in Gaius Valerius Catullus and Lucius Mamilius Turrinus.

415.2 College of Augurs] The body of 16 official Roman diviners, charged with interpreting signs of the approval or disapproval of the gods for proposed actions.

415.5 College of the Vestal Virgins] Virgins chosen from among Roman girls became part of an official cult dedicated to keeping lit an eternal flame to the ancient hearth-goddess Vesta. They were housed in seclusion next to Vesta's temple. They kept safe various sacred objects, along with the wills of prominent citizens. Once a year, they participated in a ceremony—the Vestalia, held on June 9—cleansing the temple.

415.34 new calendar] In 46 BCE, Julius Caesar instituted a reform of the solar calendar, dividing the year into twelve months and 365 days, with the addition of a leap year every fourth year. This so-called Julian calendar remained the standard until the slightly revised Gregorian calendar came into use from the 16th to the 18th century.

416.16 the mixolydian mode] Diatonic musical scale, supposedly based on one invented by Sappho.

417.24 the Battle of Cologne] In 55 BCE, because Caesar felt it beneath Roman dignity to cross a river by boat, he ordered the construction of a bridge across the Rhine, allowing his troops to attack Germanic tribes.

418.18–19 Trasteverine] Its name derived from "trans Tiberim" (Latin: across the Tiber), this Roman neighborhood lies on the west bank of the river.

419.37–38 my Cornelia . . . unborn Julia] Cornelia Cinna minor (94–69 BCE) was married to Caesar in 83 BCE and gave birth to their daughter one year later.

420.25 sumptuary laws] Laws regulating lavish consumption that were meant to curb excesses, especially in dress.

421.29 Atticus] Titus Pomponius Atticus (c. 110–32 BCE), banker and patron of the arts, with homes in Rome and Athens. He took the name Atticus because of his devotion to Greek culture. His correspondence with Cicero is celebrated.

426.2 the Alban Hills] The Albanus Mons, an area of hills and lakes outside of Rome, were popular as a rural escape from the crowded city.

426.9 Mysteries . . . *Goddess*] The Bona Dea was worshipped, especially by women and slaves, as the goddess of fertility and healing. Every December 4 secret rites were performed, attended only by women and presided over by the senior magistrate's wife assisted by the Vestal Virgins. Men and even pictures of men were banned. The desecration of these rites by Publius Clodius in 62 BCE was notorious.

427.17 Tarentum] Present-day Taranto, a coastal city in Apulia, the heel of the Italian boot. In antiquity it was connected to Rome by an extension of the Appian Way.

428.21 Epicurus] Greek philosopher (341–270 BCE), who taught that happiness was the highest good and that the universe is governed by the movement of atoms in empty space.

430.33 Baiae] A coastal resort on the Bay of Naples, dominated by the villas of the rich (including Caesar) and famous for its thermal baths.

431.29 his great ancestor] Marcus Portius Cato (234–149 BCE), Roman statesman called "the Elder" or "the Censor," renowned for his moral rigor and for having written the first history of Rome.

432.18 Anzio] A coastal resort southeast of Rome on the Tyrrhenian Sea, called Antium in antiquity.

438.20 Menander] See note 194.1–3.

448.21 Hyrcanian Tiger!] In the ancient world, Hyrcania referred to lands south of the Caspian Sea. Literary references to its fierce tigers abound, notably in Shakespeare, but seem based on exotic notions rather than fact.

450.16 Serapis] A deity of obscure Egyptian origin who in time came to recall Osiris and resemble Zeus, and who was worshipped as a worker of miracles and healer of the sick.

452.1 Cornelius Nepos] Roman biographer (c. 100–24 BCE).

452.24–25 Sirmio?" . . . Garda] Sirmio, where Catullus owned a villa, is a promontory on the southern end of Lake Garda, the largest lake in Italy, in the alpine area of the north.

455.12 Dyrrhachium] On July 10, 48 BCE, Gnaeus Pompeius Magnus defeated Julius Caesar at Dyrrhachium, in modern-day Albania, during the civil war resulting after the breakup in 53 BCE of the First Triumvirate of Caesar, Pompey, and Marcus Licinius Crassus.

455.37 *Commentaries*] Caesar wrote two histories of his military campaigns, the *Comentarii de Bello Gallico*, about the nine years of war in Gaul and Britain, and the *Comentarii de Bello Civili*, about the later Roman civil wars that ended with the death of Pompey.

465.1 Tusculum] A city in the Alban Hills favored by wealthy Romans. Cicero wrote several books at his villa there.

466.6 Anacreontic threnodies] Elegiac odes employing the seven-syllable Anacreontic line, associated with Greek lyric poet Anacreon (c. 570–c. 488 BCE).

474.16 Lucretius's poem] *De Rerum Natura* (*On the Nature of Things*), a didactic poem in six books laying out the atomic view of the universe, by Titus Lucretius Carus (c. 94–c. 55 BCE).

476.16 Ennius] Quintus Ennius (239–169 BCE), Roman author considered to be the father of Latin literature. He wrote plays and poems and is best remembered for his epic poem *Annales* (*The Annals*), a panoramic account of Roman history from the time of Aeneas.

484.31–32 assassination . . . brother-husband] Cleopatra arranged for the death of Ptolomy XII, who was both her uncle and her father, and later ordered the killing of her brother Ptolomy XIII, with whom she had first ruled as joint monarch.

488.11 Ptah . . . Cyrenaica] Ptah, Egyptian god thought to have created the world; Cyrenaica, eastern province of Libya.

488.18 Parastonium and Cyrene] Ancient cities on the north coast of Libya.

488.24 Hesta] Usually spelled Hestia, she was the Greek equivalent of the Roman Vesta, goddess of the hearth.

491.6 Sosigenes] Referred to in Pliny's *Natural History* as the Alexandrian astronomer consulted by Julius Caesar when he reformed the solar calendar (see note 415.34).

491.13 Cytheris] A celebrated Roman courtesan, mistress to several famous men, including Marc Antony.

492.27 Capua] A coastal city north of Naples.

511.30 Lusitania] Ancient Roman province consisting of modern-day Portugal and part of Spain.

519.33 Pharsalia] On August 9, 48 BCE, the forces of Caesar defeated those of Pompey at Pharsalus in central Greece, assuring an end to the civil war.

519.34 Aristobulus] Ruler of Judea, defeated by Pompey at the siege of Jerusalem in 63 BCE.

520.28 Saturnalia] Week-long, often raucous public festival in December, celebrating the dedication of the temple of Saturn.

521.15 Temple of Philae on the Nile] Ptolomeic temple on an island in the Nile, where legend had it that Osiris was buried.

533.2 Hodan, Quotan] I.e., Wotan.

533.7 Astarte and Ashtoreth] Astarte was a goddess associated with sex-
uality and war, worshipped in ancient Egypt and around the Mediterranean.
Transliterated, her name is Ashtoreth in Hebrew, Ishtar in Mesopotamian,
and eventually Aphrodite in Greek.

541.6 Lake Nemi] Small volcanic lake south of Rome, a vacation spot
for the wealthy.

546.2 Dodona] Shrine in northern Greece, home of the oldest oracle
and a grand temple to Zeus.

548.30 the Neshmet Boat] The boat belonging to the Egyptian god
Nun, which carried Osiris on the Nile from his temple to his tomb at Abydos.

564.16 Nettuno] Coastal city south of Rome, named for the god
Neptune.

570.16 Sulla and Marius] Lucius Cornelius Sulla (138–78 BCE), Roman
general and politician, was a strong and brilliant military strategist whose
eventual dictatorship—he was succeeded by Julius Caesar—foreshadowed the
Roman Empire supplanting the Republic. Roman general Gaius Marius (157–
86 BCE) was elected consul seven times. In 88 BCE the Senate chose Sulla to
head the army, and the Assembly chose Marius. Sulla quickly withdrew his
troops from Rome and in a surprise move turned and marched on the city.
Defeated, Marius fled Rome for Africa.

572.21 Praetor] A powerful position in ancient Rome, held typically by
either a magistrate of the city or a commander of the army.

575.1 [*M. Calpurnius*] Bibulus] Marcus Calpurnius Bibulus (d. 48 BCE),
a political enemy of Caesar. His second wife, Portia Catonis (c.70–43 BCE),
known as Porcia, was the daughter of Cato the Younger. She married Brutus
in 45 BCE.

577.6 Posilipo] Usually spelled Posillipo, a residential neighborhood by
Naples on the sea.

580.27–28 the eagle . . . Aeschylus] According to legend, the Greek
tragic dramatist (525–456 BCE) died when an eagle, mistaking his bald head
for a stone, dropped a tortoise on it.

584.22 Palestrina] Ancient city, once called Praeneste, east of Rome and a
summer resort for wealthy citizens of the capital.

587.25 Parthians] Parthia, which corresponded to modern-day northern
Iran, was part of Arascid Empire. Of Scythian stock, its warriors were famous
horsemen and archers.

587.26–27 The Field of Mars] The Campus Martius, an area of Rome
dedicated to the god of war, was crowded with apartment blocks and villas;

it was cleared and became a place for elections to be held and the militia to exercise.

593.5 Vercingetorix] Gallic chieftain (c. 82–46 BCE), leader of a revolt against Roman rule that was crushed by Julius Caesar.

594.14 Harmodius and Aristogiton] These male Athenian lovers planned to kill the tyrant Hippias, son of Peisistratus, during a procession, but killed his brother Hipparchus instead in 514 BCE. The couple became associated with the cause of Athenian freedom.

600.20–21 Aristedes and Themistocles] Aristedes the Just (530–468 BCE), Athenian statesman, was the hero of the battle of Marathon and a political rival of Themistocles (c. 524–459 BCE). Their conflict over naval policies led to the banishment of Aristedes. Some years later, undermined by a Spartan faction in the city, Themistocles was himself ostracized by the citizens of Athens.

EARLY STORIES

610.1 "*Spiritus Valet*"] Latin: the spirit is strong.

616.3 Nordica] American soprano Lillian Nordica (1857–1914).

620.2 *jeux*] French: games.

622.9–10 "La Bôite au Lait" and "Madame Favart,"] Operettas by German-born French composer Jacques Offenbach (1819–1880): *La Bôite au Lait* (*The Milk Box*, 1876), and *Madame Favart* (1878).

622.39 passe-partouted] Matted.

629.28 *cahier*] French: notebook.

631.1 *Précautions Inutiles*] French: useless precautions.

635.29 *mourir*] French: to die.

637.8–9 author of Mandragola] *La Mandragola* (*The Mandrake*) is the 1518 satirical play by Italian political philosopher and author Niccolò Machiavelli (1469–1527).

ESSAYS ON FICTION

645.10 Horace Walpole, the virtuoso] English author and parliamentarian Horace Walpole (1717–1797) is best remembered for his *Letters*, a vivid portrait of his era.

646.13 Violas and Imogens] The heroines of Shakespeare's *Twelfth Night* and *Cymbeline*, respectively.

646.22–24 "Out of our quarrels . . . literature."] Cf. Yeats, "Per

Amica Silentia Lunae" (1917): "We make out of the quarrel with others, rhetoric, but of the quarrel with ourselves, poetry."

646.35–36 Wesley's *Journal*] John Wesley (1703–1791), English cleric and founder of the Methodist movement. His multivolume *Journals* were fully published in 1911.

648.34 "Notre Dame des Rochers,"] French: "Our Lady of the Rocks." Walpole is alluding to Madame de Sévigné's country house in Brittany, called "Les Rochers."

649.11 St. François de Sales] French bishop, preacher, and saint (1567–1622).

652.16 Olney] English poet William Cowper (1731–1800) lived for many years in Olney, in Buckinghamshire.

652.20–21 Scott . . . chit-chat."] The remark is often attributed to Samuel Taylor Coleridge, though some claim that it was said to Coleridge by Charles Lamb.

653.10 "John Gilpin" . . . Homer] The 1782 comic ballad, "The Diverting History of John Gilpin," by William Cowper, whose translations of Homer were published in 1791.

658.14 Miss Bates] The humorous spinster in Jane Austen's novel *Emma* (1815).

658.29–30 *l'homme moyen sensuel*] The average sensual man: phrase coined by Matthew Arnold in "George Sand," essay collected in *Mixed Essays* (1879).

659.29 *Book of Kells*] Manuscript of the Gospels in Latin, made by Celtic monks around 800, famed for its virtuosic calligraphy and complex illustrations.

668.35 Mr. Owen Young] American lawyer, industrialist and diplomat (1874–1962), he helped found both RCA and NBC.

687.2 Tom Moore's *Melodies*] Irish poet and songwriter (1779–1852), whose *Irish Melodies* appeared in many editions during his lifetime.

691.1 Arnold Zweig . . . Werfel] Arnold Zweig (1887–1968), German novelist; Stefan Zweig (1881–1942), Austrian novelist and biographer; Franz Werfel (1890–1945), Czech-born Austrian novelist, poet, and dramatist.

691.4 *Dichter*] German: poet.

691.40 Guido d'Arezzo's scale] Italian Benedictine monk (c. 991–c. 1050), inventor of the modern musical system of notation.

This book is set in 10 point Linotron Galliard,
a face designed for photocomposition by Matthew Carter
and based on the sixteenth-century face Granjon. The paper
is acid-free lightweight opaque and meets the requirements
for permanence of the American National Standards Institute. The
binding material is Brillianta, a woven rayon cloth made by
Van Heek-Scholco Textielfabrieken, Holland. Compo-
sition by Dedicated Business Services. Printing by
Malloy Incorporated. Binding by Dekker Book-
binding. Designed by Bruce Campbell.